Some Praise for *Crown of Vengeance*, Book One of the Fires in Eden Series

"The book is a good blend of new ideas and Tolkien-esque imagery. Zimmer is a promising writer and I anxiously await the next installment in this series."
-Bookworm Blues

"With a compelling cast of characters, a clever use of point of view, and a well-crafted plot, Crown of Vengeance will captivate fantasy readers. Stephen Zimmer is a writer whose work I will follow for many years to come. A highly recommended book that won't disappoint."
-D. A. Adams, author of *The Brotherhood of Dwarves* and *Red Sky at Dawn*

Wonderful and detailed descriptions of the characters including their emotional state and the world of Ave and their inhabitants. The story gets more and more intriguing because you know something but you cannot see how it fits in the big frame. This is definitely a book for people who like character driven stories with gorgeous and detailed descriptions of a fantasy world and their inhabitants mixed with beings who follow devious plans who will face more resistance than expected....."
- Only the Best SciFi/Fantasy

"For me to say so many great things about a fantasy book is an accomplishment as these types of books used to be towards the bottom on my list that I was willing to read. This book with the help of Mr. Zimmer has restored my faith that fantasy makes for some thrilling reading."
-Cheryl's Book Nook

Dream of Legends

Dream of Legends

STEPHEN ZIMMER

 SEVENTH STAR PRESS

Cover art and illustrations: Matthew Perry
Cover art and illustrations in this book Copyright © 2010 Matthew Perry
& Seventh Star Press, LLC.

Editor: Karen Leet

Published by Seventh Star Press, LLC.

ISBN Number 9780983108627

Library of Congress Control Number: 2010915946

Seventh Star Press
www.seventhstarpress.com
info@seventhstarpress.com

Publisher's Note:
Dream of Legends is a work of fiction. All names, characters, and places are
the product of the author's imagination, used in fictitious manner. Any
resemblances to actual persons, places, locales, events, etc.
are purely coincidental.

Printed in the United States of America

First Edition

DEDICATION

To the One Who transcends the boundaries of time and space, without beginning and without end.

To my mother and father, who always encouraged me to follow the road that my dreams beckoned me toward.

To each and every individual who is not afraid to dream, and then to act upon those dreams.

ACKNOWLEDGEMENTS

To my editor on Dream of Legends, Karen Leet: I thank you so much for coming along with me on this literary journey, in accepting the task of becoming my editor on this book and series. Your meticulous analysis and insights really helped me to progress, and saved me from myself more than once. I can't say enough how much I appreciate all the time and effort that you put in on Dream of Legends, and I really hope that you are proud of the results. Whatever might happen, know that you will always get very last ounce of effort from me to do my best as a writer.

Matt Perry: You continue to amaze me, as your artistic wizardry reaches ever greater heights. Thanks for putting up with me and all of my weird realms yet again, and I hope that my literary worlds have offered you a fun place to play and explore with your artwork. This is another step forward, on a long journey, and the body of artwork that you have produced for both of my series is evolving into something unique and special in the realms of fantasy. Hang in there, as the best things in life do not come easy!

Mom: I thank you as always for instilling me with a love of fantasy and the courage to go after my dreams. It has been far from smooth or easy, and I know that you have had to endure some difficulties when I've stumbled along the way, but I have managed to keep moving forward, and I could not have done any of this without you.

My reader-friends: As I have always said, without readers, an author can't exist, and I am so fortunate to have such a wonderful, growing family of loyal reader-friends. A friend is one who helps someone achieve their dreams, and each and every one of you helps me towards mine, which is why you are not just readers in my eyes, but friends. I will work myself beyond the limits to bring you the best possible books and stories, and I hope that you see that you have chosen an author whose dedication to you, the reader (and friend), is paramount, absolute, and never taken for granted.

"Maybe the wildest dreams are but the
needful preludes of the truth."
-Alfred Lord Tennyson

"Courage is found in unlikely places."
-J. R. R. Tolkien

"Has this world been so kind to you that
you should leave with regret?
There are better things ahead than
any we leave behind."
C.S. Lewis

"Achieving life is not the equivalent
of avoiding death."
-Ayn Rand

section 1

AETHELSTAN

While a few shreds of clouds scudded across the night sky, there was enough luminescence for the company with Aethelstan to navigate the woods back to their encampment.

The Saxans had traveled in silence, with the exception of the snorts and steps of the horses themselves, as well as the metallic jingles and clinks from chain mail, and other metal trappings such as buckles, brooches, and elements of harness.

They returned roughly the same way that they had come, taking advantage of one of the only recognizable trails crossing through the area. Intersecting with the trail just about a league and a half from their encampment, the Saxans were able to pick up their pace.

At any other time, Aethelstan would have enjoyed the journey itself. The soft moonlight cascading down through the trees, spreading deep shadows and tranquil, bluish light, created a beautiful scene to all sides.

A silken breeze drifted through the trees, lightly caressing their leaves. Occasionally, the riders heard the sounds of forest animals jostling about the brush deeper within the woods.

Lost in his own thoughts, Aethelstan neglected to take any pleasure in the peaceable surroundings, remaining alert to them only for any signs of potential danger. As there was no conversation among the riders, he was left to wrestle with his mind all throughout the travel back.

He regretted that his two young boys, Wyglaf and Wystan, could not be with him to witness the woodland beauty, in a time of peace. Even choked by troubling thoughts, he could still imagine their excited smiles as they trotted beside him, holding their new bows, accompanying their father on a hunting sojourn in the forest.

It was never the kill of the hunt that mattered during such a time, he realized. Rather, it was the time spent with his boys that was the most important element of all. It did not matter if they returned empty-handed, as long as the bonds between Aethelstan and his sons grew in strength.

Both of his sons had been given a bit of a reprieve in their fostering with his brother, Aethelhere. Wyglaf and Wystan had been returned back to Bergton the year before, as Aethelhere had been summoned by King Alcuin to aid with the assembling of the Saxan fleet. The honor to

Aethelhere in the given task was tremendous, though it had also provided for a welcome, unexpected gift to Aethelstan as well.

Aethelstan had felt great relief over the turn of fate. The powerful thane had always envied the fact that the villagers and commoners of the land could enjoy watching their sons grow into men without interruption. Greater thanes, reeves, ealdormen, and kings were not afforded all of the treasures found in the world, he somberly realized, and regarded the unexpected truncating of his sons' fostering period as a tacit blessing from the All-Father.

He wondered how his two sons were faring in their first days adapting to life as the men of the household. His heart lightened, and a grin came to his face, as he imagined them conspiring with one of their bondservants, a big lad named Gyric, as they maneuvered to go fishing for eels under the pretext of helping him manage the swine herd in the forest.

They would probably concoct anything to get away from their uncle's eight-year-old son, Wynoth, who Aethelstan now had the joys of fostering. Little Wynoth, even Aethelstan had to admit, was indeed a bit of an annoyance. The young fellow was insatiable in his curiosity, asking questions about virtually everything. No topic was off limits, no matter how embarrassing, irreverent, or plainly boring.

It was not necessarily a bad trait, but could be a bit cumbersome at times. Even Father Wilfrid, who was always pleased to see a young and enthusiastic intellect, laughingly admitted that he had finally met his match.

Aethelhere, with a mirthful smile, had warned Aethelstan of it. Sibling pranks continued into later life, Aethelstan mused with a broader grin as he thought of his brother's look on the day that he had delivered Wynoth into his care.

Aethelstan laughed to himself, thinking of his brother and all the years that they had shared. Aethelhere had always been tenacious when the two brothers had grown up together, but now he was getting far more subtle and clever in his harassments of Aethelstan, working even through youthful surrogates that were the blood of his blood.

The reflections upon his two boys led to thoughts of his daughter, Wynflaed and his wife Gisela, and the sheer happiness that he felt whenever he returned to their hall at the end of a long day. Their warm affection was enough to erase the fatigue of even the most trying of times, his cares and troubles in administering a large burh vanishing in their hugs and smiles.

The weaving of tapestries was a subject that normally would bore him to the point of tears, yet he could not help remembering one particular moment a couple of months back.

His family had been gathered in the hall for the evening meal, taking a delight in a rich repast, complete with a recently-hunted wild boar. After a little conversation, Gisela had brought up how Wynflaed was showing a particular aptitude for working with gold and silver threads.

The genuine thrill in Wynflaed's cherubic face, as Gisela commended her growing skill, negated the dull aspects of tapestry weaving in Aethelstan's eyes. Aethelstan had then remarked how he looked forward to having one of her works hanging in the longhall, for all guests of honor to see. The little girl had beamed joyously in the recognition, matching the radiance of the sun in the pure gleam in her eyes. That look of genuinely pure happiness was a beacon to his spirit, to be remembered whenever he felt himself sinking too low.

If there was anything that he missed most of all, it was the satisfied feeling that came over him as he drifted off to sleep in Gisela's arms, within their private partition at the end of the hall.

He savored the thoughts of those restful nights with his wife in his own bedding, his three healthy children sleeping nearby in the hall, just past the tapestry that was hung at night to afford some privacy. Beyond them, his throng of unmarried household warriors and retainers slumbered along the sides of the main body of the hall. It was a most pleasant state of being, with his family and trusted warriors all together, under one roof.

Being separated, especially in light of the dark times that were sweeping over the land, only served to magnify the worries that he felt for all the members of his family.

He came out of his silent reverie with the sounds of sentries abruptly calling out, "Halt, and identify yourselves!"

Riding close to Aethelstan, Cenferth called back, "Sons of Saxany, may the blood be strong once again."

A couple of figures bearing lances moved out from the trees in front of the detachment of riders, with visibly relaxed postures in response to the utterance of correct passage words.

"I trust that you have had few disturbances?" Cenferth asked them.

"No, no disturbances. Did your travels go well?" one of the sentries asked politely.

"All are safe," Cenferth replied.

"I give thanks to the All-Father. 'Tis a blessed word you bring," the sentry responded, giving a slight bow to them.

"Good man, has anyone arrived since we departed," Aethelstan queried, bringing his horse up alongside Cenferth's.

The sentry nodded. "Yes, my lord. Some have indeed arrived back to camp since I was posted. They say we have sky steeds in the camp now, though I have not seen them yet with my own eyes. I would not leave my charge here, of course."

"And that is why Saxan blood will indeed be strong again," Aethelstan complimented the man, smiling, and already feeling hopeful at the tidings from the sentry. He remarked to Cenferth, loud enough for the guard to hear clearly, "Our guard's words were chosen with a prophet's vision, I believe."

"Thank you, my lord," the sentry replied in gratitude, giving another bow as Aethelstan spurred his horse forward.

Aethelstan's hopes rose even further as he heard the distinctive whines and grunts of the stout Himmerosen. A number of campfires were lit around the campsite, and many Saxans rose up to cheerfully greet the returning party.

Aethelstan could see the exuberance at his party's return, and knew that the men in the camp had been harboring great worries over them since they had first set out.

He paused for a moment to give some instructions to Cenferth, to convey the word of what they had seen during their journey to the other thanes. His body was tired and sore from the foray, but his spirit was buoyed by the notion that Edmund had finally arrived into the camp.

As he neared his own bell-shaped tent, he saw the outlines of the large sky steeds. He had always thought they resembled a leaner version of a war dog in their physical look. Though not quite as broad in proportion, they did bear a close likeness in the shape of their their heads and proportions.

Each time that Aethelstan saw the Himmerosen, he remembered the thrill of flying through the air while astride the wondrous creatures.

He was no sky warrior, but, in the past, Edmund had guided him up above on a small number of airborne sojourns.

The sensation of flight was incredible, and there were times that he could not help but envy the trained sky riders such as Edmund. The feeling of freedom and the perception of a much more magical, broader world was indelible in the act of soaring across the heavens.

For such truly formidable creatures, the trained Himmerosen tended to have rather gentle dispositions, and were not dangerous at all to work with, or be around. Simply riding them was not much different from riding a horse, though mastering the skills of a sky rider, and the use of weapons while in flight, required considerable training.

A couple of the creatures turned and whined playfully at Aethelstan as he walked towards them, not entirely unlike his large dogs that ran all about the grounds within Bergton.

"They are a bit too tired for a ride this evening," commented a friendly, and quite familiar, voice.

Aethelstan glanced to the left. A man of about his own age was striding toward him. His head was uncovered, and his dark hair tossed about in the crisp wind. He was clad simply in a cloak, tunic, and trousers, bearing only a sword that was sheathed at his waist.

"Edmund, Edmund. You took your time, did you not?" Aethelstan quipped, a grin sprouting upon his face, as his former trepidations at his friend's long absence fled.

A warm smile spread across Edmund's face as he drew closer. He had a thick moustache underneath his sharp nose, and his eyes sparkled with a merry glitter.

"Still not used to the beard," Edmund teased, as he stepped forward and gave a fervent embrace to Aethelstan.

"It does take some getting used to, that I confess," Aethelstan replied, laughing, reaching up and rubbing the growth that had been there for only a small portion of his life span, covering cheeks, chin, and around his mouth. "And I am far too used to your bare chin, but admittedly it is still good to see you. I was growing very worried."

"You sound like a parent. Though I know that you are a good one," Edmund replied, chuckling. "Worried about me? I cannot wait until I make Wystan or Wyglaf a sky rider. Then we will see about worry."

"You will make me grow old before my time, I fear," Aethelstan said, laughing again. His face then grew more serious. "But I really was a bit worried."

"We traveled here safely enough," Edmund replied, his own expression turning more somber. "You probably already know of enemy sky warriors appearing far too often over our land."

"Yes, I have heard of them," Aethelstan said. "And we have found where the enemy force is likely to come through. If the enemy tries a more difficult route, we could defend against them with ease. I have just returned from scouting these areas myself."

"You should leave it to your friends in the sky," Edmund remarked, an edge underlying his words.

Edmund's expression reflected some agitation, and Aethelstan knew that his friend was not thrilled about him having scouted the terrain in person. Aethelstan was the thane of greatest rank in the forces defending the borders of Wessachia, in addition to the deep, abiding frienship that he had with Edmund.

"If you were ever around," Aethelstan retorted.

"We had a muster point to reach with Aldric. He takes over six hundred sky riders to the defense on the plains, maybe seven hundred," Edmund informed him. "We were making certain of our forces, as well as our equipment and plans."

"So how many have come with you?" Aethelstan asked.

"We have around fifty here, and that is much better than I expected. Sky warriors are badly wanted at the plains, and I did not expect Aldric to spare so many for the defenses here," Edmund said.

"Then caution is to be advised, with smaller numbers," Aethelstan replied evenly.

Edmund grinned. "Caution?"

"I fear you will never cease to be a little wayward and reckless in your methods, Edmund. But heed me closely in this," Aethelstan said, his countenance becoming stern, and his voice growing firmer. "We have grown up together, and fought together. Yet we have never faced anything like the times that are upon us now. Nothing like it, ever. We have to be very, very careful."

Edmund's grin dimmed, and his face reflected his friend's grave countenance. "I need no explanation. I knew what we are facing, the moment that I saw the look upon Aldric's face. He is like the rock of a mountain ... and has the presence of one too. But I know without a doubt that I saw a flicker of fear within his eyes, as he related the word that has come to us of the approaching enemy forces."

"The best of warriors still knows fear. Fear focuses the mind, and tempers the resolve," Aethelstan commented. His expression then brightened a little. "So, have you eaten yet?"

"They had some good woodland boar for the sky riders when we arrived. It seems that some men from the general levy met with some fortune in the woods nearby," Edmund said. "To think that only nobles hunt in the forests of Avanor. My stomach gives thanks that our lands have no such laws! It is fortuitous that our levymen are hunters, not to mention valuable for our supply of archers."

"You know how to tempt an appetite, for I am starving after my own journey," Aethelstan stated. He clasped his friend's arm, just below Edmund's left shoulder. "Then join me for some food and drink, if only for company. I am famished."

"Maybe there is some meade about?" Edmund said, with evident hope in his voice.

Aethelstan laughed. "Alas, you hope too far. There is not, and if there were, it would truly be secured from the likes of you."

"My reputation precedes me always," Edmund said, laughing as he shook his head.

The two men walked to a nearby fire, where they were swiftly attended to by a couple of men from the camp.

Wooden cups and platters were brought out to them, and they were soon provided with a simple meal. Some wheat bread was served, which was just starting to toughen, and needed to be softened in a vegetable and grain pottage. A clay pitcher of ale, already strained, filled their cups more than once.

Some fresh mutton had been procured from a small village a few leagues back, and it took a little time to roast the modest amounts upon a spit. Finally, there were a few special cakes sweetened with honey.

It was not the complex fare of a feast in a longhall, but it was a welcome respite from the usual foods partaken of on a longer campaign.

"Some good fortune is with us," Aethelstan commented contentedly, as his hunger pangs were eradicated.

"Quite a good fare for a campaign," Edmund complimented, taking a long draft of ale. He smacked his lips, grinned, and held his cup out, as one of the men attending to them filled it up once again.

"Now slow yourself down a little," Aethelstan said, not entirely in jest.

"I want to enjoy times like this," Edmund said, as he glanced up, staring towards the serenity of the night sky. "Two friends sharing a good meal and ale, under a clear Saxan sky. For me that is my treasure."

"And I hope to have many more such times, once we have dealt with these Avanorans," Aethelstan said.

He could see that his friend was wrestling with a number of fears. The years had taught him much about Edmund, enough to see that underneath the Saxan's confident façade his friend was ridden with anxiety and deep foreboding about the coming struggle.

"Do not worry about me," Edmund said, almost as if he had just read Aethelstan's mind. "No matter what thoughts enter my head, I shall be at the lead of our Himmerosen come daybreak."

"No matter what is hurled against us, let us make sure that we survive together," Aethelstan said.

"No man can make such a promise. Life is a fragile thing, and war so unpredictable," Edmund stated.

"We can do everything that is left to our own power … and be as clever as we are able, fight as hard as we are capable of, and what will come, will come. Only the All-Father knows what will happen," Aethelstan said, resolve burning within him.

"You have my promise on that," Edmund replied softly, the look in his eyes unwavering.

"Then I can rest myself easier tonight," Aethelstan said, as he took notice that his eyes were growing heavy. "I do not think I am much longer for this night. My body is telling me to rest. No, rather it is commanding me to rest."

Edmund slowly yawned. "We have both done enough traveling for the moment, and I believe that my own body shares the view of yours."

"Until the morning then, my friend," Aethelstan replied, slowly rising to his feet.

While it was not the same as ending an evening surrounded by his sons, daughter, and wife, it was still a blessing to end it in the company of a true friend.

The thought was not lost on Aethelstan as he prayed within the quiet of his tent before seeking the sanctuary of sleep. With deep sincerity in his heart, he offered thanksgiving to the All-Father for the wondrous gift of friendships in life.

THE UNIFIER

The Unifier walked with a fluid stride through the center of the dense assembly. Anyone within His path quickly parted aside to create a wide channel for His unimpeded passage. Avanoran guards from the citadel's garrison were formed into two columns that followed close behind Him, as He made his way towards the far end of the Great Hall's main chamber.

The Great Hall, located on the second terrace of the huge mountain citadel within Avalos, was currently filled to capacity. Numerous emissaries hailing from many of the known kingdoms and realms across Ave, those that were ardently loyal to the Unifier, stood in rapt attendance.

It was one of several such audiences that would be taking place in the near future. The emissaries had all been directly summoned, and no excuse would have been deemed acceptable for their absence.

Had the representatives not heeded the summons, they would have found it to be a dire mistake. Their rulers knew well that a substantial price would have been paid for their absence, which would have been taken as outward defiance to the will of the Unifier.

Clad in his long tunic of immaculate white silk, the Unifier proceeded gracefully towards the raised dais of stone at the eastern end, set within a shallow recess forming an apse. A singular throne sat upon the higher stone surface, crafted of a dark, ornately carved wood. The Unifier methodically ascended the wide steps, coming to a halt just in front of the throne. He turned slowly to face the assemblage.

The violet gloaming at the cusp of evening cast little direct light through the tall, narrow windows set high in the side walls of the expansive hall. At the explicit command of the Unifier, all of the candles in the several round, layered chandeliers running down the center of the grand hall had been lit. Flames also burned within the great recessed fireplaces set intermittently down the sides of the chamber.

The effect of all the firelight within the hall was nothing short of spectacular, casting an ethereal hue about the capacious area. The deep blue ceiling looked simply magical, containing a myriad of little, silvery stars, which gleamed resplendently in the light from the flames. The intricate tapestries lining the walls with their glorious, colorful scenes of hunts and battles were brought out vividly.

Yet despite the mildness of the concluding day, and the presence of all of the flames, a deep chill reigned supreme within the hall. It left all of the attendees in a state of discomfort, one that was not just physical in nature. For the Unifier, the icy, permeating feeling suited His purpose.

It was not a time for celebration, or any other indulgence. The matter at hand was of the utmost importance. Comfort was the least of His considerations. The delegations could not be dismissed from the hall with any misinterpretations of the grave nature of the message that He had come to deliver to them.

They were there to heed His call with all their will, to bring the new age forward into its full manifestation. It was an age that they were on the very brink of achieving. A new morning star was about to make its ascension, an important step in a much greater rising.

All of the eyes in the hall were fixed intently on the Unifier, looking upon Him with a mix of both dread and anxiety. The godhead of the throng's growing wealth and worldly power stood before them in the flesh, His sharp eyes sweeping over all. Each one of the emissaries from foreign courts felt as if the Unifier was personally regarding him or her. A subdued hush fell throughout the room, as all forms of conversation thoroughly ceased.

With a clear voice that resonated all throughout the extensive hall, the Unifier finally broke the uneasy stillness.

"The world must be united as one. The world can, and will, be as one. There need no longer be any barriers to divide us. We must finish our task of ridding the world of our enemies, so that the future can be ours … and ours alone. You know of what I speak. You know that this war we fight must not fail … or even falter."

The Unifier paused, looking about the great chamber with His piercing eyes of azure brilliance. He was exceptionally fair to look upon, if not considered unrivaled among men. Yet there was no disputing the choking fear that seemed to accompany Him in rarer moments such as these. The feeling was like looking out upon a vast mass of black thunderclouds spread across the length of the horizon, billowing as they approached, and poised on the verge of hurling barrages of lightning, and torrents of wind and rain, at any given moment. It was an ominous, intimidating sensation that swept over the hearts of the assembled emissaries, causing more than one of them to reflexively blanch in their stark sense of powerlessness and diminutiveness.

The members of the elite assemblage were among the few in all of Ave who had become acquainted with this awesome, and foreboding, aspect of the Unifier. For many, especially those who were rarely around Him, the terrifying effect was inexplicable.

Those who had spent more time in closer, more regular proximity to Him understood the effect much more implicitly, though they were no less afraid. If anything, the increased knowledge fueled their fear even more.

It was a far different feeling than the one held by the common masses that had gained an opportunity to behold Him in person. The public had always been enraptured with His incredible charisma and comeliness. Mesmerized to feeling warm affection, they knew nothing of the intimidating side of the Unifier, the one that He chose to expose to the powerful that He expected binding obedience from.

"My Darroks have been unleashed upon the Five Realms … the primitive, savage tribes to the east of Gallea," the Unifier continued. "The Galleans have gathered together a great army on those borders, within the County of Talasae, and will soon surge forth to root our enemies out from those lands.

"The armies of Ehrengard, Andamoor, and Avanor now move together against Saxany. Many of you know well of this aspect of our greater war. It marks the approaching end of an age, and the beginning of the new one that we will all embrace together. The Saxans and the Five Realms … those enemies will soon be of little worry or consequence.

"The Midragardans are a different matter entirely. To bring Midragard under our authority, we must strike at them through the seas. Their lands lay far to the east, and deep to the south of here … to the far south of Kiruva, Gael, and Saxany. The wide sea is no small barrier. The seas are the heart of their power, and the soul of their people. And for that we must bring together the largest fleet that has ever been assembled on the oceans of this world. Ever!"

The Unifier's gaze swept the room again, searching for any sign of hesitation from the representatives gathered there. Only fear and acquiescence met His penetrating gaze. The recognition of that was pleasing, and He savored it intimately for a moment.

"All of your lands must contribute towards the force that we will assemble, to send against the Midragardans," He stated when He had resumed. "Ships, supplies, weapons, men, horses … all must be gathered in greater numbers at the Theonian port of Thessalas, on the edge of Garia.

"I have decided that many of My remaining Sorcerers within Avalos will be dispatched, to depart and go with you back to your own lands. You know of My blessed gifts. With My Sorcerers, to whom I have taught great and powerful arts to use in the service of mankind, you will find more help for your tasks. They will also serve as My personal representatives amongst you. As I have given you signs of My nature, so I will give you My Sorcerers."

A wave of amazement, excitement, and not a little fear passed rapidly through the assembled representatives at the unexpected announcement. The Unifier's perceptions, far transcending those of a mortal man, took in the eruption of reactions taking place within the minds of the emissaries.

Many thoughts had turned to the genesis of the Sorcerers, following the second of the Great Signs done by the Unifier during His ascension to power. Their minds were filled with remembrances of those incredible events, as well as the significance of the announcement that the Sorcerers of Avalos were to be dispersed among them.

There were countless accounts regarding manifestations of the Unifier's power throughout the years, some almost too fantastical for some to believe. Yet there were only two that stood forth throughout the allied realms, undeniable realities that enjoyed multitudes of credible, and sober, witnesses.

One of the two Great Signs had occurred during a time that only a scant few of those gathered in the assemblage were even old enough to remember. It had happened not long after the rise of the Unifier to the rule of Avanor, during the nascent period of the alliance. Only seven kingdoms had come together by that time, providing the incipient foundation of support for the Unifier's world-encompassing vision.

A great famine had spread its malignancy rampantly throughout Ehrengard, which had been one of the strongest of the initial seven kingdoms that had acquiesced to the Unifier's will. The famine had set in motion a deadly plague, leading to other tribulations as upheaval and suffering struck out at both noble and peasant alike.

Making the situation even worse, it had happened after the death of the Sacred Emperor, Lothar V, who had died without leaving an accepted heir. A fierce period of warfare had broken out because of that, further exacerbating the misery among the people. The warring among the princes and bishops of those lands had threatened to tear the Kingdom of Ehrengard, and quite possibly the entire Sacred Empire, into useless fragments, even as the great plague ravaged the populace without mercy.

Many areas were utterly devastated, as the poor were assailed from all sides. Cattle, herds of swine, and other livestock were driven off in the maelstrom of fighting, only to be devoured by the teeming packs of slavering wolves inundating the shadowy forests. There was nowhere for the peasants to run, and they had cried out desperately to the All-Father for help. It was the most horrific time that Ehrengard had ever endured, and there were few that held out any hope for the rapidly fragmenting kingdom.

The Unifier had hastened swiftly to their lands in person, taking it upon Himself publicly to respond to Ehrengard's cries. He had set about working His incredible, mysterious arts tirelessly.

Great numbers of individual examples testified to the Unifier's unrivaled capability. He invoked unusual, mystical powers in the curing of great numbers of people, summoning livestock back out from the deep woods, and dampening bitter hatreds among noble rivals. Even the hordes of wolves had slunk back into the deeper regions of the forests, no longer emboldened to assail the dwellings of humankind.

The tremendous upheaval had been suppressed, and incidents of the plague disappeared swiftly from among the people. Shaken, but intact, the Kingdom of Ehrengard had survived. It was as if the Unifier's will alone eroded the presence of the disease, and to the people, the Unifier seemed to be the direct answer to the innumerable prayers voiced to the All-Father within the churches, cathedrals, and homes all across Ehrengard. As if to accent that perception, the next harvest was extraordinarily successful, abounding more richly than it had ever done before.

A new Emperor and King, Conrad IV, had risen to acceptance in the midst of the stability. Under the Unifier's mentoring and counsel, the young emperor had set about mending the prior divisions of the kingdom. Ehrengard, one of the seven heads of the Unifier's foundation of strength, had suffered a seemingly mortal wound, and had been healed.

The tale of the second Great Sign was more recent, and almost every person in the room had heard it told from the mouths of actual eyewitnesses in Gallea to the spectacular event.

The astounding episode had happened in front of the outer gates of the Count's castle in the walled Gallean city of Troia, located in the eastern county of Chamerais. King Charles III, who was the father of the current Gallean king, Philip the Fireblade, had been investing a new bishop, Payen of Avalos, with ring and staff.

Payen enjoyed great favor within Avanor, and there were some whispers about the nature of the sudden demise of the previous Bishop, a man named Rigord. Rigord's death had been sudden, with no sign of disease or violence, despite the fact that he was far from elderly, and in the fullness of health.

Other whispers told of great influence wielded by the Unifier in regards to the Royal Bishopric and the choice of Payen. None were brave enough to voice any of the swirling suspicions in the face of the Unifier, Who had been in Troia attending the investiture ceremony.

Save for one individual.

A young and radical White Monk, Martin of Clarvas, had demonstrated enough temerity, and tenacity, to publicly confront the ascendant Avanoran ruler. The young monk had vigorously protested the nature of the Unifier's authority. He had made fantastical accusations regarding the demise of Rigord, and had even further claimed that the Unifier was actually an outright enemy of the All-Father.

The onlookers had been stunned at the fulmination of the monk, as the Unifier appeared to all to be an Archon of the light, a figure of peace and reason unprecedented in humanity's long-suffering history. More shocking, the monk was not simply some unknown renegade, or irascible malcontent that was always at odds with the people.

Martin hailed from the fabled monastery at Clarvas, where the White Monks had truly found their voice and gone on to flourish as one of the most renowned orders in Ave. Being a monk of the reform-oriented order conferred an outright status on him from the moment of his initiation, but Martin had distinguished himself prominently. Over the years, he had gained a great reputation, with many already comparing him to St. Fulbert, the fiery monk that had catalyzed the monastery at Clarvas, preached the Second Holy War, and supported by his argumentation the formation of the Knights of the High Altar. Great things had been expected in the young monk's future by many, from the ranks of commoners to the heights of the Western Church.

The stunning, abrupt confrontation in public had brought a tense, ominous pall over the vast crowd that witnessed it, such that every person's attention was fixed upon the two figures to the exclusion of everything else. The Unifier had shown no outward displeasure at the monk's heated denunciation. Wholly surprising to all of the onlookers, He actually had held a serene expression on His face, as He quietly faced the fiery and vocal young monk. He had looked entirely unconcerned with the substance of the harsh, grave accusations.

Many recalled that the Unifier had then calmly asked the monk, in a voice that all could hear, whether He could call upon nature, if He was an outright enemy to a true god. The monk had then grown hesitant, if not appearing to be a little perplexed by the Unifier's strange response.

The Unifier then had proceeded to invoke fires from the sky itself, calling for the destruction of whichever one of the two of them was not a true servant of a true god. He had made a bold statement iterating that if He was indeed the false one, then He wished for the monk to scoop His ashes from the ground that very day.

A massive column of flames had rushed down from the sky just a moment after the last word had left the Unifier's lips. The searing mass of flames had encompassed and consumed the young monk in a handful of seconds, leaving nothing remaining of him but ash that was scattered randomly about in the breezes. There was nothing for the Unifier to even scoop up, as the monk's remains were dissipated in moments upon gusts of wind that swept through the area following the stunning event.

It was a tremendous sign recognized by the people as testimony to the Unifier's authority from the heavens themselves. They had also seen it as a dire warning to any foolish enough to blaspheme His name.

The incredible story spread quickly throughout the lands, and it came to be widely regarded that the Unifier held direct, divine authority. It was the final event that catalyzed the broader union of kingdoms and realms under His guidance, an authority that had been recognized for well over two decades.

The lessons from those two Great Signs had not been ignored in the years to come, by either the soon-compliant rulers or their general populaces. It was during those formative years that the Unifier had cultivated His new brood of Sorcerers, within the heart of Avanor. When they had emerged, the rulers and people had been awestruck. The performer of the two Great Signs had brought forth an order of miracle workers.

The new Sorcerers were individuals who went beyond simple healing, communicating, or other menial types of magic, and were able to call great powers out of nature itself. There were many that felt that the new Sorcerers could possibly rival the powers of the ancient Wizards of legend and lore, who were among the First Born.

While these Sorcerers were not of the First Born, it became conspicuously obvious that they had been spared the passage of age within their bodies. They had come to be known as the Sorcerers of Avalos, and their lack of aging, and apparent grace of immortality, was seen by many as yet another vibrant demonstration of the divine favor bestowed upon the Unifier.

Yet even with the goodwill held by most, some rumors were spread that the Sorcerers' power derived from Jebaalos, the Lord of Fire and the Dark Abyss. The claims were swiftly dismissed as mere paranoia, for the Sorcerers had mainly used their powers to bring rain to parched lands, dryness to flooded ones, and a multitude of other benevolent acts serving the various kingdoms that had pledged loyalty to the Unifier.

But they had also been used in combat. The Sorcerers, during the course of the subjugation of some minor rebellions, had been used quite formidably in the art of war. They had worked some incredible feats, including such powerful acts as calling lightening down from the sky, and inducing destructive earthquakes. It was powers such as those that had kept many of the realms' leaders from airing any dissatisfactions with the emerging order, right as they watched their sovereignty erode under the will of the Unifier.

Most often, the Sorcerers were kept within Avalos, inside of the Citadel. They were rarely seen, even among the guards in the main palace fortress. For the most part, they stayed to the fifth terrace of the complex, the one closely resembling a monastic compound. From time to time, they were sent out as individuals on some charge, or appeared at assemblies within the palace.

Relatively, they were very few in number, but their concentrated presence indicated their great importance to the Unifier. None would dare speculate as to what tasks they performed deep within the chambers of the soaring mountain-palace.

That they would now be sent forth in full number, dispatched to accompany the emissaries and lend their aid in a faraway war, was a very momentous, unprecedented development. After the initial shock wave had passed through the emissaries, and more fear had swelled within them, the Unifier resumed his address.

"I know that all of you understand that my gift of the Sorcerers to you is of no small matter, and I will avail you with the greatest of My powers. Go, therefore, with haste, and send My charge to your lands. The ships will be at Thessalas. The Seven Kingdoms of the First Alliance must participate in the support and organization of the force. The Empire of Theonia must provide ships and men. The realms of the Sunlands, from my esteemed friend, Khalif Al-Hakim at Caiandria, to the Great Sultan of Saljuka, must provide supplies, more ships, and men."

At the mention of the Sunland realms, He paused to consider a particular, stately group of men gathered down below, just to the left of Him. They were clad in long, white, flowing tunics of the finest linen, edged with exquisite brocade of golden thread. Panels of fabric woven intricately with inscriptions were wrapped around their arms at the shoulder.

Over these lavish tunics they wore ornate, loose robes, made from cloth-of-gold. Their heads were also covered in turbans of a golden textile, out of which flowed a hanging length of cloth under their chins. The men wore richly jeweled necklaces of gold. On their feet, they wore an exquisitely comfortable, luxurious type of slipper-shoe.

Their dark eyes held a glint of surprise, as if they suspected that The Unifier was looking right into their thoughts. As an elite delegation from the Fahtamid Khalif, they still had one major petition remaining that they had not yet been able to bring before the Unifier, and Avanor's ruler was very conscious of that.

"And tell Khalif Al-Hakim that I know of the emergence of Ibn Amal, and of the difficulties that his rise presents to you during these times. I do not wish to become involved in your inner matters, though I will turn my attention to this Ibn Amal. It seems that he does not recognize the authority of the Khalif ... or My authority. Let it be known that I will not let him strike from his newly-inherited lands to threaten Caiandria, so that you may send more ships without worry. I shall have his full allegiance, or his destruction, soon enough.

"Those with zeal for the Holy Wars will be sent against him. It will keep the most ardent of that kind well occupied, and away from harassment of your own lands. Baron Osbern of Rocheston, in Norengal, departs with a great force of such warriors soon enough."

He looked to each of the Fahtamid delegates, to let his words sink into them. He had addressed their Khalif's greatest worries outright, before they had even spoken a single word aloud regarding them. Their sheer amazement at His uncanny perception was evident in their astonished expressions. He was channeling their sworn enemies to fight their upstart enemy, and in the process fulfilling both their Khalif's and the Unifier's will.

Looking up, His encompassing gaze swept back over the crowd once again.

"Those serving in My court will attend to each of you now, to go over particular matters involved in this campaign. From some, I will need supplies. From others, men. From others, ships. Fulfill their requests as if they came directly from Me. Move with the greatest of speed. We are on the edge of victory, and everything must be committed towards the final struggle."

The Unifier then let the first smile of the gathering creep onto His face. In form, it was the balanced, graceful expression that He displayed to public crowds, but oddly, the crowd of emissaries felt no relief at the change of countenance.

"Your reward is upon the horizon. A world of new wonders awaits you all."

The Unifier's grand words did not soothe them either, and most simply attributed it to having become too pensive, for too extended a period of time. The Unifier did not wait for any kind of subsequent response. The citadel guards falling in around Him when He reached the bottom, He descended the steps of the dais and strode gracefully from the chamber, leaving the gathered delegations and emissaries behind Him.

His heavy steps echoed in the great hall, and not one in the assembly felt any impetus to move, or even talk, until He had entirely departed. A reverent silence lingered for several more moments in the chamber, as if the Unifier's presence was still there among them.

Excited conversation finally broke the disquiet and spread rapidly throughout the gathering. The talk of a final battle to unite an entire world, the mustering of a vast naval expedition, and the word of the Sorcerers of Avalos being dispatched to their various lands was virtually overwhelming to take in at once.

Within hours, the clerks and high officers of the Unifier's court would disseminate the specific requests being made of each delegation. They would be very efficient, seeking to hasten the emissaries onward to their respective lands, Kings, Emperors, Emirs, Sultans, Princes, and Khalifs.

The emissaries found themselves quite eager to attend to their tasks, with no further delay. Thoughts of feasting and luxuries had fled from their minds. The absence of such desires was an irony, as they had all experienced great discomfort, having not eaten much in their hurry to arrive in Avalos in time for the assembly.

The Unifier's directives were all that they could think of, as the resources and peoples of many great lands were being set into motion. Such was the pervasive, and encompassing nature of the Unifier.

A great storm filling the horizons was building, soon to be loosed in full force upon the world.

DRAGOL

Dragol's Harrak, like the others in his loose formation, flew in a slow, circular pattern, far above the hilly, tree-blanketed terrain. The wings of the sky steed were spread wide, clinging to the flowing air as the Trogens drifted smoothly, carefully scanning the area below with their sharp eyes.

To any observer upon the ground, the Trogen sky riders appeared content to glide upon the gentle currents of the air. To a Saxan, they would have appeared like so many carrion birds, swirling over an espied carcass.

In truth, there was no degree of contentment within Dragol's tumultuous mind. In the depths of his thoughts, the huge warrior would have found agreement to a Saxan's comparison of the Trogens to carrion birds.

It was a loathsome feeling to see himself, and his fellow Trogens, akin to glorified carrion birds, trailing and shadowing the harbinger of impending carnage; a scavenger, not a hunter.

The hunters, what the Trogens should have been in Dragol's mind, were moving below. A substantial force from Avanor, like a vast winding serpent, was pressing towards the outermost boundary of Saxany's hilly, northwestern forests. The fast pace of the march was conducted at the direct behest of the Unifier, conveyed through the Lord Generals of Avalos. There was no toleration of delay, as the leaders of the ground forces spurred the men onward in a forced march.

Word had come to Dragol and the other sky riders that the main invasion armies were finally amassing on the border of Saxany, near a place called the Plains of Athelney. He knew that it would not be much longer before they would be engaged in heavy combat.

Other tidings he had gleaned from messengers indicated that the Saxans had levied a very formidable army of their own on the Plains to contest the imminent invasion.

A colossal clash of armies was in the offing.

The strategy of the second, comparatively much smaller Avanoran force below was simple enough, in light of the overall circumstances. Tragan had been quite clear about the scenario when he had given Dragol and the others their firm orders.

The smaller, second army of Avanor would curl through the forest, to emerge onto the Plains behind the main Saxan army. Not only would they have the opportunity to strike from behind, they would effectively drive a wedge between the Saxan front lines and any potential relief forces.

Additionally, if the Avanorans gained their desired position, it prevented any escape route for the Saxans involved in the main battle out on the Plains. The jaws of the Unifier's armies would easily be able to close down and crush the Saxans arrayed out on those Plains. The battle for the renegade kingdom that still defied the Unifier, and the emerging new world, would be over with the destruction of that army.

It would then just be a matter of occupying the many towns and villages, and destroying any lingering rebellious elements. The ensuing campaign would be done much like the way faraway Norengal was once conquered by the Avanorans. The back of the defenders broken in one giant battle, the invaders would proceed onward to stamp out the scattered, residual resistance in a harshly executed campaign.

The strategy made good, logical sense, in terms of seeking one decisive blow, and winning an entire war in one battle. Yet despite the imminent importance of the movements below, the minds of most of the Trogen warriors around Dragol were undoubtedly distracted. Other, more disturbing reports had also reached their camp, and had spread quickly amongst their kind.

The first Darrok raid on the Five Realms had ended, and the Trogens were seething at the stark reports of what had transpired. It was the first major use of Darroks in war, and the Avanorans had evidently believed that there was nothing that could challenge the flying hulks in the sky. An Avanoran viscount named Adhemar had believed that archers alone could ward the behemoths. He had concentrated on sending the Darroks forth with greater loads of stones, dismissing concerns of the tribal warriors mounting any kind of defense that could actually threaten the juggernauts.

Messengers spoke extensively of how the tribal warriors had indeed mustered a daring and effective defense in the skies. They had flown up from the forest upon their Brega to vigorously assault the unescorted Darroks. They had succeeded in driving the great creatures off before the Darroks could be fully used to strike more areas, beyond one hapless village that they had initially destroyed.

A great number of Trogen warriors had been slain, as the clever tribal warriors had concentrated their smaller numbers on one Darrok at a time. The debacle had confirmed a fear that Dragol had harbored when he had first learned that the sky warriors of the Trogen clans were being subjected to Avanoran authority.

The Trogen sky riders were left in a very foul mood, insomuch as it was inconceivable to them that anyone had allowed the slow, lumbering behemoths to go forward without the protection of escorting sky warriors. Many of their brethren had been needlessly slain as a result of Avanoran overconfidence, something that never would have been allowed to pass so easily if left to their own power and choice.

Dragol, who was already fuming over being held back from avenging his own warriors that had fallen in the border missions, was absolutely livid at the dour reports. The Trogen leader's anger was raging towards the presence of orders from humans that had left fellow Trogens so vulnerable on the exposed backs of the Darroks.

A pang of guilt now laced through him, at having followed the orders not to strike back towards those who had recently slain his own warriors. He knew that he and his brethren were increasingly compromising the ways of their kind. In light of the distressing news from the Five Realms, he wondered what his kind really was gaining in fighting this war, if they ceased to be Trogen in manner and tradition before it was over.

After centuries, the Elves still had not succeeded in destroying the Trogens. In a few short years, service to the Unifier might well accomplish what the Elves had failed to do.

The heat of those feelings was further exacerbated by the impending duties that he had recently been assigned. Earlier that morning, a small contingent of Trogen sky warriors had been chosen for another Darrok mission that would shortly issue forth. The Trogen force was being diverted from the invasion of Saxany, to accompany the next foray over the Five Realms.

Dragol was glad that the folly of the Avanoran viscount would be corrected, but the announcement was rife with its own cause for regrets and misgivings. For those who had been chosen to accompany the Darroks, the last hours shadowing the army from Avanor seemed to crawl by mercilessly.

Trogen longblades were single-edged, but what he now faced was truly reminiscent of something like the double-edged variety used by the Avanorans. Dragol, having been named commander of the new escort force, was chafing at the mix of strong emotions within him. Leaving the area of Saxany, he knew that he now would not be able to personally avenge the deaths of the warriors that had fallen to the beasts and the archer in the outer woods.

Yet he also knew that he was finally going to return to a more honorable manner of combat once again, instead of the restraint that he had been made to suffer. The Avanorans had come to their senses, and were not going to leave the Trogens laboring on the backs of the Darroks so vulnerable.

In a way, it was also a small victory in that the humans were being forced to acknowledge that the Trogens were correct in their initial misgivings. Far too often Dragol had perceived that humans regarded themselves as innately more intelligent than, and superior to, the Trogens.

Such was maddening enough, but he was simply glad that he did not understand many Avanoran words, so that he did not translate the insults that he knew were regularly uttered by humans in the presence of Trogens. Had he spoken their language and understood what they said, he would have had to lay quite a few humans low with his longblade, or his massive fists.

"The spirits of Elysium ride with you, Dragol, for fortune is with you," Goras rumbled from the back of his steed, his loud voice carrying strongly across the air between their sky mounts. Goras made no effort to hide his envy, having been commanded to remain with the other Trogens aiding the Avanoran force beneath them. "I must yet remain with my weapons bound, by the orders."

Dragol sympathized deeply with his friend. "Soon we will be fighting together once again. The savage tribesmen of the other land will swiftly fall. It is said that they are not great in number. They will not be able to stop the invasion there. The Saxans will fight very hard here, and may not fall so easily. We may yet fight them together."

"The Saxans are warriors, true warriors, and worthy opponents to overcome. We have both seen this," acknowledged Goras, "but we will still overwhelm them at the onset of the battle. The force gathered is far too powerful for the Saxans. There may be only one battle for us."

"No battle's end is truly known. Little did our brothers foresee their end in the raid upon the Five Realms," Dragol observed. He then snarled, "Though that was due to human stupidity, when Trogens warned them of the dangers."

"And of the Sorcerers of Avalos?" Goras queried. "What if they break the enemy with haste?"

Goras' concerns were valid, even if a little speculative. The deployed power of the Unifier was incredible in scale and composition, and quite capable of swiftly breaking even a great army.

The humans revered and feared the Unifier's Sorcerers, to such an extent that the Trogens took the Sorcerers very seriously, even if they were still largely a mystery to the towering warriors. Rumors abounded regarding their capabilities, though Dragol had not yet witnessed them in something like a battle. Some were said to harbor great abilities, a few Sorcerers even believed to be capable of authority over the elements. It was commonly believed that they far exceeded the powers held by the Trogens who were of the Clan of the Healers, the famed shamans of the Trogen kind. Even more foreboding, more than a few whispers attributed the skills of Avanor's Sorcerers to the practice and study of dark mysteries.

Dragol wondered whether Sorcerers could actually manipulate things such as wind and lightning, but there was much talk that several great Sorcerers had accompanied the main invasion force. If they were among the invasion force, then they were there for a specific reason. The Avanorans, for all of their haughtiness, were not frivolous.

To the Trogens, such tidings were becoming a bitter bane, especially among those such as Goras and Dragol who were being effectively fettered by Avanoran orders. At the very least, the Trogens wished to conduct all of the fighting in the skies, as they feared that there would only be a limited opportunity for it. They certainly did not want Sorcerers' arts preventing them from engaging in open combat, and taking part in the battles to come.

"It may be as you say," returned Dragol. "You still do not know what may come."

"I am ready," Goras shot back, his eyes burning with a raging intensity. "I ..."

Goras' voice trailed off as the two noticed a trio of Harraks approaching from just ahead of them. It was one of the small, high-altitude scouting groups that foraged through the upper skies, looking for any sign of new developments. Such scouts normally flew far ahead of the main positions of the armies that they accompanied, and risked much danger.

They were an undeniable example of the great bravery of Trogen warriors, especially in the current instance. The forces of Saxany were known to be able to put strong forces into the skies, and the whereabouts of enemy sky warriors were still not known. As such, the Trogen scouts were rendered very vulnerable by their scant numbers and distance from their own camps, every time that they went on a far-ranging mission over enemy territory.

"My eyes tell me that it is the farthest reaching of the scouting groups that were sent," Dragol commented, as he squinted towards the three oncoming warriors.

He recognized the lead warrior of the group as the three drew nearer. His dark iron helm, broad muzzle, and flowing, black fur cloak were unmistakable. The scouts normally wore furred cloaks, as they spent much time in the frigid, highest altitudes, but few among their entire race possessed a cloak fashioned out of the deep, black-furred hide of a Mountain Bear from the Trogen homelands.

The scouts guided their steeds straight towards Dragol and Goras, something to be expected as they were the two highest-ranking warriors within the circling contingent of Trogens. The two Trogen commanders broke away from their own formation, drifting out to meet the scouts, and bringing their steeds to hover in the air as they awaited them. Their steeds bobbed up and down in rhythm, wings beating steadily to maintain their position.

The scout in the middle of the three, the veteran Trogen that Dragol had recognized from afar as Dynagan of the Mountain Bear Clan, spoke for the group.

"The Saxans know of the approach of the army below. They have taken good positions on a ridgeline inside the borders of the forest," the scout reported. "It is the only place the Avanorans can possibly use their cavalry."

"What is their strength?" Goras inquired.

"Maybe a couple thousand strong. They have mounts, but I do not know if they are used as cavalry or not. They have some sky warriors too, for we were chased by almost ten of them out on patrol," the scout reported, his face tensing, as he grudgingly admitted to having evaded battle.

Dragol could not fault the scout for evading combat, or hold him in derision. The scouting parties' orders had been strict; the acquisition of information was of the utmost importance and priority.

Yet once again, Avanoran practicality had overcome Trogen tradition, as three Trogens against ten were not insurmountable odds in any Trogen warrior's eyes.

A spark was ignited in the eyes of both Goras and Dragol at the pronouncement.

"The skies must be taken," Dragol stated. He turned to Goras, and a slight grin turned up the corners of his mouth. On a Trogen, the look had a feral edge. "I believe that you will see fighting soon enough."

"Dragol, we must go now, to report to Tragan," the brooding scout interjected, impatient to complete his mission.

Dragol understood the scout's frustration, but was still irritated with Dynagan's abrasive manner.

"Then go," Dragol replied gruffly.

Dragol and Goras nodded as the scouts hastily departed from their presence.

"Fortunes have changed, as of a sudden, Dragol," Goras said, a wave of excited, relieved energy coursing through his deep voice.

Dragol could see that his comrade's mouth was already salivating at the succulent prospects of combat. It was as if great binding chains had been suddenly cut from him, through the words of Dynagan.

"Storm winds may reveal a clear sky," Dragol remarked, repeating a saying of his kind that illustrated the unpredictability of life.

The saying recalled the sudden shifts of weather in his homeland, including the times when what looked to be certain storms were suddenly averted, and replaced by cool and passive skies. Things in life could shift abruptly, in either direction. Yet when they changed suddenly for the better, it was truly something to savor, and be grateful for. The thunderclouds in his mind eased as he took in Goras' relief, though another part of him wished that he could fly into battle against the Saxans with him.

AETHELSTAN

"They will deliver the tidings of what they have seen to their army, you can be sure of that!" lamented Aethelstan, gazing upward into the now-empty sky. Frustration clenched him tightly, as more worries were added to the teeming cluster already present within his mind.

He ran his hand through his shoulder-length, dark brown hair, standing near the top of a ridge a few paces in front of Edmund. Behind Edmund were the other members of the small group of sky warriors that had recently arrived.

They were among the few that had been spared from the Saxan forces massing out on the Plains of Athelney. Edmund and the other sky riders intended to help Aethelstan ward their movements, by driving off or distracting enemy sky patrols and scouts.

It had been about one day since Aethelstan had returned from his own short scouting foray on horseback. He knew that the battle that they were inevitably to fight was creeping ever closer. The feeling of its imminence swelled in the air with each passing hour.

They had found good positions to tether and quarter the horses. As of now, Aethelstan, the highest-ranking thanes, and the warriors from their respective household retinues were spending the greater part of their time working with, and arraying, the levied contingents from Wessachia and the immediately surrounding areas.

DREAM OF LEGENDS

A consensus had been reached regarding the Saxan defense. They had decided upon the most advantageous place to offer battle, and doubted that the Avanorans would refuse it.

The Saxan warriors were to be deployed along the crest of a long ridgeline, set squarely in the path of the oncoming force from Avanor. Its long and gentler slope was one of the only places that offered any possible use of cavalry, without which Aethelstan knew that the Avanoran enemy would not wish to fight a battle.

The narrow channels and passes through the surrounding hills would be highly uninviting to the Avanoran leaders. Even a small force of skilled warriors familiar with the landscape could hold such narrow passages for quite some time.

There was little doubt in Aethelstan's mind that the Avanorans would seek to engage the Saxans on the broader ground of the ridge and slope, the only place where the Avanorans could bring the full weight of their forces to bear.

Most of the gathered Saxans were sleeping just behind the elongated ridge in hastily assembled tents, some just a few feet away from the positions that they would soon defend. Some older men, women, and a number of religious figures, including priests, sisters, and monks, had been arriving in small numbers to help attend to the various needs of the series of makeshift encampments.

Awaiting the coming of the enemy could easily have turned into an agony of nerves for the anxious men called forth in the General Fyrd. They were primarily farmers, with a fair number of craftsmen among their number, not given regularly to the practice of combat. Fortunately, most were using their time wisely enough, honing their fighting skills, sparring with each other, throwing spears at tree targets, trying out their slings, or practicing their archery.

Aethelstan had seen to it that many experienced warriors were dispatched among the levy men to give them additional tutelage, and instruct them further in the ways of a Saxan shield wall.

At the very least, the levy men were given a physical outlet to vent their tensions and fears. Aethelstan had no doubts that their thoughts often drifted to their families back in the villages and homesteads of Wessachia. In truth, his own thoughts returned often to his wife, daughter, and sons, and he could not condemn the levy men for dwelling upon such worries.

He was just relieved that they appeared to understand the imminent, lethal threat that was facing them all. Aethelstan urged his thanes and household guards to impress upon all of the men the vital importance of a common defense.

Aethelstan knew that many of the levy men would become very fearful when the battle finally arrived. That was nothing to deride either, as even well-experienced warriors were not immune to the icy touch of fear. Without much training, and no real experience, an enormous task was being asked of the levy men to stand firm in battle. Yet Aethelstan still had hopes that they could steel themselves enough to follow directives. The overwhelming bulk of the archers available to Aethelstan's force came from the General Fyrd, and he would need every last one of them in the battle to come.

It had been late in the afternoon when Edmund had finally arrived from his latest scouting foray, and still later when the reports of the last Trogen scouting party, and the failure to stop it, had come.

The Saxan sky patrol had come up short with the pursuit of a trio of Trogen scouts who had managed to achieve a thorough survey of the Saxan positions. The swifter Harraks were able to outrun the Himmerosen, as the Harraks' riders declined battle, outnumbered ten to three.

Aethelstan knew that the Trogens' fallback was no display of cowardice. They had gained what they had set out to acquire. Now, any elements of surprise that would have belonged to the Saxans had been eliminated.

That was a horrible enough plight for Aethelstan, who knew that the forces of Saxany would need every possible advantage that they could get in the coming struggle.

"The warriors are in position, but we can move them with little trouble to another place of your liking," Cenferth stated somberly, from where he stood to Aethelstan's right.

Aethelstan looked at the stout household warrior and had to stifle a slight grin, even in light of the grim circumstances. Cenferth had misread Aethelstan's concerns, but his presence was still a comfort.

The hardy warrior always seemed to strive towards the positives of a situation, a trait honed by the resilient and tireless ethic held among the peoples of the northern provinces. Aethelstan admired men like that, but he knew that the attitude could also become a detriment when it failed to acknowledge the realities of a given situation.

"We are in a good place to fight the Avanorans, deployed on the best ground for our purposes. I have no doubts that before us is the channel that they would take. They will accept our offered site of battle, Cenferth, and I wish to keep it that way."

"It is just that we cannot allow them to map out our positions with such impunity," Aethelstan stated. He turned back to the lean, tall warrior with sharp, blue eyes standing just behind him. "Edmund, will you be able to keep them away, from now on?"

Edmund, the leader of the available contingent of sky riders, and the highest-ranking sky warrior of Ealdorman Morcar's lands, thought carefully for a moment. His brow furrowed in concentration.

"You know that we have only a relative handful of Himmerosen for our use here. Aelfric's summons of Aldric the Stormblade called upon most of the sky warriors for the great battle looming on the plains," he answered in an even tone. "But we should still have enough warriors to fend off the scouts and small patrols escorting the oncoming enemy force. But whether they might have an even stronger force coming up behind them, I cannot yet say."

Aethelstan nodded. "Then we may yet have a chance to hide much of the disposition of our forces. We will also have several of our bowmen looking out for those foolhardy Trogens that would dare venture too low in the skies. If you encounter the enemy, and are able to drive them downward in the vicinity of this position, then we should be able to give them a Saxan greeting.

"The land itself impedes their use of cavalry. They will not have much advantage even here, where mounted warriors can be used, and where they will surely come. But they will be coming with great strength upon the ground, and our men along the ridgeline cannot worry about what might threaten from the skies."

"Then we must pray to the All-Father for deliverance," another of his thanes, a broad-shouldered, middle-aged warrior named Offa stated.

The sincerity of that simple expression of piety, another trait of the northerners, was shown in the warmth emanating from the man's eyes and the calm tone of his voice.

Aethelstan nodded in agreement. "We must always pray, Offa, though the answer may not always be to our desire. What will happen, will happen. We can only do our part, to account for who we really are. How much more time do you estimate that we have before they are here?"

"Perhaps a day, maybe two," Offa replied, just as calmly, despite the fact that the words indicated that he and the men of his homelands would soon be facing the threat of death at the hands of a foreign invader. The implications of losing the coming battle, and leaving the villages and homesteads of Wessachia vulnerable, were far too terrible to contemplate.

Aethelstan looked again towards Edmund. "My good friend, your work in the skies is of ever greater importance. You must let us know the movements of their army, for it seems that time grows short indeed."

Edmund returned Aethelstan's gaze, his eyes reflecting the loyalty and affinity that the two warriors had for each other. There was no man that Aethelstan respected more among the Saxans of Wessachia than Edmund.

Just three years before, Edmund had finally made the rank of thane, just like his father before him. His stockaded residence had a modest hall and tower within it, and Aethelstan had been instrumental in helping him complete his estate, which now encompassed over seven hides of land.

Edmund's residence was located near a quite pleasant village called Golden Meadow, a place with fertile farmlands located just north of Aethelstan's town-fort of Bergton. The village was so named due to the broad meadow that spring draped with bright, golden flora every year. Tranquil and restful, the resplendent meadow afforded a stunning view of the landscape and the shining brook that timelessly meandered through it.

This was the first year that Aethelstan had not been able to enjoy the peace and serenity of the meadow, as the call of war had taken him far from any thought of repose. It was a great and terrible regret, as Aethelstan truly looked forward to visiting his childhood friend during that wondrous time each spring when the richness of bloom and leaf accompanied the vigorous return of life, following winter's long slumber.

Aethelstan and Edmund had grown up close, and although Aethelstan was destined to be the greater thane by his lineage, subject only to Ealdorman Morcar himself, they had maintained a growing, brotherly friendship in both heart, arms, and in service to their people. From their early childhood to the present moment, their paths had long been intertwined.

Now, they would be walking along a most precarious and foreboding path together. Aethelstan was well aware that at times it would take the abilities and efforts of one to keep the other from falling, as they traversed the perilous road looming ahead.

"You will know, Aethelstan. Our hearts will not tire," Edmund stated resolutely to the great thane, with a slight nod of his head. His firm, somber tone, and iron-steady gaze conveyed the confidence within him to the man that was both his superior and his friend.

"This force will depend on the eyes of your men," Aethelstan replied stoically. "I will depend upon you."

Edmund fixed his gaze upon that of Aethelstan. "If peril should come upon you, know that somehow I will be there to make certain that you do not fall."

Aethelstan held back the smile that wished to emerge, not wanting Edmund to misinterpret his expression as taking the lesser thane lightly. Edmund's words were no boast, as Aethelstan knew that the man would go through hell itself if Aethelstan was in mortal danger.

Aethelstan was so very grateful that Edmund would be there for the coming battle. Edmund's resolve was infectious, something that was good for all the warriors, including Aethelstan. With the slightest of grins, Aethelstan patted Edmund firmly upon the shoulder.

"I know you would be there, but it is imperative that you do not fall either," Aethelstan stated. A wide smile then burst upon his face. "I will trust in Offa's estimation that we have at least a day left to us. The Trogens can learn no more today than what they have already acquired. Let us go share some ale together, and forget about this turmoil for a few precious moments."

Aethelstan glanced around at his houseguard, and the other men with Edmund. "Is there any objection?"

The men around him smiled back warmly.

"I didn't think so," Aethelstan said, with a chuckle. "Then let us not tarry further. To my tent. Let us fill some cups together! Some Saxan practices must not be ignored, even in such trying times!"

"Indeed, if there ever was the perfect Saxan thane, such a thane would only be your equal!" Edmund remarked, as he strode alongside his friend.

WULFSTAN

"They abandoned all the hill forts along the borders. The forts at the crossroads too. Pulled the cavalry right back out. The garrisons too, they say, and left 'em abandoned. Heard it with my own ears," commented a man to Wulfstan's right, as they worked to break up the hard earth and dig the wide trench rapidly forming along the outermost boundary of the sprawling encampment.

"Then it must be no small force indeed that comes at us," added a paunchy, gray-bearded man whose face was caked in sweat. He huffed with exertion as he swung his pick-axe down, scattering lumps of newly-freed earth. "If you are sayin' the Western March is emptied, that is ..."

"It had better hope to be very strong, if it is to get by us," Wulfstan riposted firmly, hearing the great anxiety beneath the man's words. His own chest heaved as he brought the iron headed pick-axe overhead, and slammed it forcefully into the ground, throwing up several substantial chunks of dirt.

The men spoke with the relaxed familiarity that came from long years of association and interaction together. None of them had ever been so far away from their home villages, but their shared past and current experiences strengthened their bonds even further.

The Saxan ranks had continued to swell considerably over the past couple of days, as large numbers of the new arrivals were put immediately to work on defenses surrounding the principle Saxan encampment.

Wulfstan was glad for the hard labor, as it gave them all something to do to pass the time and hold their deep unease at bay. Most of the men had never seen more than a handful of people gathered together, hundreds at the most. The presence of so many thousands was a bewildering sight to most levy men, looking as if the entire world was coming together in one location.

For his own part, Wulfstan was slowly working to grow used to the presence of so many people in one place. It was certainly staggering to consider the vast sights around him.

Whatever others were feeling, he knew that his own state of mind had definitely been cast awry, as his recurring dream had been coming back to him on a nightly basis. The visions of destruction and flight towards the heavens continued to permeate his mind, feeling so real that he often woke up in cold sweats, with a racing heart.

Leaning on the rough wooden shaft of the pick, he looked up at the sky. With echoes of his dreams resounding in his mind, Wulfstan almost expected to see a peculiar, and conspicuous, layer of something like a cloudmass far, far above, of the purest white radiance.

"They'll get by you for sure, dreaming while awake," jibed the first man with a chuckle, snapping Wulfstan out of his reverie.

"It is a nice day for such," the second man remarked.

Wulfstan smiled, heaving the pick back up to his shoulder. "Okay, I'm guilty, you all caught me. I'm getting back to work now, if you do not mind."

He swung the pick again with renewed force, feeling the strength unleash through the muscles of his arms, shoulders and back. Ultimately and in truth, there was little else to do, other than await the certain approach of the enemy.

"You'd face an army by yourself, says I," the first man uttered, chuckling and shaking his head as he glanced at the stout-hearted warrior.

"And what is that?" queried the second, older man, a curious lilt to his tone of voice. He rested the head of his own pick-ax on the ground, and peered out towards the plain in front of them, squinting.

"You'd better not take another break, Cenwald. Your bones are not that old. Even if you always try to make us think so. Nobody believes it during the plowing time at the village back home. We all know you are one of the best hunters and all ... and I ..." the first speaker started to say.

His jovial smile faded as fast as his words, as his own eyes rose upward and gazed out. His attention was drawn suddenly in the direction of the west, towards where Cenwald was staring.

Wulfstan followed their gazes, seeing the trepidation spreading on their faces. Out on the very edge of their vision, the men beheld the distant, swift movement of several horsemen who were circling about on the open plain to the northwest. The horsemen had just crested the low, long slope of a distant rise. It took no expert amongst them to immediately recognize that the horsemen were of a foreign nature.

The horses moved with speed and grace, flowing in harmony across the grassy plain. They looked to be smaller of build than any horses that the village men had seen before.

Overall, there were only a few of the galloping horsemen, but all of the men in the developing trench knew what their presence meant. It signified boldly that the time that they had all been inwardly dreading had arrived at last. The horsemen could be none other than the outlying scouts of the invaders, in the vanguard of the enemy force.

"From Andamoor, I'd say. The turban-wearers far from the north, across the seas. Their horses look fragile enough. We will see what kind of warriors they are soon enough," rumbled a grizzled thane, standing on the lip of the deepening trench.

The thane rested his strong, weathered hands on his hips, as he looked out with a hard gaze towards the plain.

Wulfstan looked from the thane and back out toowards the plain with increased wonder. He had heard a few gleeman tell tales of the lands far to the northwest, but had never actually seen anyone from Andamoor before with his own eyes.

He continued to marvel at the swift, slender horses that gracefully navigated the plain. He did not see anything fragile about the elegant, controlled way that the riders and horses seemed to glide in harmony across the open ground.

Instead, the sight of their dexterity was at once a thing to instill caution in him. It was the first, unmistakable sign that the enemy would be coming at them with new types of fighters and cavalry, of kinds unknown to their own lands and ways.

Something in Wulfstan's mind told him that the strange horsemen would be far from the only different element within the invading army now marching upon their lands. Yet there would be no way of knowing what was truly coming until everything was already upon them. Even then, the things that were unknown to the Saxans would be just as confusing and hard to fathom.

The enemy army would be like a dense, impenetrable storm surging relentlessly towards them, vast and mysterious in the power that it would hurl against the Saxans. In some ways, it was like the cataclysmic forces of Wulfstan's dreams. Their promises of destruction always preceded the deep, distinctive voice that Wulfstan heard in his dreams, and the subsequent flight into the skies toward a faraway, cloud-like shape.

That thought, coupled with the cognizance of the implications displayed out on the plains before his eyes, caused a slight agitation to take hold within him. He fought an impulse to look back up to the skies, to again look for a cloud-like shape of opalescent brilliance.

The horsemen showed little worry about being seen, almost as if they wanted to herald the arrival of their army. They were not worried about silence, either. The air carried their faint, distant cries across the ground. Wulfstan held little doubt that they could have easily remained hidden if they had wanted to.

"They will camp beyond the edge of our sight," added the thane, before returning his attentions to the men in the trench. "But the battle is not long off now. Something you must keep in mind. There is no time for delay. Finish this trench."

Despite the strong tone to the thane's words, there was a perceptible undercurrent of grave concern in his voice. The men needed no prodding or cajoling to achieve a greater sense of urgency.

Wulfstan barely heard the thane's words, absently nodding, as he brought his pick up and down again. In between blows to the earth, his gaze returned to the horsemen.

To the right of his field of vision, a small group of Saxan cavalry galloped in the direction of the scouts. He could see the sunlight glinting off their iron helms and the spear-blades of their long lances, pennons flapping in the wind from a couple of them.

Even from his distance, Wulfstan could assess the differences in the two types of mounts. The strong Saxan steeds were indeed hardy, but they were noticeably slower than the breed utilized by the enemy scouts. The gap still closed as the enemy horsemen circled, yelling out some unintelligible cries at the approaching Saxan warriors.

When the gap had shortened considerably, Wulfstan watched as the enemy horsemen swiftly turned their mounts and galloped back in the direction from which they had come. In an outright race on open plains, there was absolutely no danger to the horsemen of being caught by the Saxan warriors upon their slower steeds.

The enemy horsemen soon disappeared over the edge of the far horizon; a horizon that obscured a vast, oncoming storm.

GUNTHER

The majority of the Jaghuns had been recalled into Gunther's humble timber dwelling. To his best judgement, leaving them out in the open, wandering about the forest around his demesne, would do little other than to advertise their exact location.

With a little luck, he hoped that the enemy would pass by in their haste to press against the Saxans. They should have little interest in a solitary forest dweller, one that could provide nothing of advantage to their army.

The best-trained pair of his Jaghuns remained outside, Fang and Nightshadow. Both had been given firm commands to come back to Gunther if outsiders neared. They were the only two that he trusted enough to override their instincts at the sight of threatening Licanthers, and obey the order rather than attack a natural nemesis of theirs.

The others had been gathered into the main building on the entry-level floor, a few growling and whining incessantly in their agitation. Increasingly fidgety, the Jaghuns inside of Gunther's home announced in their own way that the forces of the Unifier were close. The creatures clearly seemed to sense an intruding presence within their forest.

Gunther had to frequently move among the group of Jaghuns to settle them down, from the largest male to the youngest two, Skyheart and Darkmane.

Lee and the other foreigners appeared to be astonished at the level of discomfort and nervousness being expressed among the animals. The creatures had, until most recently, exhibited calm demeanors.

"What is making them so upset?" Lee asked Gunther, standing near to the wooden staircase leading up to the second level.

Gunther looked up from where he was rubbing the head of a particularly irritated female Jaghun, Merein. He knew that her agitation was compounded by the fact that she was a mother to both Skyheart and Darkmane, and was undoubtedly feeling protective about her offspring.

Gunther had a far off look in his eye as he responded to Lee. "It is not taught so in my own faith, but I believe that the creatures of this world also choose either good or evil to serve.

"The choice of the animals was once told to me, long ago, by a man who said he was from the far northern lands, in territory now held by the followers of the Prophet. He was a man who had still not adopted the religion of the Prophet, and worshipped in an ancient way and custom. In many ways, his faith was not altogether different from my own.

"Anyway, he spoke of how the animals of the world divided

themselves in loyalty. Some siding with the good God, and the rest with the evil One. It is a strange belief, but if he was somehow right, that animals also choose sides in the struggle of good and evil, then I believe that the Jaghuns choose to serve the All-Father ... and also that the Licanthers of the enemy serve the great Adversary. It would surely explain why my Jaghuns grow so upset at their approach."

"So even the animals have free will?" murmured Erin, almost in a mocking tone.

Gunther nodded, with a slight expression of puzzlement at Erin's comment, while feeling a sharp irritation at the flippancy of her tone.

"Perhaps some do," he remarked. "Who am I to say absolutely that they do not?"

"There's only one entrance into this place, right?" ventured Ryan. He eyed the restless Jaghuns with an edgy demeanor. "There is no secret side door or anything, is there?"

"No, there is only the cave passage into the depths of the lower world. Those of the Island of Gael would say a passage to Otherworld," Gunther stated, with a trace of a grin, thinking of the hardy, devout people. "Even a large force could not pursue us there. They would soon enough learn the truth of the Stone Hides, if they had heard the old tales of the tribal lands."

His words caused all of the others to peer inquisitively towards the thick, wooden door in the back of the chamber. Anxiety flickered on their faces, as to them the doorway was one that opened upon the sheer unknown.

"Do not worry yourselves unduly. There will be no danger to you from the Unguhur. I will make certain of it. As for now, I am going to go outside, and take a look around," Gunther announced. His voice then took on a sharp edge, which brooked no question or dispute. "Do not leave here. Your lives may depend on that. If you are threatened, and I have not returned, go through that door, and do not fear the race that you will find in the depths. Tell them that you are friends of Gunther, and that he told you to seek refuge with Treas. Do not hesitate to announce that ... not for a moment ... no matter what fear may rise at the sight of the beings you will encounter beyond that door."

Without another word, he grabbed up his longbow, scabbard, and belt, and quietly left through the front door. The Jaghuns rustled about and whimpered at his departure, but did not make any move to disobey their master.

LEE

Despite the stated escape rout being within just a few short strides from them, Gunther's four guests exhibited a range of morose expressions in the aftermath of the woodsman's departure. Lee felt as if he could now relate to a cornered rat, helplessly waiting to see whether or not a hunting snake would discover the entrance to its nest, to enter and devour its trapped quarry.

The notion of another race of creatures, located within the depths of the ground, was not very reassuring either. Each moment spent within Gunther's dwelling increased the overall feeling of trepidation, though Lee was not about to question the woodsman's admonishment to remain where they were.

Lee realized without question that to try and go out into the woods by themselves would be virtually suicidal. All too recently, he and his companions had personally experienced the sheer folly of such a situation. He knew that Gunther's intervention had enabled them to survive, and, as a result, gain from the valuable lessons concerning their great vulnerabilities in Ave.

Even so, their trust was now placed with a man whom they knew very little about, in a world that they knew even less about. For four people who were not from a world that was very oriented towards trusting strangers, it was a very uneasy and burdensome predicament to be caught within. Lee could not deny that such a reality did not sit entirely well within his own heart.

Ryan paced back and forth anxiously, while Lynn and Erin sat quietly nearby on stools, with pensive expressions on their faces. All cast periodic glances at the Jaghuns, exhibiting a sustained wariness towards the woodman's formidable creatures. Lee kept to his place near the bottom rung of the staircase, leaning up against the wall as he regarded his companions, and the Jaghuns.

It could not be denied that they were all effectively prisoners of the new world, especially relating to the situation immediately at hand. Lee felt ill prepared for what was rapidly descending upon them, and knew that his three companions were faring little better as they struggled with their own inner turmoil.

After several ponderous, uncomfortably silent moments, Lee finally straightened up and meandered slowly over towards the broad door on the back wall of the dwelling. He looked at it carefully, taking in its crafting and texture. There was very little that was special about the door. It was just a plain wooden door, constructed of rough-surfaced planks, with an additional wooden plank that was used to bar it shut from the inside.

His thoughts and curiosities were fully directed to what lay just beyond the door. Lee had an instinctive feeling in his gut that they would all be crossing through that doorway soon enough. It was better to expect the worst, if only because it was a much more honest and likely expectation.

If an invading army was moving through the woodlands, Lee did not see how it could fail to find Gunther's dwelling. He knew that Gunther certainly did not intend to greet the invaders or parley with them.

"So what is going on here? Are we just going to sit around and wait to be killed?" Erin complained, fear thickly present in her edgy voice. "This is just a trap, and all of you know it. Isn't it, Lee?"

Her gaze was now riveted upon Lee, as he stood before the mysterious doorway. Ryan and Lynn looked up as they awaited Lee's reply.

Deep in a serious train of thought of his own, Lee reflexively flinched at the rather curt inquiry.

"What do you mean?" he asked, as he turned to look at her.

"You heard what he said. There's an army outside in those woods, one large enough to cause him to pull in all of his precious beasts. I suppose he can make his buildings invisible too," Erin said derisively. "And he wants us to go through that door, maybe by ourselves, and seek help from some kind of creatures that we don't know the first thing about. I think it is incredibly stupid. What happens if these ... Stone Hides ... Unguhur ... whatever they are ... do not believe we are friends of Gunther? Then what, Lee? Think they are going to be enthused about a bunch of strangers, especially if they suspect something amiss?"

"Can you be so sure of anything, anywhere around here?" Lee posed to her, exasperated by her continually obstinate manner. The lines of his face tightened with the tension that coiled tightly within him. "We've seen no reason not to trust Gunther. He knows a lot more about this world than we do, and you know damn well that he and his Jaghuns saved our own hides ... which definitely aren't made of stone, Erin. We don't have many options, and no good ones that I can see. I think we should listen to him, and risk a little trust in this case."

His sharp response clearly caught Erin off guard. Her mouth started to open, and then tightened in a mien filled with petulance. Lee had no illusions that she was barely withholding a strident retort that was perched upon her lips.

"No, there are no guarantees" she said at last, with some manifest reservation. Her voice then became firmer, as her eyes narrowed with a hint of defiance. "But the odds are a lot better when an army is not breathing down your back."

Lee nodded in full agreement. "I don't argue that, Erin. I'm sure none of us do. But still, we have to adjust as things happen. We must react. I've said what I think, so let me ask you, what options do we have? Running around on the surface through the woods? Do you really think we would last very long?"

She glared at Lee, and remained fixed in silence.

"We wouldn't do so well, and I think we all know that," Lee pressed.

Erin turned her face away from Lee, but not before he saw a sullen expression weighing down heavily upon it. She then shot Lee a thorny glance. "No, so I guess that we are just screwed … and I'm just being realistic, you know. I think we all know that."

Her last words dripped with mockery and scorn. She turned away on the wooden stool, her back now squarely facing him and the others. Lee watched her for a few seconds, both mystified and disgusted with her churlish attitude, before finally letting his eyes drift back to the others.

"Am I wrong?" Lee asked them a little plaintively.

Lynn shook her head, before answering him in a voice laden with the onerous weight of full resignation. "No. Just a lot of things going on right now. The shock of being here is wearing off, too, and I'm finding myself thinking a lot more about my friends and my family, and the life we were all taken from. It has been troubling enough for me without all of those concerns starting in on me. And now, those worries certainly are making their presence known."

"No kidding," Ryan added. "I was just wondering what Antoine might be thinking, about where I am, where I've gone. And I really wonder if I am ever going to see him again. Can't let myself have much hope now. What would be the sense in that, given all this surrounding us? Don't even really know anything anymore. So what's the use?"

The teenager looked away, and Lee did not have to go any closer to know that the young male's eyes were now moist and reddening.

A lump rose in Lee's own throat, as he thought of his elderly mother, the beloved woman who he had always been near to attend to. He thought of the brothers and sisters he was now separated from, perhaps irrevocably. The small restaurant that represented his life work, refuge, and savings could not be forgotten either.

It was almost as if all of his former life had just been a dream, all ephemeral images of the mind, with nothing of it accessible anymore. Were it not for the three people currently in the room with him, he might well have begun to sincerely doubt the reality of his memories.

Nonetheless, he kept his stronger emotions tucked deeper inside of him. He could see that Ryan and Erin were not all that far from a breaking point. Both were grasping for answers, and even if it was little more than a façade Lee had to act as if he had some bearings.

Lee could not see past the stoic demeanor that Lynn had been presenting, to see how close or how far she was from sharing their disposition. Lee was not about to assume anything in regards to her. Yet no matter whether or not the strain of everything had her at a breaking point, Lynn was absolutely right about what was beginning to happen to all of them.

The anxiety and pace of the initial hours following their stunning appearance within the new world was finally dissipating. They were all starting to get acclimated to the new world, at least enough that their minds were starting to drift back more and more to the world that they had been so shockingly taken away from.

Looming before them was a strenuous test of character, one that exceeded anything that they could ever have known. Every member of their families had been removed from their world, and every friend, and every familiar surrounding. Everything that they had come to know since the day they had been born was entirely gone.

All that they had left of their own world was each other. This overbearing climate of great loss was coupled with the daunting task of picking up the pieces of their lives and somehow finding new things to hold on to. It was imperative that they find new goals to drive them ahead, a step at a time.

In a way, Lee recognized that the cruelest aspect of their shared predicament was their very memories, but he also knew that he would not have it any other way. They might not ever find their way back to their own world. Yet just as the memories of loved ones that had passed away stayed with him, so did those of all of the people from his former world.

With both groups, those living and those who had passed away, Lee refused to deny that he would someday, and somehow, find a way to reunite with all of them. It was a very considerable element of what gave meaning to anything good that he had ever experienced in life.

Lynn was the nearest one of the other three in proximity to Lee. He took a couple of steps over to her, and placed his hands gently upon her shoulders as he smiled down at her.

She looked up to him, and though she did not smile, he could see the beginnings of a filial affection reflected in her face. Even though it was nascent, the sight encourged him greatly.

He said softly, and reassuringly, to her, "There is one thing, Lynn … Ryan … Erin … We still have us."

Quietly, he turned away from Lynn after lightly stroking her upper back. Walking over to Ryan, he put his right arm around the young man's shoulders and gave the youth a firm hug. After holding the embrace for a second, he patted the young man firmly on the right shoulder, no words needing to be said.

He then made his way over to where Erin was still sitting with her back facing him. She twitched as his hands touched her shoulders, as if about to recoil, though she did not resist as he went on to reach around her, and hug her from behind.

"Hang in there," he whispered into her ear. "Way too early to lose hope, Erin. Let's keep fighting."

As if he had broken down some sort of barricade, she abruptly turned in his arms. A glimpse at her face showed that her hardened demeanor had melted.

She wrapped her own arms around Lee and buried her face intently into the middle of his chest. He could feel her body shake as she quietly sobbed, grasping him tightly as if she was afraid that if she were to let go, he might well disappear from her life as well.

In that moment, he came to a momentous realization that required its own considerable degree of resolve. In his heart, he made a silent and sincere commitment to his three suffering companions.

He shared their fears, and shared their growing sadness, but he knew that he now had to be stronger than he had ever been in his whole life.

Lee had never been married, nor ever been a father before, but he sensed that he had, in a way, just gained three new family members within the last few moments.

DRAGOL

The huge form of Tragan loomed like a mountainous shadow within the dark confines of the central command tent. Sparse glints of light reflected off of his eyes from the couple of small torches set within the enclosed space. Though smoke escaped through the hole in the upper center of the tent, a haze now encompassed the relatively small space.

Dragol and Goras stood silently before him, their eyes lowered and heads tilted in respect before the high commander of the Unifier's sky warriors. Only Framorg himself, the legendary figure from the Mountain Bear Clan who had been chosen to be the overall War Chieftain of the Trogens, outranked the large Trogen standing before them.

They sensed that the monotony of the sky patrols was about to break, for they had been summoned firmly, urged to return with great haste. It was evident that Tragan was still boiling over the debacle in the skies over the Five Realms, and the loss of so many fine Trogen warriors.

Tragan had been venting about the matter ever since Dragol had been conducted into the tent. Tragan was still filled with resentment that the Darroks were being crewed entirely by Trogens in the first instance.

As Tragan explained it, the Avanorans wished to avail themselves of the far greater strength and stamina of the race of Trogens in comparison to men. The undeniable physical advantages of the Trogens had been a major part of the reason that had compelled the Unifier to use them in the task of manning the Darrok carriages.

Trogens were far more adept at jettisoning the great stores of large stones within the carriages affixed to the creatures' backs, both in terms of endurance as well as the girth of individual missiles. Enabling larger stones to be selected increased the destruction that could be levied upon the enemy. The average Trogen was able to lift up rocks of such size that two humans cooperating could barely carry.

Avanorans were also relative newcomers to the use of Harraks and the environment of the upper skies, having only adopted them at the Unifier's insistence, once He had come to power. It was true that Harraks had been imported to Avalos, and that a new population was being bred. It was also true that a new force ridden by Avanorans had been established, and that large numbers of human warriors were even now being trained.

Even so, as a whole, Trogens were still far more prepared and comfortable when undergoing the sensations of flight. The Trogen propensity for enduring physical hardship, and being able to withstand the highest altitudes far easier than humans, had sealed the choice of who would accompany the Darroks as their attendant crews. That choice had now been sorely abused, as the overconfident human Viscount Adhemar had left them so vulnerable.

Tragan's face had clouded with the blackest of rages as he had described in visceral terms what he would do to the viscount if he ever encountered the Avanoran. Dragol knew that it was best that the viscount remain in Avanor, as he literally would be torn limb from limb if Tragan ever got the man in his grasp.

Finally Tragan proceeded to the reasons for his summons of the two Trogen chieftains. As Dragol and Goras had perceived, their summons to Tragan's tent involved the changes that would be taking place in the wake of the debacle with the first Darrok raid.

For Goras, Tragan's wishes were not all that disruptive. Dragol, on the other hand, had to fight against mixed emotions churning within, as he listened to the orders from Tragan. A part of him was firmly bound to duty, and well pleased that the viscount's error in judgment on the first raid was being resolved with Trogen self-determination. Another part of him met the words of Tragan with chagrin, as he did not wish to be separated from Goras, and the other Trogens in Saxany, so close to the great battle.

"Dragol, you will take your warriors with you to accompany the Darroks, and defend them in their next raid upon the Five Realms. Other chieftains will join you with further sky warriors. No others among this alliance will respect Trogens. We must take control of this task by ourselves, fools that we were to think otherwise," the Trogen commander iterated acidly, his iron gaze fixated upon Dragol. "This is no order of the Lord Generals … It is mine, and they are not about to disagree. We will see that our brothers receive protection … this time."

The last words of the Trogen commander were strained and spoken through sharp, clenched teeth. Veins stood out along his thick neck and broad head, as Tragan continued to seethe.

Dragol had seen few Trogens so utterly livid as Tragan had been towards the unescorted mission that had resulted in so many slain Trogens. It had taken all of Dragol's might, and that of a few others, to restrain Tragan from going to assault one of the Lord Generals who was residing in the nearby Avanoran camp, shortly after the news had reached them.

It pleased Dragol greatly that initiative had been taken by the older Trogen commander, declaring an escort force irrespective of Avanor's desires. Like many of the higher-ranking Trogens, Dragol had felt scathing discomfort at following orders that he knew had originated from the Unifier's men.

He also felt deeply honored that Tragan had selected him for the task of protecting fellow Trogens serving upon the great Darroks. There would be no lack of resolve on his part to ensure the safety of the Trogen crews.

Tragan then turned towards Goras, and exclaimed in a thunderous voice. "The attack into the woods begins very soon. You must not allow any enemy to drive our scouts away. You must sweep any defenders from the skies, and you must be the eyes of the ground army. There can be no surprises. We must win this battle fast, so that the army can move through."

He raised his massive right hand and tightly clenched his fist, his eyes glaring at Goras. "We are to take no prisoners. The enemies of the Unifier are the enemies of us all. This is a war that will gain our land's long-desired freedom, and the liberation of so many of our brethren held all too long in bondage. For the freeing of our homelands, and our kind, go forth, now! Show them the strength of the Trogens!"

Both dismissed from Tragan's presence, Goras and Dragol nodded their heads deferentially, and swiftly strode from the inner tent. Outside of the tent, gathered nearby, were a number of veteran Trogen leaders who were anxiously awaiting their instructions.

"We go to the skies, to glories that will be remembered!" Dragol called to them, his gaze fiery with the passion burning within him. "Those with me, will go forth with the great Darroks. Those with Goras, must sweep the skies clear of our enemies. The invasion begins soon. War has come. Rely only on your weapons, your strength, and your fury! The Trogen is alone in this world, as our kind has always been, and it is only you that can speak with your arms and deeds. Speak now, with a thunderous voice!"

A loud, roaring cheer arose from the gathered Trogens, as they shouted their approval of Dragol's words with feverish intensity. Their eyes flashed with volcanic fires building towards an apex within them. They thrust their great blades and other weapons skyward, and continued their chants and shouts long after, as they thundered their consummate approval.

"Go forth, as this war begins!" bellowed Dragol, thrusting his own longblade furiously into the sky.

Without further reply, the ebullient warriors gathered around them turned and rushed off with vigor. They quickly spread the commands among the various Trogen warriors gathered into the war bands that would be commanded under Dragol and Goras.

An excitable frenzy ensued, as Trogens were soon running everywhere. Nervous Andamooran volunteers saw to the harnesses on the Harraks, as the light Andamooran horsemen currently in the adjoining camp looked on with unmistakable curiosity, from behind their face veils.

Other Trogens, scowling at being unable to immediately join their brethren, worked to aid the departing Trogen warriors with their equipment.

Arrow quivers were filled, extra bowstrings procured, supply packs buckled up, longblades sheathed in scabbards attached to baldrics, great lances and other long-hafted weapons brought forth, and rectangular shields were slung across the broad backs of the Trogen riders. The Harraks growled and pawed at the ground, as the proud creatures sensed the impatience and energy of their riders and masters.

In a brief passage of time, twenty-five Trogens were fully prepared to escort the Darroks with Dragol. Nearly seventy were readied to attend to Goras' company, all elated as they primed themselves for the beginning of the long-awaited battle for Saxany.

When all of the nearly one hundred warriors were ready and

assembled, word was swiftly conveyed to Dragol and Goras. Dragol listened to the updates regarding the disposition of the warriors, as he adjusted a newly acquired segmented iron helm in place, the attached mail aventail drooping down to rest around the sides and back of his neck. With the helm fitted upon his head, secured snugly with a leather chin-strap, Dragol turned towards Goras.

"Neither of us will be held back now," Dragol said, clamping a huge hand enthusiastically upon Goras' broad shoulder. As they were the last two to mount their steeds, the gathered warriors silently, and restlessly, awaited their commanders.

"Show them a warrior that is worthy to reside in Elysium, in the High Halls!" Goras urged Dragol with buoyant vigor.

"That both of us shall be worthy!" Dragol countered. "I shall return, and join with you, that we may smash the Saxans together."

"If I leave any for you," Goras retorted, rumbling with mirth.

"Then I will show the tribesmen a fury to behold, and I shall return in haste," Dragol replied, clasping the saddle, setting his booted foot into the bronze stirrup, and lithely mounting his Harrak, Rodor.

"For now, farewell, may the High Gods ride with you!" Goras exclaimed.

Eyes sparkling with a renewed vivacity, Dragol looked around at the throng of eager Trogen warriors around him.

"In honor of the Highest God, it begins!" he roared to a fully deafening acclamation from all the surrounding Trogens, both mounted and not.

Spurring his steed forth, he was the first to leave the ground by the power of the Harrak's great wings.

With zealous shouts, the envious Trogens remaining on the ground saluted their comrade warriors as they followed in the wake of Dragol up into the sky. Their ascent was like a rising thundercloud, blackened with ominous declarations of an imminent, violent maelstrom, that would manifest in a very short time to come.

Once the full mass of flying warriors had ascended, Dragol and Goras exchanged salutes, before separating to continue onward to their respective destinations.

As the wind whipped about his face, Dragol felt the bobbing and tilting of Rodor as the steed settled into its rhythmic pattern of flight. Dragol breathed a long, cathartic sigh of relief.

He was beginning to feel like a Trogen warrior once again.

DEGANAWIDA

The Grand Council had been convened, and for perhaps the first time since the very genesis of the Five Realms, it would not be held within a longhouse of the Onan. The damage from the attack had been too extensive on the Place of Far Seeing, and the longhouse harboring the Sacred Fire had been destroyed. There were no alternate structures left standing in a condition that could house the traditional fifty Great Sachems.

The remains of the village stood in a dismal pall under the cloud-saturated, ash-gray sky as dawn broke. The wreckage was like a lifeless corpse, once filled with the spirit of a vigilant and thriving people. The surviving Onan villagers had taken refuge within the deeper forest, aided by a diligent, tireless contingent of Onan warriors, and the calm resolve of the clan matrons.

The Onan were not alone in the upheaval. Most other villages across the lands of the Five Realms had also been abandoned, their future destruction all but conceded.

A good distance from both the village and the places where the villagers were encamped, close to the bank of a broad stream, the tribal sachems gathered in tense silence, ruminating on the dire situation.

The sachems of the Gayogohon and Onyota, the Younger Brother tribes of the great confederacy, sat together on one side of the gathering. The sachems of the Kanienke, Onan, and Onondowa, the Older Brother tribes of the confederacy, sat just opposite them.

Deganawida was greatly relieved that the Great Sachems from the other tribes had acted upon his warnings without delay, as few of the others had yet endured direct attacks upon their villages. It was a testament to the great respect that they and their village headmen, and other sachems, had for Deganawida. The Great Sachems had responded swiftly to attend the Grand Council, even as their villages were simultaneously emptied out.

A numerous force of scouts had been sent towards the western borders of the tribal lands, to patrol and search out any signs of the expected enemy intrusions. If the enemy decided to move, the sachems knew that word would have to be delivered with the greatest of haste.

The environment for the latest Grand Council was far different from what they had known before, yet it was still a surrounding that was both familiar and a part of them.

The sounds of the gentle, constant flow of water that filled the air had a soothing quality, as the broad stream coursed over the lip of a wide rock a short distance from where they were gathered. The water fell several feet down to where it resumed its forward journey once again.

The liquid sibilance was intertwined with the cracks and pops of wood within the fire that had been built in the center of the gathered sachems. Under the overcast skies, the mass of flickering red flames glowed in reflection upon their worry-ridden visages.

A welcome relief to all, the wood had been set aflame directly from the Sacred Fire. Tradition held that the Sacred Fire had been continuously tended and kept burning from the very beginning of the Five Realms, all the way to the present age.

The Sacred Fire had always been housed within a Grand Council Longhouse, located within a specially designated Onan village. It had always been carefully transferred whenever villages had been moved, and had become a deeply revered symbol of the spirit of tribal unity.

Several of the great boulders that had rained down upon Deganawida's village during the Darrok attack had smashed right through the center of the roof of the special Grand Council Longhouse. The barrage had brought the elm poles and bark panels crashing down upon the meticulously tended, and long-sustained, fire. The Grand Council Longhouse had been leveled in the torrent of direct impacts.

Where rampant fires had swiftly merged in some of the other communal longhouses, the rock, dust, and other debris had nearly smothered the Sacred Fire. A few tribal warriors had acted very rapidly, seeing what was happening, reacting with a desperate urgency. They lighted torches and even some large scraps of wood from the dying fire, hurrying onward with the cluster of small flames to start a more stable fire far beyond the base of the village's hill.

The other sachems had reacted with anguish and dismay at the dire news of how dangerously close the Sacred Fire had come to being extinguished, regarding it as a very dark omen. The air was thick with their brooding anxiety, and no amount of talk from Deganawida would easily allay their apprehensions.

It was almost indisputable that the Unifier had chosen that particular village of the Onan for a very precise reason: to be the first major target of the assault upon the tribal lands. The fact that the Sacred Fire was kept there, a symbol at the heart of all the tribes, was not lost on the other Great Sachems.

Taking place as the attack had during the night, the sachems also sensed that the Dark Brother had likely had a part in guiding the attack, or in identifying the village. That thought was very troubling, all the sachems knew that their longtime nemesis was both merciless and unpredictable. If the Dark Brother was openly aiding the Unifier, then it promised much more tragedy to come.

Those that had listened to tales of the brutal attacks from the night sky, from the mouths of those that had endured and barely survived them, were stricken to an even greater extent with a paralysis of worry. Deganawida could see the powerful grip of anxiety taking hold upon their faces.

As much as they could, the Great Sachems labored to hold onto the traditions of the Grand Council. The circumstances surrounding them were nearly overwhelming, as they started the meeting very early in the day to address the many matters at hand. They desired to gain every moment that they could when the powers of the Dark Brother were believed to be at their most reduced.

The Grand Council had passed through the early rituals, including the sharing of the symbolic tobacco pipe that was reverently passed among the tribes' Great Sachems. The convocation offered open prayers of thanksgiving to the Creator for the formation of their confederacy. Much was rendered in the form of solemn songs and chants, the singing evoking the deep emotions resonating within the tribal sachems.

The great wampum belt of the Five Realms, made of highly treasured colored shells, was prominently displayed. The rectangular belt had five images fashioned upon it. A prominent image of a white tree resided in the center of the sacred belt, symbolic of the Tree of Peace. It heralded the spirit of the Great Law, which had brought such harmony amongst the five tribes.

Two pine trees, each made up of stacked white triangles, stood upon either side of the larger tree image. All four pine tree images and the Tree of Peace depiction were set against a purple background.

The group of trees represented the endurance of the five tribes and their fellowship with one another, with the central image specifically representing the Onan as the Keepers of the Sacred Fire.

Oral tradition held that the mysterious, seemingly divine founder of their confederacy, who had vanished from among them unexpectedly, had bequeathed that very belt to their ancestors when the first Grand Council was formed. That patron Wizard had long been gone from sight, but the belt still remained, even in the wake of the recent, devastating tragedy.

Nearby there were a couple of other items on prominent display.

One featured five long strings of white wampum shells that were bundled together at one end. The individual strings had been brought together by a designated sachem of each tribe, to be ceremonially bundled at the beginning of the Grand Council. As a group, they symbolized the coming together of the Five Realms' confederacy.

Another cluster of wampum strings was also in evidence, with similar connotations. Arranged into the semblance of a complete circle, fifty separate wampum strings had been used. Each of the wampum strings signified one of the Great Sachems present, the circle complete only if all fifty were present.

Most of the Great Sachems were very familiar with each other. The golden age of harmony that had continued to exist among the five tribes of the confederacy had resulted in the continuance of many wise sachems being appointed to the Grand Council, all with a wealth of life experience.

Like those of Deganawida's own tribe, the clan matrons of the other villages and tribes, in such a climate of peace and stability, had had to make few changes or appointments of new sachems. What few appointments had been made in the recent years leading up to the attack were largely because of a particular Great Sachem's death.

With the terrible aftermath of the attack upon the village, involving the suffering of so many, and the deeply troubling omens such as the near extermination of the Sacred Fire, it was fortuitous that many of the Great Sachems held a common friendship and history together. Consensus, as at all Grand Councils, would be utterly vital before any collective action on the part of the Five Realms could be undertaken.

All who wished to speak, would be given time, and any single disagreement would be enough to bring an initiative to a complete halt.

Beyond the need for full agreement, there were some new challenges facing the Great Sachems at the makeshift Grand Council. Death, with no regard for either friendships or history, had abruptly caused the need for five new faces to be raised together to the Council for the very first time.

Subsequent attacks, taking place before the alarm had been fully spread across the woodlands, had visited several other villages. The Darroks had returned, and nothing had challenged their presence this time. Only the swift dispatch of messengers had likely spared a great number of other villages, whose matrons and sachems had wisely sought refuge in the forests before their own villages were visited with the death and devastation that had come down from the skies. The more recent attacks had caught some villages unawares, resulting in even greater burdens for the maintenance of a proper Grand Council.

The Grand Councils were normally convened once each year, with the exception of the times needed to raise a new member or to address a special, urgent situation. The deadly attacks upon the other villages had left no less than five Great Sachems dead in their wake, each of whom required a traditional ceremony and the immediate raising up of a new Council member to their place.

Beyond that immediate need for new Grand Council sachems, Deganawida's gravity regarding what the attack represented and heralded, reinforced by the signs of looming invasion, was reason enough to formally call the Grand Council together.

The clan matrons had understood the severe nature of the crisis, moving with great haste to reach consensus in appointing new sachems to the Grand Council. Despite their own losses and pain amid the sudden chaos, the clan matrons focused upon the need to repair the Grand Council to wholeness. They saw the extreme importance of preserving one of the greater traditions that bonded all of their tribes and peoples together.

The new men chosen for the Grand Council were sent with haste, to be raised up to take the place of those who had fallen. As it had always been, there had to be ten Gayogohon, nine Onyota, fourteen Onan, nine Kanienke, and eight Onondowa sachems present to complete the Grand Council. With calm hearts, and drawing upon their richness of wisdom, love for their people, and reason, the matrons had succeeded in naming five exceptional men to heal the Grand Council, and regenerate its strength and authority.

An ancient staff, carved with symbols representing the fifty sachems, had been presented at the Grand Council along with an oration covering the Great Law. In other less tumultuous times, the staff would have then been presented at the villages of the Great Sachem who had died, at which time the traditional titles of the fifty sachems would be given along with a recitation of the Great Law. Village clans that were not of the clan that the dead Great Sachem had belonged to would then come forward, to give a special oration of rebirth, consolation, and reformation. They would also serve to aid in the task of the burial of the Great Sachem, relieving the sorrowing clan of the onerous task.

It was a grand ceremony that honored the one who had fallen, cherished the unity and bonds among the tribes, and gave hope and consolation to the grieving village. It was a tradition that brought forth the compassion and fellowship that the tribes had for each other within those of their own tribe and village. In such a dark and foreboding time, it now seemed to be an absolute necessity for the great numbers who were personally grief-stricken by the devastating attacks.

It was all very unprecedented. Never before had five sachems been struck down at once. The widespread suffering among the attacked villages, including those that had not suffered the loss of a Great Sachem, created a seemingly insurmountable task for the bringing of such a ceremony to the villages.

Clans serving to arrange for burial and make the address of rebirth for the grieving clan of a slain sachem, in turn, would be the clan attended to for the loss of their own sachem. So many had been scarred that it strained the best intentions of their traditions just to provide a little comfort and spiritual healing among their people.

While there seemed to be not nearly enough time, and too many pressing needs, the Great Sachems were resolved to try and salvage as much as they could of their traditions, and the special spirit-healing ceremony. The new members of the Grand Council, at the very least, had been raised up, and a complete, restored Grand Council could now see to the needs of the Five Realms. The most urgent of those needs was about to be addressed by the greatest among the exalted sachems: the Onan Great Sachem who held the first place on the Grand Council, Deganawida.

With a bundle of five arrows in one hand, Deganawida stood

resolutely next to a raised pole, on which he had placed an elaborate belt of shells. White shells formed the outline of a man against a purple background. Within the outline of the man was a representation of a flame.

It was understood among the sachems that the image represented Deganawida's position, as the honored sachem of the Onan in whose village the Sacred Fire had been kept. The other sachems had similar belts, with varying symbols arranged in colored shells upon them, which were cradled reverently in their hands.

He stood with a solemn expression on his face and looked to each of the other tribal sachems. By the time that he stood to address what was the most precarious matter, there was not much time before night arrived, raising another cause for concern in regards to their traditions.

Grand Councils always disbanded before dark fully settled, as the night was held to be the dominion of the Dark Brother of their sacred lore. No discussions or decisions could be made at night, the sachems believed, without the risk of the Dark Brother's malignant influence.

With critical decisions of great magnitude facing them, Deganawida knew that another breach of long-held customs would be too much of a burden to levy upon the badly shaken men; especially one involving deep-seeded fears of the Dark Brother's ability to infiltrate minds and hearts, and sway them to his will.

He could only hope to gain their full consensus before the shroud of night had settled into place, for even if just one of them objected there would be no decision rendered.

"We gather together, away from our villages … as if we were a council of war. There is no Council Longhouse for us to go to. The villages themselves are no longer homes, but places of danger and death," he began in a level, strong voice, looking slowly around the full circumference of gathered sachems. "A time has come upon us that no ancestor of ours ever saw. A war is coming upon us all … it comes to destroy us … it is a matter for our war sachems … it is a matter for our Grand Council."

He paused for a moment, letting the distressing words sink in.

"This war does not come to conquer us, and seek that we may bend our knee to a new ruler of our people. As we have rejected the Unifier, so He has decided to rid us from these lands," he continued. "This war comes to slay every one of us, from the greatest of our warriors, to the child just born. It cannot be reasoned with. It cannot be traded with. It wishes to take our soul. Nothing less.

"I know that many of you cannot believe that this is happening. Yet it would be your death not to believe, and the death of those you love of your village, your tribe, your clans, and all of your greater family in the Five Realms.

"I know that many of you will have strong thoughts and feelings. I only hope that we may reach consensus in the manner of our great people."

Deganawida concluded for the time being, sensing that there were some among the throng of sachems wanting to voice the thoughts in their heads and the feelings of their hearts. As he took his wampum belt up for the moment, another member of the Grand Council rose to speak.

"Deganawida, most honored sachem of the Grand Council, and of the Onan. None would dispute that you see a terrible danger. This is no easy matter for us to understand. We have had no quarrel with Gallea. We have traded the pelts of the beaver for years with them," the new speaker stated, after hanging his own shell-belt on the pole, moments after Deganawida had taken his away.

He was a thin-featured Kanienke named Orenregowah. His antlered headdress held three prominent feathers, as did those of the other Kanienke sachems. His sharp, dark eyes held a level gaze towards Deganawida, set behind a hawk-like nose that fit well with his distinguished position as a member of the Hawk Clan.

Orenregowah continued, "They have no cause to make war upon us. They have given us the strong metal for our weapons, our arrows, and for the things of our village. We have lived alongside their lands for long ages before my father, and his father before him. There is no tale of a war with them that I know."

Quietly, he turned to sit back down, taking his wampum belt. Deganawida arose once again, and hung up his own.

"Orenregowah of the noble Kanienke, the lack of reason is what makes this so hard to understand. There is no harm ... no offense ... that we have done to Gallea or to any other. We have kept our faith with them. We have traded in good faith with them, and they with us.

"An age has come when they have surrendered their will, and we have kept ours. We have rejected the Unifier. Now the price is being paid, and a greater price is yet to be paid. Your brothers and sisters in the alliance, the Onan, have lost many, many lives. My own home village has been destroyed, as have others.

"This is only the beginning. I do not wish to see our people, our brothers and sisters from any of our tribes, slaughtered in such a way," Deganawida staunchly declared, replacing the shell-belt on the pole when finished.

The remembrance of the painful losses from the attack weighed down greatly upon his heart, riddled as it was with numerous spiritual wounds.

"What of Midragard? Do we not hold friendship and trade with them? It has been a long age since we have quarreled with them. The tales are still known among our people, but the arrow no longer flies between our peoples. They are great warriors. Do they serve this Unifier? Will they not stand with us?" a Great Sachem of the Onondowa, Shadekaronyes stated, hanging and taking down his shell-belt in the manner of the other speakers.

His large, dark eyes and stoic face regarded Deganawida closely. Deganawida could see past Shadekaronyes's outer facade, and knew that it hid the rising fears which were now assaulting his spirit and mind.

"Shadekaronyes of the Onondowa, my good friend, we do hold a deep friendship with the people of Midragard. It has long been that way. I do not think that they would serve the Unifier. Messengers have already been sent to the ones that are nearest to us, on the island in the Great Waters. We do not yet know their full reply," Deganawida admitted. He started to turn to take his shell-belt, before drawing his gaze around the faces of the gathered sachems. He then concluded with deep sincerity, "I believe ... very strongly, my brothers ... that they will stand with us if the storm should break."

Deganawida knew that his path was uncertain. It was important that questions and any challenges were spoken aloud, or he would have no chance at gaining consensus.

Always, it had been the way of the tribes to openly discuss any initiative. Deganawida had to make sure that others spoke freely. Even so, it was still a few moments before the next sachem stood to place his own shell-belt on the pole. Deganawida was not surprised at the delay, as he knew that many of the sachems were carefully working through the situation in their own minds.

"What is your counsel, Deganawida of the Onan? You have always spoken truly to us. The Light Brother and the Creator have favored you greatly with wisdom. You have spoken to us of the danger, but you have not told us of the answer to the question that faces this council. We would hear what you believe should be done," stated Deshayenah, another sachem of the Onondowa.

The confidence had not been lightly given, for Deshayenah, as Deganawida knew, was one of the wisest and eldest among the Onondowa. He was a first Great Sachem of the Onondowa, of the Firaken clan.

Eyes turned back to Deganawida as he got up once again to face them.

"I am most honored by your generous words, Deshayenah of the Onondowa. If I have been given any gift, I only hope that I use it well and return it to my Creator in a greater manner, one that has done well by our people. I shall always speak what is truly in my heart to you, my brothers. What I have to say is no easy thing. It comes with no easy price … and it brings great risk."

Deganawida paused for a moment, to take in the somber faces surrounding him. Several mouths were pensive, and many brows were furrowed in deep concern. Yet there was little that he could read in their expressions to know whether they understood the vital need for consensus, and the imminence of their peril.

"As we have always done, we must move as one will, as we have always made decisions of the Grand Council in consensus. I ask for you to listen to me now, and heed my words more than you ever have before. Know that this is the hardest counsel that I could offer you. It is a terrible thing that I ask, but there is no other path that I can see. My heart tells me that we must move our people to the south and east, towards the shores of the Great Waters," Deganawida stated, with great solemnity. He spoke slowly, letting each word settle upon the throng of Great Sachems.

"It is our only chance. The villages, as you know, are no protection. The west is not a choice, as our enemies will be striking with great power from that direction. Our nearest hope for help lies to the east. We must seek help from others beyond our lands, and we must move our people as far from harm as we can. We cannot remain here."

When Deganawida sat down again, it was with the heaviest of hearts. He realized what he was asking of all of them. An unsettling silence permeated the area, a foreboding and fearful atmosphere taking hold, as the sachems grasped exactly what he was proposing. There was an even longer silence before the next sachem rose to make the first comments following Deganawida's response.

"If we have consensus, do we bring the tribes together and then go east? Or does each tribe move on its own?" Wadondaherha queried.

He was a Great Sachem of the Gayogohon, the northernmost tribe in the Five Realms. Their lands bordered the remnants of the warlike tribal groups that had long ago held power over most of the eastern forests. It was little secret that these brutal tribes were now aligning with the enemy. The pressure upon the Gayogohon, in particular, was very considerable, as they were likely to find themselves beset from two directions at once.

"We have held our enemies back for many long years," Wadondaherha continued. He then added, before taking his seat again. "They watch us closely, and will surely seek to fall upon us as we leave our lands. It is better if we were to make haste to join our numbers with the other tribes, than to try to make the journey by ourselves, where a stalking enemy can better find a moment to strike."

Deganawida nodded as he rose up, taking his place in the center yet again.

"Together is the only chance we will have," Deganawida stated firmly. "There will be no villages left standing soon. No one tribe among us can withstand the attack that is coming. We must bring together our strength."

"And the war sachems?" a shorter, stocky sachem of the Onyota, named Ronyadashayouh, asked Deganawida. "And the Bregas? The Bregas were the greatest of gifts from this land to our people."

"Ayenwatha, a war sachem of the Onan, of the Firaken Clan, has sent messengers out with the ceremonial leaf to all the tribes. We will soon know who will join him," Deganawida said, looking to the relatively youthful Great Sachem.

Like Ayenwatha, Ronyadashayouh was a skilled sky rider, and it was no surprise that his concerns included the noble race of the Brega. The Bregas were precious to all of the tribes, and Deganawida knew that any undertaking would have to involve an attempt to preserve the winged creatures.

"The Bregas should be brought along with us. Those of the west do not know the Bregas or their ways. We must try to save them, just as we try to save our people," Deganawida answered.

"And what of the Wendaton? You have heard Wadondaherha of the Gayogohon. The Wendaton ever wait on the border of the Gayogohon. They have long hungered for all of our lands. And we have warred with all of the Anishin tribes, but it is also the Gayogohon that are next to lands where other Anishin tribes yet dwell. You know the scouts have said that several from Anishin tribes move among the enemy," Ronyadashayouh stated firmly. "The Gayogohon have suffered much to hold the Wendaton and others at bay. They will take our lands if we leave."

"They may for a time, yes," Deganawida responded bluntly, for he could not soften the words. "You know that they serve our enemy, and our enemy may reward them with our lands."

"Curses on them. They are no different than a tribe of witches," Ronyadashayouh responded, all but spitting the words out after he sprang up and took his own belt. His expression darkened, tension and frustration chiseled deeply into his face. "I do not dispute you, Deganawida. But we must defend ourselves. Still, I must ask ... what will happen when we reach the Great Waters? There is nowhere we can go then. Would it not be a trap?"

"We must keep our people alive," Deganawida replied strongly, endeavoring to remind Ronyadashayouh of the priorities facing them. "It will do us no good to have our tribes slaughtered. It is a trap if we stay here. And we can be surrounded here. I have faith that Midragard will honor our friendship, in a brave and generous manner.

"It is not as the days far in the past, when their raiders first came to our lands, and some tried to settle. As Shadekaronyes of the Onondowa has said, there has not been any war among our peoples for many long years. They are a people of great courage and will. They also do not bow their knee to this Unifier. I do not think that they will abandon us. We have little other choice than to trust them. We have hope and a chance to the south and east. I cannot see the same if we remain here."

There were many nods of assent among the gathered tribal sachems. Deganawida knew that they all felt a distinct difference in the manner of their trade with Gallea and Midragard.

The Gallean merchants were very discreet in their trade, as many of their clergy condemned association with the forest-dwellers, and their strange religious practices. To the east, many genuine friendships had risen up among the Midragardans and those of the Five Realms, including shared visits, feasting, and exchanges of gifts.

Gallea had always looked upon the Five Realms as something savage, primitive, and pagan, where Midragard's sons and daughters had recognized a proud and honorable people, with a resolute spirit. As each sachem reflected on the individual Midragardans that they knew and traded with in recent years, Deganawida was confident that they could not help but believe his judgement, as to who would remain faithful to them.

Yadajiwaken, one of the newly risen members of the Grand Council, then hung his own shell-belt for the very first time. "Some among the Anishin are not our enemies at this time. Some have vessels that can travel the Great Waters far enough to reach the first islands. We should send our elderly, and the smallest children, mothers, and the great matrons. If the Midragardans decide to help, then the ones most vulnerable can take refuge on those islands."

"You will be an excellent member of this Grand Council, Yadajiwaken of the Onan," Deganawida stated approvingly, seeing that even in one of their darkest hours, new individuals were stepping forward with wisdom guiding them. "You speak truly. There are Anishin villages out on the eastern shores who are not at war with us. It would not be difficult to reach them."

Yadajiwaken looked very pleased at Deganawida's words, though he made no reply. After he returned to his place, he was followed by several others who spoke of the difficulties facing an exodus to the southeast, though Deganawida noted that none of the others counseled anything in direct opposition to Deganawida's own advice. At last, there were no others that desired to speak.

Glancing upward, Deganawida saw that daylight was beginning to fade. The time had arrived for decision, and he hoped that there had been enough discussion. He feared for the worst, knowing that many lesser decisions of Grand Councils had taken days to deliberate and decide. What he had asked of them was monumental, and unprecedented, in comparison to those issues.

"Now, we must see if there is consensus. There is little time, and the day is nearly gone. Before we are in danger of coming under the influence of the Dark Brother, I put this matter before you to decide,"

Deganawida said. "What do you say?"

One by one, the sachems indicated their opinion on the matter. Even when the first twenty of the sachems had agreed, Deganawida knew that he could not get his hopes up, as even one sachem's disagreement was enough to negate a cohesive decision.

Yet he could not stop his hopes from rising, as the thirtieth sachem affirmed agreement, then the fortieth, and finally the forty-ninth. Ronyadashayouh, the fiery Onyota sachem, was the last.

He rose, looked toward Deganawida with a resolute expression. "I, Ronyadashayouh, sachem of the Onyota tribe and member of the Shadow Flyer clan, agree that we must act as one body, and move to the east as Deganawida has spoken wisely of. As I am the last to speak my mind on this matter, you now have full consensus."

The tension building within Deganawida dissipated instantly, and he almost sighed aloud in his sheer relief. The Five Realms had not been saved, but their chances of survivial would be much improved. There was utterly no doubt within Deganawida about that aspect.

The consensus had been reached just in time, for the light of day expired just as unanimous agreement had been attained. In a way, as dusk settled, the Light Brother passed jurisdiction over to the Dark Brother, as it had always been.

While agreement had been attained, not everything was a relief. As daylight ebbed, Deganawida still could not help but think that the light of one age was coming to an end, and that a new, much darker age beckoned.

AYENWATHA

Deeper in the forest, in a more remote part from where the villagers sheltered, another council transpired the following day. With the signs of invasion imminent, the summons had been sent out well before the momentous decision of the Grand Council.

Ayenwatha had sent the messengers afar in great haste, bearing the sacred leaf of the tobacco, and braving great danger on Brega steeds to reach all parts of the tribal lands. They had issued the invitation to the War Council being called by Ayenwatha. In all cases, the recipients of the summons had smoked the tobacco leaf with the messengers, in distinctive pipes fitted with narrow axe blades at their farther ends.

Setting out immediately for the Onan lands, tribal warriors flocked in from all around towards the Place of Far Seeing. When the designated day arrived, Ayenwatha was able to convene a very large War Council; one that was united in purpose and resolve.

Great numbers of warriors had answered the summons from all over the Five Realms. It was a concentration of the strongest, the bravest, the swiftest, and the most resolute of the able males from the five tribes. When a few contingents from the Gayogohon had arrived, and every tribe had warriors present, the ceremonies had soon gotten underway.

As with the Grand Council, the great War Council worked to keep the tribal traditions honored as much as possible. A shell-belt made up of white figures with hands joining, set against a red background, was displayed to symbolize both the presence of war and the alliance among the warriors of the confederacy.

Ayenwatha, in what was perhaps his greatest hour, was convening the largest War Council known to tribal memory. As the one who had called the War Council, Ayenwatha was accepted by those who had responded to his summons as the leader of the coming effort.

The Onan war sachem and honored member of the Firaken Clan gained widespread goodwill from the massed warriors when he named his war lieutenants. Five were chosen for the high honor, one from each of the tribes of the Five Realms. Each one was an exceptional choice, well regarded among the people of their own tribe, as well as the populaces of the other tribes.

Discussion of what was to come, and what the tribal warriors needed to achieve, then occupied the warriors for quite some time. Deliberations had focused not only on methods of conducting the defense of the tribal lands, and speculations concerning the enemy, but also about the issue of supplies for a sustained fight.

Those arriving at the War Council had come prepared, with pouches at their belts filled with corn meal, and quivers filled with arrows. Whatever remaining supplies that could be used by the warriors would be gathered up from the ruins of the stricken villages, as well as those that remained intact.

Even so, food would run low and quivers would empty if the fight dragged on for any considerable length of time. There would be few opportunities for hunting, especially with the woods filling up with battling warriors. Plans and contingencies had to be made so that warriors did not weaken from hunger, and bows still had arrows to loose.

The forest had then been filled with the sounds of chanting and rhythmic drums, as the warriors engaged in ceremonial dancing and ritual purification. There was little available for the traditional war feast, but the warriors ate what they could, and viewed the meager amounts of food in its more symbolic light.

Ayenwatha had then guided the long streams of warriors back to his destroyed village for what was to become a very contemplative moment. The long march through the woods had allowed the warriors a period of inner reflection, culminating at the site of the unprovoked, brutal attack on the Onan village where the Sacred Fire had been harbored.

Within the village was a single timber pole, painted red. It had somehow emerged unscathed from the withering storm of rocks that had showered down upon the village, and Ayenwatha was determined that it would serve its intended purpose once again.

Surrounded as it was by the broken shells of longhouses, and the ponderous silence of the abandoned village, the final stage of the preparation for war was undertaken in a very emotional and heartfelt environment. The single red pole stood unscathed as a symbol of defiance, and survival, within the terrible scene of tragedy.

At first, there was a profound silence, as the horde of warriors assembled in a great mass around the red war pole. One by one, the warriors then began to build themselves into a frenzy, drums thumping as chants rose up into the skies. Over a very long, poignant sequence, the warriors of the five tribes moved in to strike the red pole, as they would soon strike their enemies.

Hundreds upon hundreds filed by, as Ayenwatha looked over the moving ceremony, with a grim expression on his face and a maelstrom of emotion within. By the time the last warrior had struck the red pole, well over two thousand five hundred warriors had passed it.

It would be the final ritualistic act before the war band would disperse to begin their defense. The tribes no longer practiced the dog-feast that had once crowned such a ceremonial war preparation. That was from a darker period, in which the flesh of prisoners was consumed, and the enemy was seen to be no better than a dog. Ayenwatha knew very well that the Great Sachem Deganawida, as well as the Wizard named Deganawida, that had originally founded the Great Law, abhorred such practices.

Even so, Ayenwatha felt a dark rage building deep within him as he looked out over the charred, jagged husks of the longhouses in back of the throng of warriors. As far as Ayenwatha saw things, the current enemy was far lesser in stature than the least among dogs. A primal urge was burning within him, empowered by his great anger, begging for a vicious revenge that would leave a Gallean town or village in such ruins.

The black rage swelled up within Ayenwatha, until his lips began to twitch with the venomous feelings reverberating throughout him. Perhaps it would not be such a bad thing to reintroduce some of the older ways.

He would not have to go so far as to bring the eating of human flesh back, but he could at least bring back some of the extended tortures meted out to the prisoners of war, before the consuming of their flesh had taken place. As far as Ayenwatha now felt, it was the least that the attackers deserved for their unprovoked assault upon his village.

The malefic sentiments shocked Ayenwatha out of his consuming anger. Almost immediately, he admonished himself for giving life to such vile, wicked feelings. Whether or not the Dark Brother was somehow working an influence upon him, he was acquiescing to mordant passions. Summoning up the force of his will, he choked down the bile with a considerable effort.

The Gallean villagers were no more deserving of such a horrible fate, than the tribal villagers had been. Ayenwatha could not, at any cost, lose sight of that. If he did, he would be no better than the Unifier. Perhaps he would even be worse, as the Unifier was still being true to His own evil purposes, while Ayenwatha would be shaming everything that he had stood for, and embraced throughout his life.

Ayenwatha forced his emotions farther down, and brought his thoughts back to bear more fully upon the more practical matters facing him. The ranks of the tribal warriors would undoubtedly expand in the coming days, but Ayenwatha now had a very strong war band to lead. It was evident that a potent tribal force would be in place to oppose the enemy, when they drove into the forest from the west.

The tribal warriors would still be heavily outnumbered, but they would know the terrain, and would be superior in their woodland movements. Ayenwatha's warriors would need to hit the enemy hard and swiftly from the shadows.

If the warriors could avoid being caught in a conflict of brute force, then a chance remained to inflict wound after wound upon the aggressors. Even the mightiest of bears encountered in the woods could eventually be worn down.

The thought left Ayenwatha with a sliver of hope, as he exited the devastated village with a river of determined tribal warriors following in his wake.

AELFRIC

The outer scouts, those that had not been captured or slain, had brought back several more foreboding reports to the main Saxan encampment on the Plains of Athelney. The reports merely confirmed the information that Aelfric had gained already, but in another sense they revealed the sheer scale of what the Saxans were going to face, and it was far greater than any of them had ever imagined.

Incomparably vast, the enemy encampments were now rooted firmly in place. The discipline of the Saxans' enemy was also very much in evidence.

The arrival of Andamoor's huge columns had embodied both qualities. Teeming ranks of well-ordered Andamooran infantry, bearing tall shields of hide, and distinctive, long bamboo spears, had fanned out shortly after their arrival over the horizon. They had provided a warding perimeter of living fighters, while trenches were swiftly dug by other Andamoorans around the boundaries of their encampment.

The interior of the marked encampment was soon filled with the presence of thousands of warriors, horsemen, pack mules, and a huge number of the strange, hump-backed creatures that were so unique to the Andamooran contingent. Tents of a wide range of varieties, from small, simple constructs, to what looked to be ornate, lavish pavillions, were erected. Hosts of vividly colorful banners were soon waving in the breezes where they signified the location of high-ranking Andamoorans.

There had already been a few fierce skirmishes with small bands of swift, lightly armed horsemen, who were serving as auxiliaries and scouts for the Andamooran force. The brief encounters with the Andamooran outriders had drawn a little blood on both sides, though the enemy scouts were always quick to withdraw.

In and of itself, the Andamooran ranks would have constituted an invasion threat, but Aelfric was faced with the presence of no less than two other enormous contingents.

The banners of many great lords of Avanor were now flying high over the masses of tents in the middle enemy encampment.

Small bands of foraging Avanoran squires had recently been encountered by Saxan patrols, but these were swiftly driven off, wherever they were found. Squires were of little concern, as Aelfric knew the core strength of the Avanorans lay with the multitude of veteran knights quartering within the encampment.

Most daunting to Aelfric, there was considerable evidence of a great siege train being present with the Avanorans, as well as a host of wagons and supply carts filled to capacity to reinforce the Avanoran ranks. The siege train and overabundance of supplies indicated the intention of a long, thoroughly prosecuted campaign, which was exactly what Aelfric had feared.

The third force, from Ehrengard itself, was now resting at ease amid its own tents and considerable array of supply wagons. Stately, powerful bishops with strong retinues, exalted princes far removed from their lofty, crag-surmounting castles, and mighty bond-knights alike were quartered all throughout the Ehrengardian camp.

The Saxan scouts had not been able to confirm whether ranks of the dreaded Halmlander mercenaries were currently settled among the Ehrengardian camp, though Aelfric would have been very surprised if they were not there. The uncertainty was quite bothersome nonetheless, even though Aelfric was making all plans as if the murderous hirelings of Ehrengard would be arrayed against the Saxans on the very first day of battle.

Aelfric stood quietly with a pair of highly respected ealdormen, Morcar of Wessachia, and Byrtnoth of Sussachia. They listened intently to the latest scouting reports, far away from the ears of others in the camp.

A light, crisp breeze danced along the air, and the bright, clear skies above contrasted starkly with the dark essence of the growing threats on the ground, just beyond the horizon. The lazy, low-lying white clouds that traversed the sky foretold no hint of storms whatsoever, though Aelfric knew that a tremendous one was right on the verge of breaking upon all of Saxany.

It was a day that would normally have found the ealdormen and their thanes out hawking or hunting within the woods of Saxany, where the only dangers would be falling from a horse, or getting attacked by a great boar or other fierce beast caught at bay. It was not an environment reflective of the grim reports currently being given to the prominent Saxans.

"These creatures with humps, I do not know of them, or what they are called, but they seemed to be used to carry packs and men in the manner of horses," stated one of the scouts, a wiry youth named Osmod.

Aelfric saw the young scout's eyes reflecting a great wonder at witnessing the foreign dress and contents of the Andamooran ranks. The Unifier had been very wise in assembling His invasion force, as the exotic nature and appearances of the Andamoorans would undoubtedly have an unsettling effect on men who had never before beheld their like.

"If the beasts carry packs and men, then they are likely no greater threat than a horse," Aelfric responded firmly, seeking to encourage the wavering young man. "No matter how strange their appearance, there is likely little more to worry about regarding them."

"We could take the battle right to them," Morcar suggested then to Aelfric, a determined edge in his voice. "We could take our army and strike them now, before all three armies are fully settled, or can array together."

Aelfric looked over at the rough-countenanced, thickly bearded ealdorman. Like Byrtnoth and himself, Morcar was truly a likeness of the hilly, mountainous, and forested terrain that they all hailed from. They were of the blood of the older Northern Kingdom, which had so capably endured for long ages before the union with the southern realm had taken place.

The Saxan majordomo took great comfort being among his fellow men from the cherished lands spanning the north and north east of the Kingdom of Saxany. A long, hard-won heritage was shared among them, and he could fully relate to the fiery passions that drove such men.

The will to meet a challenge burned strongly indeed. There was no lack of bravery within the man, but Aelfric knew well that Morcar was very quick to judgment, and was often impatient towards any extended counsel. Aelfric did not have such a tendency, which he knew was a significant reason why he had risen to such a preeminent standing with King Alcuin.

"It would be a good course, Morcar, if we knew exactly where their full force of sky warriors was gathered. We have only seen small groups of enemy scouts in the skies around their encampments, which have harried and kept our own few back.

"Their total force is clearly growing with every incoming report. They have far more horsemen than we do. Of that there is no doubt at all. If we attack their encampments, and commit our own forces in full, they could unleash a punishing attack with a great force of horsemen on our vulnerable flanks. Here, arrayed on the plains, we can break them against our shield wall," Aelfric stated carefully.

Morcar's brows furrowed in apparent frustration, and though his mouth tightened, no argument was forthcoming. Aelfric knew that the ealdorman had inwardly accepted the reason and logic in Aelfric's reply, even if the taste of it was bitter. He could see the Ealdorman of Wessachia's discomfort in holding his passions at bay.

"You speak truly," the northern ealdorman huffed, "but this is a tremendous agony to a spirit such as mine. I would strike at their heart like a bolt of lightning from the sky … and sear it to ashes."

Aelfric allowed a thin smile to show on his face. It was one of empathic understanding, and in no way demeaning to the impulses and fires burning within Morcar.

"And I think you would indeed strike at them all by yourself, were it not for the men under your command," Aelfric responded. "There will be time enough for battle, my friend, when the enemy will surely come to know the skill of your arms, and those of the fighters of Wessachia … those here with us, and those with your great thane Aethelstan, warding the forested hills north and east of here."

Morcar straightened up a little, appearing somewhat placated by the flattering words from Aelfric. They were not spoken untruthfully, for Aelfric did indeed respect the valorous character and exceptional skill at arms of the veteran warrior before him.

"What do the scouts say of the current strength of this army from Andamoor?" Aelfric then asked of Osmod, all vestiges of mirth leaving his face, as his expression hardened again.

"Thousands upon thousands, upon more thousands," Osmod

replied somberly, his face taking on a hint of dismay as he voiced the words.

Knowing how swift the Andamooran outriders were reputed to be, Aelfric had a sinking feeling that the enemy had intentionally allowed some scouts to draw close enough to behold the colossal size of the invader's army. The conveyance of reports concerning the daunting sight among the ranks of the defenders would undoubtedly serve the invader's wishes. Fear was also a powerful weapon, and how the Saxans handled it would undeniably be a determining factor in their chances.

Yet there was one other truth that was evident in the reports of the immense size of the enemy ranks. It was paramount in Aelfric's planning.

The attack of the enemy could be expected to come very soon. Armies of such astounding size could not linger for long in the field with the constant demands for prodigious quantities of food and drink. Steeds, draft animals, warriors, and camp attendants alike needed to be sustained, and armies of the size facing the Saxans would be voracious in their requirements.

Adding to the issue of supplies, many warriors among the enemy contingents would only be expecting to serve for a certain amount of time, and a very limited one at that. It was the way of the western kingdoms, in terms of how forces that were not hired outright were levied. Obligations owed to lords were set in very defined terms, most being just around six weeks a year.

It was likely that many of the Avanoran and Ehrengardian knights that had just arrived over the horizon were of such a disposition. If the campaign lasted beyond the designated period, such knights would be in their rights to go back to their homelands. Aelfric was well aware of this reality, and it constituted a significant part of his speculation regarding the enemy's inclinations.

The enemy leaders would seek to create a major breach into the Saxan Kingdom before such knights would expect to return to their home territories. Others could be summoned, or brought up in time, and still others would remain with the tantalizing lure of acquiring new land holdings, but not all the elements among the invaders would remain intact for a sustained period of time. The longer that the Saxans could resist the enemy, the more possible it was that complications would arise within the invader's ranks.

The past few weeks were little more than a hazy blur within Aelfric's tumultuous mind. Images of all kinds rushed through his inner sight, some clear, and others more vague.

He vividly recalled the momentous confrontations with the Unifier's emissaries in Alcuin's court at Aixen, and the ensuing acceptance of the fact that war would be unavoidable with the forcible expulsion of the Unifier's representatives. He also remembered the lighting of the beacons, and the sending of numerous messengers upon horses and sky steeds throughout the lands, to spread the call to arms.

Aelfric thought about the musters and how they had swelled, and had then set out in their lengthy columns upon horse and foot. He could even now see the pennons fluttering proudly in the breezes, and hear the wagon and cart wheels creaking with the strain incurred under their heavy loads of arms and supplies.

Everything had led right up to the moment that he now found himself in, converging within the quiet, resigned intake of breath before the thunderous roar of battle sounded. Aelfric looked outward, far past Morcar, Osmod, and Byrtnoth, towards the flowing grass blanketing the open plain and stretching beyond the farthest edge of the horizon.

The cleansing air filled each breath with a sense of the blooming spring that should have been a time for uplifted spirits and hope throughout the realm; the hope of bountiful fields, a wealth of wool, and increased trade in the markets. It was a time that should have been filled with riddles and song, abundant with ale and meat.

The coming onslaught was an absolute mockery of everything that Aelfric believed that the All-Father had intended for humankind. A part of him wondered why the All-Father would even tolerate the passing of such insidious times, when so many innocents would be caught up in an inferno of war, death, and suffering.

Aelfric did not need to be reminded that mortal life was so very fragile. Only the present moment promised even a shred of stability, and even that little scrap could unravel at any time, without warning.

The great thane and Ealdorman of the Wesvald had already lost two children. Both of them should have easily outlived him, but he had been made to helplessly witness a wasting sickness, as it voraciously consumed his young son and daughter, down to their last drop of life essence. He had prayed to exhaustion, but the disease had not hesitated to devour that final spark of light within his two dear children.

He had also lost one brother, one that he had grown very close to throughout his life, due to a vicious fight over the perception of offended honor. The sorrowful and unexpected loss had happened just a month before his beloved brother was to be married to the daughter of a thane that Aelfric's family had long embraced, in warm friendship.

Aelfric's own blade had taken vengeance on the man that had slain his brother, but only a cold emptiness had been left in the wake of the act of retribution. The passage of time may have aided him in learning to live with the hole in his heart, but it had never truly gone away. The sting of the shock of the loss still resided deep within Aelfric's soul.

Life was not assured, nor did it ever seem to proceed in what Aelfric could deem to be any semblance of a sensible, understandable fashion. The empty horizon that he now beheld would shortly be filled from one end to the other with ranks of enemies, whose only purpose was to conquer and destroy the Saxan realm for all time to come.

The Saxans' own encampment was indeed enormous, a far greater mustering than Aelfric had ever imagined that the realm could gather together. Yet he could not deny that the chance of victory lay to a much greater extent with the overwhelmingly massive enemy forces arraying against them.

He shook his head in sadness, as he slowly turned his eyes away from the green, windswept plains to the west. The undulating expanse of grasses would soon be dyed crimson with the blood of Aelfric's own people, as well as the blood of so many others who were far removed from their homes and hearths.

It caused Aelfric to wonder why the invaders felt so compelled to attack, and why so many great and historic realms so willingly served the whims of such an obviously dark power, as the Unifier unmistakably was. Aelfric could not believe that the Great Vicar of his faith, Celestine IX, could tolerate such a senseless war between realms of fellow believers.

He mused that even the Grand Shepherd, residing behind the massive walls of faraway Theonium, sitting in authority over those that had broken away in the great Schism that had ruptured the once united faith of Emmanu's followers, could certainly perceive the grave injustice of this coming war.

Another part of him wondered as to whether the most adamant protest by the two sacred leaders could even bring about a moment's pause in the impending onslaught. Aelfric knew the answer to that well enough. It was a very sobering thought, to believe that the two holy leaders could not resist the will of the Unifier. The world was indeed changing fast, and not for the better.

"What troubles you?" Morcar asked quietly, grabbing Aelfric's attention before the majordomo sank into even deeper fathoms within himself.

Aelfric looked up at him, and gave a very weary sigh. "Just life … no more than that. No less than that."

"You need say no more my friend," Byrtnoth said compassionately, from Aelfric's other side. He lay a hand upon Aelfric's shoulder, as Morcar nodded his agreement with the Ealdorman of Sussachia's somber words.

AYENWATHA

Raw cries of anguish and sorrow permeated the forests of the Five Realms on the traumatic day of departure. Villages all across the woodlands were left behind, empty and purposely abandoned, as the great exodus began.

Emotional wounds suffered in the vicious attacks from the skies were ripped open even further. Most villagers had not recovered well from the sudden pronouncement of the Grand Council's decision, for the tribes to desert the villages and their lands. They could not believe that they were leaving the lands that they loved, and had inhabited for all of their lives, heading into a future fraught with instability.

There had been no time to adjust or prepare, and the tribal people were not coping well. The decision of the Grand Council had been swift in its delivery, and absolute in its urgency.

Throughout the tribal lands, each village left as a group. Plans were quickly made so that the village groups would eventually combine together into larger contingents, all along the way of the various forest trails crossing through their extensive lands.

There had been no time for proper condolences, or even for the proper, traditional burial rituals. The hastily constructed platforms holding the wrapped bodies of the dead were cleared immediately, as the bodies were hastened into great pits. It was not wholly unlike their regular practices, but it was greatly shortened in terms of ceremony, and the methodical, tribal customs, something that was considered to be a very bad omen by many of the villagers.

The only comfort to be had anywhere was found in the fact that family groups would be kept together. The villagers would still have the presence of their cherished clan matrons, clan sachems, Wise Ones, and headmen walking on the long march with them.

Even so, between the confederated tribes and villages there were many friends who were being parted from friends, and lover from lover, making the exodus one of tremendous discomfort, pain, and frustration for the sorrowing people.

The people had little time to salvage whatever they could from their villages. Those who were a part of the great Healing Societies reverently gathered together all of the ritual masks that had survived the destruction, along with ash, rattles, and other implements used in their mystical ceremonies.

Foodstuffs of all kinds were scraped up and gathered into baskets, buckets, and any method of containment that could be taken along. Weapons were also collected, with quantities of arrows distributed and placed within quivers woven of corn husks, or fashioned of hide.

Ayenwatha, fresh from the formal war council, had volunteered to keep the seven exiles with him. None of the others in the village, under the circumstances, could reasonably be expected to care for the needs of the outsiders in the midst of the terrible calamities that had been mercilessly thrust upon their own families and clans.

When he found them towards the base of the hill, at the Place of Far Seeing, it was clear that his appearance startled the exiles, for his skin was now painted red and black for the impending war.

JANUS

"We must go seek the Midragardans," Ayenwatha had quickly informed the exiles, as he guided them down to the banks of the river where the batch of long canoes were kept. "We cannot send anyone through the skies. You have already seen the dangers above. We will have to go by stream and river, even if it is slower. It does not spare us from danger, but we can defend ourselves, or turn to the banks if needed."

Ayenwatha's demeanor was resolute, but Janus knew that the war sachem was riddled with dismay and sorrow at everything that was happening to his people. The last images of the doomed village were still fresh and vivid within Janus' mind. Janus had stood at the summit of the hill and looked on from above as the villagers had started off on their long march. Taking their first steps down the narrow paths of the forest, the survivors were abandoning their homes for the shrouded mysteries of the future.

Several villagers combing through the destroyed village, in the hopes of finding some extra scraps of food or useful implements, had passed right by Janus on their way down the slope to join the others. He had kept his eyes fixed ahead as best as he could, for they were already reddening with sadness and empathy for the warm-hearted people of the Onan village. The feeling of suffering in the air was thick and oppressive, bearing down upon him without respite.

He knew that the others with him, in their own way, harbored similar feelings to his own. Even Derek's particularly stony silence and iron countenance belied his inner feelings, as he was one of the only exiles who seemed completely unwilling to look upon the departing groups of villagers.

As much as it pained him, something within Janus told him that he needed to bear witness to the terrible spectacle. Nonetheless, at one point he turned away from the villagers, having to wipe a tear away as it escaped his own eye. Even then, he discovered that he could not escape the melancholy sights.

He observed as a mother clutched two of her children tightly to her. The two children sobbed in her weary arms, as her own face struggled to maintain a façade of strength for the sake of her children. Her husband, his face drained from fatigue and grief, worked to finish filling some large pouches with dried provisions that he had been able to gather from the ruins of the village.

A couple of horses were being prepared for departure near to the family. Three men were working to affix a type of makeshift sled to them, two long poles spanned by hide, and pulled tilted up. Janus knew that they would be used to help bear along the more elderly members of the village. He had already seen a few such arrangements being put to use at the base of the hill, when the main throng had begun their march.

It was very fortuitous that a few horses had somehow survived the attack. The small horses, whose backs were loaded with packs already, stood without complaint. Their calm demeanors appeared to indicate that they were ready and willing to share in the extensive burdens of their keepers.

Janus' eyes were then stricken by the sight of an old man standing alone near the village entryway. With a hollow look, he was staring back at the shambles that had been vibrant, inhabited dwellings only a couple of days before.

Janus knew that the old man was seeing much more than the wreckage that remained of the village. His faraway look transcended the physical wreckage before him, hearkening back to a better time. There was little doubt that the man had endured grievous losses in the attack, as his listless expression testified.

When the man silently turned and walked onward to join those who were leaving the village, Janus knew that it took great strength for him to do so. To lift his legs and step forward probably called upon a level of will commiserate with the most stalwart of the tribes' warriors.

Janus' heart ached watching the man's slow steps. In that moment he knew that his heart had truly bonded with the people of the Onan village; a people attacked savagely, by an overwhelmingly powerful enemy, and left helpless and voiceless.

Janus looked around, and noticed Mershad's distant stare, where the young man stood close by him. Mershad had a haunted look about him as he regarded the destroyed village.

"Come on, Mershad," Erika then said gently, placing her hand on his arm to break Mershad out of his momentary paralysis.

Janus was not surprised at Mershad's reaction, as out of the seven exiles, Mershad probably understood the Onan villagers in ways that the rest of the exiles could not.

The villagers had been deemed as enemies, to be destroyed by a far stronger attacker. Janus knew that Mershad truly understood those ramifications, as he had family, friends, and acquaintances in his own life that had been caught up in the storm of far greater powers. Janus knew that the experience of widespread destruction and loss was something shared at a deep level between Mershad and the villagers.

When Mershad glanced towards him, as he was led away by Erika, Janus saw a depth of sadness and anger reflected in Mershad's face that pierced him to the core. As Mershad took his eyes away, Janus closed his eyes, and took a deep breath, as his sympathies for the young man threatened to burst. Steadying himself, Janus silently strode forward in the wake of the others, accompanying them out of the village and down the slope.

Ayenwatha, his body painted for war, had met them at the base of the hill, and guided them to the banks of the stream. With all seven of the exiles gathered at the edge of the flowing waters, Ayenwatha moved to help a group of warriors work to bring out the canoes. Antonio, Logan, Kent, Erika, and Derek moved forward to help them, leaving Mershad and Janus to themselves.

A few other Onan warriors subsequently joined them for the coming journey, as all were divided among the vessels. Paddles were distributed, and everyone participated in the rowing from the outset.

Muscles were soon strained to the limit, as they set off down the broad stream, propelling the vessels as fast as they could. Assumptions could not be made about the time available to them, and Ayenwatha, in the lead vessel, was embracing a sense of urgency.

Janus at least knew a little about their destination on this foray. Using tributaries, they would be making their way to a far-off bay, which opened onto the Great Waters. As Ayenwatha had explained, it was not far from that bay that a small island was located which harbored a small trading colony of Midragardans.

Far beyond that island, to the south, a few weeks-long journey by ship across the Great Waters could bring a person to Midragard itself. A land of many incredible legends, and populated by a strong and fierce people, Midragard was, according to Ayenwatha, the best ally that the tribal people could hope to reach out to.

Though incomparably dark times were befalling his people, Ayenwatha exhibited a flame of hope burning strongly within him. He had stated that the character of the Midragardans was such that the seafarers would honor their bonds with the Five Realms.

Janus took that presence of trust and hope to heart, as he put his energy into paddling the canoe, finding at its core that there was indeed a spark of inspiration to draw upon.

AETHELSTAN

Aethelstan watched the events transpiring in the sky, gripped with trepidation, and an acute sense of helplessness. The Saxan warriors that had been sent up to strike at the seemingly small Trogen patrol had suddenly found themselves facing a wide array of expectant, prepared Trogens.

A clever ruse had been enacted by the Trogens, the emergence of which had made time stand still for Aethelstan.

The Saxans had scattered apart almost immediately, which Aethelstan deemed to be a reactive decision on the part of Edmund. It was a very wise one, undoubtedly the only chance to salvage a few Saxan lives from the clamping jaws of the Trogen entrapment.

The Trogens had demonstrated a remarkable cunning, the bulk of their number waiting within the obscuring cover of the lower clouds until all of the area's defenders had been drawn forth. The bait had been well set, and a fearsome ambush had been sprung.

The actual fighting had not lasted very long. Aethelstan had witnessed in rising dismay as many brave Saxans hurtled downward with their steeds from the lofty heights. For a sky rider, one of the greatest fears once airborne was having their steed slain from under them. It doomed the rider to a horrific death, following a terrifying, dizzying descent that ended with the bludgeoning and shattering of their bodies upon tree, stone, and hard earth.

The lifeless bodies of several Saxans were being returned upon surviving steeds that had begun to trickle back in to the Saxan encampment. The steeds had been gathered and led in by Saxan scouts who were very familiar with the surrounding woods. The scouts guided them back from where they had strayed without the conscious direction of their riders, who had been slain during the battle.

Aethelstan's keen observation of the fighting revealed that only a scant few of the Trogens had been slain in the airborne melee. The ferocity of the Trogens' attack was something incredible to behold. The great thane could not begrudge the Trogens the fact that they were fearsome warriors.

They wielded long, singled-edged weapons, akin to great swords, as well as great lances, and strange long-bladed, long-hafted weapons. All were wielded with tremendous force and dexterity in their parries and strikes. They utilized their rectangular shields very capably, and also displayed exceptional control of their hardy steeds.

One against one, the Saxan warriors were at a significant disadvantage. Sorely outnumbered, as they were, the outcome of the fighting had been left little in doubt. As far as Aethelstan could surmise, only a few Saxans from the group that had ascended, and a slightly larger proportion of their steeds, had survived the gruesome combat.

Inevitably, the strongest of his worries and fears gravitated towards the fate of Edmund, without whom the surviving Saxan sky warriors would be left with no experienced leaders, for any kind of sky maneuvers. For Aethelstan, the matter was even further compounded, as it was not only the possible loss of one of their better fighting minds that concerned him. It was the potential loss of his best friend that Aethelstan feared the most, a loss that he could never hope to replace.

Aethelstan paced for what seemed to be an interminable amount of time, striding back and forth along the top of the ridge. His mood was tense as he watched new groups of Trogens appear in the skies overhead, taking up uncontested patrols that kept a regular surveillance upon the area.

His men looked up nervously around him, eyeing the gliding Trogens almost as if expecting an attack at any moment. The Saxan thane was not so lost in his thoughts and worries that he failed to perceive their agitation.

"They will not strike now, they merely serve as eyes for the army that is to come," Aethelstan said to a group of simple village men from the General Fyrd, several of whom appeared to be on the verge of panic.

More than one of them clutched tightly onto an old spear, makeshift club, or other weapon, with whitened knuckles that betrayed their inner emotions more than the stony looks upon their faces. At his words, they relaxed only slightly, a few of them nodding speechlessly in response.

They were far from alone. In this matter, those of poorer means were in union with those that possessed mail coat, helm, and sword. Even the hardier of the Wessachian thanes that Aethelstan encountered along the ridge reflected an unnerved state within the look of their eyes.

Aethelstan knew that he would have to address them all soon, as morale was always tenuous in the aftermath of a very visible loss, such as the one suffered that day.

His greatest worries were soon assuaged, when a heavily downtrodden-looking Edmund was ushered up to the ridgeline, and over to Aethelstan by a couple of warriors from his personal household retinue. The sky commander's eyes had a hollow look to them that echoed the debilitating nature of the recent defeat.

"Edmund! Praise the All-Father," Aethelstan stated exuberantly at the sight of the approaching men, striding forth quickly, and firmly embracing his friend. In his zeal and euphoric relief, Aethelstan, almost knocked the dispirited man into a nearby spruce tree. "By heaven, you were spared! I give thanks to the All-Father for that!"

Edmund shook his head slowly as they broke apart, hesitant to bring his eyes up to meet those of Aethelstan. His voice carried a bitter edge. "And the All-Father should not have spared me, least of all. I did not deserve to survive that battle. I did not consider that they might have an ambush lying in wait, letting a small patrol sit so obviously out in the open. I fell entirely for their lure, and these Trogens have shown much more skill in their tactics than I expected. I deserved to die more than any other."

Aethelstan could feel the pall of heavy guilt shrouding his friend. Knowing Edmund as well as he did, he was not surprised at all.

Aethelstan placed his hand down upon Edmund's shoulder, clasping him tightly. "None of us would have expected them to strike by force, in such a clever way. We have not seen them do such a tactic before. Why would you have expected them now?

"How could they have known that our full sky forces were not in the area? It is clear that they took a great risk as well. The tilt of fate does not render one the wiser, and the other the more foolish. It is merely that fate tilted in their favor, and not ours. Nothing more, and nothing less, Edmund."

"We could not stand and fight against that force, I could only urge them to try to survive," Edmund replied gloomily. He looked as if he needed to explain his immediate decision to fragment the cluster of badly outnumbered Saxans at the onset of the ambush, imploring them to try and escape with their lives. "The Trogens were far too many. Each one of them is a great wolf of the skies, and their steeds are no lesser. If we had stayed, I am certain that none of our men would have survived."

"None would have," Aethelstan said quickly, with firm certainty, wanting the continuing onrush of guilt to ebb and cease in his friend.

"Anyone could see that plainly enough. It was more than evident. The Trogens are no ordinary warriors, and there were several of them for each Saxan ... at least four or five to one. They fight with a fury beyond the natural order, as if possessed by the fell spirits of the Lord of Fire Himself.

"In no time you made the wisest of decisions, Edmund. Because of you, some have lived, where none would have if you had not decided to break up your formation. Each and every one of those in the skies would have been destroyed, as your own mouth has spoken."

At that moment, a Saxan fighter hurried towards Aethelstan and Edmund. He brought himself to an abrupt halt, heavy of breath as he lowered his eyes and gave a bow towards the thanes.

"What is it?" Aethelstan queried insistently of the warrior.

"I am here to report that nine sky warriors have survived the sky battle, and are now safe within the camp. Only one of them was badly wounded, but the Sister tending to him said that the wounds will not be fatal. The steeds of these men have also survived. Seven other Himmerosen have been found, or have made their way back as well. There may yet be others, but that is the latest count," the man stated.

Aethelstan turned back to face Edmund. "Then nine men owe their very lives to your decision. Nine who may come to be very important when we make our inevitable stand here, do not forget that. Only the living can be of help to us in the future. Dead warriors can do us no good."

Edmund still refrained from meeting Aethelstan's gaze, though Aethelstan saw that a little of the despondency that had been present had departed his friend's expression. Still, there was little doubt in Aethelstan's mind that his friend would yet feel deep pangs of guilt at his survival of the conflict.

It was the kind of man that Edmund was, and one of the great qualities about him. He truly was willing to meet the worst fate experienced by any one of the men that he led forth.

Sorrow would still be a ponderous weight upon Edmund's spirit, as there was also a very personal aspect to the deaths of the men that Aethelstan and Edmund led. Their forces consisted of warriors who had lived alongside each other throughout their entire lives, within the villages and burhs of Wessachia. As such, concerning those who had recently fallen, Edmund had almost certainly known several of them as long as he had been alive. As many of the deaths were so personal in nature, it made the burdens of spirit even heavier.

Aethelstan understood that onerous weight, and patted Edmund reassuringly upon the back, glad that his friend's eyes were not looking to see the sadness present in his own look.

His voice remained steady and encouraging. "Come now, Edmund. There is yet much to do, and I need your mind clear to help our people. The enemy is even now relaying our positions from the skies, and we are going to have to work hard and think cleverly to undo the damage that their constant observation of us brings. Remember, Edmund, they can only watch us. They cannot hear us, and they do not know what our plans and intentions may be."

Edmund's eyes remained downcast, but after a few moments he finally brought his gaze up. A different look was now reflected within his eyes. Aethelstan was not surprised at the change, as he knew that Edmund would swiftly come to reason.

"Let us resume our work here, Aethelstan," he said, with an edge of resolve, though his next words carried a trace of despair. "But is there not anything in this wide world that can ever work to our favor?"

Aethelstan smiled gently. "In such times it seems there is nothing going in our favor. I can only believe that there are things that happen, far and wide, which we ourselves may never know of, that work to our aid in many enduring ways."

"I would like to believe that, but I cannot see it," Edmund replied dourly.

"And neither can I, but then again, we cannot see all things, can we, Edmund?" Aethelstan queried.

He placed his hand again on Edmund's shoulder, stepping past him before the other thane could feel a need to answer Aethelstan's question. The question was intended to be more rhetorical in nature, something for Edmund to ponder as he wrestled with his turbulent emotions.

Edmund hesitated for a moment, perhaps already thinking upon the words. Aethelstan looked back, and gave a gesture to his friend to follow him to the tents.

The beleaguered sky warrior would need some food and rest, as all of his men undoubtedly would. There were physical needs to address. At least that could be achieved, even if his friend could not really hope to take his mind completely away from his inner torments.

JANUS

"Back on the water, where this all began," Janus remarked to Erika.

He leaned back closer to her, in order to gain a little privacy for their conversation. Janus was sitting just in front of her in the narrow watercraft, both of them with the haft of an oar held firmly in their hands as they made their own physical contributions to the travel.

They had been journeying down river for at least a couple of hours. Most of the earlier portion of their travel had been endured in attentive silence, individuals left to their own thoughts as they paddled in a steady rhythm. A rapid pace was still being sustained, though after the initially robust outset Ayenwatha had eased everyone back just a little to preserve strength.

A few conversations had finally broken out amongst the group, much to Janus' relief, as the interactions offset the extended monotony of the excursion.

At first, Erika returned a confused expression to Janus in response to his words. The look vanished after another moment of thought, as comprehension dawned within her eyes.

"Almost forgot about all of that," she replied in a low voice. "You were on a boat with Derek and Kent when the fog first came, weren't you?"

"Can't say I really trust the water anymore," Janus declared ruefully, as he nodded in reply, traces of a mirthless grin playing about his face.

"And I suppose I don't trust secluded university areas that are covered in grass, and surrounded by trees," Erika retorted. She grinned, a fragment of lighthearted laughter escaping her. Dipping her oar blade back into the surface of the stream, she pulled back strongly.

"But it seems we are on the water, and there are no universities close by," she stated, as she looked back to Janus again. "So it would seem the burden is greater on you."

Her smile broadened, and her eyes sparkled like the very surface of the river that they were now coursing along. For no identifiable reason, Janus immediately felt self-conscious, and not a little embarrassed at the warm, radiant smile that she had given him. He had never felt entirely settled in the presence of a woman, especially a woman with the sheer magnetism and charisma that Erika possessed.

The more that he was around her, the more he saw that she was truly a rarity among both women and men alike. She was not just imbued with a comely appearance, but also amply gifted in wit, humility, and a quiet strength. It all contributed to the strong presence that she exuded, which he admittedly found both intensely attractive, and not a little bit intimidating.

"I know I probably sounded pretty stupid there," he responded, with some hesitation.

Erika smiled again. "Janus, given what we are all going through, the issue of trust towards anything is becoming pretty muddled these days. Wouldn't you agree?"

Janus readily assented, as matters of trust struck at the core of everything that he had been struggling with. His voice took on a more somber tone as he replied to her.

"Yes it is, as you say, certainly muddled. But I miss having at least some sense of bearings, even if they are just very convincing illusions at the end of the day," Janus said. "I already have more than enough trouble trying to have faith in anything. But I need something to grasp onto everyday, even if it is a simple matter of believing that I will not suddenly find myself in another entire world. And I'm well aware now that even faith in that could fail me at any time."

"We all need a little stability to hold onto," Erika responded, her tone taking a serious tilt. "Finding yourself in a new world is rattling, to say the least."

Once again, Janus felt the awkward sensation of having just said something rather ignorant in her presence.

"Sorry, I made another obviously dumb comment," he muttered contritely. "I know I'm not the only one shaken up here."

Raising his oar back up, he dipped it back into the water with a little more vigor, the burst of exertion born out of his inner frustrations.

"Hey, it's okay to say what you feel. You need to get it out. And it lets me know I'm not alone in what I'm thinking these days," Erika said sympathetically, a smile warming her countenance.

"You are very kind," Janus said, just above a whisper, his eyes avoiding contact with hers.

His gaze drifted over towards the tree-lined banks of the river, before lowering to stare at the currents that their canoe was cutting through. Everything seemed part of an immensely nightmarish dream, the genesis of which was the crushing blow of his father's unexpected passing. His sheer foolishness in the company of a woman that he found wholly fascinating was just a sliver of the continued feeling of discordance that enveloped him.

In so many ways he was adrift, far out of harmony, and clouded by a fog far denser than the one that had unveiled this new world to him. Looking forward, he quietly watched the pathway of the river as it wended through the thick, hilly forest bordering it. Its course was quite varied, continuing straight for lengthy stretches, turning in sharp bends at other points, or angling into elongated curves to either the left or right.

Janus turned his head to look in the direction of the riverbank to the right, hearing a sudden splash of water. He saw the outward ripples marking the place where a large fish had broken the surface, and then plunged back down into the depths.

The meandering of the river, and everything else about it, was not entirely unlike the course of his life. It was a thought that gave Janus pause.

The water, the banks, the current, and the fish all formed the elements of the river that the canoe was traversing. There was a certain order to all of it, even if he had no idea as to what they might encounter around the next bend in the river.

Such was life, in a way, traveling down its own natural course, on an unceasing flow that progressed from one moment to the next within its own host of elements. Like the travelers upon the canoes, life held a considerable degree of blindness towards both the immediate and distant future. Life held its own gradual shifts in course, as well as sharper ones, and some periods that appeared rather straightforward. Yet in all cases, time drifted onward like the canoe across the water.

Janus knew that the river, and the life teeming within it, would continue onward long after he had passed through, just like the world would continue after his own life's journey had reached its ultimate end. In life, Janus was a passenger on a great and foreboding river, carried forward in the vessel of a physical body.

As helpless as some aspects of that perception might have seemed, neither could he ignore the unmistakable order to the river, which also echoed life's journey. Underlying the act of passing down the river in a canoe was a strong sense of destination.

DREAM OF LEGENDS

The recognition of the presence of a destination was a small comfort to him, even if he could not so easily liken that aspect of their physical travel to his rumination upon life. It nonetheless brought to mind thoughts of greater powers, ones that might very well lay beyond the natural design that he observed all around him.

Perhaps life had a destination as well. It was the challenge of handling the ambiguity that was the difficult part, as he could not say for certain that there was a destination, but neither could he honestly rule it out. There was just altogether too much that was deeply shrouded in mystery, and he knew that it would be entirely disingenuous, if not intellectually dishonest, to claim certainty of things that he did not have a full understanding or knowledge of.

He just wished that he could still the anxieties, especially when the world seemed to be cloaked in ashen gray. The tribal people, such as Ayenwatha, appeared to be unshaken in the things that they held to heart, and not even the immense tragedies that had been visited upon them seemed to significantly rattle their bonds of belief in something greater.

Janus both admired and envied their conviction, as it was something that he could not fathom within his own life. He realized that he had lost much of the ability to trust in even the simpler aspects of life, especially where they related to other individuals.

It was a tremendous predicament to be in, as life was anything but a solitary experience. It was undeniable that a person entered and left the world alone, but those two moments were truly aberrations during the course of a lifetime. He lived in a world that left him no chance of persisting within it if he were entirely left to his own devices. The need for at least a small amount of trust in others was paramount, as, in truth, he needed others for the survival of more than just his body; he needed others so that his spirit could endure.

"What are you thinking about?" Erika asked him, curiosity dancing in her eyes as she looked into his face.

Janus did not shy away from her gaze, as he brought himself back out of his musings. "I suppose a lot of things … great and small. Sometimes you miss the obvious, but it's better to figure something out late than never."

A slight grin broke onto his face, as he realized that at the very least he had just taken a small step. It remained to be seen whether or not he could take enough steps to come forth from the depths of shrouding darkness that had thickened around him over the past few months.

Even so, the first step in any path back towards light was the recognition of the absence of it, as well as understanding the need for it. That much, at least, he had achieved.

LOGAN

Logan paddled in sullen disquiet, feeling like cursing the very day that he had been brought into the world. Everything seemed like a mammoth mudslide to him, a slow, continual descent into a murky abyss that was neither warranted nor preventable.

Certainly, none of it involved a course that had been chosen by him, but then again, that was precisely what angered him the most. The sole missing factor in feeling like he truly had even a small degree of free will was the lack of power to make a different choice in the course that was taken.

Throughout the lands he now found himself within, there were several thousands of displaced people, all suffering a heart-wrenching exodus from their homelands. At an even farther distance, there was a dark and ambiguous threat manifesting, as an enemy force encroached upon the tribal lands. Going even farther, there was an entire world that was not all too different from the decaying one that he had once lived in.

There was simply no presence of justice, or even sanity, not when the simplest of observations was faced truthfully. The darker forces of the world held the truest advantages, in all of their forms. Their ends would always justify the means. No matter how brutal, no matter how deceitful, one who disregarded the constraints of virtues could act in any capacity to achieve a desired means.

The forces attacking the villagers were undeniable proof of that reality. Such proofs were everywhere, Logan knew, if one was willing to open his or her eyes, and see what was there for all eyes to see.

The lying merchant could smoothly gain the sale that the honest merchant could not attain. The deceptive craftsman could hide a blemish or weakness in structure, where the honest one could not. An errant laborer could twist his way out of failing a task, where the honest would willingly face consequences, with their full weight of penalty.

An invading army, without the burden of virtues, could readily annihilate their enemy, destroying civilian and warrior alike. A truly honor-bound people would be above employing widely destructive and indiscriminate tactics, and in adhering to such ways could well suffer a comprehensive defeat in the long run.

The list of examples was practically endless, demonstrating the enormous advantages that the amoral or immoral person held over the one who embraced a moral code. It was a drink most bitter to the tongue, and maddening to the mind.

In the middle of a substantial river, within a sprawling forest, in the midst of a vast new world, Logan felt himself to be little more than a speck of foreign dust on the strange planet.

He could see Erika and Janus talking together in one of the canoes just behind him. It was true that the two of them shared his unfamiliarity with the new world, as well as his familiarity with their world of origin. It was a very basic bond among the exiles, but it was one that Logan valued nonetheless.

Janus was of the silent, more contemplative type, and Logan keenly sensed that the man was wrestling with a tremendous internal struggle. Erika was undeniably an attractive woman, with a real flare of life to her. Depending on the day, it was either an irritation or enjoyable, as she was not shy about saying whatever was on her mind.

Logan was conscious of his genuine friendship with Antonio, and he was grateful that he had someone with him from his former world that he knew well.

He was also aware of the fact that Ayenwatha and his tribal people were going to great lengths to care for the small band of outsiders. The tribal people were under a tremendous burden, and still they strove to protect and guide Logan and his companions.

Yet ultimately, despite the various bonds, Logan felt quite powerless and alone. It was a weighty and forlorn emotion that threatened to douse the fires of his spirit, rendering him dead to the world. Even so, the same fires within him could not be so easily soaked, and he burned fiercely to find some possible way to seize a degree of control over the course of things.

He chanced a glance back towards Ayenwatha. The tribal leader was focused on his paddling efforts, and paid Logan no heed. The noble warrior's muscle and sinew worked in a flowing harmony, a striking example of symmetry and motion. Each instant, the tribal warrior looked like a skilled artist's sculpture, as he worked the oar with a strong posture rife with rippling striations of musculature.

Logan knew that Ayenwatha was one of the most respected and greatest warriors of his village and tribe. He was a living example of the highest values that the tribe embraced, a man disciplined in the ways of nature and of the spirit.

Even so, Ayenwatha still had been set to desperate flight, along with all of his people.

Logan turned his eyes back to the front. A determination gripped him, as he promised himself that one day he would find his way into a position where he could not easily be put to flight, or made helpless.

One day, he would make his own determinations, and not be vulnerable to the reasonless, fickle whims of fate.

LEE

Gunther's mood was severe, his face and hair caked with sweat as he bustled through the doorway into his woodland home. Lynn and Erin had watched him striding briskly towards the building, from a small window opening on the upper level. They had been alerted to his impending presence by a sudden restlessness among the Jaghuns.

Hearing the comments of the two women as they saw Gunther emerge from the forest depths, Lee and Ryan had hurried down the stairs to await the woodsman's entrance. Lee felt impatient and on edge as he waited for the door to open, and the information that he anxiously sought to be delivered.

It was difficult enough for Gunther to move into the room, given that all of the Jaghuns crowded around and pressed their bodies together, close to the thick wood planks of the front door. Gunther barely responded to the greetings of the creatures, looking both distracted and pensive as he set his great bow down.

Lee could tell at once that something was very wrong.

Gunther looked towards Lee and Ryan, not even bothering to give them a greeting. He asked bluntly "Where are the other two?"

Lee pointed upstairs.

"The two of you up there, come down, now!" Gunther yelled upwards, before turning back towards the others.

He waited tensely until the two young women had come down the steps to join them. "No luck is with us. None whatsoever. The Avanorans are coming in force straight towards this dwelling. Far too many to even think about a fight. It is certain that they will find this place, and I am not so naïve as to think that they will respect a man's dwelling. We must go!"

"How far away are they?" Erin asked.

Erin, like the others, presented anything but a calm façade. Wide-eyed panic was written all over her face as she looked to Gunther.

Lee's greatest anxieties were spawned by the deep worry etched across Gunther's face. In the short time that he had known the stalwart woodsman, there were some clear traits that rose prominently to the surface.

Gunther was not the sort of man to openly exhibit consternation, unless there was truly a very daunting reason. The entire patrol of the bestial warriors on the winged steeds had not rattled him in the slightest. He had been wholly unflappable in the aftermath of that conflict, except for the trauma at the loss of his Jaghun.

Lee knew without a doubt that fear did not come lightly to the tall, brawny woodsman. That alone, more than anything else, gave Lee the most cause to be afraid himself as he saw the agitation in Gunther.

"They are close enough. Unless you prefer to die gloriously and take a few of them with you, and hope that some gleeman sings of you one day, I would suggest that we all get moving now. As for myself, I am not seeking glory in a senseless fight, so I am leaving now. You may stay if you like, though," Gunther replied tersely.

The man was not in the mood for any edgy banter with Erin, preempting any rude responses that she might have had on her lips. For her part, Erin made no caustic reply, keeping her mouth shut.

Gunther moved swiftly, gathering up a couple of leather packs, and opening a pair of wooden chests on the ground. He rummaged through the chests quickly, withdrawing some items of clothing and other incidentals that he packed into the hide pouches.

Lee and the others were sternly exhorted by Gunther to get their weapons along with any other things that they wished to take with them.

There was not much in that regard, as Lee and the others did not have so much as a change of clothes.

Packs filled, Gunther strode over to the back of the room, heading towards the barred door, brushing roughly by Ryan in the process. Ryan was almost knocked off his feet by the brusque impact.

Lee knew that the contact was not intentional, simply a result of Gunther's mind being far away from the woodland abode. Gunther paused to glance back towards Ryan, as if in afterthought, and apparently recognized the confusion upon the younger man's face.

"There is no time. We must go without delay," he said more gently, as he lifted the wooden plank from the great door and swung it open.

What little light existed in the outer room was immediately sucked up, swallowed by the impenetrable blackness on the other side of the door. Lee reflexively shivered as a strong draft of cold air rushed out.

The cooler air had a clean moistness to it, emerging from the interior of the cave-like atmosphere. Only a tiny speck of dim light in the far depths of the blackness signified anything that he could orient upon with his eyes.

The four awaited Gunther hesitantly, looking between the entrance and the woodsman.

"The door is open for you to go through, now!" Gunther barked at them with urgency. "Walk slowly towards the light, the ground underfoot is even enough. You can feel your way along the sides if you wish, but keep your balance."

Lee started through the doorway first, giving some confidence to the others as they followed behind him. He noticed that the ground within the doorway was at a somewhat steep, downward slant, which headed straight towards the distant light.

Putting his hands out, he discovered that they were in a narrow passage, as his hands found the rough-hewn rock on the sides. Methodically, he took his first steps forward, careful to maintain his footing. The surfacing beneath his feet, though not perfectly even, did not have any large projections or dips that threatened to make him stumble or fall.

After about twenty paces in the narrow corridor, his hands could no longer touch both sides at once. He could also sense the enlargement of space in the widening corridor, yawning open above and around them.

He adjusted over to the side, to move forward along the wall to the right.

Within the surrounding blackness, he could hear the sounds of the Jaghuns padding up from behind. The creatures passed by Lee and the others in the darkness. Their presence in the passageway was undeniably reassuring to Lee, though it did not quench his sense of apprehension as they moved through the dark towards the unknown.

Lee heard the shutting of the wooden door behind them, followed by a sliding sound and a loud "pop," undoubtedly a wood plank being shoved into place from the inside.

It came as no surprise to Lee that Gunther had taken both sides of the door into consideration when he had built his dwelling. Heavy, swift footsteps then echoed into the larger part of the passageway, as Gunther hurried down the corridor. Within moments, he drew up alongside Lee.

"The enemy will find my home, but there will be no easy path for them to take to come against us down here. Remember, we are calling upon friends in a time of need," Gunther said to Lee, loud enough for the others to hear. He then spoke in an even louder voice to the quartet. "Now keep going towards that distant light."

Gunther's voice trailed off as he started forward, taking the lead. Lee and his three companions fixed their eyes upon the distant glow, still far ahead and below.

Moving slowly through the deep gloom, the rest of the descent seemed to take an eternity to complete. The light before them was a welcoming beacon, reassuring and calling to them as they carefully passed through the engulfing darkness of the downward pathway.

Gradually, the speck of light grew to become a definable circle, which in turn became an oval-shaped portal that was easily big enough for the group to walk through.

The light gradually illuminated the ground and sides around them, though it revealed little other than rock. Of all the strange things that Lee had seen in his life within two worlds, what awaited the group at the end of the passageway was perhaps the strangest yet. He had expected something unusual, but found that he was completely unprepared for the sight that finally met his eyes.

The light was not generated from any sun or artificial means.

The luminescent glow came from broad, amorphous patches spread high up the sides of a huge rock cavern that the passageway opened into. The blue-hued light was quite ample, revealing what looked to be a rather bizarre type of forest that was spread out far and wide within the gargantuan cavern.

Even at first glance, and in the midst of his great awe, Lee saw that there was some type of order to the strange forest. It was as if it had been cultivated in a highly organized arrangement, with a specific purpose. Lee's first impression was that it held the quality of a well-tended farm.

The forest was a mixture of soaring vertical growths, some varieties resembling giant mushrooms, continuing on down to much shorter stalks that were barely taller than Lee. The footing underneath was very strange, covered by algae-like growths and spongy loam. Lee could see that it was the substance of the much thicker layers that served as the foundation for the greater forest. The amount of organic material that the towering stalks were rooted in was incredible to consider.

The bright, glowing patches on the walls, and the bathing bluish light that they cast, added considerably to the mystical beauty of the extraordinary place.

Lee had come to a complete halt just a few steps into the cavern. He looked about in wonder, nearly breathless as his eyes adjusted further to the glowing light. The overall effect of the place was simply magical, and unlike anything he had ever experienced.

"I don't believe this," Lynn remarked slowly, her eyes drinking in the astonishing sights all around them.

"Unbelievable," Ryan said, craning his neck back to look up at the underbelly of one of the tall mushroom caps. Had the cap been upon the ground, all four of the companions could have stood within its circumference.

Lee hardly bothered to notice the Jaghuns grouping swiftly around them, in a protective manner. Just ahead, Gunther had come to a stop himself, though it was not out of awe for the sights around them. His eyes darted among the growths, as if searching for some sort of sign or presence.

Gunther slowly stepped back to where Lee was.

"What is it?" Lee asked him in a hushed tone.

"The Unguhur might wonder why I bring companions who can speak their language well ... as they know that I possess only a modest number of their words. It is best not to give rise to suspicions where we are needing friends," Gunther said, keeping his attention riveted upon their surroundings. "I will have to unveil everything about the four of you in time, including your amulets from the Wanderer."

"Should we take ours off?" Lynn asked him, voicing the obvious question that came to Lee's mind.

It took no great leap of logic to perceive that the Unguhur would be quite surprised to encounter four people that they had never met speaking their language without error, much more fluently than Gunther.

"They will know you are of another world no matter what you do. I may suggest that you keep your own words few at the beginning. But keep your amulets on you. At least it will help you understand what they say. We have little other choice," Gunther replied evenly. He then paused, as if thinking further on the matter. "Then again, at first it may not be deemed wise to reveal that you can speak with them, and understand them. Sometimes it is wisest to hold some things back. It could even be an advantage. They may speak more openly if they do not know you can understand their words."

Lee, Lynn, and the others nodded in understanding. Lee was relieved to know that they could retain the pendants. Once he had come to understand the nature of the amulet, he had regarded it as invaluable, if not indispensable. In a world where he knew not one of the languages spoken upon its surface, the amulet was a lifeline.

The group remained silent as Gunther continued to look out into the wondrous forest around them.

"As a friend I come," Gunther called out loudly into the stillness around them.

His voice carried far and vibrantly, echoing within the enormous space of the cavern. His words brought Lee, Lynn, Ryan, and Erin closer towards him. Lee was taken out of his enraptured state, as he looked around to see who or what Gunther was speaking to. He found himself gripped by nervous anticipation, feeling the sense of expectency coming from the woodsman.

Movement drew Lee's eyes, as a grayish shape could be seen moving amongst the growths, emerging from a deeper part of the fungus-forest and heading towards them. Several other large shapes issued from the midst of the forest growths just a few moments later.

Lee quickly realized the great size of the approaching beings, which became more apparent with each long stride that they took. Were it not for the relaxed nature of the Jaghuns and the calm disposition of Gunther, Lee and the others would likely have taken flight and run as hard as they could back towards the passage.

The hulking creatures approaching them were indeed humanoid, each one standing well over eight feet in height. They had large, triangular ears that were pressed close against the sides of their broad heads.

Their faces had a distinctive concavity. Were it not for their greatly formidable nature, Lee would have found them to have a naturally melancholic expression. Large, forward-set eyes rested deep in their wide sockets, while their prominent lower jaws jutted forward.

Their thick, bullish necks were connected to immensely muscular bodies, warning any who looked upon them of great physical strength. They were also long-limbed creatures in proportion to their powerful bodies, the considerable lengths of their arms and legs rippling with chiseled muscle.

There was little mystery as to the identity of the oncoming creatures. Lee knew that the beings striding towards them were the Unguhur.

He could see why the creatures had once been called Stone Hides. Their grayish skin did indeed have a stony texture, though up close Lee could see that the creatures had a very light growth of thin, gray hairs along the surface of their bodies.

Most of the creatures wore a type of hide-skirt, similar to a kilt, which was wrapped around their waists and hung down to just above their thick knees. A select few wore plain hide tunics along with the kilt, both items appearing to be fashioned of a thicker, different kind of leather. These Unguhur looked to be larger and even more muscular than the ones with only the kilt.

Their massive hands exhibited fingers that ended in what looked like small spear blades. The same was true of their long feet. Lee could not help but conjecture that the creatures could readily tunnel through hard-packed ground without the need for any tools.

The ones wearing tunics were armed with what appeared to be great lances. The lance blades were made of a black stone that had been shaped long and sharp, making the weapon suitable for slashing or for thrusting.

Those with just the hide-skirts carried much shorter weapons, club-sized for the scale of the beasts. The crude, mace-like weapons held a large, obsidian stone lashed tightly to the end of their thick shafts.

The creatures bearing the lances moved to the forefront of the bare-chested ones, the latter clustering behind.

Altogether, sixteen of the creatures had come to stand before Gunther's party. The huge beings made no hostile moves, though they kept some distance between the two parties. The ones in the front retained a firm grip upon their huge spears, though the sharpened points were tilted upwards, oriented towards the cavern ceiling.

Gunther turned to Lee and the others, and spoke in a lowered voice. "We must wait for one of the Unguhur leaders, versed in our language. One will come. These were the closest to us. Warriors and laborers, attending to this cavern."

Lee nodded wordlessly to Gunther. He was not about to divulge the nature of their amulets to these creatures, for there was no telling what kind of interest or alarm that the magical amulets might invoke in the brutish-looking beings. He definitely did not want to risk gaining their ire.

It seemed like an age had passed, when five more of the Unguhur finally came forth from the forest. Like those in the forefront of the group before Gunther, four were wearing the tunic-kilt combination and bore great spears. The four warriors walked in escort around the fifth member of their group, keeping the distinctive individual centered within their midst.

The protected Unguhur, alone among the twenty others of its kind in sight, was unarmed. Clad in a full-length tunic of softer material, flowing almost like a robe, the creature wore a necklace made up of an array of very long, sharp teeth. Tan-hued hide armbands were wound snugly about each of its upper arms. Each of the armbands exhibited a single line of raised scutes, presumably from the hide of whatever creature had been used to fashion them.

"Hail, Eranthus," Gunther proclaimed, lowering his head towards the approaching contingent.

"Gunther. You come. Been long. No wood? No trade? You bring others?" the robe-wearing one stated, as the last group of Unguhur finally reached the larger gathering.

Lee listened with the benefit of the amulet, but from the stilted delivery of the Unguhur, he surmised that Gunther was being addressed in the Saxan tongue. The creature spoke in a low, gravely tone of voice that fit well within the atmosphere pervading the strange underground world. It was obvious to Lee, watching the considerable deference given to the creature by its surrounding brethren, that the being held great authority amongst its kind.

It was difficult to read the expression upon the creature's broad face, but the look in the creature's eyes conveyed familiarity, and a sense of friendship, towards Gunther. The same eyes shifted to study the four humans with Gunther very closely. The creature's eyes narrowed, furrowing the skin covering the prominent ridge of its forehead, as it applied scrutiny to the human guests.

"Enemy come?" the being then asked, looking back to Gunther.

Gunther nodded, and as he spoke he used physical gestures to illustrate and emphasize his words. "Bad times come in world above. Work of Unifier. Big army comes. There are many enemy. Had to leave home. Could not stay above. Too much danger. Come to warn Unguhur. Need home with Unguhur."

At the mention of the Unifier, Eranthus' facial muscles tensed into something akin to a snarl. The lips curled back far enough to reveal that the Unguhur had very sizeable teeth, accompanied with a set of extremely prominent, sharp canines. Lee could certainly tell that there was no love lost between the Unifier and the Unguhur, something that made Lee feel much more reassured.

"You safe. In Unguhur lands now. Come now. Who friends?" Eranthus asked, his eyes looking back inquisitively at the four with Gunther.

"Will give story. Maybe prophecy. Friends. Protect from Unifier," Gunther replied.

"Gunther friends welcome. Gunther beasts welcome. Come. We go to Oranim," Eranthus said. "Watch tunnel."

Eranthus turned and spoke in a lower tone to the warriors that had escorted him. Lee picked out several words, listening as the Unguhur leader instructed the warriors to summon others, ordering them to watch over the long tunnel that led to Gunther's dwelling.

When Eranthus was finished speaking to the warriors, two of the spear-carrying Unguhur cupped their hands to their faces, and bellowed back in the direction of the bizarre forest. In mere moments, a number of other voices were raised from places near and far throughout the great cavern. A trickle of Unguhur appeared shortly, covering the ground in swift, loping strides as they hastened to the summons.

Gunther did not have to explain to Lee that each of the giant creatures was worth several human warriors, if combat were to ensue. Lee found himself intensely grateful for the fact that Gunther was regarded as a friend by the creatures, for over thirty of the Unguhur now surrounded them. If the Unguhur had decided to become hostile, there was nothing that Gunther and all of his Jaghuns combined could have done to protect Lee and his companions.

The warriors gathered together, leaving with the ones that Eranthus had instructed and heading towards the lower tunnel entrance.

Eranthus then motioned for the humans to follow, adding the invocation, "Warriors there. Now, come."

Only a couple of the warriors had remained behind, and these now escorted Eranthus, as the club-wielding Unguhur dispersed and moved back into the depths of the towering growths.

Eranthus led them on a path that meandered through the forest-like environment. Walking in silence, Lee took in the sights of the lofty stalks rising around them. They moved through many varieties of unusual growths, before they finally stepped out of the forest and entered a broad clearing.

His feet stepped once again onto a hardened surface, the ground no longer covered with the organic material that saturated the area underneath the fungal growths.

A short distance ahead of them, at the end of a gentle, downward slope, an underground river flowed. The dark waters of the river coursed with a slow current, patient and confident within the channel that it had carved out of the rock over long ages.

There was an area at the shoreline where there were a number of crude rafts, fashioned out of even lengths of some kind of thick stalk. Though Lee suspected that the stalks had been culled from something within the fungal forest, he could not tell for sure. The stalks were lashed tightly together, with lengths of hide rope.

Several large stones rested on the edge of the river's shore. The end of a long rope of hide was looped and secured around each stone, the other tied to an end of a raft. There were two such anchoring points for each individual raft, arranged so that the length of a particular raft could be tethered right alongside the landing area.

A cluster of long paddles and some considerably longer poles lay prone upon the stony shore, with even more on the rafts themselves. There were a few Unguhur standing around the rafts, all looking upon the party's approach with great interest reflected in their deep gazes.

As they neared the edge of the river, Lee and his companions hung back slightly, keeping a little distance between themselves and the flowing waters. Looking down the river, Lee could see that it traveled along the outer edge of the forest, curving out of sight into the depths of a tunnel that was not far downstream.

It was in that moment that Lynn suddenly flinched, and then aggressively nudged Lee. A startled look was displayed upon her face, and Lee followed the line of her sight to see what had suddenly unnerved her.

A distinct pair of impassive eyes was poking above the water's surface, set into two rising protrusions. The creature's pale eyes reflected the glowing light within the cavern. A modest distance in front of the eyes was what looked to be a very pale, light tan bump that broke through the surface of the water. The creature was hovering just a short few yards beyond the bobbing rafts, staring intently towards the group of newcomers and the Unguhur alike.

At first, Lee could make out very little of the organism's full form, concealed as it was within the dark waters. Finally, as realization dawned upon him, his eyes stretched wider with an upsurge of amazement and fear, wholly apprehensive.

Lee did not need to be an expert to judge the great size of the jaws belonging to the floating creature, gauging the span from the eyes to the tip of its elongated, tapering snout. He instinctively shuddered to think of the full size of the body extending beyond those unblinking eyes, easily larger than any crocodile or alligator that he had ever seen before.

"Gunther! What's that? Tell me that's not what I think it is," Erin blurted out with fearful excitement, as she became acutely aware of what had captivated Lee's and Lynn's attentions.

The Unguhur, especially Eranthus, whirled towards Erin with looks of utter surprise, even as she exhibited an expression of stunned alarm towards Gunther. It was in that moment that she realized her careless mistake, seeing that the Unguhur had understood her words perfectly.

"Wizard Gift. Will tell story soon," Gunther quickly added, while shooting Erin a highly annoyed glance.

Lee could not entirely blame Erin for the inadvisable lapse in discipline this time. The massive creature in the water was absolutely terrifying to comprehend, in proximity to the rafts that they were apparently going to board. He could not fault her for being shocked into committing the blunder.

The Unguhur leader nodded to Gunther, although some tension had now been brought between them. Its pensive voice replied to Gunther, "You tell soon. All speak?"

The leader glanced towards Gunther's companions for emphasis.

Gunther's face tensed, as he replied, "Yes, all speak."

Eranthus regarded Erin and the others with confusion apparent in his expression. "You understand my words?"

With a sigh, Gunther looked to his four human companions, and back to Eranthus, whose already large eyes had widened further.

"A Wizard Gift. It lets them speak the Unguhur language well," Gunther explained in a resigned tone. "I wanted to talk to you about this first, to explain it, so that you would not be alarmed."

"What Wizard?" Eranthus asked Gunther, with palpable apprehension.

"The Wanderer," Gunther replied firmly.

Lee could see Eranthus visibly relax at the open mention of the Wanderer.

"That is good," Eranthus commented, the edge now absent from his voice.

"Nice going, Erin," Ryan muttered under his breath, with more than a little disgust in his tone.

Lee did not reprimand the young man, as there was no use in hiding their capability anymore. Ryan had also taken notice of the cause for Erin's outburst, and his eyes glanced back to the creature in the river.

"So what are they, Gunther?" Ryan asked the woodsman uneasily.

"Those are gallidils," Gunther calmly informed Ryan and the others. "Do not be afraid of them, but be cautious. They have lived alongside the Unguhur race for much, much longer than I have."

"They are so enormous," Lynn remarked in unfettered awe.

"They are one of the greatest of their kind," Gunther replied. "There is some talk in the world above of an even larger surface kin, living somewhere within the Shadowlands. But I did not see such when I traveled through those lands. These are not of that breed, but you will likely find nothing to rival them in all of Ave."

"Doesn't surprise me," Ryan retorted.

"How can the Unguhur live so close to things like that?" Erin asked hesitantly.

"They do not have a taste for the Unguhur," Gunther said. "There is also some interaction between the Unguhur and the gallidils that would bear witness to a rudimentary level of relationship. But all of you should simply use reason. They are creatures of the wild. I will give you one solid piece of reason. Do not swim in the waters and tempt the gallidils."

Gunther grinned with a humorous sparkle to his eye, albeit brief, as he looked upon the faces of the four otherworlders. The woodsman was undeniably deriving a little personal enjoyment from the sight of their collective agitation.

"Stay out of these waters, and you will be fine enough", Gunther reiterated. "Is that clear enough?"

"That one stays by rafts often. It is a young bull of their kind. We feed him plenty enough," Eranthus remarked.

The Unguhur leader then gestured towards the cluster of his kind that had been standing down by the rafts when the party had emerged from the forest. One of the others turned, took a couple of steps to the side, and bent down to pick up the prone body of a large fish. The fish was one of a row of several rather sizeable specimens lying upon the ground, some as long as Lee was tall, near to one of the anchorage boulders.

Lee got a good look at the body of the fish as the Unghur lifted it up. The pale-hued fish was highly unusual in appearance. It had an extended dorsal fin, with a similar fin running along its underside, adding to a general form that for Lee brought to mind an eel.

Yet he knew without question that it was certainly no eel. If anything, it was something like a catfish, judging by the long, whisker-like barbs protruding from the rounded end of its rectangular head. In proportion to its body, the fish had very tiny eyes. For a creature that lived in the dark of underground waterways, the existence of a diminutive set of eyes was not a surprise to Lee.

As the Unguhur raised the bulky fish up, the gallidil immediately started drifting towards the shore, as if it was well familiar with the gesture. Lee watched the giant creature gravitate closer, gaining more of a sense of the reptilian beast's substantial girth and length. It was truly a monster, and the fact that it apparently had some sort of routine encounters with the Unguhur was of little comfort.

As the water parted and coursed around the contours of its tapering snout, Lee received some glimpses of the glistening spikes visible on the creature's exterior, lining its upper and lower jaws. The fearsome array of interlocking teeth included a veritable dagger protruding upward from the lower jaw on each side, located towards the end of the snout.

Lee did not even want to think about what it might look like when the creature opened its extensive jaws wide, but he had a feeling that he was about to. Even closed, the jaws and exposed teeth were incredibly intimidating to behold.

With a great heave, the Unguhur slung the fish carcass out towards the incoming gallidil. The creature's great jaws exploded out of the water, flashing amidst a great burst of water as they clamped down upon the offered meal.

Lee quivered at the sheer power and speed exhibited by the massive beast, even as he heard an audible gasp from Lynn, and a curt exclamation escape Ryan's lips. Erin was left in a state of near paralysis, a faint trembling having come over her body.

"Keep him eating. Keep belly full. No room for Unguhur then," Eranthus commented with a throaty rumble that Lee took to be laughter. Eranthus saw the dumbfounded expressions on the faces of the four with Gunther, and a mild look of irritation came across his face, "Second fish in short time. Now no room for Unguhur. Do you understand?"

"They do not have much humor in them right now," Gunther said wryly, chuckling. "I will explain it to them later, Eranthus. Do not take offense at their distress."

Gunther's reply caused Eranthus to suddenly break into loud laughter, accompanied by several of the other Unguhur. Thinking that they had just inadvertently caused some offense, Lee was very relieved to see the Unguhur's open mirth.

Gunther winked at his four guests, and turned back to Eranthus. "Many thanks, for keeping the gallidils full. I am not sure whether or not I would like to find out if they like the taste of humans."

The Unguhur within earshot rumbled merrily for a few more moments. The display of joviality in creatures with such robust, outwardly intimidating appearances was quite a juxtaposition to Lee's perspective. Admittedly, he expected the creatures to be far more given to other manners of expression, such as sternness, ferocity, and even anger.

The lighthearted reaction and few snippets of explanations did much to allay the fears in Lee. He could see the others with him starting to relax as well. Lee looked from Gunther back out towards the river, to see if his calming nerves would hold up at the direct sight of the gallidil.

As if no longer interested in seeking another meal, the huge gallidil had turned, and was already swimming slowly away from the raft area. The sight of the gallidil distancing itself was admittedly more reassuring than anything that Gunther or the Unguhur could say.

A couple of the Unguhur then stepped out onto the broad rafts. The rafts bobbed a little as they took the creatures' full weight, but the great size and mass of the rafts kept them fairly stable upon the water's surface.

At a gesture from one of the Unguhur upon the raft, Gunther guided his four human wards forward to the edge of the natural quay. His Jaghuns followed in a loose cluster closely behind him.

The Unguhur appeared fully relaxed, despite the fact that another gallidil manifested itself in the wake of the one that had just been fed. Lee's breath caught in his throat as he took notice of the new creature, which was significantly larger than the former one.

The tremendous creature was hovering uncomfortably close to the edge of the raft that Lee was being guided onto. It slowly crept inward, as Lee took his first step upon the lashed stalks of the raft.

The ease with which the Unguhur went about preparing the raft only marginally lessened his renewed anxiety. Erin looked as if her nerves were about to swiftly fray, as she hung back a few paces. Ryan's face held little conviction as he tried to gently coax her forward. Lynn had managed to board the raft, but her eyes were riveted downward, clearly shutting out the intimidating sight of the creature.

"Hah! Now you want extra meal, big one!" one of the Unguhur on the raft shouted to the gallidil, while slowly shaking its head.

The Unguhur's attitude showed its high annoyance, and also its familiarity, with the beast. It looked back to one of the others on the shore, continuing to shake its great head in apparent resignation. "Give him one, too."

The Unguhur's comrade snatched up another of the large fish lying upon the shoreline. The fish that was selected was a grander specimen of the same type as the first, one that was easily as big in mass and length as Lee. The Unguhur lugged it over to the shore's edge, and heaved it deeper into the river.

Swiftly, the gallidil rotated, darting off with surprising dexterity towards the ample offering as the Unguhur on the raft scowled after it. The Unguhur turned back towards the four humans with Gunther, staring quietly at them. To Lee, it seemed that the creature took notice of the great discomfort exhibited upon their faces.

"Gallidil no danger," the Unguhur pronounced. "We know that old bull, too. Do not worry. The big one is no danger."

Eranthus then gently implored them, "Go. Get on the raft. The gallidil will be no trouble."

Ryan stepped onto the raft, and turned around to help Erin. He held out his hands to her, to offer her some assistance.

Erin paused for a few more moments, right at the edge of the river, before finally grasping Ryan's hands and gingerly stepping onto the raft. A look of panic remained etched across her face, as she kept looking past Ryan towards the water. Once on the raft, she swiftly moved to join her companions towards the middle.

A second Unguhur followed Erin onto the raft, holding two of the longer poles, and two paddles. It handed one of each of the elongated implements to the other Unguhur.

The small group of Jaghuns was then divided amongst the two rafts. Gunther aided each of the quadrupeds in getting onto the floating surfaces, as they had to be cajoled one at a time.

The beasts were agitated and fidgety around the water, especially the youngest amongst them, Skyheart and Darkmane. Gunther's presence aided the younger creatures' willpower, and he kept them with him on the raft that he was to ride upon.

"Come now Fang, you are the most fearless! And yet you are little better than the pups!" Gunther commented gruffly to the greatest of his Jaghuns, as the muscular creature eased itself nervously towards the center of the raft.

The Jaghun eyed the water with great intensity. Its rippling chest muscles were taut, and its broad paws were pressed firmly into the raft, as it stoutly braced itself.

"Can't blame him at all," Lee remarked, staring out at the dark, flowing waters. It was a sight that was understandably unnerving for any terrestrial creature, especially with the knowledge of what lurked beneath the water's surface.

"No, I sure can't either," Lynn agreed at his side.

"Fang's been here before, he should know better by now," Gunther replied curtly, with a dismissive air.

The more that Lee stared, the more his mind began to conjure up visions of exaggerated depths and hidden leviathans. He pulled his attention away from the murky river to watch the rest of the group boarding, knowing that the sight of the river was doing him little good.

In a few moments, all of the passengers were finally settled aboard. The Unguhur raft pilots untied the pair of rafts from the anchoring rocks upon the shore. With a shove, and a few dips of the paddles to orient the rafts, the party was heading down the river.

The rafts, though rather simple in design, were sturdy, providing amply for the larger forms of the Unguhur. For the much smaller humans, they were more than adequate vessels. The rafts were easily able to accommodate all of the humans and Jaghuns, with plenty of space to spare. Ably handled by the Unguhur piloting them, the floating platforms remained amazingly steady within the waters, as they traveled along the slow currents towards the tunnel opening.

Lee's nerves were given little respite, however, as he was quick to notice that the rafts were accompanied by their own set of waterborne escorts. A couple more gallidils were keeping pace effortlessly, swimming in the wake of the rafts.

"We don't have any fish on this raft to give them," Erin commented to Lee laconically, in a whisper.

"We'll be fine," he murmured quietly back to her, though the sight of the pursuing giants was quite unsettling. If he could have edged any further towards the center of raft, then he would have, but he was already as far in the middle of it as he could possibly go.

While Erin kept up her watch on the gallidils, Lee relaxed his guard enough to start noticing the other aspects of their travel. They passed by the teeming stalks of the underground forest to the left, as they made their way closer towards the gaping tunnel entrance.

There was not much activity within sight, but on a few occasions Lee espied a few Unguhur a short distance from shore. They invariably came to a halt in their tasks as the rafts drifted by them, standing quietly and staring at the unusual group of visitors riding upon the vessels.

They left the huge cavern with its mystical forest behind, as the rafts entered the wide tunnel that had been burrowed out by the river. The continuous passage of water had rendered the surfaces of the tunnel walls fairly smooth. The ceiling of the passage was a little low, just barely high enough for the Unguhur to stand upright.

Patches of the glowing, algae-like substance that lit the great cavern grew at periodic places within the tunnel, swathes of it clinging to the damp walls. The regularity of positioning, and the general uniformity of the size of the patches themselves, gave strong indication that they had been purposely placed and cultivated by the Unguhur, to help with their navigation of the otherwise dark tunnel.

Lee noticed that their large hosts were not extremely talkative, even amongst themselves. He looked over to the woodsman, who was cradling Skyheart and Darkmane close to him. While the two Jaghun cubs whimpered and whined, Gunther appeared to be completely at ease, though he also shared their hosts' subdued demeanor in the sustained silence of their travel.

Deep within the rock, at the end of a prolonged stretch of river, the rafts abruptly emerged into a sprawling, gargantuan, underground lake. Like the strange forest, the sight was instantly breathtaking, only on a much greater scale.

Lee's mouth went agape at the immensity of the cavern. He was speechless as he looked out across the waters of the huge lake. On the far shore, at the end of the enormous cavern, rose up a subterranean metropolis. Even more spectacular, the mass of edifices looked to have been carved out of the very rock of the cavern itself.

Stretching from one side of the cavern all the way to the opposite end, the semi-circular city was recessed back into the rock, rising in distinctive terraces. The glowing, algae-like substance used in the forest and tunnels was applied in great quantity within the cavern, casting a considerable amount of ambient light over the city and around the lake.

A gossamer shimmering was spread like a thin, dynamic membrane all across the rock facing of the great cavern. Its glimmering nature flowed from the undulating lake surface, reflecting the cerulean light coming from the widespread swathes of luminous growths from water to rock. The effect was at once ephemeral, and dazzling, holding Lee spellbound for many moments as he gazed upon the majestic entirety of the spectacle.

Most of the luminance within the city emitted from among the

ascending terraced structures. A sprawling cascade of shadows was cast along the jagged cavern walls that bordered the city on three of its sides, as well as the rock ceiling above it.

Moving, merging, and separating, a host of lively shadows paraded across those rock surfaces, emanating from the movements of a substantial number of Unguhur, whose activity was visible all throughout the stone-carved city. A considerable number of rafts of various sizes were tethered along the far shoreline, and many others were floating out upon the surface of the expansive underground lake.

Those out upon the water were each attended by two to three Unguhur, whose purpose was immediately clear. Standing rigidly in place, as if statues, they stared intently downward, eyes fixed upon the gleaming surface of the water.

In their huge hands they gripped a type of spear that had been fashioned with a forked end. The Unguhur held the spears poised and motionless above the water, with their powerful arms drawn back, on the verge of a downward thrust. Tensed and ready, they were patiently awaiting a very specific moment.

As Lee looked on, one of them abruptly lashed out with blinding speed and force, driving the two-pronged shaft down into the water. When the Unguhur retracted the spear, a splashing form had been skewered upon its far end. The Unguhur strained with both arms as it brought the flopping, thrashing body of a large fish aboard the raft.

The fish was of a different kind than the type that had been fed earlier to the gallidils. It had a flatter head shape, provided with a lower jaw that jutted out noticeably farther than the upper. Its back and underside fins were set further back along its body. Like the other type of fish that Lee had witnessed, this fish was also very light in its coloration, its pale hue shaded by the light blue ambience radiating from the growths dotting the cavern's rock surfaces.

Though the raft was very large, the throes of the fish, and movements of the Unguhur, as it pulled the catch towards the center, caused the raft to rock significantly, sending up splashes at the edges.

Several of the Unguhur engaged in fishing, whether distracted, or having already secured a catch, paused to look up at the newcomers on the incoming rafts. They hesitated for a moment, and Lee could see a few of them getting the attention of their companions. None of them appeared to be alarmed, as they silently regarded the visitors to their subterranean domain. A few finally turned their attentions back towards the task of fishing, while the gazes of others still lingered.

Several more gallidils could be seen resting out of the water, their ample bulks pulled up on the bank in small clusters at a few points along the far shoreline. Still others were traversing the surface of the lake, their extensive masses drifting gracefully through the dark waters. The latter showed little reaction to the two rafts, though a couple of the creatures altered their courses to avoid any chance of colliding with the watercrafts.

Once they were deeper into the cavern, Eranthus' raft took the lead, edging a little ahead of the second. The Unguhur upon it paddled with strong vigor for the midpoint of the great crescent that formed the far shoreline.

One Unguhur on each raft then shifted to the longer poles as they drew closer, having reached much shallower waters. The Unguhur used the poles to aid in their final approach, as they deftly positioned the rafts, and brought them towards an area on the shoreline where several large anchorage-rocks were set down by the water's edge.

A few Unguhur, of the type wearing only the hide-kilts, hurried to the edge of the shoreline to help the arrivals secure the rafts and disembark. The Jaghuns bounded nimbly onto the shore as soon as the rafts had come to a halt, appearing more than pleased to find a solid rock surface underneath their paws. Gunther set Darkmane down, as Skyheart leaped to the solid ground behind him. The woodsman strode away several paces from the rafts, and waited quietly for Lee and the others to join him.

Lee hardly saw the woodsman, as his eyes were wide with an abundance of sheer wonder, as were those of his companions. They all stood dumbfounded, captivated and drinking in the sight of the astonishing underground city from up close.

The great terraces now towered far over them, with evenly demarcated sections running down to the left and right. The sections, to Lee's best guess, were likely groups of individual dwellings. Each section contained a series of four units, stacked upwards and positioned back within the terraced arrangement. The terrace-sections ran all the way to the ends of the crescent, where the lakeshore culminated in the cavern's walls.

It was a colossal mass of edifices that could provide for a large number of the huge Unguhur, at least a thousand or more. Lee could not begin to fathom how much effort had gone into the undertaking required to fashion the subterranean city.

Not far ahead from where they were standing was the base of a very broad set of stone-carved steps. The steps led far upwards, towards a massive and unique structure, which exhibited a smooth, curving outer facing. Whatever the rounded-faced structure was, it was set at the center of the entire metropolis, with everything else in the balance of the city's design.

A couple of the lance-bearing Unguhur wearing the tunics stood attentively to each side of the stone steps at their base. Though they had undoubtedly observed the arrival of the human and Jaghun newcomers, the expressionless Unguhur warriors made no move to come forward from their positions.

Another set of rafts was disembarking just a short distance from where Lee's group had landed. Several of the warrior-Unguhur were busy offloading the bounty of a recent hunt. Erin wrinkled her nose in distaste, as Lynn openly gawked at the unusual contents of the rafts.

Lee found the quarry of the hunters to be fascinating, giving him some more clues to the nature of the underground world that he and his companions now found themselves within. The evidence indicated a world as strange as it was daunting, and not one to be approached with a trivial attitude.

Great woven baskets rested idly on the shore, containing the forms of several huge crayfish. The great crayfish were, on average, longer than the distance from Lee's elbow to his fingertips. Lee did not want to imagine the pain that their sizable pincers could inflict.

A warrior lugged the bodies of two substantial eels to the shore, dragging the ends of their over ten foot long bodies to scrape along the stony surface. The bodies of the eels were greater around in circumference than Lee's upper leg, and the sight of them and the crayfish served to bestow a greater understanding upon Lee regarding the underground water's formidable denizens.

Two other warriors picked up a long pole, along which were strung the bodies of several very large bats, a couple of which had wingspans of well over two feet. One bearing up each end, the warriors conveyed the pole high off the ground as they moved away from the shore, heading down its edge to the right.

Three warriors labored with the massive coils of a great constrictor.

Its immense bulk and length made Lee shudder, as he realized with certainty that the giant serpent was large enough to swallow a human being. It was a creature that was not limited to either water or land, and Lee could only hope that the Unguhur hunters had rid the giant snakes from the immediate vicinity of the metropolis.

The last warrior among the rafts of the hunting party carried another carcass ashore, a creature that had a bulbous, rounded shape. Its long, thin legs were all folded and pulled in tightly against its lifeless body.

"A great cave spider. A delicacy among the Unguhur, and one that your friend probably would not appreciate," Gunther commented to Lee, nodding towards Erin with the hint of a smirk on his face.

Lee chuckled in detached amusement, as Erin proceeded to confirm Gunther's words. Having taken notice of the great spider, Erin had blanched instantly. Though he found some humor in the reaction, he did not find the idea of a great cave spider altogether appealing.

"All that is down here? In these caves?" Lee asked Gunther, as the implications of the hunters' quarry continued to dawn upon him.

"It is an enormous cave system, and this hunting party has likely been out for quite some time. It is a dangerous undertaking for them, but the Unguhur do not want to eat fish constantly," Gunther stated, another grin escaping him, as he eyed Erin's continuing discomfort. "And, like all of us, they like to test themselves, though I admit that they do indeed choose difficult tests."

"Nothing I would like to test myself with, anytime soon, or even remotely encounter," Lee said, glancing back to the forty foot length of the serpent, and the massive head at one end.

"I cannot say I disagree," Gunther replied, also looking upon the substantial creature.

Most ironically, Lee and his companions seemed to be every bit as exotic to the Unguhur as the warriors' underworld catch was to the newcomers. Lee caught the successful hunters more than once stealing curious glances towards his own party.

Though they continued in their labors, there was no mistaking that the hunters were deeply intrigued by the sight of humans. Lee surmised that it was Eranthus's presence, as an Unguhur of great authority, that prevented them from giving in further to their curiosity.

Lee then noticed that Eranthus had sent forth the two warriors that had escorted them from the cavern-forest, towards the metropolis. The two creatures headed briskly in the direction of the central flight of steps. The two lance-bearing sentries made no move to hinder them, as they drew up to the base of the climb.

The two Unguhur then ascended the steps with quick, fluid strides that looked effortless to Lee's eye. The warriors finally reached some manner of stone platform or landing at the end of the long staircase, disappearing from view as they proceeded towards the massive circular structure looming at the summit.

"Welcome to Oranim, the great city of the Unguhur," Gunther informed Lee and the others. "There are other underground forests, such as the one that you have seen, but this is the only city for this population of Unguhur. From what I have been able to tell, several hundred live here, perhaps as many as a thousand."

"This is ... amazing!" Ryan stated, looking thunderstruck as his eyes panned along the sights of the stone metropolis.

"How often have you been here?" Lee asked the woodsman.

"In the forest that you just beheld ... many times. To Oranim, only a few times," Gunther replied. "Wood is highly valued here, far under the ground. I have brought the Unguhur many select batches, over the years ... cut and prepared, as I have thinned the area around my dwelling.

"I do not often go beyond that underground forest, though. Eranthus has taken me into Oranim out of kindness and gratitude for our trade and ongoing friendship."

Gunther paused, regarding Lee with a serious countenance that was reflected in the tone of his voice as he continued.

"Believe me, you have been given a special gift ... to set your eyes upon Oranim. It is a sight that very few human eyes have ever gotten to behold. No human who was not a welcome guest of the Unguhur has done so ... that I can assure you. Consider it good fortune that you have been bestowed with this chance, even if the reason that drove us down here has nothing to do with good fortune."

Lee took the words to heart. Looking at the formidable creatures populating the city, he had no doubt that Gunther spoke accurately. He found it inconceivable that a human could reach Oranim without the blessing of the brawny, giant race of beings.

"I still hope I don't have too much more of this good fortune,"

Erin quipped with sarcasm, though her eyes continued to scan the myriad sights around them.

The spectrum of the Unguhur society was in full evidence around them, ranging from smaller offspring on up to very elderly ones of their kind. Lee realized in moments that he had only seen males of the species as of yet, as a group of basket-bearing females passed close by them.

Like the others, the females regarded the newcomers with unabashed curiosity, slowing down to observe Lee and his companions as they talked quietly amongst themselves. Not unlike humans, the females of the Unguhur race exhibited a wider hip structure, and on average were smaller in size and narrower in shoulder than the males. Their faces were a little more slender and rounded than those of their stout male counterparts, taking on a more kindly natural mien.

They wore a lighter hide garment that wrapped around their bodies, covering them down to the knees. Pins made of carved bone held the hide garments in place, and colorful fibers had been worked into the surface of the hide to form sinuous, swirling patterns that flowed from top to bottom.

An energetic commotion soon developed as a small number of young Unguhur emerged from the city. They approached steadily closer to the landing party, talking excitedly among themselves. The shortest one among the cluster of youth was at least a couple of inches taller than Lee, and most were already taller than Gunther.

The young Unguhur were a mixture of males and females, judging by the hide-kilts on the males, and the long, wrap-around garments on the females that mimicked the fashion of the adults of their kind.

They kept a wary distance from the party, mindful of the presence of the adult Unguhur warriors and the elder, Eranthus. The older Unguhur seemed to tolerate the younger ones' curiosities, paying them little heed.

With both rafts tied up to the shore and unloaded, Eranthus walked purposefully towards Gunther and the others.

"Come, we go to the Great Chamber now. The khan and khanum will want to meet you," he said, beckoning for the group to follow him.

By then, several more of the warrior Unguhur had appeared, a few having come down the high, broad staircase. Now escorted by several of the spear-carrying warriors, the group accompanied Eranthus towards the steps, proceeding with him upwards without delay.

The humans all had to exert themselves just to keep up with the longer strides of the Unguhur. Erin grimaced with dismay as they took the first steps up, and Lee immediately knew why.

The steps had been cut for the much larger Unguhur, and as such each was a very high step for a human. As the feet of the Unguhur were so much longer than were those of a human, the steps were likewise extremely deep. The height and depth of each step combined for quite a challenge, one that was imbued with awkwardness as Lee and his companions labored up the steep incline.

"It will make you stronger, and more balanced in your step," Gunther remarked, with an amused look at Erin's pouting expression.

The Jaghuns bounded up nimbly beside Gunther, and even the smallest of them had little trouble navigating the staircase. Lee envied their dexterity and balance, wishing he had a couple more legs to work with himself.

By the time they had reached the stone platform at the top, only Gunther still breathed steadily among the five humans. First to reach the landing, he looked back towards the other four as they strained to climb up the last few steps. He shook his head slowly, as if disappointed, before turning away and striding forward along the stone face of the upper platform.

Erin scowled at one of the Jaghuns, which was sitting back on its haunches, watching her as she surmounted the final step. She paused for a moment to catch her breath, and glared hotly at the relaxed-looking creature. Lee chuckled quietly at the sight of her extreme annoyance, contrasted so sharply with the utterly mellow posture of the quadruped.

"Give me four legs, and then we can talk about it," she snapped curtly to the beast. "Until then, you have no room to talk."

"I'm sure he understood you clearly," Ryan remarked, drawing a momentary glower from her.

"Okay, I know I am out of condition. ... No denying it," Lee commented to Lynn, between large, deep breaths, as he surmounted the final step.

"No disagreement here," Lynn replied between gasps of her own.

Lee stared towards the massive, rounded edifice that crowned the summit. Its surfacing was filled with what looked to be a great mural of small figures and scenes, ordered into general lines that wrapped around the semi-circular facing. Lee had no doubts that the figures and scenes that had been carved were of great significance to the Unguhur, whether historic, religious, or perhaps both.

The lofty vantage also gave Lee a tremendous view of the terrace-sections to either side of the central structure. Turning his head and looking back over his shoulder, he paused as he beheld an extraordinary overview of the lake.

"Time enough for seeing Oranim's sights later," Gunther said gently at Lee's side, bringing his attention back around.

A broad entryway was set in the middle of the rounded structure. Towards the entrance of the tall chamber, a small cluster of warriors was gathered. The armed warriors parted at the sight of Eranthus, two of them moving swiftly to separate two great hides that were draped over the opening into the chamber.

Gunther commanded the Jaghuns to remain outside. The creatures dutifully grouped together several feet to the right side of the entrance. The warriors that had been escorting them also held back, as only Eranthus and the humans moved forward, continuing on to the beckoning entrance.

"Stay close to me," Gunther said in a low voice to the four humans, as they passed into the opening behind Eranthus.

Some voluminous patches of the glowing algae-substance lighted the interior of the stone structure, placed at frequent intervals along the inner walls of the capacious chamber. A number of considerably older Unguhur were arrayed upon benches that had been carved out of the stone wall ringing the chamber's outer edge. They rested upon some manner of mats or padding set underneath them, providing cushioning against the unforgiving stone surface.

From what Lee could tell, most of the Unguhur in the chamber were attired in a manner similar to Eranthus, in extended, robe-like garments. Many likewise had armbands, or necklaces strung with an array of large, sharp teeth, though there were some noticeable variations. Some armbands had a furred outer surface, or shiny scales, while distinctly different types of teeth were present upon some of the other necklaces.

In the very center of the chamber was a large, rectangular block of ebony stone, rising up to a height approximate to the midsection of an average male Unguhur. Arranged such that its longer width faced the entrance to the chamber, it had an unmistakable altar-like appearance.

The opposite side of the chamber, directly across from the

entrance, held a raised stone platform, accessed by a short flight of stone steps that extended the width of the platorm. Upon the high dais were two great stone seats carved out of the far wall of the chamber. The seats were copiously draped in hides, some fashioned into a manner of cushioning for the apparent thrones. Two Unguhur, one male, and one female, were seated upon the great stone seats.

The male was clad in a knee-length, light-hued tunic, fashioned of a softened hide that lay loosely upon the contours of his considerable girth. The hide was woven with many delicately rendered designs, worked into the material in an abundance of colors. The remarkable tunic was bound snugly about his waist with a stout belt, the scaly surface of which gave evidence to a reptilian origin.

He wore an unusual type of head covering fashioned from some other type of hide, whose surface was covered in a very fine quality of dark fur. The head covering was almost like a cowl, draped about the male's wide shoulders.

A singular necklace was hung around his broad neck. Huge, spiky teeth were strung all along its length, save for a pair of very wicked-looking, enormous fangs. The latter were paired together at the bottom and center of the necklace, displayed prominently in the middle of his massive chest.

The female of the pair was garbed in the wrap-around style adopted by the other Unguhur females that Lee had seen. Her garment, like the tunic of her male counterpart, was fashioned from a softened, light-colored hide, and was also filled with resplendently fabricated designs of rich colors.

She wore a series of bracelets on both arms, and multiple necklaces were arrayed in a concentric fashion, as they dropped down in their various lengths between her breasts. The components of both the necklaces and the bracelets appeared to be a combination of shiny scales and glistening teeth. Some were composed entirely of one kind of scale or tooth, and others were crafted of an artfully arranged mixture of various types.

In trappings and posture, the pair of Unguhur on the dais were impressive, and undeniably regal, figures. Their expressions did not change as the newcomers were ushered into the chamber, although their large eyes slightly narrowed as they regarded them.

One of the Unguhur among those seated along the bench-line

ringing the wall, a male whose wrinkled skin surface and sunken eyes indicated a very advanced age, slowly arose as the group entered the chamber. He ambled with shuffling, ponderous steps over to Eranthus.

The elder spoke with Eranthus for a few moments in their unique, gutteral language, just loud enough for his voice to reach those that Eranthus had brought with him. Lee, and the others, wearing the pendants, could understand the discourse perfectly well.

Eranthus methodically illuminated the elder Unguhur, to the extent of his knowledge, as to the nature of the four humans, and what had transpired from the moment that Gunther had sought the Unguhur out in the cavern-forest. The elderly Unguhur listened in pensive silence, with a rigid, unreadable expression, until Eranthus had finished. The elder Unguhur slowly nodded, giving no comment before turning to walk slowly down the middle of the chamber. He came to stand at the bottom of the dais, before the two Unguhur positioned above upon the stone platform.

After another short dialogue, the distance of which prevented Lee and the others from deciphering its particulars, the elder Unguhur tediously returned back to the group.

"Bring them forward," he said to Eranthus, before moving away to take his seat along the inner curve of the wall once again.

Eranthus turned towards the five humans and said, "Come."

He led them through the center of the chamber, leading them around the rectangular, altar-like stone, and on up towards the base of the stone platform that held the two prominent Unguhur. Lee could readily feel the heavy weight of the gazes bearing down upon them, coming from the studious eyes of the elder Unguhur situated all around the chamber. The feeling in the chamber was like that of a breath held back in the lungs, willfully restrained, and pressing for release in a liberating exhale.

Eranthus halted a couple of strides before the stone platform, exclaiming, "Treas, Great Khan of the Unguhur, and Vuriant, exalted Khanum of the Unguhur. I humbly come before you, with human guests to the Unguhur Realm. A threat has risen in the world above."

Eranthus then prostrated himself, knees to the ground first and then bending over with his arms spread out wide. Gunther looked over to the other four humans, nodding to them slightly, as he proceeded to emulate the deferential gesture.

Lee signaled to the others, knowing that Gunther wanted them to follow likewise, before mimicking the movement himself. The others cooperated well enough, even Erin.

After the prostration, an action that felt very awkward to Lee, the female Unguhur upon the stone throne above inquired, "A threat, Eranthus? A threat has come to the Unguhur Realm?"

"The Unifier comes," Eranthus replied in a low tone, which Lee took to be one of respectful deference. "The Hill-Dweller warns us. A great army is coming. They attack the kingdom of humans above us."

"The kingdom above has never harmed the Unguhur Realm," the male on the stone seat declared in a very deep, sonorous tone. He paused for a moment, and looked over the four others with Gunther. His face seemed impassive, as he appraised them. "I would like to talk with the new people, and the Hill-Dweller. Speak for them, and speak to them."

Eranthus nodded, but appeared suddenly hesitant. After a moment, he ventured, "They have a Wizard Gift. It is a gift that lets them speak, and understand our words well."

A tense silence took hold almost instantly within the great chamber at the revelation.

"How possible?" asked the exalted male, with evident concern. "A Wizard gift? Tell us of this gift."

Eranthus looked over to Gunther. He nodded to the woodsman. "Tell them, Hill-Dweller."

After a short pause, Gunther responded to the request with his eyes lowered towards the ground, his voice also very deferential in tone. "Great Khan and Khanum of the Unguhur of Oranim, the gift was from the Wanderer, in the forests above. Given to these four."

Lee noted an almost immediate relaxation in the posture of the enthroned pair of Unguhur at the open mention of the Wanderer. Gunther continued to relate to the two Unguhur rulers the story of the acquisition of the pendants, at last prompting Lee to tell more concerning their arrival into Ave.

Though Lee was highly nervous, he did his part to explain how they were from another world, had been engulfed in a great mist, and had found themselves lost within an entirely new world. When Lee was finished, at Gunther's insistence, the group pulled their pendants out for the Unguhur to see.

The lengthy tale ignited some instantaneous excitement among the ranks of the onlooking elders and the two rulers. Whispers and low voices came from all directions, as those seated along the outer wall talked spiritedly amongst themselves. Even the pair upon the dais leaned in towards each other, sharing a few low comments.

"It is a great magic. We know it is good, if it came from the Wanderer. He has always served the Creator," Khan Treas exclaimed, as he leaned back in his throne, peering with great interest at the amulets held out by Lee and the others. "Let us talk further. What names do you have?"

"I am called Lee," Lee said, bowing again, though he felt somewhat awkward at the brevity of his name and lack of any lofty title. The formality of the audience with the Unguhur rulers seemed to demand something more fancy.

The other three followed in turn with their own introductions, all sounding hesitant and nervous.

"Welcome, Lee, Lynn, Erin, Ryan ... of the humans of the above world," Treas stated, carefully pronouncing each of their names.

"Welcome to our realm, and to Oranim," Vuriant added.

The khanum's voice was decidedly smoother and more melodious than that of the males, and her lips spread apart in a facial gesture that Lee took to be a smile. He could not help but notice the huge canines that were displayed as her lips pulled back, slightly offsetting the warmth in the expression.

Lee and the others bowed, inclining their heads at the extended welcome.

"Thank you, Khan Treas and Khanum Vuriant," Gunther stated.

"Belief of story is hard. Hard to think of other worlds. But the Creator has great power. Can do more than we can ever think of, Unguhur or human," Khan Treas said. "It could be as you say."

The remark by the Unguhur ruler reflected a child-like trust in whatever deity their kind served. While not appearing absolutely convinced of the story, it was clear that the khan was not rooted in inflexibility, and was willing to leave some room for the possible veracity of the tale.

"You are here in Unguhur Realm and world ... for a reason," Vuriant added, further evidencing the simple trust that Lee had perceived. "The Unguhur Realm will protect you."

She then looked toward her regal companion.

"We must help the surface kingdom," she said to Khan Treas.

"Enemy of the surface kingdom is the Unguhur's enemy. Is enemy to all."

The Unguhur Khan remained very quiet for several moments before finally replying. He turned his gaze towards Gunther, with a look that Lee interpreted as grave concern.

"Why does the enemy come to lands above?" the underworld khan asked the surface-dwelling woodsman.

"The above kingdom will not accept the rule of the Unifier," Gunther answered steadfastly. "The Unifier is trying to conquer the entire world. The Unifier wants every land under His dominion."

"Unguhur Realm is in this world, as is above kingdom. Both not accept Unifier," the khanum interjected firmly as she looked to Khan Treas, letting the obvious implications hang in the air.

The khan held her eyes for an extended moment, before looking back to Gunther once again.

"How do they attack?" the khan asked.

"The forces of the Unifier are invading Saxany. A great number attack farther away, at another place within our lands. A smaller army is now approaching the area near to your realm, coming through the land above us. They will surely find my home," Gunther replied. "We were in great danger, and could not stay there."

The Unguhur Khan and Khanum remained silent for quite some time, plainly reflecting upon the distressing news given to them by Gunther. Vuriant then raised her right arm, gesturing towards one of the elders seated to her left. As the summoned elder rose to his feet, Lee was amazed by the Unguhur's immense height.

The soaring Unguhur rose up a full foot or so above the average Unguhur warrior, easily over nine feet tall. Though clearly older in years, he still retained a powerful, bulky muscularity in his physical appearance. This was certainly not a being that had let his body soften over the course of time.

The hulking Unguhur was dressed in the manner of the other warriors, garbed in tunic and kilt. Additionally, he wore a necklace with a pair of long, curving fangs, which were of a slightly lesser size than were the similar ones upon the khan's necklace.

"Drubrell," Treas solemnly addressed the gigantic Unguhur warrior. "We must help the surface kingdom. We must protect our realm. We must act. Gather your strongest warriors. Use workers so that you have a force of many. Find the enemy. Fight the enemy if they are here, above us. Let our council know what is found."

The huge elder-warrior prostrated himself silently, showing that his aged body was still quite supple in its movements as he rose up to his feet again. Drubrell had a steely look about him, and Lee did not want to consider the fate of a human warrior that met this formidable creature under hostile circumstances.

Turning about, Drubrell then strode the length of the chamber and exited it without the slightest pause. While Drubrell was giving his respects and departing, Lee looked over to Gunther in hopes of getting some indication of the woodman's reaction to what had just transpired.

The woodsman's face had taken on an expression of great worry. Lee was taken aback at the level of concern evident in Gunther's face, suddenly becoming highly frustrated, as he could not easily question Gunther at that moment.

"Hill-Dweller, Lee, Ryan, Lynn, and Erin. Rest now. Eat to your fill. We will tell you what Drubrell finds. The Unguhur Realm protects you now. You are safe," Vuriant stated to the humans, exhibiting the strange manner of smiling that the Unguhur possessed. "You may leave now. Eranthus will see to your quarters."

The audience before the Ungahur rulers, without any doubt, had come to an end. Gunther looked over to the others with him, as he prostrated himself before the Unguhur Khan and Khanum once more.

The four in Gunther's care understood his desire well enough, and repeated the respectful gesture. As before, Lee found the act a little awkward to execute, though he managed it capably enough.

Once they were all standing, the group accompanied Eranthus back down the center of the chamber after skirting around the massive altar stone. Once again, Lee felt the weight of the stares coming from the throng of elders surrounding them, a feeling that did not dissipate entirely until he was well outside of the stone hall.

Eranthus and the spear-carrying warrior escorts guided them from the stone structure, and on to their lodgings. Their quarters were located not far from the great chamber, which came as a relief to Lee, as he was not enthused about surmounting another great flight of steps, such as the one that rose up from the shore level to the throne chamber.

The humans' quarters constituted the third and fourth terraces of one of the common dwelling structures that comprised most of the

Unguhur metropolis. Descending a few steps to one side of the landing before the great chamber, they set foot directly onto the roof of the edifice's third terrace.

A square-sided hole was set in the center of the flat roof of the third terrace. The ends of a wide ladder poked up above the nearest side of the opening, which descended down well over a dozen feet to the flooring of a large, rectangular chamber.

The far end of the roof looked out over another similar terrace just below, as well as affording any onlooker a spectacular view of the cavern and subterranean metropolis.

To the back of the third terrace's roof, there was a broad entrance, covered by a hide flap, which opened into a chamber that formed the interior body of the fourth terrace. Inside of that chamber was another high ladder that reached to another square opening in the ceiling. Lee noticed that the gaps between ladder rungs were quite wide, fashioned for the reach and size of an Unguhur.

It was not lost on Lee that he and his companions had been subtly placed in a position that would not allow for unobserved escape. To reach the ground, they would have to go back up and pass through the main landing to descend the towering flight of steps all the way to the bottom.

The only other alternative was to go through chambers and roof-holes, passing down through the lower two terraces until they reached the ground level. Lee had no doubts that the lower two terrace-chambers were occupied.

Either way, the Unguhur within the underground city would most certainly witness anyone attempting to depart.

Lynn and Erin quickly claimed the lower of the two chambers, leaving the uppermost one for Lee, Ryan, and Gunther. The two women slowly, and a little awkwardly, went down the ladder to explore the chambers that they had selected, while the males entered the higher chamber through its front entryway.

Once inside a chamber, Lee found the surroundings to be extremely oversized for a human. The height of the ceiling alone made him feel very diminutive.

The chamber with the square roof-holes was the first of two chambers situated on a given terrace level. The entry chamber appeared to be arranged for cooking and other domestic activities, provided with a shallow fire pit that was just offset from the hole in the ceiling. Like the great throne chamber, ledges had been carved into the walls that were more than adequate for sitting space.

The rear chamber was clearly intended to serve as sleeping quarters for a terrace's occupants. It was accessed by a more narrow opening than was the primary entrance, and was also fully covered with a hide flap.

Light within the two chambers was provided by a couple of flat stones that each contained a copious swathe of the bioluminescent growths on their upper surfaces. The stones were not overly large, and though they were heavy, they could be carried by a human.

As the far chamber was nearly pitch black, Lee lugged one of the stones from the forward chamber to the back to provide some ambience. Following Lee into the rear of the two chambers, Gunther located a substantial pile of softened hides in one corner, upon which the humans could rest, or use to cover themselves like blankets.

As Lee handled the thick hides, he judged that only a few of them would be necessary to make sufficient bedding. In only a few minutes, he and Gunther had sorted the hides into three roughly equivalent piles, for each of the three males to use as they wished.

Ryan moved wearily into the second chamber, and flopped down upon one pile of hides, looking very fatigued. He let out a long sigh, shutting his eyes as his chest heaved with an extended intake of breath. Lee and Gunther did not bother to disturb him, as they made their way back out into the entrance chamber.

Lee then spoke to Gunther in a lowered voice, deciding to venture one question that had been burning ceaselessly on his tongue ever since they had left the throne chamber. "I saw your face when the Unguhur said that they were going to see to the enemy forces above. Why did you look so worried? It appeared to me as if something was really bothering you."

Gunther paused, a heavy-hearted sheen coming over his eyes before answering. "It is the reason that I myself do not live in human cities. As I have long wished to be simply left alone, to live as I wish, so have the Unguhur as a race. They are not interested in the power struggles and affairs of the kingdoms of this world, or any other folly of humankind.

"In that respect, they are much like me. I want to be free to live my life the way that I choose to live ... without anyone delegating my affairs to me, or helping themselves to the fruits of my labor.

"It has always been the cooperation … the assent … of the many that have engorged the greedy appetites of the few, filling their armies and their treasuries from the lives and labors of the greater majority. It is always from the willing assent of the many that the few derive their power. The noble relies on the agreement and continued obedience of the peasant … make no mistake about that.

"Do not misunderstand me, Lee, I do not begrudge any fortune made in an honest manner, but the world has gone far beyond concerns for honor, and honest living. It is now something else entirely, and it has little to do with virtue.

"So, as I prefer to be responsible for my own fate, as I see it, in a way, so do the Unguhur. Now, both of us are being drawn ever deeper into this greater conflict. I find it abhorrent to the core of my heart, and an absolute scourge upon justice, that a benevolent race like the Unguhur is being pulled into this hellish affair spawned by the Unifier, humankind, and whatever other darkness may be behind it all.

"If you knew more about this ancient race of beings, you would know that it is no small matter that they decided so quickly to send a force of warriors to the surface … and likely determined to become part of a war openly on the side of one group of humans. What you witnessed this day was nothing short of monumental, and unprecedented, and I feel a terrible guilt for being a part of it."

Lee could hear the alternating emotions of anger and sorrow, intertwining within the words and sentiments pouring forth from the woodsman. He could not argue with Gunther, for he had often felt many similar frustrations in his own society. To live under the auspices of one's own self-determination, and to enjoy fully the fruits of one's own labor, were worthy desires that Lee could not dispute.

While Lee had never been disposed to becoming an ardent, recalcitrant, hermit, as Gunther seemed to incline towards being, he found that he could relate very well to the obstinate woodsman. Many were the times that Lee had ended a long and arduous week, wholly weary of body and mind, and burdened with many worries and concerns, only to see that he had little to nothing in the way of material rewards, or personal satisfaction, left over for himself.

He had watched the frivolous, bloated waste that was made of the revenues collected through taxes by the rulers of his own age. He knew that in reality he had only one voice among millions to ever challenge those who felt entitled to use the fruits of his labor to support much which he found repugnant, or profligate.

In many ways, he envied the defiant independence that was so manifestly evident in Gunther. Lee knew that he would never have had the strength to break away, and live largely on his own, solitary merits, as Gunther had so obviously done.

The Unguhur were still a great mystery to Lee, but he could see the powerful bond that Gunther felt with the strange race of creatures. Their motivations for remaining isolated from the surface world and human kingdoms might have some considerable differences from Gunther's own personal situation, but the presence of a desire for self-determination was unmistakable. The Unguhur were content to live out their lives in the relative seclusion of their underground society.

At the same time, Lee knew that it was almost certain that the turmoil and conflict of the upper world would mercilessly engulf both the woodsman and the Unguhur. The powers of the upper world would not hesitate for a moment to impose their will upon them. It was a loathsome truism that was present in every time, in every age, and, apparently, in every world.

Recognizing the sheer determination and strength inherent in the woodsman, and seeing the signs of similar qualities in the Unguhur during his early experience with them, Lee found that he had already grown strong in his sympathies. It was a tragic reality that the world was forcibly dragging the Unguhur, and Gunther, into conflicts not of their choosing or making, not so different from the state of affairs involving Lee and his three companions.

"I want you to know something, Gunther. We still do not know why we are here, and why we were taken away from our own world," Lee said, after an uncomfortably long span of silence. "Most of it is a complete mystery, but I do know that I did not have a choice in the matter … none at all. But we are in this world now, and we must also face its troubles. Alongside you. Alongside the Unguhur."

Lee paused for a moment, reflecting, as his eyes looked towards the brooding, somber countenance of Gunther. While undeniably bitter, the woodsman was resolved to the coerced situation facing them all.

"And then there's the thought that what we are going through together is what we were meant to do," Lee then continued, before the ponderous silence grew too weighty. "It is difficult for me to think there is no reason for all of this happening. I know that none of us have chosen this path. Certainly not you, not the Unguhur, and not us. Please, understand that, at the least, with what I now say. We will stand with you, do whatever we can to help, and we will share your risks."

Gunther nodded slowly, his expression remaining dour. "Maybe you will ... and you are well-spoken on this. But even in regards to yourself, I would question the All-Father Himself, though some would call that outright blasphemy. I cannot understand why you had to be taken from your world, and put into the middle of the terrible dangers that swarm in this one. Maybe it has some purpose, as you say, though I wish some manner of it would be revealed to both you and me. It has all confused me very much. These are indeed very dark and unpleasant times, maybe the darkest in the entire history of our world."

"Maybe in my world we were living in very dark times too ... though I, like most of the people in my world, refused to admit what was right before my eyes," Lee responded.

In that very moment, he realized more about himself than he had ever cared to face before. An obscuring haze had suddenly been burned away, before the onset of an emergent dawn, revealing things for what they were in all of their stark reality. Truth, as it was more often than not, was anything but comforting.

Lee recognized that a penetrating chill had slipped into his own world, delving far underneath the shining magnificence of the tools and trades of modernity. It was an empty heart at the center of a body whose marvels of advancement would utterly shock one such as Gunther, or anyone from Ave.

The people of his world in their masses were drifting further and further apart, like great lands being shattered and fragmented into tiny, ever-fracturing islands. They were increasingly following a siren's song, a call that subtly, and sometimes openly, promised to make them masters and gods of their mortal lives. Like whispers from sylvan tongues, notions drifted into, and resounded throughout, the general consciousness that humanity could unearth all secrets, and control their world and beyond, by turning entirely to the direction of their own will. They were promises that could never, ever be fulfilled.

A nagging emptiness, pressures, and growing anxieties had crept into Lee's own life. He could see the same things occurring in so many others, the result of an existence with increasingly unstable foundations. Like a furious storm that rapidly expended itself, so would the frenzied lifestyles so predominant in his former world. Under what was touted as the most civilized and advanced age ever was little more than a splendid, ornamented tomb, with the decaying essence of true, living humanity within.

Lee knew the stark revelation was nothing less than the reality, and it was the identity of the evasive, murky frustrations that had so often gripped him. He also saw the parallels to Gunther's own world, facing a future where enslavement and destruction of the free human spirit loomed, the willpower of a dominating few pounding the great majority in all lands into a compliant submission. The two worlds, despite their enormous differences in cultures and styles, were both going through unrivaled dark ages. It was merely the trappings and forms that differed.

The gruff, large woodsman was not so different from the comparatively diminutive, otherworld refugee standing before him. Interestingly, Lee felt a shared bond and understanding with Gunther. It was one that was forged with the fires of a shared passion, born of a mutual hunger for the desire to be free of those who had the arrogance, or malfeasance, to promise humanity a way to become their own gods.

"Maybe we are more alike than we think," Lee remarked. "The more I think about it, the more I'm sure this is so."

"Then there is little that we can do, other than to be true to each moment, as it comes," Gunther responded.

"I think both of us can say we have no idea what the future will bring. I used to think I had a good idea of the future, but I think that it goes without saying how quickly things can change," Lee said. "That much is pretty obvious."

"I used to think that I knew my general future as well," Gunther said ruefully, as a little sadness mixed into his shadowy expression. "I knew otherwise by the time that I resolved to live my days out in these woodlands. Maybe all of this is a good lesson for both of us. Even this old woodsman should not be too arrogant to think that he cannot learn something new."

The slightest hint of amusement crept onto Gunther's face at his words of self-deprecation.

"Then I guess we will learn some new things together, but I hope to learn much from you as well," Lee responded, mirroring the woodsman's grin on his own face.

Gunther leaned forward, and placed his hand gently upon Lee's shoulder. "And perhaps I will learn much from you as well. Perhaps I already have during these recent moments. And we may yet find a way through all of this. We just may."

"We may … and I'm going to think that we will," Lee responded, smiling warmly, as he saw the emboldened spirit renewing right before him like a stoked flame within Gunther.

AVANORANS

A large patrol group of Avanoran soldiers, accompanied by a few Atagar with Licanthers, discovered the woodland abode of Gunther. Their attentions were quickly turned from the small outbuildings and pen towards its main structure, set against the slope of the sizeable hill rising before them.

Very cautiously, the Avanoran fighters circled around the two-level dwelling. The Atagar kept to the outer perimeter of the woodsman's timber constructs, as the Licanthers that they tended displayed an extreme edginess around the buildings.

From their agitation, it was obvious that the feline monstrosities had picked up a wealth of distressing scents from the grounds. The hackles of the great cats were raised, and they paced about with slow, deliberate movements, muscles tensed and in a state of full alertness.

It was very apparent to the warriors that the main dwelling was in a solid, well-maintained condition, and was certainly not any long-abandoned homestead. While capably kept up, the structure was still not anything more than two levels of rough timber construction, attended by a couple of small outbuildings and the large, gated pen. In addition to the pen, there was an abundance of signs that a number of animals had been kept around the place. The huge paw prints and widespread droppings quickly told the Avanorans that the homestead had not quartered simple livestock, such as cattle, sheep, or swine. The signs also told them unmistakably that the dwelling had only very recently been deserted.

The ubiquitous tufts of fur, excrement, impressions, and other signs baffled the most experienced, knowledgeable individuals amongst the large scouting party. Not one person in the patrol could ascertain the exact nature of the creatures that had clearly been on those grounds just mere hours before.

The Licanthers provided the only comfort in those strained moments, as the muscular, feline creatures finally began to relax their rigid postures. The Avanorans inferred that the keen predators did not sense any imminent threats.

Trusting to the discernment of the cats' superior senses, the Avanorans allowed themselves to breathe just a little easier. The scouts' eyes still darted at every slight sound, their wariness continuing to be roused as they slowly made their way towards the door of the main dwelling structure.

One of the scout leaders rapped his fist hard against the thick wooden door.

"Is anyone in there?" he called out, in a commanding voice. "Show yourselves now, and you shall not be harmed!"

Empty silence met the scout's inquiry. He looked back towards the others from his party, gathered all around the grounds with weapons drawn and ready. Spears and bows were poised all throughout the grounds, and the warriors were positioned to react should an attack be sprung.

The Atagar chattered excitedly amongst themselves in their high pitched voices, drawing some fiery glares from the Avanorans. The Licanthers that the rat-men mastered were held tightly back on their long leashes.

The scouting party's leader, a tall, thin-faced warrior, then nodded towards a few men standing to his left, and gestured towards the door. The Avanoran fighters hurried up and gathered around the scout at the door, as he knocked upon it one more time. Not a sound emerged from within the building.

"Open it!" the scout leader commanded the men, who withdrew some small hand axes, and set about hacking into the planks of the door.

In a few short moments, the steel-edged blades burst through the planks, as splintered, shattered chunks of the door flew all about. The way was soon open for the Avanorans to enter the dwelling. They paused hesitantly before the heavy darkness of the interior, weapons raised, as if expecting some sort of ambush by the inhabitants of the edifice. As their eyes began to adjust more fully to the deep, shadowy interior, they carefully entered with their weapons gripped firmly in hand.

There was no sign of the occupants of the abode. The emptiness of the upper floor was discovered a few moments later, when a couple of the Avanorans guardedly ascended the wooden staircase to inspect the second level.

"There were at least four, staying up there," one of the men reported back to the party's leader.

The leader's brow furrowed in concern, as the few sparse belongings, furnishings, a couple of chests and clothes found on the first level indicated a larger-bodied, singular male. As he stood in the center of the room, he watched a couple of other men try the large door set in the back of the ground level's open chamber. At first, he paid them little attention, surmising that the door opened into some manner of storage chamber.

"Some further sign of what this place is may be in there," he said, encouraging the men endeavoring to open it. "And perhaps some supplies as well. This is not the usual Saxan dwelling."

It was swiftly discovered that the door was barred from the inside. That only meant one thing to the Avanoran leader.

"Break through it then! I care not how!" he ordered them harshly, his curiosity significantly piqued.

The men did not need any extra impetus, as they set their muscles towards breaking through the second door. Hand axes were turned again from being weapons to tools of utility. The blades impacted heavily into the planks, and bits of wood flew outward, exposing the thick timber bar that had been set in place on the opposite side. Beyond the bar was what seemed to be some kind of passageway.

"Barred from the inside. Can only mean one thing," muttered the scout leader, his sense of caution rising fast. His eyes narrowed as he stared at the doorway. He then concluded aloud, "Whoever was here has gone down that passage."

Eyes riveted to the door, he raised his spear up, and gestured for the others to gather close around him. The cracks of shattering wood resounded as the door was bashed into pieces, to fully expose the entryway into darkness.

Cool air wafted up from the dark entrance and flowed into the room, enveloping the Avanorans and causing several of them to shiver. The scout leader immediately sensed that an elongated chamber, or some kind of extended tunnel, lay beyond, far different in scale than the small storage area that he had initially expected to find.

The Avanorans hesitated nervously at the opening to the dark passage, letting their eyes adjust, even as they took notice of a far off speck of light within the blackness.

"Get some torches ready," the leader gruffly commanded the men.

As some kept their vigil at the opening, others immediately set about preparing flames and lighting short-hafted torches. When they were finally ready, the scout leader ordered a couple of fighters in the front to take a few steps inside the chilly entrance.

The torchlight seemed to be swallowed up by the encompassing darkness within, though the flames' ambience cast enough light to reveal the damp, rocky environs of a cave's interior. A short distance down, just beyond the revealing edge of the lights, it looked as if the walls were much more even than they were towards the opening. To those that looked upon the change in the surfacing, it looked uncannily as if the rock had been worked intentionally.

"Bring the dagger-tooths through, and keep your guard up, rat-men," the scout leader curtly ordered a couple of nearby Atagar.

The two rat-men that he had addressed made no reply, though the scout leader heard them chattering a few words in their strange tongue as they scurried off. They returned quickly enough, this time in the company of a couple of others of their kind that held the leashes to brawny Licanthers.

The Avanorans in the room backed up as the beasts padded forward with their handlers. Even the leader tensed for a moment, as the dark-furred cats stepped silently past him, watching their muscles rippling in their fluid, graceful motions.

At their masters' urgings, the pair moved into the mouth of the opening, one following the other into the narrow confines. The two huge cats tensed within a couple of steps, their ears flattening back against their heads, as they paused and stared into the blackness.

The Avanoran leader brusquely compelled the Atagar to move the beasts deeper into the passage, impatient to get underway before his nerves began to fray. Looking greatly irritated, the Atagar handlers complied, and cajoled the reluctant beasts forward.

Low growls rumbled from the back of the agitated beasts' throats as they started forward again. They drew up to the torchbearers in the passage and took the lead. The scout leader and several other Avanoran warriors then entered the tunnel, and followed closely behind.

A few Avanorans remained back in the dwelling, as the larger proportion of the patrol proceeded forward into the depths of the cave passage. The few torches that the party had lit did little to ease the oppressive feeling that the scout leader felt, an ominous dread that rose with each step. The blackness appeared to press in, confining the scant glow cast by the torches, and threatening to swallow the firebrands, and perhaps even their bearers, at any time.

The walls of the passage grew broader, and the scout leader knew that the ceiling had risen higher when the Licanthers started to growl more fervently, in extreme agitation. The creatures were now side by side, no longer forced to walk in single file. Their handlers were unable to coax the giant cats forward, both beasts rigidly defiant as they stood their ground.

"What is it?" the scout leader whispered sharply to the Atagar handlers, as he eased his way up to their position.

His words trailed off right at the moment when the cave walls themselves appeared to come alive. A storm of motion exploded upon the scouting party, Avanoran, Atagar, and Licanther alike.

Huge, shadowy forms erupted from the darkness, whirling about from where they had been pressed closely against the cave walls. Their rock-gray hides, rough and of gritty textures, had blended very capably with the stone as they had maneuvered themselves to fill in crevices and depressions along the course of the passageway.

Hidden in the deeper shadows, and only faintly touched by the light of the torches, they had been utterly silent, and imperceptible to the humans and Atagar. Only the Licanthers had sensed that anything was amiss, and by the time that the cats were certain of the danger, it was too late.

One of the Licanthers emitted a blood-curdling outcry, high-pitched sounds interwoven with roaring and hissing as it whirled about lithely to face the emerging threats. In a flash, four sets of claws were unsheathed, and ready to maul its imminent attackers. Two great spears were driven into the Licanther's body with relentless force before it could even loose one swipe of its deadly claws.

The second Licanther was felled by a singular thrust of staggering force. The thunderous, impaling blow knocked the creature off of its paws and slammed it down into the ground. The great cat was already lifeless when it thudded heavily onto the stone surfacing of the passage.

The frenzied stabs of the long, thick-hafted spears, at whose ends were wickedly sharp, obsidian heads, that to a human would be considered daggers in their own right, were devastating to the unarmored scouts. Even if they had worn coats of mail, it would have been of little protection against the horrific strength wielded by the hulking attackers.

Torches fell and clattered to the ground, casting a flurry of shadows amid the anguished, panicked cries of the men. The Avanorans were swiftly cut down by the massive forms, which had so suddenly arisen from the darkness. The hapless Avanorans realized with horror that their attackers had them completely surrounded. At a tremendous loss in the swirling darkness, the Avanorans' senses and skills were overwhelmed in mere seconds.

A couple of them started to run back the way they had come, dropping their weapons in terror. They only got a few strides before their path was intercepted, and they were dispatched brutally, without mercy.

The handful of Avanoran warriors that had remained behind within the woodland dwelling looked into the passageway in crippling fear, as they heard the frightened outcries and sounds of slaughter pouring out of the baleful darkness. One of them, who happened to be one of the Avanorans whose axe had hewn through the door to the passage, murmured under his breath his fervent wish that the thick timber door could be closed.

They could not see the attackers, nor could they recognize the forms of their own men. They remained frozen in place, indecision and dread paralyzing them to inaction.

The sounds of the battle ended very quickly, but it brought no cessation of their worry as they saw flickers of movements within the caliginous depths. The movements were accompanied by a flurry of scuffling, scratching noises, which seemed be rising in volume.

"Macy?" called one of the Avanorans, hoping against hope that their leader was still alive as he listened to the foreboding sounds of movement within the passage. "Macy, answer me!"

The scuffling sounds continued to build, but there was no answer forthcoming.

"Anyone? Anyone in there?" he called out frantically again, at a loss for words as he stared wide-eyed into the passage.

He instinctively took a step back from the opening, his hands faintly quivering where they gripped the shaft of his spear.

"Answer us, or we will loose arrows!" another Avanoran cried out.

Again, no answer was forthcoming as the sounds of approach drew closer. It was as if the darkness was coalescing, and rushing towards the opening. All of the Avanorans stepped back another couple of paces, their movements betraying that they had little doubt that something dreadful was almost upon them.

"Loose the arrows! Loose them!" yelled the Avanoran that had taken part in the door's shattering.

The Avanoran fighter, whether his eyes perceived truly or not, espied hints of shapes looming closer in the dark. The forms were far too immense to be those of any humans. Every primal part of his being screamed out inside that doom was imminent.

A couple of the archers among them then loosed their arrows, sending the shafts flying into the passageway. A guttural, angry cry that was anything but human answered from the darkness. An arrow had found its mark, and confirmed the presence of a grave threat.

The perilous tide continued to swell in the darkness, as it surged towards the Avanorans, the scuffles now taking the form of a multitude of heavy, rapid steps.

"Get out of here! Flee now!" one of the archers cried out frantically, to the few Avanorans in the room.

The remaining soldiers needed no encouragement as they turned and ran towards the entrance to the dwelling. In the confusion, a third Licanther with its Atagar handler, having entered the dwelling at the onset of the commotion, were the first to meet the deadly torrent rushing out from the passage.

The Licanther roared in searing pain as it took a hurled spear from the first Unguhur to emerge from the passageway. Its body crumpled to the ground with the massive shaft protruding from its neck. Its life ebbed in sickening gurgles, as its scrabbling, haphazard movements slowed.

The lone Atagar was driven through by another of the large spears, wielded swiftly by the second attacker to burst into the front room. The huge Unguhur was upon the Atagar before it could even comprehend the nature of its slayer. The Atagar's high-pitched shriek pierced through the front doorway, and carried into the grounds outside of the dwelling.

To a man, the Avanorans that had just exited the woodland abode cried out in abject fear, as they quickly beheld what was patiently awaiting them outside the building. Towering gray shapes hemmed them in at the entrance of the timber dwelling, having formed a tight semicircle that trapped the forlorn humans.

Greatly outnumbered, and facing fearsome creatures, of a type that they had never seen before, the last few Avanorans yelled out in a crazed sense of desperation and defiance. Weapons held firmly, they charged the enormous Unguhur in a maddened fury that channeled their fear.

Their wild slashes with spear, hand-axe, or dagger largely went awry, though one of the fighters did manage to drive his spear into the thick leg of an Unguhur warrior. The creature, howling in pain and rage, swung furiously through the air with its crude, mace-like weapon, black stone lashed tightly to a thick haft. The crushing blow crumpled the unfortunate man, his broken body thudding to the ground.

One against one, the Avanorans were absolutely no match for the Unguhur. With a ratio of several Unguhur for every man, the struggle was entirely hopeless for the humans. Not one Avanoran out of the large scout patrol survived the brief fight.

When the combat had ended, the Unguhur warriors dispersed. A few of the Unguhur proceeded back down the passageway from the woodsman's dwelling. They headed into the underground fungus-forest, and felled several stalks, which they then carried back into the passage. They worked to fashion a considerable barricade within the opening from the surface dwelling, stuffing the narrow part of the passage thoroughly.

Long before the obstacle was set into place, others had already gathered and dragged the bodies of the slain Avanorans into the passage and down into the lower cavern. They removed any sign of the dour fates of the Avanoran scouts and their non-human allies. In a short while, Gunther's homestead looked lonely and abandoned once again.

A number of warrior Unguhur were then set in position to keep watch within the rough-hewn, wider section of the passageway, beyond the makeshift blockade.

Others from the band of warriors wended their way through the woods on the surface, continuing back to the secondary location where they had emerged out into the open air. The small cave opening that awaited them had allowed them to circle around and set the choking trap, which had caught the remnants of the Avanoran patrol as they fled the interior of the dwelling.

Filing into the cave one by one, the warriors proceeded down another long passage that their kind's labor had widened ages ago, to allow for their great forms. The last one through pulled some brush into place that obscured the cave opening. When finished, the Unguhur warrior entered the passage, and adjusted a large stone behind it to conceal the passage entrance in the rear of the cave.

What the woodsman Gunther had known for a long while, and had gladly embraced, the Avanoran intruders had just discovered to their extreme detriment; the existence of a large population of the Unguhur race, living primarily in isolation, far underneath the outer, western forests of Saxany.

section ii

JANUS

The canoes bearing Ayenwatha, the tribal warriors, and the seven exiles traveled smoothly, gliding along the river's mild currents. Several hours had already passed, and the day had finally crossed the midpoint, though it would still be quite some time before the sunlight ebbed.

Muscles were drained to weakness, backs had become very sore, and an assortment of cramps and aches had to be ignored by the occupants of the canoes in their urgency to get down the river. Tribal warriors served as steersmen and navigators in the bows and sterns of the canoes, but the journey was a comprehensive effort. The exiles did their part from the beginning, putting their best efforts into repeatedly pulling their paddles through the water.

Ayenwatha called for one brief, merciful stop, at a broad stretch of embankment. During the respite, the Onan warriors passed out some cornmeal, sweetened by a little maple syrup, amongst the members of the tired party. After taking just a few moments to eat and catch their breaths, they were called to return the canoes to the water. The meager sustenance could not fully assuage Janus' growing hunger, or replenish his sorely depleted energy, but at the time each mouthful seemed like a precious luxury.

Constructed of panels of elm or birch bark that had been stitched together around a cedar frame, generously gummed with spruce resin, the canoes held up quite well over the pressing journey. To Janus' relief, they did not take on much water, though when landing he noticed that the warriors were cautious not to run the vessels aground, likely due to the nature of the gummed seams.

The unbroken continuum of thick forest growths hugging the edge of the embankments eventually degenerated in Janus' eyes. They changed from visions of lush, natural beauty, to repetitive monotony, especially by the time that afternoon had begun to mature.

At least, he was not left baking in the sun. The canoes glided into segments of the river that were well-shaded and cool, before emerging into stretches of direct, unimpeded sunlight that showered down warmly upon their bodies. The robust pace of their travel also sustained a cool flow of air over the canoes' occupants.

Janus was grateful for each and every small comfort that graced them, as his strength ebbed further with every passing hour. A little anxiety arose within him, as he began to labor with each strenuous pull of the cedar paddle. He was not so sure that he could endure for very much longer.

He felt a distinct sense of relief when Ayenwatha finally guided the canoes towards a large encampment situated near the edge of the shore. At first, Janus wondered which tribe of the Five Realms occupied the site, but as soon as he set his eyes on it, he could see at once that the encampment and its inhabitants exhibited many differences from Ayenwatha's people and their hill-surmounting villages.

There were a fair number of canoes in evidence within the encampment, though they were of a noticeably different style than those belonging to the Onan. A few rested upon their bellies close to the water. Others were turned upside down, propped up off the ground at one end on a bracing of lashed poles.

They were fashioned of birch bark sheaths fitted over light timber frames, a few being roughly of the same size as those of the Onan, and several that were substantially larger. Rounded at each of their extremities, the more prominent vessels all had a distinctive hump in their side profiles, located at their approximate midsections.

Several conical structures were set farther back from the river's edge. The constructs were covered in overlapping bark sheeting, laid over frames of five inward-leaning poles that had been lashed together with cording, fashioned out of strong, durable roots, towards the top. The frame formed by the lengthy poles created a broad, circular base for each of the edifices. Additional narrow wooden poles had been laid upon the outside of the structures, to help reinforce, and keep in place, the bark panels.

A flap of animal hide covered the entryways to the dwellings, which varied in size from structures that could hold just a few people, to others that could probably hold a dozen or more. There were a couple of more elongated structures, of a generally elliptical shape, that could be seen even farther back amongst the trees.

The surfacing of the bark panels on the dwellings were painted generously, with reds, yellows, blacks, and whites being among the predominant colors employed in the ornamentation. Many of the images were of natural forms, those of birds and other various animals of the forest. Janus picked out the outline of a broad-antlered moose depicted upon one of the nearer dwellings, as well as the form of a great bear on another.

Among the non-organic images that Janus identified were a considerable number of shapes that were variations based upon a common theme. These involved the use of lines that had matching, backward curving ends, which formed a kind of bracket. The brackets often served to frame other geometric designs, some being quite intricate.

The double-curving lines were oriented in a number of ways, sometimes even set back to back, with variances in the depths and angles of their curves. Whether part of a complex or simple design, the distinctive shapes appeared to be common on the surfaces of the conical structures.

A large number of people were moving among the dwellings, engaged in a wide range of activities. A few men had evidently just returned from a fishing excursion, bearing distinctive three-pronged wooden spears, fashioned with sharpened bone points. The ends of the spears had prominent, spiky extensions in the center, the latter flanked by two smaller tines, whose endpoints were angled backwards in such a way that anything skewered upon the middle prong would be gripped and held in place by the other two. The implements must have been quite effective, as two of the men in the group were struggling to carry forward what looked to be a few large salmon, which had been strung together through their gills and mouths.

Several of the inhabitants of the riverside village paused in their endeavors to watch the approach of the incoming Onan canoes. Faces both pensive and curious turned in the direction of the river, as tools and other implements were set down.

As Janus studied the village and its occupants, Ayenwatha explained to Erika, Kent, and himself that the people that they were about to meet were the "Masters of the Great Waters." They were the people of a tribe called the Lnuk. While not part of the Five Realms, the Lnuk enjoyed very good relations with Ayenwatha's people.

Their Great Saqmaw was an individual named Membertou, a very wise man for whom Deganawida and many Great Sachems of the Five Realms held a high degree of respect and trust. Membertou was now a very elderly man, but Ayenwatha indicated that many, both of Membertou's and Ayenwatha's people alike, had great confidence in his son, Tumel. Ayenwatha commented that there was little question that Tumel would be chosen to succeed Membertou by the Lnuk tribal council, after the venerable saqmaw had taken the Spirit Road of their people.

Ayenwatha then remarked to Janus and Erika that the saqmaws of the Lnuk were chosen in a manner much different than the way in which the Five Realms chose their sachems, but there was no trace of judgement in his voice. It was very evident that Ayenwatha harbored deep respect for Tumel, both as a courageous warrior, and as a future Great Saqmaw of the Lnuk tribe.

According to Ayenwatha, the tribe had once been a part of another Confederation, known as The People of the Dawn. The Lnuk had been one of the few tribes to survive a terrible period of war called the Forest Storm, which had involved the tribes of the Five Realms, and was thankfully long past.

The people of the Lnuk were divided among seven territories, each with its own saqmaw, the greatest of the territories being Membertou's region. As such, Membertou held preeminence among the seven saqmaws, which was why he was recognized as the Great Saqmaw of the Lnuk.

After the ferocious wars had finally begun to fade into history, the Lnuk had made a truce and cultivated a friendship with the Onan. It was not much longer before that friendship had spread to the other tribes of the Five Realms. The development, in Ayenwatha's eyes, proved yet again the ancient Wizard and Grand Council Founder Deganawida's wisdom; that war was not the path for a flourishing people to embrace.

The Lnuk, Ayenwatha explained, traveled and fished upon the Great Waters. He attested that the Lnuk canoes were constructed very well for traveling upon Great Waters. Ayenwatha held no doubts that the canoes of the Onan, though very capable in the streams and rivers of the tribal lands, were not suitable for the Great Waters. As he listened to Ayenwatha, it became apparent to Janus that it was the matter of vessels that had brought them to the Lnuk in the desperate hour of need.

The mention of the Great Waters, and Ayenwatha's desire to seek the help of the Lnuk to travel upon them, came as an absolute surprise to Janus. He had thought that they were simply going towards another rendezvous with a Midragardan vessel, as they had done before.

It was evident that his companions had also been caught by surprise, as different degrees of anxiety and excitement manifested in the wake of Ayenwatha's pronouncement. Despite the unexpected circumstances, there was no time to question the Onan war sachem, as the convergence of the canoes with the shoreline was imminent.

A number of Lnuk men came down to meet Ayenwatha's party, as the vessels drifted into the shallows. Several were armed, with long lances, bows, or spiky clubs, the latter fashioned from a spruce tree's taproots. A few of the warriors carried long shields, largely rectangular in shape, with rounded tops. Although they carried weapons, the men showed no sign of hostility.

A few dogs, smaller of build, with elongated heads and lengthy muzzles, scampered about the Lnuk warriors, sending up a chorus of excited howls at the sight of the newcomers.

Ayenwatha exchanged lively greetings with a few of the men at the forefront of the awaiting group, each of them obviously familiar to the Onan sachem. Each saluted the other with the phrase "My Kin Friend", words which boded well for the impending visit, in Janus' assessment.

Ayenwatha's words sounded noticeably halting in their delivery to Janus, and he quickly realized that the Onan war sachem was addressing the Lnuk in their native tongue.

For the most part, the Lnuk men were attired in hide leggings, with loincloths fashioned of a supple hide that was accompanied by a girdle about their waists, the softer hide looping over the girdles in front and back. Hide pouches were secured to the belt-like girdles, and many of the men wore sheathed knives at their breast, in a manner not unlike the Onan warriors. A few of the men had loose, knee-length outer robes of either fur or hide, worn like capes around their shoulders. All wore moccasins on their feet.

Their ebon hair was predominantly worn long, unbound, and loose to the shoulders. Only a few of them had a lock knotted at the top of their heads, the narrow leather strips securing the lock in place hanging down in back. More than one of the men wore adornments of small bird wings upon each side of their heads, while a few others exhibited one or more feathers.

Most noticeable about the men's appearances was the conspicuous glisten to the surface of their skin and hair. The sheen was unmistakably from application of some sort of oil, which left a lustrous coating in its wake. Janus wondered if such oils had a pragmatic reason behind their use, or were simply cosmetic.

The Lnuk assisted the Onan warriors and the exiles as they picked the canoes up and carried them from the water to the shore. Once the vessels had been set down upon solid ground, Ayenwatha begged leave of the exiles, to go off to talk for a few moments with the Lnuk.

Janus attentively watched the Lnuk as they interacted with Ayenwatha, gauging their moods and reactions as best he could. Their faces looked grave throughout the discussion, and there were more than a few somber glances cast back in the direction of the seven exiles. There was little mistaking the serious nature of the conversation, which was not entirely reassuring to Janus.

Ayenwatha broke away from the Lnuk, and came back to let the exiles and Onan warriors know that they could find places to rest among the trees closest to the shore for the time being. He gave no indication as to the course of his dialogue with the Lnuk, other than to say that it might be a while yet before he came back again. He then returned to resume his deep conversations with the Lnuk.

The Onan warriors and exiles moved away from the shore soon after. They kept together, gathering within some unoccupied ground among the trees, located a short distance from where Ayenwatha was engaged in his discourse with the Lnuk.

Several within Janus' party, exile and warrior alike, then saw to their physical needs in the relative privacy of the nearby woods. They stretched out tightening muscles, or took advantage of the period of respite to just sit down and relax for a little while.

Janus relieved himself first, using a large tree to shield himself from the sight of any others. He then came back to where the others were grouped, easing himself down, and bracing his back against a broad tree trunk. There was little talk among the seven, all lost in their own thoughts as they waited to learn something more about the next part of their journey.

Janus passed the time by watching the activity within the Lnuk village. He observed some village women skimming a thick substance off the top of the boiling contents within a strange kind of kettle. The kettle, as Janus came to recognize, had been fashioned of a hollowed out section of wood.

A "pot" of stitched birch bark was suspended near another open fire. Janus watched with interest, as one of the Lnuk women carefully removed a heated rock from the flames, and plopped it into the rather unusual pot.

He could see that the Lnuk utilized wicker-woven baskets made of tree shoots, as well as a distinctive style of bags fashioned from reeds, grasses, or bark. A variety of weaving patterns had been used to fabricate the various bags, which were dyed in a range of colors.

The women cast some furtive glances in the direction of the exiles and the Onan warriors. While their interest in the newcomers was apparent, they were still very careful to keep the curiosity of the encampment's children under firm control.

Janus turned his eyes towards a few village men who were making some sort of preparations by a canoe that was set down at the water's edge. They were placing a couple of long poles into the vessel, as well as what looked to be several unlit torches. Another canoe was being similarly equipped a few paces away. He had no idea what they were preparing for, but he wanted to satisfy his curiosity. He saw little harm in making an inquiry.

Turning to one of the nearby Onan warriors, Janus asked him, "What are they doing? The ones there with the canoes, the poles, and torches."

"Hunting wild geese, or ducks. This is done at night by the Lnuk hunters. Those boats will come back full of birds," the Onan warrior replied. "They will guide those canoes into the coves, where the birds gather to sleep on the water. They will rouse them with torches aflame, and then knock them out of the air as they circle about the flames in confusion. They will take up the stunned birds, finish them off, and put them in the boats, to bring them back to the village."

Janus nodded to the Onan warrior, and looked back towards the men as they continued their preparations for the night hunt.

After a little while longer, a few women from the encampment brought Ayenwatha's warriors and the exiles some food. Freshly cooked fish, a good portion of oysters and mussels, and some roots and berries formed the core of the meal.

Janus discovered at this time what was being skimmed off in the wooden kettles, a kind of butter, which he learned after questioning his Onan companions derived from the boiled fat and marrow of a moose. While he did not find the idea of the butter's origins very appetizing, it was evidently a very prized source of nutrients for the Lnuk.

Janus had become ravenous by then, and consumed the food quickly, in as polite a manner as possible. The others with him also ate rapidly in silence, displaying ample evidence of the great hunger that had grown within everyone throughout the long, arduous day.

The women of the Lnuk looked upon the strangers with great curiosity as they served them the food, though they said very little. The women of the Lnuk were clad in long garments of animal skins that were comfortably wrapped around their bodies, just under their arms. There were what appeared to be thin strips of leather over their shoulders, which acted as a kind of suspender for the wrapping garments. Snug-fitting girdles further secured the attire in place.

Leggings, moccasins, and separate sleeves of hide or fur rounded out the basic garb of the village women. Their clothing was richly decorated with a variety of materials, such as animal claws, quills, and even teeth, as well as a plethora of colorful, painted designs, many of which echoed the same forms and patterns displayed upon the outside of their dwellings.

Like the men, they wore their black tresses unbound and flowing, though they exhibited more personal adornment in the forms of earrings, necklaces, and arm and leg bracelets fashioned of quill or shell. The décor extended to their girdles as well, and a few of the women exhibited what looked to be silver coins that had been adopted to aesthetic uses.

Ayenwatha finally ended his lengthy conversation with the Lnuk, and came back to summon his waiting party. While far more extensive than the last time that they had stopped for a respite, the rest felt all too short to Janus' weary body.

There were more than a couple of protesting groans coming from among the exiles, especially from Antonio and Kent, as they labored slowly to get back up to their feet. Their momentary repose had resulted in rapidly stiffened joints, and tightly drawn muscles, causing Janus to grimace more than once as his movements mercilessly revealed each taut bodily area.

The Onan warriors displayed their usual stoic countenances, getting up much more smoothly. Janus could not fathom that the warriors would not have desired a longer rest, if the truth were to be known.

Several of the Lnuk warriors from the riverside encampment joined the Onan as they moved to requisition several new boats. A tall Lnuk warrior led Ayenwatha to where most of the Lnuk vessels were kept, singling out seven of the largest craft among those resting upon the beach. Three were sharper in profile and narrower of beam than their kin, but all were of roughly the same length.

Janus marveled at just how light the vessels were, especially in regard to their length and sturdiness, as he helped in the efforts to carry them down to the water's edge and turn them over. The men placed the canoes down in the water and slid them out with little difficulty, quickly getting into the sizeable boats as Ayenwatha's party moved to resume their trek down the river.

Paddles were soon dipping into the water, propelling the lengthy canoes. The party swiftly lost sight of the encampment behind them, but not before Janus witnessed a throng of Lnuk warriors hurrying to move some other canoes down to the water. The sight of their urgency, in the wake of his party's departure, troubled him greatly as they disappeared from view at last.

The Lnuk that had joined them in the new vessels were very welcome additions to the group, as the vessels soon attained a rapid pace that worked in harmonious concert with the flow of the river.

Ayenwatha informed the occupants of his canoe that the location of the large Lnuk camp was not far from the ocean, as the semi-nomadic Lnuk spent most of their year in the coastal areas. Janus did not know whether to be relieved or not by the tidings, as he did not know how far they intended to go once they reached the ocean. He settled into a rhythm with his paddle, knowing that time would eventually give him the answer, one way or another.

Ayenwatha pointed out one special landmark as they traveled along the river. Located up the slope of a great hill, a small cave entrance overlooked the river farther below.

"A Wizard named Kluskap, who had the great power of turning things to stone, used to reside there," Ayenwatha explained to Janus, Erika, and Kent. "That cave was the last place that he was seen in these lands, and his absence is deeply lamented by the Lnuk people ... much as Wizards who were friends to our tribe are now greatly missed. I believe it is all part of the same mystery."

Janus stared off towards the hillside cave, acutely perceiving the melancholy undertones lying just beneath Ayenwatha's words. He did not know how to respond, though he found it intriguing that the Lnuk, like the Onan, were evidently struggling with the loss of Wizards that had once befriended and aided their tribe.

Less than an hour had passed when they reached the 'Gateway to the Great Waters' that Ayenwatha had spoken of. The sight opened up dramatically to the convoy, as they passed through the last few hundred feet of flanking trees. The river emerged into a wide, expansive bay, which opened into the great seas beyond.

Sandy beaches ran up to the edge of the forest ringing the broad, crescent-shaped bay. The light of the sun, though just a scant few hours from dusk, sparkled off of the surface of the glassy waters. Whitecaps crowned small waves that rolled towards the beaches, their motions harmonious with the pull of the tides.

Many seabirds glided high overhead, drifting along the mild air currents, and sending their high-pitched calls out over the bay. Others of their avian ilk walked the lengths of the beach where the waves gently caressed the shoreline. A soothing breeze flowed off of the waters, washing across the flotilla of canoes. It was at once refreshing and invigorating, bringing a salty scent that lingered in the air.

The wondrous vision spread out before them, as they paddled out from the river and into the midst of the bay, was simply rapturous to behold. Janus was momentarily spellbound by the entirety of the timeless, beautiful scene. Though his body continued to work his paddle, he stared outward in amazement.

The undulations of the low waves were smooth and rhythmic, and the Lnuk warriors with the convoy navigated the sea-capable vessels gracefully through the bay's waters. Any tinges of fear or pent up anxieties within Janus at the prospect of heading into the ocean were quelled as the boats nimbly sliced through the rolling waters.

The broad expanse of the ocean reached forth under the clear turquoise skies to the distant horizons, beckoning to places beyond the boundaries where sky and sea flowingly intertwined. The awesome sight called powerfully to Janus, with that timeless invitation to worlds of unknown adventures and new experiences. Janus could only guess that the sensation was the deep, primal inspiration that adventurers often felt within the core of their beings, throughout all the ages of every world.

As the canoes glided across the bay, he noticed that the water itself held a different shade of color from the waters that he had seen back in his own world. Like the sky above them, the waters of the bay held a unique, greenish-blue hue. The richness of the water's color compared favorably to the luster of a rare jewel.

DREAM OF LEGENDS

The mystical allure present within the regal vision appeared to be something that strongly moved Janus' companions, as he looked around at their faces. Widened stares of wonder and excited expressions were displayed by all of the exiles, witnessing the tremendous vista spread out before them. Even the stoicism of the Onan warriors had softened, with unmistakable reverence displayed in their miens towards the majestic display of nature. Only the Lnuk warriors, who were likely well-acclimated to such a grand sight, exhibited no exceptional reactions.

Despite all of the weighty concerns, burdens, and fears within him, Janus could not help but have his spirits lifted up, as his eyes continued to take in the elegance and splendor of the dreamy setting.

The waters became rougher towards the lip of the bay, where its calmer, more sheltered waters finally met the raw expanse of the ocean. Ayenwatha's boat skillfully took the lead, helping to set the pace as it guided the seven Lnuk canoes onward.

Janus felt a reprieve, as his eyes scanned the horizons. Fortune appeared to be with them, if only for the moment, as the sky in all directions was completely clear, empty of any threats of storms.

He pulled again and again on his paddle, as the canoe rose and fell along the contours of the waves. Once past the mouth of the bay, the rhythm of the waves settled down once again, into a gentler, rolling pattern. It was as if the waves were in reality slow-moving, low-lying hills, watery terrain to be smoothly glided over.

The temperature out over the waters, buoyed by the soft breezes wafting through the air, was cool and comfortable. The time of day, with the sun now beginning to dip towards the far horizon, was also advantageous. With scant cloud cover to obstruct the rays from that fiery orb, it was fortuitous that they were not in the direct heat of the midday.

The small formation of vessels continued at a steady pace into the open sea. The shoreline behind them grew more distant, until it was just a solid, ambiguous line.

Though between two different horizons, the passage was anything but uninteresting. There were plenty of sights to see all around the convoy, the likes of which appeared to fascinate both the foreigners and the Onan. Even the Lnuk did not seem to be completely inured to the abundant signs of life.

More than once, the waters close to the canoes were agitated with the turbulent passages of large schools of fish. The vast numbers of fish moving beneath the surface churned up the ocean waters into a frothy tumult.

Numerous sea gulls hovered about in the air above the violent, choppy swathes of water, as they shadowed the passage of the schools of fish. With excited cries they awaited the aftermath of the obvious feeding taking place just below them, as the ranks of predators cleaved into masses of smaller prey.

The colorful backs of a larger variety of fish broke the surface of the water in many places, their scales refracting the light of the ebbing sun as they splashed back down into the depths.

It was during one of these episodes, when Janus knew well that the shore was far behind them, that he observed a number of immense dorsal fins cutting through the water, each one towering high into the air. The huge dorsal fins were on the outskirts of the latest schools of fish passing by, swiftly trailing the great multitudes of quarry beneath the surface.

Janus' eyes widened, and his heartbeat quickened, as he beheld the fins heralding the presence of titanic newcomers. As he was in the canoe with Ayenwatha, their vessel was one of the first to draw near to the vicinity of one of the gliding leviathans.

As Ayenwatha seemed to show no outward signs of discomfort, Janus quickly questioned him about the creatures. Ayenwatha must have sensed the panic rising in Janus, as he quickly entreated him to relax, reassuring him that there was no real danger. Ayenwatha then implored one of the Lnuks, paddling just behind Janus, to tell him of the giant sea creatures.

As the Lnuk warrior informed Janus, the large dorsal fins belonged to a huge, shark-like, sea hunter known as Shrakas. The enormous predators hunted in small packs, and the Lnuks had evidently fished and navigated their boats among them for generations.

The Lnuk warrior indicated that while they were in the boats, they had little to fear. There had been very few occasions that the great predators had shown any interest in boats. As nervous as Janus felt, he did not want to ask the warrior about those rare exceptions.

Ayenwatha reassured Janus that the creatures did not attack canoes, though the Onan war sachem displayed a little anxiety as one of the creatures swam very close to their vessel. The dorsal fin soared high above them, and Janus could easily estimate that the creature was more than three times as long as the approximately twenty-five foot boat, if not four times. It was a beast of tremendous bulk, with a girth that was much wider than the beam of the large canoe. As far as Janus was concerned, the canoe did not feel all that safe, and the extremely close proximity of the Shraka was deeply unsettling.

Yet as the Lnuk warrior had said, the Shrakas paid little heed to the watercrafts. The hulking creatures were apparently content to shadow the schools of the larger type of fish, who would quickly be making one of nature's age-old transitions from hunter to hunted.

Janus could feel the tension leaving the air as the great fins drifted away from the canoes, the triangular forms fading behind them with the churning waters from the schools of fish. Yet he barely had time to recover a normalcy of heart rate before the convoy was greeted with yet another incredible view.

About a mile beyond the sighting of the Shrakas, the occupants of the canoes all saw an immense tail fin break the surface of the water. Off to the right, a little farther off, Janus saw what looked at first to be an island. The seeming island then visibly moved, though, just as Ayenwatha enlightened them to its real nature. A moment later, Janus saw the tail fin and body of a second enormous form in the distance, the great fluke breaking above the surface as the whale plunged to feed in the lower depths.

The forms belonged to a colossal type of whale. The gigantic creatures, by Ayenwatha's description, and Janus' sight of them, were again substantially larger than their counterparts back in his former world. The sight was at once sobering and breathtaking, and his eyes remained riveted upon their tremendous forms until they too faded from sight.

With the exception of a small number of diminutive, flying reptilian creatures, which glided along the air currents overhead, the convoy encountered no more strange or daunting wildlife during their passage. Janus was not quite sure that his nerves would be able to handle many more surprises, especially considering the immense scale of some of Ave's incredible denizens.

The strange, intimidating creatures were a strong reinforcement to Janus that he still knew very little about their new world. The recognition of that reality also brought with it an increased measure of gratitude towards Ayenwatha and the Onan, for their unwavering patronage of the exiles.

It was less than an hour later that their destination finally came into view, a timely development as there was not much daylight remaining. At first, their goal was just a hazy lump on the edge of Janus' vision. Gradually, its features emerged into greater clarity, revealing a long, low island.

Ayenwatha, the warriors, and the exiles worked harder to increase their pace. The Lnuk guided the boats towards one end of the oblong island, where there was a little inlet that formed a small, natural harbor.

A small cluster of galleys was pulled up on the curving beach, their single masts lowered, and their oars resting idly on T-shaped racks rising from the decking. A broader, single-masted craft built in a similar fashion to the galleys rested just off the shore at anchor, with its square sail furled. A small rowboat containing a couple of men could be seen making its way slowly out towards the vessel.

A short distance up from the beach, there was a sprawling cluster of rectangular, timber buildings, of various lengths and construction methods. On a few of the structures, tendrils of smoke were rising lazily skyward through holes set in the middle of the roofs.

There was a flurry of activity throughout the place. The lively sounds of woodcutting, the clanging of metal, and a chorus of spirited voices carried through the air to the approaching canoes.

The ships and the people in view were just like the Midragardans that Janus had witnessed before the Darrok raids. Many wore the same, richly colored tunics, though a few had cloaks augmented with furs. Several of those attending to the beached galleys were shirtless, exhibiting the sheen of sweat elicited by heavy manual labors, even despite the cooling breezes.

In the spaces between the buildings, a cluster of Midragardan children were playing, running around in the company of a few large, wolf-like dogs. Janus could not help but chuckle at the sight of one young boy who was diligently, and futilely, chasing a sizeable, long-limbed cat with a thick coat of fur. The nimble black and white cat easily evaded the efforts of the boisterous youth, though it did not halt the spirited young fellow in his relentless pursuit.

A standard displaying a flying eagle and a running wolf was rippling high in the air over the boats at the farther edge of the village.

The banner blew proudly in the steady air currents, fully revealing the dynamic images woven into it.

At the sight of the canoes, a number of excited cries rang out among the villagers. A teeming throng of men, women, and children quickly assembled along the edge of the water, as the canoes drew nearer.

A tall blonde-haired figure with a forked beard emerged from the midst of the assemblage, proceeding to stand alone, several paces in front of the others. Janus immediately recognized the strong-looking man as Eirik, the warrior who had commanded the ship that previously met Ayenwatha and the exiles.

"Eirik!" Ayenwatha hailed in a loud voice, leaping over the side of his canoe to splash down into the shallow waters.

The other Lnuk and Onan began to get out of the canoes as well, prompting Janus and his companions to do likewise.

"Ayenwatha!" Eirik called back with equal fervor. He strode out, beckoning for others to come and help with the canoes, as the other narrow-bodied vessels drifted in alongside the first.

His eyes scanned the arrivals carefully, taking a methodical, purposeful appraisal of the entire group. His face failed to mask his astonishment at once again seeing the strange visitors that he had encountered back in the tribal lands.

"This is not an expected visit! What brings you to this far outpost, with such guests?" he queried Ayenwatha, with a look of great curiosity.

"It is very unexpected for us as well, my friend," Ayenwatha replied, his expression dampening from the initial brilliance of his greeting.

Janus strained to listen to the conversation as he helped the Lnuk, Onan, and Midragardans heave and carry the canoes up to rest on the shoreline.

"What has happened?" inquired Eirik, his voice grave, as he clearly sensed something amiss with Ayenwatha.

"I fear that the day I have long feared has finally come," Ayenwatha stated in reply.

Janus did not like the sounds of Ayenwatha's words, not in the least bit.

AYENWATHA

Ayenwatha did not have to illustrate the point any further, to convey to Eirik the deeply troubling news that the Unifier was now turning His direct attention upon the villages and lands of the Five Realms. They had spoken together often enough of his fear before, as rumors of war traveled far and wide over the lands.

"A large raid of great flying beasts has struck my village, and destroyed it. We had to warn you, seek your counsel, and ask for your help in this dark time," Ayenwatha announced to the brawny Midragardan.

"Large flying beasts?" inquired Eirik, puzzlement and concern etched into his broad face.

"Bigger than anything my eyes have ever seen in the skies. True monstrosities, perhaps even greater than dragons. These creatures can carry many upon their backs, and the Unifier has equipped them for this purpose. They carried a race of beings in this attack, beings larger than men, with fierce, dog-like faces," Ayenwatha informed Eirik, using his hands to demonstrate the height, girth, and strange, muzzled faces of the fearsome warriors that they had contended with.

Eirik's eyes widened, as he marveled at the descriptions given to him by Ayenwatha.

"I do not know the flying creatures, but I do know of the others that you describe … these beast-like warriors," Eirik stated solemnly, his brow furrowing. "Their stories are common among those we trade with in Kiruva. They are without a doubt Trogens, from the lands north and west of Kiruva. That the Unifier has them serving in His ranks is dire news indeed, for they are not known to venture beyond their homelands.… What is the state of your village?"

Ayenwatha closed his eyes for a moment, his heart sinking with the searing, inner agony evoked from the raw memories of his village's devastation. As the terrible images played vividly through his mind, he could not help but think of what might even now be occurring back in his homeland.

"Many were slain, and our dwellings were laid to waste. There is no choice left to the Onan. We are leaving the villages," Ayenwatha replied. "We have no way of defending our skies. Even were we to be scattered widely among the dense woods, we would have a better chance to survive than to remain vulnerable in the villages."

Eirik shook his head slowly, a deeply saddened expression upon his face. He looked away from Ayenwatha, staring up towards the dimming skies in silence for several weighty moments.

"You and I both know that there is little doubt regarding the attack on your village," Eirik said heavily, after the lengthy pause. "He meant to strike the first blow at the place where the Sacred Fire was tended. This is what the Unifier is, and what the world, and this age, has come to. People are forced to flee their own lands, just because they choose to live in the way that they wish to."

Disgust and bitterness were thick within the stout Midragardan's tones. His jaw was clenched with tension, as he shook his head again.

Ayenwatha nodded somberly towards his fair-skinned friend, his own voice low and leaden, as he responded, "It has indeed come to that, and I cannot deny that an invasion of our lands is about to begin. All signs tell us so. Large numbers of the enemy are gathering on our borderlands to the west. It is a great, powerful force, and there is no mistaking its purpose. The enemy has now taken control of the skies over our lands. Our own scouts on the ground are taking more risks than ever, just to keep a few eyes on the movements along our own borders."

"And what can I do?" Eirik replied forlornly, looking into Ayenwatha's gaze.

Ayenwatha did not miss the trace of hopelessness present deep within the Midragardan's voice. He knew that Eirik did not have the full might of Midragard immediately at hand. His homestead was not the smallest of estates, but it was little more than a modest village in size, merely a staging ground for the traders who interacted with the tribes of the mainland.

It was obvious that Eirik was feeling overwhelmed in the aftermath of Ayenwatha's stark tidings, not knowing exactly how he could respond in any meaningful way to the dire plight of the tribes. As it was, Eirik only had at hand a small band of his own men, a few capable bondservants, and whatever trader-warriors were currently visiting his homestead.

"Stand with us, if you would choose to do so," Ayenwatha returned firmly, "Just one man can resist wickedness."

Eirik fixed Ayenwatha, and the Onan warriors standing in back of him, with a resolute, encompassing expression. His eyes went from one man to the next, looking straight into each of their eyes, reflecting the strength of iron. He then looked away towards the Midragardans gathered around the beach, before turning his eyes to the timber structures beyond.

Ayenwatha wondered at the thoughts that were surely swirling within the Midragardan warrior's mind. The Onan sachem did not offer any further arguments or pleas, as the reality of the situation could not be any more clear.

Once the conflagration had begun, there would be no end to its ravenous hunger, until its flames had turned Eirik's own homestead to ash. Even Midragard itself would not be spared in the Unifier's coming storm. Ayenwatha hoped that Eirik understood that stark, but undeniable, truth.

Eirik turned slowly towards Ayenwatha. If the look in his eyes held the strength of iron before, it was now honed to a razor sharp edge.

"Your lands are our concern. Were our situations exchanged, I know that a respect of our own lands lies in your heart. It may not bring you the decisive help that you require, but the Midragardans will not abandon their friends in a time of need."

Eirik raised his right fist, clenching it tightly in emphasis, as his face took on a darkened scowl. Ayenwatha sensed the great, simmering anger welling up within the rugged warrior. When Eirik spoke, he seemed barely able to stifle the strong emotions heating up within him. His next words came out in a controlled fashion, though he was unable to mask the fiery look blazing in his eyes.

"If the Unifier thinks that He has made your defenses soft with His monsters in the air … and if He thinks that His forces will simply walk into tribal lands, with no challenge … then He will be most surprised. His forces will be met with fierce resistance, and the warriors of the Five Realms and Midragard will stand side by side. By the One Spirit of your people, by the All-Father of my people, and by the spirits of the brave warriors of all of our peoples, we will stand with you, Ayenwatha."

Ayenwatha was taken aback at the sudden ferocity in the tone of the Midragardan leader. The man had an inferno residing within his heart towards the dark intentions of Avanor, and those fires were being given full vent as he agreed to help the tribes.

"I am deeply thankful," Ayenwatha replied, in utmost sincerity. "My heart told me that you would stand with us."

"That I have agreed is nothing to be lauded … no more than

what our duty should always be in such times," Eirik replied. He looked back over towards the rest of those gathered with Ayenwatha. "There is much to be discussed. Come to my hall for some food and drink. Word will be sent by sky before the night ends, to King Hakon, and to others who are much closer. I will seek out my brother Gunnar immediately. If he can be reached in time, I know that he has considerable strength under his command. A small force can immediately be raised from this homestead, and hopefully there will be several others that can be gathered. You will not be abandoned to fight by yourself, Ayenwatha … it will be a great honor to stand with you."

He placed his large right hand down upon Ayenwatha's left shoulder, and squeezed firmly. "For now, come with me. We will make our enemies bitterly regret the moment that they take one step underneath your trees."

None of those present, whether Midragardans, warriors of the Five Realms or the Lnuk, or strangers from entirely different worlds, doubted the truth flowing through the words of the Midragardan warrior.

ERIN

"Leaves in the wind, that's what we've become," griped Erin sourly to Lynn, as they sat together on the carved wall-seats within their frontal chamber. "Blown helplessly in any direction that the wind cares to go."

"Afraid so," Lynn responded wearily, a dour expression spread upon her face.

"Prisoners too," Erin stated with despondence, venting her honest feelings regarding their current situation.

"Maybe, and maybe not," Lynn retorted curtly.

Erin stared down at the floor, a pout on her face. She could not believe that Lynn steadfastly refused to admit the obvious. By any reasonable definition, Erin and the others were under incarceration.

Living away from open sky and sunlight was already grating heavily upon her nerves. She was growing ever more anxious to simply take a few breaths of fresh air, and escape from the weighty confines of the shadowy, underground realm.

The food that they had been served only added to her irritation. Erin had barely been able to keep down a small portion of fish, though all the others had demonstrated quite healthy appetites. Then again, they had not been coerced into compromising their standards.

"Lynn, we are prisoners, whether you want to say it or not. And God knows where we'll find ourselves next," Erin observed, her words accelerating. "And we sure can't go home. No, we are stuck here. What I wouldn't give to just go home now, and get out of here."

Tears welled up swiftly in her eyes, as her simmering frustration reached a boil.

Lynn shot Erin a sharp look, and her next words had a noticeable edge to them. "Must I remind you that we really don't have a lot of say in the matter? We'd be dead right now, or prisoners of those invaders, if it weren't for Gunther and, now, the Unguhur. Just be very, very glad we're still free of the invaders' grasp, as things could be a whole lot worse. It is a fact that we can't do a damn thing about where we are, and we'd better start dealing with the reality that we may never get back home."

Erin looked up for a moment, taken off guard by the sobering, hard utterance from her friend. Lynn's eyes held a determined glint, but Erin found it very hard to believe that their situation was not tearing her friend apart inside.

"Never? How can you say that so easily? That you think we will never get home," Erin questioned.

"I don't know! Do you think I'm thrilled about being hidden underground among a race of giant cave dwellers?" Lynn snapped back, losing a little of her composure. "I'd like to be home right now, with my family, and my friends, just like you. But there is such a thing as reality, and it is better to confront it sooner than later."

Erin's lips trembled, as tears began to roll down her cheeks. She found herself at a great loss for words, caught in a swirl of emotions.

"Look, Erin, I don't want to sound so harsh with you, as you are my best friend ... After all I've been separated from, I still have you with me, and you being here is helping me get through this nightmare. Believe me, I'm very grateful for your friendship, and that I'm not alone in this weird place, even if I wish that you weren't having to endure this world too," Lynn said more softly. "It's just that I'm girding myself for the worst. It's all that we really can do, until we find a way out of all this."

Erin said nothing, as she looked into Lynn's face. Her friend's eyes had moistened, and her expression had softened considerably from the stony visage of moments before.

The two young women then embraced tightly, hugging the only strong tether that each of them had to their former worlds. They parted only at the sound of footsteps scraping across the roof towards the opening down into their chamber.

A moment later, Ryan and Lee stood at the edge of the roof opening, peering downward.

"Well, you're both awake, so I'm coming down," Lee announced, kneeling, turning around, and starting down the ladder.

Erin watched Lee navigate the ladder with a little difficulty, quite oversized for an average human's stature. Ryan followed closely after Lee, faring only a little better on his descent.

"So, how are we doing here?" Lee inquired, turning around to face them, when he got to the bottom.

He smiled amiably at the two women, though the lighthearted expression quickly faded as he took in their forlorn faces. Erin imagined that her tear-streaked face was quite a sight, but she made no move to turn aside, or try to mask it.

"Can't say I can really decide right now," Lynn answered through a throaty voice, laden with emotion. "Passing the time, I guess."

Erin nodded, and added in a low voice. "Passing the time … that's a good way to say it."

"We seem to be doing a lot of that, though I can't nap as well as Ryan, it turns out," Lee replied gently. "Still, our situation is better than some alternatives might have been."

Lynn nodded, as she cleared her throat. "I think you are very right about that. So, what do the two of you advise right now?"

"We rest, we eat, we wait, and maybe learn a little more about this world … and we pray that nothing disastrous comes to us," Lee commented matter-of-factly. "There really isn't much else that we can do right now."

"How is Gunther doing?" Erin queried.

"He's fishing at the moment, out on the lake," Ryan said. "You can see him from the roof, if you want to. He's not very far off."

"And the Jaghuns?" Lynn asked.

"Still in their quarters, and I'm glad he found separate ones for them," Lee said.

Erin could not disagree with Lee. As cute as the younger ones were, she did not want a bunch of animals around her at the moment, especially ones as intimidating as the Jaghuns. The more solitude that she could get, the better, as far as she was concerned.

"So we can speak a little more openly," Lynn said. "Then I guess it is safe to ask, what do you all think of him now?"

Erin bit back a few choice words that rushed to her tongue concerning the woodsman. Gunther had not hurt them, and it was undeniable that he had saved them, but he was still a brooding, abrasive man, who was altogether unpleasant to be around. He was insulting and inconsiderate, and better suited for his non-human companions than the company of people. She hoped that he stayed out fishing as long as possible, as her interactions with him were never comfortable.

"Come on, I know you all have some thoughts about Gunther. Any volunteers?" Lynn prodded.

Lee shook his head, with a rueful grin. "An enigma? I think that would be the best way to describe him. He's a very good man, I'm more certain of that than ever, but he is a man with many levels. I can understand some things about him, but others are a deep mystery. I kind of feel sorry for him, in a few ways. Don't forget, just like us, and just like the Unguhur, he has been pulled into all of this against his will."

"No real choice for any of us, is there?" Lynn responded morosely.

"Certainly not on my end," Erin muttered irritably.

"We do what we must do, when the situation presents itself," Ryan stated, walking over to take a seat next to Erin. "Moment to moment. I'm just glad that Gunther has stayed with us."

"Believe me, me too," Lee agreed quickly. "I don't know how I would feel about things right now without him."

Erin held back another acid retort.

"So, is there anything to consider doing around here?" Lynn asked.

"I was thinking about going down to the shoreline, just to watch the locals for awhile," Lee commented. "They are fascinating, you have to admit."

"That sounds like something, at least," Lynn said. "Which way are you going? Down through the chambers below, or up and down the staircase by the big landing?"

"Staircase," Lee responded. "I'm still not comfortable walking through occupied dwellings, though that does not seem to be a very bothersome matter for the Unguhur."

"They haven't heard a lot about privacy," Ryan said.

Lynn looked over to Erin. "Want to go for a stroll?"

Erin shook her head. "Not right now."

Lynn got to her feet. She gestured towards the ladder. "You first."

Lee smiled, and glanced over to Ryan.

Ryan waved him off. "Not now, I'll hang out here for a little while with Erin, if that's okay."

Ryan paused and looked over to Erin, who nodded her approval.

"I could use some company," she said.

Lee shrugged. "Have it your way."

He grinned as he turned around, and started up the ladder, followed by Lynn. When the sound of their footsteps had ebbed, Ryan looked into Erin's face.

"Hard day?" he asked.

There was a surprising degree of compassion in his voice, given his tendency for being rather boisterous most of the time.

Erin nodded, and her voice was thick with exasperation as she replied. "Not my best day. Let's see … cooped up in a big cave, with a lot of big ugly creatures that look like they just walked off the pages of some disturbing storybook. Being hustled and badgered around by a surly, ill-mannered, reclusive, foul-smelling wilderness man, and just wanting to get five minutes of breathing open air. No, Ryan, definitely not my favorite of times."

She grinned, though the expression was devoid of humor.

"Not the best of times, is it?" Ryan responded agreeably.

"So why would I want to walk down by the shore, or go anywhere around here. It's all the same stuffy cavern," Erin said in resignation. She gave a long sigh. "What I wouldn't give for a short trip to the surface."

"Probably not too hard to do that," Ryan replied, with an intriguing tone to his voice. "Gunther said that they have many passages and tunnels in other places that go up to the surface. These Unguhur have a lot of options for going to the forest, it's just that they choose not to spend time up above. They can easily access the surface, evidently, any time they want to."

"But how easy is it to get around here? Without being watched all the time, that is," Erin responded.

Ryan grinned with an edge of mischief. "Like I said a little earlier, maybe when the situation presents itself. I don't think it would do a whole lot of harm to go for a short walk outside. We don't have to go far, and I don't think we would miss the sight or sound of an invading army if they were somewhere near. If we poke our heads out, and there's any hint of an entire army about, then we just come back right away."

"I would think that an army would be pretty hard to miss," Erin concurred.

She could not deny that even if Ryan had misunderstood things, it still sparked a little hope in her. Just the thought of going above seemed to make her next breath feel more crisp to her lungs. Almost instantly, the cavern no longer seemed so confining.

"Lee and Lynn have gone for a walk ... Gunther is out fishing. I noticed a lot of rafts down by the lake, and we can talk to the Unguhur," Ryan said, with an adventurous sparkle in his eyes.

"Maybe we should go for a stroll then? A situation might present itself, perhaps?" Erin queried, seeing where Ryan was going.

"That's exactly what I was thinking," Ryan nodded, with a merry chuckle. "Or at least we can begin to form some contingency plans."

AVANOR

The mustering of the behemoths and their crews took place far to the north of Avalos, outside of the great castle of Robert Beaumaris, one of the great Barons of Avanor.

The Darroks had to be fitted well outside of the castle's walls, as even the expansive outer bailey of the castle could not hold the immense creatures and swarm of attending warriors, artisans, and other laborers attending to them.

A few plowed and planted fields had been forcibly requisitioned out of necessity, ruining a greater portion of the nascent crops for several hard-pressed farmers. It was not the first time that the peasant farmers had been forced to endure such injury to their labor. Tournament melees held by the knights and nobles of Avanor had trampled and ripped up their fields, and those of many others, on multiple occasions over the years.

As with the far-ranging tournament melees, the village farmers had to swallow their anger and pride, even more so at the present, as the Darroks were being sent forth at the behest of the Unifier. In some ways, the nature of the requisition helped to take a little of the sting out of the invasive, destructive act, as it was not just another indulgence by the Avanoran nobility. Nonetheless, the long-suffering peasant farmers quietly seethed, cursing their ill-fortunes, as they looked on incredulously from a distance at the monstrosities occupying their ruined fields.

The Darroks were outfitted with a new design of harness, one provided with a couple of additional adjustments to increase protection for the vital network of hide and iron. The group of Darroks was larger than the one used in the first strike on the Five Realms, as two more of the winged titans had been added to their number.

One of the new additions was a fully trained, matured female, while the second one was a younger male that the flight masters had just enough confidence in to dispatch for the coming task. The latter had given no indications that it would give any sort of trouble to its handlers, but it was still untested beyond its training exercises.

There was some initial hesitancy at the sight of the young male Darrok, especially by those that would have to be carried upon its back. The Trogens had to stifle their misgivings, as it was made abundantly clear that every possible resource was needed for the coming strike. It was a consequence of the tremendous pressure coming from Avalos that the final decision had been made to add the younger Darrok to the main contingent.

All but two of the Darroks were to be sent off with a full compliment of well-armed Trogens, heavily supplied with carefully sorted and selected stones for the coming bombardments. The remaining two Darroks were to carry a much lighter load of Trogens and stones, as each was to ferry a cluster of Harrak-mounted Trogen warriors. The carriages on those two Darroks were far from being filled to capacity. A considerable amount of space was left to enable the coming additions to their surfaces, as the contingent reached the outer boundaries of the Five Realms.

At the firm behest of the Trogen leaders, Avanoran skyriders would accompany the Darroks in the first part of the trek, across the skies of Gallea. Other Trogens would then join the force of Darroks in mid-flight, as the behemoths neared the Five Realms. The force of Trogens would intersect with the Darroks' path, as the former flew up from the south, where they had been deployed in Saxany. The mounted Trogens would create a formidable escort, quite capable of fending off challenges much larger in size than the one that had manifested during the first raid. This time, the raid would be conducted under the auspices of the Trogen chieftains, and the tribes of the Five Realms were not going to be underestimated again.

The take-off of the Darroks was a sight to behold, and even the peasant farmers forgot about their troubles as they observed the creatures taking to flight. With tremendous exertions of force, the Darroks plodded across a considerable distance of open ground, building up speed. Massive wings beat the air powerfully, as their bodies lurched off the ground.

It seemed as if they hovered in place for a moment, just before their forms began to lumber slowly up into the sky. Once all of them were airborne, the Darroks consolidated into a loose formation as they flew in the direction of Avalos.

In no more than an hour, the Darroks passed over the great city itself, before turning towards the west, to set out for the forestlands of the Five Realms. The enormous flotilla cast sprawling, dark shadows over the city as they soared across the skies high above it.

Far below, whether a market, craft shop, or street, activity ceased entirely, as many thousands of eyes peered skyward at the passing juggernauts. It was only recently that they had seen a similar formation heading over the city, on its way to the distant war zone.

The passage of the Darroks once again sent a reflexive flutter through many hearts, as men and women hurriedly whispered prayers of thanksgiving that they were under the protection of the Unifier. The purpose of the creatures was a mystery to most observers, but it was understood by all that it was much more advantageous to be aligned with the Unifier, than to remain defiant.

AYENWATHA

Several days passed by idly upon the small island where Eirik's homestead was located. The exiles appeared to be in much better spirits within the atmosphere of relative serenity, especially following the tumult and horror of the Darrok raid.

Ayenwatha was glad for the stability, knowing that several of the exiles felt guilt at the mere sight of himself and the other tribal warriors. He had been adamant with them that his choice to convey them to the island was both a free choice and one that he saw as absolutely necessary.

Nonetheless, several of the exiles had openly expressed deep regrets that concerns for their well-being had taken Ayenwatha and the other Onan warriors away from their own people during such an uncertain time. While he did not regret his choice, Ayenwatha could not deny that the exiles had touched upon one very sensitive aspect of the mission.

There was so much unknown, the cognizance of which plagued his mind relentlessly. Bringing the exiles under the protection of Eirik did not lessen for a moment the sting of Ayenwatha's incessant worries over the fate of his people.

Ayenwatha had put on a stoic demeanor whenever he was in front of the exiles, not wishing to add further to their burdens, but there was no denying that he was deeply restless. His mind was constantly distracted, consumed with thoughts about his people, and the threats that they were facing back in the Five Realms.

He had chosen full silence on the matter, striving to keep his worries about his peoples' upheaval and sufferings to himself. The foreigners were bewildered enough with everything that they had been unwillingly thrust into. Ayenwatha knew in his heart that they had no part in bringing the deadly ordeal from the skies upon the Five Realms.

Even so, Ayenwatha could not fully mask the pensive expression that spread across his face during a few unguarded moments. The distress was tearing at him without respite, from deep inside, but he continued to await the arrival of word that King Hakon, and other Midragardan leaders in closer locales, had been informed of the burgeoning plight facing the Five Realms.

Several of the Onan warriors who had initially helped to escort the exiles had been sent back to the mainland, leaving the morning after their arrival with the Lnuk warriors and their large, seagoing canoes. A few of the departed Onan warriors had since returned back to the island, this time flying in upon Brega sky steeds, as Ayenwatha had requested them to do.

He had then sent them as scouts, dispatched to discover whatever tidings they could gather, and to bring back any updates concerning the mass exodus of the tribal people from their villages.

After two more days, the far-ranging scouts had returned by sky steed to the Midragardan village, bearing word that there had been no major developments since Ayenwatha had reached the island. They did carry with them some troubling reports that the enemy's army was now fully encamped on the western edges of the tribal lands, and its numbers were swelling by the day.

At the very least, no fighting had broken out as of yet, and no more death had rained down from the skies, but Ayenwatha could take no heart from the absence of violence. The enemy was like a coiling snake, tensing to lash forward with blinding speed and fearsome power, and it would strike at the moment that it chose.

Each day rattled Ayenwatha's nerves even more, as he knew that it would not be much longer before the full force of the enemy was unleashed upon the tribal lands. Making matters even worse was the daily worry that the attack had already occurred, and that Ayenwatha would find out about it only after it was well underway.

He decided to remain upon the island for the time being, even after several reports of the massing enemy forces indicated that the invasion was worrisomely close. Gaining assistance from the Midragardans was paramount to the hopes of his people, as without it, Ayenwatha knew that they stood no chance. He also realized that he did not know the full truth regarding the exiles, but his heart told him that he had to try to keep them out of the Unifier's clutches, as best he could.

JANUS

The exiles had all inferred that there had to be an imperative reason as to why the Onan war sachem continued to remain with them on the island. The observation was never openly raised to Ayenwatha, but Janus, Logan, and some of the others had discussed the issue at length amongst themselves.

On the eighth day of their stay on the island, two stout

Midgragardan warriors arrived in the early morning at the quarters that had been given over to their use. Politely, but firmly, they summoned Ayenwatha and all of the exiles.

Once Ayenwatha and the exiles had been gathered together outside, the stocky, bearded warriors wasted no time, escorting the group through the buildings of the seaside homestead towards the open grounds spreading beyond it. They marched out from the buildings and proceeded into a wide, cleared field, which had been set aside to lay fallow for the current growing season. Several incredible sights were awaiting the exiles when they arrived in the cleared expanse.

A gathering of armed Midragardan warriors was assembled around Eirik. Their cloaks blowing about in the chill winds, they regarded the newcomers quietly, as the group approached them across the open field.

Janus paid the Midragardan warriors no heed, as his eyes were riveted upon the amazing vision consuming all of his attention. Magnificent and striking, the creatures gathered in the midst of the field were breathtaking to behold. Most of them were standing upon their four long legs, but a couple of the beasts were resting their bodies on the ground.

The collective sight of the beasts rendered Janus utterly speechless. They were the essence of imaginative myth made into flesh and blood, living, breathing legends right before his eyes.

In the body, the creatures were akin to immense wolves. At the shoulder, the shortest of them was at least as tall as the height of an average human. The creatures had a noticeably elongated profile, with relatively narrow backs that ended in muscular hindquarters, out of which extended long, bushy tails.

Their burly chests swelled with a pronounced muscularity that flowed up and around to a pronounced hump just beyond the back of their necks. The heads of the creatures were incredibly wolf-like, with lengthy muzzles, broad faces, and upright, triangular ears. Their piercing, golden eyes seemed to look right through Janus, as the creatures regarded the approaching newcomers.

Their legs were longer and leaner in proportion to their bodies than were those of a terrestrial wolf. The legs ended in broad paws that were each equipped with a set of rather stout, very durable-looking claws.

A pair of very broad wings connected into the bulging muscle mass located down past the base of their necks. Tucked in at their sides,

the wings were covered with an extremely fine layer of fur. The latter did not fully obscure the extensive network of veins lining the surface of the expansive appendages.

A thicker coat of lustrous fur covered the rest of their bodies, giving each of the creatures a particularly striking appearance. For most, the coats were of a silvery, gray hue. The luxuriant sheen of the silver coats in the sunlight made it look at a glance as if their fur was composed of the precious metal itself. A couple of the others were black-furred, and one was snow white, imbued with either an ebon or opal richness that fully matched the grandeur inherent in the coats of their silvery counterparts.

All of the creatures had harnesses and saddles for the accommodation of riders, both elements being noticeably different in fashion from those used by the tribal people on their Brega steeds. The leather breast straps were wide and thick, as compared with the long, thinner crupper straps crafted for the elongated forms of the wolf-like creatures.

The wood-framed saddles featured a lower pommel and cantle, and were fitted with a few additional, loose-hanging straps, a couple of which ended in metal buckles, for securing the rider to the seat. Hanging down from the saddles were sets of wide iron stirrups, a few of which had silver filigree ornamentation that showed brilliantly against the dark iron used to fashion them.

Around twenty-five of the impressive creatures were present within the field, exceeding the number of Midragardan warriors currently gathered there. Janus did not know what to say, as it was all that he could do just to continue walking alongside his companions while he stared awestruck at the winged creatures.

"The Fenraren are beautiful creatures, with a great heart and strength," Ayenwatha said to Erika, just behind Janus, as they drew nearer to the gathered warriors. "You already know of our Brega. These are the sky steeds of the Midragardans. The Brega and the Fenraren are both of the Skiantha, the precious flying steeds of this world."

"Absolutely beautiful," Erika answered him with reverence in her voice.

Janus had to call up some additional willpower to take his eyes off of the stunning creatures, and glance over to Erika. Her eyes were filled with sheer wonderment as she gazed upon the winged beasts. She looked positively enraptured, such that she did not even appear to take notice of Janus looking at her.

Janus then saw that the other exiles were all standing still, closely gathered around Janus, Ayenwatha, and Erika, with similarly awed expressions.

"Fast and powerful ... the Fenraren are a most special creature of the One Spirit," Ayenwatha continued, in obvious admiration of the creatures himself. "They can soar like the great birds of the air, and they have the kinship, nobility, and ferocity of the wolf of the forest."

When they neared the cluster of Midragardan warriors and Fenraren, Eirik strode forth to meet them. His tall, proud posture complimented his broad-shouldered frame, casting a dignified, resolute air about him.

He looked to Ayenwatha, and glanced towards the seven exiles. Janus noted the intense interest in his brief look towards them, a look that had not been present in his eyes when they had first arrived at the island.

AYENWATHA

Eirik looked intently at Ayenwatha, and the Onan warrior could see the deep tension splayed across the Midragardan's face.

"My friend, the times are indeed urgent! King Hakon has sent for you, to come in person, without delay," Eirik informed Ayenwatha, his voice grave and insistent. "He has provided an escort for you, of some of the best sky warriors in all of Midragard. You and any warriors that you choose to bring with you will be provided with Fenraren steeds.

"The journey will not be an easy one, and only you and tribal warriors of your choosing are to take this path. King Hakon insists that the seven exiles must not be risked. There are some small islands along the way, where we may gain some rest and sustenance ... and I will be going with you as well."

Eirik's demeanor and timbre left no doubt in Ayenwatha's mind that the Midragardan would not accept a refusal of the journey.

"What has happened? Why is there such haste?" Ayenwatha asked Eirik.

The Midragardan's attitude was such an anomaly in comparison to his normal disposition. Something was seriously amiss, and given recent events Ayenwatha was not feeling overly patient.

"I know little more than what you already know, Ayenwatha. The king is very troubled at the news of the brutal attacks upon your villages. He is also greatly troubled by the news of the seven that you found in your lands. He does not want to risk the loss of time, not even a moment," Eirik stated, the insistence surging again within the warrior's voice.

"Very well, I shall go with you then," Ayenwatha replied after a moment's consideration, giving his acquiescence with a single, purposeful nod.

"King Hakon also asks that you allow him to keep the outlanders safe within the Midragardan lands," Eirik said. "But they must not travel upon Fenraren."

This unexpected request gave Ayenwatha some initial pause, but Eirik continued speaking before the Onan war sachem had a chance to reply.

"We do not know who they are, for certain. But if they are sought by our enemies, then the skies will be far more dangerous to traverse than the seas," Eirik stated, his voice firm. "It is advised that the outlanders travel upon our longships, for any journey to Midragard. Their path will be slower, but there will be less chance of them being discovered. And once in our lands, they will be much safer than in yours. No enemies muster upon our borders, and any enemy desiring to harm Midragard will have to cross the seas first."

The Midragardan looked a little reticent, if not regretful. Ayenwatha perceived that Eirik was feeling a great aversion at having to openly speak of the threats to Ayenwatha's own homelands. He fell silent for several long moments, as he pondered the solemn words of Eirik. A momentous decision lay before Ayenwatha, and he had to make it quickly.

There was no reason to mistrust the Midragardan King, and nothing that Eirik had said sounded unwise. The friendship between Midragard and the Five Realms had been strong and fruitful for a great many years. The reputation of King Hakon's wisdom and integrity stood far beyond that of any foreign leader that Ayenwatha's ears had ever heard account of, with the possible exception of the latest King of Saxany.

Ayenwatha therefore regarded Eirik's message in a spirit of genuine goodwill. Its origin was from the very mouth of a king who was beloved by his own people, and well-respected by others. The king's effect upon his people had been transforming. That, more than anything else, spoke the loudest concerning the king's nature.

The legendary raiding tendencies of the Midragardans were now very diminished from what they had been many years before. Occasional Midragardan freebooters and pirates still existed, but were much reduced in number. Under King Hakon's leadership, they were rooted out and subdued wherever they were found.

King Hakon was effectively ushering in a new age for Midragard. It said much about the man that he had reined in the heated impulses of young, landless warriors, who had formed the greater proportion of the devastating raiding fleets in ages past. Ayenwatha could relate to such a profound period of change, as the Wizard Deganawida had revealed a higher vision for his own ancestors.

Adding to Ayenwatha's conviction about King Hakon was the fact that there was no real good reason for Midragard to lead the tribes of the Five Realms astray. Even when Midragard had been ruled by a mosaic of warrior chieftains and petty kings, when raiding both each other and foreign lands was a common pursuit, the Five Realms had held little attraction for the ravenous appetites of the seaborne raiders. The two lands did not share the same passion for precious metals, forged weapons, or jewels. The western lands with their considerable material wealth were much more inviting targets, abundant in gold, silver, and captives.

Learning very quickly that they would face a formidable enemy and gain little to nothing in plunder for their efforts, Midragard's raiders soon turned away from conflict with the tribes. There was continued contact, and the roots of trade had gradually developed. The Midragardans no longer referred to the tribal peoples by the slightly derogatory term of skraelings, but instead began to identify the native peoples according to their individual tribes.

Friendship between the two peoples had thus grown and prospered. Trade had expanded, with the Five Realms providing primarily furs, in return for the Midragardans providing forged arrowheads, spearheads, axe-heads, and other forms of metal work that were of practical use to the tribal people.

In the time of King Hakon, that relationship had never been better. If there was ever a chance to gain significant help for the Five Realms, Ayenwatha knew that the possibility lay the strongest with King Hakon.

Also weighing heavily upon his inner deliberation was the matter of the seven exiles. He had heard of the legends regarding visitors from other worlds, tales that were common in the west, and known to the Midragardans as well. While it was true that the seven foreigners might not be the ones prophesied in those ancient stories, Ayenwatha did not want to take any chances, or make any loose assumptions, within the increasingly dark, turbulent age.

Above all, he could not deny the stark realities facing his own lands, the conditions involving Midragard, and the level of threats likely to face each of them in the near future. The Midragardans were unquestioned masters of the sea, and were the only peoples occupying their far southern lands. They resided very far from Avalos, and Eirik was absolutely correct in saying that any future threat would have to cross the seas first.

Ayenwatha's own lands, by contrast, were under a massive, immediate threat. It was already to the point where his people were being effectively exiled from their own tribal lands. There was no question at all that, of the two places, the safest refuge for the exiles would be in Midragard; if they could be safely conveyed there.

The answer was fairly simple, even if Ayenwatha had felt the responsibility to carefully deliberate it. Ayenwatha took a deep breath, and looked Eirik squarely in the eyes.

"It will be done as you wish, my friend," Ayenwatha announced, clasping Eirik's forearm, in the tradition of the Midragardan people. With his answer, Ayenwatha put an unprecedented amount of trust in the Midragardans.

"I will stand by you in all things, my friend. Never forget that. We share the same enemies, and we will face them together. But let us make haste now. We must waste no more time," Eirik stated with urgency.

Ayenwatha nodded, and turned quickly to explain the situation to the others with him. Confused expressions met him as he began to address the exiles, and the looks did not entirely leave their faces when he finished.

"To Midragard?" asked Antonio in apparent disbelief. "We'll be leaving your people behind?"

Ayenwatha watched the paunchy young man look over at the rough-looking assemblage of Midragardan warriors nearby. Ayenwatha had to remind himself that while he was entirely at ease with the Midragardans, it was not surprising that one who was very unfamiliar with the fierce southern warriors could react with such outward anxiety.

"Then what will happen with you? Or your people?" Erika asked, her voice demonstrating that she was much more concerned than nervous.

Ayenwatha smiled kindly at the tough young woman, appreciating her regard for his people and himself. "Who can know the future? Who can say what will happen when a new day rises? I must go to seek help for my people, and you must be safeguarded from danger. My people can no longer offer you any refuge."

"Then why should we not fly with you?" the brooding, dark-haired one named Logan asked.

"Eirik speaks truly," Ayenwatha replied. "A long flight such as this is very dangerous. The steeds will be very hard pressed, and not in a great enough number that we can resist a concentrated attack. No, we will be very vulnerable, and the risk of taking you through the skies is far too great. I must take this risk myself, as I seek to return quickly to my people. But this is no journey for you. We must take all precautions, in getting you to Midragard without harm."

Logan scowled in the wake of Ayenwatha's answer, and his brow furrowed.

"So what is it with us? There is something about us that you know, and are not saying. Am I right?" he asked sharply.

"You are," Derek said abruptly to Logan, before turning towards Ayenwatha. "You wish to take no risks with us, and take such great cautions, when your own people are under such a terrible plight. Why? What compels you to do this?"

Ayenwatha looked slowly from Logan to Derek, holding their unwavering gazes for a few moments, and then glanced towards the rest of the exiles.

"I cannot lie to you," he said. "I do not know for sure about such things, as they are mysterious to me, but it is just possible that you may be the ones who have been foreseen."

"Foreseen? You mean prophesied?" Mershad asked, his tone full of obvious incredulity.

Mershad was not alone in his reaction, as Ayenwatha could see that the others viewed the notion as preposterous.

"In the book of the new religion," interjected Eirik. "I have heard such things spoken of by priests and monks. It is always said that we should look out for those who come from another world."

"What does this … book … say?" Logan inquired slowly, his face somber, and his curiosity clearly piqued. He eyed Eirik and Ayenwatha with great expectancy.

"I do not read, so I have not read this book for myself," Eirik replied. "I only know what has been spoken of by those who can. It speaks of the end times, an End of Days, and the coming of those from a very foreign land, understood to be a different world."

"It is not unlike some legends of our own," Ayenwatha then added. "These tales speak of many signs. I remember little of the stories that I have heard in my youth regarding this, but I have heard some of the tales of this book of the new religion more recently. They speak of many strange things. They speak of those who will come from another world, who will break the barriers between worlds. They will help to bring about the power of the One Spirit, the Sky Lord, as we see the Creator, into this world … to undo the work of evil. It is said that a new, undying age will then come."

"These stories also speak of the great threat of Jebaalos, the Dark Ruler of the Abyss," Eirik then commented bluntly. "All the legends are clear that those who come from another world must not be claimed by Jebaalos. It is said that Jebaalos will tirelessly hunt them down, to control them for His own purposes."

The words were plainly not the ones that the outlanders wanted to hear. Ayenwatha could see that reflected in their subdued, tense expressions in the wake of Eirik's words, as well as the lightened pallor that came to more than one of their faces.

While they might find it entirely incomprehensible to believe that they could have specifically been prophesied, Ayenwatha could see the dilemma that they were facing. He could see they understood that if others merely believed such a thing, that they were the result of a prophecy, then they would still have to deal with the consequences.

In such a context, Ayenwatha certainly could not blame them for their trepidation. The daunting idea that a dark ruler of the abyss would be actively searching for them, and assiduously endeavoring to take hold of them, was no doubt more than unsettling.

"So you think that the prophecy is really talking about … us?" Kent asked hesitantly.

"Who can say? It is said that no man knows of the time when the All-Father will manifest His Power in the world again, to bring an end to this world. I have even heard it said that even Emmanu Himself did not know when this moment would occur," Eirik said in a lowered voice.

"I have known no others such as you," Ayenwatha told the exiles. "I cannot say that you are here because of these prophetic visions. But I also cannot say that you are not. I also do know that it would be unwise to think that I know for certain that you are not. The consequences of being wrong are far too terrible to imagine, and I will not take any risks."

"Well, I'm not part of any prophecy, nor do I ever want to be," Janus said, a sharp edge of resentment in his voice. "I never asked for any of this, not for a moment."

"Nor did my people," Ayenwatha replied gently. "What is … still is."

Janus abruptly looked downward, and cursed under his breath. Ayenwatha could see that the man felt ashamed for speaking so suddenly.

"It is okay, Janus. There are times when none of us want what is given to us in this life. They say that the Sky Lord has reasons for all things, but I do not believe that the Sky Lord chooses ill for some of us," Ayenwatha replied. "The world must take its course, whatever course that may be. It means that great evil can exist. It means terrible things can happen unexpectedly. It also means that great good can exist, and great good can happen unexpectedly too."

"And I, for one, will fight to defend what is good," Eirik interjected.

"And I will too," Janus added gently, nodding his agreement with Eirik.

"What else do these prophecies say?" Mershad then questioned.

"You will have to ask one of the priests," Eirik replied with a shrug. "I only know a little. I know that King Hakon believes that our situation is very serious. I know also that you would not wish to be taken captive by the Unifier."

"What do you wish to do?" Ayenwatha asked the exiles suddenly.

Eirik was about to comment, but held back, keeping silent at a brief, forceful gesture from Ayenwatha.

The seven otherworlders looked back at Ayenwatha, apparently taken off guard by the bluntness of the question. Gradually, they started to look at each other, and Ayenwatha knew that they were realizing that none of them had any other viable alternative to offer for deliberation. He wanted them to come to that conclusion on their own.

"It is a choice to go nearer to a war, or to go away from one," Mershad remarked in a low voice.

Being that he was one of the quietest of the exiles, Ayenwatha was a little surprised that he had ventured the first opinion. Janus then clenched his teeth, with a look that reflected some unspoken realization that had taken place inside of him.

Janus queried in a voice that was just above a whisper, "Choice? Do any of Ayenwatha's people have the choice that we have?"

"There is no choice for Ayenwatha's people," Derek stated somberly. "But we could take our chances in the Five Realms with them. I am fine with either decision. There is no guarantee of safety anywhere in this world for us."

Ayenwatha gazed at Janus, seeing the turmoil swirling in his eyes. The image contrasted greatly with the look of curiosity and excitement that had graced his countenance when he had accompanied Ayenwatha on the Brega steeds to the tribal villages.

Ayenwatha had little doubt that Janus would indeed be willing to face whatever the tribal people were made to face, even if that meant destruction. It was not the conclusion that Ayenwatha was hoping for.

"Then I want to stay with Ayenwatha's people. I will gladly take my chances with them," Janus announced in a steady voice, to Ayenwatha's chagrin.

"I wish to go to Midragard. I cannot lie to myself, or to any of you," Mershad said, though he averted his gaze from meeting Ayenwatha as he spoke. "I will go wherever everyone else goes, but I say that we go onward to Midragard."

Ayenwatha respected Mershad's honesty, knowing that it was not cowardice to speak one's true feelings. He looked over towards those that had not yet spoken.

"I don't mind going to Midragard," Kent muttered quickly, glancing over at Mershad first, and then looking to the rest of his comrades. "What about all of you?"

Only Antonio, Erika, and Logan remained.

"I'm with Logan, whatever he feels," Antonio said, shrugging his shoulders, as if resigned to the winds of chance. "He's my friend, and I will go where he goes. I already have lost enough in coming to this world, and I'm sure as hell not going to lose my closest friend."

"And it does not matter what I think, I am sure," Logan stated a little abrasively. A slight glare came to his eyes, as he looked around at the others. "And it does not really matter what any of us think. We will be going where we are pulled to go. We certainly can't set off all by ourselves. You all know that. Better to get that out right now. I'm sure we will be told where we will be going soon enough."

Erika looked to Ayenwatha, who was listening intently to each of their answers. Hers was the final response.

"I would stay with your people too, Ayenwatha," she stated with resonant conviction. "Even if others think that would be a crazy decision. But I have one question for you…. What choice by us would help you the most, Ayenwatha?"

Her gaze searched his face, as she listened patiently for his answer.

Ayenwatha's own eyes threatened to tear for a fleeting moment, as he looked to her, Janus, and Derek. He felt a deep wave of emotion roll over him at their brave, generous replies, expressing willingness to go back to the tribal lands. He was moved by the gestures, even if he found them to be foolhardy, given what they were all facing.

His eyes roved among the three particular exiles as he responded. "It would be my true wish to see all of you safe in Midragard. If you are the ones spoken of by these prophecies and tales, then everything possible must be done to keep you away from the Unifier. If you are not the ones spoken of, then you would still have a greater chance of being kept from the Unifier's grasp by sending you to Midragard. Either way, this path to Midragard is the best choice for you to take, and the better one regarding my own hopes for you. I would not have to worry myself over your fate, if I knew you were there. I say to you truly, going to Midragard is what I would want for you to do."

He then looked towards Logan, and fixed him with a level stare.

"And know that the choice is truly yours. After I return from my own journey to Midragard, I will take you back with me to the tribal lands, if that is the choice you should make," Ayenwatha added.

After a long moment of silence, the others began to look to each other. As if something unspoken passed among them, they gradually began to nod to each other.

Erika finally replied to Ayenwatha, as if speaking for the entire group. "From what I see here, we will choose to do as you wish. We choose to go to Midragard, if that is what you truly want for us."

Ayenwatha smiled at her, grateful and relieved that they had assented to his own hopes, of their own accord.

The others quietly watched Ayenwatha, as he turned to speak to Eirik. "Then it is time for us to go, Eirik. You will have to take a moment for some instruction, as my warriors do not know the particular ways of your steeds."

Eirik nodded, though not before glancing towards Erika, Derek, and Janus. He also spared a noticeably separate glance towards Antonio. Ayenwatha understood the look, and recognized the sincere respect in Eirik's eye towards the four exiles, though the Midragardan did not give voice to any of the sentiments he was feeling.

"Then we must tell your warriors about our steeds," Eirik replied evenly to Ayenwatha. "Though you will not find them too unfamiliar from the Brega of your own lands. Who is to go?"

Ayenwatha looked to each of his warriors, who one by one acknowledged his glance with slight nods of their own.

"All of the warriors here will go with me," Ayenwatha finally answered.

Eirik then had the tribal warriors gather around him, and guided them towards one of the nearby Fenraren. He spent some time speaking with Ayenwatha's warriors, being the only one that could really do so, as he was one of the few Midragardans present that could adequately speak the language of the Five Realms.

He told them of the special commands, both verbal and physical, for handling the Fenraren. The verbal commands were in the Midragardan tongue, so Eirik had the tribal warriors repeat the instructions back to him several times, making sure of their pronunciation and memorization. Ayenwatha knew that it was vital that the tribal warriors remembered everything exactly, on the chance that they were disrupted or dispersed at some point during their lengthy travel.

At the end of the instruction, Ayenwatha and his warriors mounted their new steeds. They were given some extra time to adjust to the markedly different form of saddle and harness. Ayenwatha had to admit that he was much more comfortable with the more sparse arrangement that the tribal people employed upon the Brega.

Ayenwatha then bid the exiles well, fully confident that he was leaving them in good keeping. They would be underway soon enough, embarking upon a sea voyage that would take them to far less threatened environs in the distant south. All of the exiles exchanged farewells with him, each in their own way.

Janus was the last to approach Ayenwatha.

"I am sorry for speaking so quickly, Ayenwatha," Janus said in a low, apologetic voice that was meant for his ears alone. "I want you to know that I would have gladly stayed with your people."

"I know that you would have," Ayenwatha replied, giving him a smile. "But you stay safe, for me. I would be much happier that way."

"As best I can," Janus replied, before backing slowly away.

All of those standing around them on the ground cleared back several paces, creating a wide berth for the Onan and Midgardan warriors mounted upon the Fenraren.

Once a wide path was made, at a command from Eirik, the foremost of the riders spurred their steeds into motion. The Fenraren spread their wings broadly, and began loping forward. After a few initial, easy strides, the creatures bounded vigorously across the ground for several paces before leaping upwards. Their wings snapped out and downward with great power, lifting both creature and rider up into the air.

Ayenwatha followed in the wake of Eirik and a few other Midragardans, feeling the sensation of flight take hold as his steed began its ascent. The rest of the group, both Midragardan and Onan alike, followed behind.

In a very short time, those watching them from the ground looked like mere specks. The island soon became an aberrant patch of brown and green within the glistening waters of the sea, limned with ephemeral streaks of white, where waves crashed down upon its shoreline.

Ayenwatha settled into the saddle, making himself more comfortable as the formation of Fenraren moved away from the island. Starting off at a modest pace across the seas, they began their journey towards the Midragardan lands lying to the far south.

Ayenwatha had never set his eyes upon the storied lands of

Midragard, and despite the circumstances, a part of him felt a little thrill of adventure about the impending journey. Yet at the same time, the reason they were taking him to Midragard were never out of mind, even for a moment.

His heart remained in the lands that he was leaving behind, in the hands of his people, but he knew that he had a chance to gain aid for them. King Hakon had responded swiftly, as Ayenwatha had thought that the Midragardan king would.

Ayenwatha had no idea as to what to expect when he arrived in Midragard. Having heard a few of their epic stories, a part of his mind was fed by wild imaginings of mythic warriors and fantastical creatures of lore.

He could not be certain about anything, but he did know that he was going to an audience with someone who had eyes to see, and ears to hear; to Ayenwatha's view, that fact alone represented more than enough of a hope.

JANUS

A pair of rather uneventful days had passed on the small island since Eirik, Ayenwatha, and the others had left upon the incredible, wolf-like sky steeds. The seven exiles were patiently awaiting the arrival of a pair of Midragardan longships, which were to take them to Midragard itself. The ships were said to be coming from the north, and that was the direction in which their eyes were often turned, in hopeful anticipation.

Janus largely kept to himself as they waited for the expected longships. He found himself often walking down to the water's edge and looking out to sea, staring off towards the empty horizon. More than once he believed that he saw something in the distance, only to discover that there was nothing approaching the island. Whether the occasional sights were mirages or something of substance, they were certainly not what he was looking for.

With Ayenwatha and the tribal warriors gone, what little familiarity Janus had with the new world had been carried off on the wings of the Fenraren. A decline in familiarity was one of the last things that he needed at the moment, feeling alone enough as it was.

Janus' vigil at the shore's edge was not necessary in a practical sense. Their Midragardan hosts were keeping up a diligent watch on the sea's horizon. Janus could sense the rising tension within the homestead, ever since the departure of Eirik, Ayenwatha, and the others. It was never openly spoken of, but was plainly written on the faces of every man and woman, and those of many of the homestead's older children.

At long last, on the third day after Ayenwatha had left, a great commotion was raised within the homestead. Janus had already espied the source of the excitement, a little before anyone else had.

The shapes had taken form on the edge of the horizon, moving steadily towards the settlement. They were not illusions, but rather were objects rooted in solidity. Gradually, the forms had grown more distinct, and Janus knew from their outline that they were the promised longships.

Cutting through the waters, each was narrow of body, with single masts rising high, and square sails unfurled; unquestionably Midragardan.

Running back hurriedly towards the settlement from the shoreline, Janus quickly found Erika, where she was sitting and conversing with Mershad. They both leaped up in initial alarm at his hurried approach, and he swiftly related the news to them.

It was about that moment that the air was filled with the cries of Midragardans who had finally spotted the incoming vessels. Janus, Erika, and Mershad proceeded immediately to gather the others in their group. They led them without delay down to the shoreline, to await the arrival of the longships. By the time they all stood upon the edge of the ocean waters, the longships had drawn much closer on the power of their oars.

The square woolen sails of the vessels had been furled since Janus had first sighted the ships, no longer needed, as the longships glided towards berths on the shore. One of the longships had twenty oars on each side, and the second one was a slightly longer vessel, with twenty-five oars per side. Round shields were lined up in colorful arrays, set in battens running down the sides of each of the ships, just outside their top strakes.

Their oars rowed in steady unison as the ships pulled ever nearer, dipping and pulling through the water in rhythmic harmony. The men manning the broad-bladed steering oars, affixed to the starboard side of the stern, made a few adjustments as the crews maneuvered the two vessels up towards the beach.

The narrow ships sliced so effortlessly through the waters, cleaving the surface like great, sea-borne blades. Their low draught enabled the Midragardans to bring the graceful, elegant galleys right up onto the beach itself, with little difficulty.

A number of people from the settlement had gathered with Janus and the other exiles to greet the two ships right at the water's edge. Several of them stepped forward to help the crew of the vessels, as the latter hopped down over the sides of the longships. The men from the ships splashed down into the shallow waters, moving to join the volunteers from the settlement as they all found grips along the ships' strakes, pushing and dragging the vessels up more securely onto the land.

Once the vessels were brought to a full halt upon solid ground, spirited greetings were made, and long gangway planks were lowered at their sides. It was abundantly clear that the Midragardans from the ships were not there for any extended visit, as they immediately set about restocking their provisions. Chests and sacks were removed from the ships, while replacements were soon being carried aboard, with the help of several men from the homestead.

There was an undercurrent of urgency to the crewmen's movements. It was apparent that the men from the ships did not wish to waste even a moment more than was necessary to gain additional supplies for the resumption of their voyage. Their anxious demeanors unnerved Janus more than a little, as he knew that the Midragardans were not the kind of people who were easily distressed.

Janus and his companions stood idly nearby at first, trying to stay out of the way of the stream of individuals involved in loading supplies onto the pair of ships. As he waited, he gazed upon the remarkable vessels, finding that he was becoming more familiarized with their attributes.

Averaging around sixty to seventy feet in length, the vessels were both warships. In the bow, they each featured an intricately carved prow, employing a thematic design that rose up and outward from the forefront of the ships. One ship's prow was fashioned with the snarling visage of a wolf, and the other displayed a roaring dragon. The designs were echoed in the ornamentation of the sterns, providing appropriate tails for the creatures whose motifs graced the ships.

The hulls did not go very deep, constructed out of thin, horizontal planks of wood that overlapped downwards. Their main decking was comprised of loose timber planking, spanning between small, raised platforms at stern and bow.

They were both ships that had been designed efficiently for speed. The sleek forms had been expertly honed and crafted, reflecting the kind of workmanship developed over long years, spent by multitudes of seafarers traversing both ocean and river. As Janus could plainly see, the most formidable aspect of the ships' design was the fact that they were usable in either river or ocean settings, lending their crews an advantageous level of flexibility not afforded to vessels confined to just one type of water environment.

Despite his interest in the details of the longships, soon Janus had become very uncomfortable standing around and watching all of the Midragardans laboring. He could see the fidgety signs of growing discomfort reflected in his companions as well.

Erika caught Janus' eyes, her eyes narrowing as she asked him, "What's wrong?"

"Couldn't we help them? With the loading, that is," Janus asked. "We're healthy and rested enough, and they look like they are in a real hurry. We're not doing much else right now."

"Only one way to find out," Erika responded with a shrug, and a slight grin.

She approached one of Eirik's warriors, an affable fellow who had been left behind to accompany the exiles on their sea journey. She stopped him before he could pick up a cask that had been carried down to the shore by another man. Once she had the warrior's attention, she inquired as to whether the exiles could help out with the loading of the ships.

The warrior readily agreed to her proposal, and none of the other Midragrdans nearby seemed opposed to the offer of help either. Within moments, Janus and the others were busy loading wooden chests, sacks, and barrels onto the ships.

Janus was eminently glad for the physical activity, as the labor gave him a welcome distraction from everything else that was plaguing his mind. He lugged a chest, trudging slowly up the wooden gangway from the beach to the ship. It was a tedious effort, and he felt the tautness in his arms and back as he slogged up the plank to the body of the ship.

Once aboard, Janus got a better look at the longship's two small raised decks, as well as the loose, lower deck planking arrayed in between them, running most of the length of the ship. There were no benches on the flat lower decking. After making an inquiry of one of the ship's crew, Janus learned that those rowing used the type of chests that he was carrying to sit upon when working the oars. They were perfectly sized for the position of the oar ports that ran down the ship's sides at regular intervals. As the ports were not in use, circular, timber coverings affixed to the strakes slid down to close off the openings.

The seven exiles gradually settled into a sustained period of activity, one born of muscle and sweat. Janus assisted Logan in bringing a heavy barrel full of ale aboard, which he quickly found to be quite a laborious task.

Janus listened casually, as Logan began to strike up conversations with some of the Midragardans that had arrived with the two vessels. Logan was indulging his curiosities about the backgrounds of the ships that they were loading, and their crews, but Janus was most interested in the discourse as it revealed several new things about their Midragardan patrons, and Ave itself.

The Midragardans talked about the journeys that they had been about to undertake, just before they were diverted to bring the exiles back to Midragard. They spoke of a land called Kiruva, an extensive realm located to the east that had been their ultimate trading destination. They described it as a land of innumerable rivers, great forests, and vast, open steppes.

The Midragardans had been looking forward to reaching a large town or city there called Novgrad, in which a special section had been designated as quarters for Midragardan merchants. The men had evidently been looking forward to bringing back a good quantity of silver from the new season's trading, a hope that was now placed in jeopardy due to their summons to convey the exiles to Midragard.

Yet despite the potential loss of trade, the men apparently had not been relishing the long river journey necessary to reach Novgrad. As Logan pressed them for more details, the men commented that the trek to the Kiruvan town would involve making it through at least one portage site.

The traders described how they would have to disembark the vessels at such locations, and take their ships over a short stretch of land to bypass violent, rocky stretches of the river, which were too dangerous to navigate. Rolling galleys across a series of logs that were shuffled constantly from the rear to the front, they would methodically bring the vessels across the solid ground, to where they could place them back in the water.

The men also appeared to be highly relieved that they were not going to be putting the vessels into shore to visit a particular man who lived in the eastern region of an island realm called Gael.

Janus quickly grew very fascinated with Gael, as one of the men lamented, "Who knows what is in the waters near there? Whether it is the islands with the water horses that are on the way … or the seal people and the fish people in the waters just off the coasts of Gael … nothing is what it seems in those lands. You would find few human women as fair as some among the strange creatures that live in those lands and waters. The foolhardy man has often learned the truths of such beings, far too late.

"It is no wonder that the people of that land are so devout in their religion, and fierce in their devotion to their kin. There is so much that can deceive them and bring them to ruin. Great beauty is perilous, and even the fairy folk that dwell within Gael can be very wicked."

A thousand questions and curiosities rushed into Janus' mind, but he kept his thoughts silent, and contented himself with listening to the ongoing conversations.

As Janus and Logan went with the men to retrieve a few more casks, the Midragardans spoke in hushed tones of a fearsome, wailing female spirit that they had come perilously close to encountering on their last sojourn to the lands of Gael. The demonic entity evidently inhabited a boggy area situated uncomfortably close to a crannog, which by their description appeared to be a fortified homestead of some sort, in which the Gael man that regularly traded with the Midragardans resided. It was very clear that the men believed that they would have met with certain death had they simply set their eyes upon the spectral entity.

Seeing the fear openly reflected in the hardy Midragardan men, during their discussion of the dark spirit haunting the bog land, Janus hoped that he would never have the ill fortune of personally encountering such a malevolent, supernatural being. It was certainly not very comforting to learn of the worrisome reality that such beings existed in the world that Janus inhabited.

Listening to all of their incredible stories, it seemed that the time would pass quickly enough, until they were finally ready to set off on their way to Midragard. They were almost finished loading the ships, when an unwelcome disturbance occurred.

An agitated murmur arose suddenly among the Midragardans, soon turning into clamorous outcries of distress and warning. The seven exiles, and those loading the boats, stopped what they were doing immediately. Janus and the others, exile and Midragardan alike, followed the frantic gestures of an old man who was looking out towards the sea, with a very distraught expression on his face.

"Enemies! They are coming!" the older man cried out in a raspy, fearful voice. "We must move inland! Now! It is an enemy that approaches!"

The words buffeted like an icy, biting wind, freezing Janus' blood. He and the others standing in the middle of the longship's deck looked out to sea, where they beheld several more shapes approaching the shore across the waters.

The outlines were unmistakably different from those of the longships, though they were rowed galleys. The oncoming vessels were formed into a broad line.

The differences in the approaching galleys manifested more clearly as they drew closer. The galleys were two-masted, fitted with very lengthy yards from which great lateen sails were suspended. The masts were each crowned with small lookout nests.

Banners of blue and gold flapped from the bows and sterns of the vessels. Shields with surface ornamentation similar to the image on the banners were also positioned at the front and rear of the ships.

The bow of each galley featured a broad forecastle, with timber railing around the sides. Upon the raised platform, a number of archers and crossbowmen were gathered, weapons at the ready. A great spur projected from the front of the ship, carried above the waterline like the end of a menacing spear.

Though low to the water, the galleys were a little higher than the Midragardan ships, as well as being broader of beam. Staggered pairs of long oars ran down the length of the galleys, with over twenty-five such pairs per side.

The sterns of the galleys were fitted with another railed, raised platform. As with the forecastle, throngs of warriors arrayed for battle were situated on their surfaces.

Even more daunting, the line of rowed galleys were not the only vessels approaching the shoreline. Coming up just behind the galleys were a couple of slower-moving, round-bodied sailing vessels. The ships were much broader of beam, with a freeboard far exceeding that of the low-draught galleys. High platforms with battlement-like enclosures of wood had been affixed near bow and stern on the sailing ships, bristling with armed men. The sailing vessels carried banners and pennons that matched those upon the galleys.

Janus knew that there would not be much more time before the first of the oncoming ships drew near to the shoreline. A sense of grave danger flooded the air, washing over exile and Midragardan alike.

"We cannot take to the water," a younger Midragardan warrior shouted out from the deck of the other prone longship. He moved over and lifted up one of the round shields from its resting place along the outer railing. "Those ships fly the symbol of Avanor. We must move fast. We...."

The young man's words were suddenly cut off by an arrow that embedded itself deeply into his chest, fired from the direction of the beach. The warrior pitched over the side of the longship and fell onto the shore, at the water's edge, as an incoming wave lapped across his body.

Janus turned swiftly, just as a large number of fearsome-looking creatures burst out into the open. They charged towards the shore, pouring forth from amongst the buildings of the Midragardan homestead.

The creatures wielded long, sword-like weapons, great spears, and lengthy two-handed war implements, fitted with elongated, single edged blades. Those with the sword-like weapons carried rectangular shields. Some had their heads bared, several wore what looked to be protective cap-helms of boiled leather, while one or two of the bestial figures exhibited rounded, iron half-helms.

Janus was thunderstruck by their fierce visages, which were locked into feral, snarling masks of battle fury, as they bore down upon the Midragardans.

Janus, Logan, Antonio, and Erika dived for cover along the deck of the longship. They all began to reach around in desperation, for anything that they could use as a weapon, as Janus listened to the throaty, guttural war cries of the attackers drawing closer.

Janus caught a brief glimpse of Mershad, Derek, and Kent as he peeked over the top strake of the longship to assess the enemy's positions. The three had just been about to retrieve some chests along the shore to take aboard the ships, and were now forced to scramble away from the onslaught. Janus watched anxiously as the three raced towards the body of the second longship. They disappeared from view a moment later, maneuvering behind the farther side of the other vessel.

The Midragardans had been taken completely by surprise, and few were armed for conflict at the outset of the fight. They grabbed at whatever they could to defend themselves, some using tools, and a few others fortunate enough to be near weapons such as axes, swords, or spears. Others finding themselves more isolated quickly grasped the hilts of the single-edged knives sheathed at their waists.

There was no hint of surrender within the air, and as Janus looked out it appeared as if the entire homestead was girding to fight back with everything they had. Everyone, young and old alike, man or woman, strove to defend themselves, with the lone exception being the smallest of children.

The tall, burly beast-men reached the shore area and set upon the Midragardans ravenously, hacking, stabbing, and slashing at all within their reach. More arrows, coming from some of their comrades that had climbed up onto the thatch roofs of the timber buildings, continued to find targets within the growing melee.

Janus gnashed his teeth in helpless rage, as he saw one of the dog-faced entities pull a longbow back, and let a black-shafted arrow fly to pierce an old Midragardan man through the neck. The man's eyes widened in desperation as he gurgled and gasped. He clutched at the arrow shaft in a vain attempt to stem the outflow of life-giving blood, before falling over at last.

Janus had spent over an hour alone with that very same old man, just the previous day, listening to some fascinating tales of Midragardan lore. The man was an old thrall, soft-spoken and kind-hearted, and in no way did he deserve such a brutal end.

A new round of furious cries arose from the combatants on both sides, as the first clashes of steel ripped through the air. It was almost impossible to imagine the pervading tranquility that had existed mere minutes before.

From the deck of the first ship, Janus shifted his position, and slid up the covering to peer through one of the oar holes spaced between two shields set in the outer pine-batten. The fighting among the two larger, beached longships was erupting at a furious pace, as more and more combatants were brought together in the deadly clash.

The Midragardans were responding strongly, having recovered from the initial shock of the unexpected attack. Several of the more experienced warriors among them had been able to reach their weapons by now, and they were fighting back with a vengeful fury.

An abrupt, heavy thudding noise just behind Janus caused him to whirl about. A huge beast-warrior had jumped aboard the ship. It did not hesitate for a moment, bearing down upon Janus with a look of unfettered malice.

The snarling creature had one of the imposing, two-handed weapons, like an axe, lance, and sword fused together, raised over its head, corded muscle bulging throughout its arms. Both of its massive, dark hands gripped the elongated haft, from which the heavy, lengthy, single-edged blade extended. The fearsome weapon was poised to crash down upon Janus' exposed head.

Even though the gesture seemed entirely futile, Janus brought up a small hammer, of the kind that would have normally been used to strike a chisel for wood-carving. He moved to swing it at the knees of his powerful assailant, the only action that came to his mind in the split-second of time left to him.

Before the heavy steel blade could be brought down to bear upon him, a very large dog or wolf slammed into the beast-man from the side. The brawny warrior tumbled down onto the deck several feet away, knocked entirely off its feet. The inhuman figure cried out in rage at the interference, teeth bared in a particularly rabid expression that froze Janus' breath in his lungs. It twirled about with astonishing litheness to get back on its feet and meet its attacker.

Janus caught the deep gaze of the wolf-like dog for only a moment, as its penetrating, golden stare caught his eyes. The dog had not continued its attack upon the Trogen, instead remaining close to Janus. Without a sound, it bounded fluidly towards the side of the ship, leaping high over the top to disappear from sight.

There was no time to indulge any curiosities, or even pause to consider the bizarre intervention. The enemy creature was on its feet with its imposing weapon in hand, its eyes exuding a murderous intent.

Janus crawled, scrabbled, and lunged hurriedly for the bow of the boat, doing everything that he could to reach Erika while keeping his body below the top strakes of the vessel. She was crouched down, holding tightly onto a spear that she had retrieved from the equipment brought aboard the longship. He glanced back for any sign of the strange dog, but there was nothing to be seen of his canine savior.

The beast-warrior had its sights set squarely upon the two of them. The enemy warrior shook with rage, its powerful muscles flexing and bulging with its tightening grip upon the shaft of its great weapon. Janus felt lightheaded, as he saw the sharp canines now openly bared towards him, set just forward of a baleful gaze. The enemy warrior tramped resolutely forward across the decking of the longship, its heavy steps thumping on the wooden surface.

Janus stayed with Erika as they held their ground, for there were no good options left. Janus gripped the iron-headed hammer, while Erika clutched her spear. The beast-man strode rapidly down the length of the deck, readying its great, heavy blade to strike.

Using every bit of her might, Erika suddenly lunged forward and thrust the spear outward. Seeing her fast, desperate move, Janus reacted by hurling himself low, swinging the hammer at the creature's knees with all of the strength that he could muster.

The hammer and spear attacks both met with success, catching the creature by complete surprise. The warrior emitted an angered, pained cry as it stumbled forward. The spear was lodged deep in its unprotected throat, blood draining in rivulets down the leather jerkin covering its upper body. Its broken knee, having caught the full force of the hammer blow, caused the creature to buckle and topple onto the deck.

Neither Erika nor Janus paused to regard the success or failure of their first strikes. As Erika pulled the spear free, and stabbed again, Janus moved upward and pounded the hammer down into the face of the beast-man. The two of them did not cease, raining successive blows upon the creature's body, even after it became still and unresponsive to their attacks.

Pulling the spear free from her last stab, Erika straightened up, and looked out to the shore. "The enemy galleys are nearing the land now," she reported, a wide, anxious look in her eye.

Janus listened to her words with his heart beating fast from the adrenaline coursing throughout him. He gripped the hammer tightly, his hand shaking, now finished with his grisly task.

Janus followed her gaze and saw that the incoming ships were now indeed very close to the shore. Their decks were filled with armed human warriors, all of whom looked eager to join the fray. Fore and aft platforms in the galleys were packed with archers and crossbowmen. With an elevated position to fire their missiles from, they trained their sights on various targets. Janus knew in his heart that the situation was worsening rapidly.

"What do you say we should do?" Janus asked Erika, casting her a brief glance.

Erika met his gaze, and looked back out to the water. "We must get to the others. Where are Antonio and Logan?"

Janus looked around frantically. He saw the other two at the far end of the longship, where they were slashing and hacking with short-hafted hand axes at a couple of beast-warriors that were trying to climb over the sides of the ship.

"Antonio, Logan!" Janus called, attracting their attention. "Get over here now!"

The other two, their eyes reflecting fear and a heightened state of alertness, kept low as they hurriedly crawled across the deck towards Janus and Erika. An arrow sank into the wood close to Logan's head, just as the two men passed the mid-point of the ship. It was a very narrow miss, making Janus' breath catch in his throat.

Logan cast a furtive glance at the lodged arrow, as he spurred himself forward more quickly. Antonio hustled in Logan's wake, having also taken note of his friend's close call.

"We have to try and get to the others," Erika said, peering cautiously over the sides of the vessel again. She then added, with a sharp look of worry, "Once we can find them."

At that moment, a few Midragardans clamored up over the sides towards the middle of the ship. Janus felt the longship lurch and begin to move, as it was pushed into the water. The haggard warriors were all armed well, with spears, swords, and one who bore a great two-handed axe, which had a prominent, downward-extended blade, cut to a flat edge at its lower extremity.

"To the water! The water!" a loud cry came from a stout warrior at the center of the longship. "Get this ship out there! Hurry! We must run for it! With all speed!"

The men tensed momentarily, as their eyes fell upon Janus and his other three companions, but the Midragardans immediately relaxed their postures as they recognized the four exiles.

"We have others on the shore still!" Erika cried out to them, as the boat was pushed further out into the water.

Most did not seem to hear her, as the Midragardans were lending their hands to help several others climb aboard the vessel.

"We are not going back!" the stout warrior cried out emphatically, as the others grabbed up oars from where they lay upon t-shaped racks, rapidly situating themselves along the sides of the ship. Chests scraped upon the planks and thudded as they were hurriedly moved into place.

The ship started to glide out into the sea. At the burly warrior's orders, the oars were set down to the water.

Erika ran to the apparent leader of the Midragardans, as Janus hurried up behind her. Her tone was adamant, as she shouted. "We must go back!"

"No!" he roared back at her, equally forceful, as the ship pulled away from the shore.

"Tryggvi, enemy galleys are bearing down upon us!" cried another of the warriors, looking out as he pulled back on his oar.

Erika, Janus, and Tryggvi looked out to sea, where a large enemy galley was rushing towards them, parting the waters as it was propelled forward by a full complement of rowers. It was swiftly closing the distance between the ships, drawing nearer with every passing second.

Tryggvi cursed loudly at the development. "If we had a full crew, we might have had a chance to outrun her.... Crew or not, we must try anyway!"

Janus looked back out towards the oncoming galley. He could see a throng of archers and crossbowmen readying themselves at the bow to loose their missiles at the longship. The galley was higher of freeboard than was the Midragardan vessel, rising out of the water to a height that allowed the forecastle at the bow to have an open, unobstructed shot at any occupants of the longship. There was not a place on the longship that would not be reachable by the impending enemy volley.

Erika looked back to Janus, and he saw the unmistakable fear in her eyes. Yet the fear did not freeze her to inaction, as she turned and called back to Logan and Antonio. She urged everyone to pull up a shield from where they were set along the timber railing on the side of the ship.

In their desperation, they did not question Erika, not even the caustic Logan. The two men each yanked a shield free from the outer rack. Antonio's trembling hands dropped the first one that he grabbed, and it splashed into the water. He immediately grabbed for another, and was more careful with the second one as he lifted it free.

"What do you have in mind?" Janus asked her, also following her directive, as he heaved a shield up and free from the outer rail.

The large wooden shield was fairly heavy. Janus grabbed onto the short iron bar set in the back of the small, dome-like protrusion of iron that was fitted in the shield's center.

"We need to make a wall of shields, if we want to live!" Erika responded, loudly enough for all to hear her. "Follow me now!"

Having lifted a shield free for herself, she broke into a run towards the stern. Janus followed close behind her, as the others converged with them. He listened to her rapid instructions regarding the idea that she had.

With their backs turned to the raised deck at the longship's stern, they proceeded to huddle together, allowing the round shields to overlap in front of them, forming a protective wall. Scant moments later they heard anxious cries from the men on the ship, as the horrific hiss of arrows and bolts filled the air.

More than once, Janus' body was jolted as missiles slammed into the thick wood planking of the shield. Two arrows and a bolt burrowed solidly into the shield, as splinters and small chunks of wood flew free. He flinched as an arrow deflected off the iron boss of Erika's shield.

The sickening sound of shafts piercing clothing, flesh, bone, and muscle carried to his ears, an eerie sound that Janus would not soon forget. What in reality took just mere seconds to pass seemed like a timeless gulf to Janus, as the missiles loosed from the enemy galley raked through the entire length of the longship. The screams from the Midragardan warriors were soon transformed into ebbing moans and rasps of death, as the torrents of arrows and bolts finally ceased.

A number of strange voices grew louder, as Janus and the others remained behind their makeshift wall of round shields. A tremendous force then shook the longship, as the two galleys impacted. In the aftermath of the collision, there was a great outcry proclaiming "With the Hand of God!" from the assaulting galley.

It was like having a herald at the cusp of an avalanche. The longship rocked violently, as many attackers jumped aboard the undermanned ship. A cascade of tremors passed through the longship, as numerous feet continued to heavily strike the deck.

The sounds of a furious, desperate fight erupted at the other end of the ship. There were several cries, thuds, clangs of steel, and splashes, but in a few moments the surface of the deck fell into a numbing silence.

"Come out from behind the shields. The rest are dead, and we can kill you easily enough, if we want to," announced a gruff voice, outside the cluster of shields.

Janus heard a number of weighty footsteps approaching them slowly, striding down the length of the deck. He decided to lower his shield slightly. With nowhere to run, he felt resigned, and a strange calm fell over him as he knew that fate would have to take its course.

A number of armed men stood on the deck of the vessel, weapons in hand, and squared towards them. Many wore mail and half-helms, bearing an assortment of spears, swords, and short-hafted axes.

Others, primarily archers and crossbowmen, wore no armor, and had just cloth caps upon their heads. Several drawn bows and crossbows were trained upon Janus and his companions, both from the main deck and the high platform at the bow of the other ship.

As his gaze swept the ship, Janus saw that there was not a single Midragardan warrior left alive. Many bloodied bodies were strewn about the deck, exhibiting gruesome-looking wounds. The Midragardans had evidently acquitted themselves well in the short, furious fighting, as the casualties in view reflected both sides about evenly.

The warriors that had boarded the longship had distinctive accents, and were notably clean-shaven. Their demeanors appeared hard and unforgiving, and there was little doubt that they would have few misgivings about slaying Janus and the others, if provoked. The heightened tension was unyielding, as Janus waited to see what would happen.

"These appear to be foreign," a deep voice pronounced.

The speaker was a man who looked to be a more prominent warrior among the group, with a hauberk of mail over a padded gambeson. The end of a long blue tunic poked out from beneath the protective attire, richly embroidered. The circular pommel of a sword surmounted the scabbard at his waist. Mail mittens hung loosely back from his exposed right hand, which rested on the hilt of the sword. His other hand held up a broad-topped kite shield, whose half-yellow and half-blue facing was crossed by banded iron strips, the latter arranged like a radiating star.

A full iron face mask, with a bluish hue, extended down from the brow of a yellow, round half-helm. The warrior carried himself with a straight, authoritative posture that set him apart from the men around him.

"Your barbaric allies have been defeated, look upon their destruction yourselves," the figure chided them in an icy tone. Though he could not see the warrior's eyes, Janus keenly felt the weight of the man's stare.

At that moment, a low, gurgling cough broke out from one of the seemingly dead Midragardan warriors close to Janus' group. The man had no less than three arrow shafts sticking out of his body.

Swiftly, the warrior with the iron face mask drew his sword, and slashed it downward with great violence upon the dying Midragardan. Blood spraying into the air by the sheer force of the blow spattered onto the mask of his helm. The warrior turned his head back towards Janus and his companions, a single drop of blood dripping down off the edge of his face mask, and falling to the deck.

"Such is the cost of resisting the will of the Unifier," the leader continued in his chilly tone. "And it might be the price you may yet pay."

He turned away, facing towards a few men to his immediate right. He addressed them in a commanding tone. "Take these prisoners by sky steed back to the fleet, and deliver them into the hands of Bohemond. While they are here, they are under my ward, and are not to be harmed. As for the rest, do with them as you wish."

"Understood, Lord William," replied one of the other warriors.

Erika, whose eyes remained fixed upon Lord William, was mercifully spared the unfettered lust within the eyes of a few nearby warriors. Disappointment came to their faces, as their nascent plans for her were plainly thwarted by the leader's command. Janus had not missed the salacious expressions, and a burning anger flared within him. He could only hope that she kept her eyes averted.

Having received the leader's approval, several warriors set at once to looting the fallen Midragardans of their weapons, rings, arm bands, pendants, and anything else of value that they had on their bodies. Janus closed his eyes to the brazen violations of the courageous, fallen warriors, hating each and every moment that he was made to endure the disrespectful ordeal.

While several crossbows and bows remained fixed upon the prisoners, a few of the other warriors strode forward. Unceremoniously, using narrow rope, they proceeded to bind the captives' hands behind their backs. There was little use in resisting, as Janus and his companions were surrounded on the captured longship, with skillfully managed arrows and bolts trained upon them. With rough force, the prisoners were then shoved and jostled forward. Hands clutched them, and it was difficult to keep their feet under them as they were nearly dragged onto the other galley.

Janus felt a host of stares as they were herded towards the stern of the galley. They were guided to the aft-castle, and up a flight of timber steps onto its surface.

"Do as I say … an we 'av no troubles," one of their captors, a dark eyed, leathery-skinned man told them. "You 'av done well so far. Lord William's sword did not have to drink your blood. Don't give my dagger reason to."

Nearby was a wiry-looking man, whose deep-set, cold eyes peered out from an elongated face, one that Janus found was not altogether unlike that of a large rodent. The lean man regarded Logan with a haughty expression, verging on a sneer. He stuck the tip of his spear close to Logan's face, letting the point lightly scratch his skin. To his credit, Logan remained firmly in place, doing nothing to provoke the man.

"Do not much like the looks of this 'un. Think of somethin' ya want to try, lad. Go ahead. Do it," the slender warrior hissed at Logan, clearly inviting him to lose his composure.

The smile that then spread across the warrior's face was devoid of any speck of kindness, instead hinting at a hungry desire for cruelty. Janus did not want to know what kind of thoughts had conjured the icy expression.

Still another warrior, a medium-sized man with a bulbous nose, drew a dagger, and traced a short cut down the front of Erika's clothes. "Were it not for Lord William, I could think of somethin' to try with this one."

The staccato cackle of the cold-eyed man, and the unsettling chortle of the leathery-skinned one, joined the thicker-set one's raspy laughter.

"Try it then," Erika retorted through clenched teeth, her eyes casting daggers, unable to withhold her fury.

Her lips trembled with pulsating anger, and Janus instantly feared for her. He tensed, ready to throw caution to the wind to intervene on her behalf. There was not much he could do with his hands tied behind his back, but he was not going to stand by if the degenerate men threatened harm to her.

The face of the man with the dagger grew taut with visible rage, though he was not able to keep his eyes level with her molten stare.

"Leave them alone. They are the wards of Lord William. You had ears to hear," interjected another voice, carrying the power of authority within its confident timbre.

With a small nose, large round cheeks, and a weak chin, he did not look nearly as intimidating in appearance as the other three men. Though wearing no helm at the moment, he was dressed in a similar fashion to Lord William. He had full length mail sleeves, with mail mittens hanging at the end, and a blue surcoat worn over a mail-coat and padded gambeson. He was a little shorter and narrower of shoulder than Lord William had been, but he carried the same kind of resolute posture.

Despite his non-threatening demeanor, the three other men ceased their harassment immediately. They quickly backed away from their taunting of the prisoners, keeping their eyes lowered and clearing the way for the newcomer to approach.

"My name is Robert of Mirar, liege knight to Lord William, of the Viscounty of Talais, in the Duchy of Avanor," he said calmly, curiosity evident within his eyes. He spoke with a formal air, one that was much more fluid and articulate than the rougher manner of the warriors that had deferred to him. "Here is my advice to you, and I suggest that you heed it faithfully. Cooperation will be the best course for your well-being. If you cooperate, I will make sure no harm comes to you. Simple enough?"

He slowly regarded the men around him, and Janus caught the sharp glare that he cast each of warriors before he walked away, continuing down to the main deck. While more glances were forthcoming in the wake of Robert of Mirar's departure, including several more lascivious ones cast Erika's way, the other warriors on the ship kept their distance from the prisoners, and went about their tasks.

Once the recovery of their own dead and the despoilment of the longship had taken place, the large galley was prepared for cast off from the doomed longship. Slanted benches were occupied in good order, by pairs of men that took up the ends of long oars.

Robert of Mirar's next orders were then relayed down the length of the galley. Janus listened idly to the firm directive as it was conveyed all over the vessel. There was no use for the conquered longship, and as the victors did not want it to fall into enemy hands again, they had to sink it before departing.

A couple of men labored to swivel the yard arm of the mizzen mast outward, bringing it over the interior of the Midragardan vessel at about midship. A large, heavy shaft of wood, bound by stout, iron studs, was attached to the extremity of the yard arm.

The iron-studded shaft descended in a plunging free-fall, ending with a tremendous, crashing blow, as shards of wood exploded high into the air. Water was already rushing into the belly of the longship by the time that the crew had pulled the tethered shaft of wood back up to the yard arm. Moments later, a little further down the longship, they let it plummet to another smashing impact.

The crew then swiveled the long yard arm away from the other deck. It was not long before the longship began to sag beneath the lapping waves.

The galley crew labored quickly to remove the shaft. A rhythmic chant broke out, as the oarsmen dipped their wooden blades into the seas, and began to pull away from the submerging longship. Not wanting to watch the elegant longship lower into the depths, Janus watched the men as they rowed, using a sit and stand method.

A short time later, more orders were disseminated, and the crew worked the halyards on the two great masts to lower a pair of huge, triangular sails. The wind had grown in strength as the galley moved farther away from the island, and the sails were adjusted to use the natural force to the ship's advantage.

The four captives sat together miserably, unable to look back towards the fading shore, or to inquire into the matter of the other three from their world. Logan retreated into a dark silence, a scowl weighing heavily upon his face, while Antonio looked about wide-eyed, his face a mask of anxiety. His hands shook as he tried in vain to clasp them to stillness.

To Antonio's right, Erika looked downcast, staring at the wooden boards of the aft-castle. The hardened defiance of a few minutes earlier had deflated into a numbed placidity.

Janus closed his eyes and breathed in deeply. They were all prisoners within their own private worlds, as well as that of the world that they dwelled within. The only mercy was that there were no great ocean swells for the galley to contend with, and the gentle, low-rolling waters that they passed through did little to unsettle him.

In time, excited outcries from the vessel's crew broke the monotony of the travel. A number of large winged steeds descended from the sky, coming into the captive's view as they landed upon the forecastle platform of the galley.

Janus recognized the riders, if not their robust steeds.

"The Trogen'r here for ya!" exclaimed one of the men, in a jeering, derisive manner. "Bet ya like those tidings."

The riders were unmistakably of the kind that had attacked Janus and the others on the shore, hulking brutes with pronounced, canid visages, and bristling with muscularity. Their steeds were similar in many respects to the Brega and Fenraren that Janus had come to know. They were winged, four legged mammals, of a decidedly predatory nature.

There were several characteristics that distinguished them from the steeds of the tribal warriors and Midragardans. Janus took notice of the distinctive slant to their bodily profile, from head to haunches, even as he beheld their broad jaws, and large, triangular ears. Thick, coarse fur, of varying dark brown and black hairs, covered the formidable-looking creatures, with the fur of their legs ascending in rings of contrasting light and dark hues, all the way up to their underbellies.

One of the Trogens dismounted, and walked over to talk privately with Lord William. Janus could not make out what the bestial creature was saying, as its voice carried across to him as a low rumble.

Fear rippled through Janus, as he thought of the frothing, enraged, non-human warriors that had ambushed them on the beach. The feral-looking creatures' mere appearance was disconcerting enough, and not just to the captives. Several of the crewmen cast nervous, furtive glances towards the Trogens. The creatures apparently were in alliance with the humans, but there was not a trace of affinity to be found. Of all the men that Janus could see, only Lord William appeared to be completely at ease in the Trogens' presence.

The conversation came to an end, and the Trogen shifted to face its still-mounted comrades. It commanded the other four Trogens to dismount.

Lord William of Talais strode briskly down the deck towards the captives, with Robert of Mirar to his right side, keeping about a stride's length back. He wasted no time when he reached the quartet, stating "You are to go with the Trogens, upon their Harrak steeds. They will keep you safe, as they convey you onward. Your destination is eventually to be Avalos itself. Consider it an honor that you will be escorted and protected in a journey to the great city."

"Your safe passage there is desired by the Unifier. You have nothing to fear from the Trogens," Robert of Mirar said, when Lord William had finished. Janus followed Robert of Mirar's sideward gaze, to see that Antonio was pressing nervously against the sides of the ship, as the towering beast-men strode up to the aft-castle and came to the platform to join them.

The Trogen leader looked upon the bound captives, and warned them in a growling tone, ill-humored and thick with severity, "Do not harm the Harraks. Or try to escape. You will find that you cannot fly."

The Trogens then hauled and dragged the captives in a rough manner away from the aft-castle, prodding them down the length of the galley towards the waiting Harraks. With their wrists still bound, the captives were lifted up onto the saddles of the beasts, hoisted as if they were little more than sacks of grain. Leather straps attached to the saddles were used to tie them down.

Once the captives were affixed to the saddles, the Trogens freed their hands, much to Janus' immense relief. The Trogen warrior that had addressed them on the aft-castle of the ship then reminded them, in a very harsh timbre, not to entertain any ideas of resistance, or evasion.

Janus, who had ridden upon the Brega, took immediate account of the greater size and much edgier temperament of the Harraks. The steed that he was mounted upon rotated its head, emitting a throaty snarl, its sneering mouth revealing razor-sharp, huge canines. Janus could only take a deep breath as his heart sped up rapidly, drawing upon every shred of his experience with the Brega, as he awaited their departure.

A total of seven Trogens had been provided to escort them, two of which had been circling about in the sky, high above the galleys, as the captives were attended to. The one that seemed to be the leader of the small band finally called out a loud command, when all of the captives and Trogens were saddled up. One by one, the winged steeds leapt from the bow of the ship, dipping down sharply towards the ocean's surface, before lurching upward violently, with vigorous, rapid flaps of their great wings.

The awkward takeoff was instantly disconcerting to Janus, his throat feeling like it was merging with his stomach in a dizzying embrace. He held his composure as best he could, as they began to climb steadily into the air. He spared a glance back, to see how his companions were faring. Within the angle of the steep incline, the effect was more than a little disorienting as he craned his neck around.

Farthest behind, Antonio had finally succumbed to a wave of fear-driven nausea, retching and vomiting copiously. He had closed his eyes tightly, patently unable to bear the sights of the tumultuous ascension.

Though Logan maintained a stony expression, his eyes bore straight into the neck of his steed, never straying away from where his gaze was locked. Janus knew that the rigid stare betrayed Logan's own rattled nerves.

Erika looked to Janus as she flew up behind him. She managed a weak grin in his direction, though her hands were drained of color where she clenched tightly onto the reins of her steed. He held her eyes for a moment, and gave her a nod of reassurance, before a gust of wind brought his head back around, as his steed was buffeted about for a moment.

Awash with their fears, the captives kept their eyes trained forward as they began their flight over the blue expanse of the ocean. Only Janus cast a few furtive glances backwards, already feeling sharp pangs of anxiety concerning the unknown fates of the friends that they had left behind. There was no hope of gaining any answers, as the Midragardan island was an indistinct speck at the outset of the flight, before swiftly becoming lost to his eyes.

The Trogens oriented the flight of the group westward, heading directly towards the coastline of the Five Realms. Janus watched the waves coursing along the ocean's surface far below, looking up occasionally, to watch the stark lines of the coast and hills beyond the water drawing ever nearer on the horizon.

When they were on the cusp of the outer borders, and could see the coast and the tribal lands spread far ahead of them, the Trogens adjusted their flight path once again. The cluster of sky steeds turned sharply to the right, keeping roughly above the line where the land met the waters of the sea. The Trogens spurred the Harraks to pick up more speed, shouting loudly in their gruff voices.

The beasts repeatedly beat their wings down with great force, tilting their bodies a little forward in the exertion. The journey soon became a rush through the air, one that was undoubtedly very discomfiting for Janus' inexperienced companions. It was unsettling enough for himself, even with the flying experience that he had gained with Ayenwatha. Janus turned his head away from the winds streaming into his face, and looked towards his comrades.

If it were not for the leather straps holding him in, Antonio looked as if he would have lost his balance from the saddle in those moments, as he swooned and swayed, shortly succumbing to another wave of sickness. The contents of his latest bout of nausea were sprayed out to the winds on one side of his Harrak. Fortunately, no others were immediately behind him.

Janus, the only one of them that had ridden in the sky before, came to appreciate the great strength and speed of the Harraks. Sturdy, powerful steeds, the creatures matched their imposing Trogen masters well.

Janus estimated that they had flown for less than an hour up the coastline when they came into sight of a few vessels, including several galleys. The ships were lumbering along the coastline, the elongated galleys accompanying a couple of larger, two-masted transport vessels.

It was not long before Janus' group caught up to the small flotilla. The galleys and transports had their sails filled to capacity, taking advantage of the winds that labored to push the vessels onward.

The Trogens brought the Harraks into a descent towards one of the two sailing vessels. It was a hulking, round-bodied ship, with high, raised platforms set at either end, the rear graced by two curving spurs that rose high into the air.

Pennons flew aloft from the vessel, bearing a red spear set against a white background. A sizeable crew was diligently attending to an assortment of tasks, especially with regards to the two lateen sails hanging from enormous yard arms. The crew was human in nature, which in itself was a relief to Janus.

A number of warriors and ship hands surrounded the Trogens and their captives the instant that they landed on the raised aft deck. The four prisoners were regarded with great interest, curiosity emblazoned upon the faces of every observer.

"What task brings you here? This ship is under the command of the Order of the High Altar," came the firm, unfriendly words of a tall, bearded man, whose gray eyes held an icy gaze.

He was clad in a long white mantle, which displayed a red, spear-like shape over the left breast, matching the images on the pennons. The mantle covered a long, black garment underneath, and he wore a soft black cap atop his head.

"Prisoners, captured from the Midragardans," the lead Trogen responded. "This ship is bound for the north. Lord William of Talais says these prisoners are for the Unifier."

The tall man regarded the prisoners quietly for a moment, his cold eyes studying them with keen intent.

"You will find Brother Bohemond below deck, in his compartment. He is still attending to the business of the horses that we are taking to the Sunlands," the bearded man replied, the hair extending down from his cap blowing in the steady breezes. "Brother Bohemond and those assisting him still have to review some records, but you may take these captives below decks right away."

The Trogens dismounted, and proceeded to get the four prisoners off of their steeds. As before, they cared little for politeness or comfort in the manner that they handled the captives. Janus winced, as he felt the hard nails of a Trogen's hands dig into his sides, as he was brought down from the saddle. The freedom of his hands was then taken away, as they were once again bound behind his back.

With grips like iron, the Trogens tugged them forward, towards the wooden stairway to the main deck of the ship. Janus cast a quick glance around. Just off the port side was one of the war galleys, a great, mounted crossbow resting on its forecastle deck.

They continued below through an opening in the main deck, descending a short flight of wooden stairs. Janus' nostrils were greeted instantly by the pungent scent of animals. The air was thick to breathe, as compared to the open air that they had just left above them.

A moment later, Janus' ears caught several neighs and whinnies from somewhere within the lower depths of the ship. Given their considerable height, the Trogens had to hunch over to walk in the tighter confines below deck. The ship's timbers creaked as the vessel rode the waves, and Janus could feel the ocean's movements in his shaky balance, made worse with his bindings. He was simply grateful that the waves were not choppy or turbulent, keeping to a calm, rhythmic pattern.

There were a couple of voices engaged in discussion, the words of which were understandable as Janus stepped forward carefully along the lower deck.

"They all look healthy, and we have enough provisions to easily cover the leagues until we reach a friendly port," came a low, deferential voice.

"Then so be it, as our brothers in the Sunlands are forced to use what would be pack animals as war horses. Such are the shortages along the coast there," replied a deep voice.

"I understand, and I will work to make sure that every horse on this ship reaches the Sunlands, in a healthy condition," said the other.

"So this record accounts for all transactions?" the deep voice said.

"It does," confirmed the other. "We will secure the records right away."

A low growl heralded the approach of the Trogens with their prisoners, just as they neared the doorway to a small compartment, which Janus estimated to be at the bow of the ship.

"Yes, I know you are there, come in," called the deep voice, with a hint of irritation.

The foremost Trogen opened the creaky wooden door, letting light spill out into the gloom around them. The deep-throated growl came again, louder, and more menacing.

The light of the lamp inside the compartment seemed to be swallowed by the black fur of the huge cat sprawled out on the timber planks. Its gold-hued eyes reflected brightly in the light, fixed upon the incoming group. It was then that Janus took note of the light reflecting off of two immense canines, descending from the broad upper jaws of the beast. Like unsheathed blades, their bared presence cast a fearsome aura.

Janus' heart nearly stopped, until he noticed that a metal chain secured the great feline.

"And I should presume that new tidings or prisoners have arrived. It is not often that we are visited by the like of Trogens," the strong, low voice proclaimed, as the speaker came into view. "At ease, Shadow."

The great cat eased downward at the man's words, though its gleaming orbs remained riveted upon the prisoners and Trogens. The light from the suspended lantern was enough to reveal a man clad in a white mantle, also displaying the red spear ensign. From his crouched posture, Janus could tell that had the man been standing, his height might well come close to that of the Trogens.

His squared jaw, furrowed brow, and coal black eyes complimented a natural scowl. His hair was cropped just below his ears, and a thick black beard grew along his chin and jaws. He wore a dark, soft cap, like that gracing the head of the man on the aft castle.

He was seated on a wooden bench, and had been pouring over some parchments with another man, of medium build, who wore a black mantle with a red spear ensign. As they came into the light, the first man set the documents down upon a chest in front of him. He regarded the incoming prisoners with scrutiny.

As they gathered before him, he folded his arms across his broad chest. Janus did not doubt that the man's menacing visage had troubled and intimidated many men before. With a hardened expression, and focused gaze, he studied the prisoners closely, for several moments, before speaking.

"And who might they be?" he addressed the Trogens, though he kept his eyes fixed firmly upon the quartet.

"Captured in battle with the Midragardans. A raid led by Lord William of Talais," the Trogen dutifully responded, in its rumbling voice. "Lord William said to bring them here. That they are foreign. That the Unifier has interest in them."

The other man nodded, as he studied the four carefully. His eyes lingered upon the matching pendants that the prisoners wore. He was not the sort of man prone to give away his intentions by his expression, but Janus caught a moment of recognition in the man, as he stared at the pendants.

Although he did not smile, it was clear to Janus that he was pleased with the decision by Lord William to send the prisoners to him. His interest shifted immediately from worries about horses to rest in full upon the prisoners.

"There is something unusual here," the man mused aloud, addressing the foursome. "It goes without saying the words. I have been around all kinds, in escorting pilgrims to the Sunlands. I have traveled far on the business of my Order. In time, we will find out who you are, and where you are from. For now, know that you are in the ward of Bohemond, of the Order of the High Altar."

The man gave them a smile entirely devoid of welcome or warmth. He glanced back towards the Trogens.

"I have few enough men as it is. Keep them bound, and hold them above deck, where all can keep their eyes upon them. I hold you responsible. I will decide the best way to convey them to Avalos," Bohemond commanded, making a motion of dismissal. "I must finish my business here."

"As you wish," the Trogen replied with a nod, though visibly irritated at the order.

The four prisoners were pushed and jostled out of Bohemond's presence, and led all the way back, out onto the open deck where they were unceremoniously shoved to the right. They were guided to the stern of the ship, taken beneath the wide, raised half-deck augmented by the two curving sternposts.

The prisoners were then thrust down onto the hard wooden surface, hitting it with a series of thuds. They were able to brace their backs on the side, their heads coming to rest just below the gunwale.

A number of the ship's men paused to regard the strangers as they passed by. Hard, warning stares from the Trogens compelled them to resume their business with the rigging and the other tasks of the large vessel. The ship's crew kept a wide berth from the upper level with the Harraks.

The sun was still high, but theirs was a shaded section of the ship. The air was comfortable enough, with cool, salty breezes wafting off of the sea waters. Janus could feel the graceful movement of the sailing vessel through the waters. In any other time, the conditions would have been ideal for such a voyage, but there was no mistaking the powerless nature of their incarceration.

"Stay strong," Erika said quietly to Antonio, the first real words among them since they had gone into the skies.

Antonio looked positively terrible, with a pasty, clammy sheen to his skin. He had not recovered from the flight at all. He still shook with tremors from the great terror that he endured during the trip, and Janus knew that there was nothing left in the poor young man's stomach.

"I mean it. Hold together, Antonio," she told him gently. "We are together."

His wide, glistening eyes locked onto hers, and he slowly swallowed, and nodded his head.

Janus, on the other side of Antonio, gently added. "They still think we are important. We need to make sure it stays that way. If it does, they are not going to harm us."

Antonio looked back at him and nodded, but mustered no verbal reply.

To Janus' left, Logan looked sullen and angry, as he stared down at the hard wood of the deck, unable to express any counsel to Antonio. He did his best just to keep quiet every time he felt the weight of a stare upon him, glowering at everyone, captor or companion.

They had effectively been captives for much of the time since they had entered the new world. Only now, their captors were exhibiting a much lower degree of goodwill than had the tribal people. Janus could not even put a hand on Antonio's shoulder to console the young man.

Once again, Janus and his companions were going to be sorely tested, on many different levels. As he had said to Antonio, he could only hope that they remained important in the eyes of their captors. He knew without a doubt that things would indeed turn for the worse if he and his comrades were deemed unnecessary.

Yet at the same time, he was not so sure that he wanted to be regarded as important enough to be taken to the Unifier; the individual that the Midragardans and five tribes so despised.

MERSHAD

Mershad, Kent, and Derek carefully made their way to the cover of the second longship, before quickly moving onward. They continued to the last ship of the group resting along the shore. It was one of the homestead's vessels, which had been there prior to the arrival of the pair that was to take the exiles on to Midragard.

Located down the beach, it was farther removed from the core of the intensive fighting. The ringing clang of steel on steel filled Mershad's ears, along with the frenzied cries of the combatants behind them, both human and inhuman.

"Mershad, get a weapon!" Derek shouted at him, in the sharp tone of a command. A short-hafted hand axe was clenched in Derek's own right fist. While it was an axe intended for woodworking, it could certainly serve as a weapon.

Kent held onto a long, single-edged knife, and had also managed to grab up a round shield from the beach. He gripped both shield and knife tightly, though he carried the latter awkwardly.

At the least, Kent had some means of protection and self-defense. Mershad could not say the same for himself. His mind had gone entirely blank during the initial stages of the attack. It was all that he could do to stay close to Derek and Kent, as they raced away from the shoreline.

It was fortunate that they had done so, as the huge, feral-looking attackers had swarmed over the area soon after. Their roaring battle cries filled the air, as they descended with fury upon the Midragardans.

Mershad looked around frenetically. He knew that he could not climb up on the longship to their side, as the risk of exposing their position to enemy eyes was far too great. Similarly, it was even more dangerous to stray out into the open. In a way, they were trapped.

"There is nothing here!" he stammered back to Derek, a feeling of panic swiftly building up within him.

Without a weapon in hand, he felt vulnerable. One of the most basic rights of a person, to defend his or her own life, was in serious jeopardy for Mershad, as he was totally bereft of the means to fight back against any potential assailants.

"Then stay close, right by me!" Derek ordered him curtly.

Derek chanced a glance around the narrow end of the longship, where they were gathered at its bow. Mershad edged forward to take a look from just behind him. Hand to hand fighting raged up and down the length of the shore. A number of bodies from both sides lay strewn about the increasingly chaotic landscape.

"You three, come with me! Now!" cried out a loud voice from a few paces behind them.

Mershad and the others whirled about at the sound of the voice. Derek and Kent brought up their weapons, readying to defend themselves.

The grips upon both Derek's axe and Kent's seax were slightly relaxed a moment later, as the three otherworlders recognized the Midragardan who had escorted them to the last meeting with Eirik and Ayenwatha.

The lower part of the Midragardan's face was smeared with streaks of sweat and blood, and his tunic displayed a substantial gash, where he had already received a small, grazing wound. He held a sword and shield, and he had managed to don a half-helm as well. The iron helm was fashioned with a spectacle-like eye guard projecting down from the front rim, an extension meant to protect his eyes and nose. It gave the warrior a decidedly grim, dispassionate look, as he faced the three exiles.

He beckoned urgently to the trio, eyes darting about as he trotted away from the end of the longship with a slight limp to his movements. The man's labored gait drew Mershad's attention to another openly bleeding wound on the warrior's right thigh.

"Come with me! If you want to live, come now! It's clear!" the Midragardan repeated emphatically, again signaling them to follow.

Mershad looked to Derek and Kent, as Derek nodded back to both of them. Without a better strategy of their own in the offing, they set out quickly after the wounded warrior.

The Midragardan guided them around the outskirts of the homestead buildings, heading back toward a long, low structure located a couple hundred yards away. The edifice sat towards the back of the homestead, on its northernmost edge.

Out in the open again, Mershad could not resist peering back over his shoulder towards the shoreline, expecting either pursuit or arrow fire. His heart pounded in his chest with every stride, but there was no outcry, or other indication of pursuit.

In a sliver of good fortune, the four men were able to cross the open ground and reach the elongated building without incident. The combat had engulfed everyone by the ships and water's edge, confining it to that area for the time being. Even the enemy archers that had taken some shots from the rooftops of the Midragardan buildings had descended from their perches to join the intense shoreline fray.

The Midragardan warrior hastily drew the three otherworlders into the shadowy interior of the building. Almost at once, Mershad found himself sheltered away from the battle outside, the sounds of combat seeming much more distant. While his mind was swirling, he drew some security from the fact that they were no longer so exposed out in the open.

As Mershad caught his breath, he sensed the presence of animals nearby. A powerful musk filled the languid air, coursing into his nostrils with each breath. A moment later, he heard a few low growls and whines coming from deeper within the shadows of the rectangular structure.

The nature of the sounds surprised him, as he had expected to hear the whinny of horses, or possibly the bellows of oxen. He had seen both creatures being used for the labors of the Midragardan estate.

"I am Einar. My brother, now looking for your friends, is Sigurd. We cleared this byre, and kept a few Fenraren hidden in here, from the group that was sent with the warriors from the tribes," the warrior swiftly explained, as quizzical looks were turned towards him. "These few were left behind for us, by Eirik's private order. This was done the night before the morning that you saw the rest of the steeds. It was known only to a few of us, for the possibility of a time just such as this. I am a skilled sky rider, and Eirik personally charged my brother and I with your safety. We must get off this island right now. I can take you towards the Midragardan lands. Going by sea is no longer a choice left to us, but remaining here is certain death or captivity."

"And what about the others?" Derek asked, with an edge to his tone. "We cannot leave them here."

The warrior fixed Derek with a hard, unflinching gaze. His steady, firm voice conveyed the severe gravity and logic of the situation at hand. "My brother seeks them out as we speak, as I have told you. We cannot wait to gather the full group together here. We have no time. He will try to guide them here, and we hope to meet them on the way to Midragard. Listen to me. There is no further time. We must get underway now."

Derek made no reply, nor did Einar await one. The Midragardan turned away, moving deeper into the byre.

As Mershad's eyes adjusted to the darker interior, the forms of several Fenraren became more visible amongst the dim shadows. There were around ten of the creatures within the byre, as far as Mershad could tell. Their dark forms looked even larger in the confines of the byre, which was structured for the stout, smaller Midragardan horses, and the oxen.

Speaking softly, and working quickly, Einar labored to saddle up four of the creatures. During the pensive moments, the Midragardan kept glancing back towards the byre's entrance, where Derek was keeping a steady lookout for any threat of enemy approach.

"Is there any sign of them?" Einar asked, as he finished saddling the third steed.

"None yet," replied Derek, gazing outward. "The fighting is still down along the shore."

Mershad looked from Derek to the Midragardan.

The two men were keeping up strong appearances that obscured their truer feelings. Underneath the hard tones in their voices, Mershad recognized that one was greatly worried for his friends, and the other was anxious for news of his endangered brother. Only their honed discipline kept them focused upon the tasks at hand.

The four steeds were finally saddled up, and Einar helped Mershad and the others to mount the winged creatures. He hurriedly secured the long leather straps that served to tether them to the saddle.

Under any other circumstances, the chance to ride such gallant creatures would have been the experience of a lifetime. Mershad had envied Janus' opportunity to go skyward on the Brega with Ayenwatha. He could see the thrill of the experience reflected in Janus' eyes, as he had spoken later of the adventure. But the circumstances deprived Mershad of any enjoyment regarding his own impending experience.

Einar mounted the fourth and last steed, wasting no time in leading the quartet out of the stable's entryway. The thick, pungent scents were cleared the moment they stepped out into the open air, as was any feeling of concealment. Mershad instantly felt vulnerable, as the sounds coming from the beach and waters were no longer muffled.

"We need to get the others," Derek said, echoing the thoughts that gripped Mershad's mind.

Mershad looked towards the shoreline, his eyes searching fruitlessly among the combatants down along the water's edge for any sign of their companions. He quickly noticed that there was one solitary longship that had been pushed off the beach since they had gone into the byre. It was now rowing out to sea, and the modest distance prevented him from discerning the identity of any of the forms on the longship. As far as he could tell, all of the figures on the ship were Midragardans.

His heart then caught in his throat. The longship was not alone on the open waters. It was in great peril, beset by a much larger enemy galley that was swiftly overtaking it. Mershad watched in great anxiety, as an initial shower of arrows and bolts rained down from the attacking galley upon the exposed deck of the longship.

Several Midragardans fell to the planking, as the deadly missiles riddled the deck. A couple of the men tumbled over the sides of the ship during the terrible hail, plunging lifelessly into the waters. At the bow and stern of the attacking galley, bows and crossbows were readied for another volley. There was no doubt that the Midragardan longship was doomed.

"We need to find them," Derek stated, in a very strained voice.

"Do you not think that I wish to find my own brother?" the Midragardan warrior snapped at Derek.

The look in Einar's eyes penetrated deeply into Mershad's stalwart comrade, and Mershad felt the surging presence of a challenge. The Midragardan's look conveyed a horrible pain that the man was struggling to stifle, and Mershad could see he was barely able to choke his emotions back.

"You must live, and I am the only one you have here to guide you. To the skies!" Einar shouted forcefully at Derek.

Mershad could hear the regret and restraint underneath the clarion call for duty. Einar turned the steed about, so that it was facing the open ground in back of the byre, oriented away from the shore. The other three steeds followed, as they stepped away from the building.

At a cry and signal from Einar, the four Fenraren lurched forward with explosive bursts of motion. They propelled forward into a run for several steps, and then took off to the sky with prodigious leaps and wing beats. The three ridden by Derek, Kent, and Mershad followed the lead of the Midragardan's steed, as Einar climbed upward and set off across the island.

Mershad felt himself at a great loss, as he did not know the means of guiding his steed. It occurred to him that the lack of instruction was precisely what the Midragardan had wanted. Einar had purposely left the otherworlders ill-prepared, as an extra safeguard, in the case of reticence or resistance during a situation like the present. Even Derek was locked into the course set for them by Einar. Among his capabilities, the Midragardan warrior was certainly gifted with foresight and shrewdness.

Einar led them on a route that meandered up north, taking them along the western side of the island. It seemed like a long and circuitous route to take, but Mershad surmised that the warrior had his reasons.

They continued to gain altitude as they flew. Mershad kept his feet pressed firmly into the iron stirrups, even as he felt the pressure increasing on his lower back where he was thrust back by the steep incline. Mershad's heart raced, and he found himself glancing back over his shoulder time and time again. He hoped that there were no errors with the saddle straps, fearing that he would slide off the back of the Fenraren at any moment.

There was no pursuit, much to the relief of Mershad's flayed nerves. The quartet of riders proceeded at a moderate pace, as Einar turned them to the right, continuing along the northern edge of the island until the landmass turned south along its eastern side. At that juncture, the Midgardan guided them straight ahead, leaving the island behind as the glittering sea sprawled out far underneath them.

They hastened towards the east, as the island dropped farther away. Mershad watched the island shrinking in periodic increments, casting occasional glances over his shoulder, half-expecting to see signs of pursuit. Thankfully, each time he looked, Mershad beheld no such indications.

Gradually, Einar guided them into a long, looping arc, which finally turned the group due south. As they began the curve, the steeds took a level path, ceasing in their ascent. They had attained a tremendous altitude, at least as far as Mershad was concerned. His stomach fluttered, and his head swam as the steed bobbed and jostled about in the high, flowing breezes.

The group traveled onward in a brooding, tense silence. Each one of them was left to wrestle with his own thoughts and fears, not the least of which was the mode of travel they were experiencing. Yet there was one issue that was paramount in Mershad's mind, and he knew without asking that it was much the same for his comrades.

He was already tormented by thoughts of the friends and companions left somewhere behind. He could barely imagine the agonizing thoughts plaguing Einar, who undoubtedly was consumed with worry about his own brother's unknown fate. Great turmoil lay beneath the warrior's rigid, stoic facade.

While Mershad desperately wished that they would meet up reasonably soon with the others, he held out little hope of it actually happening. He knew that it would do him no good to stake his hopes on a swift reunion. With the ferocity of the attack, and their own narrow escape, Mershad knew that the likelihood of rejoining the others anytime soon was very small.

His spirit was weighed down heavily as he ruminated upon his companions' fate. He closed his eyes, taking several breaths to calm himself, as he thought about Erika, and wondered about the plight she was facing. She might well have been captured, or even be dead, both seeming much more plausible outcomes than the idea that she had escaped. The thought of her dying was gut-wrenching, inflicting a sharp constriction upon his heart.

She was Mershad's lone friend from his home world. The uncertainty of her fate evoked a helpless, overwhelmed feeling within him. He had to fight back a muster of tears that threatened to burst forth. He wished that he could just know if she had survived, even if that meant that she and the others had been taken captive.

Of the others he had been separated from, he feared for Janus most especially. Mershad had come to see him as a very thoughtful, compassionate individual, one who was barely withstanding a great level of inner torment.

Mershad also felt anxiety over the trusting and kind-hearted Antonio. He even sincerely hoped that Antonio's surly, abrasive friend, Logan, was unharmed. He admittedly had to trust that there was something good that Logan's friend could see in the brooding man. Mershad had yet to find much to convince him that Logan was anything other than unfriendly, and largely self-absorbed.

Heading southward, Mershad surmised that Einar must have judged it necessary to take the excessively long passage around the island, and make the huge arc to turn south, so that they could reduce their chances of being seen while escaping.

The Fenraren, for their part, had taken vigorously to the skies, exuberant to be released from their dim confines within the stuffy byre. They flew swiftly and steadily, with league after league of open ocean waters passing far below. From the high vantage, the sea looked like rolling fields of deep blue, a beautiful and daunting vision.

After some time, Einar guided the group into a more modest pace, and gradually the quartet fanned out a little, such that they flew in a staggered line. Mershad turned his attention to his immediate companions, shivering a little from the touch of the chilly, high-altitude winds.

Mershad was barely in a position to observe it, but he was nonetheless shaken by what he beheld on Derek's face. As Mershad looked on, glistening moisture in Derek's eyes broke open with a single tear that escaped, only to be blown off a moment later by the beating winds.

Likewise, Mershad fathomed that the Midragardan warriors that had known Einar would probably have been troubled at his expression. At the lead of the group, Sigurd's brother stared forward with a hollow look. Einar's face was almost completely hidden, deeply obscuring a few tears that ran down from his own eyes, to be cleared away by the cold, rushing air. Pulling close to even with Einar's steed, for a few moments, Mershad caught an unobstructed glimpse of the man's sorrowful visage. He tactfully looked away, before Einar realized that Mershad had observed the Midragardan's grief.

Mershad could sense the immense sorrow shaking both of the stalwart men to the core. Their postures remained stiff, and they kept their faces forward.

Glancing over towards Kent, Mershad quickly looked away, as he saw the sheer misery spread upon the young man's face. Both Kent and Derek had just been separated from their friend Janus, a relationship that Mershad knew was much closer than was his own with Erika.

It was abundantly clear that the hearts and minds of Mershad, Derek, Kent, and their Midragardan guide had been left behind, with the unknown fates of those that they cared for. There was not even a sliver of a feeling of joy present at having escaped the island attack.

Mershad shifted in his saddle, adjusting into a more comfortable position. It was very early in the journey, but he could already feel the first signs of soreness, as well as a little stiffness beginning to form in his lower back. He did not even want to begin to think about how his body would feel at the end of their lengthy journey.

He tightened his grip upon the leather reins of the sky steed, though the action was more for his own reassurance. The creature was dutifully keeping pace with Einar's steed, staying close abreast, or allowing the other a slight lead.

Mershad slowly allowed himself to grow numb in thought, caught in the melancholic grasp of his current disposition. Without focusing on anything in particular, he stared ahead, to the far horizons, the winds whistling in his ears.

Midragard lay somewhere beyond the edge of sight. It offered a pledge of refuge to the three rattled exiles. Midragard would be an entirely new land for Mershad, Derek, and Kent, filled with a host of new sights and people. Based upon the impressions that Mershad held of the Midragardans that he had already encountered, he felt very good about their prospects within the new land.

With everything that had already happened to them, Mershad recognized that it was best to at least have a little shard of encouragement to hold onto, as they headed into a highly uncertain future.

DRAGOL

Dragol, accompanied by his war band, joined up successfully with the Darrok formation, as it flew towards the lands of the Five Realms. Dragol and his warriors had kept to a hard-pressed pace to reach the rendezvous zone. They had greatly taxed their Harraks in the process, but their robust steeds were more than equal to the arduous task.

At last, the paths of the two flying contingents finally intersected, the Darroks heading east, and the others coming up from the south. The spirits of Dragol's warriors were all buoyed at the first sight of the looming monstrosities approaching through the skies.

Excited shouts rang out, as Dragol yelled out final commands. The war band spurred their steeds forward, for one final burst, covering the remaining distance between the two formations hurriedly. To a distant observer upon the ground, the Harraks would have appeared like little more than small flies buzzing near the flanks of some mammoth beast, as they drew up in the air over the largest Darrok, leading the incoming formation.

At close proximity, Dragol's mind was teetering on the edge of becoming overwhelmed by the sheer size of the Darroks. He had seen them from the ground level, in the encampment inside Saxany's borders. He already knew well enough that they were like nothing that he had ever encountered before.

Now that he was actually approaching one of the juggernauts, he was struck with a very unsettling sense of disbelief that such massive creatures could possibly remain airborne. The only thing that he could think of in comparison were the dragons in some of the oral tales told in his youth. Even regarding those barely-remembered tales, he had never gotten the sense that the dragons were of the size of the winged behemoth that he was now guiding his Harrak towards.

The elongated back of the great creature was narrow in proportion to its own form, but wide for the size of a Trogen. It carried a platform constructed of timber that ran from its neck to just behind its vast wings. The platform was fitted with a railing, and the entire construct was secured by a plethora of harness ropes that snaked down the creature's sides to its underbelly.

Currently, the platform was occupied by only a few figures, a mixture of Harraks, men, and Trogens. The sight of the Harraks upon the back of the Darrok was a firm assurance to Dragol that the grave oversights leading to the debacle of the first raid were not happening again. Dragol and his war band were further living proof of that.

Landing upon the moving Darroks was a bit of a challenge. Trogen sky riders had a sense of alighting upon moving objects, as they had gained skills in setting down upon sea borne watercraft, whether long galleys or the bulkier, sail-driven transports used by humans.

Yet despite their prior training, the mastery of such a manner of landing was truly dependent upon a keen awareness and sensitivity with their steeds, borne upon years of flying experience. Not unlike the elite horsemen of the Sunlands, or those on the steppes to the east of Kiruva, the veteran Trogens developed a very close bonding over time between steed and rider. It was one that enabled Trogen and Harrak to move as one mind and body, as if one was merely the extension of the other.

After keeping a steady pace with the Darrok, becoming more attuned to the giant's speed, Dragol guided Rodor downward, to land smoothly upon an open swathe of the platform. He had timed the movement of the Darrok and his own Harrak to near perfection. There was only a little disorientation, as his steed tucked its wings in and touched down upon the platform, the Darrok lurching up for a moment following a mighty down-flap of its huge wings.

Behind Dragol, one after another, the other Trogens landed with little trouble. As if it were some kind of cue, the humans upon the Darrok mounted other Harraks, and began to take off in the wake of Dragol's landing. In Dragol's eyes, the humans simply wanted to depart, now that their escorting task was finished. They clearly did not want to waste a moment more than was necessary, and Dragol caught the hard glares in several of their eyes, before the Avanoran riders departed the platform.

Dismounting from his own saddle, Dragol gave a gentle pat to his Harrak, stroking Rodor softly on the side of its thick-furred neck. It was an affectionate gesture, meant to show gratitude to the creature for its tremendous exertion. Rodor rubbed its head against Dragol, exhibiting some lather about its mouth, as its sides heaved. As fiery as

Dragol tended to be while on a war campaign, he embraced the close relationship with his flying steed. It was something that grew naturally between an adept rider and a capable steed, extending a proper respect to the creature that enabled a Trogen warrior to take to the skies.

Not infrequently, such a relationship was the very difference between life and death in the volatile environment of sky combat. Riders and steeds attuned well to each other's temperaments and tendencies held a distinct advantage in such an atmosphere.

"Dragol?" inquired the deep, gravely voice of another Trogen, walking up from behind him.

"I am Dragol … of the Thunder Wolf clan…," Dragol started to reply in the way of introduction, turning towards the speaker.

His eyes widened in reflex as he beheld the particular Trogen to whom the resonant voice belonged. The Trogen was an older warrior, a little shorter of height, and somewhat broader of build, than Dragol. His great rank was outwardly indicated by the thick, braided tassels, woven of long hairs from a Harrak, hanging down from the upper, central tip of the iron half-helm that he wore atop his large head.

At his side was a single-edged longblade of the Trogen style, though it was unlike most Trogen longblades in that the weapon exhibited some ornamentation. It bore a silver gilt pommel of a triangular shape, which only Trogens of very elite status tended to have. Similarly, the grip of the weapon was fashioned of bone, the origin of which Dragol could not tell.

The Trogen's leather cuirass had what looked to be deep black claw marks painted across his chest, as if the massive paw of a predatory beast had raked him. A thin neck ring of silver displayed what looked to be several individual claws, or talons, affixed to its length in the front. They were all symbols and decorations representing a very capable, accomplished warrior in the Trogen realms, one whose reputation was well-known throughout all Trogen lands.

The warrior's skin was drawn a little tighter, and appeared much more weathered, than did Dragol's. Some noticeable strands of gray could be seen within the warrior's cascading locks of hair, which descended to the middle of his back. A few small scars of various lengths, collected from violent past encounters, graced his face. Though many years older than Dragol, his distinctive gray eyes were as alert and vibrant as any warrior in their physical prime.

"I am Tirok of the Black Tigers. You are very welcome here,

Dragol of the Thunder Wolves," the older Trogen greeted him warmly. "Your name has reached my ears before. They say that strong blood flows in you."

Tirok had not needed to introduce himself, and Dragol was incredibly flattered that the vaunted Trogen warrior had openly indicated foreknowledge of him. The two clamped their right hands down strongly upon the other's left shoulder, in the Trogen manner of greeting a respected comrade.

"I have heard many great tales of Tirok, chieftain of the honored Black Tiger Clan. Your victories are celebrated among the Thunder Wolf Clan. It is a deep honor to fight at your side," Dragol stated deferentially, with no small degree of enthusiasm.

He had known that there would be a Trogen of high rank accompanying the Darroks, but he had never expected it to be one of the most exalted warriors of all of their clans.

"Come with me … I would speak with you now, as there is a little time before we bring these winged titans to rest upon the ground," Tirok said, a slight grin parting his lips to reveal his still-sharp canines. He gestured for Dragol to walk with him. "I would like to know more of you, Dragol of the Thunder Wolf Clan, before we go together into battle … and that will be happening soon enough."

The two warriors strode over to the wooden railing warding the perimeter of the large carriage. Dragol removed his helm, and let the robust breezes strengthened by the Darrok's flight run through his thick, coarse locks of hair. His heated skin, suddenly freed from the confines of the helm, cooled rapidly under the soothing touch of the winds. His sweat-matted hair was buffeted, as if the strands were eager to stretch themselves out. The feeling was refreshing and invigorating, and he took a deep breath of the crisp air.

The vapors of some low clouds were scudding by just above them, while the lands under the Darroks spread far and wide underneath the oncoming violet light, heralding the transition of day to night. Dragol could tell that the air was markedly thinner at the level of the Darroks, than at the usual heights that Trogens rode their Harraks. Yet their altitude was still well below the dangerous levels where one could no longer draw a healthy breath. As it was, the journey was still being undertaken at a pace and altitude that was tolerable to the body of a Trogen.

The scene underneath and around them was breathtaking and

expansive, a view rarely afforded to any of the denizens living within the world of Ave. The entire world seemed quiet and still, and nothing moved near the tops of the abundant forest growths below. It was as if the Trogens and Darroks were the only elements of creation moving through time itself.

Though it was far from being a hard level of exertion for the Darroks, Dragol quickly assessed that they were covering a significant distance with alacrity. It would not be very long before they reached their destination, and were able to rest for the night.

The atmosphere contrasted sharply with the troubled mindset churning within the chieftain from the Thunder Wolf Clan. Even so, Dragol was not so buried in his concerns that he was entirely incapable of admiring the magnificent vistas revealed to his eyes. He was always inspired by the grandeur of the natural world. There were many such views afforded to him within his homelands, ones that he often indulged, and the current one was incredible to behold.

Yet at the present, he was not as stirred as he might otherwise have been, as his focus had grown quite singular. He could think of little else other than to be well underway in the struggle to conquer the Five Realms, as it was a necessary obstacle on a much greater quest.

The sooner that the Unifier's wars could be resolved, the sooner that the Trogens could gain aid for the greatest struggle of their own kind: to free their lands from the oppressions and persecutions of the Northern Elves.

"A whole world, all falling under the power of the Unifier," Tirok muttered, peering out across the vast lands. "Maybe that is what was always needed in this world … a greater power, a power that no land, or race, can deny. One that has authority over the affairs of the world."

He glanced towards Dragol, his eyes narrowing. His voice then lowered, to a level that could be heard only between Dragol and himself. His expression was unreadable, giving no hint as to his purpose.

The old Trogen chieftain asked Dragol slowly, in a very deliberate tone, "What do you think of this war? The one that we fly to now, the one that you have just come from, which is not truly our war? Our clans have agreed to fight in this war, in return for a promise. That is why we are here. A promise. With that promise fulfilled, this war becomes a part of our own struggle.

"But if the promise is not fulfilled, then this war was never a part of our own struggle. Do you think this promise will be broken? Will this war be a part of our struggle as well? Or will this war be something that is not part of our struggle, making it a terrible, dishonorable war for us, the moment we know the promise would not be fulfilled."

Dragol's eyes ran past the massive wings of the Darrok, looking towards the other Darroks that were flying just a short distance behind them. He could see the numerous Trogens and Harraks standing about idly upon the other carriages.

He paused a few moments before answering, gathering his thoughts carefully. A part of him wondered why the old, legendary Trogen would ask him such direct, weighty questions. He knew that they were not casually voiced, as Tirok was not the kind to engage in useless banter.

Dragol's reply came out low and even, as he held Tirok's steady gaze. "It is almost a reality, this victory the Unifier seeks. It is close to His grasp. So many lands fight for Him. He will win this war, with or without Trogens fighting for Him. If we did not fight, we would know without doubt that no help would come for our own plight ... and maybe even bring harm to our kind.

"If we fight ... we may hope for help. And the Unifier may fulfill the promise. Then our own lands would no longer be denied. The past will be set to rights, and our kind will have back what was ours in the beginning. We have never asked for anything more.

"But if we did not fight, we could expect only failure in all of our hopes. It is because we fight, that we have hope. I think we had little choice. There was only one path for the Trogens to take in this war," Dragol finished, keeping his gaze locked to the older Trogen.

Tirok continued holding his eyes to Dragol's gaze without blinking. There was a flicker of amazement that crossed Tirok's expression, ever so brief, but still undeniable. Dragol got the impression that Tirok approved of the younger Trogen's answer.

"Your words speak very true, Dragol. There is wisdom in them. You would make a wise Great Chieftain in the Thunder Wolf Clan. Soon there will be no resistance to the Unifier. The Unifier can then help us. We cannot know if the promise will be fulfilled, until that time comes, but we will have done our part. We may soon be able to fight the final, great war of our kind, and free those held long in bondage."

"And then no more wars? A part of me wonders ... maybe that

is not a good path," Dragol mused, looking downward, towards the thick forests that stretched on and on, covering the low, rolling landscape.

The other Trogen turned towards Dragol with a look of understanding. As Tirok, Dragol, and all Trogens had had instilled in them from their earliest youth, wars were the most effective means of measuring a Trogen's courage, resolve, and skill. A world without wars could only result in Trogens that were untested, unproven, and whose honor could never be known or measured. It was not a world that would be easy to contemplate for any Trogen, and certainly not one that Dragol could really grasp himself.

"No, maybe it will not be," Tirok concurred in a solemn voice. "Maybe our kind will weaken in the absence of war. You have seen the men of Theonia."

"The riches thin their blood ... even those that claim to be warriors," Dragol rumbled, exhibiting the significant disgust that he harbored for the Theonians.

He had heard wisps of reports that the Unifier had been forced to undertake great measures to help protect a Theonian port town. Though few Trogens could be spared on the verge of the onslaughts against the Five Realms and Saxany, some Trogen warriors had evidently been diverted to assist in the protection of the port city of Thessalas.

It was all because the Theonians could not fight off a rebellion started by a rabble of semi-nomadic people who were far inferior in wealth and weapons. If anything, the reports indicated that the Theonians had been rapidly crumbling prior to the Unifier's intervention. In Dragol's eyes, the Unifier should have allowed the Theonians to be crushed. It was what they truly deserved, having given over the strength of their persons and honor for mere vanities, trinkets, and baubles.

"A wealthy Trogen may forget what it is to be a Trogen," Tirok added provocatively. He glanced towards Dragol, with a look that showed that such a possibility was one of the very few things that the old Trogen truly feared. "May it never be so, even were great material wealth to come into our possession."

"It would be a dangerous path for our kind to follow. This age we have been given, we must grab and pull to ourselves, with an iron grip," Dragol stated resolutely, taking a another deep, cleansing breath of the cool, early evening air. He clenched his fist, and gestured towards the horizon, as if he meant to strike out at the future itself. "Another day may come, when what we fear may come to pass…. There is little we can do once we leave this world and go to the eternal dwellings of our fathers in Elysium.

"It is nothing to worry about today. We must do everything to break the hold upon our lands. Even if it is fighting for others, as we do now. The Unifier is the first to offer to help our kind. No other, even the Kiruvans who have long bordered our lands, have ever offered such aid to us. Our part in this war is the risk we have taken. I will descend with fury on those that stand in the way of ending the long suffering that our kind has endured. We do not seek to conquer, only to regain what was stolen from us, and to free many of our brethren who live in slavery."

A searing flame surged within Tirok's gaze. He appeared visibly moved by Dragol's words, and was not the only one affected by the declarative affirmation.

The Thunder Wolf warrior had reminded himself what was best about their kind. He had spoken of it during a time when all of the experience and wisdom gained through the years, even that gleaned from periods of folly, had called so many questions to mind.

Though often hidden from Dragol, such moments reminded him that he was deeply conflicted about having entered a war that even had a small chance of becoming a war without justification to the Trogens. If the Unifier did not fulfill His promise to the Trogens, once they had shed their blood in His service, this war would become precisely what he most loathed; a war that was dishonorable, and wholly unpalatable, to any worthy Trogen.

A race of beings fierce in war, and a race that derived great value from the experiences of war, Trogens were not ones to fight a war without strong reasons, based upon legitimate needs for their kind. Whether an imminent threat, or a path to liberation, such as in the current instance, war had to be pursued for an honorable reason.

Ages spent living under horrific strains within their own homelands had rendered the Trogen kind vulnerable to risking a reasonless war. It was not a small worry for Dragol to wrestle with, and he saw that the matter was little different for Tirok.

Tirok turned towards Dragol after another short period of silence. He spoke with a rising voice, one that was buoyed by his clearly rekindled spirit. "And if there will be no more wars, when we are no longer here to show our kind an honorable way, then it is we who must now be the greatest of our kind. We must leave a legacy that will last throughout the long ages to follow."

A broad grin broke out upon Dragol's face, showing his own large, sharp teeth. Encountering Tirok had been a most unexpected end to his long day of flight, but it certainly was a most welcome one. Dragol's eyes burned with a barely-restrained intensity, and he felt an exhilarating mixture of reverence, awe, and pride that he was being treated as both a comrade and a peer by the renowned Tirok, the Great Chieftain of the noble Black Tiger Clan.

"Then such a legacy we will leave," Dragol stated proudly, and with great conviction, as the winds brushed across his face.

section iii

MERSHAD

Mershad's body was permeated with soreness, thoroughly chafed from the prolonged saddle ride, as the group finally reached the outskirts of Midragard. Becoming more attuned to the two companions from his home world, he could see that neither had been immune to the harsh effects of the lengthy journey. Kent's grumbling had increased significantly over the past few hours, while Derek's unwavering, stoic demeanor was a telltale sign of the discomforts that he was enduring.

While Mershad was aware that they were all enraptured by the electrifying sensations and spectacular views afforded by the high altitude, open-air flight, he knew that his companions were anything but upset that the journey's end was finally within reach. As for himself, he was more than ready to feel the reassuring presence of solid ground lying directly beneath his feet.

The lands of Midragard initially appeared as a sprawling haze on the far horizon, the sight instantly raising the spirits of their stalwart Midragardan guide, Einar. Prior to that moment, Einar was shrouded in a deep, brooding silence, even during the few times when the group had landed for the night, to rest themselves and their hard-pressed steeds.

The first such respite had taken place at a small farm and homestead, situated upon an island that was not much bigger than the one that they had escaped from. Mershad and his comrades had consumed a little food, and then had barely gotten a few hours rest when Einar had brusquely pressed them onward, much to the protest of their generous hosts. Kent had shared the reluctance, as the farmstead's occupants were more than willing to share ale and meat with their visitors. He had held his tongue, which did not surprise Mershad, even as boisterous as Kent had shown himself to be, as Einar's blackened mood stifled any arguments on the matter.

A couple of layovers later, they had caused much more of a commotion within a market town that was located on a sizeable island, which they had learned was not all that far from Midragard itself. The great jarl of that large hall, a demonstrative, haughty man named Atli, had nearly come to physical blows with Einar at being denied a good tale and the opportunity for some time spent with the exotic foreign travelers.

The surly giant of a man was held back only by the slim thread of a fact that Einar was taking them directly to King Hakon, at the king's firm request. Mershad was relieved that things had not worsened. Even though Einar was a strong man, the glittering, crazed look that flared within the jarl's eyes heralded the presence of a very dangerous individual. Had the argument broken down into a melee, Mershad was not all that certain that Einar would have emerged in a condition capable of continuing their flight together.

The air had cooled precipitously as they proceeded deeper southward. At Einar's behest, the party had all been provided with fur-lined cloaks for the last stretches of travel.

Mershad had encountered some trouble donning his own cloak, fumbling with the pin of the bronze ring-brooch, as he worked to clasp the woolen cloak at his right shoulder. He had no difficulty motivating himself to pull the cloak more snugly about his body within the brisk, icy winds that they encountered when climbing up into the airy heights. He found himself pulling the front of his tunic up like a makeshift mask for his face, his skin having become slightly numb with the incessant flow of chilly air against it.

Mershad had no choice but to set his mind firmly against the cold as they continued onward. Eventually, and mercifully, he found himself becoming more inured to the chill. He was settled well into that state on the afternoon that the outskirts of Midragard had drawn into sight.

The hazy, shadowy forms spanning the distant horizon were soon revealed to be a great land front. The broad boundary was marked by an expansive stretch of high crags, cliffs, and mountains, their continuity broken up by deep channels and rivulets that cut far into them from the sea.

The Fenraren and their riders were no longer the lone occupants of the air, as a number of seabirds flew about in the skies all around them. A few curious gulls shadowed Mershad's party from a safe distance, loosing excited cries, as if extending the incoming party a boisterous welcome. The sight of the birds and the land brought a smile to Mershad's face, raising his attentiveness to take in the full spectrum of their approach.

Their avian visitors continued to glide and dart around the Fenraren, as if providing a kind of escort. The winged steeds paid the seabirds little heed, and were not distracted in the least by their sustained chorus of squawks and cries. The Fenraren kept their loose formation and did not react, other than to growl whenever one of the birds drifted too near.

"There!" Einar suddenly yelled out to the party, pointing downward with a burst of enthusiasm, of a kind that had not been present during the entire journey.

Mershad looked down to see a number of shapes darting swiftly along the surface of the water, their small, triangular dorsal fins the only part of their bodies that cleaved the ocean's surface. The porpoises moved with a swift, elegant grace, powerfully cutting through the water as they swam in a unified cluster.

Not long after they sighted the porpoises, a massive explosion of spray denoted the presence of a behemoth that had just surfaced for breath. Mershad looked down in sheer wonderment, as the huge fin whale descended towards the depths once again, its enormous tail briefly lifting out from the water, and coming down with a thunderous splash. Another fin whale, a monstrosity well over seventy-five feet in length, surfaced just a moment later, replenishing its own breath and sending a fountain of water soaring into the air before submerging to join its oceanic companion.

Soon after, Mershad sighted a pod of around fifteen whales, of a markedly different type with distinctly rounded heads. On average, they were only a fourth of the size of the great fin whales.

"Now they have the right idea," Einar exclaimed loudly, as an assortment of skerries came into view, breaking up the blue of the ocean. The small, rocky islands were scattered all across the surface of the water, rendered in a wide array of irregular shapes. "What I would not give to just lie around, and indulge myself in as much herring as my belly could hold!"

Einar's eyes were fixed upon a host of life forms that had taken occupancy of the skerries, basking in the open sun on the broad rock surfaces. A few of the seals flopped into the water as Mershad gazed down on them.

"Best they be careful though," Einar then added, gesturing off towards the right.

A few tall, ebony dorsal fins protruded far out of the water, mixed with ones of a lower profile. They were spaced well apart, and attached to massive bodies lurking just beneath the waves. The killer whales were large, some being nearly thirty feet in length. The pack of predators were still a good distance away from the main concentration of seals, but

Mershad did not doubt that the bulky hunters were well aware of the seals' territory.

A series of high escarpments met the sea a short distance beyond the end of the staggered array of skerries. The expanse of cliffs was riddled with crevices, ledges, and nooks, where a host of seabirds had made their homes. Vegetation was scanty around the first series of cliffs and mountains, with very sparse tree growth visible. Lichens clung to rock facings, coating them with a deep green.

Still at their lead, Einar turned his steed to the left, so that their course shadowed the cliff facings. The jagged facades defiantly withstood the ocean and its crashing waves, which boomed thunderously into their bases. The passage of the Fenraren stirred up a number of the cliff-side denizens, stoking the seabirds' more cautious, protective instincts around their nesting sites. A few throaty rumbles and bared teeth from the Fenraren prevented the seabirds from becoming overly bold in warding their nests.

The quartet soon passed into a more mountainous area, where regal fjords reached deeper into the landmass. The fjords, mountains, and other natural elements were incredible to behold. Mershad glimpsed thickly forested valleys nestled among the towering heights. Flashes of vibrant gold broke up the rich green blanketing the valleys, exposing meadows gilded in golden, floral brilliance. The group had continued by a few gleaming channels, before a particularly broad channel beckoned to them, from up ahead to the right.

"The Silver Fjord!" Einar shouted. "This is where we pass into the heart of Midragard!"

Einar guided them down from the upper heights, turning them to the right as they descended through the air over the center of the great fjord. The wide, sparkling waters indeed looked like a silvery pathway, as the great fjord reflected the light of the sun with a jewel's splendor.

The steep, elevated heights flanking the fjord looked foreboding and uninhabitable. Yet not everything within the confines of the fjord and its bordering rises was inhospitable. Once flying down the length of the fjord, Mershad espied some relatively narrow stretches of flatter, greener land hugging the water's edge, some of the expanses reaching a little farther back than others.

On more than one of the larger swathes, Mershad observed the rectangular structures and cleared land that indicated the presence of modest farmsteads. Clusters of sheep and cattle grazed idly out in the open air, taking little notice of the group as they passed overhead.

The first signs of ships then began to come into sight, as Mershad beheld some vessels pulled up onto the shorelines of the farmsteads, and a few out upon the fjord waters. The forms of the ships became increasingly clearer to the eye, as Mershad's group descended lower. Some were simply very small rowing vessels, while others were longships, provided with both a mast and square sail.

Mershad looked farther ahead, and was instantly struck by the sheer magnitude and beauty of the majestic fjord. Tree growth had increased substantially, conifers such as spruce and pine rising up from the steep slopes, some clinging tenaciously to sparse holds along the minimal rocky ledges and crevices.

The resplendent waters continued forward between two particularly massive mountains, just a short distance ahead. The great rises flanked the water, looking like mirror images of each other.

"The Great Helms! You can see why they are named so," Einar called to Mershad and the others, gesturing towards the two towering rock formations, which did resemble the profile of the conical helms worn by the Midragardans. "Old tales say great giants that are the offspring of gods stand beneath them to this day, awaiting the final battle of Ragaras-Narok."

Mershad had almost no idea of what Einar was referring to, but was fascinated by the claim nonetheless. The huge mountains were certainly of a size capable of containing giants, if such beings even existed.

The party was then blessed with an unfettered view of the gorgeous scenes spread all around them, as the sun broke out fully from the scudding clouds far overhead. The clear skies allowed for dramatic effects from the sun's radiance, as the mountains along the fjord broke the beaming rays up. Striking contrasts were created instantly, as the greater portion of a mountain's facing on one side was left draped in shadow, while the areas opposite it, across the fjord, were bathed in an abundance of golden light.

More than once, the quartet passed by dazzling waterfalls that tumbled and cascaded with silvery grace down the facings of towering escarpments. Some falls looked like long staircases carved into the sides of the lofty mountains, while others poured over the lips of high ledges, to plummet great distances into pools far below.

A few of the great mountains were still crowned in pure white, their summits reaching high enough that snows could continue to resist the onset of spring.

Einar drew the Fenraren even lower as they passed down the Silver Fjord, until Mershad was able to make out the faces of the people on the ships and settlements that they encountered along their path. The water and land collaborated to form a dizzying array of offshoots, nooks, and crannies, but Einar had no trouble in navigating the seeming maze, as they kept faithfully to the main channel of the fjord.

The Silver Fjord twisted and turned as it drove ever deeper into the Midragardan lands. Mershad sat back in his saddle, wholly content to relax, and take in the surrounding sights. He noticed that the traffic on the water was picking up considerably, with a much greater frequency of boats visible.

He also noticed that the mountains were gradually lowering in height, some more aptly described as great hills. His suspicions that they were approaching a larger settlement, or series of settlements, were confirmed not long afterwards. Expecting a larger estate or a small town, Mershad realized that he had greatly underestimated in his conjecture, as a very large market town loomed into sight. An expanse filled with edifices, the market town was spread out ahead of them, from the left side of the fjord.

A vast, semi-circular earthen rampart and timber palisade shielded the market town's landward side. A ditch and moat paralleled the course of the rampart, reinforcing the protective elements. The curving outer wall was pierced by three main gates, providing access into the town. Each gate was provided with timber bridges that spanned the exterior ditch and moat. Stout wooden towers of a square profile were perched atop the gates. Armed warriors stood upon the upper platforms of the towers, overseeing the principle entrance and exit points of the large market town.

An amalgam of packhorses, pedestrians, and carts could be seen in the process of approaching, or departing from, the market town. Many were moving along the earthen pathways running across the neighboring lands up to the market town, and all manner of traffic was entering and exiting through the three main gates. The town itself was awash with vibrant activity. Narrow streets surfaced with wooden planking were lined on the sides by a variety of timber-built structures. Low fences demarcated larger plots of land, upon which multiple buildings had been erected.

The fjord's waters around the market town teemed with numerous ships, of a great range of sizes. The area was itself provided with a kind of palisade, which formed a large crescent extending far out into the water from the town's edge.

Some of the vessels were the size of great warships, long and elegant in profile, while others were much broader of beam, resting at anchor farther out in the water. There were more than a few small rowboats, which could be manned by just one or two persons.

Visible a short distance outside the walls of the market town, and standing atop its own great hill, was what appeared to be a circular fort. Looking over the town, its elevated position was marked by its tall earthen rampart, and thick crowning of wooden palisades. The fort did not seem to have much, if any, activity occurring within it, though there were some wooden structures within its protective circumference.

Einar led the party further inland, taking them around the outskirts of the market-town, and slowing down their pace, which allowed Mershad to take in the sights more easily.

"Hedirka, the great market town under King Hakon," Einar yelled out, as they continued their passage around the town. "You will visit it soon enough! But we have pressing business with the king, and we cannot delay."

After curling around Hedirka, they broke away from the market town and headed farther to the southeast. A roadway of hard packed dirt, cleaved by many continuous lines of wagon tracks, stretched onward beneath them. They shadowed the roadway from above as it reached out from the walled market town and meandered deep into the Midragardan lands, leaving the fjord increasingly farther behind.

The airborne party covered several more leagues before an expansive swathe of flatter, open ground came into view, upon which a large cluster of buildings was located. There were some trees dotting the area, turning into a much denser mass where the ground sloped up far behind the homestead to the east, ascending towards the top of a great ridge overlooking the estate.

A lake could be seen to the eastern side of the homestead, nestled serenely within the shadow of the prominent ridge. The lake was ornamented all around its edges by an abundance of purple, gold, and white, as a wealth of blooming flowers brought the richness of spring to grace the gleaming body of water.

Mershad was transfixed for a moment by the striking beauty of the sight, but his eyes were soon drawn toward the throng of structures that they were fast approaching. A hall of exceptional size was located at the center of the various timber edifices and outbuildings. The great hall drew the eye immediately, its gable ends decorated by crossing extensions that projected well above the apex of the roofline, shaped into what looked to be animal forms. Tendrils of smoke lazily wafted out of a sheltered opening placed midway down the ridge of the steeply-pitched roof.

Mershad's gaze then roved onward, scanning the surrounding edifices and land around the regal hall that so clearly anchored the estate. There were fenced pens with attendant byres, as well as a number of smaller buildings and open-faced structures, which Mershad guessed were either workshops, or buildings for storage.

Other hall-shaped buildings, which also had covered smoke-holes in their rooftops, identified likely dwellings. They were of various lengths, but even the largest of them was much lesser in stature and appearance than the main hall.

Telltale furrows marked the location of thoroughly plowed fields, obviously put in use for the current growing season. The unbroken surfaces of other fields announced that they had been left fallow, or perhaps were to be used for grazing. The various fields spread out far from the large homestead.

A few minor structures, of the square, open-faced type, were scattered within the sprawling expanses of fields. A few of the fields were encompassed with a perimeter of low, wattle-and-daub fencing, while others were left entirely open.

Einar guided the group sharply downward, towards the open ground on the nearest side of the main cluster of edifices. The wolfish steeds landed surprisingly gently upon the ground, and Mershad silently rejoiced at the first feelings of solid ground underneath.

Einar immediately freed the protective straps that held the rider tight to the saddle, prompting the other three to do likewise. Mershad fumbled for a moment with the buckles of his own straps, but in a few seconds the hide lengths fell loosely to the sides of the Fenraren.

Kent winced and moaned as he slowly got down out of his saddle.

Mershad could not blame him for the display of discomfort, as his own body was riddled with a pervasive aching and stiffness. He clenched his teeth tightly as he eased himself carefully down to the ground, his lower back crying out for relief.

It was a little disorienting to suddenly feel the ground directly beneath his feet, a strange period of adjustment that he was only beginning to get used to following extensive periods aloft upon the sky steeds. The bobbing and shifting of flight, some movements subtle, and others not quite so gentle, depending upon the level of turbulence, were a constant when airborne. To suddenly go from an environment of wobbles and sways to one of rigid solidity was admittedly jarring to Mershad's senses.

Derek bore whatever soreness he harbored with no outward change of expression, though Mershad fathomed that it was no less comfortable for him.

A few men rushed up to the travelers as they stood waiting upon the ground.

"Hail, Einar, welcome back to our lands!" a rather stout man with reddish blond hair greeted amiably.

"Hail, Onund! It is good to be back in King Hakon's stead. These are guests of high honor, expected by the king, and will remain with me. Please see to it that our steeds are well-fed and given shelter," Einar instructed him firmly.

Onund gestured to the men standing around him. They hurried to the sides of the Fenraren, taking up their tethers and leading the fatigued, hungry creatures off in the direction of what looked to be a byre.

Einar glanced towards Onund, and continued, "I wish we could request to be well-fed in your home, as that good wife of yours knows few equals in the preparation of food."

Onund grinned, and patted the rounded paunch of his belly. "I always carry the proof of her skills with me."

The two men laughed together, and Mershad could not help but grin at the self-deprecation.

"Einar!" shouted a resonant voice, coming from the right.

A tall, broad-shouldered man of modest build approached them. He possessed sparkling blue eyes, and his bright, blond tresses hung down loosely, to rest just below the tops of his shoulders. A well-groomed beard ornamented his angular face, and though he radiated confidence and strength, he had a very kindly look about him.

He wore a deep blue tunic, richly brocaded in gold threads that looked striking set against the darker blue, woolen fabric. He wore a bright red cloak over the tunic, adding to the vivid contrasts, and lushness, of color.

The glint of silver and gold came from several circular arm bands and an assortment of rings gracing his fingers. He carried a sword sheathed at his left side, the pommel of which was gilt in silver, as was the band around the mouth of his scabbard.

Mershad knew at once that this was a man of high standing, as his fine trappings allowed for nothing less.

"Svein!" Einar responded in genuine elation at the blond man's approach, striding forward immediately and embracing the other tightly.

"Einar, you rascal! These eyes do not see you often enough, now that you ply the waters to the far north," Svein greeted warmly, and Mershad could see the sincere affinity that the two men held for each other.

"The path of trade leads far," Einar replied. "Perhaps too far, though."

The smile faded, as a serious mien crossed Einar's face and took hold.

"What concern burdens you?" asked Svein, growing solemn at the change in Einar's mood.

"There is much to tell, Svein. More than I can begin to say here. These men should be brought before King Hakon now, and I feel that they should be protected by Midragard," Einar replied firmly.

"Indeed, you have brought unusual guests," Svein commented, as his eyes settled upon them, taking in the sight of Einar's foreign companions. His eyes narrowed in scrutiny as he gazed upon Mershad and Derek. "Of the Sunlands, yes? Then they are very far indeed from their homelands."

"No, I do not think they are of the Sunlands, and their tale may be hard to believe," Einar responded. "But I have reason to believe that they speak truthfully, as do many others."

"Then my curiosity is awakened," Svein remarked. He turned to face the newcomers squarely, and took a couple steps towards them. He gave them an affable smile. "My name is Svein, a loyal retainer in service to good King Hakon, King of all Midragard."

The three exiles proceeded to introduce themselves in turn, but there was no further delay, as Svein quickly heeded Einar's advice. He led them into the midst of the complex of buildings, striding directly towards the large, prominent hall at the center.

On closer inspection, Mershad saw that most of the edifices were stave built or wood-framed, with wattle-and-daub panels, while a few were horizontal. All were wholly fashioned of timber, and roofed in thatch.

Children giggled and looked upon the newcomers with wide, curious eyes, though they kept to a respectful distance. A cat of considerable size, long legged and coated in black and white fur, paused to momentarily regard the party, before traipsing around the side of a nearby building.

Mershad soon gained a much better view of the animal forms looming above the apex of the main hall's sharp-sloped roof. The crossing extensions at the gable end were fashioned by elaborate carving into vivid representations of two fierce wolves. Their dark, snarling visages radiated pride and ferocity, outlined starkly against the smooth, aqua sky.

The broad doors underneath the gables were open, and a couple of spear-armed warriors stood attentively to each side of the entrance. The warriors made no effort to impede the newcomers, as Svein led them directly into the large structure.

While the outside of the hall was not overly elaborate, the inside of the structure was stunning to behold. Towering circular posts of wood ran down each side of the hall, intricately carved with the highest levels of craftsmanship. The intertwining patterns snaking up the thick posts were comprised of a variety of geometric designs and representations of animals, both familiar and fantastical. The floor underneath their feet was hard-packed earth, provided with a layering of fresh rushes spread copiously over its surface.

An elongated hearth ran through the center of the hall, and a number of men and women were standing close to the warmth of the robust fire blazing within it. There were also a few lit oil lamps placed about the hall, bolstering the light coming from the hearth's flames. The interior of the hall was filled with flickering shadows from the multiple sources of firelight.

Overall, the ambience was dim, as there were no side windows open to allow the sun's light to enter. Only the entrance let some of the day's light spill inside the great hall.

There was one opening in the middle of the roof, with a timber covering set just above it to keep out the rain. The billowing smoke from the fires could exit through it, but it did not rid the hall entirely of excess smoke. A haze lingered among the rafters, and the air inside was thicker, with a smoky scent.

At the far end of the hall was a raised platform, with a great wooden settle resting upon it, the back and arms of which were ornamented richly with exquisite carvings. Two short wooden pillars, which looked to Mershad's eye to be freestanding, flanked the elaborate settle.

Seated upon the settle was an older man with a long white beard, who was engaged in conversation with a couple of fierce-looking men standing to his left, at the base of the low platform. To each side of the platform, set just in back of it, were a pair of closed doors. Judging by the full size of the hall, and estimating the interior space that they were now standing within, Mershad guessed that the doors opened into some manner of chambers or spaces beyond.

Though clearly advanced in years, the man upon the platform was still very erect in his posture, showing that age had not yet sapped him of a proud bearing. He was broad of frame, though the ready access to food and drink that a king enjoyed had evidently added a little padded girth to his body.

He was dressed in a manner similar to most of the others, with a long cloak over a tunic, the former being of a blue-green color, and the latter being of red with silvery brocade. The cloak was richly lined with fur. A blue-green headband, also embroidered in silver thread, held his snowy locks in place. His weathered hands, resting on the edges of the ornate wooden settle, showed the glint of gold and silver rings upon his long fingers.

Sprawled out on the ground before the platform was a great black wolf, with luminous golden eyes. The huge wolf raised its head as Einar and the others entered, and at the first sight of the creature, Mershad's breath caught in his throat. Its penetrating gaze and triangular ears focused upon them as the newcomers approached.

There were a few large dogs loitering around the hall, though they kept to the shadows around the sides. Their ears also perked up, as their eyes riveted upon the incoming party.

Svein and Einar quietly led the three foreigners down the length of the hall, striding along the right side of the hearth. It did not take very long at all for the three exiles to attract the full attention of those around them. All conversations gradually ceased, as the Midragardans in the hall took account of the entrants.

Svein and Einar guided Mershad and his companions up to the right side of the platform, where they deferentially waited quietly as the older man on the throne finished up his conversation with the two strong-looking men. He had not yet taken notice of the newcomers, or at least had not indicated that he had. It would not have been entirely surprising to Mershad if he had remained engrossed in the conversation, as there seemed to be an open, flowing atmosphere within the hall.

"We will ride to my two easternmost estates, as there is some business there that I personally need to see to, and then we shall proceed onward to the Great Gathering," the old man said to the two men in a low, steady voice. He had an authoritative cadence, slow and purposeful, as if he was the kind of man who gave careful thought to each word loosed from his mouth. "You may tell Thorolf that I will speak to him at length before then, about taking ward of his son on one of my estates, perhaps one of those two eastern ones. Tell him not to worry himself over the matter, as he has long done well by me, and I will certainly do well by him. There is much to attend to with the market town coming to full life, and Thorolf must see to it now that a good year begins. Spring is here and trade will be flourishing again. The trading fleets are well-poised to the north as we speak."

"According to your will," one of the men responded, a particularly fierce-looking individual who bore more than one substantial scar upon his craggy, well-weathered face.

The king then dismissed the pair.

With a low bow, the man and his companion took their leaves, turned, and started off down the hall with long, balanced strides. They paused in momentary surprise when they glanced over at the three guests accompanying Einar and Svein, but quickly continued onward.

By then, the old man on the platform had taken full notice of the new arrivals. His eyes appeared to sparkle with a merry light for a moment, as he regarded Einar. A slight smile was evident, even behind his thick beard.

"You have certainly come a good distance, Einar. It is still amazing how far one can go upon a sky steed. Is that brother of yours well? You

and Sigurd are reflections of your father Olaf," the old man stated in a tone both kindly and familiar. The informality gave light to a personal, amiable relationship existing between the old man, Einar, his brother, and their father, something that gave some comfort to Mershad in the strange environs. "I hope that trade to the north goes richly. It is now time for all the convoys to go north, to bring back the abundance of Kiruva, and even farther abroad. What I would not give to gain some youth back to make such a voyage on river and sea, though memory looks upon hard journeys much more fondly than when one is undertaking them."

Einar looked downcast as he raised his eyes to the old man. His timbre matched his expression. "My king, I wish I could be the bearer of better tidings, but I bring you dire words. We were attacked suddenly, at Eirik's settlement in the north, just east of the Five Realms.

"Those that struck us were from Avanor, and they attacked in great strength from sea and sky. I had to rescue the three that I bring before you today. You were expecting them and others of their group to come by sea, but desperation drove us to take the skies. The others of their number likely fell into the grasp of Avanor's warriors. We know nothing of their fate.

"Their importance is great, though I do not understand it fully … I am also fearful for my brother, as I do not know what has happened to him."

It was as if a dark shadow passed across the face of the old king. His eyes moved purposely from Einar to the three young men with him. Though they were dressed in the garb of Midragardans, his eyes scrutinized them assiduously, and Mershad knew that the king could not fail to miss their foreign nature.

"They understand our language, and can speak it," Einar then interjected in a low voice, as the king quietly studied them.

"Then welcome to my hall," the king stated, taking the news in stride. If anything, the king seemed to relax slightly when Einar announced the lack of a language barrier. "I am King Hakon, and the three of you will be my personal guests here in Midragard. By what names are you each called?"

Mershad and the others each gave their names in a polite manner, the introductions accompanied by low bows. They waited silently and respectfully for the king to respond once they had done so.

"I know that all of you must be very tired after your long journey, but please endure with me a few moments more," the king said, with the trace of apology to his words. He looked to Einar with an expression of grave concern. "Tell me what you have learned of them, and I would hear their story from their own lips as well."

Einar proceeded to explain everything that he knew about Mershad and his companions, and all three of the guests were given several opportunities to speak, as they described their harrowing stay within Ave. The king listened intently as the incredible story was told, not commenting or reacting in any way until they had all finished.

"The All-Father has a purpose for them. I am afraid only the ones that are learned in the ancient knowledge would have the wisdom to know what must be done," King Hakon said to Einar. "I know little myself, but I do know of the things that have been foretold for our world. It is enough to know that you were indeed wise to bring them here without delay, though I am much relieved that you passed through the skies safely. It was a dangerous passage that you undertook, if Avanor's eyes are searching for them.

"Know that they will be accorded all privileges as my guests, and know that they are placed under my firm protection. They must be taken to the province moot, to the Great Gathering, for Heimdall will be joining us there. I am certain that he will know more of what to do."

The King then looked steadfastly at the three newcomers. "As you are my guests, you shall be fed, clothed, and well-protected. All of your needs and comforts will be provided for out of my dominion. I do not know you as of yet, but I freely offer my friendship, and ask only that you do nothing that would make us think ill of you."

His kindly tone took on an edge at the latter words, showing that although he had a generous, kindly demeanor, there was a very serious, resolute nature within the king. Mershad was not about to underestimate the old king, as he knew that a weak, dottering old man could never have been accepted as king by the tough, stalwart people of Midragard. Only a fool would risk underestimating the figure upon the settle, and there was no doubt in Mershad's mind that King Hakon was an extraordinary individual, a man to be respected and obeyed.

"They will be under my eye as well, my king," added Svein, nodding respectfully from where he stood at Mershad's side.

"I will remain to help here, if you need," Einar then added.

The older man smiled with sudden mirth, his tone softening once again. "I may need all of you after the mead flows, to help me make it back to my bed for the night! Among all of us, we should still be able to keep one eye out on behalf of our new guests, but I insist that the mead flows in rivers this very evening. While it is late this day, and though I do not wish to burden the good women of my homestead, I must call for a feast on behalf of Einar and my new guests."

Mershad could see the mood brightening immediately as the throng in the hall took in the king's words, though he wondered how Einar felt regarding the announcement of a feast. He knew that the Midragardan was heavily burdened by thoughts of his brother's uncertain fate.

Evidently, the king had the same concern. The king had paused, as his gaze took in Einar. Mershad was struck by the subtle shift in the king that then occurred, bringing a decidedly compassionate air to his demeanor and words.

"This world is filled with sorrows enough," the king stated. "And I know that your heart is heavy, Einar. Mine is not light either, but we must not forget to celebrate and embrace the good in this life … and seeing you again in my hall is indeed a good thing, one that is worthy of rejoicing over. I wish to welcome you, and to welcome three new friends of Midragard, to my home and hearth."

Einar seemed to be very moved by the king's words, as he lowered his eyes and gave a slight bow. The expression on his face could only have been motivated by genuine affection, and a feeling of gratitude, towards the king.

"And there is more good fortune for us all, in that Aun's recent elk hunt was not the only hunt that met with success," the king added, in a louder voice, looking to the others assembled within the hall. "Grettir landed a monster of a boar on his own recent foray into the woods, which will be served this very night!"

"Not such a difficult task for Grettir, my king, as I hear that the beast died from fright after looking upon Grettir's face!" jested one of the other Midragardans.

Svein, Einar, and several others in the hall laughed heartily, as many cheered the king's pronouncement. Seeing the spirited reactions, Mershad strongly suspected that Midragardans were the type who readily embraced any occasion as justification for a prodigious feast. The surge of levity throughout the hall admittedly felt wonderful, after having endured all the hardship and uncertainty that had flooded the past few days.

"Have you tasted the life water of our people? That which we call mead?" asked Svein, grinning, looking back at the three guests who were now formally in his stead.

All three shook their heads to the negative, though Kent displayed a spark of highly piqued interest at Svein's words.

"Then we will remedy that shortcoming this very night! You must not wait any longer to imbibe the nectar of Midragard!" Svein replied with great enthusiasm, much to Kent's apparent satisfaction. Mershad almost chuckled at the anticipatory look that spread across Kent's face. "And it is an opportune time for you, as the waters of the rivers and sea have been generous, and the hunting rich. In addition to this news of a great boar being brought down by Grettir, the largest salmon in years will grace our table, and even a great elk bull that was just brought down by Aun shall be roasted to honor our new guests."

"You will make us very hungry with more talk such as that," the king remarked, with a warm smile. He looked again towards the newcomers. "Welcome to Midragard, and to my great hall. I look forward to speaking with each of you more in times to come."

The king glanced over towards Svein. "Svein, please see our honored guests to their new quarters. I know that they must be tired. They have been patient in coming here immediately, without protest, after their hard journey."

Einar, Svein, and the others bowed to the king once again. Svein guided them back out of the hall, and before they were outside, Mershad could already hear the king taking up the next matter of business, with one of the other parties that had been standing inside the hall.

Once they were in the open air again, the group strode across the grounds and made their way into the midst of the surrounding timber structures. The grounds were alive with activity, crisscrossed by bond-servants, retainers, women, and children alike.

The distinctive clank of hammers upon metal emitted from one structure set a little apart from the other buildings. A stream of dark smoke wafted upward from the opening in its roof. Mershad listened to the steady pounding of iron upon iron, though he could not see the blacksmith, as the front entrance to the workshop was obscured from view.

They continued onward, heading towards one of the smaller rectangular structures provided with a roof vent. Svein opened the door leading into it, standing aside and gesturing for the others to enter.

The interior was revealed to be a relatively cramped space, with little more than a central hearth dug into the middle of a primary front room with raised earthen sides. An additional small room was set adjacent, separated by a timber partition from the main chamber.

"It is fortunate that the visitors from the tribal lands were just here, as we already have enough stored within these quarters to accommodate the three of you," Svein said. "Einar will be staying in different quarters. There are enough pallets in the back room for the three of you to sleep on, and enough coverings to keep you warm."

As far as Mershad was concerned, it was a luxurious accommodation, offering the greatest degree of privacy that he and the others had enjoyed since coming into the new lands.

Svein looked around the room, and commented. "I will have an extra supply of wood brought in for the fire. Relax, and adjust yourselves for the moment. I will return to summon you for the evening feast."

"And I will rejoin you then as well," Einar said, as he began to turn to leave.

"Thank you … for everything," Mershad interjected, addressing gratitude to both Svein and Einar. The latter stopped before he had exited through the door, and rotated to face them.

"You are welcome," Einar replied, with deep sincerity in his gaze.

"Yes, thank you so much for what you have done for us, Einar," Kent added, entirely serious in his expression and tone.

"We would be in a lot of trouble without all of you," Derek stated, looking to the two Midragardans, before settling fully on Einar. His voice lowered. "And you have given much of yourself to see us here, Einar. I understand that … and I thank you."

Einar made no verbal reply to Derek, but instead gave him a slow bow of his head, as an understanding passed between the two men. As both were warriors, Mershad knew that they related to each other on a unique level.

"We could not in good conscience offer you anything less," Svein replied, with a nod of his head.

The two Midragardans then begged leave, proceeding out of the small hall-house. Kent walked to the edge of one of the raised earthen sides and plopped down heavily, his right hand clasping his left forearm, as he wrapped his arms just below his tucked-in knees. Derek strolled over to the opening that led into the smaller chamber, and peered inside. Walking in, he reappeared a moment later, with a pallet in his clutches.

He dragged it up on the side that Kent was sitting upon, kneeled down, and then situated himself, so that he was lying on his back upon the mattress. He loosed a long, extended sigh.

"Feels so good just to lie down for a second," he commented, his voice echoing fatigue.

"Not a bad idea, Derek," Mershad replied.

"It will take them awhile to ready a feast. We have some time, if you all want to get a little shut-eye. Speaking for myself, I sure do," Derek said. "Not too much to look at in here anyway."

"A nap sounds very, very good," Kent agreed, pushing himself up to his feet, and getting his own pallet from the small storage room. He returned to the chamber, and came back with a woolen blanket and a couple of furs.

"I'll take this side, so we have some more space," Mershad said, claiming the other raised earthen platform for his own bedding space. He felt more comfortable with that arrangement anyway, as Derek and Kent knew each other so well, and he preferred being more solitary.

After a couple of trips, he had a woolen blanket, fur, and a down-stuffed mattress set up on the opposite side from Derek and Kent. He lay down upon the mattress gingerly, but found it to be surprisingly comfortable. Then again, a lot of things would have felt very comfortable at that moment, after having endured sitting in the saddle of a sky steed for so many hours.

Kent's light snores a few minutes later were the first indications that the weary travelers had begun to succumb to the welcome invitations of sleep. It was not much longer before all three of the otherworlders were deep in slumber. Mershad drifted off smoothly, descending down into the fathoms of a dreamless repose.

Svein found them all fast asleep when he returned a few hours later, to summon them for the feast called by the king. Mershad woke up groggily, though immensely glad for the hours of precious, continuous rest. By that time, his stomach had built up quite an appetite, and he was more than ready to go to a feast.

First, though, he would attend to prayers, the undertaking of which had gone haphazardly over the past few days of travel. It was important to him to reestablish his routine as much as possible, knowing that under the circumstances it would be very easy to forget about his obligations. Following prayers, though, food would be the very next thing occupying his thoughts.

DRAGOL

Dragol was filled with anxiety and discontentment as he sat upon the back of his steadfast Harrak. As always, Rodor stood with a proud bearing, supporting its brave rider with a strong posture that seemed to exude great esteem in being the steed of such an honored Trogen warrior.

The creature was larger, bolder, and more aggressive than most of its formidable brethren, traits that Dragol took no small amount of pride in himself. The exceptional nature of his personal steed reflected the growing standing of its master among his own kind, a matter that all Trogens familiar with Dragol could readily agree upon.

The beast growled and shifted, highly impatient, and eager to be relieved of the tedious journey that Dragol had again forced upon it. Restrained from stretching its wings and flying, it had become exceedingly restless. As with the previous Darrok raids that had leveled so many tribal villages, Dragol was saving his steed's energy for what was to come.

Nearby, Tirok and over twenty other Trogens sat astride their steeds in full readiness, spread down the upper back of the hulking Darrok. Likewise, numerous Trogens on the other Darroks were saddled and armed, as the moment of attack approached at last. Rested and refreshed, they were all eager to set into the skies, and challenge anything that might come up to oppose them.

The lands populated and ruled by the tribes of the Five Realms were spread out directly beneath them, following the short flight from the encampment located a few leagues west in Gallean lands. Their formation had just drawn over an open break in the trees, exposing the top of a broad ridge revealing yet another one of the enemy's palisade-surrounded villages.

Dragol heard the curt horn blasts carrying through the air,

drawing his attention forward. Just ahead of him, dismounted Trogen warriors on the other Darroks began to levy a massive bombardment of stones down upon the exposed village.

Peering ahead, it was yet another trying experience for Dragol to watch the methods of war utilizing the gigantic Darroks. Before coming to Gallea and the Five Realms, he had never witnessed a weapon with such devastating potential. Once again, he witnessed the assault unfolding with a look of awe spread across his face, as the incredible power of the Darroks was unleashed.

Attached to the Darrok's carriages were connected panels of curved timber, riveted together with iron fastenings. They could be pulled up to the carriage in flight, and lowered when needed. Each series of panels was carefully shaped and formed into flexible chutes, which guided the stones of various sizes into a vertical free fall as they were discharged. The extending length of the rough chutes released the stone loads safely below the wing level of the Darroks.

From their lofty height, the showering bombardments reduced the wooden edifices within the village of the Five Realms to little more than piles of shards and splinters. Even the great trebuchets that Dragol had seen, the mightiest of the siege and war machines of Avanor and Gallea, could not wreak so much damage within such a very short amount of time. The thunderous display of destruction was undeniably impressive, daunting, and even intimidating to observe.

Tirok looked over towards Dragol, raising a clenched fist to his right ear. Dragol responded to the gesture in similar fashion. The two senior Trogen warriors then took up the large signaling horns hanging loose at their sides, swiftly raising the ends to their lips. With a deep intake of breath, both of the chieftains blew forcefully upon the narrow ends, and the horns blared in loud unison.

The deep, resonant blasts loosed the mounted Trogens off the back of the Darrok. In moments, many riders and steeds had lifted up and spread out into the surrounding air. The signal from Dragol's and Tirok's Darrok was spread quickly amongst the other Darroks in the formation. Several other groups of Trogens rose up upon their Harrak steeds, and all of them slowly converged, forming a veritable cloud of sky warriors. If there was to be any response or sudden surprises coming from the defenders, the Trogens were ready, and more than willing to meet them.

Dragol gave another distinctive signal upon his horn, and guided a small detachment of Trogens up and away from the main Darrok formation, in order to survey the lands immediately below them. He seized upon the benefits brought by the high, unobstructed altitude, giving him a tremendous vantage from which to scan the tree-shrouded land.

He momentarily eyed the tight Darrok formation proceeding ahead of them, now a good distance away, underneath the position of the hovering sky riders. The slow-moving brutes looked to be creeping forward to Dragol's perspective, and the Trogen chieftain had no worries about closing the distance if they got too far ahead.

Dragol's new position also lent him a full view of the unfolding destruction. Deadly, weighty stone missiles continued to be sent hurtling towards the earth in a pummeling cascade by the diligent strain and exertion of Trogen muscle. Yet all was not in harmony as he watched the pulverizing attack.

He worked to stifle the return of revulsion at the barbaric method of warfare. He still found it so very hard to even conceive how the Unifier and the humans that had developed the new war tactic saw any honor in such a practice. More than ever, he could barely stomach Trogen warriors serving upon the Darroks, made to execute such a craven manner of attack.

In the deep privacy of his heart, Dragol hoped that the enemy tribal warriors had vacated the village that was being assaulted, and would soon be coming up to match their martial skills against Dragol and the other Trogen riders. That was a method of warfare that he could sanction, where enemies looked each other face to face, and matched blade against blade.

He did not want to face the rising notion within him that the Darrok bombardment was, in truth, a cowardly way of making war, striking from such a high altitude with the enemy having no means to defend itself. The ways of Avanor and those of the Trogens were so very different.

Dragol's head turned slowly from side to side, distracting his mind a little, as he passed his intensive gaze across the rolling landscape. Trees within the older regions of the forests covering the Five Realms grew thickly together, their upper tangles of foliage serving to cover hilltop, slope, valley and other terrain elements alike. The natural, largely unbroken mass of dense growth also served to make the enemy villages much easier to spot from the higher skies.

With their locations on higher ground, in areas extensively cleared of trees, the tribal villages were very easy to idenfity, from leagues away. Virtually any significant break in the forest canopy revealed the presence of telltale corn fields, or the villages often located very close to them. Both were easy, static targets for the voluminous loads of stone being jettisoned by the Darrok onslaught.

Dragol hovered and watched as the Darrok formation flew onward, nearing another intact, vulnerable village. He spurred his steed into a slow rate of flight, bringing it a little closer to the vicinity of the doomed village.

Though disliking the manner of attack, Dragol could still not help but be almost mesmerized by the utter ferocity unleashed in the new type of warfare. He had never witnessed such blistering, quick destruction, other than the unpredictable times when the earth itself shook from terrible, unknown forces deep within it.

His eyes drifted, as if in a detached daydream, towards the numerous varieties of longhouses within the large village that was situated along the crest of a sizeable ridge. There were no signs of movement within the outer palisades, and his ears picked up no sounds of alarm or terror at the imminent approach of the giant airborne formation.

That did not come entirely as a surprise to Dragol, for he had not believed that they would have been able to catch any villager unaware after so many attacks. The first Darrok raid would have taught a harsh lesson, eliciting wariness and perhaps even the instigation of a full lookout system among the tribal peoples of the Five Realms. The following attacks would have solidified and reinforced such efforts.

The longhouses were nothing but deathtraps for the kind of attack that the Darroks brought. Dragol had mused that the tribes would have long since left their villages as a precautionary measure against the spreading air attacks, seeking the safer harbor of the sheltering woods.

Despite his burgeoning misgivings concerning the tactics, Dragol implicitly understood the dispassionate rationale of the Avanorans. The tribal villages would have to be destroyed, so that the enemy would have no fortifications to return to once the ground assault into the forest region was underway. The air assaults were preliminary attacks, employed to uproot and soften the enemy.

It would save the impending invasion forces substantial amounts of time and numerous lives, both of which would otherwise have been consumed in much greater measures over the course of a multitude of difficult village sieges. The campaign to subdue the tribes and take their lands would be rendered swifter and smoother if the Five Realms were cast into fearful disarray, almost a surety with the widespread destruction of their villages. Displaced and scattered into makeshift communities, the tribal people would be left with no significant fortifications to use in resisting the invasion force sweeping in from the west.

While there was little denying that the greatest honor for a Trogen, or any type of warrior, was in single combat, Dragol could not argue the logic and effectiveness of the strategy in attaining the Avanoran goals. The Avanorans were merciless and coldly practical in Dragol's estimation. Even if they embraced methods that he viewed as dishonorable, and difficult to understand, the huge Trogen still realized that great passions for war burned within the blood of Avanor's warriors.

The Darroks slowly passed directly over the second doomed village. The first large stones crashed and thudded amid the trees farther down the slope, and then the buildings within the outer circumference of high timber stakes. Bark panels, rough planks, framing poles, and many other elements exploded into jagged bits with each ruthless impact.

The vicious sounds of collision between rock and timber transformed swiftly into a cacophony of bark and wood shattering, as the elongated village structures were relentlessly crushed under the hail of rock.

Dragol brought his steed into another hovering, static position, in close proximity to the stricken village. He watched as the Darroks looped about in a wide, ponderously slow arc, for another ruinous pass over the village. A very small number of structures that had somehow avoided the destruction of the first pass were annihilated by the second.

A spotter upon one of the Darrok carriages, deeming the destruction to be thorough enough, loosed a distinctive horn signal of several deep, staggered notes. The large behemoths then continued onward, leaving the wrecked village behind, as the enormous, airborne flotilla headed away to search out the next village to target.

Dragol then cried out a firm command to the small formation attending him, leading them into a wide arc that shadowed the ponderous Darrok formation at a distance. They descended a little lower, though they remained well out of the bow-shot range of any enemy archer lurking amongst the trees below.

The keen eyes of Dragol and his Trogens scanned the trees intensely for even the slightest sign of the tribal people. They kept in mind the spirited resistance that had taken to the skies the first time the Darroks had attacked.

Dragol was careful not to stray too far from the Darroks, speeding his group onward before the gap between the winged juggernauts and the escorting sky riders grew too much. He refused to be caught unawares, or too far away from the Darroks, if resistance did emerge.

It was not long before a host of loud cracks filled the air once again, as yet another Five Realms village was relentlessly demolished under torrents of plummeting rock. Not a building was spared, and only a few trees in the immediate vicinity avoided being broken, smashed, and snapped apart by the unforgiving, indiscriminate attack.

The area showered by the massive deluge of stone, though crudely targeted, was as devastated as the previous village in only two passes. Dragol quietly witnessed yet another validation that a Darrok bombardment was thorough and comprehensive in its maleficent effect.

Just moments later, another few short blasts of a horn filled the air, following the dissonant signals coming from the spotter responsible for determining that an attacking run had been completed.

The newer blasts were signals from Tirok. The other Trogen's group was located on the farther side of the Darrok formation, though they were situated much closer to the core of the bombardment site than Dragol's war band was.

Dragol reacted to the distinctive signal by rallying his Trogens around him. With Dragol at their lead, they soared through the skies to position themselves closer to the main formation.

Several were then distpatched from his group, and Dragol looked on as these warriors alighted carefully upon the backs of the Darroks, so that the winged leviathans could ferry them to the next chosen attack site. A portion of the steeds would be kept well-rested, but a small number remained to keep up the escort of the formation on both sides, shadowing the flying titans.

Dragol spurred Rodor forward, drawing up to the frontal areas of the lumbering formation. Leaning forward at the base of the lead Darrok's neck, where the handlers were located, a very sharp-eyed Trogen named Dagorda, of the Forest Wolverine clan, peered towards the far horizons. Dragol patiently waited, as the keen-eyed Trogen remained motionless, studying the skyline and terrain intensively. Dagorda abruptly straightened up, and called out vigorously, after just a few moments of assiduous scrutiny.

A hulking Trogen standing just to the right of the highly regarded searcher shifted the Darrok's great reins that he held in his hands. Following Dagorda's directive, he adjusted the creature's path towards the next unconformity sighted within the dark, green sea of tree cover.

Though it took a moment, Dragol finally saw what Dagorda had espied. The patch of cleared ground was a good distance away, but Dragol had no doubts regarding its nature.

As they drew closer, it was indeed revealed to be another tribal village site. Extensive areas cleared for crops sat just off of the base of a very large hill, which was surmounted by one of the largest villages that Dragol had yet seen. As with the last village, Dragol saw no signs of life within the crop areas, or amid the village structures.

With a few more signals, all of the warriors that had rested their steeds for a short while lifted off the Darroks to rejoin Dragol and the others. Once regrouped, they all fanned outward, keeping a tight vigil upon the areas being bludgeoned by the new assault.

The villages were being destroyed well beyond any reasonable hope of utilization. A tremendous amount of destruction was also levied upon the areas abundant with nascent growths of crops, which were undoubtedly ruined.

Despite the unobstructed, methodical achievement of Avanor's objectives, Dragol continued to chafe at the method. The Thunder Wolf chieftain's hopes of engaging the enemy in an honorable way were fading precipitously, with every new encounter of an abandoned village.

With numerous horn signals echoing far across the forestlands, their massive formation was certainly no secret. With the long span of time spent in the skies over the tribal lands, and the distances that they had covered, Dragol highly doubted that their presence was not well known to the enemy by then. Somewhere underneath the trees, perhaps in a number of locations, the enemy's eyes were watching them.

As was the growing trend, the enemy warriors had not been engaged that day. The only conclusion that Dragol could come to was that they were intentionally refusing to come up into the skies to challenge the Trogens. Perhaps they did not have enough steeds, as all reports indicated that the tribal warriors were fierce, brave fighters.

Of even further frustration, there was still no sign of the non-combatants of the five tribes either. A couple of false alarms had been raised, brought on by overanxious warriors, perhaps espying a bounding deer herd that had been startled by the formation's passage. Yet no signs had been found to indicate the whereabouts of the great numbers of villagers undeniably dislodged from their villages. Where they had sought refuge, Dragol and the other Trogens had not an inkling.

To Dragol, it was a very unsettling, increasingly tense atmosphere to endure, fraught with uncertainty. It was not a matter of fear, but rather the inner conflict in Dragol that was sustained by the enemy's refusal to challenge the Darrok formation.

The day laboriously dragged onward, as the Trogens continued to strike at a couple more of the empty villages, while others such as Dragol continued in their assiduous search for the location of the tribal people's havens. Many villages and crop fields were ravaged by the time that the ample stores of stones carried upon the Darroks were finally emptied. Yet the day ended to no avail, as far as Dragol was concerned, centered as he was on the declining hopes of encountering the enemy defenders, and meeting them in a clash of arms.

The lack of fighting left a feeling of disgust in Dragol and the fiery Trogen warriors at the end of the day, in addition to the tremendous sense of frustration that was being multiplied with every passing day. It was a gloomy, irritated mood that encompassed the Trogens returning from the skies back to their new encampment, when the day's raids were declared over.

Anyone viewing the snarling, brooding warriors climbing down from the carriages on the Darroks would not have guessed that they had just dealt another heavy blow to the tribal lands. They would not have suspected that the Trogens had just accomplished all the aims that they had been sent to execute, without losing so much as one warrior in the process.

The encampment itself was located a good distance away from the forests of the tribal lands, as a large expanse of open, treeless ground was necessary for Darroks to take off and land. The swathe of terrain was positioned at the midpoint of the Five Realms' outermost, western border, within Gallean territory. Open, rolling grasslands spread westward from the edge of the Five Realms, broken up randomly by copses of trees.

The designated site was a superb place to ward the Darroks, as well as being situated favorably for the missions at hand. The encampment was almost impossible to approach undetected, as important an attribute as the fact that it was within relatively easy reach of the enemy targets.

A modest force of Trogens had come loaded with supplies, weapons, and materials to set up the encampment. A broad mass of hide tents, erected in the Trogen style, was now fully arrayed. Armed Trogen sentinels were positioned around the outskirts of the camp, and a couple of small patrols were circling in the skies overhead.

There were no Andamoorans in this camp, only Trogens, which was one thing that gave a small shred of comfort to Dragol's greatly troubled mind. The Andamoorans seemed to be fairly skilled with their horses, but their strange rituals, which they performed five times each day to their strange god, were thoroughly alien to him. He had found himself becoming increasingly more aware of their hardened stares, and had never been entirely comfortable while in their midst. The feeling was quite mutual, as the Andamoorans were always on edge when he was in their immediate presence.

He was not afraid of them in the least, but it was far more palatable to know that the new encampment was entirely populated by Trogens. It eliminated distractions and tensions that were not necessary in the first place.

Dragol and the other mounted Trogens took their Harraks up off the Darroks and into the sky, as they approached the sprawling grounds. Beyond the encampment was a tremendous length of open ground used for the quartering, launching, and landing of the Darroks. Hovering high above, Dragol and the other Trogens watched as the Darroks slowly descended to land.

The expanse of open ground was great enough that the creatures could come in two at a time, spread far apart from each other. The Darroks making up the second and third rank in the approach were staggered a good distance apart by their handlers, allowing for each of the gargantuan beasts to land without undue risk of collision.

Despite all of the precautions and care, the winged giants still set down somewhat awkwardly, lumbering forward as their four clawed appendages touched down on the solid ground. Dragol noticed that more than a few Trogens on the carriages completely lost their footing, as each of the behemoth creatures alighted upon the ground. The carriages were jarred violently from side to side before the Darroks fully steadied themselves, and Dragol had little doubt that keeping balance was a harrowing task for the carriages' occupants.

Fortunately, each of the Trogens was secured by a single hide rope that they had tied about their waists, which in turn was tied to the carriage railing. If they lost their grips on the carriage rails in the process of being violently jostled about, they would not get thrown off to the ground, which was a far distance from the back of the titans that they rode upon. It was a method that also helped if the Darroks were caught suddenly within great turbulence while airborne. Dragol noticed a couple such individuals pulling themselves back up, after having been thrown over the side of the railing during the tumultuous landing.

A horde of Trogens swarmed out of the nearby encampment, immediately attending to the Darroks and the Trogens that had remained upon the carriages. With the Darroks all safely landed, Dragol, Tirok, and the sky riders brought their steeds down a short distance away from the monstrosities.

Dragol heard the low rumbles and resonant snorts coming from the weary Darroks, and he hoped that their temperaments were as stable as he had heard. He was in no disposition to witness what the imposing giants were capable of if they became irritated enough to lash out.

It was very evident that the creatures had been pressed very hard, and were in great need of sustenance and rest. He hoped that the former was attended to without delay, and that the latter was adequately provided for in the war planning.

Rodor was still in moderately good condition when they landed, and the Harrak whined affectionately, turning its head to nuzzle Dragol as he dismounted. At the very least, Dragol could rest assured that Rodor would be well tended. The hardy steed deserved every comfort and provision, in Dragol's mind.

He patted the great beast's side, feeling its calming breathing as he took notice of the slight lather clinging to its stout muzzle. Reaching up, he scratched Rodor behind its upright, triangular ears, which were attentively taking in the flurry of sounds coming from the swirling activity surrounding the creature.

Dragol continued to scratch and pet his ardent steed, as he concentrated on the feeling of solid ground beneath his leather boots. It was indeed good to be adjusting to being on land again, after long hours spent in the constantly vacillating realm of flight.

A few Trogens from the camp finally reached Dragol and the other mounted Trogens. One immediately strode up to Dragol, to attend to the steed of the chieftain. Dragol handed Rodor's tethers off to the Trogen, and gave the warrior some verbal instructions regarding treatment of the outstanding steed. Dragol then walked off towards the main body of the encampment.

An excited commotion greeted the attacking force upon its return, though it quickly turned towards disappointment. The Trogens streaming from the encampment became quiet and subdued as they beheld the countenances of their dour, frustrated brethren.

The returning Trogens climbed down the ladders of hemp rope from the carriages, turning with scowling miens, as they headed towards their tents. Some exchanged a few brief words with the Trogens that had emerged from the camp, but a pensive hush soon lingered all around the area.

Even so, the Trogens moving to attend to the Darroks would go about their routines with pride and diligence. They had all been brought to understand the importance of this new weapon of war. Whether the method of attack that the Darroks enabled was found to be disgraceful, the care of the rare creatures that had been fully entrusted to the Trogens was indeed an honor.

Avanor had very few of the giant beasts at its disposal, and it was not lost upon Dragol and his kind that the crewing and care of the Darroks had not been given over to humans. The Trogens carried out their duties with the utmost attention, cognizant of the great respect that had been afforded them by Avanor.

Yet Dragol and other Trogen leaders never forgot that there were also very practical reasons for the arrangement. Trogens could endure for much longer in the thinner environment of the highest altitudes, without showing adverse effects. They had also long demonstrated their great aptitude for handling and breeding what was generally regarded as the greatest of the Skiantha, the Harraks. Therefore, it was not much of a surprise that Avanor had chosen the Trogens to guide and care for the Unifier's potent new weapons. Trogen crewing of the beasts was to Avanor's best interests by far.

More ladders of hempen rope were unfurled from the carriages, as attendants and some of the remaining Darrok crews unloaded supplies and weapons. The loads for the Darroks had been much lighter for the return flight, with the considerable stocks of great stones having been fully discharged during the day's events. The tired Trogen crews and mounted escorts had disembarked with hearty appetites, which begged to be sated despite the disappointments that the Trogens felt at failing to draw up the tribal defenders from the forests. Dragol's mouth began salivating as he caught the first scents of roasting meat coming from the encampment.

Dragol turned his head to idly watch the Trogens working around the Darroks, as he passed them on his way to the encampment. Dragol and those not involved in tasks regarding the Darroks found that it was wise to keep a very wide berth during feeding times.

Darroks regularly exhibited a voracious appetite, and as a group they were quite capable of consuming a great number of cattle or sheep at one feeding. The Trogens attending to the behemoths took great precautions to avoid accidentally becoming part of the meal during the feeding process, and Dragol did not envy them in the least.

Dragol twisted and stretched as he walked, gradually working out the deep stiffness in his muscles from the long day endured in the saddle. He removed his iron half-helm, carrying it under his right arm, as he let the cool air of the early evening massage his skin and provide a soothing feeling of relief.

When he reached the camp's edge, he glanced up to watch the sky patrols circling the vicinity, still visible in the dimming light. The patrols would keep a vigilant eye on the lands approaching the campsite, even beyond the inevitable transitions from dusk to night.

He then noticed that Tirok was walking up from behind him, and Dragol acknowledged the fabled Black Tiger Chieftain with a prolonged nod of the head.

"Another day without much event," Tirok remarked curtly, as he strode up to stand next to Dragol.

"No sign of the tribes at all. Not one warrior came up in defense. Where could they be?" Dragol queried in a low, tense voice, unable to suppress the bitter frustration boiling within him.

Tirok shook his head, the dark look in his eyes showing that he fully shared Dragol's sentiments. "No signs. Not even one! They hide from us. It can only mean they have few steeds now. They had the courage to come up on the first raid, and their effort was met with success that time. I know it was not cowardice that kept them hidden this day."

"They let their villages be destroyed, with no resistance," Dragol countered.

"They could not defend the villages against the Darroks. They mean to draw us under the trees. If you had flown low, I am certain that you would have drawn many arrows your way," Tirok replied.

"There were times when I sensed their eyes upon us, but I felt that such was only because of my own hopes," Dragol said.

"They were there, somewhere under those trees," Tirok assured Dragol.

"Then only warriors on the ground can hope to find a warrior's honor in this attack," Dragol growled in reply.

Tirok did not reply, but the look on his face revealed his agreement with Dragol's conclusion.

The two quietly looked out over the wide, spacious grassland, and the random copses of trees farther away. They were a few leagues from where the massive forests started to the east.

Taking his eyes off the darkening horizon, straining to see far away into the depths of the Five Realms, Dragol finally turned back towards Tirok.

"When the new day comes, I know we shall begin again. We must scout better. Maybe we should think about dropping stones in places other than the villages, even randomly. If we do that, we may find a sign of where they are hiding. We know that the tribes are still in the forests, and they will fight, if they are brought forth."

Tirok nodded. "Your words have truth to them."

Dragol then said with increasing tension in his voice. "The battle for Saxany will begin soon. The blood of warriors will soon flow as great rivers, from fighters on both sides. Many of our own will gain great glory in Saxany, and only they would be worthy of the feasts of the high gods, and a place in Elysium. It is not that way here. I do not wish to rise each day to stare at trees. It is like we are seeking ghosts."

"The ghosts of today may yet turn into warriors tomorrow. We do not know what they will do," Tirok replied evenly.

Dragol looked towards the old Trogen warrior. He relished the thought of intense battle, one that was open and honest, with combatants matching their skills, warrior to warrior. Dragol was plagued with growing anxiety and trepidation at the thought of spending more days like the one that had just mercifully ended.

It was only through an honorable fight that Dragol could prove the conquest of his fears, and establish the measure of himself. Such determinations could only come through the direct facing of an enemy. The greater the skill of the enemy, the greater the honor that could be gained, and the greater the chance that Dragol could become the warrior that he had set out to become. The tribesmen were said to be fighters of great skill, and if they were, then they could most certainly deliver him this chance; if only they would emerge to fight.

Dragol hoped that they were truly formidable warriors, by whose overcoming he could take pride and gain genuine honor. If he were to fall, then he hoped that the tribal warrior that bested him would be of such greatness that Dragol's own death would not prevent him an exalted place in the afterworld.

His greatest fear, like that of any Trogen, was that he would never be given the truest test to discover what measure of heart, strength, bravery, and skill he possessed. To be denied that opportunity was one of the few terrors that a Trogen warrior could experience.

It was not the lure of wealth, or the possession of new lands that drove Dragol, or any Trogen warrior. In this, the Trogens were vastly different from the humans that Dragol had witnessed in service to the Unifier.

Rather, Dragol and other Trogen warriors simply wanted the chance to measure themselves on an individual level. Only in a war, one with a strong and vigorous opponent, could that be achieved beyond doubt.

Whether the tribal warriors remained similar to ephemeral ghosts, or manifested as worthy opponents, remained to be seen.

The muscular, towering figure slowly turned his head back towards Tirok. At last, Dragol replied to Tirok's words. His response came out almost as a menacing growl, as his frustrations flowed within his words. His voice was heavily laden with the swirling fears and aspirations that resided inside of him, and his eyes flashed intensely in the gathering dusk.

"Then there is only one thing we must do … we must find the tribesmen … and we must bring them to battle."

One of the last rays of sunlight glinted off the long canines in the snarling visage of the Trogen warrior. It gave him a particularly feral appearance, which was not far from how he felt, as he pondered the dilemma facing the Trogens accompanying the Darroks.

The enemy had to somehow be cajoled into coming out to fight, in order for the Trogens to prove themselves true warriors from the Darrok forays.

Another part of Dragol cried out that the Trogens were simply being used to carry out the will of the Unifier. The thought, no matter how much Dragol wished to dismiss it, tugged darkly at the edges of his conscience.

Dragol was beginning to realize that it was a disturbance that he would have to learn to live with. He would not be able to fully rest his mind until the Unifier's assistance manifested to aid the Trogens in their own war and struggle for their homelands.

Until that day, he would have his misgivings, and he could only hope that the negative feelings did not come to cloud his judgements.

Tirok continued to silently regard Dragol with an impassive expression, but a steely, resolved look had flared up within the venerated Trogen's eyes. Dragol knew that there would be no argument from the other Trogen. Tirok was a living embodiment of everything a Trogen could become, and most certainly understood the fires burning so hotly in Dragol. They were core feelings that any genuine Trogen warrior would relate to.

AETHELSTAN

Scouts returning to Aethelstan's camp reported that the enemy force's current dispositions indicated a strong likelihood of imminent attack.

Adding to the growing tensions was the reality that there was no easy way of finding out how their fellow Saxan warriors, massed in their many thousands out upon the Plains of Athelney, were faring. Aethelstan and the smaller, second force in the westernmost hills of Wessachia did not even know if the battle out on the plains was underway or not.

Aethelstan did not have to be reminded of what his warriors were up against, and why they had to stop the invaders in their tracks. He recognized the enemy's hopes, and what they intended to do if they were able to get beyond Aethelstan's force.

The Saxans had no option but to hold their ground and resist, with every last shred of strength that they had available. If the enemy slithered deeper inside their lands, great havoc would inevitably be wreaked upon Wessachia. The rear and the flank of the main Saxan army would be left exposed and vulnerable.

If the Avanorans were able to successfully exploit such an opening, the results would be simply too disastrous for Aethelstan to even ponder. Everything was at stake, and Aethelstan knew that he could not live with himself if he failed in his effort.

Things were certainly getting no easier for the Saxan thane, as accumulating word of the enemy's capabilities reinforced his fears. More word had arrived that the attacking force was well-prepared for all manner of eventualities.

Segments of siege engines were being carried along with the baggage train of the enemy army. Aethelstan had learned the daunting facts regarding the siege equipment from a particularly brave scout, who had nearly paid with his life to gain the discovery.

The presence of man-powered, stone-throwing devices and giant crossbows had been confirmed, and it would not surprise Aethelstan if the enemy force also possessed the devastating stone-throwing devices that worked off of counterweights. Aethelstan had heard tales about such incredible weapons, and how they could batter down thick stone walls, reducing them to rubble with no need to sacrifice men in scaling them with ladders. There was no doubt that timber palisades surrounding burhs would be no match for such formidable devices.

The Unifier's army coming towards his force, Aethelstan was quickly learning to his chagrin, possessed the capability of shifting its tactics to assault the lightly defended burhs and villages. With the vast depletion of hale fighting men caused by the General Fyrd, such sieges would present little in the way of a challenge to Avanor's might. Without question, Aethelstan's modest forces comprised the thin line that would have to hold at all costs.

During the deeper hours of night, Saxan efforts were much more shielded from the monitoring eyes of the airborne Trogen scouts. Under the cloaking darkness, they had strained to achieve whatever they could, from the setting of lookouts to pickets. The Saxans had labored carefully to disguise the positions, to make them harder to discern in daylight, when the eyes of the airborne enemy scouts would be shadowing them incessantly.

For his own part, Aethelstan had spent the better part of the previous afternoon and evening taking careful accounts of the strength at his disposal. He had assiduously taken stock of all of those who had been levied from Ealdorman Morcar's territory, most especially those who were men of experience in arms.

The final assessment, after all the various musters had been appraised, gave him a little more encouragement. He had discovered that there were a fair number of experienced, trained warriors within the masses summoned up in the General Fyrd.

Many of them possessed good quality weapons, and even some armor, such as shield and helm. Most of the better-equipped men had periodically served as garrison guards for thanes within their burhs or fortified residences.

Likewise, the ceorls of greater rank were almost all found to have well-maintained shields, swords, spears, mail shirts, and half-helms. Even more fortuitous, there were also many more ceorls than Aethelstan had initially expected would be available to him.

Yet once again, the area of concern that had been regularly plaguing his mind came back to the fore. It tamped down all of the welcome discoveries, as it regarded the greater majority of his entire force.

The greater proportion of the broad levy was a rabble of common men who had very few good arms, and even less skill. Aethelstan tried to gain a little encouragement from the fact that the northern and eastern territories of the Saxan realm were made up of very hardy, tough men.

Many hailed from a lineage that had survived the dark times when Midragardans had visited several vicious raids upon the Saxan lands. The Midragardan raiders had made no distinctions in those distant times, as monks, villagers, ceorls, and thanes alike had been beset.

The villagers had risen many times to meet the seaborne threats, acquitting themselves surprisingly well in many storied instances. They had often shown courage, and they also demonstrated that they were not without their own strengths either.

There was some hope in that regard for the present time. Many northern Saxans, even simple villagers, were fairly good hunters. Hunting required a degree of diligence and patience, as well as competency with weapons such as the bow. Aethelstan could therefore expect to find at least a few quality fighters among the men of the mass levies, though inexperienced, and modestly armed at best.

Yet there was much to be concerned about, things that Aethelstan could not afford to deny. In normal times, men of the General Fyrd would have been called forth only to defend their market towns, or immediate villages. The extraordinary circumstances that the Saxan Kingdom now faced called for these levies to leave home and hearth, to march to the front lines far away, to meet a threat that was common to all. Adding to the burden, much of the commoners' better equipment was old, some being ancient family heirlooms, but it would have to serve them as best it could against the well-armed Avanorans marching upon them.

The thanes, and those of their immediate household would be in a much different situation. Most possessed mail shirts, as did some of the warriors from the primary, Select Fyrd. They also had the best condition shields, helms, and practically all of the swords available.

As with their traditional methods of warfare, Aethelstan would array the better equipped warriors along the front lines of their formation. They were to be positioned among the general levy men of their own territories, to provide leadership and encouragement for the others.

The rest of the common levy, with only a smattering of helms and dilapidated shields, and mostly armed with spears, bows, makeshift war clubs, slings, and farming tools, would be mainly deployed in the ranks set in back of the shield wall.

Before he got too daunted, Aethelstan reminded himself once again that at least the General Fyrd provided his force with a good number of capable archers. Years of hunting in the mountains, hills, and valleys of the north and northwestern forests of the Saxan Kingdom had honed their skills with the bow.

Also of slight comfort, the terrain that Aethelstan's force would be fighting in would not be advantageous for cavalry, whether from friend or foe. This was not a hindrance for Aethelstan, as most of Saxany's mounted warriors were from the southern provinces, and would now be fighting with the main army out on the Plains of Athelney.

Horses were nonetheless a concern to Aethelstan in terms of his own force. The thanes, their household and garrison guards, and many of the higher-status freemen had arrived at the camp with Aethelstan on horseback. Unlike a cavalry force, they dismounted to fight, and were not trained for effective fighting from horseback.

As such, there were many horses quartered within the main Wessachian encampment, and it was imperative that they did not fall into the hands of the enemy. There were many stories of the times when the Midragardan raiders had captured horses, using them to move quickly into the heart of the kingdom during the legendary incursions launched from sea or river.

Not only would the enemy be able to move faster with more horses available, but their knights, trained to fight both on foot and horse, would surely benefit from an influx of extra mounts.

The skies above would also be to the Saxans' distinct disadvantage. The few Himmerosen that were still available to Aethelstan had been grouped with Edmund, prepared to respond to a desperate, emergency situation. They would be quickly overwhelmed if they tried to challenge the more numerous Trogens now in regular evidence high above them.

The enemy forces assaulting them on the ground would undoubtedly have a greater number of weapons and armor, a much larger proportion of well-trained warriors, and considerably more numbers overall.

The enemy had both heavy and light cavalry available, as well as the vicious Licanthers, with their nimble Atagar handlers. Both heavy and light infantry had been reported as well, as had the presence of a few horrifically strong, massive Gigans.

It was a force with flexibility, power, and speed, and one that gave their commanders all manner of options.

Despite the clear burdens, and the enemy advantages, Aethelstan was not about to even come close to conceding the coming battle. He knew that the situation did not bode well from the perspective of a commander, but he set his mind only to one pursuit; discovering a way to victory.

The principle task would be to hold off each enemy wave, while simultaneously fending off harassment from the air. They would have to wear the Avanorans down and delay them, until dwindling supplies forced them to have no choice but to pull back. It was perhaps the only chance the Saxans would have, though Aethelstan knew that it was truly much easier in conception than in achievement.

Aethelstan knew that his men would fight well together, as they were comprised of friends, family, and pledged relations, all from the same general region. Many had grown up with each other since birth, and there were many brothers, sons, and fathers up and down the ranks of both the select and general levies. Ties of blood knitted an inspiring pennon to rally around, forging the links of an incomparably strong, resolute coat of mail that would serve the Saxans well in the coming fight.

All sentry posts and scouts had been placed on a full state of alertness, for the incoming forces of the Unifier were capable of a powerful, swift strike. It would also not be unheard of for the enemy to attack at night, and diligent watches were maintained at all hours, as Aethelstan was not about to take any chances.

At the end of his inspections, Aethelstan was pleased with the general disposition of the men, a feeling shared by the higher thanes within his force. His Wessachian forces were as prepared as they could be, barring any hidden surprises.

As a quiet peace descended over the Saxan camp, and many of the men took to much-needed rest, Aethelstan made his way back to his own tent. He wanted to be left alone for a few minutes of solitude, to immerse himself in his own thoughts and reflections.

He had urged his higher thanes to spend the evening in prayer and rest. Before he set his own head down to sleep, he would be spending some time with a priest from his own parish, Father Wilfrid. The great thane feared for the lives of all of his men, and intended to beseech the priest's blessing and prayers for his warriors.

The coming clash was unavoidable, and it was also a likely reality that many now resting in the camp would not live to see the onset of the very next night. It was possible that number would include Aethelstan himself, a fact that he was very well aware of.

As he sat amid the thick shadows of his tent, the thought of not seeing his wife and family again flashed in the back of his mind. A wave of emotion threatened to power those fears all throughout his mind, but he was able to push them back. Yet he knew that the inner demon born of those fears would not leave him until he stood clear of the battle, and knew that he had survived it.

He also feared what might happen to Gisela, Wynflaed, Wyglaf, and Wystan if he and his men did fail; and by doing so leave their homelands wide open to the ravagings of the enemy forces.

His wife and children lived inside the walls of the large market town of Bergton, and he was angrily cognizant of what vile traditions the Avanorans would uphold if they were to sack it. It was likely that a victorious Avanoran army would be given dispensation to plunder and indulge their lusts for three entire days; three days of unbridled terror unleashed among his kin, friends, wife, and children.

The torturous thoughts brought a cold chill seeping throughout him, causing him to physically tense to hold the dire thoughts back at the darker edges of his mind. He wiped the beaded sweat that had built up on his forehead, and turned his heart towards thoughts of his faith in the Creator. He took several deep breaths in the stillness of the tent, and once again steeled his mind with conviction, faith, and purpose.

He understood what was at stake very well, and knew what cost would come with failure. Despite the great dread that stretched its claws into his mind and heart, he made sure that the fears were kept hidden and private. He knew that he was more than just a man to those that followed him. He was a leader, and a symbol of the order that held their worlds together. He could do no less than keep a steady countenance for his men, whether they were a greater thane or the most poverty-stricken peasant among the men of the general levy. It was the very least that he could do for them, and to do any less would be to weaken them, and put them all at even greater risk.

WULFSTAN

His stomach full from a meal of bread, cheese, and a good portion of salted pork, washed down with an equally ample portion of ale, Wulfstan made his way back towards his tent. A good majority of the men were engaging in a mild fast, as was encouraged by many of the greater thanes, ealdormen, and counts, but he felt that he would fight better with the strength gained from a full meal. He did not believe that the Creator would begrudge him that view, if he was to put his life on the line for his homelands and fellow Saxans. He was certain that Father Dunstan would not begrudge him that indulgence either.

The word had been passed to everyone that they would be forming up for battle at the cusp of morning. The coming of the enemy army looked to be inevitable once the dawn struck, and the orders had been quickly disseminated.

Preparations had been made. The main encampment was now bounded by a trench, a raised earthen wall, and stakes, and there had been some time to do a little drilling with the more inexperienced commoners. Most contingents had arrived and were accounted for.

Prince Aidan's dragon banner now flew high over his large tent, situated near to the center of the encampment, fluttering proud and defiant against the coming onslaught. He brought the vigor of youth into the royal line, serving as the representative for the aged King Alcuin.

The Prince's arrival had brought much excitement from the camp, and was a true bolster to morale. He had been accompanied by a few hundred of his elite household guards, also known as huscarles. Armed with great, two-handed axes, the King's Guard would be a very formidable addition to the Saxan force.

Wulfstan regretted that he had been working on the far boundary of the trench and earthen wall when the Prince had arrived. By the time that he had jogged back into the camp, the Prince had already reached the center, and had retired to a tent with a few of the counts and ealdormen.

Like numerous villagers in the Saxan Kingdom, Wulfstan and his comrades had never actually seen the Prince, or even his father King Alcuin, for that matter. It was a sharp disappointment, and Wulfstan hoped to gain another chance to see the Prince of the realm before battle ensued.

There were few signs of the enemy, with the exception of some airborne scouts that kept to the edges of the horizon, and a couple more appearances of the bold, lithe horsemen from Andamoor.

The main enemy encampments, some leagues away, could not be seen, even on the clearest of days. If it were not for the scouts that constantly moved in and out of the camp, and their enemy counterparts, Wulfstan and many others would have been inclined to wonder if any army was encamped in strength over the calm horizon.

Though a little colder, the weather had continued to remain clear and steady. The cloud cover was sporadic, with only a few light gray formations holding even the slightest hint of rain.

It was a momentous time, and one that Wulfstan was very conscious of. Everyone was well aware that the force that they were a part of was easily the largest army that had ever been gathered in Saxany, or even in the former time of the Two Kingdoms.

He looked into countless eyes as he passed by the openings to tents and the many blazing campfires. The voices and instruments used to give life to low, somber songs wafted over the camp, as did the scrapes and clanks from men adjusting equipment, or sharpening weapons.

It was a scene far removed from the initial spirits that accompanied their arrival. After the euphoria of the Prince's arrival, a very heavy atmosphere had settled down upon the sprawling encampment and taken firm hold. The light of dawn would finally bring all of them the day that they had known was inevitable.

The eyes that Wulfstan looked into conveyed a wide spectrum of emotions. Some conveyed unmistakable fear, such as one young lad who was visibly shaking as he gripped a crude war club in his callused hands. The older man next to him had placed a comforting hand on his shoulder, but the boy did not see the fear in his comforter's eyes, when the gray-haired fellow glanced up at the passing Wulfstan.

The vision lingered in Wulfstan's mind as he passed by numerous tents, many with variations of similar scenes taking place. Some men prayed together, some were in their tents trying to retire, and others sat with melancholy expressions, lost in their own thoughts as they sharpened sword, seax, or spear point.

Cenwald was seated on the ground in front of the opening to his tent, set adjacent to Wulfstan's. He had his head down, with his beard gripped between tensed hands. His shield and spear were before him, upon the ground, along with his long, single-edged seax. He had clearly been going through his equipment, as he habitually tended to do each night.

"Not an easy night, says I," he muttered, as he saw Wulfstan returning.

"No, it is not. I do not think that many will find rest this night," Wulfstan replied, as he sat down slowly next to Cenwald.

"Each with his own thoughts," Cenwald commented. "We do not know what tomorrow may bring."

"We face it nonetheless," Wulfstan responded, seeing the deep worry etched into the other's face.

As Cenwald looked back towards the ground, Wulfstan thought about the eerie stillness in the air. A number of thoughts raced through his mind. Perhaps the enemy would not form up for battle, or maybe a treaty would be forged at the last minute. The enemy might yet wait another day before drawing up their ranks, though that would just be a delay in the inevitable.

These types of thoughts were mixed with the thoughts of the forests near his home. Spring had now taken hold in the woods, as the winter faded behind. The hills and dells would be awash with the color of flowers. Children would be running about in the village, playing with each other and their dogs. They would do just as their mothers and fathers, and grandfathers and grandmothers before them, had done. Every generation of their bloodline had played within the very same village grounds and surrounding woods, when they were young.

The air would be filled with the urgent shouts of mothers as they ran off the village's cats, slinking around and eager to sample the fresh milk that was being reserved for the making of cheese. The men and older boys would be off tending to the common pasturage, or seeing to the fields where the plowing had just been completed. Swineherds would be leaning back against the trunks of trees, as their snorting, four-legged charges rooted about the forest floor.

Wulfstan could not count how many times he had looked forward to the end of the day, when he gathered with his friends and kin to sample a fresh batch of ale, trade riddles, and sing songs. His own mother had been one of the best at making ale, a warm thought that made him smile, as he thought about how he had become one of the village's best at consuming it.

A good night's rest in the village might be followed up by a trip with Hadwald and Edgar into the forest, hunting bows in hand. Sometimes that brought even more reason to celebrate in the village, if they were lucky enough to down a large stag, or one of the rancorous, huge boars that still lived in the depths of the woods.

None of them were quite up to taking a boar with just sword and shield, as some thanes were reputed to do, but it took a lot of courage to simply hunt the fearsome beasts. The village was always ready to recognize the bravery that brought such succulent meat to their table.

The thought brought a wistful smile to Wulstan's face, as he thought about what was really the best aspect of a hunt. The villagers would surely have named the confrontation with the quarry, and the challenge of life and death.

Wulfstan would have offered a much different opinion on the matter. It was not so much the kill itself that he enjoyed as much as it was bantering with Hadwald and Edgar, and taking in the fresh, soothing air of a clear, sunny day spent in the woods. Friendship and free-spiritedness were what Wulfstan valued.

"You are smilin'," the thick voice of Cenwald abruptly entered his mental refuge. "What are ya thinkin' of?"

Wulfstan slowly opened his eyes, and turned to look at his companion. "What all of us must do before the battle begins. Think of the reasons we must fight, and the reasons why we must fight hard, and survive this."

The thoughts gave him a little peace, before he gave himself over to sleep, and the inevitable dream images; of a great conflagration, and his own passage up into a sunny sky, like the one that he had seen that day.

Words that he always heard in the dream, 'Bring them into the world,' resonated in his memory, even if the only thing he could ever think of involved old dragon tales.

He truly wished that he could bring dragons to join their armies. Creatures out of myth and legend would be quite a wonderful addition to the Saxan cause, and would be a powerful way for him to honor the reasons for his own part in the coming war.

The thought made him feel a little melancholy, as the only contribution that he would be bringing to the battlefield would be his own life, and his single sword. Yet that would still be the least that he could do for everything and everyone that he loved, even if he deeply wished that he could do much more.

GUNTHER

The word spread quickly among the Unguhur populace about the victory over the enemy forces up on the surface. The Unguhur of the underground stone city had never before interfered in the affairs of the upper world, but they all recognized the common threat that they and the Saxans were facing.

An ebullient mood fanned rapidly amongst the great creatures, though the celebrations were tempered by the sobering notion that there would be much more yet to face. All were aware that they were facing an implacable, determined enemy, but they still allowed themselves a little period of enjoyment after having won the first encounter so thoroughly. From the ambush in the dark passageway, to the trap set out in the forest for the fleeing Avanorans and their allies, it was undeniably a resounding success.

Even with the apprehensions plaguing him, the tidings lifted Gunther's spirits out of the gloomy mood that he had remained in since he had come to the aid of the outlanders, in the outer forest region of Wessachia.

Adding to the upswing in his feelings was the fact that his Jaghuns were being well cared for, and were exhibiting better demeanors than he would have expected, given that they had been removed from their natural environment. He had just finished spending a good length of time with them, wrestling and playing with the boisterous creatures.

Gunther had been reassured to see that they all had very full bellies due to the beneficence of the Unguhur. Gunther admittedly hated leaving them behind, and the creatures displayed a little agitation when he had departed, but he knew that they would be a hindrance for what he was about to do.

Gunther's step was a little lighter, and his head felt much clearer, as he ascended the ladder to the roof opening just above him. At the top, he pushed himself up, to come to stand in the forward-most area of one of the Unguhur terrace-dwellings.

He walked straight ahead, moving towards the stone-carved entrance to the dwelling's frontal chamber. The woodsman paused at the opening, poking his head partially into the dark interior. He was relieved to see that all of his new wards were gathered together in the interior of the chamber, and that he would not have to track any of them down.

"Come, there are some things that I would like to retrieve up in my home, now that the invading vermin have been driven back for a time," Gunther promptly informed the four exiles.

They were spread apart, seated on the smooth stone ledges along the walls. Their faces were barely lit by the small amount of light filtering down through the opening in the middle of the ceiling. Gunther mused that they must have been content to sit in the dimness, as he did not see any of the portable stones with the glowing fungus within the chamber.

"I thought that you might like to take a walk, and get away from Oranim for a little while," Gunther then added, a little less curtly.

Erin and Ryan politely declined the offer. Gunther could see that the two were displaying undeniable, physical evidence of fatigue, though he found their rejection to be a little unusual, as they seemed to be the two who had been chafing the most for a surface excursion.

Lee and Lynn, though looking quite tired themselves, still appeared eager enough to engage in some activity, as both accepted the invitation with manifest enthusiasm. The two got to their feet, Lee's back popping audibly as he arched backwards and stretched it out.

"To be in my twenties again," Lee remarked, as he looked to the others with a grin. He then nodded towards Gunther. "I'm good to go."

Lee and Lynn then walked out of the chamber behind Gunther, leaving their other companions behind. They continued over to the square opening to the next lower chamber, Gunther taking the lead as they proceeded down through the lower dwellings.

Gunther noticed their hesitancy as they moved through the lower dwellings, one of which was occupied by an Unguhur female who was just about to engage in cooking a meal of fish. She barely cast them a glance as they moved through, as the Unguhur were well-used to those of the higher terraces moving through the lower dwellings on their way to the ground level.

Gunther found the apprehension of the exiles a little strange, adding to a number of other indications that reinforced the notion that they came from a world that held an unsual amount of privacy for individuals. By their own words, the exiles were not of the nobility of their world, yet they behaved as if they had regularly enjoyed the kinds of privileges that only kings, queens, and greater nobles were afforded in Ave. Gunther intended to discuss that particular matter in depth with them, at a later time, as he found it immensely intriguing.

After exiting the dwelling at the ground level, Gunther led the others straight down towards the waterside. The lake looked as placid as ever, as the cool waters gently lapped at the rocky shoreline. The water surface shimmered all around the huge lake, casting its ethereal, dynamic tapestry upon the cavern's rock surfaces.

A few of the Unguhur's giant rafts were moored just a short distance down the shore to the left. They floated lightly, where they were tethered securely by fiber ropes looped around large rocks resting just out of the water's reach. The rafts were attended casually by a trio of the humans' hulking benefactors, who were sitting on the ground a few strides away from the mooring rocks.

They had a portable slab of flat rock in their midst, upon which they were casting handfuls of bones in a variety of shapes. It was an Unguhur game that Gunther had not yet learned the specifics of, though he guessed that it probably had some elements familiar to the games of dice played by humans.

The three Unguhur ceased in their play, quickly rising at the approach of the human trio. They towered over Gunther as he drew nearer, silently regarding him with their naturally melancholic expressions.

After a short inquiry, Gunther secured the assistance of one of the Unguhur to guide them by raft. He explained to the creature that their desire was to go back to the mushroom forest which rested at the base of the carved rock passage leading up to his home.

The Unguhur agreed without hesitation, and then enlisted one of its companions to assist in the trip. Gunther, Lee, and Lynn boarded the nearest raft, and in a few moments the watercraft was being paddled across the lake.

They continued past several other rafts, whose occupants were engaged in fishing activities. As always, several of the other Unguhur paused and looked upon the surface folk with great curiosity.

The few gallidils that were around paid them little heed as the lengthy creatures drifted along the lake surface. Always interested in creatures of the wild, Gunther marveled at more than one enormous specimen that he espied gliding within the dark waters.

There were a couple of other rafts that were also heading in the direction of the underground forest. The pilot of Gunther's raft had to slow down considerably as they came very close to bumping the rear of one of the other rafts, just within the narrow tunnel that led from the lake cavern to the fungal forest. They barely avoided a collision with the raft, and proceeded through the tunnel at a slower rate. At last, they entered the cavern with the unusual forest that the Unguhur had cultivated so painstakingly, entailing extraordinary amounts of labor.

Their guide maneuvered them towards an open berth on the right shorefront, near to where the other rafts were already coming to rest. The raft pilot tossed a thick fibrous rope to another Unguhur who was standing on the shore. Catching it, the creature tied the other end around a boulder-sized rock, before catching a second rope, and repeating the process with another boulder. The raft was fairly snug against the natural rock quay when it came to rest in its final position.

Gunther cast his gaze into the fungal forest beyond the landing, and saw the presence of large numbers of Unguhur within the glowing cavern. By their garb, Gunther knew that they were full-fledged warriors. They were gathered in small groups, scattered amid the teeming arrays of mushroom stalks.

Most were seated upon the ground, arranged into rough circles as they conversed amongst themselves. They had stacked their long spears together, near to where they were positioned, leaning them against fungal stalks so that it would be easy to grasp the weapons if the need suddenly arose.

The prevailing mood among the warriors was very relaxed, a general spirit that was comforting to Gunther as they made their way from the shore. The human trio strode up the long pathway through the towering stalks, heading towards the passage opening on the far side of the cavern.

The warriors conveyed no indication of immediate worries or cautions in their postures or expressions, dispositions that certainly would have been in evidence if there was even a remote chance of an impending strike. Gunther took increasing reassurance from the sight. As skilled and resourceful as the Unguhur were in the nuances of cave dwelling and surviving in a sunless world, they were also quite formidable scouts and trackers. Nothing could easily come within their vicinity without the creatures being aware of it well in advance, especially when they were in a very heightened state of alertness.

The Unguhur warriors, while recognizing the presence of the three humans in their midst, paid them little attention and made no move to obstruct their passage. The humans continued upward, trekking through the far end of the cavern and heading directly into the darkened tunnel beyond.

Several Unguhur warriors cooperated readily after the humans had traversed the incline, and neared the top of the passage. They pulled aside blockading materials in order to open up a tiny passageway to allow access to Gunther's surface dwelling. Gunther and his companions worked through the narrow channel carefully, having to squeeze through with a concerted effort at some points.

Interacting with a couple of the warriors, Gunther learned that the Unguhur had several eyes watching on the surface, and that no enemies threatened at the moment. The warriors cautioned them to return with haste if the enemy suddenly arrived, as they would not be able to hold off for long before reforming the dense barricade of the lower passage.

After having scraped and shouldered their way through the tight passage, the trio walked unimpeded through the rear opening into Gunther's home. The initial sight that met him was disheartening.

Lynn and Lee appeared to be even more unnerved than Gunther about the condition of the main room, as looks of dismay rapidly spread upon their faces. Gunther's mouth tensed into the foundation of a rigid, stony demeanor, which forcibly suppressed the open venting of painful feelings inside. He effectively felt stabbed in the spirit, and was not a little angered at the brazen violation of his home.

The place had incurred considerable damage from the invaders, as the few wooden furnishings that Gunther owned had been smashed into fragments. The beaten earth floor, which still had the old straw strewn about it, was covered with numerous chunks and splinters of wood.

"I still have myself in one piece ... even if my possessions are not," Gunther stated tersely to the others, noticing their expressions at the stark vision of vandalism.

They looked back at Gunther with a significant degree of disbelief. He quickly rationalized that they were half-expecting him to vent, and outwardly express some sort of sorrow or frustration.

Gunther, though far from joyous, kept an unmoving, serious mien fixed on his face, as he made his way slowly across the room towards the front door. His leather shoes crunched on the shards and pieces of wood underfoot, as he felt the iron of a broken-off chest hinge bite into his right sole.

Withdrawing his single-edged dagger from a sheath at his hip, he knelt down by a patch of ground that was just to the right of the entrance. Almost at once, he began hacking away at the tightly packed earth. Chunks of dirt went flying, the likes of which prompted him to perodically pause in his digging to clear away from a widening hole.

After several minutes of excavating, his dagger finally struck something solid. The tip stuck in place with the jarring impact. Gunther tugged the dagger free with a jerk, and began to chip away more carefully at the dirt.

Fastidiously, the process dragging on, Gunther proceeded to remove the debris slowly, revealing the form of a rectangular chest that had been buried beneath the earthen floor. Gunther carved and scooped around the sides of the timber chest, piling up dirt on all sides as the hole deepened around the container. With a few jostles, and extra scooping out around the bottom edges, the chest finally came loose.

Gunther gripped the chest at its far ends and pulled it free from the ground. He turned and set the chest down on the floor by the edge of the new hole.

"They did not get this," Gunther stated with a bittersweet countenance on his face, feeling both melancholy and triumphant as he looked down upon the iron-banded chest. He then repeated more softly, "They did not get this."

"What is in there?" Lee questioned in a low voice, stepping up to Gunther's side.

Gunther's eyes remained riveted upon the small chest for many minutes, and the two with him did not press any further for answers. He was grateful for their respect, as he was wrestling with his own emotions at the sight of the carefully hidden chest.

Finally, he answered Lee in a voice that was just above a whisper. "These are some very special belongings of mine. They are the kind that I could not afford to keep out in my home ... if a day like this ever should have come. Such a day has indeed come to pass, and it seems that I judged well to have buried this chest."

Gunther stopped and took a deep breath. Slowly, he looked over towards the others, and gestured at the outer door.

"You might as well get a few breaths of fresh air. The area is safe at this time," he told them. "We might remain long underground after we return, or we might not, but you should take advantage of the moment that is in hand. The future is never for certain."

Lee looked towards Lynn, who nodded silently back to him, as an understanding passed between them. He looked to Gunther and replied gently, "Might as well take advantage of it while we can, like you said."

His words said one thing, but Gunther could tell that both had been perceptive enough to realize that the woodsman needed some time to himself. Gunther appreciated their keen awareness greatly, even if he did not express his sentiments.

The two filed quietly past Gunther and headed outside. Gunther rose in silence, and looked beyond the front doorway, just to make certain that the two foreigners were not alone.

He could see that there was another small contingent of Unguhur warriors gathered amongst the trees outside of his dwelling, all armed with the type of spear that was commonly used by their kind.

Though obviously alert, the Unguhur body language was just as relaxed as that of the warriors down in the cavern below. They came to a slight start as the two humans walked out into the dappled sunlight around the dwelling, but clearly recognized them, eased, and resumed their quiet watch.

Taking a few steps back into his abode, Gunther dropped to his knees before the chest. He reached down and ran his finger along the latch of the container. There was small keyhole on the iron padlock that secured it, to which a barrel-key in the pouch at his waist fit. He fit the stout key into the lock and turned it, the sharp sounds of the lock's release rising to his ears an instant later. Gunther then opened the chest, carefully lifting the lid of the container.

Inside the receptacle were items that spanned the course of Gunther's life. Coins of silver, and a few of gold, some gleaned from the wide travels that he had made with his father as a youth, lay randomly inside. A couple of small silken weavings were neatly folded, and tightly packed to one side, saved from places that still remained very near to his heart.

A small, wood-carved figurine of a Jaghun brought some wetness to Gunther's eyes, though nobody was there to witness the surge of emotion overwhelming the stoic man. An uncle had given the finely detailed figure to him during his youth. Neither Gunther nor his uncle had known how portentous that gift was to be, for what was to come later in Gunther's life.

It had been carved by his uncle's skilled hand, based upon a male Jaghun that he had once seen, which had been purchased by a castellan knight from an old Sunland trader in Paleria. The creature was an absolute rarity, brought from far to the east, where the trader had acquired it in the Sunlands.

Paleria still held a significant population of followers of the Great Prophet, who hearkened from times when their ancestors had once conquered the island kingdom. The rulers of the island kingdom following that age had been Avanorans who had been led there by a mercenary adventurer. The Avanoran kings of Paleria had then given way to the blood of Ehrengard in the person of the Sacred Emperor.

Despite all of the changes in rule, the Prophet-following families still endured, having survived throughout the many bitter struggles. They had also maintained continuing ties to the east, which was what enabled the Sun Land trader to bring a living Jaghun to Paleria, to be purchased by a knight of the west.

Gunther remembered how he had often listened in fascination to the tales of the Sun Lands, including stories of birds of incredible size, oil lamps with spirits dwelling in them, and many other fantastical tales that concerned a particularly brave sailor. Yet it was the old trader that had brought the most amazing and wondrous sight to his uncle's eyes, the resonance of which had continued in Gunther's life from the day that he had received the carved likeness.

He remembered his very first friends among the four-legged race of Jaghuns, as if those times of many long years before were the present day. Gunther was swiftly taken on an interior journey, as a recollection of the past paraded before his mind's eye. He did not waver in the face of the swell of memories and images, even as more recent wounds were opened fresh, to bleed once again.

Triker and Jarka had been the most beautiful and loyal of creatures, from their discovery as a pair of vulnerable cubs in the Shadowlands, to the day that they breathed their last in Saxany. Gunther wished bitterly that the Jaghuns, like all of their kind, had a lifespan long enough to outlive the years that the Almighty had granted to the woodsman.

It was almost treacherous, in his view, that the years given to most beasts, especially the ones that were close companions to humankind, were so relatively scant. The creatures that showed friendship to mankind possessed lives so much shorter than those afforded to humans; at least those men and women who managed to avoid disease and violent death.

Gunther loved his first Jaghuns in a special way, as virtually a brother and a sister to him. The deeper sense of kinship and affection had steadily expanded as time went on, once kindled with Triker and Jarka. It had built up stronger with each successive Jaghun that had entered his life. The relationships blossomed in a shining continuum that led right up to the majestic animal that had recently been slain in the forest, Mianta.

The unfettered, enthusiastic love and loyalty shown to him by Mianta, from such a young age, had contrasted mightily with the human world that whirled in seeming chaos all around the woodsman. The impressions made by the starkly contrasting experiences were profound in their impact upon Gunther.

In his life, he had witnessed cutthroats, liars, cheaters, thieves, and countless other disreputable men and women, many of whom were held in popular esteem, and possessed of comfort and wealth. His travels had taken him far across the face of the world. The various lands that he had visited were all consistent in that nobility were so very rarely noble, either in deed or spirit.

As Gunther had gotten older, he had come to recognize more and more of the contrasts between truth and facade among the merchants, ruling classes, and even prominent religious figures, until he was firmly convinced that the human world was plagued with a malignant disease that was only getting worse. More often than not, a beautiful edifice adorned with gold and jewels masked a diseased and corrupt interior, among both groups and individuals.

A kind of maxim had taken root within Gunther, a metaphor for the living reality that he could testify to; a splendid and ornate tomb was still nothing more than a container for a rotting, dead organism.

The ways of humankind had changed much even in the course of his own lifetime. A sense of honor and a tendency for looking out for one another were rapidly becoming nothing more than mere words, which once spoken dissipated in the wind.

A world of tranquil villages and farmsteads was giving way to the power of ever-larger cities, as families were uprooted and dispersed. Gunther had strongly come to believe that the people flocking to the cities were chasing phantoms, fleeting and ephemeral delusions of hoped for wealth and comforts that would never be realized. The truth was that most were chasing after a wealth that would always concentrate itself in the great guilds of the west, and the nobles and rulers that chartered the towns that they occupied; powers that effectively controlled the lives of the urban populaces with an ironclad will.

The Unifier's precipitous rise to such great heights of power had been one of the final events that had pushed Gunther to go into the east. He had sought escape and seclusion in a part of the world that he had hoped was not yet fully tainted with the decay that he saw so prevalent in the west. That hope had been naïve, for he had quickly discovered that the same forces flowed in the east as in the west. Even more dismaying, his sojourn had led him straight to his most onerous, soul-wrenching experience of all.

Gunther could never forget the last, long journey that he had undertaken. He had finally departed the east, broken-hearted and weary, working his way through a meandering journey back to Ehrengard. He had then taken the overland route to the east, reaching the edge of his homeland, then crossing over the borders of Saxany.

He had found nothing to help alleviate the heaviness in his heart, having held a sliver of hope that at least some things would be different in the storied land. The Saxans were good enough as a people, but the disease that he had seen in the other lands was beginning to show itself there too.

Though King Alcuin and many respectable thanes still stood tall and strong upon the foundation of the values that they, and those before them, held dear, a malignancy was indeed present among the people. Many in the populace now openly whispered their desire that the realm look to the ways of the western lands, and seek relations with the Unifier, in order to secure more prosperity for themselves. Those subtle murmurs, Gunther knew well enough, could easily transform into shouted advocacy in a very short time.

During his first months within the new land, Gunther had traveled all about the kingdom. News and tales had come in with the merchants that traded with the edge of the western kingdoms, and Gunther had heard a host of opinions, as conversations bandied about the burhs and greater towns of Saxany.

For every individual such as Aethelstan, there were three others who harbored a reluctance to oppose the Unifier, in Gunther's final assessment. Those kinds of individuals seemed to hold freedom in very light regard, as something not worthy of struggle if, by accepting the Unifier's will and authority, they could fill their bellies and coin pouches easier.

Gunther had promised himself then to hold little pity for the latter types of people, if the preeminence of the Unifier ever fell upon the Saxan lands. He had come to the rueful conclusion that there was no mistaking the eventual course of things, in that the Saxan lands would fall by conquest or acquiescence.

The kind of people propogating across the world, who had started to define what was evil as good, and what was good as evil, were woefully incapable of seeing below the surface of such a powerful, cunning entity as the Unifier indeed was.

Gunther had come to Saxany with initial thoughts of living around a village or town, but his further disgust with many of its inhabitants had pushed him to embrace the idea of a largely solitary existence. At the end of it all, he only desired a hideaway deep in the woods, far removed from the travails and storms encompassing humankind. Only then, in such an isolated environment, did he think that he could begin to heal.

The dark stream of thoughts caused Gunther to close his eyes for a few moments. The madness that was gripping mankind was only getting worse in a world turning itself upside down. Gunther found that he could hardly stomach what he could never even begin to truly comprehend.

Looking back into the chest, his eyes went from the Jaghun figurine to a golden arm bracelet. The look on his face softened even further, the very instant that his eyes alighted upon the bracelet. The wetness in his eyes swelled, until a lone tear escaped, and ran along a slow course down his right cheek.

Irene.

She was perhaps the greatest reason that his faith in people had been almost completely shattered. She was the prime reason why he had essentially fled the east, with such an aggrieved, disillusioned heart.

Irene was the first and only love that he had ever had. To him, she was so perfect, beautiful, and eternal. As a younger man of twenty-six, filled with new hopes and aspirations as he arrived in the east, he had thought that the whole world was ahead of him. After his life had intertwined with hers soon after, he had thought that he had found everything that he was looking for, and that she would always be by his side.

He was certainly of a marriageable age, and his mind and heart were fixated upon only one person in the entire world. Gunther vividly remembered how he had always been captivated by her warm eyes and soft smile, a look whose memory now evoked only pain within his heart.

Gunther had found his true love in the heart of distant Theonia, or so he had thought at the time. It had seemed that a great blessing had come into his life, in the form of the daughter of one of the Empire's authorized dyers of purple silks. In Gunther's eyes, the precious, regal color, derived from a highly valuable, rarer breed of sea snails within the region's oceans, was unfit for his own beautiful empress.

The young woman's father often visited the vast and ornate palace complexes within the Empire's great capital city of Theonium. Gunther had gotten to know him well, and had felt confident that he had the man's favor, in the courting of the merchant's youngest daughter.

At the end of each day, when Gunther was banged up with the effects of an education by trial and error concering the ways of the world and fighting arts, Irene had always performed her own little miracles upon him, lifting the aches and pains away. Often, it was accomplished by merely her close presence to him.

She had soon professed that she would be there for him forever, and he had promised the same in return. Irene had been the one who had lied, as it was not long after that she had broken her vow.

Unbeknownst to him, a local officer, in one of the native units of the central, elite Tagmata force, had caught her affections. Gunther had no indication that the relationship with the officer had developed so strongly and quickly, until Irene had abruptly informed him one day that their courtship was over.

Leaden, cold rains had been poured into his world without warning. He had not seen so much as even a hint of one gray cloud on the horizon, to herald the sudden change in the skies of his life.

Gunther found it all so very hard to believe at the time, thinking that he was in the grip of some terrible nightmare from which he would awaken at any moment. Stunned, and shocked, he was frozen to inaction and sadness for many terrible days, as he began to realize that he would never truly awaken from the nightmare.

One of the harder things about the experience was that he did not even know of the other man when their courtship had been broken off. In truth, Gunther had learned nothing of the reality until they had already been split apart for many days. The recognition of the lengthy deception by Irene dug ever deeper into his raw wounds.

Irene had claimed earlier that the reason for breaking off the courtship was that she needed to find her soul, and to contemplate her faith. Though shocked, he had tried to understand that as much as he could. He agreed with her that everyone needed to find some bearing in regards to who they were, in order for them to contribute to the life of another. He had not wanted to press her much on the matter, being that he had come from the Western Church, and she was under the Eastern one, with its Grand Shepherd.

The shock and betrayal coalesced and transformed into a sheer torrent of anger when, in the coming month following their severance, the actuality of what had happened became clear. In a fit of rage, Gunther had sought after the Tagmata officer, to crush the serpentine thief that had slithered into the paradise of his life. Friends of his in the Emperor's vaunted bodyguard, the Vargi, had forcibly restrained him. It had taken many of them to do so, and more than one had incurred a heavy blow in the process.

It was only the stark realization that Irene was as much of a part of the betrayal as the officer that finally kept Gunther from committing an atrocity, one that he would have greatly rued in time. Though barely, he was able to keep control of his vitriol and heated emotions, culminating in a steely resolve to survive the terrible betrayal.

As it was, he did not undertake any action that would have caused him to face the heavy justice of Theonia, even though he was wracked in awful torments at the mere sight of the two of them. Even though he was in the Emperor's bodyguard at the time, he was still a foreigner, and the Tagmata officer held favor with many of the elite families within the massive, lavish city. Had Gunther given in to his volcanic urges, he would not have found pardon in the Imperial courts.

He had still paid a terrible price. Having long been reticent to trust others, even before that time, the damage done to his perception of the world in the aftermath of the horrid deception was tremendous.

In comparison to anyone he had ever known, he had sincerely thought that he could at least trust Irene, and that he really knew her. After the terrible revelation, he was left in a state of mind that degenerated quickly to a level where he never really trusted anyone from that time onward. Gunther now felt strongly that the only being that he could put all of his faith in was the Creator.

That darker, pessimistic state of mind that had taken hold in those former times had never softened for Gunther, and he had chosen to keep the bracelet, to visibly remind him of that jarring betrayal.

Mianta and Irene.

The two individuals, one a Jaghun, and the other a human, had taught him important lessons in the path of life. Both had involved their own experiences of joys and heartaches, and both had left scars, for very different reasons. Yet the past and the present were still very much the same in essence at the end of the day, as they both left him bleeding inside.

DREAM OF LEGENDS

A part of Gunther bitterly wished that he could regain at least a modicum of the innocence and confidence that he had enjoyed as a youth. Life had seemed so much more full and sunlit in those distant days, times that seemed ever more like an ephemeral dream.

Nevertheless, Gunther realized that he had grown, learned much, and had come to realize how much more he did not know. It was all a part of living life, and he knew that it would continue throughout the remainder of his years, in one form or another. The small items in the chest were indeed important reminders of the various facets of that reality, and he did not regret keeping any of them. As such, Gunther was not about to let the powerful, highly personal symbols ever be forgotten, or, if he could help it, become lost.

There was one last principle item in the chest that attracted his attention. It was a pendant that was fastened to a long, thin leather strip that could be worn around the neck. Gunther had obtained the pendant shortly after he had established his new dwelling place in Saxany. He had finally found a place of refuge in the western forests of Wessachia, lands that had once been a border territory of the old Northern Kingdom. In those days, he had continued to make a few journeys to the easternmost parts of Saxany, going to the great port city of Landahn as he began the phase in life that continued up to the present moment.

A stranger traveling through the woodlands had given the silver pendant to him. Gunther had come across the stranger under quite unusual circumstances, during his return from one of those long sojourns to Landahn.

Gunther had been cutting through the woods, taking a shortcut off of the narrow forest trails that oriented him more directly towards his newly-built timber home. A skilled woodsman, he was not daunted by brush, wild animals, or more difficult terrain, and simply wanted to be back in his dwelling sooner than later.

Gunther had encountered the mysterious stranger shortly thereafter. The individual that he came upon was an elderly gentleman, who had appeared to be on the verge of complete exhaustion. The stranger was far off the few beaten paths that the Saxans used to pass between their villages and towns, and he was entirely alone.

The man had looked to be in tremendous need, right on the verge of collapse as he leaned against a tree. Even though Gunther had finally achieved a place intended for his own solitude, he had not hesitated to come to the man's aid.

Gunther carefully helped and guided the elderly stranger back to his simple abode, taking some circuitous paths to lessen the strain on the old man. The woodsman had proceeded to provide the old man with a full meal, and an evening's worth of rest and shelter.

The following morning, to Gunther's utter amazement, the old man had insisted on resuming his journey. He looked spry, and was warmly engaging in his manner. Had Gunther not known better, he would have found it very hard to believe that the old man was in a very downtrodden state mere hours before. There was a spritely youthfulness within the old man's eyes that Gunther had never forgotten since.

The two of them had then proceed to share a warm meal and a period of spirited conversation together. It soon became evident that the old man's travels far exceeded Gunther's own substantial experiences, deepening the mystery of it all.

The more that Gunther looked upon him, the more that he recognized physical characteristics about the man that hearkened to the people that lived in the lands where the Holy City was located. The angle of his face, his dark eyes, his prominent nose, and the tone of his skin indicated a life that had originated in those hallowed regions of the Sunlands.

The man was evasive about his origins, much to Gunther's frustration, but the woodsman was not about to disparage anyone for leaving elements of their life in the past. Before he had departed, the old man had expressed his heartfelt gratitude for Gunther's kindness and generosity. It was then that he had given Gunther the silver pendant, retrieving it out of a pouch that had been hanging at his waist.

He had never forgotten the old man's voice, as the stranger had given the pendant to Gunther. The resonant words echoed across time itself. "In time, wear this, as it will give you strength for going back among the world of men. You will see in time that not all is lost, even when you feel far more alone and betrayed than you do now."

Gunther had been quite confused by the old man's words, but the old man had gently reassured him that they would make sense in his future. Gunther had smiled amiably in response, dismissing the gesture at the moment as the whims of a senile old man trying to express his gratitude.

Gunther had spoken no further about the matter to the old man, as the morning visit had drawn to an end, and the stranger prepared to depart. After the old man had taken his leave, and set off again on his path, Gunther had stood just outside of his front doorway, savoring the serenity of his immediate surroundings. His heart felt very peaceful as he listened to the rustling of the leaves, and he had never felt more convinced that he had selected the ideal place to live out the rest of his years.

He had then held the medallion up by its leather cord, and taken his first close examination of the small pendant. It was nothing exceedingly ornate, but it held a decided elegance within its simplicity. It was a circular, silver medallion with the upward-pointing, spear-shaped symbol of the Redeemer worked into one of its facings. The opposite side was entirely smooth, devoid of any symbol or other manner of design.

Gunther breathed a heavy sigh, thinking back on those old memories, especially of the moment that the flesh of his fingers had first touched the silver object. The instant that Gunther's skin had made contact with the cool metal, he had felt a sudden wave of light-headedness roll over him. He had also felt a deep-penetrating tingle that had coursed throughout his body, from head to foot.

Whether it was just mere coincidence, or there was some sort of strange power emanating from the amulet, Gunther did not know. He had been around magic often enough by that point in his life, and had already seen its power work for good and for ill.

His preference had eventually become to avoid the risk of magic altogether, at least when he had a choice in the matter. He was not about to begin altering his ways, even when there was an element of doubt. Whatever power the pendant might have possessed, Gunther had decided to stow the medallion away, and keep it safely out of sight.

His distrust of magic had only strengthened and deepened in the following years. He had even refused the villagers' simple charms and amulets, which a few of them had offered as gifts to him after he had begun to interact periodically with the inhabitants of a few nearby locales. Gunther did not want to court any effects of magic during the mundane endeavors that he undertook, while in his self-imposed exile from the world at large. As such, the pendant had remained firmly hidden away, as year followed year.

Now, looking down upon the pendant, as if for the first time, Gunther wondered why it had not graced his neck ever since that long past day. The world had been dark enough to reach him even here, right in the heart of his refuge within the lonely outer forests of western Saxany. He knew more than ever that the world would never respect his wish to be left alone.

Tenderly, he picked up the medallion for the first time in many years, and looped the thin leather strap around his neck. He shut his eyes to steady himself as dizziness again rushed to his head, the very moment that the pendant rested against his chest. A tingling sensation permeated him, causing Gunther to physically quiver.

As if it were just seconds before, Gunther vividly remembered that very first time that he had touched the pendant. The sensations passed in due course, and a few moments later he felt like his normal self once again. Gunther wondered momentarily whether his mind had instigated the strange feelings, perhaps inventing the puissant sensations based upon his memories.

There was also the alternative view, the one that he had first feared. Perhaps his mind had nothing to do with the sensations, and the medallion really did hold some sort of hidden strength within it.

This time, however, he was not cowed by the thoughts of magic, and decided to keep the medallion on him. Closing the timber chest, he locked it up once again with the barrel-key. Digging around his dwelling, he managed to come up with some lengths of hempen rope. With them, he fabricated a makeshift harness that would allow him to carry the chest across his back.

Though rather crude in contrivance, he found that the harness insured that the chest would cause him no great strain to carry back down to Oranim. There would be time enough to find a new home or hiding place for the chest, but Gunther knew that its current location would not suffice anymore.

He conceded in his heart that, unless a wave of unexpected good fortune struck soon, he was likely going to be leaving his modest dwelling at the hillside far behind.

With a deep, melancholic exhale, Gunther stood up, shouldered the newly added weight, and went to summon the two exiles that he had brought up to the surface with him. It was time to go back into the depths.

DEGANAWIDA

Deep within the cool shadows, underneath the thick covering of the forest, the Grand Council of the Five Realms met once again. Uneasiness and great concern were visibly splayed upon the faces of many of those present, and the rest had simply managed to retain a stoic facade. Even though the sun's rays beamed down upon the forest, the clear day brought little comfort to the troubled souls of the Great Sachems seated amongst the trees.

Fifty strings of white shell-beads were again displayed in the center of the gathering, arranged in an unbroken circle. The array of strings were placed near to the large, rectangular shell-bead belt, with its design of purple and white, the prominent symbol of their collective unity. Also present was the bundle of five wampum strings.

Fifty sachems, bearing their ageless, hereditary titles, were gathered into two groupings on each side of a great fire. Many more of their number since the last gathering had received word that their villages had been reduced to rubble and splinters by the intense bombardments of stone from the returning Darroks.

The proud confederacy, which clung loyally to the One Spirit, was being pushed farther eastward to avoid the rain of death and destruction from the air. There would be no miraculous defense. The tribes were greatly reduced in terms of the warriors available who had mastered the use of sky steeds.

Even if there had been enough sky warriors to muster a defence, the enemy had come back this time with a strong escorting force of their own. It was no feeble guard either, as the new force of Trogen warriors mounted upon Harraks would have been more than enough to throw back the counterattack led by Ayenwatha during the enemy's first assault.

A few of the more heated minds among the warriors of the tribes had advocated the immediate seeking of vengeance, but the cooler mindsets of Ayenwatha and others had fortunately prevailed at the War Councils. The hearts of most of the beleagured tribal people, warrior or not, were increasingly focused upon petition to the One Spirit for answers and for deliverance.

The darkest of tidings had arrived just a few hours earlier, hastening a meeting of the Grand Council. It had also spurred an emergency meeting of Ayenwatha and the lieutenants that had been chosen at the War Council following the initial Darrok attack.

Border scouts that bravely, and vigorously, kept watch on the adjacent lands controlled by the massive Gallean force had returned with urgency. Every word coming from their lips had carried a dire sense of warning. The tidings that they brought gave further life to the malevolent darkness now casting its shadows upon the hearts of the tribal people, as it fed ravenously off of the maelstrom of fear and sorrow that wafted through the forests of the Five Realms like a poisonous mist.

Enemy forces had begun to marshal, for what plainly appeared to be the final stages before the anticipated attack upon the outer boundaries of the Five Realms. The star insignia of the Unifier was being flown high from every area of the huge, diverse force's encampment. Great numbers of warriors, both human and non-human, were assembling for impending war. A coalescing threat, like no other that the five tribes had ever faced before, was about to be unleashed upon them.

There were even signs that the weakened Anishin tribes to the north were mustering to join in the rapidly approaching assault. To many, the news would have been disheartening in the extreme, but Deganawida knew that he had to keep his mind still in order to execute his duties effectively as a Great Sachem. He was well aware of the fact that he was not the only leader whose limits would be sorely challenged, even among those of his own village.

He knew that Ayenwatha had numerous burdens to assume in carrying out the defense of the retreating tribal people. The task before the hardy war sachem was exceedingly difficult, and Deganawida felt an abiding sympathy for the ardent warrior.

Fighting humans was one matter, but all kinds of possibilities were inherent within the invading force. It made planning for defense all the more complicated, with many more elements to constantly keep in mind.

The Trogens, the brutish race that thrived upon drinking copiously from the cup of war, would be abundant in the skies above. With unfettered access to the high skies, the enemy would be able to ceaselessly watch for all movements being undertaken by the tribal defenders. That factor alone gave the enemy a tremendous advantage.

A small force of Gigans accompanying the enemy forces would also have to be closely watched. Much depended upon exactly where the immense beings would be bringing their legendary strength and fury.

Concentrated, the towering, grotesque beings could punch through a massed defense all by themselves.

The formidable Atagar, the strange, rodent-like race whose odd anatomy allowed for fluid, subtle shifts between four and two legged stances, would present a host of problems within the dense, woodland environment; not the least of which were the huge, dagger-toothed cats that they brought along with them.

It was undeniably a potent, gravely threatening array of force, one that boded nothing but ill-fortune towards the future of the Five Realms.

"And what do the scouts determine?" Deganawida had asked a young, sharp-faced warrior, who had been summoned to address the Grand Council and act as a speaker for his fellow scouts.

The scout had replied to Deganawida's query in a subdued voice, and the Great Sachem could tell that the scout deeply disliked being the bearer of such ill-tidings. "The enemy forces are ready for fighting within our forests. They are very numerous, and what disadvantages that the Galleans may have had in the forest they have planned for well, with the enlisting of the rat-men, the Gigans, and the Anishin tribes."

"Is there any sign of exactly when they will strike?" asked a portly figure named Dehonareken, the fifth Great Sachem of the Onondowa tribe.

"To our eyes, the attack will occur at any moment … maybe it has already happened," the scout answered gloomily. "When I left, their numbers were gathering in full strength."

"Then the time is upon us to defend our lands and our ways," Deganawida stated with absolute certainty. "There is no other choice for us to take."

There was no hesitation in the Great Sachem's voice. He walked closer to the fire, and slowly looked across the faces of the individuals on either side, brushing them with his own fiery gaze. The people of Deganawida's tribe, the Onan, were known as the Keepers of the Sacred Fire. In that moment, it looked as if some of those very flames burned within the depth of his eyes.

There was not one trace of disagreement to be found amongst the gathered Great Sachems during that momentous hour. They were not about to bow to the demands of the Unifier, and they were also not about to leave their families and fellow tribal members exposed and defenseless.

The powerful statement of Deganawida was merely a reflection of their already hardened resolve.

"Go back, and tell Ayenwatha that we must all prepare for battle," Deganawida said to the scout. "The moment that they move against us, we must close our bite down upon them, with powerful jaws."

The scout balked for a moment, cowed by the icy, steely gaze from Deganawida. He recovered swiftly, and bowed his head in a gesture of deep respect, before ushering himself out of the Council's sight, to begin the task that had been delegated to him.

Deganawida himself bowed to the others of the Council, and the assemblage was brought to a close a short time later. Deganawida lingered for a few moments afterwards to remove his deer-antler headdress, giving it, his own shell-belt, and the bundle of five arrows that he had held during the Council over to a trusted Onan man for safekeeping. When he was finished, Deganawida strode outward from the Council fire, heading in the general direction that the scout had gone.

Once away from the site of the Council, he looked towards a couple of warriors from his village, who were standing idly just a short distance away. Both were awaiting his presence, having been assigned to attend to the venerable sachem at the express desire of Ayenwatha. Deganawida did not delay in his purpose, quickly asking for them to bring forth his Brega steed, Coramm.

The warriors hurried off, returning quickly with the mighty winged beast that Deganawida had trusted implicitly for more than eight years. The creature was already fitted out with a blanket, low padded saddle, and harness. The warriors handed Deganawida his tribal war club, which they had kept in their care during the Grand Council assembly.

The Brega then lowered itself down to the ground so that Deganawida could get situated upon its back. Once Deganawida was seated, the Brega rose up and trotted forth under the Great Sachem's guidance. Deganawida acknowledged the two warriors with a nod, bidding them well as he moved past them.

The intertwining labyrinth of branches overhead effectively blocked any chance of upward passage, forcing rider and steed to search out a suitable place for ascent. It was one of the great limitations of using the Brega in the woodlands, especially when the tribal people no longer had any access to their hill-top villages.

After less than half a league, they came to a small break in the forest's naturally interwoven ceiling. It was an open space that was just large enough to allow the Brega and Deganawida a passage of escape up into the heights.

Starting farther back under the tangle of overhead tree branches, Deganawida urged Coramm forward into a run. The creature rapidly built up speed, such that it was bounding by the time it reached the small clearing.

As soon as it was clear of the trees, Coramm leapt upward. With powerful flexing of its broad wings, the Brega pulled itself above the trees, rising through the opening. The creature's calculation was precise, as the Brega was in no danger of grazing the treetops on the farther side of the clearing.

The Brega then angled itself downward almost immediately, at Deganawida's behest, to keep a lower course that was more aligned with the treeline. Deganawida felt that there was little use in flying at a high altitude, especially when he could easily be seen, and then cut off, by marauding Trogen patrols. There were few good places to bring the steed down now that he was over the forest, which increased the risk of the solitary flight. Deganawida kept his gaze sweeping about, knowing that he was now under a constant threat of danger.

The Brega streaked swiftly onward, gracefully soaring just a few feet above the treetops as it rapidly covered the distance between the Council site and the outer borders of the Five Realms. Daylight was now ebbing towards dusk as rider and steed headed westward. Thicker cloud cover and a mild climate reigned in the upper skies, and Deganawida kept up an alert watch for any hint of the enemy.

The border was not all that far away through the air, giving Deganawida a slightly queasy feeling as he realized just how close the Grand Council was to the massing enemy invaders. The stalwart Brega soon neared the forest's edge, prompting Deganawida to slow the fleet creature down to a near-hover.

At the very edges of the Five Realms, where the thinning trees gradually gave way to the open grassland of the plains beyond, Deganawida's sharp eyes took in the fires from multitudinous campsites dotting the lands up and down the border.

Deganawida brought the Brega down to land upon the solid earth, just beyond the last trees of the forest, dismounting the sky steed with little effort. The hard ground met his feet, and he took in a full breath of the approaching evening's cooling air.

He looked up into the darker blue-green shades of the sky, now fading towards the rich, violet gloaming of twilight that Deganawida normally found so enchanting. The skies of the western horizon were patchy with clouds, larger masses broken up by wispy, sporadic vapors in between.

The sounds of insects filled his ears. Deganawida envied the creatures, in that they felt no threat at the moment. Deganawida's heart felt very weighed down. He knew that he had to get away from the somber Council before he gave away the feelings that were tearing at his heart. Though he never dismissed the impossible, for he believed that all things were indeed possible in the One Spirit, his sense of reason shouted out to him that the end of the Five Realms was truly imminent.

It was the reason why he did not deem the flight that he had just taken as an unnecessary risk. He wanted to see the border area for himself, and to take in the sight of the enemy campfires, all the while contemplating the ominous situation at hand.

The lands that had been the heritage of generation after generation of Onan were now about to succumb to the insatiable appetite of the Unifier, a hunger that could only have been born out of the ravenous Darkness. Like the great, brilliant bolts of energy that flashed down from the skies during violent storms, often bringing fiery destruction to the woods in their wake, so was the presence of the enemy army.

It was a vast, terrible storm teetering on the border region, filled with a host of searing bolts; all about to be discharged without mercy upon Deganawida's homeland.

Deganawida thought for a moment that this was perhaps the last time that his ears would listen to the gentle sounds of the evening, as a weary day lay itself down to rest. It was quite possibly the last evening that he would have in the knowledge and confidence that the lands surrounding him were those of the Onan, and the fellow tribes of the great confederacy.

Even so, he felt honored at the truth that he was part of a people who were willing to remain steadfastly loyal to the One Spirit, even at the risk of their lives, and everything that they had ever known. He knew that they could have avoided the coming horror with great ease, as many kingdoms and lands already had, having simply agreed to accept the supreme sovereignty and authority of the Unifier.

He knew that such a path was no choice for those of the Five Realms, and he took a fiercely intensive pride in the knowledge that his people had steadfastly rejected such a course. In the eyes of eternity, Deganawida knew that he was playing an infinitesimally small part in an unimaginably immense cosmic battle. He had seen so much during his long life, and there was nothing in his memories to dispute his current sentiments. It was all part of an ecompassing conflict between good and evil, waged amongst a spectrum of mortals and immortals.

It was not an eternal struggle, he intimately knew. The war would be brought to an end some day. Perhaps that fateful hour would come sooner, or perhaps it would come later, but it would arrive nonetheless.

Whatever the outcome might be, Deganawida was committed to fulfilling his own part in the terrible fight. The fires dotting the plains before him showed Deganawida that a final stand was likely in the offing for him and many of his people. In his heart, he was girded and ready. The least that he felt that he could do for the One Spirit would be to lay down his life in the defense of his people and their lands.

The thought brought some further images to the forefront of his mind. Deganawida bit down on his lower lip as sadness welled up sharply within him. He was only one man, and he could not possibly stop the dark tides gathering against his people. He was braced for the worst that could happen to his own person, but women, children, and the elderly would likely be put to the claw, fang, and the sword very soon.

Suddenly, the huge number of enemy campfires seemed to be overwhelmingly daunting in the cold, unforgiving light of that knowledge. Deganawida wished that he could give up his life a thousand times over, so that his people might be spared the coming doom. He inwardly quivered at the thoughts of the terror that would soon be visited upon innocents, whose only fault was to be in the wrong place, at the wrong time.

He knew well enough that theirs was always the greatest of tragedies within wars over the long ages. The blood of innocents flowed into the umber depths of war's abyss. The sorrow that emerged from such a chasmic darkness was thunderous indeed, accompanied by a deafening chorus of unrequited cries for justice.

Whether or not such galling inequity would ever be put to rights was wholly in the hands of the One Spirit. It was something far beyond the power of humankind, or even the greatest of Wizards, for that matter.

Deganawida could not long ponder such things, lest he give in to the overwhelming power of despair. Each simply had to choose whether or not to do their own tiny part in the greater fight, even without the comfort of truly knowing the nature of the path's destination.

"Have strength, ageless one," a gentle voice called forth from the growths behind him.

Deganawida whirled about in alarm, reflexively raising up his war club to face the intrusion, not knowing whether the person that had spoken was friend or foe. As close as he was to the enemy encampments, Deganawida's instinctive inclination was to assume the latter.

A subtle glow deep among the trees limned the dark forms of two tall figures, one of which took a slow step forward, to where Deganawida could see the individual better.

"Who are you?" Deganawida queried, with an edge of challenge to his voice.

He doubted that the figures could even understand him, and hoped that they could at least perceive his wariness and tone if they somehow intended no harm.

"Rejectors of the Unifier, and certainly not part of that great rabble out there," the figure replied calmly, and articulately, again in the Quoian tongue used by the five tribes. The sudden development was one that Deganawida certainly did not expect.

Deganawida peered at the man more carefully, though his companion still lingered back at the edge of the brush, with the mysterious glow coming steadily from farther behind. Full bearded, with long dark hair, the man's head was circled about by a headband that held several narrow, wavy lines, woven of a silvery thread that reflected the moonlight. From what Deganawida could tell, the man was clad in a knee-length tunic and trousers. To Deganawida's initial impression, the man looked every bit a Midragardan.

Deganawida did not know whether or not it was some hallucination brought on by the dimming light, but the man's eyes seemed to sparkle with an energetic flare, as he looked with placid countenance towards Deganawida.

Deganawida also noticed that his Brega was not disturbed in the least by the two figures. If anything, Coramm was exhibiting signs of friendly excitement. Coramm had always had an uncanny sense for danger, so Deganawida could not help but take the reaction as a favorable indication.

Even so, Deganawida kept his war club gripped firmly in a readied position, and his feet in a well-balanced stance. He was fully prepared to show these strangers that he could wield the weapon capably, and move much better than his older appearance might have connotated.

"Who are you?" Deganawida inquired again of them.

"It is not important who we are, as much as it is what we are doing," the figure answered enigmatically. "We are friends and allies of the one that you call the Wanderer.... We are searching to find that which has been lost, and walking on a path of restoration. The Unifier is not the only one who is on the move in this troubled age."

"And your place in this war, which is to break upon my lands soon?" Deganawida asked the stranger, with an even sharper edge to his voice.

"Be assured that all that we do opposes the designs of those that bring darkness upon your lands," the stranger replied firmly, meeting Deganawida's stare without blinking.

"You should leave these lands immediately then. It is very dangerous at this moment," Deganawida said earnestly, even as part of him sensed that the man before him held no fear, or other anxiety. "This war is not one that we have chosen. The Unifier brings this war upon us, and will not allow us to live in peace. All signs are that the attack is about to commence, and some would say that it was foolish even for me to come gaze upon this border."

"The Father of the Unifier was a murderer from the beginning, my friend," the stranger responded cryptically. "What approaches is the fruit of the vine of death."

"I would not argue with you on that," Deganawida said. "It is indeed a great evil, but I try to keep such things out of my mind. I do not wish to be a beacon to such vile powers with my thoughts."

"Your road goes ever on, and the Unifier may yet meet a very unpleasant end to His own road," a new voice interjected, deeper and even more resonant than that of the first speaker.

The second figure then moved forward slowly from the shadows. Taller and broader than the first individual, he was clad in a very similar fashion. In his right hand, he gripped a long spear, whose angular blade shined brightly in the moonlight.

His face looked tense and stern, with his broad jawline taut as he peered out over the grassland and the teeming campfires farther beyond.

Whatever he was searching for, he appeared to be satisfied a moment later as his eyes looked back to Deganawida.

"The final battles have not taken place, and the world cannot yet say the outcome, at least as we can understand it," the second man continued somberly. "But you have given good account of yourself in all things, Deganawida. Stay true to your own course, and find the strength in yourself."

"Are you Wizards then?" Deganawida asked suddenly, looking from one to the other. Finally, he allowed himself to ease his weapon down, figuring that the great spear held before him would already have been put to use if the men harbored ill intent towards him. Some of the tension in the air that had been raised at the Great Sachem's sudden alarm also began to settle.

The hint of a smile crept onto the face of the first figure.

"It is you who say that we are, Deganawida," he replied.

"I see that you are going to give no easy answers," Deganawida responded, growing a little frustrated. "I can see why you are friends of the Wanderer."

The remark brought a low chuckle from both of the figures. They were not devoid of a sense of humor, at least.

"I hope that you are Wizards, then, because I do not wish to see you caught between the jaws of this looming war," Deganawida continued. "I hope that you have good means of travel out of here."

The first figure reached into a pouch attached to the belt at his waist, drawing out what looked to be a folded piece of cloth. Holding it up higher, so that the light could catch the cloth better, he carefully undid the first fold.

The cloth was unmistakably fashioned in the shape of a Midragardan longship.

"We can avoid them easily enough," the figure stated, glancing out with a nod towards the enemy campfires, "At least long enough to find a watercourse."

"You are Wizards," Deganawida then declared, gazing with interest upon the unique stretch of cloth, which held many more folds in its form.

The first figure smiled at Deganawida, as he folded the cloth over to its original state, and returned it back to the pouch.

"I wish that our people had such a means to evade this wicked design of the Unifier," Deganawida said forlornly.

"Perhaps they do, in a place that you do not expect, one that is not so far from you," the second, stoic figure stated.

"The Wizards that used to be amongst our people are nowhere to be found, and I am not confident that the Dark Brother has disappeared," Deganawida replied ruefully. "The Light Brother. Deganawida, from whom I derived my own name. Hino. Gunnodoyak. The World Mother, the greatest of all of these. Where are they in these dark times? Tell me, if you are Wizards."

The looks in the eyes of the two figures softened at Deganawida's desperate, insistent words, unmistakable compassion and sympathy on their faces.

"The Enemy's designs have long been set into motion, and in truth the invasion that you speak of has already been underway for many years," the first figure said in a low voice.

"Then you know something of the fates of these Wizards?" Deganawida asked, growing more dismayed.

Both of the figures nodded. "Just something of their fates. Like I said, we are searching, to try and undo what has been done from the shadows and the darkness."

"Many great wrongs have lingered over many long ages," the second figure added. "And I have not always chosen well myself."

At that moment, he brought up his left hand, so that Deganawida could see clearly where the man's forearm was truncated into a stump. Deganawida said nothing, though the man did not volunteer any explanation as to how he had lost his hand.

"We are all on a path of restoration, and redemption," the man finally said. "And some, more than most, on a path of discovery."

Deganawida took the words in quietly, saying nothing in reply, as he looked from the spear-holder back to his companion.

"We must continue on our own path, for now," the first figure interjected. "We must take our leave of you, Deganawida."

"Are you alone? Or are there others with you?" Deganawida asked, casting a glance towards the strange, golden glow that could be seen a little deeper in the brush.

"If you would trust us, you may see our third companion before we depart," the first figure said.

Deganawida nodded, knowing that if anything was really amiss, it would have surfaced long before then. All of his considerable instincts told Deganawida that these two figures were indeed no threat to him.

The spear-carrying figure then turned and walked off with long strides into the brush without another word, with Deganawida following behind, alongside the other stranger.

The spear-carrier pushed by some low brush growing near to the outer edge, where the thinner placement of trees allowed more light to reach the forest floor. The glow steadily grew brighter as they moved into the woods, the details of its source becoming clearer by the moment.

Deganawida stared in wonder at the creature standing just ahead of him, which radiated the golden light from its thick, bristly mane. Brawny of build, long of leg, and equipped with a fearsome set of tusks, the largest boar that Deganawida had ever beheld in the woodlands was standing just a few short paces away.

Such creatures were extremely dangerous in the wilds, but this magnificent animal made no sign of aggression as it regarded Deganawida and the others approaching it. Deganawida realized that it was great enough of stature that it could be ridden.

"This is our third companion," the first figure announced.

"Who does not have a name either, I presume," Deganawida retorted.

"It is not important who we are, at this time," the first one responded. "It is better that you know who you are, more so than you know who we are."

Deganawida just stared back at the confounding man, and shook his head.

"Well, such an incredible creature I have never seen before," Deganawida said.

The glowing mane's radiance was sufficient enough to light the way in the darkness for those with the creature.

"We shall see you again, of that I am certain," the first man stated. "Remain strong, Deganawida, and allow yourself to discover the help for your people that you seek. I assure you, it is not as far as you think."

The second figure with the spear gave a slight bow to Deganawida, as the two Wizards and the boar turned to walk off together into the forest. Deganawida watched them stride away, though it was quite some time before the forest's darkness swallowed the last of the great boar's golden glow.

Deganawida was left behind in an utterly mystified state. He had not given the Wizards his name, but they had known it all the same. They were, in all likelihood, what they said they were; friends and allies of the Wanderer. The Midragardan style of their attire and the spear were further evidence of that.

With slow, purposeful steps, Deganawida returned to where his Brega steed was still dutifully awaiting him, standing on the edge of the forest. Deganawida paused as he neared the noble creature, turning his attention back towards the fires burning off in the distance.

Deganawida took one more deep, calming breath of the night air, and relished the gentle peace that permeated the woods and grasses around him. He knew that the tranquility was not going to last, and the fires on the horizon were a grim harbinger of that dark reality. With a heavy heart, and much to ponder, he remounted his Brega and took hold of its reins.

He then set Coramm forward again, and they took off into the skies a few loping strides later. Once airborne, Deganawida turned the Brega sharply about, leaving the outermost borders of his lands behind, as he headed back eastward.

An aching rose within his gut that told the Onan sachem that it was the last time that he would set his eyes upon the border of the tribal lands. He could only hope that he was in error on the unsettling perception, though every ounce of his being told him otherwise.

Deganawida wished that he could stay for just a little while longer, but there was no time to tarry. The next day would arrive soon enough, and Deganawida's people would need his focus and guidance, with all of the vitality that he could possibly muster.

Deganawida was of a singular purpose as he flew back to where the Onan were gathered. In the innermost part of his soul, Deganawida knew that he was wholeheartedly committed to his people.

He had the resolve to do whatever was needed of him, and was ready to make whatever sacrifices had to be made. Deganawida only hoped that he could find the help for his people that he sought in time, especially if it was truly as near as the two enigmatic Wizards had claimed.

THE UNIFIER

The Unifier's infinitely deep, blue eyes absorbed the vision of worldly power gathered before Him.

The massed gathering of generals, nobles, lords, barons, counts, emirs, ambassadors, boyars, chieftains, prelates, bishops, and other various powers of humankind were assembled within the Great Hall, the stately edifice located on the second level of His towering mountain citadel.

The environment was much different from the last time the Unifier had convened a similar gathering, commanding the presence of emissaries and representatives of the secular, ecclesiastical, and other religious powers of Ave. That convocation had been just another routine audience with the Unifier, a time to deliver tributes, express loyalties, curry favors, and be issued expectations and commands. This occasion was much more than that. It carried the vibrant atmosphere of a formal celebration, on the eve of a grand new era, the air buzzing with energy born of anticipation and desire. It was a very befitting space for such a prominent, momentous assembly to occur.

The side walls of the long, rectangular hall were richly adorned with tapestries from many lands across the world. They were interspersed with the magnificent, recessed fireplaces that lent a further elegance to the hall. The various scenes of battles, eminent figures, and hunts played out splendidly upon the suspended cloths, the vivid, colorful designs woven by the most skillful of hands to be found within Ave.

Sunlight bathed the resplendent hall through the high clerestory windows, where the arched openings were set farther above in the walls. The light reached far into the shadows, revealing the hall in all of its grandeur.

Intermittent pilasters soared up the side walls to support intricately carved capitals, which in turn served to support the elaborate ribs of the vaulting gracefully fanning out across the ceiling far overhead. The ceiling itself was painted a deep blue, and dotted abundantly with stars of reflective silver. The series of chandeliers down the midst of the hall, whose multitudes of beeswax candles brought forth a scene of splendor from that ceiling when lit, were devoid of flames, but added to the stateliness of the environs nonetheless.

The brilliant painting of a white star wreathed in red flame graced the dark background of the apse, where the high dais was located. All eyes were turned towards the elevated stone platform holding the singular throne set into that apse, at the end of the majestic hall.

Standing upon the stone surface before the ornately carved throne, His head crowned in a bright golden circlet, was the Unifier. His piercing eyes seemed to look into each and every person in the room. He was clad in a long tunic of pure white silk, secured with a white belt brocaded with golden thread that was tied about His waist.

A sword rested in an ornate scabbard attached to the belt, the silver and gold inlaid hilt, circular pommel, and wide, upturned crossguard gleaming brightly. His rich locks of dark hair shined luxuriantly, with a slightly wavy texture. To those gathered, The Unifier was a living personification of strength and authority.

A few paces behind the Unifier, echoing the strength of His presence, were the members of His High Council; Gyriel, Morrigan, Niketas Palaeologos, Dragone of Girosan, Reginald FitzOsbern, Lothario Dandolo, and Ahriman.

The seven eminent figures were gathered in a semicircle upon the dais. Great warriors, Wizards, sages, and sorcerers, male and female, the members of the High Council were greatly feared by all who were familiar with them. They had the power to shake kingdoms to their foundations, able to speak with the unsurpassed authority of the Unifier. It was no secret that each one of them held great favor with the Unifier, more so than any king or emperor within all of Ave.

It was also lost on no man or woman present as to from whom the members of the High Council derived their lofty authority. While the seven of the High Council were rarely seen gathered all together before a large audience, none of those crowding the length of the hall were distracted from the singular reason for their collective presence.

The hall, from the bottom edge of the dais' steps to the great, iron-banded pair of oaken doors in the back, was filled to capacity with representatives from lands that had placed their will into the hands of the Unifier. Many had come on very short notice, from the farthest reaches of the known world.

Most were very sore and exhausted from long travel by sea, air, or land, worn out by the forced pace of travel needed to reach Avalos in time for the imperative assembly. There were many who looked forward to the feast that would be placed before them that very evening, and to the undisturbed rest that would soon follow the prodigious repast.

Yet such thoughts were pushed far to the back of their minds. For the moment, their attentions were fully focused upon the perpetually rising world ruler elevated before them.

Their eyes looked upon Him with a mix of fear, awe, respect, and loyalty in varying degrees. The Unifier had first risen with the authority of the seven great western kingdoms behind Him, and He was now crafting and nurturing the ascension of an unprecedented new order, all across the entire world.

As the vision of this new age was being unveiled, many believed that it was to be the most advanced and flourishing empire that any scholar had ever witnessed or written of. The Unifier's power knew no boundaries, and it was becoming evident that no land or populace could stand in open opposition to Him.

The submission to His greater authority was not without reward, as the wealth and power of the high lords, leaders, and rich merchants of loyal realms were expanded to ever greater degrees. Wars had decreased, and trade had expanded, even if the former had not altogether ceased.

That the age had grown more difficult for millions of commoners in the kingdoms and empires, however, was of little or no concern to most of the prominent figures in the Great Hall.

With the Unifier's seemingly mythical ability to lead, gain consensus, vanquish enemies, and expand power, it seemed to most that He was beyond human. Whatever deity or god any of them prayed to, they had no doubts that the Unifier curried the favor of the divinities themselves.

He did not age, He did not get sick, and He trod upon a path of astounding success, one that left His enemies broken and conquered in its wake.

The belief continued to be ingrained that no mere man could wield such power and authority. No ruler could possibly be graced with the incomparable victories that The Unifier had enjoyed, without having the greatest of blessings from a Creator or gods alike.

"Loyal generals, lords, kings, ambassadors, great merchants, emirs, boyars, and nobles, a profound time is at hand," the Unifier began, His voice rising to a crescendo as it expanded to saturate the capacious hall with its melodious resonance.

His articulate, smooth voice was understood in all languages spoken by those within the Great Hall, a tremendous phenomenon that was further attributed to divine favor. One of the earliest stories in the Sacred Writings spoke of the disintegration of communication amongst the enemies of the All-Father in a distant age, as they tried to build a great tower to reach the heavens themselves. To have one voice that was understood by all, each in their very own tongue, was nothing short of a miracle, whose nature could not possibly have been derived from any dark source.

"I have called all of you here, as we begin the first step of our final struggle. Our armies are now massed to strike upon Saxany and the Five Realms. You have responded well to My call, as another great army and fleet is forming rapidly … growing with each day that passes … in the port at Thessalas.

"It will not be much longer before we move to attack Midragard. The end to this dying age, and a dying history, is now within sight. The time is soon coming when the greatest achievement in the entire existence of this world will be attained. An order such as has never been seen before will be brought to the whole world.

"You shall all be the richer for it. You will see that our paths go together, as one, in unity and common purpose. That which you seek is gained from the path that I guide you forward upon. It is a wide path, paved in gold, which brings together so many other paths. Only one narrow path, that of folly, does not join this triumphant way. Only the misguided and the foolish trod upon it with their archaic ways. Your destination lies just ahead with Me, and is now within sight.

"One world. One focus. One Great Authority."

Some in the audience felt a deep tinge of unease at the Unifier's bold, elegent words, but not one of them was about to speak out in protest. As if absolutely nothing radical had been said, the Unifier smiled resplendently at His audience, seeming to exude the warmth of an invitation to a great feast upon each of them. The effect was simply mesmerizing, encompassing all who beheld Him.

Though inexplicit, their minds viewed him as the living embodiment of all their hopes, as well as the incarnate change that needed to transpire to realize those lofty ambitions. When He continued with His oration, they were hanging upon His every word, as if He was speaking to them personally.

"You have no doubts of My intentions towards each of you. You have greater wealth, power, and resources than you have ever known. I have always given a strong hand to crush and suppress any that would be enemies of those who have given their full allegiance to Me. History testifies that this is true.

"This path has not always been easy. But I have never led you astray. I have healed your lands. I have shown you the folly of fighting amongst yourselves ... and you have all tasted the great power that we can bring forth together. The future will be no different for My loyal vassals, or for My enemies. The choice is each man and woman's to make, an exercise of one's own free will."

The Unifier's words thundered from His mouth, His voice having swelled again to fill the hall and the ears of His rapt audience.

"From the Seven Western Kingdoms, who have always stood as one behind Me, to the lands that have since pledged themselves as allies, to those that stand here this very day, know that the path ahead will still be difficult. But know also that it will lead to a world the likes of which none of you have ever before dreamed could exist ... a world that you can only barely imagine."

As the sound of His voice trailed off, a broad smile formed upon His face. His full lips spread wide to show His perfect, opal-pure set of teeth.

To a few of those standing nearest to the base of the dais, those teeth appeared at that moment to be unnaturally sharp and long. Those very same people dismissed the perception a moment later as being a mere trick of the light, spurred by their own nervousness in the sheer radiance of His overwhelming presence.

Though they knew not the reason, others in the hall who were not yet wholly subservient in heart and mind to the Unifier felt a coldness permeate their bodies. Their skin felt clammy before the chill sank deeper within them, causing them to visibly shudder in the wake of the Unifier's open mention of that future world.

Among this small number were two Kiruvan boyars, whose senses were still struggling to adjust to the bold display of might and power all around them. There was something very foreboding and threatening underneath the brilliantly adorned images that most were holding fast to within their minds. Without the same anchoring grasp as those who were given over fully to the Unifier, the awkward sensation that these boyars endured only heightened their anxiety.

Yet as with the others, they were also not about to speak out, knowing that their voices would be shrill and tiny in the face of such regal authority. It was as if a force compelled them to remain complacent and silent.

For most, that unsettling feeling passed like wisps of smoke in a gust of wind, as the Unifier continued with His address once again.

"We are ending religious conflict. We are feeding the populations of great kingdoms and smaller lands. We are bringing an end to all wars. It is going to be an unrivaled golden age, and you will share with Me in the glory for bringing it about. Let no enemy stand in our way!" The Unifier boomed, His powerful voice thundering through the hall, as He thrust His clenched right fist high into the air.

The spontaneous gesture brought forth a vigorous roar of adulation from the gathered powers, representing countless armies, uncountable wealth, and immense populations from all across the surface of Ave. There was not one being in the room that would have doubted for a moment then that nothing in the world could stand in the way of the Unifier's aims. All were caught in the throes of the intoxicating moment, as if a flood of euphoria and enlightenment was coursing thoughout the Great Hall.

Seeing the assembled powers that they were in communion with inside the Great Hall, many of the lesser lords and representatives of smaller lands felt a tremendous sense of relief that they had chosen to submit themselves to the rising Lord of Avanor.

It could be seen by all that it was sheer folly to stand against the Unifier. All of those gathered could not help but marvel at the great power of the Unifier, now expanded far beyond the initial collective power wielded by the Seven Western Kingdoms.

They could not see how anyone could even remotely hope to wage war against the exalted Eminence standing upon the great dais. There were even a few within the spellbound crowd who already had begun to feel pity for the Saxans, the tribes of the Five Realms, and Midragard.

Of that diminutive group that had still managed to retain a little compassion, in the face of all the exhilaration and unrestrained ambition, there were those two Kiruvan boyars, more than any other, that felt deep misgivings about the fates of the three targeted lands.

section iv

DRAGOL

Dragol sauntered across the ground in relative silence, the only sounds of his passage the rustling of the grasses beneath his feet. He eventually reached an open expanse of ground, well beyond the outer boundaries of the encampment. He risked no great danger, as the area was still well within the perimeter guarded by the scouts and patrols, who labored so persistently to ward the sprawling mass of tents, supplies, steeds, and weapons.

Night had drawn richly upon the wellsprings of darkness, as the large and small moons of Ave endeavored to make their appointed journeys across the velvety, ebon sky. Scattered swathes of clouds blotted out bright clusters of stars as they drifted overhead, but otherwise the evening was clear, and comfortably cool to the touch.

The giant Darroks were now deep in their slumber, the outline of their behemoth forms easily mistaken for moderately-sized hills under the shrouding veil of night. Only the rectangular carriages still affixed to their backs broke the temporal illusion.

Within the shadows of the Darrok's looming forms, a number of broad tents housed both Harraks and their Trogen riders, resting in anticipation of the coming day's exertions.

Clad only in a dark woolen tunic, coarse trousers, and a pair of leather boots, Dragol had left the better part of his protective clothing and equipment back within the confines of his tent. One exception was his cherished longblade, whose lengthy scabbard hung from the baldric resting snugly around his right shoulder. His left hand rested for the time being upon the leather-wrapped hilt, as he strolled by spear-carrying Trogen sentries, both of whom nodded respectfully towards Dragol as he passed.

He inhaled deeply, taking in several breaths of the crisp air, feeling it swiftly descend into his lungs. Breathing out was an equally pleasant experience, and the rhythmic pattern brought his entire body into a more relaxed state.

Looking skyward, and carefully studying the horizon, Dragol's intense gaze quickly registered the shadowy form of a large Trogen patrol passing in the distance, faintly outlined against the dark sky. He could see that the patrol's course was set just along the edge of the forest line to the east, precisely where the Trogens had to conduct themselves with the greatest caution.

Dragol wondered if they had espied anything at all, given that the enemy forces were not likely to mark themselves carelessly, with open campfires that would serve as stark beacons from leagues around.

The sky patrols were, in essence, performing a routine. It was highly doubtful that there would be any strikes against the encampments on the open grasslands.

Just a few leagues to the north from the Trogens was a massive, Gallean-led encampment. Its swelling numbers contained the invasion forces now poised to assault the lands of the Five Realms.

The two encampments, viewed from north to south, ran along a new kind of boundary, directly parallel to the first trees of the sprawling forests, hills, and multitudinous waterways of the Five Realms. The invasion force was positioned at the mid-point of the dark woodlands sheltering the enemy tribes, like a spear about to be thrust into the heart of a hunter's quarry.

The Trogens, such as Dragol, with instincts sharply honed in the forges of a harsh existence within their homeland, were not about to underestimate their cautious, concealed adversary. The Trogen sky patrols were diligently maintained, as if there was always an imminent threat. Dragol and the other chieftains had seen to it that new routes were implemented wherever there was the slightest concern of vulnerabilities in the areas that the patrols warded.

With clearer skies and a pair of bright moons, any significant enemy force would be easily espied from the upper heights of the sky. Before an adversary ever got close to the encampments, the sonorous warnings of Trogen horns would have already roused a multitude of warriors, alert and prepared to resist any attack.

Though his physical eyesight scanned the wide spaces ahead of him, his mind's eye was roving elsewhere. His heart was weighing heavily upon him, grappling with unyielding cares and resentments. He was not about to shy away from the inner tumult, as it was a favorable night to ponder the things that were bothering him.

Dragol continued to envy the Trogens that were soon to take part in the momentous battle for Saxany. He thought of Goras, his longtime comrade, companion, and fellow member of the Thunder Wolf Clan. Goras was on the verge of participating in the greatest battle that the world had yet known.

Dragol was not so envious that he wished otherwise for his stalwart comrade. He wanted nothing less for Goras, and was genuinely happy that the hardy warrior would have such an incredible opportunity to bring tremendous renown to the Thunder Wolf clan.

Nevertheless, Dragol's own isolation from the impending battle, right at the cusp of participating in it himself, chafed sorely within him. The troubling thoughts caused him to clench his jaws tightly within his short muzzle, the tensions further stiffening his already taut neck and shoulder muscles.

Realizing that he was allowing himself to fall back into a strained inner state, so soon after easing himself down, he consciously focused upon relaxing his body again. Shaking out his powerful arms, and breathing in deeply, Dragol quieted his mind as much as he could. In a few moments, the Trogen warrior gradually felt the tightness ebb once again from his arms, shoulders, and neck.

Yet even if he could loosen the physical symptoms, it was all that Dragol could do to refrain from shouting out at the top of his lungs, erupting in a raucous cry of frustration and rage. Few warriors who had shown as much worthiness as Dragol, especially among his rugged, courageous kind, would ever have been restricted from the chance to measure themselves against such an unrivaled challenge. In the western marches of Saxany, upon the Plains of Athelney, two massive, determined armies would clash with titanic thunder.

Dragol could not deceive himself, in that the battle for the Five Realms was shaping up to be a conflict that would be much different in nature. It was far from what he had hoped for, when he had first arrived at the border region. Hiding and wary, the tribal warriors were scattered throughout the densely forested lands. It would be absolutely impossible to force the tribes into open battle, of a similar nature to the impending clash in Saxany.

Dragol knew that the tribesmen could not forever evade the Unifier's combined forces, whose multitudes would be swarming into the depths of the woods once the command was given. Once they had penetrated the forests and began to spread throughout them, their reach would be too extensive for the enemy tribes to avoid.

Even worse for the enemy tribes, the ranks of the invaders included some elements that were very well-suited for the forested environs. Very recently, more than one Trogen sky warrior returning from airborne patrols had spoken of very unusual entities sighted within the allied forces encamped to the north. Word had rapidly spread among the Trogens that a war band of the fabled Atagar had been brought in for the impending battle. The Atagar hearkened from the mysterious land of Yanith, located across the seas to the west of Kiruva. Filled with its legendary, towering forests, Yanith was reputed to be an exceptionally dangerous woodland environment, and the Atagar had thrived within it for generations. The strange, rodent-like beings were undoubtedly being utilized for their exceptional skills and experience within a woodland environment, one that paled in comparison to those of their homelands.

The stories of Yanith intrigued the Trogen chieftain enough that he desired to see the Atagar homeland for himself one day. He could only imagine the kinds of creatures that lurked within the depths of those dense, colossal woods, both upon the ground and within the lofty boughs of the enormous trees said to populate Yanith's forests. A vivid hint of the nature of those denizens came in the form of the brawny, predatory cats with the sabre-like teeth that the Atagar raised and trained, called Licanthers.

Though a part of Dragol regarded the Atagar as little more than glorified rat-men, he could understand their tremendous value for the very different type of fight that would be facing the invaders of the tribal lands. The enemy tribesmen intimately knew the pathways, ridges, hills, creeks, rivers, trees, rocks and every other natural feature within their lands. From evasion to ambushes, the advantages would certainly lie with the defenders due to their knowledge of the terrain.

The coming invasion would take speed, dexterity, and the ability to navigate, and swiftly learn, such a terrain, to bring the battle to the enemy quickly. The Atagar, at the very least, would be formidable adversaries within any forest environment. As scouts, they would be invaluable.

In addition to the Atagar, there were also recent reports of a small number of Gigans being present within the Gallean camp. The hulking Gigans were far less of a mystery than the Atagar, as Dragol's own homelands bordered the native lands of the Gigan clans to the east. Both the Trogen and Gigan territories lay just north of the broad principalities of Kiruvar, with the ranges inhabited by the great Mountain Trolls completing that boundary.

The brutish creatures, as a race, were relatively stupid and simple in Dragol's estimation. Over the years, he had become well acquainted with their ways and tendencies, though he was still perplexed by their reclusive nature.

Their unmatched strength could have won them far larger territories than their clans now occupied. As it was, while there were occasional skirmishes in the border regions with Trogen clans and the Kiruvans, the Gigan clans remained quite content to hunt within their own territories, and war amongst themselves.

The announcement of the Gigan presence within the invasion force had given Dragol great pause, as it was unprecedented. No outside ruler had ever been able to harness the Gigans' fearsome strength for their purposes. Dragol knew that no human king would have hesitated for a moment to bestow an abundance of riches to employ the ferocious creatures in their service.

It was quite an anomaly to Dragol that the Unifier had been able to secure the use of Gigans in such a fashion, gaining an immediate advantage in almost any battlefield scenario. Whatever had transpired between the Unifier and the Gigan clans, the circumstances of the Gigans going forth from their homelands, to be used in foreign wars, mystified Dragol.

It defied all precedents, as the Gigans cared for so little beyond hunting and the inner matters concerning their clans. They were rather crude artisans when it came to the making of weapons, clothing, or tools, and they knew little to nothing of metalwork or trade. The Gigans dwelled amid towering mountains and deep gorges, natural barriers that sequestered their homelands, apparently satisfied with plentiful game and their ancient clan traditions.

The relations between Trogens and Gigans had been fairly benign over the years, seldomly declining to outright enmity. Though encounters and communications were random, scattered irregularly between the neighboring Trogens and Gigans, their interactions had most often been of an amicable manner. There were only a few times when renegade elements of Gigan or Trogen clans had battled along the border regions of the two races. The bloody, costly ends of those incursions and skirmishes had been more than enough to stifle any notions of outright war, if such thoughts were ever held by individuals of either race.

As the invasion of the Five Realms and Saxany loomed, the Unifier had somehow been able to bring the Gigans down in force from their mountainous homelands, and pull them far away. The only reason that Dragol could fathom was that the Gigans participated for very similar reasons to those that had secured the involvement of the Trogens. Both had long suffered at the hands of a venemous, powerful enemy, even if the brunt of that long-standing oppression had fallen upon the Trogen clans.

The Northern Elves often marauded in force from their protected islands, off the northwestern shores of both Trogen and Gigan lands. Their cruel raids were also launched from a couple of very valuable areas of mainland taken in the past from the Trogens and Gigans.

Most disturbing and agitating to all Trogens, a population of Trogens had been cut off from the rest of their kind in the taking of those lands long ago. Those unfortunate Trogens now lived in thrall to the Northern Elves. They were made to labor unendingly for the vile beings, whose pallid appearance echoed the cold, pitilessness of their hearts.

There was nothing that the Trogen slaves could ever hope to appeal to, as the ageless Elves saw themselves as the first fruits of creation itself, imbued by the Creator with a preeminent position over all creatures dwelling in Ave. The cruder, mortal Trogens were viewed as mere fodder, to be used in the service of such blessed, exalted beings. Dragol's kind were considered to be sentient, expendable cattle, to be used however the Elves deemed fit.

Despite possessing lethal martial skills, honed over long ages, a Northern Elf did not enjoy any significant advantages in single combat with a fully-trained, seasoned Trogen warrior, much less one of the towering Gigans. Exceptional at archery and the use of crossbows, the Elves fought most often from a distance, less inclined to risk their enduring, age-defying lives by setting blade against blade. Moving nimbly through shadows, they had culled many Gigans and Trogens alike from positions of concealment, sending poison-tipped shafts deep into the flesh of victims that were not given a chance to acquit themselves in battle.

Their mastery of the two mortal races relied upon their long-established naval power, and their own teeming masses of sky-steeds. Their advanced shipbuilding had resulted in the creation of a formidable fleet, whose constant pressure over the years had successfully prevented the Trogens from ever fielding, or even developing the skill to fashion, larger watercraft. The Northern Elves had trained and developed large numbers of a very special, fearsome kind of Skiantha. With appearances like winged lions, they were ferociously hostile to the Harraks, as if an inherited enmity existed between the two.

With the advantage of having existed long before Trogens or Gigans had taken a single step upon the face of the world, the Northern Elves possessed the luxury of abundant time. It had allowed them to develop advancements in fortification that tremendously augmented their predominance.

When the discovery of great iron deposits, veins of silver, and some particularly bountiful coastal areas, teeming with many kinds of fish, occurred centuries after the Trogen and Gigan Clans had come into existence, the Northern Elves had moved with self-annointed impunity. They had conducted a huge campaign to occupy and fortify the portion of mainland necessary to secure the valuable resources.

Once considerable fortifications had been erected to shield the newly-acquired areas, the Elves had used them as bases for sending raiding parties deeper into Trogen and Gigan lands. They culled meat and furs from the wild herds of animals that the Trogens and Gigans relied upon, as well as levying destruction upon any cropland areas or dwelling sites that they could reach.

The intention was unmistakably punitive, calculated to create hardship and suffering among the other two races, and keep them in a perpetually weakened state. Withdrawing behind their massive fortifications, or retreating to their sleek war galleys, safely beyond the shoreline, the Elves had never been made to feel the pain that they delivered so regularly to others.

Elvish raids had occasionally brought about a few desperate incidents that had temporarily bonded Trogens and Gigans in a united cause. In an hour of common affliction, the two races had reached a higher level of solidarity, gained through the necessity of fighting side by side against a mutual adversary.

If used appropriately within the forests, the Gigans would be immensely effective warriors, able to batter and break through any defenses that the invaders might encounter, or reduce any obstructions erected to slow advances through the forest. The stomping approach of bellowing Gigans, battle-maddened and swinging great war-axes and maces, would challenge the resolve of even the most hardened veteran among human warriors. Dragol conceded that such a sight was unsettling enough to a battle-seasoned Trogen.

The full assault would be foreshadowed by a massive bombardment of great stones loosed from the backs of the Darroks. The monstrous hailstorm would be levied upon the areas around the invaders' planned routes, allowing for a swifter initial surge into the forest.

Dragol and Tirok's charge during that time would be very straightforward. They had been ordered to see to the protection of the Darroks, to scout for enemy movements, and to provide regular reports on anything of interest sighted from the higher skies.

Dragol could only hope that the attack proceeded quickly enough to subdue resistance, reducing it to such a miniscule level that the occupation of the Five Realms did not require the sustained involvement of large, concentrated forces. He wished that he and the other Trogens would somehow be called away to the battle marshalling far to the south, out on the Plains of Athelney.

Yet Dragol was only one Trogen, standing alone on a swathe of windswept grasses just outside of his encampment. He could not begin to see how he could possibly tilt the course of things to a better direction. Everything already seemed to be so heavily weighed against his most deeply held desires. The feeling of helplessness was becoming more overwhelming with each passing day.

His focus was slowly drawn upward, to the moons high above. Dragol took up a familiar stone disc in the palm of his right hand. Suspended from the long, leather thong around his neck, the pendant was caressed gently by the silvery light.

He peered intently at the distinct profile of a wolf's head, carved into its surface. A singular, large tooth, taken from the skull of a long-dead Thunder Wolf, was set in place across the middle of the stone disc, the sharp fang aligned with the thick neck of the wolf image. The pendant honored the apex of the moons' cycles, when both orbs were manifested in their fullness within the night skies, while also cradling the sacred image and relic of the Thunder Wolves within its circumference.

The moons were a very special part of his clan's symbolism, as were the great Thunder Wolves of old. For many ages, the Thunder Wolves had howled vigorously towards the moons when they had reached their zeniths, extending the radiant orbs hailing tributes of timeless reverence.

Dragol clenched the sacred pendant tightly in his balled fist. He closed his eyes, feeling the ache that welled up inside as he realized once again that he had never heard that sound with his own ears. Nor had he ever set his eyes, for even a moment, upon the very creature that his own clan was a living, proud homage to. Theirs was the only Trogen clan to carry such a terrible burden.

The Thunder Wolves had long ago been driven into extinction by the Northern Elves, one of the greatest travesties ever visited upon the Trogen race by their longtime tormentors. The Thunder Wolf clan had carried on ever since, refusing to choose a new clan symbol, even though the noble creatures had vanished from their lands.

Dragol slowly looked back up to the larger of the two moons, musing for a few moments that Goras and his other Thunder Wolf brethren in Saxany might well be looking up towards it at that very moment. If the Thunder Wolves could no longer gaze upon that silvered moon, then the Trogens of the clan honoring the legendary creatures still could; and always would, as long as even one of them drew breath.

The large, glowing night traveler and its smaller companion had not been stopped by the Elves. The luminous orbs would continue on their ancient journey over both Saxany and the borderlands between Gallea and the Five Realms, as they would also over Trogen lands. The celestial bodies would remain firmly in place, no matter what the Elves might otherwise wish. That thought, at the very least, was a source of comfort.

For the moment, Dragol pushed back the rancorous thoughts of the Northern Elves from his mind. He tried to replace them with thoughts of the more positive things that the sight of the moons evoked, bringing to the fore the idea that Goras and his fellow Thunder Wolf clan brethren were even now gazing upon its sylvan luminance.

Dragol reflected that both the Trogens and the moons were engaged in a timeless natural procession. While the moons already possessed an ancient legacy, the current generation of Trogens was just about to begin their own journey across the skies of the life cycle.

As the moons fulfilled their determined part in the natural order, so would the Trogens, fueled by the fires of spirit that burned fiercely within them. The blazing spirit of their kind would drive them to meet their challenges directly, to face all fears with their utmost courage and skill, and to find their measure within the enduring, growing legacy of their race.

That was the true way of a Trogen warrior, and whether the

Unifier wanted to recognize that or not, Dragol did not entirely care. It was a special inheritance reserved for his own kind, to be honored and continued, and he only hoped that he would not be denied his own chance to see where his individual place stood among his peers and ancestors.

That hope was the greatest reason why he felt disconcerted as he ruminated in silence, staring up at the skies that he would fly across the very next day. His slow exhalations merged with the soft breezes, as if the winds themselves would carry his worries to the ears of some greater power that might listen, and address his inward anxieties.

Dragol knew that he could watch a thousand Darroks drop a torrential cascade of stones for days on end, and he would come no closer to knowing his own measure. He had to be given the chance to fight a worthy adversary, blade to blade, in the skies or upon the ground. It was truly that simple, though the realization of it seemed so maddeningly elusive.

Another faint, dark thought continued to nag at the fringes of his conscience, even in the face of his incessant worrying over being able to take measure of himself in combat. It was a troubling thought, one that he dare not voice to other Trogens, as everything that they did in service of the Unifier's forces hinged solely upon the promises that had been made to their kind.

Rising doubts had taken firmer root, revealing themselves to Dragol with greater frequency. The meddlesome concerns nonetheless had momentous implications: If the Unifier did not fulfill His promises to the Trogens, then the war that they were fighting would become unjustifiable.

The terrible prospect represented a conundrum for Dragol, as it acknowledged the possibility that all of the Trogens' combined involvement could ultimately be for naught. The possibility loomed that every Trogen fighting in this war could return to their homelands tainted with disgrace, having participated in a baseless war that carried no legitimacy under a Trogen warrior's code of honor.

With a low, audible growl of frustration, the Trogen shut his eyes once again, laboring to chase the new swarm of worrying thoughts out of his head.

There was only one thing to think about, in light of what Dragol could, and could not, control. He was on the threshold of a new era.

While not denying the uncertainty encompassing him, the Trogen chieftain had to believe that somehow great honor would be gained, both for his race and for himself. It was the only way that he could go forward, with all of his strength and conviction intact.

He needed only to concentrate upon the charges that he and his warriors had been given, and to execute them flawlessly, helping to conclude the battle for the Five Realms swiftly. Everything beyond those imminent tasks was well out of his control.

There was also the possibility that welcome surprises could emerge within the course of the approaching battle. The full nature of the tribesmen was still to be revealed, and if the daring resistance displayed in the first Darrok raid was any indication, then the invaders would be well advised not to underestimate their opponent.

As the main attack would be launched with overwhelming force, a part of Dragol could not help but wonder why the tribesmen did not surrender, or at least parley. But the fact that they had not elevated his respect for them even more.

The tribes lacked the numbers and quality of weapons and armor that the invaders would bring to bear. Yet like a proud black tiger from the Trogen homelands, when cornered, the tribal warriors would undoubtedly fight back with fury. Dragol's instincts told him that the overly confident Galleans were going to be in for much more than they expected, at the very least.

Dragol's attention returned back to the present, as he opened his eyes with a markedly calmer mind. The stone disc pendant was still clutched within his hand, he suddenly realized. Gently, he lowered his right hand, letting the symbol of his clan come to rest against his muscular chest. He knew that when the new day rose, he would face the enemy as a Trogen warrior of the Thunder Wolf clan, come whatever may.

He then looked off in the direction of the dark outlines that indicated the forest's outer boundary, well off in the distance. He was not altogether certain what it was that he was looking for, but he scanned the boundary from horizon to horizon nonetheless. It was a tense stillness that met his rigid gaze, and in that moment he felt in his gut that the fight on the coming day would not be easy.

The dark, shrouded forest revealed nothing of what the future would be, yet, in a way, it represented the gateway to everything that he would become in the future. One way or another, the answers that addressed the innermost core of his being would be found somewhere within that impenetrable line of shadow spread before him.

Turning away from the concealed boundary region, Dragol strode calmly back towards the encampment. The night had not yet aged to where he needed to turn in to his tent, and take some rest. There was still time enough to join with some of the other Trogens for some meat and drink. Perhaps, if he were fortunate, there would even be time to engage in further conversation with Tirok.

Most of the other Trogens not assigned to patrol or sentry duty would likely be settling in for the night. There was always a chance during such a period to hear some good tales from members of other clans. It was an opportunity not often afforded when Dragol was back in his own clan's territory.

The legacies of the Thunder Wolf clan, and all of the clans, were like the iron ingots worked by Trogen artisans to fashion one singular Trogen longblade. That collective blade was about to be labored upon further, in the coming days and weeks.

Dragol's heart was lifted as he gazed upon three Trogen warriors immersed in conversation, relaxed and confident in their demeanor as they sat around a blazing campfire. Seeing him, the warriors called for him to join them, offering him cooked meat and ale without hesitation. As he drew closer, Dragol saw that they were of three different clans, but the bonds of a warrior brotherhood flowed among all of them.

The sight filled him with confidence, as he took a place with them, representing a fourth clan in their ongoing discussion. Trials lay ahead, of that he was certain. Yet when all was finished, and no matter what it took, Dragol believed fervently that the blade of the Trogens' spirit would ultimately come out sharper, and more robust, than ever before.

FRAMORG

Far, far away from the encampments poised on the eastern edge of Gallea, a couple of hours after the two moons of Ave had drawn to the culmination of their nightly sojourn, a mass of Trogens were soaring high through the Saxan skies, upon stout Harrak steeds. The sun now reigned fully within the skies of the new day, casting its golden luminance all across the Saxan lands.

Just beyond daybreak, the contingent of Trogen warriors had mounted their steeds and taken flight. They were a potent war band, comprised of many renowned fighters that had been carefully selected from the various clans. The prominent force was dutifully escorting a hulking warrior in their midst, the supreme Trogen war chieftain, Framorg, the most eminent member of the revered Mountain Bear clan.

Flying at a lofty altitude, Framorg looked down with an unmitigated sense of awe. A vast, deadly array of force was spread out over the grassy lands passing underneath their steeds. Thousands upon thousands of tents dotted the open plain, and throughout the multitudinous dwellings a teeming mass of activity was commencing.

It was a cool morning, and an abundance of white cloudcover was rolling in from the horizon. The sharp air was being pushed along by a considerable breeze, which bit into the exposed faces of the Trogen riders. The brawny Harraks handled the mild turbulence well enough, largely gliding through the sky as they afforded their masters an unsurpassable view of the gigantic invasion force.

The lines of three distinct encampments could be discerned from the elevated heights. Each was separated from the other by narrow spaces of open ground, which were constantly being criss-crossed by personnel and beasts.

Framorg's eyes scanned the ground with wonder. The prominent Trogen war chieftain had never witnessed anything like it, a concentration of numbers and organization far beyond anything that he had ever experienced before. The power gathered upon the Plains of Athelney was staggering to contemplate, and it was not lost on Framorg what kind of power the Unifier had assembled to do His bidding.

While the Trogens had their reasons for fighting within the Unifier's ranks, Framorg also knew that the Trogens really had no choice. He did not want to think even for a moment of the consequences of rejecting a being that could muster, and send forth, such a colossal force.

He had no doubts that the Saxans were going to discover the terrible cost of bluntly rejecting the Unifier's overtures. The unceremonious expulsion of the Unifier's emissaries was soon going to be washed away with torrents of blood.

To the left of Framorg's current vantage point was the Andamooran force, hailing from lands to the north of Gallea. Situated at the heart of the three primary armies were the Avanorans. Located on the right was the huge army brought from neighboring Ehrengard.

Just to the back of the mammoth Avanoran encampment, covering the area now directly underneath the airborne Trogen contingent, was a concentrated mass of supply wagons and carts. Now idle, they had carried in the vast quanities of food, weapons, and other supplies necessary to sustain the needs of the seemingly innumerable forces. Carried along with foodstuffs and supplies were also several large, timber components of great siege engines, though Framorg knew that such mighty weapons were not yet needed in the invasion campaign. The first battle would be an open clash of arms, and it was likely that once the main Saxan force was crushed, most walled towns and fortresses would throw open their gates, rather than endure the devastation of a prolonged siege.

Great multitudes of draft animals, from clusters of oxen to herds of stout, brawny horses, were grouped together within several areas of the sprawling Avanoran camp. Given leave of their labors at the present, the throngs of animals were grazing calmly under the open sky.

Framorg twisted in his saddle to get a better look at everything, sweeping his gaze all about. His vision traveled farther back, catching a glimpse of the other great assemblage of wagons and tents set well behind the Avanoran warriors. It was enough to evoke a growl from the back of his throat.

The presence of merchants was always disconcerting to Framorg, and time was not dulling the bitter taste that the sight of them invoked. The stark feeling reflected a cultural chasm between Trogens and humans. Framorg did not understand why the Avanorans tolerated such obvious leeches, men who merely followed the army, latching onto it to gain wealth, and were not willing to fight with it. The cowardly merchants always located themselves well out of harm's way, far to the back of encampments.

To Framorg, it was more than a good thing that the Trogens of his homeland had no such merchants, or even used coinage, a human means of trade that had probably given rise to such a loathsome batch of miscreants. The Trogen warrior knew that his longblade would not have remained dry for long if he ever came across his own kind engaged in such dishonorable pursuits.

As the Trogens passed beyond the masses of carts and wagons, they entered the airspace over a spectacular mass of small field tents, which hosted the bulk of the Avanoran foot-soldiers. A great number of men could be seen gathered around the openings to the tents in pairs and clusters, many heads turning upward to stare at the Trogens as they passed by overhead. Some were grouped around fire-pits, engaged in conversing and eating, while others were sitting more to themselves, attending to personal weapons and other assorted gear.

Blacksmiths and other skilled craftsmen, such as leatherworkers and woodworkers, had set up temporary worksites throughout the teeming masses of tents. Tendrils of smoke wafted up from several such locations, as the artisans labored diligently to repair weapons, armor, or other various elements of equipment.

The Avanoran encampment was a very dynamic sight, crawling with movements of ever more diverse elements. Mounted contingents of men passed down pathways through the midst of the tents, as numerous carts were pulled through by stout draft animals and throngs of foot-soldiers marched out towards the frontal areas. Others were gathered within open, clearly demarcated areas, practicing their skills at arms.

Framorg then looked down upon a few clusters of horses that he could tell were not mere draft animals. A fair number of camp attendants were moving busily about in the midst of palfreys and packhorses, which were quartered in close proximity to the knights that owned them.

Also belonging to the elite knights, the human warriors that Framorg respected the most, were the great war stallions that they rode into battle. Tended to in a much more individual capacity than the other steeds, the muscular war horses were living symbols of the stature of those that possessed them. Dedicated Avanoran squires, assigned to the service of individual knights, cared diligently for the majestic creatures.

It was one area in which Framorg could relate more clearly to the humans, as the better Harrak steeds reflected the level of prestige held by their Trogen riders. Framorg's own Argazen, a true lord of the skies, had no rival amongst the other Trogen steeds.

Tall banners, some crafted in a half-moon shape, and others more triangular in form, fluttered and snapped proudly in the wind from the tops of long timber poles. A forest of the most prominent ones stood vigil over the much more sizeable central tents, both pavilion and hall-shaped. The prominent tents included the quarters of higher-ranking Avanoran commanders, chapel tents, mess tents, and the field residences of higher clergy accompanying the massive campaign. This area, Framorg well knew, was the true heart of the Avanoran camp.

The land just beyond the front of the Avanoran encampment was watched over thoroughly, for a substantial distance. Small bands of Atagar, accompanied by Licanthers, pickets of Avanoran sentries, and periodic mounted patrols could be seen within a great zone covering at least a couple of leagues past the forward boundaries of the main encampment.

Even the skies over this zone were warded. Around Framorg's own formation, circling far above the patrols and sentries on the ground, were several groups of Trogens.

The location of the enemy Saxan war camp was far to the edge of the horizon. It was situated well past the eyesight of the camps below, hidden behind the undulations of the rolling grasslands.

Yet even with the fair distance, Framorg and the other riders could make out signs of the sizeable army now blocking the invasion force's path into the heart of Saxany. Numerous thin columns of smoke rose up from the fires within the distant enemy encampment. They reached towards the sky as if to block Framorg's way.

To Framorg, the sight was nonetheless a comforting one. There was going to be little worry about drawing the enemy into open battle. The Saxans were gathered in strength, waiting for the onset of the invasion, and clearly intending to meet it with muscle and steel. It was a response that Framorg respected, as it was the one that any Trogen clan would have taken in similar circumstances.

Frustratingly, it was still too far of a distance to get an accurate view of the entire magnitude, or types of forces, that were positioned to resist the impending invasion. Framorg led his escorting contingent of warriors as far forward as he could, but not far enough that he could alleviate his intense curiosity regarding the Saxan camp.

At long last, Framorg reluctantly ordered the signal to be sounded to turn his escorting force around. A Trogen warrior to his right blared out an extended, deep note upon his curving war horn. The formation curled about in a great, arcing path, and reversed course. With a sharp nudge from his heels, Framorg spurred Argazen forward, setting a faster pace for the return.

There were a few different staging areas for Trogen sky warriors located throughout the three principle camps, as the Trogens held responsibility for the skies over all of the Unifier's forces. Framorg's own tent was located within a small encampment set just to the northern side of the Avanoran forces, not far from the front edge. It was close to the freshly dug ditches bordering the outermost perimeter of the Andamooran camp, which was positioned to the immediate north of Framorg's tent.

Another sonorous horn blast emitted from a rider near Framorg's right side, giving the signal to descend and land. The throng of riders guided their steeds into a sharp, downward approach, angling for the open space of ground set within a ring of Trogen tents. Those in the forefront of the group landed a few moments later, while those coming behind flew just over their heads, alighting a short distance beyond. The staggered landing was orderly and efficient, well-practiced amongst the Trogens.

The instant that the entire contingent was on the ground, Framorg could sense the surge of excitement, confidence, and anticipation running throughout the Trogen camp. A number of Trogens hurried from the tents towards them, gathering around to see the arrival of the great Trogen leader and so many renowned warriors.

At the edges of the clearing, the camp activity continued feverishly, as other Harraks were saddled, and harnesses were adjusted. Trogens moved back and forth on appointed tasks, bearing weapons, armor, sacks of supplies, waterskins, buckets, and any other implement necessary to fulfill their chores. A couple of the gargantuan Gigans lumbered by on the far edge of the clearing, huge war axes carried in their massive hands as they trudged towards the front lines.

A couple of Trogens strode up to attend to Argazen, bowing their heads low in deference as they waited patiently for Framorg to dismount. Without a word, Framorg handed them the reins to his steed.

The Trogen leader walked briskly towards the opening of a long, tall tent that served as his personal headquarters. He could feel the curious, elated gazes from the throng of Trogen warriors watching him approach the tent, on the eve of the great battle.

An extraordinarily massive, brown-furred bear was lounging just outside the entrance, tethered securely with great chains. Upon seeing Framorg, the bear roused itself, and shifted its bulk onto its huge, clawed feet. The exceptional creature ambled over to meet Framorg, lowering its great snout to look into Framorg's face. The creature's eyes reflected affection and eagerness.

"Barondas, you are always a welcome sight to my eyes," Framorg greeted the immense animal as he came to a stop, reaching up with both of his hands to vigorously pat and rub the bear's enormous head.

The creature had been brought to the west by an Avanoran round ship at great difficulty. Nothing else was acceptable, however, as Framorg was not about to endure a long campaign without such a pure, visible representation of his clan.

He also had a personal obligation to Barondas, as the creature had been orphaned as a cub when Framorg had been attacked by its mother while on a hunt during his youth. Framorg had gained both a companion and a great reputation within his clan, and others, after slaying the raging mother all by himself. It was an incredible act, witnessed by the others of his hunting party. While the killing of a Mountain Bear was born out of the necessity of self-defense, Framorg was not about to abandon the young, lonely cub whose kind were the living symbols of his clan. He had taken the cub that very day, and had raised it dutifully, garnering a growing respect within his clan due to the close bond that he forged with the creature. Having a Mountain Bear had certainly not harmed his own mystique during his rise to becoming the clan's unanimously acclaimed war chieftain.

Framorg ruffled the fur of the bear's head, and stroked its muzzle for many moments, speaking soothing words to the beast before finally continuing into the tent.

"Chieftain Framorg!" a huge Trogen greeted him enthusiastically, upon his entrance.

The Trogen that had spoken was standing over a map, the face of which was illuminated by light from a brazier. Inked upon parchment, the map was spread out across the surface of a long, timber plank, supported at each end by broad wooden tuns.

Five other high-ranking sky warriors had evidently been going over the map with the large Trogen prior to Framorg's entrance. He knew all of them, and which clans they represented. Three were from Framorg's own Mountain Bear clan, one was from the Sea Wolf Clan, and one came from the Dark Serpent clan. The one that had addressed him was from the Thunder Wolf clan.

All of the Trogens were hardened, veteran warriors, worthy of high command at Framorg's side. All came to an abrupt silence at his appearance, and respectfully lowered their heads in acknowledgement of his presence.

Framorg slightly bowed his head in reply, and remembered his new pledges. "In the service of the Unifier, for the service of the Trogen clans."

"The last of the sky warriors who are to fight in this coming invasion have arrived in the camp," the large Trogen, whose name was Ondayon, announced.

Framorg then inquired, knowing full well who they had all been waiting upon, "And all is well with Pythora?"

The other Trogen nodded in the affirmative. "As good as can be, on the edge of such a great war. But he is here in the camp with his warriors, and he hopes that we attack very soon."

"We have suffered the longer delay in this camp, and he is the one who speaks of being impatient," Framorg remarked curtly. "Tell him his hopes will be met. The order has come that the great battle will indeed be launched tomorrow, at the breaking of the dawn."

Framorg's skin tingled with a deep-felt excitement as he uttered the savored words. The arduous waiting was finally over. The chains that had bound all of his kind were about to be cut loose.

He looked to the other Trogen commanders, and could recognize the subtle energies swelling within them, like a force of water about to burst through a weakened dam. Once the word had been spread, there would not be a Trogen in the entire camp that would be able to endure the coming night without a feeling of absolute restlessness.

The battle coming on the next day would be larger than any battle that any Trogen in the entire existence of their race had participated in. As a race that saw war as an ultimate test of their very being, such a notion was staggering to even contemplate.

"That is a great relief, to all of us," Ondayon replied, his extended canines showing brightly in his broad grin.

"We will win the skies with the might of the Trogens, as many of our brothers will earn great honor in the fighting on the ground," Framorg stated. "We will take the skies from the enemy at the beginning, even as the ground forces surge."

"If we can draw their sky warriors into an open fight," Ondayon responded somberly.

"We will go up to meet them from the beginning. They will not have to look for us," Framorg replied firmly.

The lesser commanders bowed their heads, Ondayon uttering with conviction, "It shall be done."

That was all that Framorg wanted to hear. The only way was forward, and the only option was victory.

His own lips parted to reveal a slight grin, a very rare expression on his usually stoic face.

"Then shall we talk about our deployments now?" he asked, sweeping his gaze over them.

All were eager to set their minds towards details of the coming battle, greatly buoyed by the declaration that the waiting was finally over.

AETHELSTAN

Darkness had barely begun to ebb, the pre-dawn still rich with damp mists that would soon burn away with the rays of the ascending sun. A heavy, palpable tension filled the air, as Aethelstan's warriors stoically awaited the attack that they all knew would come that day.

Their patience was not sorely tested. As they expected, the attack broke upon them with the first light of dawn. It was heralded by the fierce shouts of men, and the clamor of numerous horns, both resounding within the misty, cool dawn unveiling around the Saxan lines.

The enemy forces were somewhere just ahead of them, and a multitude of Saxan eyes was fixed resolutely in that direction. Hands tensed on the shafts of spears and axes, the hilts of swords, and the grips of large round shields, as the Saxan warriors awaited the first visible sign of the enemy approach.

Aethelstan stood tall near the center of the formation, surrounded by his household guard, an epicenter of fiery determination. The Saxan line straddled a low, tree-covered ridge, right at the edge of the downward slope. The shield wall was set in place. Their placement on the rising ground, amid trees, would certainly blunt the ability of the Avanorans to use their famed heavy cavalry.

Aethelstan's adrenaline was surging, making his long mail-shirt seem like it was fashioned out of thin cloth, and his sword feel like a shaft of wheat. A righteous fury swirled within him, filling him with strength for the coming fight.

He had walked along the entire length of the shield wall in the dim, fog-shrouded grayness of the earliest light. The scarred, bearded, hardened faces of mailed veterans were intermixed with the visibly frightened, sweating expressions of levied youths, anxiously gripping their spears in the second and third ranks.

If it were not for the presence of the thanes, with their veteran household guards and retainers, Aethelstan knew that many of the extended levies would quickly break in their discipline when the real fighting began. The veterans were the supports that kept the structure of their entire defense together.

During his foray, he had stopped many times to utter a personal word of encouragement, pat on the shoulder, clasp on the arm, or other gesture of reassurance, to both veteran and inexperienced levy man alike, whether in the front, second, or third rank. All were facing the same menace, and as Aethelstan respected the proven warriors, so also did he respect the untrained levy man, who conquered his own fear to stand in the line, and face the new, terrifying experience of battle with resolve.

Earnest nods, verbal encouragements, and nervous smiles met his various gestures. A number of monks and priests followed and preceded him, the dark-robed clerics speaking prayers of absolution, and tossing blessed water out over the arrayed warriors.

Aethelstan was deeply moved by the pious concern reflected in the faces of the monks and priests. He stopped to watch one particular priest, who was addressing a levy group that clearly had come from the villages that he had long-ministered to.

The older man's face was outwardly calm, but his eyes were wet from the powerful emotions that he was feeling in looking upon the men that he had married and anointed in the Western Faith. It was likely that he had tended to some of the younger men of the group from the very day that they had been born.

Aethelstan knew that it took a great effort for the priest to hold back such powerful emotions, knowing that many of those who his blessed water fell upon would not live to see the dusk. Priests such as that older man had come as shepherds after the most endangered members of their flocks, willing to stand with them, and also face the risks, to whatever end. While they were not ones to fight with spear and sword, they were invaluable to morale. They lifted up the spirits of the men in the midst of the dark hour, giving them the kind of reinforcement that was greater than any warrior's speech.

The priest moved in and placed his hands gently upon a particularly young man's head, exchanging some quiet, private words with him. Aethelstan could see the wide-eyed young man nodding at the words, as the priest traced the shape of the Redeemer's spear upon the youth's forehead.

Aethelstan's sharp eyes did not miss the priest's face as he turned away from the young man, acting as if he was glancing back in the direction of the enemy lines. He saw the old priest's eyes close for a moment, pain echoing in the expression, as he took that moment to regain his composure.

The emotive expression spoke of something that Aethelstan deeply understood, and he tightened his mouth and steeled his eyes as he moved onward. An overwhelming majority of the young to older males from his own burh were standing with him in those very lines, having followed him on the march out to the west. The reality was that a great majority of the able-bodied males from the region around the burh were now standing resolute behind his command, gathered from all the surrounding villages and thanes' estates.

There were more than a few of them who he had witnessed transform from child to young man, just as the priest had experienced. He had shared countless life experiences with men from both his town and the greater province of Wessachia. They had shared his tables, his feasts, his hunts, his trade, and his travels. There were several that could be considered family, being of his own bloodline.

He recognized some that were brothers, resolutely standing beside their siblings within the battle line. He also saw several instances of fathers positioned close by their sons, each ready to ward the other with their lives. Many were closely related to each other, or had shared lifelong friendships.

Each and every death of a Saxan would exact a very high, irreplaceable price. Aethelstan could see in their eyes that the men before him were fully cognizant that they might be facing the last day alongside a son, brother, or friend. It mattered not whether they fell themselves, or survived and were separated from those who had fallen by the veil between this world and the next.

As he looked into each of their eyes, each rife with dreams and ambitions of their own, he knew that many would be still, glazed and lifeless by the day's end. It was by far the hardest reality to endure, and it was one that he had the most trouble accepting, but as a commander of warriors he had to face such immutable truths in a poisoned world.

Even more demanding, he could not show them any sign of fear or emotion within himself, or he would be hurting them when they needed as much confidence as they could possibly muster. They had to feel as strong and assured in him as possible, as well as themselves, for any of them to have a chance of making it through the coming fury of battle.

It was still a difficult thing to do, as dark thoughts tormented him, like demonic whisperings empowered by icy truths. If he were to survive the battle, he would see many dead faces that would bring him right back to these quiet moments before the storm, as he walked down the battle lines in the early morning mists.

The thoughts were still running through his head after he had taken his position at the center of the Saxan line, listening to the sounds of the enemy advance. A chorus of horn blasts shook the ridge and surrounding hills again, as a light tremor ran through the ground. Aethelstan glanced to his left and right, at the throng of axe-bearing household guards around him.

Many boisterous shouts rose up from the Saxan ranks, as a wall of men emerged in the evaporating wisps of lingering mist, a rhythmic tramp sounding as they made their way steadily towards the ridgeline. They were lightly armored archers and crossbowmen, most wearing soft caps, and only a smattering with iron helms. They were garbed in little more than tunics or padded gambesons as they approached the base of the ridge, and Aethelstan knew that they would not be sent against the shield wall.

Behind them, another wall was coming, one more heavily armed. But Aethelstan knew that the first flurries of battle would come from the vanguard bearing the missile weapons below.

Without a tremendous quantity of arrows, Aethelstan did not want to loose the Saxans' own barrages wildly, and he dispatched commands up and down the lines for the Saxans to brace themselves, and to keep the shield wall in place.

The front rank, largely comprised of well-experienced fighters, overlapped their round shields, as others below put forth shields to protect the lower parts of their bodies.

Where clusters of household guards gripped their long war axes, others by them held forth taller, triangular shields. The shields would protect the axe-wielders, so that they could be free to use both hands in wielding the broad, devastating blades.

More horn signals erupted, as the line of Avanoran archers and crossbowmen came to a halt not far from the base of the low ridge. There was a rumbling noise, which broke out into a crashing roar, hurling a few words in the Avanoran tongue that Aethelstan could not understand.

The Avanorans notched arrows or brought loaded crossbows to bear upon the long shield wall above them. A long, resonant horn blast then ensued, as a torrent of bolts and arrows were loosed towards the Saxan defenders. Hissing and tearing through the air, the shafts streaked towards the shield wall.

The fighting was now underway.

The great battle for all of Saxany had begun.

A number of screams and cries broke out from the Saxan lines, coming from those caught in the deadly wake of the volley. Only a few missiles had found gaps in the shield wall, or sailed into the second or third ranks, but the grim toll of war had begun to mount.

Behind the archers and crossbowmen, the next wall of Avanorans was coming into full view, as they marched up behind the front line. The archers, meanwhile, had notched new arrows, readied, and loosed them again at the shield wall. Their barrage of arrows soared through the air in unison, like a dense flock of ravens bringing a pronouncement of death.

The Saxan line held strong once again, as the shields were tightly overlapped, and held firmly in place. Most of the shower of arrows buried into the planks of wooden shields, or embedded themselves harmlessly into trees or the ground.

A few more men cried out in pain after the second volley's impact, several clutching at feathered shafts as they fell over dead, or badly wounded.

Aethelstan could see that the crossbowmen were almost reloaded for their second shot, pulling the strings up with their arms, while keeping the end of the bow braced on the ground by an iron foot stirrup affixed to the weapon's end. The archers were nearly prepared for their third wave.

Aethelstan could not let them continue unabated, without incurring some cost. Waving his sword, he cried out for a Saxan volley, which set off a number of horn blasts in the lines along the ridge.

The scattered Saxan archers up and down the lines released their own wave of arrows, from the advantage of the higher ground. The height of the Saxan position also enabled a number of javelin throwers and stone slingers to hurl their own missiles forward.

Aethelstan watched the combined Saxan volley as it descended swiftly, stones, javelins, and arrows arcing towards the front rank of Avanorans. Several archers and crossbowmen fell to the ground, or to their knees, and whether wounded or dead they were removed from the fighting.

The enemy then released their own shafts and bolts, beginning a small pattern in which Aethelstan had a Saxan round loosed for every couple that the Avanorans sent towards the ridgeline. He did not want to run low on missiles when the main enemy thrust occurred. Perhaps there was even a chance that they could run the enemy low on arrows and bolts, without taking too many casualties in return.

"When will they come, Thane Aethelstan?" one of the younger members of his household guard asked him, after the two sides had traded a markedly uneven number of blows.

"Soon enough. The Avanorans are fierce in battle, and will soon test the shield wall," Aethelstan replied. He gave the young man a brief smile. "We will be able to fight them back with our full strength soon. Keep your axe at the ready."

The young soldier nervously returned the smile, and looked back out from behind his shield. The few rounds of missiles that the Saxans had levied had indeed weathered down the foremost line of Avanorans, bodies lying on the ground peppering the full length of their ranks.

As Aethelstan had predicted, the enemy did not wait overly long to challenge the shield wall. A braying chorus of horns sounded, and the following ranks surged forward at once. A wall of warriors engulfed the archers and crossbowmen, leaving them behind as the solid rank of infantry marched in long strides up the incline of the ridge. A thick mass of triangular shields and long spears crept steadily forward, approaching the shield wall.

Light glinted off iron helms and coats of mail. Aethelstan knew that these warriors were no lesser levies. They were heavy infantry, well-equipped with excellent weapons and armor. They were likely bolstered by dismounted knights, as Aethelstan could see a number of men with swords withdrawn, trudging up just behind the front line of spears.

"Get ready!" Aethelstan called out down the Saxan lines. "They come!"

A host of long spears were lowered along the shield wall, points facing down the slope, extending well beyond the overlapping shields.

"Fight for your lands! Fight for your families! Fight for your Faith!" Aethelstan shouted, as the Saxans braced behind the wall of spears and shields for the imminent clash.

"Out! Out!" thundered the Saxan ranks towards the invaders.

Just before the lines clashed, the deeper ranks of the Saxans released a thick hail of javelins, arrows, and sling-stones into the masses of oncoming Avanorans. Despite the heavy, tall shields, helms, and coats of mail, the missiles were coming at full force, from a much closer range. A number of advancing spearmen crumpled to the ground, some even tumbling backwards down the slope, and knocking still others awry.

The shield wall then met the impact of the oncoming Avanoran line, as a cacophonous din erupted throughout the wooded hills. The attackers were not limited to just spears, as the swordsmen and others bearing hand axes worked feverishly to puncture holes in the Saxan shield wall. Shields shattered, steel rang against steel, and men loosed cries of pain or fury. The deadly hiss of missiles continued to pass overhead, some heading down the hill and others passing up it.

At a few points along the Saxan line, wherever there was tight coordination between thanes and their household warriors, the men swinging the long-hafted war axes lashed out fiercely into the Avanoran ranks. The shield bearers by them protected their exposed sides, as the axe-wielders attacked with unimitigated furor. Even mail was of little use in stopping one of the broad axe blades, swung with such determined power. Like trees being felled, many enemy warriors were swiftly cut down wherever the axe-bearing household guards fought.

Aethelstan could not hold back for long himself. Sword raised, he dived into a couple of places where Avanoran knights appeared to be making inroads towards forcing a gap in the shield wall.

Wherever men in the front Saxan lines fell, the more inexperienced men of the levies patched up the gaps. With cruder weapons, some wielding nothing more than wooden clubs, and largely devoid of armor, the levy men presented a much easier opponent for the highly-skilled Avanoran knights. Once they moved into a breach, it did not take long for the knights to begin to hack a swathe through the Saxan defenders.

The ferociously swung war axes of Aethelstan's household guards and the heavy sword blades of the thanes quickly turned the momentum back in places where the enemy was making a little headway. Aethelstan gripped his shield tightly, swinging his sword in his right hand, as he found himself at the front of the line after driving a number of Avanoran spearmen and a few knights back from one gap.

Aethelstan's shield soon began to grow heavy, as it was embedded with the upper part of a lance, as well as a couple of arrows from below. He would soon be forced to discard it, if he could not take the time to cut the hafts off to tiny stumps, but he had little time to think as a number of spears, axes, and swords were bearing down on them again.

After two more arrows struck, the great Saxan thane was forced to discard the sorely riddled shield in back of the shield wall. He turned just in time to engage two mailed warriors, one a knight, and one a spearman. The Avanoran fighters had just broken through the shield wall, just to the left of him.

Rotating, he raised his sword with a passionate cry and advanced. Catching the spearman unawares, Aethelstan dropped him with a crashing blow to the side. He then traded two powerful strikes with the knight, sword to sword, before landing a clean slash to the neck that hewed the Avanoran down.

Whipping back to his right, he brought a heavy blow to bear on the mailed side of a third opponent, who was about to thrust a spear at him. The man had a look of utter shock on his face, as he collapsed to the ground in the wake of the crushing impact.

Without hesitation, Aethelstan turned the grip on his sword, and stabbed it straight downwards to finish the fallen warrior off. He instinctively grabbed the triangular shield of the dead man, clean of any shafts in its hide-covered surface.

Though different in design than the shields he was used to, with a wide, rounded top, narrowing sharply in convergence downward into a small, rounded lower end, the shield nonetheless provided him ample protection for the moment.

He used the Avanoran shield to deflect an oncoming sword strike, swiftly putting his weight forward and thrusting his own blade out, catching another knight of Avanor flush in the chest.

A gasping, desperate cry arose from next to him, as his eyes took in the sight of the young Saxan who had spoken to him just before the Avanoran infantry had pressed forward. The young man's eyes were already glazing over as he slumped to the ground. A short-hafted axe had been buried deep in his neck, and the attacker was stooping down to wrench it free.

With an enraged outcry, Aethelstan slew the young man's killer, bringing his strongest blow yet to bear on the man's own neck. The Avanoran did not free the axe, nor did he threaten any more Saxans, falling lifeless to the ground.

Another rumbling ran through the ground underfoot, but this time it was from a small, mounted group of Saxans that Aethelstan had cleverly placed behind a rise on the far end of the right flank. They were from Annenheim, cavalry men that had been spared for Aethelstan's use while most of their brethren had proceeded onward to the great muster at the Plains of Athelney.

With the battle fully enjoined, the riders had emerged and were now bearing down upon the enemy forces. There was no time for the enemy to erect a shield wall of their own.

The mass of horsemen curved back inward, falling upon the left flank of the enemy, thrusting spears, slashing swords, and vigorously swinging axes until their weapons were drenched in the blood of their enemies. The stallions they rode exacted a toll of their own amongst the enemy ranks, using their lashing hooves.

Aethelstan's men in the front lines, seeing the enemy's left flank folding, fought with renewed vigor. A loud roar emerged up and down the Saxan ranks as they hewed, stabbed, and thrust. In just a few moments, the battle was tilting back towards their favor.

A number of frenzied horn blasts again filled the air, the sound of which brought feverish commands from enemy officers spread throughout the forward ranks. The enemy forces, wherever they could disengage, fell back in a disorganized flurry. The temptation to pursue and attempt a route was very inviting. For a great many Saxans, it was impossible to resist, and they charged down the hill at the heels of the retreating enemy.

"Hold! Hold!" Aethelstan cried, and his commands were repeated up and down the ranks. Horn signals were sounded, holding the small group of cavalry and the bulk of his front lines from continuing their pursuit of the retreating enemy warriors.

Shooting a glance upwards, he could see the Harraks flying above. He knew that they possessed a full scope of the Saxan troop movements, and would help the enemy ground forces to engulf any pursuit. What might start as a rout of Avanor's forces could well end up in a decisive defeat of the Saxans. However tantalizing the situation appeared to be, it was not a risk that Aethelstan could afford.

Turning, he shouted, gesturing urgently back towards some men who blew out a series of horn signals a moment later. The Saxan forces, including most of those that had begun to pursue the Avanorans, tightened up, reforming into denser lines a little farther up from the base of the ridge. Well out of arrow range now, they reorganized to form another strong shield wall.

Aethelstan looked out to the battleground before him, down the slope and towards the stretch of land spreading beyond it. Dead and dying from both sides filled the ground. He steeled his gaze, peering out towards the enemy lines, which he could barely make out through the trees.

His ears were then filled with great shouts, thumps, and clinks of metal, as a huge wave of enemy cavalry rolled towards them. The enemy horse riders were followed by a rushing mass of armed warriors. The forms of a few monstrous creatures, bearing great war axes, could be seen interspersed within the enemy ranks. Had the men who were low on the ridge's slope continued in their pursuit, they would have been decimated.

"Hold the wall!" Aethelstan cried, his command echoed by some further Saxan horn bursts.

The enemy cavalry soon turned and raced alongside the front facing of the shield wall, hurling javelins upon them, even as a second rank of archers fired over the cavalry's heads to strike deeper into the Saxan forces. The shield wall was effective, holding strong through the thick exchange, and few new casualties were incurred. Many of the men jeered derisively from behind their round shields at the passing Avanoran cavalry.

As the cavalry pulled away, a replenished mass of troops followed, and the two sides clashed in hand to hand combat once again. Mailed warriors of Avanor were mixed with a large force of lightly armored spearmen, most bearing rounded shields, lances, leather jerkins, and leather caps.

Aethelstan withheld his small cavalry force, as the melee ensued in strength again. The giant beasts, where they lumbered up, were the worst elements of the second attack by far. Their powerful axes cleaved through mail or jerkin alike, although their clumsy movements often resulted in maimed or killed soldiers from their own side.

Archers, spear-throwers, and those with slings concentrated upon the immense targets, as the front line of the defenders rallied another stalwart defense, repelling the attackers' momentum again.

A couple of the towering, tusked creatures were soon dead, while the remaining ones roared defiantly, though they obeyed the Avanoran commands to retreat, along with the rest of the attackers. The shield wall was intact. The senior warriors, knowing Aethelstan's wishes, did not charge when the enemy offered a second, inviting pursuit.

A loud cry was generated among the Saxan forces, as they realized the success of their initial defenses. They shook their weapons at the retreating enemy ranks, taunting them. Those who had lost shields or weapons scrambled to grab replacements from the dead. Others pulled wounded comrades away from the front areas of the battle, along with those of the enemy that did not exhibit mortal wounds.

"At the least, the Avanorans know it will not be an easy fight," Aethelstan stated firmly to the squat, thick-chested warrior standing to his right.

"They have a fight on their hands, though we have fewer surprises to meet them with the next time," Cenferth, one of the guards of his own household, commented. His long, two-handed axe, helm, shield, and knee-length mail coat were spattered copiously in blood.

"We need to win more time, whatever the outcome may be. If this army gets through, they will fall upon an unprotected flank of Aelfric's army at the Entrance," Aethelstan replied.

"Then we must hold," Cenferth stated resolutely.

Aethelstan looked out towards the enemy, and saw that their full ranks, including all archers, crossbowmen, and infantry, had retreated well out of sight.

"It has suddenly grown very quiet out there. I wonder how long we have until their next attack?" Cenferth asked him, after a pause.

"They have tried two methods and failed," Aethelstan commented. "My thought is that their commander will take a moment to be cautious, and will ponder strategies for the next strike. Those from Avanor are not rash. They know, as we did not pursue their retreats, that we are not rash either. That will give them something to consider.

"I think we will have some time before they strike again. Even so, keep the form of the lines together and ready. If some food can be brought up to those in the lines, then have it done now. Have scouts out there immediately. If they attack again, it will be with little notice. We need every moment."

"I shall, my lord," Cenferth answered dutifully.

"Also, have our men strip the enemy of their mail shirts, helms and forged weapons, as well as from our own that have fallen. Try to retrieve as many swords as we can. Our levies could make use of them," Aethelstan ordered. The task was grim, but practical. "If we win this battle, know that I will give all warriors an honorable burial. But the living must take what can be used."

"Well spoken," Cenferth replied, nodding, and already turning to begin delegating the order.

SAXANY

Though the morning favored the eyes of the defenders, the sunlight cascading from behind them towards the western horizon, there was a perceptible heaviness in the air as the Saxan forces marched out and deployed into a massive, living wall.

There was no sense of the characteristic joviality of the Saxan people present out on the great plain. No riddles to be uttered, or songs to be sung, even the most spirited of the Saxans had a grave sense of the reality facing them on that fateful morning.

Many priests, a number of monks, and even some bishops moved among the men, praying solemnly and issuing a host of blessings over the thousands who had moved out to stare into the very face of destruction. Both the warriors and clergy alike knew that all across Saxany, within a multitude of monasteries, hosts of monks would be sending up heartfelt chants and hymns to the heavens on behalf of King Alcuin's gathered army.

All hoped desperately that the All-Father would look kindly upon them, as they defended their land against rapacious agressors.

Save for non-combatants, and a sparse few warriors that would keep watch, the vast, palisaded encampment that the Saxans had so diligently readied had been emptied out. A sprawling city of tents had been left all but vacant, their owners rallying and responding to the low, blaring tones of battle horns, and the loud shouts of thanes.

The merchants, who had been more than happy to interact with the Saxans up to that morning, had withdrawn far behind the encampment to the east. Some had already headed well away from the battlefield, content with the monies that they had already made.

The time for shield-sellers had passed, as the time for the use of shields had arrived.

Many more non-combatants, from older men, to women, to more priests, and even some children, were gathering themselves with grim determination behind the massing lines, setting their minds towards the gruesome tasks that lay just ahead. They were wary and alert, saying countless prayers on their nervous lips as they prepared to receive the wounded and dying that could be gathered during the battle, and brought back to be tended to.

Their own resolve was not entirely unlike that of the experienced warrior, as those who had seen war before knew that many terrible, nightmarish sights would fill their eyes before the day was over. Their efforts would meet with little reward, and mostly sorrow. A great many of the wounded would die; if not immediately, then from the diseases that gripped so many of the wounded in the aftermath of battle.

A small army of riding horses, which had borne forth the thanes and their household warriors, to various points along the vast line, had been returned to where they were quartered with a sprawling mass of packhorses, mules, and oxen.

Each minute that passed from the brink of dawn onward seemed to be an eternity. As the extensive forces filed out and deployed along the course of the battlefield, many thousands of eyes searched the horizon for any sign of the coming enemy. The invaders were definitely expected. Many brave scouts had died, but some had been able to bring word that all signs pointed to a full-scale attack that morning.

Not to be caught off guard in any way, the Saxan commanders had decided upon full deployment at morning's first light. Steel would be met with steel, arrayed in all the strength that the Saxans could gather.

The numerous contingents had formed up with good order, with large formations of cavalry gathering upon each far flank, and a thick shield wall spanning the greath length between them. As far as the eye could see up and down the ranks, running from north to south, the round shields with their central iron bosses were presented in overlapping fashion to the enemy as one continuous, adamant boundary.

Hosts of banners and pennons marked the places in Saxany where the various contingents of men had come from, fluttering defiantly in the calm before the looming storm.

The front ranks were filled with the most stalwart and skilled of the defenders, save for some that were being held back with Prince Aidan and his reserve force under the renowned Dragon Standard.

Great thanes, well-equipped ceorls, and many elite warriors, of the retinues of both thanes and counts alike, served to harden the shield wall. Their iron helms and the prevalent coats of mail amongst them reflected the pure light of the new day, glittering brightly. Swords and finely crafted spears, with shafts of quality ash, were held within the grips of their experienced hands.

Wherever the thanes' retinues could be found were the great axe-bearing household guards, perhaps the mightiest of the Saxan infantry arrayed upon the battlefield. A large number of men were deployed to bear the long, rounded-top, triangular shields to protect the axe-wielding household warriors. They were well-trained to work in close unison with the axe-fighters, providing defense while the household warriors unleashed fearsome, two-handed strikes with their great war axes.

Deep ranks of levies massed behind the front shield rank, summoned from all parts of the Saxan kingdom. Some were just above being children, most were of true fighting age, and a good number of the remainder were older men well past their prime. Most of them had traveled farther than they had ever been before in their lives, most determined to meet the enemy threat despite the terrible fears residing within them.

Few of the iron helms so visible in the first line of the shield wall were present in this secondary mass, as most of those in the levies wore wool caps or headgear of hardened leather. Likewise, they wore their own woolen tunics on the outside, in the place of the mail-coats worn by the thanes, retainers, and household guards in the forefront. A very few of their number had old mail shirts, mostly multi-generational family inheritances, and nearly every one of those was in need of repair.

A large number of men in the back ranks carried spears, but many were armed with a wide assortment of weapons. Some wielded makeshift war clubs made of stones lashed to shafts by leather thongs. Even the common tools of the farm were now being utilized as implements of war. Instead of well-crafted and maintained swords, axes, and lances, they wielded picks, scythes, hand axes, and other such farm tools. They were nonetheless lethal enough, when used in such a manner. Slings, javelins, and crude wooden clubs rounded out much of the rest of the weaponry.

There were a number of wooden shields in evidence amongst the secondary ranks. A few very fortunate men sprinkled amongst the General Fyrd ranks did possess some better weapons such as swords, whether ancient family heirlooms, or obtained by rare gift or act of trade. Broad, single-edged knives, called seaxes, some with lengths nearing that of a sword, could also be espied among the levy forces.

A good number of the levy men bore bows, with most archers of the Saxan army deriving from its poorer ranks. The bowmen were widespread amid the massed levy formations. Skills honed by years of hunting in the extensive forests of Saxany, their lack of wealth was no impediment to their deadly aim and ability with their bows. Out of all the secondary ranks, these were by far the most valuable fighters for the early stages of the impending battle.

Though possessing little land, and without the best of arms, the General Fyrd's offered participation, and risk incurred, was no less than any warrior of the household guards, or any province lord standing in the foremost ranks.

At the far flanks, the cavalry had gathered in strength, in preparation for the coming fight. Most of the mounted force was gathered from the horse-abundant southeastern provinces of the Kingdom, which were also home to storied reputations of horsemanship.

Count Leidrad of Poitaine's mounted ranks were clustered primarily on the left flank, with Count Gerard II of Bretica's force serving to anchor the right. Count Einhard of Annenheim's contingent, many of which were more lightly armed than the heavier cavalry of Leidrad and Gerard II, were being held back in reserve, near to the great Dragon Standard of the Saxan kingdom.

On both flanks, the numerous, sturdy horses neighed and snorted, as their riders gave them pats, speaking gentle words to ease their agitation.

Of the Saxans' own force of sky steeds, there was as yet no sign in the sky, save for a few solitary scouts shadowing the assembling Saxan force.

There had never been such an enormous, diverse gathering of force in the history of the realm, before or after the union of the Northern and Southern kingdoms. Whether it would be enough to counter the strength of the enemy that was coming remained to be seen.

As morning advanced, the horizon continued to remain clear, save for the distant, drifting forms of enemy air scouts. While the Saxans did not expect the enemy to go into battle with the sun directly in their eyes, they did expect the enemy to array themselves early in the day.

As the main force of Saxans settled into their positions, a daunting stillness hung thickly in the air. The clink of armor, horses whinnying, and the murmur of voices, as men prayed or encouraged one another, created a tense backdrop against the oppressive silence looming over the western horizon.

The minutes continued to crawl by, laboriously slowly, while tensions and anxieties mounted.

THE ANDAMOORANS

A steady tremor reverberated through the ground, rhythmic and foreboding, as a haze began to rise and take form in the distance to the west. Saxan eyes were immediately riveted towards the stark line of the horizon, many tightly gripping their weapons, as they waited for the inevitable presence of the force causing the ground itself to shake.

The noise and tremors swelled into a steady, building rumble, as the steps of teeming thousands of horses and men combined with the thunder erupting from great numbers of booming, sonorous war drums.

Facing the Saxan right flank, and serving as the left flank of the attacking force, was an Andamooran force of such prodigious strength that it could have served alone as the invasion force. A host of vibrant banners, red, green, white and black, billowed in the air as the Andamooran juggernaut crested the edge of the horizon. The massive ranks emerged into full view, marching resolutely towards the Saxan lines in a cohesive order.

The Andamoorans had departed their native lands amid the

splendor of great flag ceremonies, and the majestic nature of their appearance was no accident. The sea of colored banners were made of luxuriant fabrics, displaying geometric patterns and inscriptions worked into them with golden thread, taken directly from the Prophet's Sacred Revelation. The elegant standards billowed proudly from their high perches at the end of long poles and lances.

The Andamooran force reflected the diversity of its many territories and heritages, stretching from the western-most parts of the Sunlands, areas that included the sacred city of Marracca, to the wealthy territories occupying nearly half of Eberias' lands.

In Eberias, Andamooran territory included bountiful lands, boasting of opulent palaces and elegant, walled cities. Lush and fertile river valleys alternated with broad, open plains, and mountainous terrain, bestowing lands that were quite varied and conducive to new farming techniques, crops, and irrigation methods brought in from the Sunlands.

Over in the Sunlands themselves, the territories held by Andamoor expanded from mountain ranges rising across the strait from Eberias to drier climes of desert and shrubland.

Andamoor was truly an expansive realm, one that possessed elements from a wide range of origins. Eberian foundations in an older Empire, and later in the Western Church, had long ago given way to successive waves of conquerors from the Sunlands. Those conquerors, while all adhering steadfastly to the revelations of the Prophet, were diverse themselves. They ranged from earlier rulers that had enabled art and learning to flourish, to the latest, dominant wave, which was as strict and austere as the arid climates that they had crossed over from.

The warriors assembled within the massive invasion force reflected styles and influences derived from all the areas of Andamoor, both from Eberias and the lands facing it across the ocean waters to the north. It was from across those waters that the latest ruling class of Andamoor had manifested, to subdue the fragmented kingdoms that had come dangerously close to being reconquered by the despised infidel kings located in the south of Eberias. A strict, fundamentalist flame burned strongly within this latest influx of followers of the Prophet.

Advancing in the foremost rank of the oncoming Andamooran tide were dedicated, fanatical warriors, who originally hailed from the lands of the latest ruling class of Andamoor. Their faces and heads were covered by the revered, distinctive litham veil-turban, which was wrapped in such a manner that only the wearer's eyes were exposed. Despite having most of their faces covered by the dark cloth, there was no mistaking the measured gazes that lanced forth from their iron-hard eyes.

Their focused, disciplined motivations were further reflected in the simplicity of their dress, as they were clothed in long tunics, trousers, and the hooded robe-cloaks known as burnus.

The veiled spearmen clutched a unique kind of tall, rectangular-shaped shields, which were composed of several layers of toughened antelope hide. They carried a nearly uniform compliment of weapons, from long lances made of bamboo, to throwing javelins, as well as sharp daggers for close-quarters fighting.

Behind the veiled spearmen were deep contingents of infantry, bearing an array of vivid banners representing their various regional units. They exhibited a wide variety of armor and helms, the former including quilted styles, coats of mail, and scale armors, and the latter ranging from simple conical designs to more elaborate ones, with downward extensions from the brow that held horizontal plates at their ends to protect mouth and chin. Their shields were different than those of the veiled spearmen, as they were a mixture of round shields, oval shields, and another, quite distinctive kind, with wide, twin lobes along their top widths. A majority of the shields featured a few distinctive, downward-hanging tassels affixed to their front facings.

All of the infantry were formed into a broad, dense front, with lines extending straight back from the ends of each flank, so as to form a giant, moving square.

The litham-wearing spearmen with the tall shields in the outermost ranks lent a great functionality to the formation. The warriors with their elongated, bamboo spears enabled the vast phalanx to present a thicket of lances, and a barrier of high shields, to attacks coming from any direction.

A host of archers were drawn up behind the broad, frontline elements, armed with the angular, composite bows that were very popular with the Andamoorans. Protected by little more than small, leather round shields, wearing a type of cotton quilted armor, and bearing only long, single-edged daggers for close-quarters combat, the archers were dependent upon the other infantry to keep enemy fighters from reaching them.

A modest force of crossbowmen, whose primary weapon was

a simple manner of crossbow, one that was both unique in form and common to Andamoor, accompanied the archers, mixed amongst them in small units. They were more properly outfitted to fight as infantry if the need arose, equipped with mail and shield, and bearing swords at their sides. Rudimentary white turban-cloths were wound around their heads.

A great number of lightly-equipped men massed close behind the archers and crossbowmen, filling up a good portion of the greater square formation. Very few had any type of body armor, and only a very small fraction of their number even carried shields. Armed with a mixed assortment of weapons, some crude, others of low quality, and only a few of a good make, they were the least equipped element among the Andamooran ranks; the religious, zealous volunteers that had chosen to serve in the armies of Andamoor.

Though from markedly more humble origins than most others within the broader force, they were filled with a fiery motivation, fueled by their deep faith in the Prophet's Revelations. What they lacked in arms and armor they compensated for in fierce determination. For them, this was not a war of worldly affairs, but rather a holy war.

The very center of the massive square was filled with a great multitude of cavalry, also divided into separate units represented individually by their own unique banners.

Some were heavily armed warriors, whose family legacies connected directly to the former, more opulent rulers of Andamoor, before fragmentation and disunion had invited waves of fundamentalist warriors across the northern seas, to roll back the threats of the southern Eberian kingdoms that embraced the faith of the Western Church. With white turbans wound around their iron helms, and mail hauberks covered in a type of quilted, padded armor, they gripped tall lances made of hard wood, evidencing the manner of heavy, shock tactics that they were well capable of fighting with. Many lances held aloft battle flags and banners that were intricately inscribed with their bright golden weaves, often complimenting the sacred inscriptions worn on colored bands visible on the riders' upper arms.

In these cavalrymen's appearances were the echoes of the lavishness woven into their palaces, rich gardens, and grand centers of worship across the former Eberian territory now firmly ruled by Andamoor. Even their horses exhibited a magnificently attired harness, complete with numerous, shining bronze buckles and medallions strung along its length.

Other cavalry were attired very similarly to the veiled spearmen, wearing the litham veil-turbans, and carrying hide shields and bamboo lances, to go along with their straight swords and tapering daggers. Some of these wore a type of armor constructed of sheets of felt, with colored sashes wound around their waists, with others clad in simple, blanket-like garments, wrapped around their long tunics and cotton trousers.

A third throng of cavalry bore elongated lances with hafts of bamboo, as well as long maces and swords. Quilted, padded armor, or jubbahs, protected their bodies, and a similar fashion of soft armor was used on their horses as well. They wore their turbans in a different fashion from the fundamentalist elite, with a length of cloth hanging down in front.

The main cavalry forces were rounded out by a fourth group, a few hundred in number, who were singularly unusual amongst all of the rest. Their mounts were a very sturdy breed of steppe pony, creatures imbued with considerable stamina, as well as a particularly advantageous ability to endure periods of minimal sustenance that would rapidly debilitate larger breeds of warhorses. The stalwart horses' tails were tied in knots, with a leather collar ornamented with pierced bronze medallions, from which dangled a horsehair neck tassel in a bronze holder.

The warriors astride the ponies carried smoothly recurved composite bows, kept in bowcases hanging off their belts at their side. They also bore maces, single-edged sabers, and small round shields that hung from long guige straps about the neck. The riders were positioned farther forward on their mounts than most cavalrymen, utilizing shorter stirrups to situate themselves at the horse's shoulders, as opposed to the backs of the animals.

Simple iron helms were hidden beneath silk and felt coverings, with an upturned leather plate at the front, and the brim lined with fur. The riders' hair hung long down their backs in braided fashions. They wore cuirasses of a lamellar construct that was, in turn, laced into a jacket of felt placed over their colored tunics, and had high, soft leather boots encasing their lower legs and feet.

Riding upon camels and mules, in a condensed disposition near the center and rear of the broad ranks, were a large corps of drummers. The drums themselves were made of stretched hide, spanning various sizes of green and gold cases. The smaller drums were double-ended, sitting horizontal in front of the mounted drummers in such a manner that they could strike them at each end.

Others were enormous constructs, several yards in circumference, which resounded with deep, resonant booms upon being hit. The drummers were dark-skinned men, whose facial features were hidden behind the wrappings of their litham veil-turbans. They kept a tight formation, executing a deep, rhythmic cadence, as the huge ranks of the Andamoorans steadily marched across the plain and toward the field of battle.

Close to the rear of the Andamooran ranks was Abu Yaqub Battuta himself, the exalted, powerful Emir of Andamoor. He was second only in influence to the Great Emir of the Faithful, Yusuf Ibn Tumart, and rode upon a magnificent white stallion. His standard, a particularly ornate, red banner, carried high next to him by a dedicated bearer.

His elite bodyguard, a force that was five hundred strong, and which carried a most fearsome reputation, surrounded him. These ebony-skinned warriors from the Sunlands wore sleeveless padded armor over their mail, sittiing astride exquisite mounts.

Strangest of all to Saxan eyes that day were the mounts of a huge number of warriors, many of the litham-wearing variety, who came to fight not as cavalry, but as infantry. Held in reserve, the warriors sat upon the hump-backed forms of camels, animals utterly foreign to the Saxans, and quite bizarre to their eyes.

As the Saxan defenders looked on, several openings suddenly formed in the wall of spearmen, at the forefront of the square Andamooran formation.

The singular group of horsemen riding the steppe ponies, bearing the curved, composite bows, emerged into the open before the massive Andamooran force. Their mounts moved with a grace that evidenced considerable swiftness and dexterity, breaking into a fluid stream that surged towards the Saxan lines along their right flank.

"The bells of your churches will be the lamps that light our temples!" cried a fierce-looking horse archer, riding at the lead of the forward-most element of the galloping horsemen.

Though the Saxans could not understand the horseman's foreign tongue, the threat was far from being an undocumented, unknown practice on the part of the Andamoorans. Many who had fought in the long wars between the followers of the Prophet and the followers of Emmanu in Eberia had experienced it fully, in the ebb and flow of churches and temples caught amidst the fierce struggles of that contested land. Church bells that once tolled for the faithful of Emmanu had often ended up as war mementos, converted into lamps in the Temples of the Prophet, which were themselves often constructed right on the sites of the conquered churches.

Nonetheless, the Saxan warriors could recognize the words as being a taunting boast. The mocking horseman, and those following him, remained just out of Saxan bowshot, though some of the angrier men of the levy just behind the shield wall loosed some futile arrows at the haughty leader, before enduring the stern reprimands of nearby thanes or ceorls.

Those Saxans familiar with horses marveled at the unison of motion that seemed to blend rider and steed, as the small force of enemy horse-archers streamed down the length of their lines. The horse-archers readied their bows as they reached the area that marked the end of the front line of Andamooran spearmen. They curled about in a tight arc, and returned back down the Saxan lines.

On the second pass, they notched their arrows, drawing the bowstrings with well-practiced smoothness, and then letting them fly from the saddles of their racing steeds.

With the arrows flying towards the Saxans, the battle on the Plains of Athelney was underway.

THE EHRENGARDIANS

A land of legend, mist, and mountain, rich in ancient forests, and graced with majestic, castle-studded rivers, Ehrengard was the heart of the Sacred Empire.

Called upon by the authority of the Sacred Emperor, the heralded land had poured forth its might in the service of the Unifier, forging it into the massive right flank of the three principle formations facing the Saxan defenders.

A fiery people, whose hardiness echoed the rock of the great mountains that rose proudly within their lands, their storied heritage went far before them onto any battlefield in Ave.

At their roots, they were a people that had tamed a dangerous wilderness. As older tribes had grown into kingdoms, they had demonstrated a courage and resilience that few lands could rival. As the Sacred Empire coalesced, and stability broadened, an aptitude had been shown for trade, learning, politics, and spiritual matters.

A burgeoning populace, thriving within prosperous trade leagues and urban communes, continually expanded the successes and influence of the Sacred Empire.

The prosperity also translated into force of arms. The lords of Ehrengard, its margraves, counts, dukes, abbots, and bishops, commanded knightly retinues significantly more numerous in scale than those of Gallea, or even Norengal.

The Sacred Empire spanned a great number of territories, including a number of powerful duchies, the kingdom of Boehman, a number of cities in the north of Lombar, and even the Kingdom of Paleria. The Sacred Empire had long possessed a formidable level of power, one that had often unnerved the Great Vicars in Liantenum.

Yet even in spite of the enormous strength available in the Sacred Empire, the mustering of a great military force was not always a certainty in the course of any war. The dukes and lords of Ehrengard often held to their own designs over that of the emperor.

Serving as Electors for new emperors, they tended to assert themselves much more independently than did the lords of other kingdoms. The climate was constantly changing in the Sacred Empire's power centers, as the authority of the emperor versus that of the various princes and dukes shifted back and forth.

A few Sacred Emperors had enjoyed a near unity of authority, while others struggled to the point of outright civil wars to maintain a semblance of preeminence. As such, Ehrengard had never reached the kind of power that a contiguous unity might have brought to it, perhaps even reaching a level that could have rivaled Avanor itself.

The banners of Duke Manfred of Sachia, displaying two blue axe heads facing outward on a red background, and the ensigns of the powerful Archbishop Rainald of Maizen, were quickly recognized by several of the Saxan leaders on the opposing side of the battlefield. The sight dashed any slim hopes that some Saxans still held concerning the ebb and flow of intentions, loyalties, and acquiescence of the tumultuous

Ehrengardian nobility with respect to the emperor.

Manfred's family line, the Uelf, had long fostered coalitions that frustrated the plans of the current imperial family, the Staffes, which was now manifested in the person of the current emperor, Heinrich VIII. Archbishop Rainald himself, in his younger days, had lent great ecclesiastical authority to the powers countering the emperor, nearly having toppled the Staffes line in the process.

Ominously for the Saxans, their proudly waving banners and ensigns were now seen within the same host that included the presence of powers more traditionally loyal to the Staffes line. These included the Duke of Schueva, the Margrave of Holsheim, the Duke of Thurgian, the Bishop Thangbrand of Augenberg, and the King of Boehm.

Seen all together, the sight sent an unmistakable, daunting message to the Saxans who were more astute about Ehrengard's power structures. The enormous force represented an Ehrengard that was standing in full strength behind Heinrich VIII, whose designs toward Saxany were now conjoined to those of the Unifier.

The center and left portions of Ehrengard's host were teeming with several thousand spearmen, mixed in with several contingents of archers and crossbowmen. Equipped simply, with just conical helms and long shields, their short cloaks billowed and whipped about, caught in the morning's alternating breezes and gusts as they tramped solidly towards the Saxan lines.

A number of banners marked the origins of many of the units, and it could be discerned that the Duchies of Baraban, Thurgian, Sachia, and the Margraviate of Holsheim had provided a great portion of the foot soldiers within the Ehrengardian forces.

The concentrated units of archers amongst them were easy to identify, as they were wearing distinctive, kettle-shaped helms. With a little scrutiny, the positions of the crossbowmen could also be ascertained, as they strode forward carrying their heavy weapons in both hands, telltale hooks hanging down from their belts for reloading the weapons.

The right side of the host of Ehrengard, where the striking part of an Ehrengardian force was often deployed, was the area that attracted the most attention and dread from the watching Saxan defenders.

A deadly forest of elongated spears seemed to crawl across the grassland, covering it like a dark tide sweeping menacingly towards the Saxan ranks. In the midst of this huge formation flew ebon banners, and within each was woven the image of a single, red blade. Many thousands marched proudly and boldly under the black and red ensigns, at the forefront of the right flank of the hosts of Ehrengard.

These were the Halmlander, greatly feared and despised far beyond the lands of the Sacred Empire.

Though nominally from the lands of the Duchy of Baraban, the Halmlander were a storied mercenary company, whose skill was more than equal to the high cost that it took to bring them into a war. Many infamous mercenary captains had led their great companies, serving under many kings over the years.

The legendary exploits of Mercad, serving a Norengal monarch, and Adoc, for a Gallean king, were two such examples. Now, a grizzled, brutal man named Gerhoch had come at the behest, and generous pay, of the Sacred Emperor, bringing his foreboding, ravenous horde along with him.

Overflowing in ferocity, and maintaining discipline in battle, the Halmlander's mere presence had been enough to scatter more than one significant enemy force. Those that they fought knew fully well the dire consequences to villages and towns should the defenders fail to stop them. Even so, many forces had willfully chosen not to oppose the living plague, while knowing that the malignant horde would ravage their lands nonetheless.

Without ties to homes of their own, the Halmlander gave great advantage to those who sought their services. Unlike regular levies, and those contingents under feudal obligations, the Halmlander could be kept for overly extended periods in the field, as long as wages were paid when promised. Their home was wherever they were, and a king who had coffers full enough could depend on the Halmlander from the start to the finish of an entire campaign.

The mercenaries were men who had fled from the law, fortune seekers, heretical clergymen, disloyal knights, and other rootless men who found a haven in concentrating together as one force. Together, all past histories no longer mattered, and they could enthusiastically indulge in bloodlust and rapaciousness.

They were men that needed to be constantly employed in a state of war. If they were not being used, they often turned upon the very populaces that they dwelled amongst.

The history of Gallea, Norengal, Ehrengardian principalities, and many other lands could testify to the horror of the ravenous appetites for blood and violence that the Halmlander possessed. Such was the menace, and chilling deadliness, of the Halmlander.

Bearing their long lances, the foot-soldiers of the Halmlander were spurred forward by the few rogue knights that helped to command their great company. The seemingly innumerable shafts with their deadly points served to create a dense hedge of protection for the force of mounted knights that was coming up just behind them.

The knights comprising the force located in back of the Halmlander, on the farthest right of the Ehrengardian force, were truly among the most prime warriors in all of Ehrengard.

The symbols of the Duke of Schueva, from which the imperial Staffes family line had come, the Duke Leopold of Aestrius, and the Duke of Baraban, from whose lands the Halmlander themselves had been hired, were visible on the shields, surcoats, and pennons amongst the great knights.

Imperial banners, showing a great, black dragon, with wings outstretched wide, set against a field of gold, flew from the contingents from Schueva, as their widely renowned Duke possessed the unique honor to display the imperial ensigns.

There was a sense of elegance to the attire of these greater knights. A good number of their helms were fashioned with an aesthetic fluting, whose graceful contours beautified a design that carried great practicality, resulting in perhaps the strongest helms found in any realm. Others wore helms with full iron visors affixed to the brow, protecting their entire faces. A few still wore older, conical designs, which had little more than a nasal guard extending down for facial protection.

Over their mail coats, several knights wore finely fashioned surcoats, complete with "V" shaped necks, and drooping, pendant sleeves. Exquisitely crafted swords rested in gilded sheaths, tied into belts whose ends were split into slits, and then knotted together in a fashion common across the lands of Ehrengard.

Their shields were largely of the variety prevalent among Ehrengard's knights. Broad in width, with the two top ends rounded and extending downward, they narrowed gradually into a narrow, curved bottom that evoked a shorter, wider rendition of the elongated kite-shields carried by so many of the foot soldiers.

Even their robust war stallions carried an elite aura about them, many being covered in quilted trappers, richly colored to match the colors on their riders' shields and surcoats.

The majestic appearance of knights was not limited just to those in the rear on the right side of the line, but were spread among the other mounted elite of Ehrengard that followed the masses of infantry in the center and left.

The imperial dragons flying in the center of the formation heralded the presence of Heinrich VIII's most powerful Oath Knight, Markward of Augenberg. The powerful, proud form of the great knight sat astride a regal war steed, covered in a spectacular trapper, fashioned entirely of glinting chain mail.

Markward wore a fully encompassing great helm, surrounding his face and all parts of his head with iron, a new style of helm that had just started to be crafted and used. He was surrounded by a host of lower-ranking Oath Knights, all of whom were bonded to Emperor Heinrich.

Not far from Markward, was the Archbishop Anno of Colgonach, one of the Empire's greatest ecclesiastical princes. Like Markward, he was also mounted on a great warhorse that was clad in a full mail trapper.

A distinctive type of leather mitre-cap, with two vertical extensions, curving gradually to rounding summits, one rising in the front and one at the rear of the mitre-cap, crowned his iron great helm. The mitre-cap was snow-white, with curling red patterns interwoven on it. The two facings in the front and rear were curved slightly outward on the edges of the great helm, forming an open space between the two extensions.

The cap was held in place by a circular base that wrapped tightly around the top of the helm, with a white cloth mantling hanging down in the rear, covering the back of the great helm.

The Archbishop was a vision very different from that of a humble rural clergyman or monk, the latter two striving to distance themselves from the temporal world. His tall stature was covered from head to foot in a finely fashioned suit of mail, surmounted by a blood-red, sleeveless surcoat that was split up to the waist in the front and back.

He carried a mace with flanged head that was not intended for any act of faith. One would have presumed that the mace, in a great stretch of the proper intentions, addressed the commonly held belief that the clergy of the Creator should not shed blood. Such a notion was imminently refuted by the presence of a prominent sword, fit with an ornate pommel, resting in a finely-crafted, silver gilt scabbard hanging outside his surcoat at his waist.

Like many of the martial bishops and archbishops of Ehrengard, Archbishop Anno had brought a mighty contingent with him, and would not hesitate to lead them into the thick of the fighting.

Though a few drops of water could do little to alleviate a parched desert of dismay, the notable absence of black spear blades on white backgrounds amid the Ehrengardian host was a welcome recognition among the Saxan leaders.

The Order of the Sacred Lady, whose fierce monk-knights bore forth the legendary, black spear blade ensigns during their countless struggles, had evidently not deemed the Saxans to be apostate foes of the Western Church.

It was an exceptional absence in light of the great force arrayed against the Saxans, as the Order's high masters had gained the status of Imperial Princes during the reign of Gerard III, the grandfather of the current Emperor, Heinrich VIII.

With the apparent cohesion among the great princely and ecclesiastical powers of Ehrengard, the addition of the Order of the Sacred Lady to the force would have been nearly too much to bear for a defending army whose apprehensions were already being pushed to their outermost limits.

THE AVANORANS

A host of blaring horns heralded the coming of Avanor's force in the heart of the three primary forces, scant moments before they surmounted the horizon. Their line of pennons and gonfalons proudly rose up and spanned the edge where the world touched the sky.

They faced the middle of the Saxan line, connecting the army of Ehrengardians on the Avanoran's right flank to the massive force from Andamoor on their left. A continuous wall of lethal intent now confronted the Saxan ranks.

A solid line of foot soldiers advanced at the forefront, well equipped with long triangular shields, solid lances, and conical helms, and an ample portion of them wore coats of mail. They were no mere peasant rabble, but rather professional soldiers, filling feudal obligations and receiving steady pay in return.

Marching just behind the line of spearmen were sizeable numbers of archers and crossbowmen. Mostly without armor, and armed with little else save a dagger, they shielded themselves for the moment behind the ranks of heavy infantry, at least until the need for their deadly missiles was required.

An unrelenting rumble filled the air, as another mass of warriors then came into view, causing many Saxan observers to feel their breath catch in their throats. Rank upon rank of heavy cavalry followed closely behind the front lines of Avanoran foot soldiers, archers, and crossbowmen.

This new formation held the most feared element of the Avanoran force, and perhaps the most formidable amongst all of the forces gathered upon the battlefield.

The middle and rear ranks of the cavalry formation were filled with a thick mass of stout warriors, comprised primarily of mounted sergeants and squires. Many dedicated contingents of sergeants had come from ecclesiastical lands, equipped and supplied under the order of bishops or abbots, to fulfill the clergymen's feudal obligations to Avanor, as any lord would be required. The greater part of the sergeants were hardy, experienced warriors, armed capably with cavalry maces, lances, swords, and shields. Yet as tough fighters as they were, the sergeants were not the ones that elicited an instant dread at their mere presence on the battlefield.

The squires were also fiercely dedicated men, some on their way to becoming knights, and others fully content to serve as squires. Whatever path their future held, every squire assiduously attended to the needs of his master.

Beyond attending to equipment and war horses, they formed foraging parties in hostile lands, and conducted wood gathering forays. Many had received considerable training in the arts of war, so that when they stood on a battlefield, they were staunch opponents in their own right, if they were made to engage the enemy.

Their purpose during a battle was dual in nature, for as much as they could fight, they kept up a close watch on the masters they served, bringing spare horses to knights whenever their steeds were injured or killed under them. Such was the deadly duty that required much courage to execute, and a mass of squires was a force not to be underestimated, imbued with great bravery and solid, martial skill. Still, like the sergeants, they also evoked little outright fear within experienced, defending ranks.

The ones feared were those whom the squires served, and the sergeants rode behind, the warriors whose lofty status soared far above even the best of fighters among the latter. These men were located right at the front of the mass of heavy cavalry, positioned there for all opponents to see without obstruction.

The great knights in the cavalry formation rode upon mighty war stallions. The elite steeds were given diligent care, resulting in coats exhibiting a rich sheen, one that effectively displayed the sculpted contours of their impressive musculatures. Never before had there been such a concentrated, luxurious display of well-bred destriers, such as the mustering of Avanoran war horses upon the battlefield that day.

Carefully cultivated from stock once brought from Andamoor, which itself reached back to bloodlines originating from the Sunlands, the Avanoran breed of war horses were exceptional creatures. Compared to any mount within the Saxan ranks, even among the absolute best of the defender's cavalry, the Avanoran warhorses had noticeably longer backs, thicker hindquarters, and substantially greater body mass and height. They even had longer manes, now flowing free and unbraided after their journey by sea.

The vaunted human bloodline of Avanor was represented in its most elite, potent incarnation in the knights astride the magnificent steeds. Men of prowess, they hailed from a land that had spawned a great many conquerors and renowned warriors, ranging from Norengal to Paleria, and even extending to the coastal kingdoms in the Sunlands.

They bore their lances high, the pennons signifying the positions of smaller units, called conrois, that had trained, lived, and fought together until they could flow as if one body upon a battlefield.

Saxans who knew of the Avanoran methods of war, and had knowledge of the accounts of their battles, knew the grave danger inherent in those upright lances when in the hands of such skilled warriors. Leveled, with shaft gripped just under the arm's pit, and carried forward at a force ranging from a brisk canter to full charge, there was little to nothing that could withstand such an assault, if ever the Saxan shield wall was broken.

Some of the knights held authority over strong counties, others presided over a single castle, and many served in simplicity as household knights for their lords, but all were of a storied, proud brotherhood of arms. A great many were knights that had honed and exhibited their skills at the great tournament melees held within Gallea, many gaining considerable fame for their proficiency at arms. Most were knights who had already seen, and excelled in, the face of war, and had thoroughly bloodied both sword and lance.

All of the knights, whether a higher lord or household knight, whether possessing fame garnered from war or tournaments, or just newly ordained into knighthood on the eve of battle, were Avanoran. The legacy of that mythic heritage flowed amongst, around, and before them onto any battlefield, Athelney being no exception.

It was an energy and sense of threat that was felt by friend and foe alike, from the Ehrengardians to their right, to the Andamooran's on their left, and to the Saxan lines that they were marching towards.

WULFSTAN

Wulftsan stood in position towards the front of the shield wall, able to gain a clear sight of the colossal storm approaching. The thunder of drums boomed, as he felt the ground rattling beneath the leather soles of his shoes. He looked to his left and right, and could see the trepidation displayed on the faces all around him.

Just ahead of him, Saxan thanes, ceorls, and other strong warriors held their shields firmly in place. Despite their stoic, hardened postures, Wulfstan knew that they struggled with their nerves at the terrible sight of immense forces pouring over the horizon and shaking the ground, surging towards them with murderous intent.

"We are the wall! If they do not break this wall, all of that means nothing! Keep your hearts strong!" Wulfstan cried out to the men around him, most of whom were from the villages and burhs of his home territory. He could have identified nearly every one of them. "Cenwald, you hold strong, too!"

Standing close to him, and clearly looking frightened, Cenwald glanced quickly towards Wulfstan and nodded.

"All of you, if the enemy has come with an intent from hell, then give them a taste of the hell that drives them!" Wulfstan called out to his comrades.

His bold words caused a large number of men around him to erupt with raucous cries, even as the ground continued to vibrate from the tread of the oncoming forces.

Wulfstan gripped the leather-wrapped hilt of his old sword tightly, and raised his round shield up a little higher. He clenched the narrow iron bar that spanned the inside of the raised shield boss.

Turning his head, and looking back, he saw that Father Dunstan was standing with the levy men towards the rear of the ranks, even though he did not bear a weapon himself. The mere sight of the loyal priest slowed Wulfstan's anxious heart down a couple of beats. The old priest was making the spear-shaped gesture over the men around him, and would continue to give out his blessing when enemy arrows began to fall amongst them; and Wulfstan knew even that would not stop the old priest.

Such a perilous moment, of sharp iron rain, would not be long in coming. The enemy battle ranks were drawing ever nearer, such that Wulfstan could vividly see the lines of shrouded heads behind the strange, tall shields that the enemy fighters bore along with them. The resonance of the pounding war drums engulfed the Saxans, the booming, pulsating beats eliciting further nervousness from many within the Saxan ranks.

Behind the approaching line of shields, it looked like an ocean of men was flowing in their wake. Were it not for the circumstances, Wulfstan might even have found something aesthetic about the sights arrayed upon the plains before him. There were great numbers of colorful, bright battle flags and banners held aloft within the enemy ranks.

He halfway imagined that if he could get up into the sky, perhaps on one of the Saxan sky steeds, a sight echoing one from the natural world would greet him. The grand effect of the massive enemy army would probably have looked like a menacing storm, sweeping across open plains, blotting out a clear sky.

The only difference would be that he would look down upon it, rather than up at it.

The sky steeds were said to feel like horses in some ways. Wulfstan believed that he could remain strong during the sensation of flight. A tinge of regret cut through his adrenalized nerves; if only there was the time to explore his strange, repeating dream.

A bitter chuckle threatened to break his expression, as at the brink of an immense battle his thoughts of recurring dreams were still at the very forefront of his mind.

Girding himself, he fixed his stare on the foremost enemy ranks, right as they drew to a halt just a short distance before the Saxan lines.

FRAMORG

The air was crackling with martial energy, and a soaring euphoria erupted within Framorg as he lifted his great longblade high above him. The weapon's newly-honed edge gleamed in the bright light of the new day, as yet unstained by the blood of enemies.

A deafening roar broke out from the assembled Trogen ranks before him, mounted proudly upon their well-rested, saddled sky steeds. Their eyes burned with the fires surging within each of them, and every single warrior looked ready to take the measure of himself in the ages-old test of combat.

"The hour is now! We fight this day to free our lands! We do this for all of our Clans! We do this for all time!" Framorg thundered, feeling the swell of anticipation emitting from the Trogen warriors. They could be held back no longer. The time for battle was upon them all. "My brothers, take to the skies!"

With a flurry of spreading wings, the massive force of riders surged forward upon their Harraks. The front ranks bounded ahead, and lifted off the ground, followed a few moments later by the second line, and then the next. One rank after another, the Trogens flowed in an orderly manner off the open grounds leading away from the eastern edge of the encampment, where they had concentrated earlier that morning.

It was as if a broad, elongated cloud was wafting up from the ground, as never before had so many Trogen sky riders set off in one, extended formation, into the skies. Framorg felt fires racing through his blood, as Argazen soared rapidly upward, flying at the tip of the vast, ascending throng. The battlefield spread out before his eyes, expanding in its scope as they reached higher and higher.

Initially, the Trogen war chieftain felt a shadow of disappointment as he peered forward, as there was absolutely no sign of the enemy's sky warriors. A few minor skirmishes in the days leading up to the titanic clash had shown the skill of the Saxan sky warriors, and their Himmerosen steeds had proven to be a very capable breed of Skiantha. Framorg greatly anticipated engaging a large mass of them head to head, all across the skies.

He had to remind himself that they would likely come soon enough, probably in direct response to the Trogens now marshaling in the skies over the battlefield. For the time being, he turned his attentions towards studying the battle spread out upon the ground, if only to occupy his thoughts until the enemy sent something up to challenge the Trogens.

What he saw before him was beyond colossal in scale. He knew that few, if any, Trogen war chieftains or human kings in all of history had ever had the privilege of looking upon such an incredible vision of war. The battle that was unfolding was like nothing that he had ever witnessed or, for that matter, even imagined. While he had been amazed at the sheer size of the encampments on both sides as the conflict approached, nothing could have prepared him for the spectacular array of martial force now unfurled upon the plains.

Winds of war rippled through the standards and banners of both sides, undulating and defiant where they rose above their respective throngs of warriors. Resonant drums and horns heralded the movements of the dense ranks of the invasion forces, mounted and on foot, as the open ground between the two sides diminished.

From his lofty perch, Framorg could see the three main divisions of the invading forces distinctly. Ahead of them was the long, unbroken line of the defenders, which was like a living wall that stubbornly blocked the path into Saxany. If that wall could be breached, and broken into rubble, then all of Saxany would fall quickly enough.

Sprouting abundantly, like a colorful foliage of greens, reds, and other hues, the banners marking the Andamoorans constituting the left division of the invaders glided along within the massive square formation that they had assumed. The giant square had drawn to a halt not far from the Saxan line, though some shifts and flows were still occurring within it, as the teeming masses of warriors settled into place.

The tiny forms of Andamooran horsemen could already be seen racing down the front of the Saxan wall of warriors. The last few of the mounted contingent were still sallying forth from behind a protective line of shields.

The Trogen chieftain saw that the Saxan line facing them remained rigidly in place, and no horsemen of their own emerged to engage the harassing Andamooran riders. The Saxans were already exhibiting considerable discipline, not falling for the bait being set tantalizingly before them, a ruse designed to open early rifts in their cohesive ranks.

To his right, Framorg saw that the ranks of Ehrengard were moving forward in another condensed mass. For the most part, heavy cavalry were moving up behind an extensive screen of infantry. The ranks of infantry were numerous, and Framorg espied large groups of archers and crossbowmen within their ranks.

Located on the farthest right of Ehrengard's formation, a core of mounted warriors was conspicuously moving up behind an impenetrable hedge of long pikes, carried forth by warriors on foot. They were heavily armored knights, with great helms encasing their heads, covered head to foot in mail, and even provided with additional protection for their thighs and knees. The comprehensive armor was not wasted upon those who wore it, as Framorg knew that the knights of Ehrengard were brave warriors given to individual feats of valor. Of all the human factions that he had been exposed to during his time on the campaign, he had come to increasingly like the Ehrengardians the more that he was around them.

Their horses were very well-protected, many in extensive trappers, and some in bards crafted entirely of chain mail. The uniformity in the colors and patterns on the trappers, shields, lance pennons, and surcoats of a given knight made for quite a mosaic behind the thick, dark hedge of pikemen.

Opposite them, right behind the Saxan's living wall, another great mass of mounted fighters had gathered. Though not as heavily armored as the Ehrengardian knights, the Saxan riders looked prepared for any attempt by the invaders to skirt their left flank.

Framorg's gaze then drifted left down the Saxan shield wall, funneling towards a sizeable assemblage of Saxan fighters set a short distance in back of their line's center. They were gathered around a single, large standard, a windsock as opposed to the usual type of banners and pennons. Billowing in a steady breeze, it was fashioned into the form of some kind of winged animal figure.

As the Avanoran leadership was concentrated in an equivalent formation within the invading force, Framorg strongly suspected that the

Saxan of greatest rank was located somewhere close to the animal-shaped standard. Much in the developing battle would depend upon the kind of mettle, savvy, and discipline contained within that particular Saxan leader. Framorg doubted that any Saxan within the opposing ranks had ever been measured against a threat as monstrous as the one below. The Saxan leader was about to be given a tremendous, unprecedented test, and was certainly not going to receive any graces or conciliation from Avanor's commanders.

War was a ruthless, cold judge, and nothing about its evaluations was based upon a sense of fairness. War was ultimately quite simple and direct, in one way of looking at it. The Saxan leader would either prevail, or he would not, no matter what advantages or disadvantages were present.

Still, even if the Saxans were overwhelmed, the Saxan leader could yet acquit himself honorably in defeat. It would not be much of a consolation in the tattered aftermath of a battlefield defeat, but it was one that the Trogens had to embrace often within their own hard-pressed lands.

Framorg could respect and sympathize with that melancholy reality. All too often, Trogens had incurred the loss of many noble, heroic warriors, who had been caught within an overpowering Elven swarm, and had still fought on despite the absence of hope. In soaking an Elven victory in their own blood, such Trogen warriors had become far greater inspirations than those who had triumphed in much more balanced situations. In such a way, the Saxan leader could become a similar figure for the people of Saxany in years to come.

Framorg then looked down upon the Avanoran formation. Pennons of blue and gold flew in great numbers within the strong reserve below, as the leaders within it carefully watched the battle developing before them. Spread out immediately before the Avanoran reserve was the great might of the central division.

A thick screening line of infantry had been deployed before a large number of archers with longbows, as well as crossbowmen. The infantry and missile troops together constituted a mobile shield for the most valuable element of the Avanoran ranks.

Stretched into a compacted line were the knights of Avanor. Bristling with weapons and armor, the knights were bringing their powerful warhorses forward at a slow walk in the wake of the advancing lines on foot. There was a great cohesiveness in the knights' postures, as well as in the carrying of their lances, hinting at shared training, and a close familiarity with each other.

Light gleamed from a multitude of small, dazzling implements, reflections from the metallic ornamentation dangling from the warhorses' breast straps. The horses walked so tightly together that Framorg believed that he could drop a wedge of cheese anywhere along the line of knights without having the worry of it hitting the ground.

Other lines of mounted warriors were coming up immediately behind the knights. The strict cohesion of the first line was absent in this group, which Framorg knew to be the Avanoran sergeants and squires.

In Framorg's view, the squires had the worst of it by far, regarding the two groups of lesser rank. They had to concern themselves both with the fighting, as well as keeping attention upon the knights that they served, to rearm them or provide replacement mounts if a warhorse was brought down. The dual role of being a fighter and an attendant was a burden that Framorg did not wish upon any of his Trogens. Each and every warrior needed to be fully focused on battle, and battle alone. A distracted focus could mean death in an eye's blink.

With the knights at the spearhead, the full mass of Avanoran knights, squires, and sergeants comprised a potent cavalry force positioned at the heart of the battlefield. Framorg knew that in any victory scenario, they would play a decisive role.

Framorg brought his eyes up to look ahead again, and clenched his jaws in frustration and disappointment, as the skies before the Trogens were still empty, save for a couple of distant enemy scouts. The enemy sky riders could not have missed the gathering of the Trogens in the sky, and Framorg wondered what was keeping them waiting. He could see the increasing agitation on the faces of the warriors around him, as none of them wanted to be mere spectators in a battle as gigantic and momentous as the one breaking out right below them.

"Keep all eyes outward, and have signals given the moment that any enemy is seen in these skies," Framorg instructed the Trogens immediately with him, who then disseminated his orders quickly to messengers that would speed to all ends of the broad airborne formation.

Framorg looked back down to watch the progress of the battle. A commotion was now occurring within the right division from Ehrengard. Sunlight sparkling off of the tips of thousands of weapons, the Ehrengardian division was now resolutely advancing towards the Saxan left flank. The horde of tramping pikemen anchoring the right flank of Ehrengard's force moved forward, abounding in piercing, iron points. The force of knights sheltered by the pikemen looked quite content to avail themselves of the forest of sharp pikes, as they walked their horses slowly in the wake of the protective shield.

A host of horns called out suddenly to the heavens, backed by the bass rumble of great kettle-drums being struck repeatedly. The rhythmic booming and braying horns swelled from the left division of the invaders, drawing Framorg's attention away from Ehrengard's force.

Seas of colorful banners suddenly seemed like the crests of rolling, oceanic waves, as an immense number of warriors surged into motion. The giant Andamooran square resumed its forward path, soon blanketing the territory where the small numbers of horse archers had been galloping.

Another wave of horns sounded, as the drums continued to thunder. Framorg eyed the large cluster of mounted, black-skinned drummers, their faces hidden behind veils. They beat vigorously upon a variety of drums, ranging in size from smaller, horizontally-lying drums, with polygonal ends, to huge, upright kettle-drums, in vivid green and gold casements.

The Andamooran square was again brought to a full halt. The air between the Andamoorans and Saxans was momentarily distorted, as if by a darker haze, which Framorg recognized at once as a torrent of arrows and javelins.

For just a moment, the arrows were traveling in one direction, but the air between the two forces grew darker, as the Saxans unleashed their own barrage. Arrows and other missiles rushed by each other in the gap between the ranks, pouring down into the opposing forces.

Blood was rapidly drawn upon both sides, and Framorg knew that it would not be much longer before the Saxan wall was tested. He eyed a multitude of Saxan cavalry that was assembling at the edge of their right flank. The mass of horsemen was swelling past the end of the shield wall, looking as if it was about to enter the fray.

His keen eyes caught a distinctive force of heavier cavalry gathering behind the mounted assemblage, containing horses shining in armor of iron scales. Framorg was intrigued, wondering what the Saxans were about to attempt. He knew that the volley of missiles would extend for a little longer, as the two sides softened each other up, before attempting a more forceful blow.

Framorg's eyes flicked back towards the Avanorans, though this time he took account of the small contingents that were not a part of the three primary divisions. The narrow ranks plugging the gaps between the human forces were comprised of a much more familiar, non-human element.

To either side of the Avanorans were Trogen warriors under Berandas and Murithenum. Framorg had full confidence in the two stalwart Trogens, the former of the Storm Hawk clan, and the latter from the Water Dragon Clan. Both were exceptional warriors, who commanded great respect from those that they led.

The Trogens were not the only participant in the flank-protecting forces. Towering over the Trogens, and aggressively brandishing weapons that no human or Trogen could hope to wield, were several of Ardas's hulking brawlers. Ardas, who was of a comparable authority to Framorg within his own Gigan contingents, was an anomaly among his formidable kind. Unrivaled in ferocity and size, Ardas was also gifted with an uncommon degree of cunning and foresight. Framorg had about as good of a relationship with Ardas as a Trogen could have with the cruder, far more temperamental Gigans.

Ardas delegated through a band of barbarous chieftains that acted as his war captains, keeping his cadre of enormous warriors somewhat orderly and disciplined. Framorg had never seen any Gigan chieftain achieve any better control, or even equal the level that Ardas was able to maintain.

Framorg had known something was different about Ardas the moment that he first met the Gigan. It was not the exceedingly prominent lower tusks that so many others took immediate notice of. Nor was it the creature's menacing countenance, as a mere glower coming from Ardas's harsh visage was enough to bring weakness to the knees of most warriors. Rather, it was the alert, glittering look in Ardas's eye that caught Framorg's initial attention.

Ardas was quite capable of reaching a frothing battle rage, but it was one that was governed by intelligence and discipline. Such made for an extremely fearsome combination, when added to the excessive amount of physical power and size that a Gigan possessed. It was a relief that Ardas was a rarity among his kind, or Trogen history would likely have been much bloodier.

From the sky, Framorg could see the truest purpose of the Avanorans exposed, regarding how they had deployed Framorg's brethren and the Gigans. The Trogens, with the Gigans in their midst, only occupied a narrow front, but they extended far enough back to flank the thick ranks of Avanoran heavy cavalry.

Framorg chafed a little as he eyed his fellow Trogens. Berandas and Murithenum were carrying out a role that was more protective in nature. They would not constitute the main thrusts of the developing battle plan, but at the least they were taking part in the fighting.

Framorg's blood rose in heat as he stared again towards the empty horizon before him. It was all that he could do to refrain from trying to bait the enemy sky riders to come forth, but he was under rigidly strict orders from the Avanoran commanders, to maintain a defensive cloak over the ground formations. He could only hope that he would not have to wait much longer for the enemy to appear.

A chorus of Saxan horns then arose from Framorg's far left, coming from the end of the Saxan right flank. It cleaved through the booming war drums of the Andamoorans, rising sharp and clear, up into the skies where Framorg hovered.

His head turned towards the vibrant sound, keenly interested to know what strategy the Saxans were loosing, and whether it now involved the massed cavalry forces that he had espied just moments before.

AELFRIC

Aelfric rode out from the center, as the Saxans identified the Halmlander positioned on the enemy's far right flank of the mind-numbingly huge battle line coming straight towards the shield wall. At all costs, the Halmlander would have to be stopped.

Adrenaline flowing within his veins, Aelfric was escorted by a small number of thanes and household warriors as they raced down the back of their lines, galloping towards the farthest edge of the Saxan left flank.

Behind the rigid shield wall, at the extremity of the left flank, Count Leidrad was gathered with a mass of cavalry. They were in full readiness, to counter any enemy maneuver to try to outflank the Saxan forces, or to counterattack, if the opportunity arose in the pending combat.

Never had Aelfric been so glad that the old kingdoms of the past had united, as the Northern Kingdom had never enjoyed such richness in cavalry. Every last bit of mounted force available would be sorely needed now. With so much hanging in the balance, and his worst fears about the Halmlander presence confirmed, he took an appraisal of Leidrad's riders.

The long blades of their lances, with short, protruding lugs at their bases, were held in strong, eager hands. Their unobstructed faces exhibited a high degree of determination, as they sat with firm postures, garbed in their coats of mail.

Their heads were topped by segmented helms of a rounded type, or another kind which contained a down-tilting, prominently flaring rearward extension. A few had thin nasal guards, and some with the round-style helm also had the added protection of mail aventails, which guarded their necks all around the back of their heads, starting from the sides of their faces. A small number of the better-equipped horsemen had iron vambraces and greaves, echoes of older styles whose influence hailed from an earlier age of faraway Theonia.

Complimented with straight, broad, single-edged daggers at their right hips, in sheaths looped around their belts, three leather straps suspended their sword scabbards on their left sides. The quillons of long swords, with broad fullers and blades that tapered little, rested up against the bronze chapes crowning the top of the scabbards.

Turned downward around the tops, their high leather boots held bronze prick-spurs towards the base of their heels. They carried round wooden shields, covered in leather, fitted with iron grips, and an iron reinforcement bar across the back.

They were well-drilled, and Aelfric had witnessed many of their mock combats, as groups of cavalry charged and hurled spear shafts with tips removed, only to feign flight and be pursued by the other group. The men mustered before him were possessed of excellent skill on horseback, and he had little doubt they would have quite a part to play in the coming battle; perhaps very soon.

There was not much time left before the opposing sides clashed when Aelfric finally reached the back of the left flank. The black sea of Halmlander warriors were visible now, within just a few hundred yards of the Saxan shield wall.

Thanes on the ground were boisterously shouting orders to the archers, slingers, and javelin men in the deeper part of the ranks, urging the men to ready themselves. Many of the household guards in the front lines were shouting in a building frenzy at the oncoming Halmlander, shaking their two-handed axes high in the air, in gestures of defiant resolve.

"Out! Out! Out! OUT!" erupted the pulsing Saxan chant, from the massed ranks along the shield wall.

An even louder roar of "By the Almighty!" then surged and ascended, as the front lines of Saxans whipped themselves into a fury, to meet the the brutal Halmlander with sharpened steel.

Aelfric could also feel the vibrations underneath his feet, as well as the swelling chants delivered in thick Ehrengardian words, both increasing in force as the enemy host neared.

By now, Aelfric knew that every man along that shield wall recognized who it was that marched towards them. The Saxans comprehended that only their bodies stood between the murderous ranks of Halmander and the undefended villages spread across the lands behind them.

In a way, an enduring fight was about to continue, that between heaven and hell, as the rightful, defending Saxans steeled themselves to confront the fury of the predacious Halmlander warriors.

Espying a particular pennon held high above Leidrad's cavalry, looking almost like an axe blade, Aelfric made his way towards the great Count.

Count Leidrad hailed Aelfric loudly, as soon as he saw him. "So it begins! Poitaine is ready with a storm of steel to greet these churls!"

"And you will need to be!" Aelfric shouted back, navigating his horse through cavalrymen that were parting to allow him passage through. "We must be ready when the right moment arrives, to strike a fatal blow to these vile Halmlander."

Count Leidrad's face darkened with a simmering anger. He spoke with the growl of a wolf. "They will not set their torches to one peasant hut, Aelfric. By the All-Father, those monsters will not get past these plains. The grassland shall quench its thirst in their blood!"

Aelfric was very encouraged by what he saw. When the full strength of the enemy forces had finally been revealed, he was not entirely sure how the outnumbered Saxan ranks would react. Yet he knew that if every man echoed the blazing sentiments displayed by the great Count before him, the Saxans might yet have a chance.

FIVE REALMS

Far away from the great conflict bursting within Saxany, at the onset of the new day, a second invasion commenced with unmitigated fury.

With no warning other than the outbreak of horns, blasting all across the adjacent forest, teeming masses of armed Gallean warriors strode forth, from where they had drawn up early that morning into well-ordered ranks. In an extensive, unified line, the Galleans approached the forest across the open grassland, striding boldly alongside small groups of Atagar and Gigan allies.

The first ones to penetrate the line of trees marking the edge of the forest were the Atagar. Though few in number, in comparison to the main force, the nearly two hundred Atagar located at the invasion's spearhead were more than enough to execute their appointed tasks; serving as both a vanguard and scouting force.

With their lengthy arms, sharp claws, and light, elongated bodies, the deft creatures could scurry up the trunks of trees and move along high branches, or nimbly navigate the varying contours of the forest floor. Their darker fur blended extremely well with their immediate surroundings, as they skillfully kept to the shadows, avoiding sunbeams and larger pools of direct light within the forest's sun-dappled interior. Fast and dexterous, they were soon well ahead of the main attack force.

After piercing the outermost reaches of the forest, the Atagar invaders barely had time to sense the presence of the land's defenders before they were attacked themselves. A few Atagar frantically blared upon signal horns, as arrows streaked in amongst them, sending their resonant warnings back towards the commanders within the forces coming up right behind them. Bounding and diving for cover, most sought protection behind trees, or in the beds of a couple of streams in their path. A few concealed themselves behind lower brush.

The Atagar carried small, simply fashioned crossbows, or straight bows, using missiles sized somewhere between a dart and a bolt for a human counterpart. They also carried long, curved daggers for hand to hand combat, with the blades sharply honed on both edges.

A few of the Atagar were felled quickly during the first outbreaks of resistance, but most managed to reach places of relative safety. Swiftly, if not fully accurately, they loosed a flurry of missiles back towards those that had ambushed them.

There were a few that hastened up the trunks of high trees to gain a better line of sight, as the tribal defenders were well concealed within the trees ahead of them.

After the first wave of Atagar had encountered the enemy, at a signal, a mass of regular Gallean soldiers, joined by a few Gigans, trodded forth. The Galleans marched forward with shields up and lances angled forward, combing over the surface of the forest as they neared the area where the Atagar advance had stalled.

More archers and crossbowmen behind them peered upward, into the branches of the trees surrounding them. The dense formation promised to ferret out any Five Realms warriors that tried to maneuver around them, or endeavored to conceal themselves in the foliated upper boughs of a tree.

The early resistance was sporadic in some parts, and fiercer in others. With limited numbers of warriors at their disposal, the Five Realms war sachems had planned their defenses strategically, and cautiously. The bulk of the tribal defenses centered around protecting access to the Shimmering River, the great water channel by which the open seas to the east could be reached.

In the best of circumstances, it provided a route for any potential help to arrive. At worst, if it could be held, it allowed the tribes a way of escape.

Swiftly moving squads of tribal warriors traversed the woodlands, all along the front of the invaders, harassing their enemy with arrows and adroitly fading away, before any concentrated response could be mustered. The tribesmen wended through the forest growth as if they were an extension of it, giving no warning to the probing enemy fighters that fell victim to their ambushes.

A heavier blow would not be delivered, as there were no efforts to engage the enemy in a massed force. The tribesmen also avoided recklessness in contesting the lithe Atagar.

The tribal warriors quickly recognized the capable nature of the unfamiliar beings. Looking to the warriors like huge rodents, the peculiar creatures ran equally well over the ground on two legs or four, and their ability to flow between the trees using the overhead maze of branches was stunning to behold. They could even make use of branches that would not hold the weight of a lighter human, giving them an even further advantage.

If the Atagar had come in great numbers, the tribal warriors knew that they would have presented a tremendous challenge, but their overall threat was negated to a marginal level as they began to suffer losses to their already small numbers. Knowing the Atagar's value to the invaders, the leaders of the Five Realms defenders began to station more sharp-eyed archers in the trees themselves, wherever they believed the Atagar would try to move.

Whether surprised from above while moving along the ground, or jumping into view on a branch level with an archer waiting in a nearby tree, several of the Atagar toppled lifelessly to the forest floor, with an arrow protruding from their bodies.

The tribal war sachems did not dare to blunder into the main strengths of the oncoming force. The war bands of tribal fighters gave way wherever the primary line of invaders moved forward, after claiming a few of the attackers with skillfully loosed arrows.

Flexible and fast striking, the defenders were able to instill some caution in the invaders, and effectively slow their advances. Using the quick, bursting attacks, they threw several segments of the invading lines into momentary panic and disarray.

The brief stabs into the enemy lines revealed some further areas for the defender's exploitation. The men coming up just behind the foremost contingents were nowhere near as resolved as their companions.

While fairly well-armed, with an assortment of short-hafted axes, longer guisarmes, spears, and hand bows, they were more lightly armored, in quilted jerkins and iron caps. On the few occasions when Five Realms warriors broke through far enough to engage some of the men in the second rank, the invaders exhibited a swift tendency to break and pull back. Like the porcupines that the tribesmen were so familiar with, it became apparent that the enemy had a softer underbelly. The challenge lay in how to expose it.

AYENWATHA

Within one of the more heavily contested areas along the front lines, Ayenwatha, along with several Onan warriors, fell back hastily, to regroup and await another enemy surge. They took up a position on the top of a small hill. Far behind them, a few leagues away, was the first of several locations where the refugees from the various tribes and villages were gathering. Gratefully for Ayenwatha, the rendezvous site was still far away from the battle, and it would be quite some time before it was threatened.

Nevertheless, Ayenwatha knew that everything possible had to be done to inflict delays on the invaders. Enemy probes had to be cut off, and where flanking a forward advance could be executed, the defenders had to be ready to maneuver rapidly, to maul the softer ranks behind the tough, mailed enemy fighters in the forefront.

Ayenwatha carefully notched an arrow, lowering himself to one knee. He espied some movements in the trees just beyond the base of the hill. Steadying his body and hands, he focused himself, training his sight upon an Atagar skittering nimbly across the low branch of a tree. The dexterous creature jumped down to the ground as it neared the base of the hill, landing with perfect balance. Ayenwatha had to admit that the creatures were extraordinary, but they were invaders. The Atagar must have thought that it was safely behind the protection of a tree trunk, as it came to a halt, and began working to load a small bolt into its crossbow.

From his position, Ayenwatha had an unobstructed angle on the creature. His body remaining rigid, he let the arrow fly with his breath, as if the feathered shaft were an extension of himself. The arrow tore through the air, and the Atagar emitted a muffled cry as the iron tip embedded deeply into its body, driving the shaft far into its flesh. The creature slumped over, and its crossbow fell harmlessly to the ground.

As a number of combatants moved into sight below, Ayenwatha realized that the Atagar had been skirting around a small, pitched battle, presumably intending to pick off some unwary tribesmen with its crossbow. A number of Gallean soldiers were locked in a struggle with a fair number of tribesmen in the melee, one of the few points along the broad front where the numbers were fairly even.

The Five Realms warriors involved were falling back in relatively good order. Swinging war clubs, they cried out with righteous fury.

The wooden clubs, their slender handles arcing outward along a shaft culminating in a dense, heavy ball of wood, were deadly in their impact upon the heads and bodies of Gallean warriors. Other tribal warriors wielded hand axes, and a few used spears, but above all the attackers were quickly coming to fear, and respect, the devastating effects of the unique war clubs wielded by the heavily painted defenders.

A pair of huge forms then crashed through the brush, bellowing as they stomped forward. Their sudden appearance brought an outcry from the Onan on the hill-top around Ayenwatha. Without a further thought, archers readied arrows and let them fly, loosing them in a dense hail at the two Gigans heading swiftly towards the swarming melee. Several arrows found their large targets, as the two hulking Gigans stumbled, and then crumpled down in lifeless, arrow-ridden heaps.

"It is fortunate that they make such big targets," Ayenwatha remarked dourly to his brother, Hawk Eyes, who was standing to his right.

Ayenwatha retrieved another arrow from his corn-husk quiver, and soon took another careful shot into the fighting below. The arrow whizzed by the body of a Gallean fighter, almost grazing him. The warrior was oblivious to the miss, unaware of just how close to death he had just come. In what turned out to be a quite fortuitous move on his part, he had lunged forward just a split second after Ayenwatha had released the tension on the bowstring.

"A lucky one," Hawk Eyes replied, having watched Ayenwatha's shot, before letting an arrow of his own fly at the attackers.

Ayenwatha watched his brother's arrow strike one of the mailed spearmen in the leg. The man howled in pain, and fell onto the ground, clutching at the arrow shaft impaling him. A tribal warrior leaped at the man with a shrill cry, his war club swooshing through the air in a great arc that ended with it smashing into the Gallean's head.

The two siblings had not fought together in combat in many years, ever since Hawk Eyes had married, and gone off to live in another village, residing in the longhouse of the mother of his wife. The last time that they had stood together in a time of war was years ago, when the tribes of the Anishin had pushed an ill-fated conflict into the demesnes of the five tribes. The shattered Anishin tribes had since been confined to a more remote part of the forest lands to the far north, no longer a threat to the Five Realms.

It was not lost on Ayenwatha that his people would soon face those remnants once again. He was aware that the Anishin had formed friendly relations with the Galleans, even allowing monks and priests of the Western Church to come into their villages, to convert them to the western faith.

Though not yet present in the fighting, the remaining warriors of the Anishin would undoubtedly be seeking chances for vengeance in the midst of the maelstrom caused by the invading army. For them, it would be an irresistable opportunity.

"Ayenwatha!" called a voice from a short distance behind him, coming from the other side of the hill, opposite the fighting.

Ayenwatha swiveled in time to see a young warrior mounted upon a Brega, with a bow in one hand, trotting around the summit of the hill towards his position. At the warrior's side was another Brega, without a rider. The young warrior led the second Brega on an elongated tether of hide, which had been tied to the creature's simple harnessing.

"Speak, what is it?" Ayenwatha implored quickly, his eyes darting back to the battle on the other side of the hill. The tribal warriors had driven the enemy back again, and those that survived were now trekking steadily up the hillside to join their comrades, some laboring to help the wounded get up the slope.

"Atotarho seeks help in guiding the Midragardan force, to take them where they will be most needed," the warrior stated, as he neared Ayenwatha.

A sudden surge of energy and anticipation filled Ayenwatha as the words sounded in his ears. Atotarho, an elderly Onan Sachem with a place on the Grand Council, had been sent away earlier with a small escort of warriors. Their task was to watch for the arrival of any possible reinforcements. The words of the young warrior conveyed great hope to Ayenwatha, which raced through him, instantly invigorating his belabored spirit.

"Midragard has come?" Ayenwatha asked. Having yearned for even a shred of favorable tidings, he wanted to hear everything that the young warrior had to report.

The young warrior did not disappoint Ayenwatha in the least. "Our scouts report that many sea vessels, bearing a large force of armed Midragardans, has already entered the Shimmering River. The dragon ships row up its waters even now. Many, many boats."

A strange look came upon the young warrior's face, and Ayenwatha recognized it as a look of fascination. The warrior looked almost giddy, and his eyes gleamed with excitement.

"What is it? What holds your tongue?" Ayenwatha urged the young man, impatiently.

The warrior paused a moment, taking a deep breath before replying. "There are also many Midragardan warriors riding Fenraren, coming through the skies. But that is not all. It is said that there are even several wolf-skins, and a bear-shirt or two, among those arriving on the longships … Wolf-skins and bear-shirts … here in our lands, answering our call!"

The look of wonder had grown further upon the young warrior's face as he related the last words regarding the legendary wolf-skins and bear-shirts of Midragard. Ayenwatha's own eyes grew wider as he listened to the news, as even more hope welled up within him.

"And it is true that our friends of Midragard have sent a force upon sky steeds?"

The warrior nodded again, looking pleased to see the optimism reflected in the face of the heralded war sachem. "Yes, Ayenwatha. Of this there is no doubt. A good number of riders on Fenraren cross our skies."

Ayenwatha glanced over towards Hawk Eyes, to see his brother grinning broadly by his side. The shining smile on Hawk Eyes' face, displayed on a hardened visage painted half black and half red, looked almost surreal.

"There may be hope yet to keep our homelands," Ayenwatha said to his brother.

"A force of sky steeds? Another force arriving on boats with bear-shirts and wolf-skins amongst them? There is a chance," Hawk Eyes replied confidently. "Leave here now, and hurry to guide them in, before any more time is wasted. We will give the enemy reason to slow further."

Ayenwatha smiled back at his brother, striding over to the riderless steed by the message-bearing warrior. Bracing his hands on the back of the creature, he displayed the limberness and strength within his body as he sprung up lightly to the back of the creature.

The messenger released the tether into Ayenwatha's control, as he adjusted himself in his own saddle. Ayenwatha tugged on the reins of his Brega, and the two maneuvered their steeds to a place where they could launch themselves off the hill. Finding a short stretch of open ground, they spurred their steeds, which sprang into motion and bounded forward.

Once in the air, looking back, Ayenwatha could see that there were a number of enemy sky steeds far to the west. Many were flying low in altitude, but they were too far away to interfere with Ayenwatha's travel.

With an icy stab of trepidation, Ayenwatha saw that off to the south were the enormous flying beasts that had served to level so many tribal villages. He could see the streams of heavy rocks falling from them; a black, deadly rain that he could only hope was falling upon emptied villages. From what he could tell, the winged titans looked to be heading north.

Even more troubling, the beasts had delved much deeper into the woodland realm, flying far away from the front lines of the invading forces on the ground. That recognition brought one baleful thought to the fore of Ayenwatha's mind, and his heart sank as he fathomed their purpose; the Darroks were being used to target masses of people, and not villages. The staging areas for the tribal refugees would be disernable from the air, and highly vulnerable.

Dismay wiped away the enthusiastic burst that had gripped him only moments before. Not a thing could be done to slow or stop the Darroks, as there were not enough sky warriors of their own left to present any obstacle to the beasts. Ayenwatha hoped desperately that the report of approaching Midragardans upon sky steeds was indeed true, as that represented the only real chance to halt the deadly hail falling from the behemoth terrors.

Angered in helpless frustration, he guided his steed on a lower course, as the warrior behind him followed suit, steadying his path at a height a short distance above the tops of the trees. There, the forms of the two Onan were not set so starkly against the sky. At the very least, it would be a little harder to be discovered by enemy sky warriors. The pair of riders accelerated their pace as they continued forward, speeding on their way towards the Shimmering River.

DRAGOL

Dragol and a couple hundred Trogen warriors adhered strictly to their given orders, as the gigantic Darroks cruised uncontested through the skies over the Five Realms. Renewed bombardment with heavy stones had commenced, and there was ample evidence that they had struck their long-sought targets this time.

Loud cries and wails, and large numbers of tribal people scattering through the sporadic breaks in the forest's dense ceiling below, indicated that the Trogens had uncovered one concentrated gathering of their enemies. The stones thudded amongst people this time, rather than the empty villages that they had encountered on their most recent foray.

The heavy tree cover allowed Trogen observers to only see flashes of movement, but it was very apparent that a considerable number of humans were fleeing in all directions below the Darroks. The falling stones crashed through the trees, breaking branches, and spreading chaos and death.

A few small squads of Trogens had already taken to the air upon their Harraks, leaving the backs of the Darroks that had ferried them eastward. They had been dispatched to loose arrows into the tree cover, wherever they saw any signs of significant movement. The archers were careful to keep their steeds high in elevation, positioned safely away from any chance of return arrow fire. Not even the unknown bowman back in Saxany would have had enough range to threaten the Trogen archers where they hovered.

Following orders, Dragol drew no satisfaction from the one-sided affair. He could not deceive himself, or soften the bile he felt building within him. There was absolutley no honor in such a manner of fighting. Something felt terribly wrong deep inside him, a matter of spirit, and not flesh.

He was still chafing with envy regarding the Trogens who were taking part in the invasion of Saxany. They were likely engaged in a truly honorable manner of fighting; warrior against warrior, face to face.

He and Tirok, as Trogen commanders, still remained on the backs of the Darroks, along with a few clusters of mounted warriors that were being held in reserve, just in case the enemy had any airborne surprises waiting to throw suddenly at them.

"We have the insects stirred up," remarked Tirok, with some

apparent disgust, as he looked out over the side of the wooden railing.

Dragol knew that Tirok was also miserable about the manner of war that they were engaged in. It was never the way of the Trogens to avoid facing an enemy blade to blade. The cold truth was that this form of war, levied from high in the sky against defenseless targets, was a coward's war.

The only thing that had kept Tirok and Dragol from turning the Darroks about was the promise that, at the end of the war, many generations of torment and tragedy inflicted upon Trogen kind would finally be brought to an end. Yet even with that momentous bargain with the Unifier, set to secure the long-awaited help that was needed to overcome their terrible oppression, Dragol still felt very uneasy inside. He knew, without asking, that Tirok did as well.

Close by, a number of Trogens labored to offload a pile of moderately-sized rocks over the side of the Darrok. Each rock was fairly heavy, even for the considerable strength of a hale Trogen, lifting with both arms. The rocks had been selected for a strictly Trogen crew, as no human crew would have been able to maneuver the heavy missiles.

"Yes, they are moving about under the trees, but you and I know that nothing will come up to challenge us … they do not have the steeds to fight in the sky. Their warriors can only fight on the ground," Dragol bitterly replied.

He knew that the limited number of Bregas left to the tribesmen would not be sacrificed futilely, trying to stop the formidable array of Darroks and Trogens. The tribesmen had already shown that they were warriors with the courage to embark upon a flight in the face of death, but they were not foolhardy. They would not carelessly throw their lives away, certainly not while they had their elderly, women, and young to guide forward.

"It is hard to say how the enemy warriors fare upon the ground. They may be overwhelmed, or they may put up a good fight. The attack is a powerful one," Tirok replied, referencing the immense border attack that had been initiated, just shortly after the Darroks had taken to the skies.

The Darroks, with their numerous Trogen escorts, had been sent to the furthest edge of the attack to the south. They had begun their strike deep over the woods to the east, proceeding in a line that worked back up north. It was very difficult to observe what was happening within the woods, or to gain any insight regarding the fighting occurring further to the north.

"Do not worry yourself, Dragol. Very soon, you and I will be flying together in the skies over Saxany," Tirok continued. "There are enough sky steeds in the Saxan ranks that we will be challenged blade to blade."

"May your words come true, soon," Dragol practically hissed, glaring in his frustration at the older commander whom he had such immense reverence for.

The chance to fight alongside one as honored among Trogens as Tirok did not come often. Dragol's current predicament would be little different if he and Tirok were chained to the Darrok's back. The effect was the same. He was held back from the Trogen way of war, and an opportunity to go into battle by the side of one as eminent as Tirok.

"Dragol, Tirok!" an insistent Trogen interrupted, with obvious urgency.

"What is it?" snapped Dragol, now engulfed in a black mood.

The Trogen, wide-eyed and excited, pointed out towards the horizon, off the right side of the Darrok. He shouted his words, as he directed their attentions. "Out there! Look! In the skies!"

Dragol and Tirok followed the insistent gestures of the Trogen warrior. To his great surprise, Dragol saw what appeared to be a dark cloud moving steadfastly towards them.

It was no cloud of the natural order, as the sky around them was very clear. In truth, the skies were largely devoid of cloud cover, all the way up to the heights that a Harrak could not reach. What little could be seen was snow white in hue.

"What is that? A cloud that moves towards us?" Tirok asked, as a grin started to spread across his face. He cast a knowing glance towards Dragol, as sparks erupted within his deepset eyes.

"I would guess a great number of sky steeds, Tirok," Dragol observed, squinting towards the apparition to the east. "We must find out whose side they are on. They are still too far away to tell."

His hopes for redemption from the current, loathsome way of conducting a war were rising.

"Are there any more Harraks in this area? And why would they come from the east?" Tirok asked.

"Are we to be allowed an honorable fight at last?" Dragol offered, giving voice to his escalating hopes.

Tirok cried out, with no hesitation, "To the skies, Dragol! All forces, to the skies!"

The two Trogen commanders hurriedly issued directives that were conveyed by horn signal to the mounted Trogens upon all the Darroks to take to the skies. The short blasts were a welcome music to Dragol, and the orders were disseminated quickly along the backs of every Darrok. Within moments, several streams of Harraks were flying up into the air, taking positions above the huge creatures.

On the backs of the Darroks, most of the other Trogens stopped carrying the great rocks, or pushing them down the timber chutes from the carriages. They scrambled to grab up their longbows, readying quivers of arrows as they prepared for defense.

The sky warriors then converged together, gathering into one great mass. Dragol and Tirok hovered side by side in the air, set just in front of the assembling muster.

The Darroks were then guided away from the area by their handlers, who altered their courses sharply to the west and north. The shift placed the Trogen sky formation squarely before the unknown, oncoming force, in a perfect position to intercept them.

The two commanders were content to maintain the buffer zone between the Darroks and the approaching cloud of unidentified sky warriors. Dragol kept straining his eyes to ascertain the nature of the approaching riders, but the distance was still too great.

"And if what is in that cloud outnumbers us greatly?" Tirok asked.

"Then we should fly closer to the Darroks, and draw the attackers in, to where our warriors on the platforms can loose arrows at them," Dragol suggested.

Like Tirok, he could discern how the Trogens could be split and engulfed if the enemy numbers were overwhelming. Still, he far preferred such a concern over what he had been forced to endure while idle on the back of the Darroks.

"We must protect the Darroks, at all cost. Those are the orders," Tirok reiterated.

Tirok echoed the primacy among the commands that had been delivered to the Trogens just at the onset of daybreak, while the sky warriors were busy double-checking the harnessing on their steeds. The priorities had been made perfectly clear, repeated to the point of irritation.

"That can be done best if we have the help of the archers on the backs of the Darroks, if the enemy numbers are too many for us to entangle here," Dragol remarked. "The enemy will not be able to do much harm to the beasts, as long as we are also flying amongst them."

Tirok grew silent, staring off at the swiftly approaching cloud, while he pondered Dragol's suggestion.

"If the numbers look to be too great, then we will draw back," Tirok replied firmly. "Until then, we will remain here, to give them a proper Trogen greeting."

Dragol nodded as he sat back in his saddle, grasping the leather grip on the hilt of his Trogen longblade, sliding the weapon purposefully out of the scabbard. The smooth movement felt reassuring, and as the blade was freed he felt a surge of anticipation course through him. In his left hand, he took up the grip on his wooden shield, from where it had been resting on his back by the guige strap. He grasped the iron bar in the center, along with a segment of his Harrak's reins.

Everything depended on the identity of the approaching sky steeds. Dragol was all but certain that they would be foes, but he still did not know what kind of warriors constituted their numbers, or what manner of weapons they wielded.

Shifting his full attention back to the nearing cloud, Dragol allowed the fires of anticipated battle to build up within him. They burned throughout his being, flaring up as all of his thoughts narrowed towards a singular focus on the impending combat.

Ahead, the dark cloud kept increasing in size, as it grew closer. Finally, individual shapes could vaguely be made out.

There was the faintest possibility that it was a contingent of Harrak-mounted Trogens that Dragol and Tirok had not been aware of, coming in to reinforce their efforts over the Five Realms. Further numbers would certainly increase the havoc that was being wreaked far behind the enemy lines, spreading it over a much wider area.

A few Trogens were now engaged in executing scouting duties over other areas of the battlefront, either alone or in pairs, but the overwhelming majority of available sky warriors had already been concentrated in the task of protecting the valuable Darroks. Dragol strongly doubted that there was even a shred of a chance that the incoming force would be Trogens.

The possibility that it was a horde of defenders from the Five Realms, mounted upon Bregas, also seemed quite unlikely. If there had been a large contingent of Bregas still available to the defenders, in numbers that could constitute any real threat to the Darrok juggernauts, then they would have long since made their presence felt. The tribal warriors had already demonstrated their mettle, and it was not lacking in any measure.

Turning his head, he looked back over his shoulder. He saw that the Darroks had covered quite a distance as he and Tirok waited, having drifted much farther to the north in the intervening time. The Trogen archers on their backs must have gauged that they had ample time to respond to attacks, as a small level of bombardment had resumed. Dragol watched the Darroks for a few moments, as several rivulets of dense rock were unloaded and sent towards the ground below.

Dragol surmised that the Darrok crews must have discovered an inviting target, though he knew that all of the Trogens involved would rather be with Tirok and Dragol.

Loud outcries jerked his attention back around towards the front.

"Fenraren! Midragardans!" an excited shout loudly proclaimed, from just to his right.

Dragol stared back out towards the living cloud coming from the east. It had drawn close enough for him now to make out the triangular ears and elongated muzzles of the storied Fenraren from Midragard. The morning sun glinted off the iron helms of their riders, and he could hear their exuberant shouts, as they streaked towards the Trogens with deadly intent.

The sight thrilled him, as Midragardans were no cowards, and were certainly the manner of fighters that brought great merit to those that overcame them. Dragol's grip on his longblade tightened, as an adrenalized feeling washed over him. At last, he was being set free.

Yet his rush of excitement did not overwhelm his sensibilities. Ominiously, Dragol could clearly see that there were several ranks of mounted Midragardans flying tightly behind the others that had formed the main cloud outline from a distance. The Midragardans had taken a direct approach, on a roughly even line with the Trogens, holding a formation that had effectively masked their true numbers.

Tirok's spoken concern was now a very grim reality. The Midragardans did indeed have them heavily outnumbered.

Dragol swiftly glanced over to Tirok, whose eyes were narrowed as he studied the enemy sky riders, now that they were close enough to scrutinize.

In Dragol's mind, it would be much better to have the support of the archers on the back of the Darroks. There would be some risk of a few Trogen sky warriors being hit by the arrows, but the enemy cloud would be divided up, and prevented from easily concentrating. A chaotic melee, in Dragol's judgement, would serve the Trogens much better. It would reduce the advantage of far superior numbers, and allow the Trogens to chip away at the Midragardan force, piece by piece.

"You see the numbers they have. What do you say?" Dragol asked Tirok. "Should we hasten to the Darroks?"

The more he thought about the situation, the more Dragol realized that they must not abandon the Darroks. The Midragardans were great enough in number that they could engage all the riders in the sky, and still have a considerable number to spare for sending after the Darroks.

The last thing that needed to happen was to have the Trogens in the sky separated from the Darroks. Dragol scanned the oncoming force, and a part of him felt that such an idea was very likely within the minds of the enemy's leaders. One force would engulf Dragol and Tirok's group, while another would race after the Darroks.

Tirok's knuckles whitened as he firmly gripped the shaft of his long lance, lowering the broad, socketed blade at its end. The traces of a crazed look were spreading in his dark eyes. Tirok had long been renowned as a living maelstrom in battle, and Dragol was undoubtedly witnessing the calm before the storm.

"Midragardans ... a day to remember arrives. Not too many! We will fight them!" Tirok rumbled in a low, growling voice, his face taking on a dangerous hue, as his eyes flashed fiercely.

Consumed by the searing heat of the moment, given a chance to match arms with skilled riders upon the legendary Fenraren of Midragard, Tirok raised his war shield and shouted a bellowing war cry. With a dig of his heels to the sides of his mount, he spurred his Harrak forward, into the airborne semblance of a charge.

Before Dragol could do anything to stem the outright madness, and temper the older warrior's battle rage, the multitude of Trogens directly under Tirok followed suit. They drew their longblades, or adjusted the grip and position of their lances, before roaring their own war cries and hurtling forth towards the oncoming Midragardans upon their Fenraren.

Those under Dragol's direct command looked towards him with shock and disbelief, as if they could not believe he was not following after the legendary Tirok.

The second warrior in command, a burly Trogen of the Sea Wolf clan named Gavnar, whose face was streaked with scars gained from many fights, cried out in dismay, "We must charge! Dragol, Tirok has moved!"

Dragol held up on the reins of his Harrak. He was bold, passionate, and eager, almost without rival, but he was also no fool. Nor was he suicidal. The insanity that had suddenly gripped Tirok had transferred to the sorely outnumbered Trogen ranks, beckoning to take all of them on a path to what would undoubtedly be their doom, and leave the Darroks unprotected.

If the Darroks were isolated, the Unifier's prized creatures could be overcome, and Dragol did not want to think of what the consequences would be if that happened. The Avanoran leaders had been very clear about the vital importance of the Darroks to the Unifier. The Unifier might well disregard His promises in the face of such a great loss, and then all the Trogen sacrifice in the war would come to absolutely nothing.

"We must fall back to the Darroks!" Dragol roared out. "We must split up the enemy, and protect the Darroks. We will fight them there, blade to blade, but not foolishly!"

"We must go, now! After Tirok," Gavnar shouted urgently.

"The Midragardans want us to! They want to keep us away from the Darroks. They have the numbers to do this! I tell you, Gavnar, we will fight them! But we will fight them by the Darroks!" Dragol thundered back.

Gavnar snarled openly at him. The thick-headed Trogen screamed back in a near delirium, one that was devoid of any rational consideration. "You coward! You are unfit to lead. All with me, after Tirok! To battle, now!"

Before Dragol could strike the insubordinate Gavanar down, the lower-ranking Trogen warrior broke ranks and urged his Harrak forward. Dragol looked on in sheer disbelief, as all of those under his command were swept up in their heated passions and mutinied, following in the wake of Gavnar. Their feelings had overridden all of their discipline and senses. Caught up in the apex of emotion, and the shadow of the storied Tirok, they had abandoned Dragol.

He looked onward, frozen in incredulity that his fellow Trogens had openly defied his authority. His dismay far overshadowed any rage that he felt towards Gavnar's tremendous insult. In an instant, he was alone, as the second group of Trogens raced after Tirok's contingent.

Despite being called a coward, quite possibly the worst accusation that could be rendered from one Trogen to another, Dragol mastered his emotions. As clarity seeped back into his mind, he felt pity towards Gavnar and the other Trogens.

A cold, dizzying feeling then came over him, as fresh doubts tugged inside. Dragol suddenly feared that he had failed a test of himself. The disconcerting moment passed swiftly, as there was only time to react. No matter which way he looked at it, there were more than enough Midragardans to engage the Trogen sky warriors and to continue onward, to assail the now vulnerable Darroks.

Taking a quick look behind him, Dragol saw that the Darrok formation, with a group of archers readied on every carriage, had progressed a little further to the north. Isolated, and with enemies riding upon swift Fenraren, he realized with a sickening feeling that he would be overwhelmed by numbers alone before he could even reach the Darroks, and help to command the defense.

Even as he took measure of his own situation, and the exposed nature of the Darroks, the Midragardans were spreading outward. They flowed into a swiftly expanding array, taking full advantage of their greater numbers in a shape that would soon engulf the sides of the foolhardy Trogens streaking towards them.

They were doing exactly what Dragol had thought they would do. He was about to be caught himself in the widening, airborne jaws, and for all practical purposes he might as well have been dead in his saddle.

He had desired a time for valor, but his keener senses screamed out for intelligent discretion under the circumstances. Dragol had long been trusting of his deeper instincts, which shouted out louder to him than they ever had before.

To remain in place was to die in vain, utterly useless to his clan and his homeland, the victim of one's outright foolishness, and another's rebellious disobedience. There was no honor in such a futile death, and he knew that he would never reach the Darroks in time to be of any use to their defense.

There was no other option available to the Trogen warrior than downward. He knew that he only needed to gain some time. There was a little hope that the Midragardan numbers could be worn down enough such that the archers on the back of the Darroks could fend the surviving fighters off. In that way, Tirok's suicidal charge might produce some good yet.

If Dragol reemerged from the forest, after the Midragardans had been fought off, he could likely make it back to the main encampment, or join the Darroks en route. Once back in the encampment, he would have word of Tirok's bout of insanity carried to Tragan, who would immediately question why Dragol had not remained in the fight.

Dragol could only hope that Tragan would eventually realize Tirok's sheer rashness. The fact that the Darroks had been left undefended by the other's reckless action, and that many had disobeyed Dragol in his own efforts to adhere to Tragan's firm orders regarding that task, would not likely be well received by the stern Trogen commander.

Even so, the mutiny would probably serve to undermine Dragol's own future viability as a commander. Yet it was a chance that he would have to take.

The ground below was still fraught with risk, as he was far ahead of the advancing Gallean lines, well within the range controlled by the tribal warriors. He knew that he had to gain some distance from the areas where the Darroks had recently bombarded, or he might be setting down amongst an enraged mass of tribal people, aching for revenge.

He had to risk that danger, nonetheless, if he wanted to have any hope of surviving the day. Death he did not fear, but dying for sheer foolhardiness had to be averted.

Taking a deep breath, he clenched Rodor's reins, and guided his Harrak into a swooping, diagonal course towards the trees. It carried him farther away from the bombarded area, and also put a little more distance between himself and the oncoming Midragardans.

His mount slowed down considerably as he neared the vicinity of the forest's upper canopy, gliding smoothly into a level path of flight. Dragol cruised slowly, as he searched anxiously for an open meadow or other break in the trees. In an older forest, such as the one below, there were several places where storms or the passing of time created such holes in treecover. Exhaling a sustained breath of relief, he finally espied such an opening, and angled Rodor for it right away.

The fissure in the sea of trees was large enough for Dragol to comfortably descend through it upon his Harrak, though he maneuvered the steed down as carefully as he could. The leaves of the nearby trees rustled as the Harrak's broad wings beat hard, clipping some leaves on the edges of a few branches.

The Harrak landed relatively smoothly upon the forest floor, off to the side of a long-rotted, fallen tree, which was now little more than a softening, decomposing mass. The trees ringing the small clearing obstructed much of his view of the skies above. Not knowing when the Midragardan warriors might pass over the place where he had landed, he knew that he had to take immediate cover.

Dragol's eyes darted about, cursing the deep shadows of the forest. The dimmer depths of the woods encompassing him required a few moments of time for his eyes to adjust from the bright skies that he had left behind.

As his eyes began to pierce the dappled gloom, he was relieved to find that there were no signs of Five Realms warriors present, or any other imminent threats. Dragol had little doubt that the tribesmen would not be in the mood to extend him a warm welcome.

Grabbing the reins to his steed, he strode forward, leading Rodor into the trees. No longer exposed in the open, he turned and lowered into a crouch behind some brush, staring back up to the skies through the clearing.

Though distant, and high in altitude, the winds carried the sounds of the furious, ongoing clash between the Trogens and Midragardans. Another pang of guilt struck him, as part of him wished that he was slashing through the Midragardan warriors, rather than slinking about the forest floor in the middle of the Five Realms. Dragol was not a Trogen who shirked from fighting any opponent, and even if his choice made strategic sense, it still left him conflicted.

His blood boiling with anger and frustration, he reminded himself once again of the undeniable circumstances regarding the situation above. The badly outnumbered Trogen warriors under his command had openly defied his order and authority, and, by doing so, had ultimately opposed Tragan's firm directives. Disobedience to a chieftain, or a warrior delegated to command, was a great transgression. It was one that Dragol was not guilty of in any way, as he had dutifully honored Tragan's orders. Gavnar and the others had sorely violated the ages-old tradition, and Dragol knew that he bore no guilt for their senseless choice.

Even so, the grave infraction had been committed by a number of Trogens from the Thunder Wolf clan, among those who had been hovering with Dragol. They had effectively abandoned a chieftain of their own clan, which made it all the more painful and confusing to him.

Dragol was not about to second guess his decision, knowing in his heart that he had made the wiser choice. The sudden mutiny would have just carried him to certain destruction, if he had chosen to follow after the other Trogens by himself. He had known without a doubt that they were about to be swarmed by the much larger Midragardan force, and those under his command should have trusted his judgement.

Their abandonment, and defiance of him, had tempered any regrets that he might otherwise have had. After what they had done, he would never have been able to feel affinity towards any of them again.

Further, if Gavnar and any Thunder Wolves survived the battle, he would have simply challenged all of them to single combat. He would have slain them one at a time, his longblade quenching its thirst on their rebellious blood.

Dragol had been very clear to Gavnar and the others that they would still fight in the Trogen way, under his plan. He was simply not inclined to throw those under his command away in futility. Gaining the most advantageous position for battle was not a wrongdoing, nor was it avoidance. It offered a more propitious fight, fully honorable in nature, and, though the chances were still very slim, it offered the only real prospects for victory.

Jaws clenched within the severe tension that his ruminations invoked, such that his neck muscles bulged, he turned and got back to his feet. Taking the lead, he guided his mount deeper through the trees. He took the creature in a direction that he estimated would be leading away from the main courses of bombardment.

He had to move quickly, as the result of the combat in the sky was a foregone conclusion. It was very possible that enemy riders had seen him descending. In such numbers as they had, he could still find himself casting his life away vainly, even if he took many down with him.

Dying in such a manner would not bring any benefit to the Trogens, or aid their longtime struggle. Survival was the only choice for him to pursue, even if those chances were far from good.

Keeping the reins of the Harrak in his left hand, clenched firmly along his shield grip, he grasped his Trogen longblade in his right. Eyes peeled, peering with rigid scrutiny into the shadows of the forest, he was sensitive to any movements. Nothing of alarm was forthcoming as he continued, and he eventually came upon a wide, shallow stream. In a turn of fortune, the stream's route continued more or less in the direction that he had chosen. The water flowed calmly and timelessly, as if nothing was amiss in the woods, or above in the skies.

With a little cajoling, Dragol guided his steed into the midst of the shallow water in order to eliminate the existence of a scented trail for potential pursuers. His leather boots sank into the mud of the stream's bedding, as the cool water soaked through to his skin. The cold liquid almost mirrored the brooding, chaotic thoughts that kept penetrating, and permeating, his tumultuous mind.

His eyes scanned for any rock surface breaking clear of the water, but there was very little to be found. Their scents might be covered, but he had tracked and hunted enough animals to know that the soft mud beneath the soles of his boots, and the clawed feet of his steed, were leaving some very visible signs for anyone, or anything, with perceptive, experienced eyes.

He had to keep going forward, as it was most imperative to get away from the clearing where he had landed. Despite any concerns that he harbored about tracks, he knew that he had to press forward to achieve as much distance as possible.

The sounds of battle overhead soon faded away, as Dragol covered a significant amount of ground. At last, he came to a halt, and decided to address his concerns a little. Using his longblade, he cut off a thin, overhanging branch from a tree perched on the edge of the bank to his right. Securing his Harrak for a moment to the same tree, he doubled back to use the branch to brush the bottom of the stream over a long section of their trail.

He also spared a few moments to make some false tracks of his own at the onset of the cleared segment, giving the appearance that he had climbed out of the stream where the previous signs had ended. The time spent disguising their passage gave him some further peace of mind. Under the weighty circumstances, that slight easement was a great boon to his spirit.

There were still no signs of enemy pursuit, the tribal fighters, or even the allied, invading force, as he methodically worked back to his Harrak and untied it, to resume their sojourn. Dragol began to entertain the notion of risking a climb above the tree line, in order to see if the skies were clear.

Scanning the surrounding trees, he looked for ones that appeared promising for a dedicated climb by a heavy-bodied Trogen. The forest possessed a variety of trees, and there were several old, stout sentinels in view, whose branches would bear his weight capably high above.

Determining upon one such tree, he led the Harrak back out of the water. The mud sucked at his boots as he pulled his legs up from the stream, and strode over the embankment. He drew near to the old oak tree, and was about to tether the Harrak to the lower branch of a smaller tree close by when several bird cries broke the heavy silence of the forest.

Instinctively honing in upon the subtlest aspects of the sounds, he suspected that the bird cries had not been generated by any manner of feathered entities. There was just something a little different in tone about the cries, even though they sounded very authentic.

Hunting a variety of creatures within his own homelands, many of them perilous, he had become very attuned to the nuances of animal and bird sounds. Birds sometimes heralded the presence of a dangerous animal moving in the vicinity, alerting the surrounding forest. The cries reaching Dragol's ears did indeed proclaim a presence, but they were not testifying to the approach of a forest predator.

The elvish raiders that plagued Dragol's own homelands used animal cries when they undertook their intrusive forays. Dragol was still alive because he had long ago learned to discern the differences between an Elf mimicking a bird or animal, and the genuine bird or animal itself.

He stroked the neck of his Harrak, working to keep Rodor calm as he led the creature up a little rise to the right, where there was an area of low, thickly-grown brush. When they reached the brush, he found a small space that they could pass through. Once through, he used both hands to tug gently on the reins in a way that prompted the Harrak to lay down flat upon the ground.

Dutifully, as the Harrak had been trained, Rodor obeyed, and Dragol lowered himself down beside the prone creature. Becoming as still as stone, Dragol peered through small gaps in the growth towards the area where the bird calls seemed to be coming from.

DREAM OF LEGENDS

His sharp ears picked up a couple of light crackles, as something stepped upon dry, fallen leaves. Using the sounds as a reference, he reoriented his watch along the other side of the stream, expecting some kind of forms to emerge into sight at any moment.

While not perfect, the steps of those approaching were achieved with an extremely skillful silence. Dragol realized that whomever, or whatever, was approaching, they were very adept at moving within a forest environment. As one used to forest lands himself, and highly skilled in traversing them, he greatly respected their demonstrated ability, knowing at once that it would be folly to take them lightly.

"Stay!" Dragol whispered firmly to Rodor, as he lay his shield flat upon the ground. He gave the creature a pat on the flank as he shifted silently away, painstakingly taking step by step in a crouched position.

With slow, deliberate steps, he paced over to a tree possessing an expansive girth. He straightened up to his full height behind the trunk of it, so that he was completely hidden by the tree's form.

A few more bird calls, a snap of a twig, and another low crunch of a leaf indicated that those approaching had not yet reached the stream. With the utmost care, Dragol brought the edge of his face around the trunk until his peripheral vision could take in the ground beyond the channel of water.

Dragol then got his first look at the enemy tribesmen from the ground level. A small party of Five Realms warriors was moving through the trees, drawing near to the bank of the stream. As far as he could tell, he could make out the forms of about fifteen of the silent, gracefully-moving warriors. They all had a somber, hardened look about them. A particularly muscular, older warrior walked at the forefront of the loose formation, in which each warrior was spread well apart from the others.

Their heads were shaven, save for tufts of hair sprouting from the center, several with the feathers of birds affixed. Many had noses or ears decorated with some kind of small implements that appeared to pierce the flesh.

Most of the warriors had their upper bodies bared, wearing hide leggings and a type of short, buckskin kilt. A kind of leather shoe covered their feet, the top edge turned downward into a flap. They traveled lightly, carrying little more than their weapons and leather pouches, the latter richly embroidered, hanging at their waists from straps running across their chests from the opposite shoulder.

A few of their hand weapons were short-hafted axes and spears. Both had steel affixed to their ends, the former a single edged blade, and the other an elongated, sharp point. Most carried a kind of curving war club, shaped out of a length of wood.

A couple bore shields made of thin rods lashed together by hide thongs. Several had a kind of dagger sheathed in a hide case, woven with designs, hanging down to rest just below their chest from a leather cord worn about the neck.

At first, Dragol perceived that they had the most unusual skin tones of any being that he had ever encountered, until he fathomed that they were covered in body paint. It had been applied in a purposeful symmetry that covered one half of their body in red, and the other in black. Dragol quickly observed that the red and black combination enhanced their ability to blend with shadows and foliage.

As warriors of lands with a low population, Dragol did not have to confront them to know that they were very likely to be capable fighters. Alone, he did not stand much of a chance against fifteen of them, especially in light of the fact that several were also carrying longbows.

The warriors with bows had full quivers at their shoulders, hanging from straps similar to those that held their pouches. The quivers were fashioned from some kind of woven vegetable husks, or bark. It did not take much imagination for Dragol to envision the archers fanning out all around him, picking him off easily from the shadows with well-aimed shafts.

He could tell by their positioning that they were not moving towards a specific destination. The group proceeded as if they expected to encounter opposition with every step that they took. Their weapons were kept at the ready, and their heads remained as still as their rigid gazes.

The arrangement and number of the war party, within an obviously contested area, also told him something more of their nature of war. The tribesmen, as he had guessed, were disposed towards a method of warfare utilizing smaller contingents of warriors.

A group such as the one before him was not structured to clash directly with the much more numerous forces of the Galleans. Instead, the tribesmen could strike swiftly and with cohesion, chipping away at a massed enemy, rather than engaging them openly.

Dragol understood both types of warfare, as the Trogens employed each type in their contests amongst each other, against marauding Elves, and in the few conflicts that had occurred with the Kiruvans to the south.

Understanding the Five Realms' methods of war and surviving the moment were still two different matters, though, and Dragol had only one real option before him. If discovered, with nowhere to run, and no clearings through which he could take his Harrak upwards, he would have to fight.

He was more than resolved to try and surmount the incredible odds. Determined to face whatever befell him, he edged his longblade up until he felt the cold steel blade close to the right side of his face.

He hoped that the enemy warriors would cross the stream and continue on past him, bringing the tree he was behind into line with the middle of their formation. At the least, if his position was uncovered, he could fall upon them swiftly.

If he could assault the tribesmen by manifesting abruptly within their midst, he just might be able to delay their use of bows, and perhaps slay several before a concerted counterattack could be made. His blade would have to be swung powerfully and true, and he would have to execute his attack with lightning speed. It was a close to impossible chance, but it was still a chance nonetheless.

The muffled sounds of cries echoed in the distance, erupting from somewhere far off to his left. They immediately drew his attention away from the warriors, as a flash of worry over being caught in the middle of a battle breaking out from all sides struck him. A second later, he returned his gaze back to watching the war party, taking into account the remoteness of the sounds.

The faraway noises had brought the warriors to a complete halt. After the warrior at their lead conferred in whispers with the two tribesmen next to him, he called out a couple of the bird cry signals. Almost as one body, the tribal warriors broke into a run, taking swift, loping strides, as they moved off in a hurry towards the direction of the sounds.

With extreme patience, Dragol waited until they had passed far beyond his sight. For a few extra moments, he stared in the direction that the war party had come from, to see if any other groups of tribesmen were coming up behind the first.

Satisfied that the area was clear for the time being, he carefully lowered himself into a crouch, and moved back to where his Harrak had kept a silent vigil. Reaching out, he gave the creature a slow, affectionate stroke on the neck.

"Good, Rodor ... very good," he whispered, as the creature brought its great head around to nuzzle its master.

Dragol then waited behind the cover of the forest undergrowth for a little longer as a precaution, watching and listening carefully. The forest remained still, and ultimately he was satisfied that he could attempt to move forward again.

"Rise!" Dragol whispered sharply, prodding the Harrak to get back up to its feet.

For the size that it was, the creature responded almost without a sound. Its front legs pushed straight up, and then the Harrak got its hind legs underneath, as it leaned forward, rising up smoothly to its full height.

Picking up his shield from the ground, Dragol clutched the reins lightly in his left hand again and started forward. The two resumed their trek on the path that they had been taking before the tribal warriors' simulated bird calls had suspended their progress. The route would take them away from the place where the war party had passed, and they were also heading in the opposite direction from where the distant shouts had come.

It seemed that Dragol's ongoing caution had transferred to his steed, as both Harrak and Trogen moved soundlessly through the woodlands. Nothing could be assumed in a chaotic environment where invader and defender were crossing throughout, and furiously contesting the region. The presence of the war party, and the audible cries of distant battle, confirmed that stark reality.

Dragol took each step with great care. It was as if just one mistake, such as a branch snapping loudly enough, could result in the termination of his mortal life.

After passing no more than a league, the hackles on the back of his neck began to rise. He slowed his step gradually, as the uneasy feeling intensified, finally bringing himself to a complete halt.

Dragol's senses were at the highest level of alertness that he could muster. Physical and instinctive, they conveyed a deeply unsettling dread, that something sentient was observing him. Looking about, he vigilantly surveyed the area around him. The focused scrutiny was to little avail, as nothing could be found to justify the foreboding feelings swirling within him.

Making him worry even more that his mind was now playing tricks on him was the demeanor of his steed. The Harrak, whose sensitive nature was even more acutely refined than his, appeared to be perfectly relaxed, as it followed Dragol's lead through the forest.

Dragol began to wonder whether the shackles of a full-fledged paranoia had finally been clamped down upon him. He knew those shackles had been threatening to do so for some time. They had teetered at the edges of his existence ever since he had stepped beyond the Trogen lands to take part in this foreign campaign. Cultivated steadily after the sudden immersion into the foreign territories, after spending all of his previous years within his homelands, the mounting climate of distrust and apprehension had quite possibly reaped a bitter harvest.

Moving his head very slowly, he swept his gaze once again across the still surroundings. He spent a few more moments looking cautiously behind him, off in the direction where the enemy war party had been sighted.

There was not even the slightest outward hint of anything amiss among the trees, as gentle breezes swished through their leaves, gently swaying some of the upper branches to and fro. A few small birds chirped merrily from their high perches, apparently unconcerned by anything in the vicinity. Nonetheless, the distinctive feeling of being closely watched did not diminish, in even the slightest.

Restless and troubled, Dragol grudgingly resumed his hike. The Harrak continued to maintain an extremely calm bearing, and Dragol strove to derive some conscious encouragement from the steed's unalarmed disposition.

Keeping a constant watch about him, the Trogen was nevertheless reluctant to relax his mind fully, for fear of giving some unknown enemy a gate of opportunity through which to strike at him.

As he continued to move farther and farther along, the general feelings of disquiet still did not abate in the least. If anything, the discomfiture increased slightly. Dragol had an inclination that he would not find his mind settled until he was back among his own kind, safely within the encampment outside of the forest's borders.

As Dragol had done before the encounter with the tribal war party, he started to look for a place where he could surmount the upper heights of a tree, to take a look above the forest canopy at the skies.

He also hoped to come across another opening or meadow, as he had a similarly increasing urge to take Rodor up for a brief foray.

Taking the Harrak into the sky would certainly carry Dragol beyond the reach of whatever was causing him such extreme unease. Though he had long been very guarded in his thoughts, ever since he had left the Trogen lands, he did not think that his own mind was deceiving him. The gut instincts that protected him so often, and had just warded him in the skies above the Five Realms, were rarely wrong.

Something was out there among the trees, present within the stillness, and shadowing his every move.

AETHELSTAN

The shield wall continued to hold, though many had fallen in the tempestuous furor of the battle. The slope running up to the top of the ridge was now littered with the bodies of slain Avanorans. The ground near the top of the ridge was so cluttered with the dead of both sides that the fallen bodies created obstacles and hazards, threatening every step that a warrior took.

Aethelstan issued commands for the shield wall to pull back just far enough so that the Saxan warriors could achieve better footing. The enemy was much more numerous, and kept climbing, stumbling, and maneuvering through the fallen bodies to hack and slash at the shield wall.

Many who had begun the day in the deeper ranks of the Saxan defenders had now moved forward to fill up gaps, reinforcing the places where those in the front had fallen. The stream of arrows and other missiles between both sides had lessened, as more casualties took their toll, and the number of remaining arrows, bolts, and stones decreased. The archers, slingers, and crossbowmen were being much more selective in the targets that they aimed at, and those who had thrown javelins had nothing more to hurl after the early exchanges.

Aethelstan's eyes stung harshly from the sweat and blood covering his face, and his arms had grown very weary. His entire body felt heavy and slow, his chest heaving as he took an assessment of the course of the battle. Another Saxan shield that he had taken up was now missing about a quarter of its size, no longer fully round, as many chunks had been cut and smashed out of it during the intensive fighting.

An excited, deafening cry erupted from the right of the Saxan line. Aethelstan saw that the enemy was falling back in a loose and disorganized mass; or at least it seemed so.

Though many signals throughout the battle were being delivered by Avanoran horns, he had not failed to perceive the three distinctive, short blasts that had just preceded the mass fallback.

He was also quick to observe the forms of a large number of horsemen manifesting quietly as they moved up towards the front areas of the battlefield, across from the Saxan right flank. The trees below had, to a large extent, screened the riders' movements until they emerged into the view of those along the ridgetop, as the riders pressed forward in an orderly line.

The horsemen bore long lances, some bearing pennons, and were well-protected with mail shirts, helms, and lengthy kite-shields. The muscular destriers that they rode snorted and pawed at the ground, as the ranks drew to a halt, waiting and watching.

A small number of Saxan warriors broke off individually from places along the right flank of the shield wall, to head downhill after the chaotically retreating Avanoran warriors. It was just a trickle at the present moment, but could soon become a torrent that would threaten the stability of the entire Saxan line.

The appearance of the enemy's resolve breaking was far too tantalizing for many of the thanes and household warriors who were looking for a decisive moment to carry the hard-fought day. Tiring and bloodied, they were undoubtedly hungry to bring the battle to a conclusive end, and the scent of potential victory made the opportunity far too tempting to contemplate.

It was exactly what the Avanoran leaders were counting upon. Before the dam broke, Aethelstan had to move with haste to keep the shield wall stable, and the discipline of the men in place.

"A ruse! A ruse! Hold the shield wall! Obey my command!" Aethelstan shouted out urgently.

The men close around him hurriedly signaled upon horns, while others shouted, relaying his orders onward with alacrity and volume. The thanes down on the right side of the line, who yet remained in their positions, urgently yelled out at the few who had left the lines. Elated and vigorous, those latter warriors were slashing and stabbing as if victory was imminently within grasp, striking at the rear of the enemy warriors who were still retreating haphazardly back down the slope.

Several of the men paused and looked back up the hill, hearing the insistent shouts and horns. Their expressions held disbelief, outwardly stunned and dismayed that so few were taking advantage of the apparent fracture in the enemy lines.

As exhausted as he was, Aethelstan called upon a few last reservoirs of energy, running expeditiously down the back of the shield wall, and exhorting the men of the line to continue recalling the pursuers.

The lives of every man that had left the shield wall was now under the gravest peril. Aethelstan knew that the instant that those men reached just beyond the base of the hill, they would hear another horn blast, as a vicious trap was sprung.

The retreating enemy footsoldiers would suddenly come to a halt, and the sound of hoof beats would fill the trees as a host of knights cantered forward upon their warhorses. The encroaching, mounted force, which had only recently come within view deep in the trees, would then descend on the stranded, tired Saxans. No quarter would be extended to any warrior that the intended ruse had so ably manipulated away from the shield wall.

"Call them back! Call them back now! Their lives depend on it, do not tarry!" Aethelstan shouted at the upper limits of his lungs.

The men of the front and rear ranks took up his cry, calling on their fellow fighters to hurry back to the shield wall. The sense of alarm was rife in their tones, as their calls reached out to the warriors descending the slope.

Realizing that most of their number had stayed above along the ridge, and hearing the dire urgency in the outcries, the strayed fighters ceased in their pursuit. Most of them were a little more than halfway down the ridge, close upon the enemy, but not yet far enough along to spring the waiting trap.

They took one more frustrated hack or jab in the direction of the fleeing enemy warriors, before turning back and trudging reluctantly up the slope. Disgruntled and not entirely understanding what faced them, they made slow, half-hearted progress at first. They were spurred into haste just a moment later, as horns blared angrily from the forest below.

The Avanorans, in frustration, moved their mounted force

forward, vibrating the ground as the fleeing Avanoran warriors on foot came to an abrupt halt, turned, and started back after the now-retreating Saxans.

Casting some quick glances over their shoulders, and frantically picking up their pace, a stark realization dawned upon the returning Saxans. They now saw what had been waiting for them a short distance from the base of the ridge's slope, and knew that they had been saved from certain death by their comrades' persistent warnings.

Aethelstan called earnestly for any archers on the right flank to come forward with him. The Saxans coming back toward the wall still had about a fourth of the length of the ridge's frontal slope remaining for them to surmount. The mixed Avanoran force, of mounted cavalry and the returning lines of foot soldiers, were now climbing steadily up the slope of the hill, rapidly shortening the gap between them and the tiring Saxans.

"Archers through, send one volley on my signal, then fall back!" Aethelstan shouted.

The shields in the front were parted to allow the archers through to the outer edge of the ridge top. Aethelstan raised his sword high into the air, passing between two stout thanes, whose mail and helms were spattered copiously with blood.

"Hold!" Aethelstan called, as the warriors hurrying up the hill finally reached the top, passing in relative safety back within the confines of the shield wall. The instant that Aethelstan saw the last few men reach the refuge of the shield wall, he brought the sword down in a forward slash, crying out, "Loose arrows!"

The concentrated volley greeted the regrouped Avanoran pursuers, striking indiscriminately into the ranks of the forward-most spearmen. There were some arrows that found fleshy targets a little further behind, bringing down a few horses and riders.

"Behind the shield wall! Archers fall back!" Aethelstan called loudly.

The peasant archers needed little prompting, with the oncoming Avanoran warriors, as they hurried back with Aethelstan, hustling between the masses of round shields through channels that remained parted to allow them through. The shields then overlapped once again, as the Saxans of the front line closed their ranks.

It was not much longer before the right flank was engaged by the Avanorans, who had been thwarted in their designs for easy quarry. The ridge on that end had a more gentle slope, and the enemy's horses continued their ascent, pacing their steeds up behind the screen of foot soldiers.

Their attempt offered Aethelstan the first opportunity of the day to strike hard at the core strength of the enemy force; the mounted knights.

Aethelstan wished that he had archers with full quivers available at that moment. He commanded the men of the back ranks who had anything that they could use as a missile to ready themselves. As the clash of steel resumed along the right flank, and the cries of battle carried through the air, Aethelstan called for another volley to be loosed.

A horde of projectiles went flying, ranging from arrows, to stones, to makeshift missiles, the latter consisting of everything from crude war clubs, with stones lashed by leather thongs to short wooden shafts, to hand axes once used for farm duties. The deadly, arcing cloud soared overhead, showering down upon the mounted Avanoran ranks.

Combined with vicious axe, lance, and sword thrusts along the front of the shield wall, the enemy's left flank was gored. The Avanoran spearmen, having greatly tired themselves in the retreat down the hill, and the pressing climb back up it, splintered quickly. The mounted fighters, unable to use the full strengths afforded a mounted warrior, were stalled in their advance, providing ample targets for missiles and hand weapons. Horns called out urgently from the enemy ranks, and the spearmen and mounted warriors began backing down the slope.

"Hold!" Aethelstan called out forcefully, seeing the enemy retreat. "Hold the line!"

He hurried back up to the ridge's apex, to get a better look. The enemy forces were pulling back en masse, and the pause in the fighting afforded the Saxans a prime opportunity to regroup.

His own men had suffered heavy casualties, and were in dire need of a respite after an extended period of hand to hand combat. The wounded were helped away from the shield wall, as both clergy and non-combatants from the areas behind the battle lines hustled forward to assist.

As the din of battle was suspended, the sickening sounds of groans and cries from wounded men reached Aethelstan's ears. They were terrible noises that jabbed right into his inner heart.

Keeping his face steady, he rapidly disseminated orders that the men were to remain along the ridge-top. As with the last lull in the fighting, they were also to set about acquiring whatever weapons, shields, helms and even mail coats that could be retrieved easily from the fallen of both sides.

Each break in the fighting provided a grisly opportunity, but they were ones that could not be overlooked. The men of the General Fyrd could now arm themselves with something much better than makeshift clubs, low quality spears, harvest tools, and long knives. The men of the Select Fyrd could replace shattered shields, and broken swords and axes. Stripping the dead was a repulsive, unwelcome chore, but given the dire circumstances, Aethelstan believed that the Saxans would be forgiven for the mild violation of the corpses.

Aethelstan then repeated a very strict dictate that he had issued before the fighting had begun, that if any Avanoran wounded were come across, they were to be tended to. He knew that there would likely be moments of personal vengeance, as men who had just lost kin and dear friends came across enemy wounded, but the great thane hoped to keep bloody revenge to a minimum. Though his hope was rooted in sheer idealism, mercy was one of the ways that the Saxans could distinguish themselves further from the invaders.

Men from among the peasant levies were then ordered to gather up any arrows that they could find intact, as many of the Avanoran arrows that had missed their intended targets could be pulled out of the ground, from trees, or picked up in a reusable condition.

Aethelstan strode down the length of the Saxan front, heading back towards center where his standard still flew unscathed. Cenferth rushed forward to greet him eagerly upon his return.

"Thane Aethelstan! The right flank was saved, The Almighty is indeed with you this day!" Cenferth exclaimed, in excited tones.

"For now, Cenferth," Aethelstan replied calmly, clasping his household warrior on the shoulder. "The marauders will be back soon enough. But we have some time, as even they need some rest."

"How long do you think we have this time, before they attack again?" Cenferth asked, running a grime-covered finger over the five-lobed sword pommel jutting up from his scabbard.

"A handful of moments? An hour? Maybe they will simply retreat back to Avanor. Could we not hope for that?" Aethelstan asked, with a sad, regretful smile. He wished it could be so simple.

Aethelstan glanced towards the skies. The airborne scouts for the Avanoran force continued to circle in wide, gliding patterns overhead. In the midst of so much death, Aethelstan found that they now resembled carrion birds, readying to descend for a gruesome feast.

Relatively few in number, the sky riders would not be a great threat to the Saxan force, but they would convey to the enemy commanders that the Saxans were still concentrated along the ridge line. Any movement the Saxans tried to undertake in any numbers would be easily spotted during daylight. Edmund had so few Himmerosen available to him that the enemy presence in the skies would go uncontested. There was no hope of reinforcement, with the overwhelming majority of sky steeds requisitioned for the massive battle out on the Plains of Athelney.

Aethelstan knew that time was working at cross-purposes for the Saxans, both in their favor and against them. The longer that the Saxans held out on the ridge line, the more that the chances of the enemy's goals being achieved would dwindle. There was little doubt that the force before them intended to pass through and strike the flank or rear of the Saxan forces out on the Plains of Athelney.

The battle before them, on the other hand, would likely be lost in a struggle of unrelenting attrition. Aethelstan would not have been surprised to learn that he had already lost one in four men to death or serious injury.

He turned back towards Cenferth, who was awaiting him patiently. "Yes, we could hope that they decide to retreat. Come, let us take a walk together."

Cenferth quietly fell in with Aethelstan as they strode along the back of the ridge. Just past the center, a large group of levied peasants were sitting down and taking a rest. They looked haggard and weary, no longer unfamiliar with the horrors and agonies of battle. Aethelstan knew that for a great many of them, their outlook on life had been changed irrevocably, in just a few short hours.

A few had fallen asleep, having slumped down to the ground where they stretched out without concern for cover. Some seemed to be in a silence of their own, while still others passed the time talking with each other in low, subdued voices. Some wept openly over the losses of comrades and kin, as others sought to comfort them, speaking gently or putting an arm around their shoulders.

Aethelstan's heart ached at the mournful sights. Though phyiscally unscathed, with only a few cuts and bruises incurred in the fighting, the men were profusely bleeding in spirit.

A little more reassuring, Aethelstan could see that several peasants had procured shields, helms, swords, and other well-made weapons. One man of more advanced years was wriggling into a mail shirt, though the blood-stained, punctured iron links in the chest area spoke volumes as to what had happened to its former owner. Nevertheless, the man seemed eager to don the mail coat without delay.

Several of the men glanced in his direction as he walked through their midst. A few chewed upon pieces of salt meat or hard bread, and a barrel of ale had been tapped. A couple of men were handing out water skins, which had been filled from the stream that traveled through the low ground behind the ridge. Men cupped their hands and splashed water on their faces, working to clean off the filth and blood from the battle.

A couple of monks were assisting some men with their lighter wounds. They carefully poured water over the bleeding injuries to clean them out, before wrapping strips of cloth to temporarily bandage them.

The lessons of war were woven into the vivid images spread all around Aethelstan. Levels of fatigue and adequate food and drink were all central to the morale of an army. Food was perhaps the highest factor of them all, as empty stomachs deteriorated spirits within a force extremely quickly. In some ways, the elements of rest and sustenance were a much greater concern than all of the knights, war horses, arrows, and swords of the Avanoran invaders.

"Great Thane, you must eat too," an older, grizzled-looking man interjected in a gruff voice, breaking Aethelstan away from his dark, inner ponderings.

The scraggly, bearded man went by the name of Bothelm, a leather worker who plied his trade in Bergton. Bothelm had a look of deep concern on his weathered face.

He extended a large chunk of bread in one hand, and a wooden cup filled with ale in the other. "The ale is from a new barrel just brought up from the camp. Not the best ... not nearly as good as my wife brews ... but it is the nectar of heaven right now."

At first, Aethelstan hesitated, as he wanted to make sure that all of the men were getting a chance to get some food and ale before he worried about his own needs. Yet Aethelstan understood the look of worry in the eyes of the older man. It was the kind of expression that transcended the more worldly matters of simple artisans and high-ranking thanes.

"Thane Aethelstan, if your strength is not kept, then how can you lead us?" the older man urged, as he pushed the food and ale cup forward. "We all need you to keep your strength."

"Thank you, my friend," Aethelstan replied, smiling amiably, as he accepted the proffered bread and ale.

He took a deep draught of the ale cup, finishing about half of it in the first gulp. He had to restrain from downing all of the vessel's contents in his great thirst.

In normal times, he certainly would have questioned the skill of the brewer, but, as Bothelm had said, the circumstances of the moment made it taste as sweet as anything that had ever touched his lips. A small sigh escaped Aethelstan, as he breathed out slowly in the wake of the long swig.

The older man smiled warmly at him. "Thank you, Great Thane. When you take your needs to heart, know that you take our needs to heart. Do not refuse yourself what your body needs."

With a slight bow, the old man turned, and rejoined a nearby group of companions. Aethelstan stood a little entranced by the warm words and sentiments of the man, a beacon of light in the midst of such a terrible struggle. Even in the most daunting of times, such rays of light pierced his inner laments, reminding Aethelstan what they were all really fighting for.

After a moment's pause, he tore off a piece of the bread and placed it in his mouth. He let the rough bread soften for a moment before beginning to chew it. Cenferth had been served with some bread, dried meat, and ale from some other men close by.

He held a chunk of the salty meat out to Aethelstan, talking through a mouth full of food, "Some meat would do you good as well. A man cannot live on bread alone."

"I think your concerns about bread have been used in a different context by the priests, but thank you anyway," Aethelstan replied with a grin, taking it from him. "If there is one that I am not worried about finding ample food, it is you, Cenferth. You have a nose for it, better than the most capable hunting dog in all of Saxany."

Though he tried to slow his pace, he wolfed down the salted

meat, and the rest of the ale and bread in a few moments. The heat of the battle had obscured his hunger, but now that his senses could turn towards other needs, he found that he was as famished as he was parched.

The sound of a horse galloping, coming from somewhere behind them at great speed, abruptly attracted his attention. He heard the sentries down on the other side of the ridge calling out challenges. He drew his eyes to the sight of the rider, just as a few armed warriors stepped aside to let the mounted figure through.

Approaching slowly up the back slope of the ridge was a man upon a gray horse, whose flanks were sleek with lather from an arduous jaunt. The man was lightly garbed, with a brown cloak clasped by a silver pin at the right shoulder, over a tunic and breeches of a similar color. His face was drawn and careworn, as much as his hair was disheveled. Aethelstan knew from the first glance that the rider had pressed both himself and his mount to the outer limits of their endurance.

The horseman bore a rolled up parchment in his right hand, clutched protectively, as he neared Aethelstan and slowed the horse down.

"Thane Aethelstan," the rider addressed him without delay, pulling the reins up on the horse a couple of feet away from the Saxan commander.

"Yes?" Aethelstan replied.

"The reply from Arubandel," the rider responded, with a leaden expression, extending the parchment towards Aethelstan.

Aethelstan accepted the parchment from the somber rider, and fingered the unbroken wax seal on it. The man's countenance had already communicated the contents of the parchment, though Aethelstan still had to read the actual words inscribed upon it.

He turned towards Cenferth, "Get this man to our rear encampment. He has risked much to reach Arubandel and return back here. See that he is given food, drink, and any rations he may desire, if he should need to depart."

The man looked back over at the ridgeline, where a good number of men idled along the course of the shield wall. They were looking out with shields and lances within easy reach, awaiting the expected return of the enemy.

His eyes swiveled back to Aethelstan. "Thane Aethelstan, great thane of Bergton, I can speak for myself, but not for my steed. My horse has been driven hard, and I will not begrudge him some much earned rest, but I would like to rejoin those of my home village on the line, if you will allow me to."

Aethelstan regarded the exhausted man for a moment, before nodding. "If that is what you wish."

"I cannot rest, as long as the day has not been decided," he said, as he swung his back leg around, and dismounted the horse. "Can you have one of your men guide me to the place where the men from Oak Crossing are gathered?"

"I will take him, Thane Aethelstan," Cenferth volunteered immediately. "I know that the men from Oak Crossing were placed on the left flank. Come with me."

Cenferth beckoned to the rider, and the man started to go with him, as another Saxan took control of his horse and led it away. Before the man had gone more than a stride, Aethelstan took a sudden step forward and put a hand upon the man's shoulder, halting him momentarily. "Before you go, I must have your name."

The man replied, "Ceolfrid, a ceorl that has served in the garrison in the Burh at Sudborton, to the east."

"Sudborton … there is excellent boar hunting around there, I am told," Aethelstan said with a wistful grin, thinking of better times and pursuits.

The rider's mouth turned up into a slight grin. It was a welcome relief to see the trace of levity dawn upon his forlorn, exhausted face. "Yes, Thane Aethelstan. It is indeed exceptional hunting there."

"If we should live to see other days, and better ones at that, then I should like to come and hunt with you there. I will also make certain that you have at least five hides of land bestowed upon you," Aethelstan said, with a smile of his own. "You have the blood of a worthy thane flowing in you. Fight well, Ceolfrid, and let us see better days together."

"Thank you, Thane Aethelstan," Ceolfrid replied in a low voice, nodding, with a look of surprise reflected in his eyes. The Saxan was hesitant, tongue-tied at the sudden bequest by Aethelstan.

Cenferth cast Aethelstan a grin, and led the stunned rider off down the line towards the area where the people of Oak's Crossing were located. Aethelstan watched the rider go onward to his fellow men, willing to stand with them immediately after having endured a dangerous, hard-pressed ride alone through enemy-riddled land. As quickly as life could be cut short, Aethelstan could brook no delays in recognizing the worthiness of the brave Saxan. He deeply hoped that Ceolfrid survived to realize the reward.

Turning, Aethelstan walked away a few steps to where he stood by himself, and looked down at the parchment. The wax seal of Saxany and of Arubandel, a confirmation of the genuine nature of the message within, bound the parchment.

The nearest burh to the ridge, about ten leagues away to the south, Arubandel was one of several places to which Aethelstan had dispatched riders in a desperate need to scrape up as many additional men as could be found in the area.

Aethelstan paused a little longer, looking down at the reddish wax seals with trepidation, before delicately breaking them with his fingers and spreading the document out.

It was a direct message, reading;

'Aethelstan, Thane of Bergton, serving Ealdorman Morcar of Wessachia, in loyal service of King Alcuin of Saxany:

On behalf of my lord, Thane Hathufrith of Arubandel, in loyal service to Ealdorman Byrtnoth of Sussachia, loyal servant of King Alcuin of Saxany, I regret that I cannot send you good tidings. All of our males, and even some of our women who could walk the distance, have gone to the great muster to the west. We have only the youngest of boys and the oldest of men, and can barely lock our gates or keep a watch on our ramparts. We regrettably have nothing to send to you in the way of more people for your levy. It is not our choice. All who could carry any weapons have already left in the great levy and afterwards. We are truly sorry.

-your brother in the Almighty,
Father Stigand

The message, one of several such correspondences that had returned over the past couple of days, caused Aethelstan's heart to drop immeasurably, though he kept his face resolute. He knew that many other eyes were watching his reaction to the apparent message, many of them knowing that he had sent out calls for more help.

He was not surprised in the least by Father Stigand's answer, having fathomed what the answer was before he even cracked the wax sealing the parchment. Even so, it did not make reading the heavy words any easier. Every rejection dampened his hopes further, the frustration mounting while standing on a battle position that he could not abandon.

Aethelstan turned and strode swiftly back towards the ridge. Closing his eyes for a few seconds, he whispered a silent prayer to the Almighty to provide him with strength. He uttered a petition that he could somehow be a source of inspiration to his warriors in the hours that they would need him most.

As he contemplated the words, the prayer filled him with a calmness that took the frayed edge from his nerves. When his eyelids finally parted, any man that looked into his face would see a composed, focused individual. He knew that they must not become aware of the despondence growing deep inside him, as he struggled with the daunting realities.

If any man among the Saxans looked a little closer, however, not every sign of his inner worries was so well-masked. The parchment in his right hand was clenched tightly, to the extent that the eyes of any that bothered to look could have easily perceived the whiteness of his knuckles.

section v

DRAGOL

Dragol pressed onward through the eerily silent forest, still laden with the disconcerting feeling that other eyes were upon him. His body, underneath his hide cuirass, was now caked with sweat, which ran in thin rivulets down from his perspiring brow, trickling around his short muzzle. Dragol's robust muscles were finally drained of their normally prodigious reserves of strength.

Even if he were a typical Trogen warrior, such an exhausted state would have required considerable amounts of exertion to reach. As one of the more exceptional specimens of his race, it testified to the fact that Dragol had undergone a most arduous struggle.

The gloaming of the settling dusk had begun to permeate the forest around him, overtaking the dappled light from the late afternoon's sun. The shadows were filling in and deepening among the trees all around, the overall ambience progressively dimming.

For quite some time, his throat had been parched for drink, and his body ached for more solid sustenance. Yet Dragol was not about to worry about issues such as those. Every stride that he could take, and every league that he could traverse, would place him farther and farther beyond the swirling chaos in the region being pierced by the invasion.

A couple of ascensions to the top of aged, soaring oak trees had given him a propitious view of the situation above the forest's ceiling. The skies were largely calm, and he could see no signs of either friend or foe, whether Darroks, Trogens, or enemy Midragardans.

His own Harrak was not yet faring badly, although the stalwart steed was clearly beginning to show fatigue. Rodor was a hardy animal, to an exceptional degree, but Dragol would worry about its needs well before taking care of his own.

Just over a gentle rise, they came within sight of a woodland brook that was flowing with crisp, translucent waters. The sight was virtually irresistible, prompting Dragol to trudge slowly forward, heading down the embankment.

He removed his helm as he neared the water's edge, feeling the rush of cool air engulf his heated, sweat-matted head. Sheathing his longblade, and setting his shield down on the bank next to him, he sank to his knees by the water's edge.

Both Trogen and Harrak were shortly drinking in ample gulps of the welcome, invigorating liquid. The cool water washed down Dragol's dry throat, beginning to quench his deep thirst and renew his depleted body. Though tired, and with a seemingly bottomless desire for the water, he maintained enough presence of mind to keep his consumption controlled, maintaining his awareness for any signs of threats.

With one cupped hand, he scooped up some of the water and splashed it on his broad forehead. A few more douses with the water were sufficient to remove the stickiness caused by the sweat and dirt that had caked upon his face.

He breathed a deep sigh of relief, as the water dripped off of his protruding face, allowing himself a brief moment of enjoyment in the midst of the struggles that had enveloped his existence. As he allowed his body its first moments of rest in some time, the fatigue building inside finally began to catch up fully with him. A less rational part of him felt like collapsing in a heap on the bank, and going to sleep for awhile.

Ordering his swiftly tightening leg muscles to stand again, he slowly walked over to a tree just beyond the bank of the brook. Leaning his shield against it, Dragol slumped down wearily against the base of the trunk. He felt his eyelids growing very heavy while he watched his steed finish satiating its thirst.

The gloom in the woods had deepened considerably, growing significantly murkier as day edged upon the brink of night. Nothing stirred within the woods, and Dragol could not deny that a short rest would certainly do his body well. The prospect of rest was so powerfully inviting, so seductive that he almost pushed his cares aside and gave in to the inclination.

Cursing sharply at himself for entertaining such weakness, he roused himself back up, stretching his muscles and taking in several deep breaths to stave off the laborious fatigue. His Harrak had just finished drinking, and looked as if it was about to settle down along the embankment.

The distinctive feeling of being watched still hung ominously in the air. He had almost fallen asleep out in the open, without regard for shelter or his steed, he angrily realized. If something with harmful intent had been watching, then it would have had plenty of opportunity to launch a surprise attack.

Carefully, he panned his eyes around the forest, with a focus so intent and penetrating that his gaze threatened to see through solid objects. His search was left unsatisfied, at least in finding a physical cause for the bothersome feelings. Shaking his head, he turned to relieve himself near one of the adjacent trees, his bladder already filled, and now being added to with the weight of the water that he had just imbibed from the brook.

As he was finishing, a few flickers of movement off to his right suddenly caught his eye. As he snapped to attention, turning to focus in that direction, there were some other flickers of motion just off to his left, this time accompanied with some faint rustlings in the underbrush. Keeping his head rigid and his eyes still, he reached out with his left arm and picked his shield back up, settling his grip around the straight iron bar midway up the back.

Swiftly, he withdrew his longblade, quietly stepping forward and standing alongside his Harrak. A surge of adrenaline pushed back a good portion of his weariness, enabling a keener wariness to come forth in its wake.

As some other shadows moved off to the right, emitting the sounds of more rustlings and scrapes, the Harrak tucked its wings close and squared its body towards the movements. Rodor's large ears twitched and shifted, as they diligently tracked the sounds.

The steed's eyes and nostrils flared, as it picked up the scent of whatever was moving among the trees. A low growl emanated deep from within the sky steed's throat, as its clawed feet shuffled and scratched the ground. It bared its sharp teeth menacingly, clenched firmly within its extremely powerful jaws.

Seeing the Harrak's agitation, Dragol knew that there were serious threats fanning out in the woods around them. His fears were further confirmed just a few moments later, as forms moved in a swift blur to the left and right of his periphery, a little closer than before.

The worst aspect of it was that he had no idea what the gathering threat was, though he surmised from the sounds and rapid bursts of movement that it was some kind of wild animal. The movements were far too quick to have been executed by any human, or even one of the rat-men from Yanith.

"Guard," Dragol whispered forcibly to his Harrak, a command that set the sky steed into a trained combat mode, ready to slash and bite should anything of a foreign nature come upon them.

He slowly retreated backwards a couple more steps towards the side of his Harrak, feeling its body pressed against his back. Quickly, he spared a glance upward, to see what desperate options might lay above.

There was no clearing big enough to afford them an easy escape, even if he had wished to try to break through in an outright emergency and risk injury to Rodor. The old trees had grown a sprawling web of thick, strong branches over the years, interlaced and spread out all over, forming a continuous, dense cover. The matter of whether or not Dragol was willing to risk the Harrak's injury was entirely inconsequential, as the forest canopy was completely impassable, blocking his steed from the safer haven of the sky.

The forest grew deadly silent, as Dragol steeled his resolve for the coming attack. As if a shadow was coming to life, one of the entities openly walked out of the brush off to the right. It was about the size of a normal wolf, although Dragol could tell right away that there were many differences.

The creature's head was flatter and longer than that of a wolf, with eyes set low in its skull. The animal's open jaws exhibited a set of elongated, thin canines, as it snarled and growled at the Trogen and Harrak.

The beast had a heavily built, muscular body, walking on shorter, thick limbs that ended in large feet. Dragol could see no claws at the ends of its feet, and it appeared to walk with a more upright, flatter step than other forest hunters, such as wolves.

Not showing any fear of Dragol or the Harrak, the creature took a few more steps forward, fixing them with its feral gaze. Three other similar forms then issued forth from the surrounding trees, another to his right, one to his left, and one a little behind him.

There was little use for any further pretenses. A fight for life was about to begin.

The Harrak had turned toward the two approaching predators off to the right, hissing and growling defiantly towards them. Dragol rotated a little so that he could keep a full eye upon both of the others, as they stepped closer and closer.

Dragol waved his sword and roared a battle cry at them. Subtleties were forgotten, and would only become a concern again if he survived the impending fight.

The creatures rushed in from all sides, as Dragol braced himself for the impact. He angled his shield towards the one that had been closing from behind while he prepared to strike at the other with the longblade.

He heard the raucous cry of his Harrak, just as the two creatures on his side finally reached him. With another loud cry, Dragol brought the longblade chopping down in an incredibly forceful blow, timing the strike perfectly.

The blade cleaved deep into the creature, burying itself far into the base of its skull. The creature's momentum carried it a little further, but it flopped down heavily on the ground, killed instantly by the robust blow.

The creature that he was shielding against thudded heavily into the wooden barrier, its dense body and speed knocking Dragol backwards. He had just a split second between the time that he had lodged his longblade in the flesh and bone of the other creature and the impact of the second. The great force of the collision caused him to lose his grip on the hilt of the longblade, as he tumbled back.

With a quick glance, he saw that he had almost been knocked into the maelstrom behind him, as the Harrak's arsenal of teeth and claws were pitted against the snapping, shearing jaws of the two beasts besetting it.

Just a few feet to his left, the creature that had hit his shield had scrambled back to its feet, and was in the motion of charging in again. Dragol had no weapon in his hand to strike it with, and instead braced his legs, readying to thrust the shield outward.

As the creature came within a couple feet of him, he put his body behind a strong shove, and smashed the creature in the end of its long snout with the rigid wood of the shield. Rapid yelps and cries of pain erupted from the creature as it stumbled aside, its snout bloodied from the vigorous strike.

Dragol kept to his feet, and saw that the beast had lost much of its boldness, as it whined and snarled in a mixture of anger and pain. Out of the corner of his eye, he saw that the hilt of his longblade was sticking up just a few feet to his right.

Keeping his eyes largely riveted upon the wounded creature before him, and casting quick glances behind him, just in case one of the other beasts had broken free of the ongoing tumult, he edged over to the body of the fallen beast. Gripping the hilt of the longblade, he placed his right boot on the dead animal's head, wrenching the longblade free with a forceful yank.

Now one against one, he squared his shield towards the surviving beast, and stomped forward with his blade raised in his right hand. The creature snarled and backpedaled at his aggressive advance.

Dragol bellowed another war cry at it, as he surged forward behind the shield and brought his longblade up for a sweeping attack. The beast had evidently had enough of the struggle and Dragol's surge of aggression, as it whirled, leaped, and bounded off into the depths of the forest.

Hot with rage, Dragol cursed the fleeing beast and turned around to go to the aid of his Harrak.

The steed was still fending off the other two remaining predators. Its neck, sides, and flanks had been raked by the attacker's slashing, snapping teeth, its body rife with seeping wounds, but it had inflicted several gashes of its own upon its two muscular tormenters.

One creature was positioned in front of the Harrak, and one was edging behind, as the battle had drawn to a temporary stalemate. There was plenty of fight left in the Harrak, as it snapped viciously in the direction of the creature in front of it.

The Harraks had extraordinary jaw strength, possessing bone-crunching power. The reflexes of the two predators must have been very capable to avoid being caught in the Harrak's devastating bite.

Dragol took off at a charge towards his steed, but everything developed at a dizzyingly fast pace. The two beasts moved in near unison upon his steed, to resume their attack.

The Harrak cried out as the creature behind it clamped its jaws down upon one of its hind legs, tearing at the muscle and flesh. Given a slight opening as the Harrak lurched up in pain, the creature in front of it lunged forward, bringing its jaws down upon one of the Harrak's forelegs. The two predators intended to cripple the much larger Harrak, and then wear it down in a struggle of attrition.

Dragol did not hesitate as he neared the engaged predators and his wounded steed. With a raging outcry at the point of attack, Dragol caught the beast at the front of his steed completely by surprise. He slashed down vigorously, empowered with unrelenting fury as the blade met the exposed back of the creature. It would not aggrieve his steed any further, as the blade cleaved right through its spine.

Not pausing to evaluate the damage, Dragol unceremoniously

ripped the blade free, shifted his grip, and brought it down with all the force that he could muster. The strike impaled the stricken creature, finishing off whatever scant shreds of life that may have lingered within it.

Once again, Dragol had driven the blade deep, and had to take a couple of moments to free the longblade, stepping on the carcass of the predator. Rearing up, and with the longblade readied again, he turned immediately to see what had become of the last remaining predator.

Rodor had spun around to face the other creature, but the predator had somehow gotten underneath the Harrak's lower jaw. It had been able to bring its elongated snout, and long, narrow canines to bear down onto the neck of his loyal steed.

The image called up an unsurpassed furor within the Trogen warrior. Dragol moved with lightning speed and slew the final creature with one tremendous blow.

The strike severed the creature's head from its neck, though its jaws were still embedded in the throat of his beleaguered steed. Dragol fell forward and pulled the jaws of the dead creature wide, slinging the head aside, so that he could free the neck of his sorely wounded steed.

To his great dismay and deep anguish, the final predator had delivered a mortal wound to his cherished Harrak, Rodor. The fatally wounded sky steed collapsed on the ground, as its life ebbed rapidly. Time seemed to halt as its sides heaved a couple more times, just before the last breath fled its body.

To a Trogen sky rider, Harrak steeds were an extension of the rider. A bond of great trust and affection grew between a longtime steed and rider, as each came to know the other's mannerisms and nuances, as if they were one.

The steeds carried their riders across the skies at distances above the ground that would allow for no mistakes. In combat the steeds had to fight and respond to the directives of their riders without any room for error, as a stricken steed meant certain death for the rider. Such a close dependence bred a relationship that far surpassed that of most Trogen friendships.

Rodor had been with Dragol for several years, and the sudden loss of his sky steed wrenched deep emotions from within him. Not inclined to tears of sorrow, the Trogen warrior responded in a great burst of anger and helpless frustration.

"No enemy maggots will feast upon you, Rodor ... not one! Even if it causes the death of me!" Dragol seethed, through tightly clenched teeth.

Despite every effort to hold back the deepest of his emotions, his eyes misted over hotly, with a burning sadness. He reached out and caressed the muzzle of his loyal, fallen sky steed.

The overwhelming feeling of emptiness gaping within him prompted some actions that would have seemed to be very ill-advised, especially within a foreign land caught in the chaotic, deadly grip of war. Not even bothering to think of the possible consequences, looking out through eyes white hot, and fueled by several passions, Dragol set about fashioning a makeshift funeral pyre. His sense of caution gave way to recklessness, as he barely paused to worry about the possibility of dangerous wild animals or enemy tribesmen, despite having recently come across both in his journey through the unfamiliar woods.

In a way, he hoped that the last of the predators came back, so that he could take his time and hack it apart piece by piece, for each injury suffered by Rodor, even the slightest scratch.

He cleared out a wide space upon the forest floor, setting wood and dry brush around the body of his steed. Dutifully, he removed all of the items that could still be used from the Harrak, leaving its harnessing and saddle on it.

Dragol retrieved some flint from one of the leather pouches that had been affixed to the harnessing. With a little effort, he started a fire, and watched with a leaden heart as the flames took to life, spreading around the body of his loyal sky steed. Neither the smoke from the fire, though stinging his eyes, nor the pungent scent of burning flesh, which filled his nostrils, could do so much as budge him, as he stared dourly into the depths of the consuming flames.

His thoughts dwelled upon Rodor's steadfast loyalty and companionship. Dragol reflected upon a host of adventures that they had shared together, as the smoke wafted up. It was the least of tributes that he could give to a creature that had shared so much of his life.

"Goodbye, Rodor. Were it possible that we meet again, then I would most gladly," Dragol murmured, as the flames were finishing up with their appointed task. "Fly high across the Elysian Fields, Rodor ... fly free and far, to every horizon."

Only when the flames were dying out did the thought finally

cross his mind that the smoke from the pyre and scent of the burned flesh might attract unwelcome attention. Feeling as hollow as he ever had before, he mustered his resolve and trudged onward, following the course of the stream along its bank. He was now bearing a couple of leather bags in addition to his weapons, and the progress was slower and more taxing. He had barely proceeded more than one league before he needed to stop and rest for a few moments.

Leaning up against a tree, he set his shield down to lean against his thigh. He fumbled about in one of the packs for some hard bread and dried meat. In his sorrow, he did not feel hungry, but knew that his body needed something now if he hoped to have enough strength to hunt later.

The darkness was much thicker now, and the silvery light of the two moons filtered down in thin rays through the overhead canopy. The descending light gave a spectral cast to the environs, though after what he had been through Dragol was not unnerved in the least. He looked at the woods around him, though his mind was far from where he could even appreciate the aesthetic nature of the scene.

Yet in that moment, a sense of alertness flooded back into his conscious mind, as another feeling of being closely watched surfaced.

Whether it was due to the great fatigue accumulated through the battle, the ordeals in the forest, and the debilitating, emotional loss of his sky steed, or perhaps some deeper insight, he did not experience the sense of threat that had accompanied his prior feelings. He let the bread and meat fall back into the saddle pouch, and then let it and the other leather pack that he carried fall to the ground. Picking up his shield again, his chest heaved with deep breaths, as he girded his resolve once more.

He was beyond caring, and felt that he would rather not delay a moment more, and get whatever fight was coming over with. Gripping his Thunder Wolf amulet on the leather cord about his neck, he spoke aloud an oath that he would die well, in a way that would honor the Trogen race.

Placing the amulet back down to rest upon his chest, he reached down and slid his longblade out of its sheath once again.

Breathing in a deep draught of air, he shouted loudly into the forest. "Who is it that comes now? I know that you are there. Reveal yourself! Fight me if you will! Beast or man, I do not care!"

His glistening, sorrowful eyes peered out into the shadows,

awaiting a response. After several long moments, in which it seemed as if nothing more would happen, a solitary figure moved out from among the trees just across the brook. The beams of moonlight revealed that the figure was dressed in a flowing cloak that draped the being from the neck nearly to the ground. On the figure's head was a wide-brimmed, round-topped hat.

"It is not safe in this area. Especially for a Trogen," a deep, yet gentle, voice emerged from the being. It was a decidedly non-threatening tone, one that contrasted mightily with everything that Dragol had felt and experienced since deciding to land his steed in the forest. Even more surprising, the words had been spoken fluently in the Trogen language.

"Who are you?" Dragol queried, utterly surprised at the presence of a stranger, clearly not of his own kind, speaking in the Trogen tongue.

"One of past, present, and future," returned the cryptic reply, again in perfectly rendered Trogen. From what Dragol could judge, the individual was a human male.

"Are you of the Five Realms?" Dragol asked.

"No, for my loyalty is only given to one Kingdom, though my path has taken me through many," the other stated calmly.

"Which Kingdom is that?" Dragol asked, his curiosity rising.

"A Kingdom not of this world, though it still resides in the hearts of many who yet walk the face of this world," the other replied.

The figure walked to the edge of the brook, pulling his cloak up as he stepped through the shallow waters to reach the bank on the other side. The strange figure surmounted the bank and stepped towards Dragol, approaching closely enough for the Trogen to make out some further details.

Underneath the broad brim of the hat was the face of an old man, with thick, flowing locks of white hair, and a copious, white beard that reached down to the middle of his chest. The old man wore a patch covering one eye, while the lone, exposed eye seemed to sparkle, even in the dim environs.

Despite the outward signs of advanced age on the human, Dragol noticed that the man moved with a certain litheness that belied the elderly appearance. He also had fairly broad shoulders, carried well, in good posture. The man exhibited none of the frailty that old humans usually showed.

"I have heard of no such Kingdom," Dragol countered, not

knowing what to make of the peculiar figure. His hand remained tight upon the hilt of his longblade, though his instincts still perceived no trace of threat. Nevertheless, he warned the man sternly, "Go no farther."

The old man halted, about ten feet away from where Dragol stood. There was no hint of aggression in the man's posture or face.

"Why are you in these woods? This is far from those under your command, Dragol," the old man addressed him, as if they were merely sharing a casual conversation.

The words caused the Trogen chieftain to pause. His body was tired, and his mind was probably very dulled after all of the recent, arduous trials, but he had not completely lost his wits.

Dragol wondered immediately how the old man knew his name and that he was a commander of warriors. It was even stranger than the fact that the man spoke the Trogen language with fluency, and moved with far more suppleness than a human of advanced years normally did. Whatever the explanation was, it was apparent that the man likely possessed some sort of mystical power.

Dragol could not afford to assume otherwise, or he was sure to find himself in even greater peril. The huge Trogen's grip tightened further on the leather-wrapped hilt of his longblade. He was not one with inclinations to trust Wizards, for that is what he perceived the man to be.

"There is no need for alarm, Dragol. No harm shall come to you from me," the old man said, as if he had just read Dragol's thoughts.

The old man then grew quiet for a moment, his attention distracted, momentarily intent on another, unspoken matter. He suddenly brought his head up and looked at Dragol. "Another patrol of tribal warriors is coming this way."

A few moments later, Dragol's sharp ears caught the sounds of a group approaching through the trees. Deftly, he snatched up the saddlebags and moved to the side, taking refuge behind a large tree.

He took his eyes off of the old man for only an instant. When his eyes reverted back to where the old man had been standing, he gnashed his teeth in frustration and rising anxiety. The old man was no longer in sight.

A few hushed voices indicated that the oncoming entities were even closer. Not knowing whether he had been betrayed or warned by the old man, Dragol quietly awaited his fate.

Straightening up, he became as still as the wide trunk of the tree that he stood next to. Moments later, a party of tribal warriors passed by, sweeping through the trees from the right. Dragol found himself marveling at their considerable ability to melt in and out of shadows. In all, there were about forty warriors, and Dragol quietly edged around the tree as they passed down the near bank of the brook.

It was a very large war patrol, and fully armed. Dragol stood no chance against them if discovered. He held his breath as a few of the warriors passed within just ten paces of his position. The warriors did not seem overly intent upon a search, and they soon passed beyond his position, heading deeper into the woods.

Long after Dragol could no longer make out any sounds of the warrior group, he slowly came out from behind the tree trunk. He looked around for the strange old man, wondering if he was still in the vicinity.

"A large patrol, and concerned with other business than finding you, but that may not last much longer," the voice of an old man remarked, breaking the stillness.

Dragol whirled about, raising up his shield and deadly blade in the same movement. The old man was standing about twenty feet behind him, in full sight. He bore no weapons, and held no threatening posture, but Dragol still remained very cautious. The Trogen's eyes darted about for signs of others, just in case the old man was trying to distract him.

"They are sure to come across the bodies of those Pahyna that you slew, and the remains of the fire," the old man continued in a relaxed manner, not even flinching at Dragol's swift movements. "It would not be wise for you to tarry here much longer."

Dragol felt speechless, stunned at the man's appearance and audacity.

"If you are wondering why I did not assist you, I arrived after your fight was already over. I am very sorry over the loss of your good steed," the man said, in a voice that seemed entirely sincere. A compassionate smile came to the man's face. "Just know that Rodor will not forget you, and that he spreads his wings in another place."

"Who are you?" Dragol queried again, with an edge to his voice at the open mention of Rodor. Dragol was incredulous at the man's unbelievable ability to move imperceptibly. He was equally shocked at the man's highly personal knowledge regarding Dragol, having just openly named his fallen steed. He then added, with exasperation, "What do you want of me?"

The old man smiled warmly, a radiance that seemed to evoke light amid the deep shadows of the forest. His singular eye appeared to glint with amusement.

"Want from you? Or want for you? The two questions are different, and perhaps you should ask the latter," the elderly man replied. "I see good fortune in our paths crossing. In time, you will understand. I believe you are set for a greater path, if you choose, and if you survive to set foot on it. Take heed of yourself. I was not expecting to meet you, as I am in these woods for other purposes, but I will endeavor to return to you. For now, I must go onward."

"Go, now?" replied a sorely rankled Dragol.

"Look to the things of your heart. Is that not the way of your kind? It does not always come easy, to gain wisdom, nor should it be easy," the old man said reflectively, his lone eye holding Dragol firmly in place. "Draw strength from your heart, and find the truths that have taken root there, and grown over time. Often, we have already learned the answers to what we seek, only we have not realized how to ask ourselves the right questions to discover those answers within us."

"The questions?" Dragol responded, now thoroughly perplexed.

"When you first learned to use your longblade, were there ever times where a lesson or a movement seemed difficult?" the old man asked him.

Dragol nodded slowly, remembering the many ordeals of being a youth training to be proficient with the longblade. It had been a very painful trial, and he had incurred innumerable bruises during the process. Many were the nights that he went to sleep with his muscles wracked with soreness, and his body feeling as heavy as mountain stone. Sparring, learning defensive movements, body stances, striking techniques, and everything else involved with the mastery of the Trogen longblade had been an extended process that had taken many years, and Dragol knew that he could still get better.

"And did you not have days where a lesson that once seemed mystifying suddenly made sense to you? Or a movement that was once awkward and clumsy suddenly came much easier to you?" the old man asked him.

Again, Dragol had to agree, remembering his own amazement during such moments. "Yes, I remember."

"What I speak of is a different matter, but it is not unlike the times when realizations suddenly came to you, long ago, as you learned the use of your longblade," the old man said. "There are things that you know you are struggling with, and there are also struggles going on within you, that you do not know are happening. Perhaps these things will all become clear to you in time, as things became clear to you over time when you were learning to wield the longblade. I do not wish to depart, but I must go now. I will try to return to you soon."

Without a further word, the old man smiled, before turning abruptly and walking off into the depths of the forest. A bewildered and amazed Dragol watched quietly until the old man disappeared into the thick, woodland growths.

As the old man vanished into the young night, Dragol found himself wondering if he had just experienced his first personal encounter with a Wizard. A very sobering thought then struck him in the midst of his wonderment. If the man was indeed a Wizard, then Dragol was either being faced with a wondrous boon, or a very grave danger. Only time would discern which of the two it was.

AYENWATHA

Ayenwatha, accompanied by an entourage of Onan warriors, strode briskly down towards the bank of the Shimmering River. Resting farther up on the shore, and streaming in towards it, were an abundant number of sleek Midragardan longships.

Atotarho was already standing close to the water's edge with another welcoming party, which, to Ayenwatha's delight, also included Deganawida. Upon looking up, and seeing Ayenwatha, Deganawida gave him a warm smile as he approached.

Both Atotarho and Deganawida were wearing the traditional hide caps upon their heads, graced with two eagle feathers, one pointed up, and one down. Deer antlers were affixed to each side of the caps, to display their status as Onan sachems.

The armada of warships was an exquisitely welcome sight for Ayenwatha to behold, almost bringing tears of joy to his eyes. The prows of many of the graceful ships were carved into the forms of fierce beasts, including an array of dragons, wolves, serpents, and other formidable creatures revered by Midragardans.

The designs of the prows were often echoed in the stern, whether the coiled end of a serpent, or the tail of a dragon or wolf. The effect that the war-girded ships had on the Onan warriors and sachems, standing along the shoreline, was immense relief, rather than the alarm that they would have brought to enemies.

It was truly the sign of a different age, as in truth the sight of Midragardan longships was far from a welcome sight to the tribal peoples living in Ayenwatha's lands in earlier ages.

The arrival also heralded something beyond just the presence of physical assistance itself. The numerous warships sent a clear, resolute message, that other men, who were not themselves blood members of any of the five main tribes, would stand side to side with the people of the Five Realms. They would share the risks and dangers that the tribesmen faced. The Five Realms was no longer isolated in its fight with the Galleans and their allied invaders, and this alone would bring the tribesmen an enormous boost in morale.

Ayenwatha basked in the reassurance that the ships represented, even as his vision flowed over the features of the incredible vessels. Swiveling gently, and looking almost like axe heads, whether perched at the top of the main masts of some vessels, or affixed at the forward prow of still other ships, were shining, gilt-bronze weathervanes, inscribed with intricate designs.

The great square sails of the longships had been furled already, but the sides of the boats were lined with round shields, resting in the wooden battens running along the sides. Whether their facings were leather-covered or bare wood, the shields were colorfully painted in a variety of patterns and forms, their circular iron bosses glinting in the center.

There was a defined color scheme to some of the ships, reflected in the colors of their prows, their sails, and even the displayed shields, demarcating which ships belonged to which Midragardan chieftains. From the color schemes, Ayenwatha could tell that the fleet represented a variety of leaders and chieftains among the Midgragardans. Some of the leaders commanded just a few ships, and many had just one, but all of them were united in purpose.

Warriors in a state of full readiness for combat occupied the ships. Most of the men on the boats offshore were still helping to row and steer the longships to berths along the shoreline, but all would have been prepared if the group welcoming them on the bank were enemy fighters, and not tribesmen from the Five Realms.

A majority of the warriors were wearing conical iron helms upon their heads, a good number with stout nasal guards projecting downward. Most wore some sort of protection on their upper bodies, as only a small number of warriors were equipped with just helm and shield. Several had donned a distinct type of leather jerkin, crafted from the hide of a unique kind of deer from their own lands. Others wore padded leather jerkins, which displayed a raised, checkered pattern. A small number of warriors possessed coats of chain mail. Their stern visages, visible underneath their shining helms, revealed their hardened readiness to fight from the moment that they landed upon the riverbank.

The ones that had landed their craft on the beach had already removed their shields from the racks along the outer strakes, and had armed themselves with an assortment of wide-bladed spears, broad axes, swords, and bows.

"A time to stand together, as brothers, against an enemy we all share," called out a huge Midragardan warrior, in Quoian, the language of the Five Realms.

The sound of the booming voice further brightened Ayenwatha's spirits. Familiar and well-trusted, the voice belonged to one of the few men that could speak rather fluently in the tongue of the Five Realms. The Midragardan warrior who had spoken was standing next to a sizeable, beached longship. Ayenwatha did not fail to notice that the longship was perhaps the greatest in size among the vessels in the wide river's curving bend.

Behind the huge Midragardan was another particularly large warrior, who had disembarked from the same exceptional warship. The second man bore a standard upright, steadying it with his massive right hand.

Ayenwatha recognized the standard instantly. It was the standard of Gunnar, a great black banner pierced by a long, forked streak of white lightning. Almost the reverse of the standard of the great Jarl Bjorn Magnusson back in Midragard, it showed the deep respect held by the seafaring Midragardans for the great power of the weather itself.

The black and white color pattern was repeated on the serpent head of his warship, the shields still set within the side rails, and other small elements of the warship. The color pattern was likewise reflected in four other Midragardan longships beached nearby, all of which were under the authority of Gunnar.

"Truly spoken, Gunnar!" Ayenwatha exclaimed, walking over towards the powerful Midragardan. "You are a welcome sight to these eyes."

Right behind them, another longship coasted up onto the beach. Several Onan warriors hurried forward to assist some Midragardans in pulling the ship snugly onto the solid ground of the riverbank. The shallow draught of the boat, with its narrow oak keel, enabled its amazing efficiency in landing. Ayenwatha could never cease being impressed at how the wondrous vessels were so capable in navigating both river and open sea.

Gunnar, with a wide grin, took several long strides up to Ayenwatha. He took the revered Onan war sachem into a tight embrace that would likely have squeezed all the air out of a lesser man. As it was, it still squeezed most of the breath out of Ayenwatha.

The Midragardan chieftain was a full head taller than Ayenwatha, and significantly broader of shoulder. His thick, blond hair blew chaotically about his lion-like face, save for a single, tightly wound plait that hung down each side of his head.

The short crossguard of his sword rested against the bronze chape of a leather-covered scabbard, hanging at his waist from a baldric looped over his opposite shoulder. The lobed pommel and crossguard were ornately decorated, covered in golden foil, and inlaid with spiraling, intertwining designs. Between them was a grip fashioned from the purest ivory. It was a sword crafted splendidly in artistry and functionality, and did not wear its name of Golden Fury lightly.

The sharp point of Gunnar's large nose, and a set of piercing blue eyes, stood out prominently above his thick, blonde beard. The latter was braided into one lock that fell from the bottom of his chin to the middle of his chest. He was clad in a short-sleeved chain mail shirt, worn over a green tunic with silver brocade along the hem. Beneath were brown trousers, the lower part bound to his legs by long straps of fabric wound up between ankle and knee.

The snug-fitting mail shirt revealed the contours of his broad shoulders, and very sizeable upper body. The bulges of his powerful build made it seem as if the man's flesh underneath was carved out of stone. A lone, spear-shaped silver pendant was resting upon his chest, from the end of a leather thong.

"You look as strong as ever, Gunnar. If not bigger than I ever remembered you before," Deganawida stated, having come over to join them. "It has been some time, my friend."

"Have to keep the louts in line, and the edge on my better men. No small task, I assure you," the other replied, with a hearty laugh, as he took up the older sachem in a somewhat less boisterous embrace than the Midragardan had applied to Ayenwatha. "You look well yourself, Deganawida. I must apologize that we have the carved prows affixed to our ships, but we could not be sure that we would not land in the midst of a battle, or be welcomed by a hostile bunch of Galleans."

Ayenwatha glanced back towards the beaching Midragrdan longships, recalling the fact that they normally removed the fearsome visages from the bows of their ships when landing in friendly harbors. The carvings were symbols reserved for the uncertainties of war, and he did not blame the Midragardans for keeping the carvings displayed so deep in Five Realms territory.

"No harm has been done, Gunnar. Our lands are no longer filled by those with an intent of friendship," Ayenwatha replied, with a trace of melancholy in his voice. "I am here greeting you with the colors of war on my own body."

"How many have come with you?" Deganawida inquired, glancing past Gunnar, to where several other boats had found slots on the muddy bank and were now being unloaded.

The air was filled with the sounds of spirited shouts, talking, water splashing, and metallic clinks, as well as a host of other noises as the embankment began to fill up with ships and warriors. A number of timber gangplanks had been set over the sides of the ships, and men were already offloading chests, the elements of tent frames, haversacks, wooden kegs, and many other containers and implements.

Ayenwatha could not help but marvel at the striking collection of colors evident on the men. Unlike his own people, whose war attire blended in well with their surroundings, the Midragardans seemed to desire the most conspicuous attire, as if seeking to proclaim their presence with boldness.

"Over thirty ships, with more than twelve hundreds … of good men," Gunnar stated, with some visible pride as he announced the number that he had been able to muster on such short notice.

"Twelve hundreds?" Ayenwatha repeated, in elated surprise.

"Yes, and you are lucky that ships were gathering for trade this summer in the islands near Gael, Gael itself, and our quarters in the Kiruvan towns," Gunnar replied. "It doesn't take much to turn us from traders to fighters, unlike those western merchants. Just be grateful that your eastern shores are located close to the ship routes."

"Believe me, I am," Ayenwatha responded.

"I also hope that word has reached you that a full war band of sky warriors upon Fenraren has arrived in your lands. Over four hundred strong. King Hakon's been keeping more of them to the north … maybe he foresaw the storms approaching. Our brethren on the Fenraren will rid your skies of those who would seek to harass and assault you from the air.

Gunnar's tone then lowered, taking on a tenor of compassion.

"I am sorry to hear of your terrible losses and suffering. It would be my wish that you had hundreds of Bregas, and as many riders for them. They are good, hardy steeds, and as Skiantha they are family to the Fenraren."

He glanced past Ayenwatha, to where the two Bregas that Ayenwatha had come with were standing. Ayenwatha followed his gaze.

"They are indeed hardy steeds," Ayenwatha commented, in admiration, though he felt a pang of lament at the remembrance of the costly air battle. There had been only a small number of the winged creatures that were fully trained amongst the five tribes, and a large portion of those had been quartered where the Sacred Fire was tended and guarded. Now, even fewer capable steeds remained, and the breeding herd would be very vulnerable during all of the upheaval.

"But I did not come here to speak of sorrowful things," Gunnar remarked, with a lilt to his voice.

Ayenwatha turned his head back, and saw that a mischievous grin had spread across Gunnar's face. "The ships, the warriors, and the Fenraren are not all that I bring to you, my woodland friends. We have also brought some of the wolf-skins, and a bear-shirt, along with us. Ulfhednar, and Berzerk, in our tongue. Each of those fellows is worth fifty good warriors."

With a glance, he gestured towards another longship now

advancing towards the embankment, having almost reached the shoreline. Many of its occupants were much different in appearance than those on the surrounding ships.

Standing on the unsecured, pine planks of the longship's decking were five huge, very barbaric-looking men. Unlike most of the other Midragardans, they were clad very simply. Their appearance was devoid of any silver or gold, save for a singular, hammer-shaped amulet, made of silver, hanging upside down from a cord about their necks.

The unusual-looking warriors wore no armor, covered in nothing more than coarse woolen tunics over their burly upper bodies. Over the tunics were cloaks made of a thick, silvery fur that faced outward, clasped with large silver pins. Ayenwatha's perceptive eyes swiftly recognized the fur as being from wolves.

Their long hair flowed freely about their shoulders, unbound by headband, woolen cap, or iron helm. Their expressions conveyed that these were men who were much different in nature from their comrades. They had a severe, very hardened mien, the kind of look that was forged through years of discipline and trial. A fiery, maniacal gaze flickered within the depths of their unsettling eyes. There was something decidedly feral about them, a quality that a veteran hunter like Ayenwatha could quickly perceive.

It was then that his eyes traveled a little farther down the boat, to where a hulk of a man stood on the small portion of raised deck at the stern. In many ways he was like the other five, with the exception that a brown fur-skin, that of a great bear, was draped over his massive body. Ayenwatha did not think that he had ever seen such an immense human.

"Can I believe my own eyes?" Ayenwatha murmured in wonder, as he knew many tales of the roughly-clad warriors. "Never have I seen the wolf-skins or bear-shirts of your people."

"And it is good that you have never seen them in opposition to you," Gunnar replied, matter-of-factly. "Those five men would take on five hundred, and the one at the end an additional hundred, by himself. Those that have invaded your land will soon learn what they are capable of, and it will be a very frightening, very painful lesson for them indeed."

Ayenwatha watched as the strange men disembarked from their ship. He was astonished that they showed an easy rapport with the other warriors around them, for their fierce countenances, and intimidating appearances, would seem to have inferred otherwise.

He came to an understanding in those moments, while observing their relatively casual manner with the other men of their land, that they were warriors who loved Midragard and its people with a deep, abiding passion. It gave Ayenwatha some comfort, as he hoped there would be no difficulties involving their interactions with the tribal warriors. It looked pretty clear that their legendary, fanatical fury would only be directed at the enemies of Midragard and its allies.

All of the sights spread about them, and the good tidings from Gunnar, invigorated Ayenwatha, snatching him up from sinking deeper into the morass of dimming confidence and hope.

"You have brought our people something to hold fast to. We may never be able to thank you in the way that you deserve," Deganawida then stated, echoing Ayenwatha's feelings.

"We do not do this for any reward," replied Gunnar, his expression growing serious again. "We stand with you as we would for any friend of ours. No man is a friend who does not go to aid another in dire need. As we live our lives to the fullest in our lands, as you do in yours, we are here to respect and honor such a right with our blood, if need be."

Deganawida's countenance then turned a shade more somber. "As we would stand with you. As to the war at hand, there is little time, for the forests are already being flooded with the minions of the Unifier. Ayenwatha has just returned from the front areas of the fighting, and may be able to tell you more."

Ayenwatha nodded, and added, "We have slowed them, but they are very many, too many to hold back for long. Galleans, rat-men from Yanith, and even some enormous, beast-like beings, which the enemy calls Gigans."

A rueful smile spread on Gunnar's face, though sparks came to his eyes. "Atagar and Gigans too? What type of feast have we been invited too? You are giving us Midragardans a real opportunity to test our skills against rarely encountered creatures. We will be more than happy to see if these rat-men and big brutes measure up to the iron of Midragard."

The large Midragardan then shook his head, and when he resumed, his voice lost its boastful edge.

"This is no minor incursion by the Unifier's miscreants. You are right, Deganawida, we should not wait further. We are ready to march with you now. A small number of warriors will be left behind to guard the longships here, but the rest can come now. Lead us to the site of battle. We can talk more along the way."

Taking leave of the sachems, Gunnar then took a few moments to summon the other chieftains and ship captains together. After explaining the situation in the Five Realms to the other leaders, the orders were disseminated to march without delay. There was not a word of protest from the Midragardans, as they hurried to take up foodstuffs and weapons.

Ayenwatha and Deganawida fell in with Gunnar shortly afterwards, as the three headed away from the line of longships, striding towards the forest's edge. Over a thousand warriors followed in their wake, as the call of friends in grave danger was answered.

AETHELSTAN

The hiss of arrows and bolts thinned, before finally ebbing into silence. The burst of malignant rain had claimed few additional lives, as the bulk of the Saxan defenders were over the top of the ridge, and those in the front had steadfastly kept their shields overlapped. Though only a handful had been killed or wounded, the stillness beyond the line of Avanoran archers and crossbowmen below was discomforting, filled with dire omen.

The expected resumption of the enemy's frontal assault was then unleashed. Several faint cries cascaded down from the skies far above the Saxans. Looking up with an expression of helpless frustration, Aethelstan watched the Harrak-mounted scouts circling lower, their movements imbued with venomous purpose.

The cries were followed by several horn signals, a portion coming from the ground level, and others coming from the skyward riders above. Aethelstan could do nothing to stop the aerial scouts, though he knew fully well that they were conveying word of his force's disposition, and their arrangement along the ridge-top.

"Ready yourselves!" Aethelstan shouted out at the top of his lungs.

The higher-ranking thanes up and down the lines cried out to their men in turn, from the more veteran and hardened warriors in the front, to the slingers, archers, and more lightly-armed, general levy members massed at the rear.

A clamorous, challenging roar broke out from the Avanorans as they emerged into view, marching in a broad, deep line that reached the base of the hill and started up its slope. Well-equipped foot soldiers strode alongside dismounted knights, in a mass of fighters that as a whole was larger, more skilled, and much better-equipped than were the Saxan defenders awaiting them.

Aethelstan knew that the enemy was throwing the full weight of their numbers against the defenders, who were bereft of surprises of their own. It was going to be a contest of sheer force, in which the enemy would seek to bludgeon and pound the defenders with overwhelming strength.

When the assaulting ranks had proceeded a third of the way up the slope, the order to loose missiles was given to the Saxan ranks. Stones, arrows, and javelins were sent streaking towards the enemy, over the shield wall. Arcing downward, the missiles riddled the dense, oncoming ranks. Many Avanorans fell, but the stalwart knights spurred the infantry around them onwards, with fiery, harsh shouts.

The short-lived torrent of missiles quickly slowed to a trickle, as quivers were emptied, and the sorely depleted stocks of javelins and other throwing weapons were drained to the last drop. The gap between the two lines shrank, until it was closed with the ear-splitting din of clashing steel, throaty cries, and cracking timber, as the two sides slammed together once again. Aethelstan, with a sword in his right hand, and a shield in his left, cried out words of encouragement to his men.

The thick mass of spears, slashing swords, and whipping axes mixed with the yells and screams of men, as they fought with fury and died in agony. Aethelstan braced himself as an Avanoran knight brought his sword crashing down upon his shield. The heavy blow reverberated throughout his body, spraying wood shards and splinters out from the area of impact. Reacting, Aethelstan lunged forward with his shield, putting his entire body weight into the movement, and smashing the iron shield boss directly into his opponent's face.

The stunned, bloodied knight did not even see the sword slashing down from above, the broad, heavy blade as much a crushing weapon as a cutting one. The enemy fighter fell to the ground, slain instantly by the sundering blow.

Frenzied horn calls erupted from the bottom of the slope, and the attacking line began to pull backwards. Aethelstan was caught up in the surge, as the Saxan line pressed forward to seize the momentum, hacking and stabbing at the retreating Avanoran force. A vigorous cry erupted from the Saxans up and down the line.

"Hold! Hold!" Aethelstan shouted with all of the energy he could muster, seeing the Avanorans trying to employ yet another feigned flight. "Hold the line!"

Though in the blistering heat of battle, the greater thanes were not so consumed as to ignore Aethelstan's order. They saw an enemy that was turning back, exposed and vulnerable, but they also remembered the last feints attempted by the Avanorans. Many of them did not need Aethelstan's warning, recognizing the tactic themselves.

As expected, the enemy warriors did not go very far, reforming their lines at the bottom of the slope, as a new volley of arrows arched overhead. A flock of crossbow bolts then sped up the slope towards the front of the Saxan ranks.

The Saxan archers had almost nothing left to answer with, and the thanes had to command the defenders to absorb the volley without a response. A tense pause ensued, followed by a few energetic horn blasts, and then the ground rumbled.

A line of mounted warriors cantered up behind the Avanoran infantry, and immediately began to ascend the ridge. Knights and sergeants alike proceeded towards the Saxans, lances lowered with points extended well in front. With so very few arrows or other missiles left to the Saxans, Aethelstan then understood that the broad assault by the men on foot had not been a feint as before. It had been conducted to exhaust the Saxans' diminished supply of missiles, for the moment now at hand.

The mounted Avanorans brought their lances to bear upon the Saxan shields, as their horses dug their hooves in, pressing their power and weight forward. The Saxans were already worn down, and many were thrown back in the ensuing moments, stumbling or falling haphazardly as they were overpowered by the robust stallions. The mounted knights and sergeants were not yet striking at the Saxans, but instead using the considerable strength of the horses to shove and jostle the men of the shield wall back, creating gaps in the defensive line.

The effort did not come without cost, as some of the Saxan household guards wielded their long, deadly broad axes against the enemy's steeds. The axes were swung with such force that one blow could decapitate a warhorse, and the grisly reality of that capability was demonstrated more than once, as the Avanorans prodded their way into the Saxan lines.

Aethelstan agilely stepped down the line, quickly working his way down to where one such breach was being opened. He rushed in to strike at an Avanoran rider who was delving deeper into the Saxan ranks. With a blurring, slashing stroke, Aethelstan slew the warrior before he even was aware of the thane's presence.

Ducking, Aethelstan avoided the blow of a cleaving axe, before reflexively driving his sword upward, skewering a second horseman with a vicious thrust into the exposed part of his face that was left unprotected by his nasal guard. To his dismay, several more of the Avanorans had pushed through the widening opening, and were now fighting just behind him.

The thick scents of horses, and the sounds of their neighs and snorts, filled the air. The former mixed with the noxious odors of grievously wounded men, such as a young Saxan who had been disemboweled right by Aethelstan's side. The progress of the mounted fighters forged a larger path for others to follow, like rivulets of water breaking through a weakening dam.

With a brief glance, Aethelstan saw that several foot soldiers were pouring through the breach, as well as a few other horsemen that had been able to maneuver their steeds down the shield wall to reach the gap. Other enemy fighters were now turning to the sides, to vigorously beset the defenders from inside the gaps, protecting the flanks of those pushing forward.

It did not take long for him to see that the fate of the defenders was being written in stone. The war of numbers and attrition was not going to end in the Saxans' favor, no matter how hard they fought. The sheer weight of numbers was a specter far greater than they were able to handle. It was a debilitating, but undeniable, reality. Even so, Aethelstan was determined to fight on, as were all of the Saxan fighters.

"Together!" Aethelstan shouted. "Stay together!"

Many Saxans hastened to his call, forming large pockets of defense that were not so easily overwhelmed, as the shield wall fractured, and began to collapse. Archers and slingers, wherever possible, found their way to the centers of the defensive pockets. Out of arrows and stones, they looked around for anything that they could take up and wield, beyond the single-edged seaxes that a few of them carried.

The weight of the enemy attack rapidly increased, and the spirits of the attackers were buoyed by the stark shift in momentum. Many of the pockets were completely encircled, as the battle transformed into a chaotic melee. Some Avanorans raced onward, as nothing stood between the battle lines and the non-combatants with the Saxan baggage train.

Aethelstan looked on in horror, as an Avanoran knight brutally struck down a priest in the heat of his bloodlust, felling the clergyman even as he labored to assist a wounded Saxan. As if the knight's battle-rage was not satiated by the vicious slaying, the Avanoran brought his mace up again, bringing it crashing down upon the head of the injured, defenseless Saxan. The impact emitted a sickening crunch that made Aethelstan's blood run cold.

As he struck down yet another enemy warrior, Aethelstan felt as if he was in the midst of a dark, terrible nightmare. It seemed as if time itself had come to a complete standstill. His eyes blazing with righteous fire, his sword flashed in the air, hewing down still another enemy fighter. Yet for every one brought down, it seemed as if two or three more rose to take their place.

Another exuberant roar filled the air of the forest, and a quick look from the edge of the ridge showed another broad mass of enemy infantry charging up the slope. Aethelstan's heart sank even lower. The enemy commander had seen that no surprises were forthcoming, and was now committing all of his reserves to finish off the Saxans in a decisive, pulverizing blow.

It seemed as if there was no end to the swarming enemy force, and finally Aethelstan began to feel the drain of fatigue, as his body gradually wore down from the relentless fighting. His mind mercifully blocked out the situation, keeping a narrow vision focused towards the now-hopeless task at hand.

He cried out in pain as the tip of an enemy sword glanced off his tiring defenses, opening a wide gash in his arm. The searing agony and loss of blood from the wound only compounded Aethelstan's difficulties.

His sword felt as if it grew heavier with each moment that passed, but a wellspring of resolve, bolstered by desperation and outrage, remained within him. Crying out with all of the fury that he could muster, he returned the blow with one of his own. A moment later, the

Avanoran that had drawn his blood toppled to the ground lifeless.

EDMUND

"Aethelstan!"

Edmund, along with every Himmeros rider left at his command, surged over the ridge on the Saxan right flank. They launched a ferocious attack upon the exposed enemy left flank. They charged along the ground, surprising the Trogens far over them, who had been trying to draw them up into the air.

The Himmerosens' talons and jaws, combined with the sharp lances and swords of their battle-fevered riders, were brought to bear heavily upon the Avanorans. Frantic cries and more horn signals filled the air, as the left flank of Avanor was shattered in the unrelenting wrath of the attack. Men scattered and dived aside, most trying to avoid the small band of riders upon Himmerosen. A few offered resistance, but any that were foolish enough to remain in the direct path of the Saxan tempest were cut down without mercy.

Edmund guided his Himmeros swiftly towards Aethelstan, espying the Saxan thane trapped in a swirl of combat. Aethelstan's wild eyes and matted hair gave testimony to the battle frenzy that had risen up within him. He gazed up at Edmund in the respite brought about by the Avanorans giving way to the sudden Himmerosen's charge. Edmund knew that it would not last long.

"Aethelstan, I will not leave you here! You must come with me!" Edmund shouted emphatically, in the tone of both an order as well as a plea.

Aethelstan stared into Edmund's eyes, and shook his head vigorously. He clenched his blood-drenched sword, and proceeded to stride right past Edmund, heading towards the regrouping Avanorans that had been splintered apart by the Himmeros-riding band.

"Aethelstan, get on my Himmeros, now!" Edmund reiterated, reaching out to grasp the great thane's shoulder.

"I will fight on with my warriors!" Aethelstan growled at Edmund, forcefully shrugging off the grip.

"We need your mind, Aethelstan! If you do not survive, then

countless more Saxans will die because you needlessly fell here!" Edmund hastily pleaded.

His impassioned entreaty was to no avail, as Aethelstan broke into a trot, closing with a few Avanoran horsemen that were besetting a patch of Saxan levymen. Aethelstan plunged into the fray, first slaying a mounted warrior, and then cutting down a foot soldier. His slowing reflexes allowed another glancing sword blow through, tearing across his left thigh.

Edmund, frozen in indecision behind the battle, momentarily did not know how to proceed. His lord and dear friend, as close as a brother, was openly bleeding, and would soon fall beneath exhaustion and the weight of the far too numerous enemy. Frantic, he cast his eyes about to see where the other Himmeros-mounted warriors were located. Seeing two nearby, who were not yet engaged heavily in the fighting, he spurred his mount towards them.

"Defend Aethelstan, I will get him out of here!" Edmund shouted at the pair.

The two warriors moved with alacrity to attend to the task, getting their steeds into a position where they were on either side of Aethelstan. Using their lances, they drove back a number of enemy warriors. Edmund guided his Himmeros in closer behind Aethelstan, who continued to strike fiercely at the enemy fighters.

He was slowing down as Edmund watched, and would not be able to sustain his effectiveness for much longer. A killing blow could land at any instant, the likelihood greatly increased as Aethelstan's defenses continued to deteriorate.

Edmund' heart nearly stopped, for as he drew near, an enemy axe narrowly missed Aethelstan's neck. As the gallant warrior stood up from where he had crouched to avoid the strike, a blow from a short-handled axe held by another mounted warrior caught him on the left side of his helm.

Fortunately, the blow was not direct, or balanced, and did not impact fully. Aethelstan, rendered unconscious nonetheless, instantly had his legs fall out from under him as he crumpled heavily to the ground.

"Protect him!" Edmund frantically implored.

The two warriors to either side of Aethelstan attacked the enemy soldier who had landed the blow. Their selfless movement, though, left them exposed for a brief moment to enemy attack. One of the Saxan sky riders was struck with a mortal blow, from a spear wielded by one of the enemy's infantry, but not before the axe-wielder was stilled.

Edmund gripped the reins of his Himmeros tightly, guiding the creature up to where Aethelstan lay oblivious. Hopping off of his saddle, he gingerly gripped his lord and comrade, lifting the great thane with a burst of exertion borne from sheer desperation. Edmund lay Aethelstan across the back of his steed, placing him just in front of where the sky warrior sat in his saddle. Carefully, Edmund remounted, and did not waste another moment as he turned his steed. He knew that he could not likely go up into the sky, but the steed was more than strong enough to bear the additional weight along the ground level.

Upon sight of Edmund being occupied with Aethelstan's inert body, several other Himmeros-mounted warriors moved in, providing him with a makeshift escort of seven. Risking arrows, but keeping to the back of the ridge, the group of eight turned their backs as they trotted away from the edge of the maelstrom. Building up speed, they streaked deeper into the forest, soon bounding amongst the trees.

Their hurried movements did not go unnoticed by the Trogens monitoring the battle overhead, however, as was evidenced by a new round of cries emanating from the airborne observers. Several Trogens upon Harraks streamed downwards, intent on cutting into their Saxan counterparts.

They had seen the group of Himmerosen moving to escape together, positioned around the rider bearing the wounded warrior. It took little insight to assume the importance of the coordinated movement.

Five of the Saxans, knowing that they could gain some additional time for Edmund, whirled about to meet the oncoming Trogens. The other two continued forward with Edmund, who was eager to put more distance between them.

The ploy worked, as each of the five Saxans put up a furious fight, in an ultimate sacrifice, taking a few of the landing Trogens with them as they fell one by one into death's embrace. Their resistance stalled the pursuit long enough so that Edmund and the others were able to continue forward under the denser tree cover. Once under the more solid canopy of foliage away from the ridge, their movements were well-shielded from the searching eyes of the Trogens remaining above in the sky.

After some time had passed, and the steeds were breathing heavily, Edmund gave the command for the trio to slow down as he espied the emergency landmark that he had kept embedded within his mind, ever since an earlier scouting foray. Seeing the small cave opening set towards the bottom of a hillside, he dismounted, and asked for one of the others to assist him in helping to carry Aethelstan over to the mouth of the cave.

They moved with as much haste as possible, not knowing how long they had until the Trogens located them again. Edmund hoped that the Trogens had lost interest, or were more tethered to the main battle site.

The cave was just big enough for the warriors and their steeds to enter. For the time being, they would be safe from the enemy forces, if they had not been tracked from the sky, but Edmund knew that it would not be a permanent refuge.

Having traveled along the ground, the Himmerosen had undoubtedly left distinctive tracks behind. After the enemy had concluded the fighting along the ridge, the unique imprints would be found sooner or later, and they would lead the enemy right to the maw of the cave. Nevertheless, Edmund had to see to the state of Aethelstan's condition, and needed a little time to regroup his thoughts.

As fast as they could, taking packs and cloaks from their steeds, the Saxans fashioned a crude bed upon which Aethelstan could rest. They gently carried their unconscious leader, entirely a dead weight, over to the makeshift bed, and lay him down upon it.

Almost at once, Edmund began to tend to Aethelstan's wounds, working to bandage them, and stem the bleeding. The other two warriors kept a constant eye on the mouth of the cave. Edmund feared that at any moment the sound of angry Trogens, successfully discovering their hiding place, would reach his ears.

The fighters' weapons were out and close at hand, although they would be of little use if they were all cornered within the cave. Edmund now keenly understood the awful plight of the rabbit facing the cunning fox.

Perhaps they would be passed over for the moment, if they were very still. If they were discovered anytime soon, then Edmund knew that they would have little chance of survival.

WULFSTAN

Many Saxans fell under the hail of arrows, including several from the villages within Wulfstan's home region. The enemy horse archers had made many deadly passes, evoking a tremendous respect for their skill, dexterity, and the great power of their smaller recurved bows.

The composite bows used by the enemy archers, both mounted and within the hosts of infantry, were devastating weapons. Wulfstan witnessed several instances where arrows from such bows had pierced right through iron mail, despite being loosed from what he would have initially thought to be a reasonably safe distance for the Saxans. More than one thane had been grievously wounded or killed by the mail-penetrating shafts.

The thundering drums continued to roll as the veiled spearmen in the front ranks maintained their wall of tall hide shields. They provided a refuge for the horse archers sallying forth to harass the Saxans, as well as a barricade for the infantry bowmen engaged in showering the defenders with a lethal rain.

Just when it seemed to Wulfstan that the Saxans would have to outlast the enemy's supply of arrows, the timbre of the drumming changed. A rhythmic surge of powerful booms accompanied the sonorous braying of horns, and Wulfstan knew that a marked shift in the attack was about to occur.

The horse archers swiftly looped back around, and re-entered the narrow openings in the shield wall created for them by the spearmen. The latter promptly closed their ranks when the last of the horses were securely through.

The huge wall of spearmen lurched into motion, tromping forward in a disciplined line, as the tremors rippling through the ground grew beneath Wulfstan's feet. The foremost ranks of the enemy drew to a halt several paces before coming into contact with the Saxan lines, as warriors deeper in their ranks began to add hurled javelins to the mass of arrows still soaring overhead.

With the closer positioning of the enemy lines, the impressive range of their composite bows reached even deeper into the Saxan ranks, as the first of the javelins flew in high arcs over the shield wall. The head of one javelin buried itself in the small gap of space between Wulfstan and Cenwald, who flinched at the quick hiss and ensuing thud of the impact.

DREAM OF LEGENDS

The narrowing of ground between the opposing forces also benefitted the Saxans, who were finally able to draw blood. Saxan horns blasted, and the shouts of thanes went up, as their own archers, slingers, and javelin throwers unleashed a ferocious response. Flurries of missiles arced high over the tall shields of the enemy line to fall down within the Andamooran ranks. Cries of pain erupted in the wake of the retaliating hail, and a deafening cheer went up among the Saxans.

Wulfstan's sword grip was on the edge of turning his knuckles white, as he was still largely helpless during the current course of the battle. He kept his mind steeled upon keeping his shield raised up, knowing that even a moment's lapse in concentration could be deadly.

The shield itself was already a little heavier, as an arrow shaft was embedded into one of the lime-wood planks. The thwack of the arrow, as it burrowed into the wood, had caused Wulfstan's heart to skip a beat. He had uttered a brief prayer of thanks to the All-Father for having the good fortune to possess a shield of modest quality.

He could only imagine what the highly exposed, vulnerable levy men towards the rear of the Saxan lines were going through in their minds. There were probably several men huddling together under each of the few old, battered shields held amongst their ranks.

After the first wave of javelins, Wulfstan angled his shield a little higher. The downward trajectory of the javelin stuck in the ground by his right leg prompted him to make the adjustment, as it would have made it past the rim of his shield in its former position, had the thrower's aim been a little more to the right. Another deep thud of steel into wood sounded. A quick sideways glance revealed a wide-eyed Cenwald, who had just caught one of the thrown missiles with his own shield.

"It can do you no harm, while you keep behind your shield," Wulfstan said to Cenwald, while trying to keep his own nerves steady.

Just in front of him, he could see the tensed forms of many axe-bearing household guards, who were tantalizingly close to being able to strike at the enemy. Thanes cried out exhortations to keep the shield wall tight.

The sky above was blurred with the streams of missiles flying back and forth. There was little to do but wait, for either the thanes to call for a march forward, or for the enemy to do something similar. The inaction was torturous to endure, as the lethal torrents continued to exact a bloody toll upon the Saxans. The only consolation was that cries continued to arise from the enemy's ranks, too, derived from Saxan arrows, javelins, and sling-stones.

The sound of a muffled gasp emitted suddenly from behind Wulfstan, as a javelin claimed the life of a man with gray-streaked locks of hair. He felt the man's body bump against the back of his legs, as the dead Saxan slumped to the ground.

Wulfstan recognized the fallen levyman. He had known the family, and he was aware of the terrible price that had just been paid. In one flashing moment, seven Saxan children had lost their father, and a generous, warm-hearted woman had lost a caring, hard-working husband.

Wulfstan hardened his mind, as the pang of sorrow bit sharply into him, forcing himself to keep his focus squarely on the battle at hand. There would be time enough to agonize over the horrible fragility of life, and the mounting losses around him that were far from over. He quickly reset his feet, sliding about half a pace to his left. Tripping on a fallen body, in the midst of combat, could easily mean a quick death.

"Watch your step," he called to Cenwald with a downward glance towards the body. Cenwald's expression showed that he understood the warning, as he nodded back to Wulfstan.

The ground then reverberated with the thrumming sound of a great mass of hooves striking the earth. Wulfstan chanced a glance around the edge of his shield, elated to see a force of Saxan horsemen charging into the zone between the two opposing forces. He could see the mounted warriors flowing across his view, just above the heads of the Saxan warriors forming the front line.

The mounted Saxans hurled javelins as they neared the enemy, bringing the horses around quickly to angle back for the Saxan ranks. Wulfstan watched their arms rear back and snap forward, sending iron-tipped shafts whistling into the dense, enemy ranks.

Simultaneously, as if it was the signal the enemy had been waiting for, the wall of spearmen surged forward to engage the Saxan cavalry. Bait had been taken, as Wulfstan witnessed a keen strategy unfurling.

The famed warriors of Bretica, bearing the proud standards of Count Gerard II, suddenly emerged from behind the lighter, javelin-throwing horsemen. Their horses, resplendent and proud in their trappers of iron scales, gleamed brightly as they bore down heavily upon the freshly-opened channels in the Andamooran ranks. Their stalwart riders, mirroring the steeds in their own scale armor, held spears in high overhand grips, or underhanded ones out from their bodies. Others carried swords, holding them high in the air as they cried out loudly, charging into the fray.

The Bretican horsemen's eyes blazed as they sliced through the fissures in the Andamooran ranks, scattering panicking infantry spearmen. Wulfstan eyed a lone Bretican pennon that seemed to glide forward above the melee. The white horse on its green field appeared to fly defiantly above the fury of the battle.

Buoyed by the strong, sudden shift in momentum, the Saxan forces around Wulfstan could not be restrained any longer. A clamor arose as thanes and household warriors alike shouted, and the Saxan shield wall rushed forward in an outpouring of martial ardor. They fell furiously upon the breaking ranks of the Andamoorans, swinging axes and swords with reckless abandon.

Wulfstan and those around him hurried forward within the massive outflow, swiftly finding themselves amongst the enemy warriors. Reacting fast, he knocked aside a spear thrust from one of the veiled fighters, before bringing his sword back in a slaying blow to the attacker's neck.

A helmed enemy warrior, armed with a long-bladed, single-edged weapon, then charged him. Wulfstan smashed his shield into the man's face, driving the iron boss into flesh and bone, and knocking the man backwards. A half-maddened Saxan ceorl in the grip of a fiery bloodlust pinned the man to the ground with a frenzied spear thrust, before Wulfstan could even move to finish off his stunned enemy.

The ceorl glanced towards Wulfstan with a wild look dancing in his eyes, giving a loud outcry as he ripped the spear loose, and shook it defiantly in the air. He charged off into the depths of the uproar spreading around them.

The enemy's front ranks were clearly disintegrating, and the Saxans were making tremendous progress, following in the wake of Count Gerard's elite heavy cavalry. The Bretican cavalry had pressed deeper into the teeming enemy, cutting a broad swathe through ranks of lightly armed fighters. A more determined, heavier-armed force of enemy cavalry, consisting of dark-skinned men with fierce countenances, would soon be matching blades with the Breticans.

Indescribable exhilaration filled Wulfstan as he flowed along with his battle-maddened Saxan brethren. The left flank of the overall enemy force was in the process of being eroded. The Andamooran ranks were teetering on the edge of a widespread breakdown in morale, which would lead almost certainly to the flank being rolled up entirely.

Many of the Andamoorans bravely accounted for themselves as they were swept up within the Saxan swarm. Wulfstan engaged in a few blistering moments of combat himself along the way, but it was plain to all eyes that the great mass of Andamoorans were being driven steadily backwards.

Wulfstan saw a household warrior bring his two-handed axe crashing down on an enemy swordsman. The sheer power inflicted by the blow elicited a wince from Wulfstan, as the heavy axe blade cleaved deep into the hapless Andamooran's body.

Wulfstan then caught sight of a thane vigorously assailing two of the veiled Andamoorans. Whether they were archers, or spearmen who had lost their main weapons and shields in the fighting, the pair wielded nothing more than long daggers. They had an enormous disadvantage against the thane's robust, heavy sword blade.

The two Andamoorans rushed at the thane, who deftly thwarted one of them with an outward shield-thrust, while lancing his sword with accuracy and power up under the chin of the second man. A couple of heavy, hacking blows later, the first Andamooran was sent by the thane to join his comrade in whatever afterlife beckoned to them.

Flurries of blows transpired all around, as Wulfstan hurried by with a number of Saxans to fall upon several dagger-armed, veiled warriors, standing amid a number of composite bows that had been hurriedly cast aside. The sight of the bows lying all around told Wulfstan everything that he needed to bring himself into an inferno of rage.

The Andamooran archers that had killed so many Saxans from a distance were now engulfed in a maelstrom of vengeance, as Wulfstan and others cut viciously into them. With their small round shields, lack of armor, and daggers, they were hewn down rapidly, as the Saxans moved through them like brushfire through drought-parched grasses.

One Andamooran howled in agony, as a heavy, chopping cut of Wulfstan's sword removed the hand that had pulled arrows and a bowstring back so very recently. The Andamooran was given no time to contemplate the disastrous wound, as Wulfstan condemned him to lasting silence with a brutal slash.

Wulfstan squared off with another, striking out from behind his round shield and bringing the Andamooran down with a cutting stroke below the man's left knee. Another Saxan pierced the Andamooran with a heavy spear, as the man lay writhing, and crippled, upon the ground.

Resistance dropped precipitously, as a great panic began to spread and take hold throughout the splintering Andamooran ranks.

Wulfstan was afforded a few moments to glance around at the progress of the Saxan attack. His eyes widened, as he took his first close look at the strange, hump-backed mounts that the Andamoorans had brought along with them, all the way from their distant homelands.

They were odd-shaped creatures, each with singular, distinctive humps, elongated necks, and strange facial features. To Wulfstan's eyes, the beasts looked quite ungainly in form, though it was clear that the animals were well-accustomed to riders and saddles.

The horses of the Saxans reared as they drew near to the unfamiliar mounts of the enemy. The infantry riding the humped beasts had dismounted to form up ranks, utilizing their mounts as a type of makeshift, living field fortification. It was a manner of fighting that they were evidently well accustomed to, as Wulfstsan watched the enemy fighters hastening to create a fallback position.

The sounds of more horns filled the air, coming from the south. The ground rumbled anew with the pounding resonance of approaching horses, as Wulfstan and the other Saxans heard their own side's distinctive horn signals rising into the air. The Saxan signals carried an edge of urgency, commanding an immediate fallback.

Wulfstan looked over towards the weird, humped beasts massed just a short distance ahead. The hastily assembling ranks of Andamooran spearmen were allowing their retreating brethren to stream through their ranks, while their cavalry labored to slow the vigorous Saxan advance. Though still very numerous, the spirit of the Andamoorans had been broken, and a heavy blow to the invaders was now within the Saxans' grasp.

The rumbling drew steadily nearer, as the Saxan horn calls were redoubled. The Bretican warriors, their once-gleaming armor now anointed in the blood of the aggressors, began pulling away from engagements with the Andamooran cavalry.

Wulfstan eyed a mass of dark-skinned warriors, arrayed tightly around a proud-looking man, mounted upon an exquisite-looking steed. His bearing, attire, and the vivid, ornate standards around him announced to all that he was a man of great importance, and that the men around him were serving as a type of bodyguard.

The sight of the obvious Andamooran leader, almost within reach of Saxan swords, was tantalizing. The Saxans were so close to finishing off the Andamoorans, and the loss of their leader would break the back of their pummeled morale.

Wulfstan knew that the Saxan cavalry, and especially the elite Bretican forces, would not pull away from such a bounteous opportunity unless a dire situation loomed. He cursed the abrupt twist of fortune, but shouted out to the men around him.

"Fall back," he cried out. "Fall back, Saxans, now!"

The Saxans near to Wulfstan began pulling back with reluctance, as he noticed the Bretican cavalry moving off towards the south, where the reverberations were growing in intensity.

Wulfstan realized then that the enemy was falling upon them from the center. The deep Saxan penetration into the Andamooran ranks had overreached, leaving an inviting, highly exposed flank to the Avanorans occupying the center of the invasion force.

Understanding what was happening, Wulfstan broke into a full run back towards the Saxan lines. He gestured and called out urgently to Saxan warriors wherever he could, warning them of the fast-approaching threat.

Many Saxans were still mopping up trapped pockets of Andamoorans scattered across the battlefield behind him, and there were also a number of individual combats sprinkled amid the chaos. Wulfstan slowed down as he came upon one such melee.

He slashed his sword down upon an unsuspecting Andamooran from behind, where two of them had been embroiled with a lone Saxan thane. With one less opponent, the thane quickly finished off the remaining Andamooran, as Wulfstan exhorted the thane to fall back.

Wulfstan looked farther ahead, shouting as he gestured with his sword towards a great number of Saxans in the distance, ahead of him. His heart leapt and his fears spiraled as he saw hand axes and picks of the type used on village farms, and set his eyes upon even more crude weapons, such as stones lashed to stout clubs of wood.

A sizeable contingent of Saxans from the general levy had spread deeper into the battlefield, most in the process of gaining their first taste of battle. Against fragments of the enemy infantry, their overwhelming numbers offset their lack of skills and good quality weaponry. But in the face of mounted Avanoran knights, they were little more than plump sheep standing before an oncoming horde of ravenous wolves.

As nervous and timid as many of them were, the levymen needed little encouragement to begin a hasty retreat. Hearing the cries of those such as Wulfstan, and seeing the Saxan ceorls, thanes and other veterans hurrying back, the levymen shouted out to each other, with panicked countenances. Turning, they rushed away in a sprawling cavalcade before Wulfstan.

Wulfstan glanced to his right, and his heart caught in his throat as he saw Avanoran horsemen amongst the Saxans. The muscular stallions and their heavily-armored riders were a deadly, terrible combination. The Avanorans leveled their spears in a technique whereby the far ends of the long shafts were held securely beneath their arm pits, orienting the shining, sharply-honed tips towards Saxan flesh.

Caught out in the open, and in disarray, it did not matter whether one was a household warrior, a thane, a ceorl, or a simple farming peasant from the General Fyrd. The brushfire was now blowing back onto Saxan grass.

Wulfstan cast his lot with a number of mailed household guards and thanes that had gathered around a fallen warrior, whose blood-caked chain mail was rent in more than one place. The older warrior's helm still lay upon his head, but his eyes stared lifelessly skyward, as if gazing into another world.

"Lay as befits a thane, at his lord's side! Fight to the last!" roared one of the other thanes defiantly, delivering the words with a booming passion that smote the very air around them.

From all appearances, fighting to the last was exactly what the small band was intending to do, but Wulfstan did not have any other options if he wanted even a remote chance to survive. The forward elements of the oncoming Avanoran cavalry now surrounded them.

Wulfstan had never before witnessed the Avanorans up close, but now saw why they possessed such a legendary reputation. Their discipline was extraordinary, as they maintained tight, small units that appeared to act as if they were of one mind.

The knights among them were easy to spot. Had they not been wearing colorful surcoats, they would have displayed bodies entirely covered in chain mail. Mail hose covered their legs and feet, long-sleeved mail coats encased their upper bodies, with mail mittens protecting the backs of their hands.

Some wore conical helms with nasal guards, but several looked impassive and foreboding in their flat-topped, cylindrical helms. Iron visors affixed to the brows extended downward, covering their faces, and giving them cold, expressionless visages of war. Only horizontal eye slits, and tiny holes piercing the iron visors for ventilation, broke the metallic surfaces.

The barrel-chested destriers, to Wulfstan's dismay, showed themselves to be well-trained for combat as they drew near the Saxans. Biting and lashing out with their hooves, the tall, robust horses created a menacing combination with the armored riders skillfully wielding weapons from their backs. Wulfstan watched several Saxans die horribly under the explosive hooves of the war horses. The gruesome sight instantly erased any qualms that he might otherwise have had about driving his own sword into the body of one of the majestic beasts.

Behind the enemy knights came a mass of other mounted fighters. The accompanying Avanoran squires and sergeants were not as encompassed in iron links as were the knights they followed into battle. Yet, for the most part, they were equipped as well, or better, than virtually any Saxan that they engaged. Most of these secondary fighters wore helms with iron nasal guards, and a large majority had their upper bodies sheathed in coats of mail.

As a whole, their horses were not as dangerous or powerful as the brawny, ferocious stallions of the knights, being a little smaller in size, and less aggressive.

The initial strikes of the knights were made with lowered, couched lances. Several Saxans caught on open ground were brutally impaled upon the long shafts, as the great power of the warhorses' momentum coursed into lethal, deeply penetrating blows.

Once the long lances were lodged into their victims, or were abandoned by necessity in close-quarters fighting, most of the knights resorted to secondary weapons. Wulfstan saw that most of these weapons were long, tapering swords, while a few were flanged, bronze-headed maces, of a kind that could deal crushingly powerful blows.

Even though the Avanorans displayed a propensity for aggression, they were not foolhardy. They rapidly showed great wariness for the long, two-handed Saxan axes that indiscriminately slew horse or rider, whichever offered a better target for the axe-wielders.

The caution allowed a few Saxans caught within the killing ground to reach their comrades. A few peasants and ceorls, finding refuge in the presence of the small island of Saxans around Wulfstan, held their long spears outward to ward against sudden charges, allowing thanes and household guards to emerge to strike at the enemy with sword and axe.

Seeing yet another Saxan run down by a mounted knight, who drove a lance right through the unfortunate man's body, Wulfstan was relieved that even the staunchest of the warhorses were loathe to rush upon a concentration of lowered spears.

In front of Wulfstan, several Avanorans whipped their heads about, as a cluster of Saxan horns sounded from just beyond them. With his back, left, and right amply protected, Wulfstan risked taking a couple of paces forward.

A horseman directly in front of him, likely a sergeant, was holding a lance above his head, as Wulfstan advanced upon the horse's right side. Wulfstan kept his shield raised, acting as if he were about to strike the horse with a forward thrust of his sword. The Avanoran reacted to the perceived threat, twisting in his saddle to thrust his spear downward at Wulfstan.

Wulfstan side-stepped quickly to the left, sliding by the shoulder of the horse as the spear jabbed nothing but air a few scant inches behind him. He brought his sword racing up in a sweeping, backhanded slash, feeling the crashing impact of the heavy blade into the exposed side of the Avanoran warrior. A mail coat could not stop the bludgeoning impact, and the large, heavy Saxan swords could pulverize as much as they could sever.

Absorbing the entire force of the blow, the shocked Avanoran sergeant collapsed forward in his saddle. Wulfstan whipped his sword around, bringing it up, over, and downward in a thunderous, cleaving blow that found a narrow space between the hapless man's iron helm and mail coat. The horse was left riderless, as the sergeant's maimed body slid to the side, toppling heavily to the ground.

The Avanoran knights, sergeants, and squires were now reeling backwards, finding themselves beset from both sides in the sudden shift of battle. Other Saxans had rallied, streaking to the aid of the throng gathered around Wulfstan, arriving in force at a most unexpected moment.

It was one of the most welcome sights that Wulfstan had ever seen. Saxan cavalry charged down from the left, rugged men from the lands of Count Einhard. Medium and light cavalry were both thrown into the desperate fighting, penetrating into the swirling chaos to stem the Avanoran tide, and prevent the Saxan right flank from being destroyed.

While not as heavily equipped as the mail-encased Avanoran knights with their full visors, the Saxan cavalry's spears and swords could still deliver lethal blows to any opponent. The broad, drawn out spear blades of the Saxan riders, with their short, lateral wings protruding from the bases of the blades, were wielded in a variety of ways. One-handed and two-handed techniques were employed, using both thrusting and slashing methods.

While the Avanoran knights were the equal of virtually any warrior standing upon the battlefield, the squires and sergeants were not quite as prepared for the encompassing Saxan onslaught.

Thanes, household guards, and others around Wulfstan responded quickly to the beckoning openings. They levied several more casualties on the Avanorans, before turning their attention to the cleared channels across the battlefield back towards the Saxan shield wall.

Given a miraculous reprieve on the apparent finality of just a few moments before, the energy born of anger and desperation was replaced by a surging hope. Most of the ceorls, and all the peasants, broke into a vigorous run through the cleared ground, as the rest of the Saxan riders passed by them.

The household guards and thanes moved more slowly and orderly. A couple of their number gently lifted and carried the body of the high-ranking thane that they had been warding, and for whom they were willing to lay down their lives.

In one's and two's, other Saxans that had been stranded in the no-man's land streamed around Wulfstan's methodical group, sprinting for the harbor of the Saxan shield wall. Other cohesive clusters of thanes and household guards also began to emerge in the wake of the Saxan cavalry. Like the ones near to Wulfstan, they kept close together as they moved, with weapons readied as they backed up towards the Saxan lines.

On the cusp of a route, the Avanorans now found themselves in the midst of a little chaos themselves. Count Einhard's cavalry hurled javelins, and engaged the Avanorans with spear and sword wherever they could. Hand axes loomed up, as if out of thin air, swung in deadly arcs towards the enemy riders.

Yet after the initial shock of the influx of Saxan cavalry, the Avanoran knights threatened to rally, stem the counterattack, and roll it back. Evincing their steely discipline once again, they began to regroup, bringing the lesser-skilled squires and sergeants back in from the far-flung reaches of the fighting.

Wulfstan witnessed the unsettling skill of the Avanoran knights as they wielded their blades, felling many of Einhard's warriors. Their tapering swords were every bit as devastating in blurring-fast, piercing thrusts, as they were when slashing.

Glancing blows upon the mail-encased Avanorans did little, as only the heaviest of strikes could unhorse them, or have a chance at mortally wounding them. Their taller, more powerful steeds also lent the enemy riders further advantages.

But just when the knights were almost reassembled, and had begun to stiffen their resistance, they were beset from an entirely new direction. The Bretican force, which had been thwarted from reaching the Andamooran leader, was now furiously cleaving its way back through to the Saxan lines. In a unified body, the Breticans burrowed relentlessly into the Avanoran riders.

Horns were immediately sounded amongst the Avanorans, as the heavy cavalrymen of Count Gerard gored them. Denied their chance to finish off the Andamooran force, the Bretican warriors took out their tremendous frustrations in a searing assault that swiftly began to claim the lives of Avanoran knights, in addition to many squires and sergeants.

Nothing had ever looked better to Wulfstan, as the shiny scales on the Bretican horse armor made the formation look like a massive sword as it drove into the ranks of their enemies. The incoming Breticans eliminated any further notions of attack that the Avanoran knights might have entertained, as the enemy riders began to fall back towards the center.

The Avanorans were still quite dangerous in retreat, and both Breticans and riders from Annenheim were slain as the Saxans harried the knights, and kept pressure upon them. When the Avanorans were pushed back farther towards the center, both Count Einhard's and Count Gerard's mounted warriors withdrew from pressing the attack, cantering back in broad masses along the face of the Saxan shield wall.

By that juncture, Wulfstan had reached the face of the shield wall. Before he slipped through one of the openings created for the retreating Saxan warriors, he took a moment to watch throngs of Saxan horsemen stream by. The rumble under his feet now felt welcome, as he looked with gratitude and pride upon the brave warriors that had delivered him and the other Saxans from certain entrapment and death.

The course of battle was so unpredictable, and fickle. Just as the Andamoorans had thought they had achieved a prime opening to strike a crushing blow to the Saxans, they had been splintered apart. When the Saxans had been poised to route the Andamoorans, they had themselves been pummeled by the Avanorans from the center. Likewise, the Avanorans had seen a decisive blow snatched out of their own grasp by the warriors of Count Einhard and Count Gerard.

It was a sobering, frightening lesson, regarding the abrupt ebbs and flows of a large-scale battle. Crescendos of exhilarating hope, flavored with the taste of victory, were juxtaposed with terrifying abysses of despair.

The Andamooran spearman swallowed up in the surge of the Saxan ranks was no different than the Saxan ceorl or levyman that found himself stranded amongst charging Avanoran knights. Hopes of surviving the battle could suddenly be revealed to be false, ephemeral illusions.

In a very short time, Wulfstan himself had experienced the tremendous swings of fate, brought face to face with a death that he feared was imminent, as the Avanorans swept around his position. The whims of circumstance had left him free to walk between the Saxan shields, when so many had fallen behind him on the blood-drenched battlefield. He was not so arrogant to think that he had been singled out to be spared by the All-Father, when so many men who were far more devout than Wulfstan had met such brutal, agonizing ends. Such dour thoughts brought a degree of hollowness to Wulfstan's relief at his survival, as he edged wearily through the Saxan ranks, trudging towards the back of their line.

"Wulfstan!"

The voice was like a piercing light in the growing, dark cavern inside his heart, snatching his attention as he was about to sink deeper into a grimmer state. He reached for that ray of light, as it blocked the darkness beginning to shroud him.

Stained and caked in filth, the face of Cenwald looked simply beautiful to his eyes. His shield was a jagged wreck, and he had evidently lost his spear, as he had only a seaxe in his hand. Cenwald set his shield down, and then lay the single-edged blade upon it, as Wulfstan placed his own shield and sword upon the ground. Without a word, Wulfstan strode up and embraced his friend tightly.

"I made it back, Wulfstan … don't know how, but I got back here," Cenwald said, when they had disengaged.

Wulfstan did not dwell upon thoughts of the many from his homeland that had already fallen that day. He knew that the coming hours and days would bring awful tidings of men that he had known for years. The losses would continue to mount, and there were no guarantees that Wulfstan and Cenwald would avoid similar fates.

For the moment, Wulfstan chose to savor the radiant uplift of a sudden reunion with a friend who had survived. Discovering that Cenwald had made it through the fighting so far transported Wulfstan's spirits far away from the battlefield surrounding him. There were no immediate threats to the Saxan right flank, with the Andamooran ranks decimated, and driven back. The din of continued fighting in the center and on the Saxan left flank seemed far off. The precious few moments of relief from the terrors and sorrows of the ongoing battle were a blessing from the highest levels of Palladium.

"Cenwald, never have I deemed your face a thing of beauty, but you are a sight to behold, on this day," Wulfstan jested, as a slight grin escaped his leaden countenance.

"And you still have the looks that the village maidens find favorable," Cenwald replied, with a laugh that beamed through the gloomy pallor of his dirty, blood-streaked face.

Wulfstan glanced towards the back of the shield wall. "Until the enemy withdraws fully, we should not stray too far, but we need to find you more than a broken shield and a short blade."

Cenwald nodded grimly. "I was thinking the same thing."

Cenwald bent over and picked up his seaxe, returning it to the horizontal sheath at his waist. He left the badly-gouged shield where it lay.

Wulfstan looked over to where several bodies lay on the ground, with arrows protruding from them. Abandoned weapons, and more than a few shields, littered the ground around the fallen Saxans.

"We won't have far to look," Wulfstan commented ruefully,

recognizing the body of a young man.

He was a ceorl like himself, from a village called Whispering Fork, which was located near the confluence of a stream that joined the river that Wulfstan's own village rested by.

Wulfstan was pierced by sorrow as he looked upon the lifeless body of the young man, who had been at the onset of his prime years. Wulfstan closed his eyes for a moment, girding himself for what was about to unfold. The tragic tidings of death, coming from the witness of his eyes, to the word of his fellow Saxans, had only just begun.

FRAMORG

The day had grown much older, but the main battle lines had not shifted. Framorg, sitting high in the saddle of his Harrak mount, had watched the battle from the onset.

It was a maddening feeling, being situated so close to such a massive battle and having to idly watch it transpire. Framorg often found himself cursing his fortunes, as the Saxan sky riders refused to manifest in the skies.

For the most part, the Trogens had remained out of the battle, except for the occasional messenger dispatched to the Avanoran leadership, which was positioned with the reserve contingent a short distance back from the direct center of the battle lines. Framorg allowed the Trogens to vent some of their frustrations by loosing arrows from the heights towards the massed Saxan ranks. For his own part, he steeled his mind towards a keen observation of the movements within the battlefield. At the least, he hoped that he could gain some further insights into the conduct of war on such an incredible scale.

He could see the three main attacking formations demarcated clearly enough; Ehrengard on the right, Avanor in the center, and Andamoor on the left. The left flank of the invasion forces, and then the right, had already probed the corresponding Saxan flanks.

The rhythmic booming of Andamooran drums, as hosts of warriors surged forward, had sounded like thunder coming up from the ground. The dense masses of Andamoorans looked like human waves, rolling towards a Saxan shore.

A short time later, the chorus of horns blaring from Ehrengard's hosts on the right sent a tingle down Framorg's spine. The long, unified blasts shook the air, as if echoing the thunder of the Andamooran drums far down the line.

The roar of the fighting itself carried up into the heavens, as the two sides clashed furiously, on either end of the immense battle line. The swelling tides of sound, coalescing into an incessant roaring, encompassed the Trogen sky riders.

Framorg felt the energy crackling through the chorus of battle, yet he and his riders were still left alone, and idle, in uneventful skies. The invigorating sensations brought on by watching and hearing the titanic battle unfolding beneath them only served to increase the Trogen leader's agitation.

From the initial stages of the battle, Framorg saw quickly that it would not be an easy fight. The Saxans had drawn masses of cavalry up on the left and right flanks of a long, dense shield wall. They were well positioned to counter any attempts to circle around the edges of their extended line. In the center, positioned a little further back from the ranks of the shield wall, a large reserve force had mustered, presumably the Saxan Prince Aidan and the royal household guard that the Avanoran leaders had oft spoken of.

As utterly massive as the attacking force was, and despite the great strength that Andamoor and Ehrengard had hurled forth, the living wall of Saxans had not yet given way. The main Avanoran force in the center, upon the failures of the left and right flanks to make any kind of headway against the Saxan defenders, had yet to fully engage in combat.

Framorg could not help but respect the valor of the Saxans. Their stalwart courage made him look forward even more to engaging them in the skies. He just wondered how he could get them to come up to fight.

After about another hour had passed, with nothing stirring within the clear skies, Framorg had to grudgingly call for a rotation. As exceptional in endurance as Harraks were, the steeds were not inexhaustible in their energy. The last thing that he wanted to see happen was for fresh Saxan sky warriors to assail his Trogens, right when their Harrak steeds were too depleted to execute the directives of their riders.

At a signal from Framorg, a Trogen to the left, and another to the right, brought up horns and blasted out summons for the sky riders to return back to the encampment. Turning Argazen about, Framorg spurred his steed back over the teeming ranks of the Avanoran force. With a tight clutch upon the reins, he guided the creature sharply downward, heading towards the open space in the midst of the Trogen encampment.

The miniscule figures scurrying about rapidly grew larger as the ground swiftly approached. He pulled up on the reins towards the end, bringing the Harrak to alight upon the ground smoothly, with only a little jarring to his own body.

A Trogen ran up and held the reins for Framorg, keeping his steed steady, as he unfastened the buckles on the straps securing him to the saddle. Bringing his leg around, Framorg dismounted and strode off towards his command tent.

With his feet touching the ground, he could feel the powerful vibrations resonating along the surface from the battle lines just to the east. The feeling fired his blood, as well as his regrets.

He cast his gaze out towards the eastern horizon, watching as a new mass of Trogen warriors ascended the skies upon fresh steeds. Most were arrayed in a compact formation, with a string of stragglers bringing up the rear. The sky riders almost looked like a cloud drifting across the skies, with a few tendrils of vapor trailing behind.

The return of Framorg's warriors elicited an eruption of activity within the camp, as a great number of Trogens raced to attend to the tired steeds. The animals were led off on their tethers to be fed and cared for without delay, while their riders sought a little food and rest.

A few Andamooran healers, who the Avanoran leadership had insisted were unparalleled in their arts, came forth with the Trogens. With no combat in the sky, no injuries had yet been suffered by the sky riders, and the healers were quickly, and a little abrasively, dismissed.

Framorg was still suspicious of the bearded men in their long, flowing clothes, but he was not about to ignore any possible benefits for his warriors. The Andamooran healers were reputed to be amongst the best healers in the world, filled with knowledge regarding the treatment of wounds and the prevention of them festering into something worse.

The forces from Ehrengard and Avanor, for the most part, shunned the Andamoorans because of the stark religious divides between their lands and Andamoor. With the great importance of his sky warriors, and the fact that the Andamoorans were not welcome in the other camps, Framorg had not hesitated to accept the Andamooran healers' services when they had been offered.

Framorg could not afford to partake in any rest himself, as the first day of the great battle approached the middle of the day. He had nothing to show for the Trogens' presence, either in aiding the ground assault, or defending the skies against the still-absent Saxan sky warriors.

Yet he knew that the enemy sky steeds were out there somewhere, and he had to figure out what they were plotting. The full strength of the Saxan Kingdom looked to be arrayed along the opposing battle lines, a notion underscored more than once during his observations hovering far above the rolling plains.

Accompanied by an entourage of ardent Trogen chieftains, who streamed in from the open landing space, Framorg made his way toward his spacious tent. A few others who had been idly waiting joined their number at the sight of Framorg's return, falling into line behind him.

Framorg's huge Mountain Bear was not there to greet him this time, having been sequestered farther away on his order. With the unpredictable nature of war, Framorg did not want any mishaps to occur with his precious bear. Under Trogen watch, and removed to an area not trafficked by humans, Barondas would be safeguarded from encounters with Avanorans not aware of the creature's presence, or association with Framorg.

The brown hide flaps covering the opening were watched over by two very muscular Trogens bearing extensive lances. There was little worry of enemy infiltration, but Framorg wanted no one to disturb his quarters while he was away.

The two guards pulled back the flaps, clearing the opening for him as he approached. Inside the tent, a large brazier in the center had been kept burning, its twisting columns of smoke stretching up and out of the hole in the center of the tent. Other than the light cast around the brazier, the interior was very dim, contrasting sharply with the bright day outside.

The Trogen chieftains ushered in close behind him, as Framorg adjusted his eyes to the relative gloom. He took his place on the other side of the long plank trestle table set near the center. He waited patiently, gazing upon each Trogen that filed into the space, as they took their own places around the table.

Framorg wasted little time in getting started with his address. "The battle proceeds, as you have seen. The skies are ours. They go unchallenged by the Saxans. But we have not made ourselves felt in this battle. We know the enemy sky riders are out there, but no word comes from any of the scouts we have sent. I ask those of you that were not up in the skies just now … has there been any new word?"

A Trogen who had not been among those returning with Framorg answered, "There is still no sight or word of the enemy sky riders."

"No signs of where they might be?" Framorg asked, his voice carrying a faint edge of exasperation.

"None, yet," the Trogen replied somberly.

An immediate tension welled up in the room. The continued absence of the enemy sky forces was troubling enough, but to not have even one hint as to their location was unnerving. Framorg glared around at the chieftains, letting them know his extreme displeasure.

"Then there are two tasks at hand. We must find out what has become of them, and we must make our presence felt on this battlefield," Framorg stated unequivocally.

The front flap of his tent then opened, and a lone figure walked through. Outlined by the light from outside, Framorg could see at once that the figure was not a Trogen. Lean of build, the individual was just barely six feet tall. Irritation surged within Framorg at the unannounced intrusion by a human, though he restrained himself from an open outburst.

As the flap closed, and his eyes readjusted, Framorg identified the human as Renaud de Bracy, a baron of Avanor. The brother of Avanor's Seneschal Guerin de Bracy, the baron held considerable authority. While not a Lord General of Avalos, Renaud possessed a wide swathe of land within the Querrelan region in the eastern part of Avanor. Several manor estates, a couple of small towns, and a few strategic castles were directly under his control.

His dark locks had a wavy texture to them, cropped neatly where they fell to an even line just above his shoulders. His brow was trimmed into bangs, forming a tight frame around his sharp, thin face, which was adorned with a substantial nose. Renaud had a wide mouth and thin lips that were currently pressed together in anger, as his protruding eyes fixed on Framorg.

The huge Trogen took further umbrage at the brazen attitude of the human, but the man's stature held back his burning urge to berate the man for his insolent entrance. It was yet another price to pay for the eventual help of the Unifier in the liberation of Trogen lands.

"All are engaged in battle, but what will the Trogens do to break the enemy lines?" Renaud asked coolly.

Framorg bristled at the baron's inference, as a hot bile bit at the back of his throat. His lips threatened to pull back in a snarl, but he concentrated until they merely twitched in his surging anger.

"The enemy has not yet challenged the skies," Framorg replied in a steady, deliberate tone, showing his improved ability to speak the Avanoran's tongue.

Only a few of the others in the room understood even a smattering of the baron's words. It was probably for the best that they did not. The questioning of a Trogen's courage was not something taken lightly, and Framorg could not have guaranteed that all in the room could have held themselves back as he had. Had all of them understood the baron, it was more than likely that the man's head would have been separated from his shoulders with a longblade.

"And the enemy may never challenge the skies, hoping to keep you lingering, waiting for them," Renaud responded, his eyes sweeping past the faces of the gathered Trogens. "They seek to take you out of the battle, yes?"

"They may be, but caution is sometimes advised," Framorg responded. He thought of the unending stream of lessons learned in fighting the immensely clever Elven raiding parties that haunted the northwest regions of the Trogen lands. "A trap can be well-disguised, Renaud."

"If you desire aid in the matter of your Elven oppressors, then you will fight in this battle," Renaud replied in a haughty manner.

Framorg's mind turned to the two enormous Darroks that were in an open meadow, just a few leagues behind the encampments. They were currently resting, following an arduous journey, having recently ferried in an Avanoran Lord General with several of his household knights and their squires.

Their main destriers had also been brought with them, albeit with great trouble. The horses had been wide-eyed with fear, kicking and nearly uncontrollable as they were led down a long gangway. Their tails, braided for the long travel, looked to be the only part of the stallions that was unperturbed. A few squires and camp attendants had suffered injuries, some quite severe, while trying to calm the nerve-wracked equines. The idea of transporting ground steeds had not yet been perfected, but the movement of infantry could certainly be accomplished.

"I could strike the enemy heavily with the use of the Darroks, with Avanor's authority," Framorg finally replied.

An amused grin arose upon Renaud's face. "The Darroks? There are only two here, and the Unifier will not want to have Darroks used recklessly. There are not many available to us."

"You admonish me for not taking a reckless chance with the full sky strength of the Trogens? Then you advise me against using Darroks, in a much wiser manner, with far less risk?" Framorg snapped back, his sharp, confrontational mien causing the Avanoran to take a sudden step backwards.

Several rumbling murmurs broke out among the chieftains in the room. Though they had understood very few of the words between Framorg and Renaud, it was evident that a great transgression had taken place. The baron quickly regrouped, and Framorg saw that the man was not so arrogant as to misread the abrupt change in atmosphere within the tent. The human straightened up, and looked Framorg in the eyes.

"A wise risk? With a Darrok? Tell me how this is so," he asked Framorg, a little more evenly.

"Have you never used them to carry warriors during a battle?" Framorg stated, as the idea formed more clearly within his mind. "A number of our warriors, fully armed, could be taken forth by the Darroks. They could be flown at a high altitude behind the Saxan lines, where the Darroks would land, setting down a force of Trogen warriors to cause a disruption and distraction in the enemy rear.

"Before the enemy is aware of this use of Darroks, we would be cutting into their soft underbelly. It would give them even more to guard against, and it may spread them thinner. Maybe your Avanorans could break through their shield wall then."

It was plain that the mocking edge girding Framorg's last words was not lost on Renaud, as the petulant baron's face visibly flushed. This time, it was Framorg's turn to display an amused smile, as his lips curled back to reveal his large, gleaming canines.

Renaud did not try to provoke Framorg any further, evidently seeing some promise in the Trogen's plan. The Avanoran took a deep breath, regaining his composure as the color in his face returned to a normal state. Framorg noticed that a glimmer of realization flickered in the depths of the human's eyes, and even the arrogance faded from his expression.

"You have your authority, Trogen. But I warn you, do not lose even one Darrok. Be sure that messages are sent to the reserve area of our forces. I want to be informed of everything that happens," he retorted, curtly.

"And you shall," Framorg responded, just as tersely.

Renaud turned, and strode away from the table. The light from the outside engulfed his silhouette for a moment, and then the flaps were set gently back down into place.

Framorg swept his gaze around the room, looking upon some of the best warriors from all the clans dwelling within the Trogen lands. Some of the fiercest warriors from clans such as the Sea Wolves, the Dark Serpents, the Black Tigers, the Thunder Wolves, and the Blood Boars were standing before him, awaiting his initiative. He was not about to be daunted by the attitudes of an arrogant Avanoran lord, and certainly not when it was within the power and abilities of the Trogens to affect the great battle.

As Ondayon had led the latest batch of riders up into the sky, when Framorg had called for a rotation, he decided to choose Goras for his next delegation of authority. Like Ondayon, Goras was another Thunder Wolf who was highly regarded by Trogens of all clans. It was a tragic irony that the Thunder Wolf clan was the only one that still had no living example of their clan's symbol within their homelands.

The Northern Elves had driven the great Thunder Wolves to extinction long ago, but the Thunder Wolves' spirit had infused the blood of the clan that had bonded their identity with the majestic beasts. Ondayon and Goras were exceptional warriors, as was another, named Dragol, who was off with the forces ordered to support the Gallean invasion of the Five Realms. All had repeatedly come into his notice, far from a common occurrence, given Framorg's lofty standards.

In a position where he was temporarily wielding authority over the members of all the various clans, he strived not to favor any one clan over another. Yet he was not about to dismiss remarkable skill and ardor in favor of assuaging the feelings of a particular clan. The Thunder Wolves had simply produced several capable battle leaders, proven and trusted. Regardless of whether the others were expecting him to choose one from their own clan, Framorg always selected the best leader of warriors that was immediately available to him.

"Goras, I will go see to the Darroks, and I will leave it in your stead to command the next rotation, when Ondayon returns," Framorg ordered, looking at the burly Trogen standing directly across from him.

Goras nodded quietly, as he accepted the charge. Framorg's eyes slowly looked around the other faces, but he saw no significant reactions in the miens of the others. The complete absence of resentment was a glowing tribute to the reputation that Goras had earned.

Pythora, the member of the Black Tiger clan whose contingent had been among the last to arrive to the muster, before the battle had started, then asked, "Is this attack to take place at once?"

"As soon as our forces are gathered," Framorg responded firmly.

"What of the night? We could surprise them at night, if the clouds favor us," Pythora queried.

"Night? When their rear encampment is filled with warriors? Even in the darkest, cloud-filled night, the campfires of an army would make the Darroks visible," Framorg replied. "And if the enemy sky steeds are hidden near that camp, and have some warning? We would be wasting Trogen lives for no gain. We would likely lose one or both Darroks, and then all of this will be a waste. No, we strike now, at their back, when their army is tired, and arrayed in their shield wall. We can also see their sky steeds coming from a distance now … if they are out there."

Murmurs of agreement coursed through the room, and Pythora nodded in clear deference to Framorg's rationale.

"Then our way is chosen," Framorg continued. "Kayadeon, of the brave Blood Boars, go at once to Eigon. Have him and his ground-fighting brawlers move out at once, to the rear of the camp, where the Darroks are kept. They are to gather with full arms and shields."

A Trogen to his right inclined his head, thumped his chest twice with his right fist, and briskly marched off, departing through the tent opening.

"Herag, of the Sea Wolves, form fifteen patrols, of no more than five Trogen warriors each. Every patrol with at least one signaling horn. If the enemy sky riders come, make certain the alarm is raised," Framorg ordered another Trogen, who stood just off to his left.

Herag did as Kayadeon had done, giving a slight bow and striking his chest twice with a closed fist, before leaving to fulfill Framorg's wishes.

"Goras, to the skies, at the next rotation. I shall join you soon enough. We may yet send a panic through the enemy … a panic that will lead to the breaking of their will. If the Unifier sees that it is the Trogens who have won this great battle for His forces, then we can demand our reward, and free our lands of the Elven menace sooner."

A raucous cry broke out from the elite Trogen warriors, and their eyes were bright with a fiery desire. Framorg felt the eruption of energy pouring from them, echoes of the dreams of countless thousands of Trogens from across so many long, difficult generations. The end of a tremendous, age-old ordeal was in sight, once they fulfilled the desires of the Unifier.

As the Trogens cheered Framorg, he strode through their midst and continued out the opening to his tent. A number of Trogens outside were looking towards the tent, having heard the excited outcries coming from within. At Framorg's emergence, they immediately lowered their eyes in respect to the exalted war chieftain.

Framorg sent a couple of them off to procure one of his alternate steeds, a feisty young male Harrak named Gasa. The steed had already been harnessed and saddled, prepared for flying before Framorg had even returned from the skies over the battlefield. It was not a new practice, as a fresh, alternate steed was kept readied at all times for the huge Trogen.

He was not kept waiting long, as two Trogens led his steed into the clearing surrounded by the tents. The muscular Harrak jerked one of the Trogens back with a quick flick of its large head. It growled deeply, glaring hotly at the other walking by its side.

As the tempermental creature was Framorg's steed, the Trogen holding the tether, after regaining his balance, held his tongue. The Trogen gripped the long leather cord more firmly, as he tugged the steed forward.

"You will not wait much longer to spread your wings, Gasa," Framorg said to the Harrak, running his hand down the creature's snout, stopping right above a formidable array of sharp teeth powered by bone-crushing jaw force. It was a very confident gesture, with such a cantankerous male Harrak. "Do not envy Argazen, for you are just beginning your years, Gasa."

He gave the creature a firm pat on the side of its neck, as he moved alongside its body and prepared to climb up into the saddle. In his presence, the creature seemed to relax, and did not give the other two Trogens any more difficulties.

Framorg placed his left foot into the bronze stirrup, pushing upward as he hoisted himself into the saddle. He noticed that his legs were forced a little wider, as Gasa was a little larger in breadth than Argazen. He secured the iron buckles of the leather straps holding him into the saddle.

With a vibrant cry, he urged Gasa to take flight. The creature spread its wings, flapping them powerfully as it took a couple of hops forward, bounded for a few paces, and then leaped high. The outstretched wings clutched the air, thrusting downward, lifting rider and steed skyward.

Framorg guided Gasa away from the direction of the battlefield, soaring ever higher as they headed towards the west. It was not long before the sounds of the battle, with its cacophony of cries, drums, horns, clashing steel, pounding hooves, and shattering wood, began to fade behind him.

Only a couple of warrior escorts flew alongside him, spread far apart to either side. Despite the light guard, he felt very secure in the open sky. With several patrols already dispatched to the rear and flanks of the main encampments, and those about to be bolstered further by Herag's forces, the ground that he was flying over was adequately warded.

Eyeing his destination, Framorg began a gradual descent on the Harrak towards a prodigious expanse of flatter ground, whose surface looked to be broken only by a throng of tents, and two small, black hills. The "hills" were the forms of two Darroks resting upon the ground, with their gigantic bodies stretched out lengthwise. A number of Trogens gathered as soon as Framorg's Harrak drew closer to the soft, billowing grasses and wildflowers blanketing the swathe of ground.

Harnessed and readied for flight, the two Darroks were slumbering lazily, and paid little heed to the three newcomers. Climbing ladders were suspended down their sides, leading up to the timber, railed platforms affixed to their backs by a criss-crossing network of hide ropes and iron buckles.

One of the Trogens from the throng around the landing area stepped forward. A large, fanning emblem, fabricated of serpent scales, hung down from around his neck. Framorg recognized the warrior as Laruga, of the Dark Serpent clan. For a Trogen, he was a little shorter and leaner of build than most, but he had great cunning, and was diligent when given commands.

"War Chieftain Framorg," Laruga greeted, going into a deep

bow, as Framorg unbuckled himself and dismounted Gasa.

He turned towards Laruga, towering over the warrior.

"Are the Darroks prepared to fly?" Framorg asked.

"Yes," Laruga replied without hesitation. "They are rested enough."

"They are both to be sent forward, once Eigon's ground fighters arrive," Framorg stated. "They will carry Eigon's warriors as high as you can go, across the Saxan forces. Land the Darroks on the other side of their camp. If you can, land the Darroks far enough that they are just out of sight from the rear of the enemy camp. Eigon is to then lead a raid upon the Saxan encampment. He is to pull back, and you are to return, after striking a heavy blow. Do not wait for the Saxans to gather an overwhelming force."

Laruga nodded.

Framorg eyed some open cookfires nearby. He walked across the ground towards them, and requisitioned a bowl of pottage, which was quickly provided for him by a Trogen warrior. Once he had obtained a crude wooden spoon, he began to quickly scoop up the contents of the bowl. There would not be many opportunities to get a meal during the first day of a major battle.

When he had eaten a greater portion of the pottage within the bowl, a number of cries called Framorg away from the campfire. He set the bowl down, striding swiftly to meet a familiar Trogen figure. The Trogen warrior was at the forefront of a large mass of armed Trogens that had just arrived, all of them slowing down from running at a modest pace.

A brown-furred cloak flowed from his back, and at his neck he wore a prominent necklace. The latter threaded through five claws, which had likely once belonged to the same Mountain Bear that had possessed the fur of the cloak. Eigon, during his rite of passage, had gone to stay in the thick brush lands where Mountain Bears often came down to snare fish from the streams and rivers cutting through the area.

Most Trogens of the Mountain Bear Clan kept their distance from the great Mountain Bears, contemplating the characteristics of the massive beasts before returning as full-fledged warriors. Eigon's fate had been otherwise; he had been given the ultimate test, as an old, ravenous male bear had beset him.

In a feat worthy of tales similar to Framorg's own encounter with the clan's animal patron, Eigon had fought against the bear, agilely dodging its mauliing swipes and rushes. Seeing a brief opening, he had thrust his spear out, driving the point deep into the bear, earning the claws and cloak that he had worn from that day on.

Something of that raging bear had transferred into Eigon, as he had become a ferocious land warrior, who shunned taking the wings of a sky rider. Eigon was the ideal Trogen to lead any kind of ground raid upon the Saxans.

Over two hundred Trogens behind him were armed with a mixture of lances, longblades, and the long-hafted weapons known as scythens. A few carried strung great bows over their shoulders, the extensive bows not much shorter than the warriors that bore them.

Many carried the tall, rectangular shields, made of stout planks of wood covered with hide, that Trogen infantry typically were equipped with. Most wore cuirasses of toughened hide, to go with either iron helms or hardened leather caps, the latter made of the same kind of boiled hide as that which protected their upper bodies.

The signs of many different clans were in evidence from the pendants, amulets, emblems, and other accoutrements visible upon the various warriors. The members of a similar clan were often grouped together within the broader force. Eagerness shone from the eyes of all of the warriors, as they looked expectantly upon Framorg and Eigon.

Framorg spread his arms wide, as did Eigon, and the two met with a great clench, embracing each other in an exaggerated manner reminiscent of the great Mountain Bears. The dramatic embrace was a special gesture, displaying a high level of respect for a storied, fellow clan member.

"Eigon, it is good to see you again," Framorg greeted warmly.

"I understand that you are to free us from this torture of idleness," Eigon replied, in a deep, scratchy voice. Vigor danced within his eyes as he gazed back at Framorg.

"Yes, I am. And you may strike a great blow that turns the entire battle to our favor," Framorg said.

Eigon's eyes sparked, and his canines gleamed. "These are good tidings, War Chieftain Framorg."

"The Darroks will bear you over the battlefield, landing on the other side. Strike at the enemy encampment, and inflict a deep wound upon them, but return before you are overrun with their great numbers.

We must not be foolish. We must not needlessly sacrifice Trogen warriors. But let us create great worry among them, and make them stretch their forces thinner."

As if instinctively, Eigon's large left hand shifted down to grasp the hide-bound hilt of his longblade.

"I will give them a great wound," Eigon replied evenly, his voice as iron hard as the blade he wielded.

"Do not let yourself be caught when the enemy becomes aware of what is happening, their numbers will overwhelm any skill or bravery," Framorg again cautioned his fellow clan member, knowing well how Trogens could be in the heat of a battle.

"The Mountain Bear shows caution on the hunt, even though it is the biggest, and strongest, of predators," Eigon responded.

Framorg clasped him on the shoulder, pleased with the response. "Then waste no more time, go at once. Go with Laruga, and have your warriors mount the Darroks."

Eigon gave Framorg a bow, saluted with two thumps to his own chest, and turned to accompany Laruga. Framorg watched as Eigon signaled for the band of infantry to follow him. The mass of Trogen warriors streamed towards the ladders hanging down from the carriages surmounting the massive Darroks.

It took a little while for the warriors to climb up onto the platforms. Once at the ladder's summit, the Trogens spread out down the length of the vast creatures, so that room could be made for those coming up from below. Once they had taken their places, the warriors began to tie themselves to the carriage using lengths of stout hide rope, most often securing one arm, with a few looping around the waist. Eventually, Eigon's entire force was standing prepared for going skyward on the backs of the massive pair of creatures. The Trogens on the ground were then ordered to give the creatures a wide berth.

Framorg strode away, achieving a considerable distance himself, as the Darrok handlers were the last to ascend the ladders. The ladders were drawn up behind the handlers, as the latter moved to the front of the carriage to take up the ends of the long reins that the Darroks had been acclimated to. The creatures were impeccably well-trained, though they responded slowly, as they were brought out of their deep slumber.

The Trogens on the platform shifted about, grabbing onto the railings, or one of the teeming mass of tethers and straps that were tied to the wooden structure, as the creatures heaved and lurched ponderously into a standing position. Framorg noticed that a few of the Trogens fell to their knees. It was to be expected, as the infantry rarely felt the sensation of the very surface beneath their feet moving so violently.

The huge nostrils at the end of the Darroks' elongated heads snorted, as the winged titans shifted and raked at the ground, tearing great clods of earth up as they dug deep furrows. To Framorg, it had always been mystifying as to how the creatures could carry so much weight. Yet watching them in person, it became obvious that the additional weight placed on the Darroks was of little consequence to their ability to fly.

Though he had never inspected the skeleton of a Darrok, he suspected strongly that their bones had the unusual quality of the Harraks. Hollowed out, a Harrak's bones were very light in weight, but the bone itself was much stronger than that of any other animal that Framorg was familiar with.

The Darroks had very long, lean bodies, with utterly colossal wings attached to an unbelievably powerful musculature. The wings were placed at a point on the creature's body where another set of legs might otherwise have been located.

The sight reminded Framorg of old legends, which spoke of dragon-kind that were flightless. The creatures of those tales were said to have walked upon the face of the world with three pairs of legs. If the wings of the Darroks were transformed into legs, Framorg could easily envision such creatures of those old stories, standing and breathing right before him.

The combined weight of the Trogens arrayed along the Darroks' extensive length was not enough to inhibit them from climbing into the skies, but the great beasts still needed a considerable expanse of ground to begin their initial surge.

It was perhaps one of the few limitations, and perhaps vulnerabilities, regarding the Darroks, as they needed ample amounts of space, both to rest and for building momentum whenever they took to flight. The war being pressed in Saxany, and the one engulfing the western edge of the Five Realms, were both fortuitous for such substantial needs. Open grasslands were adjacent to both of the principle invasion sites.

Framorg watched in sheer fascination, as one of the creatures lumbered forward and flared its great wings outward. The ground rumbled with its mighty steps, the shaking reverberations accelerating as the creature built up speed. The wings began beating up and down as it ran faster. After it had crossed a lengthy stretch, the creature at last thrust itself up and forward. The enormous wings pumped up and down with a force and speed that Framorg could barely imagine coming from a creature of such immense size.

The Darrok seemed to hover in place just above the ground, as it began to drift forward in the air. Its wings worked forcefully, the whooshing sounds of their movements resounding through the air. Gradually, the Darrok began to lift higher and higher into the sky.

The vibrations did not leave the ground, as when the first Darrok's feet had lifted up from the surface, to tuck its legs against its underbelly, the second Darrok surged into motion. Like the first, it also required several moments to gain enough speed to engage in a powerful, launching leap. It also appeared to be suspended just above the ground at first, as its wings fought to gain altitude and momentum.

Once both were airborne, the two Darroks gained height as their handlers steered them towards the west. The handlers made certain that their quest to gain higher altitudes did not carry them recklessly out over the battlefield, just to the east.

It took a fairly long time before the Darroks reached the upper skies. Even then, their forms were still large to the eye. In the lofty heights, the creatures took on a certain grace, flapping only occasionally to maintain their bearings. The beasts seemed increasingly content to glide upon their outstretched wings, conserving their strength as they circled about in a broad arc and started towards the east.

Framorg watched them heading toward the other horizon. It was not much longer before he observed them beginning their descent, far in the distance.

The two Darroks lowering towards the surface, behind the Saxan encampment, represented a part of something much greater. The shadows of dreams were transforming within the embrace of a new light, no longer mere reflections of hopes, but the beginning vestiges of a reality that all Trogens hungered for.

Framorg's own time had finally arrived, to reach for heights that few Trogens had ever attained. Perhaps he would even go beyond, soaring to uncharted regions for a Trogen. Though he tried to keep it all at the back of his mind, he could not help but remember the great prophecies that were passed on from generation to generation among his kind.

A Liberator would one day rise among the Trogens. A warrior and leader without equal, of an unprecedented spirit, would arrive to break the bindings of enslavement that the Elves had placed upon so many. The Liberator would be a Trogen whose radiant light would drive the baleful darkness of the Elven menace out from their lands.

If Framorg rose within the eyes of Avanor, and could bring the kind of might that he had seen that day on the battlefield to the aid of his own lands, the Elves could not hope to withstand the Trogen clans. Framorg already knew that he had no equals amongst the Trogens in skill of arms or strength, which had been one reason why he was so quickly put forward to be the Supreme War Chieftain of the Trogen clans for the campaign with Avanor.

A light, dizzying feeling came over him, as he wondered whether he might be the Liberator that had been spoken of for so many long years. One Trogen was to be the embodiment of a hope that had been passed from elders to the young, woven into the deepest traditions of their kind.

In some ways, the story was similar to the religion of most of the human kingdoms and lands that Framorg knew of. As the holy men of that religion spoke of their Redeemer, who had come to break the chains of death, so would the Liberator of the Trogens come forward to sunder the bindings of a terrible oppression.

The implications were staggering, when seen in light of the Trogen's ancient history, and Framorg closed his eyes for a moment to regain his full equilibrium. When he opened them again, the forms of the Darroks had vanished from the western skies. It would not be much longer before the results of Eigon's raid became known.

Framorg called for Gasa to be returned to him, as there were many other matters to look into. There was little use speculating upon ancient prophecies when the Trogens were in the throes of such a great battle.

Goras would lead the next rotation capably. Herag would have many more eyes watching the perimeter of the region that the invading army occupied. Yet Framorg was not about to rest. He had never been a commander content to wait idly for word to be brought to him. He wanted to see whatever he could with his own eyes. It had always been his way.

DEGANAWIDA

Many leagues had been covered in a forced march, exhausting to those that undertook it, but there could be no thoughts of letting up on the pace. Save for a few of the hardiest warriors, virtually none of the people in the mass movement had ever been put through even a fraction of the exertion that they were made to endure.

The lethal hail of stones from the Darroks in the onset of the attack, and the rapid influx of enemy forces into the forest, made it imperative that the tribes put as much distance as possible between themselves and the western border areas of the Five Realms.

In one of the crueler twists of irony, stopping for extended rests would have meant that the tribal matrons and sachems were willing to unnecessarily risk the deaths of their own people. The onerous decision to coerce the tribal peoples forward, heavily taxing the energy of so many of the elderly, pregnant women, and children, to the edges of their health and strength, was done precisely because of the great love that the tribal leaders had for their people. The danger that pursued them did so with a murderous, merciless intent, and time was of the most critical essence.

Ayenwatha, Deganawida, and Gunnar walked ahead of a column streaming in the opposite direction of the main body of tribal people. They had also marched a very long way, and had only recently come into contact with the teeming horde of refugees heading southeast. At the moment, they were nearing the rear of the mass of refugees. Like the matrons, village sachems, and headmen, Deganawida felt a deep, inner pain within his heart at the sight of the strenuous odyssey occurring all around him.

The last ranks of refugees were entirely comprised of people. The few horses that had been salvaged from the villages were located in the middle to front of the trudging mass, and Deganawida had been relieved to see that most were holding up fairly well.

In a small glimmer of light, the fact that the Five Realms used horses primarily for bearing weighty burdens, and not commonly for riding, had the animals prepared more fully for the hardships that were now being asked of them. They were being made to carry baskets, bark casks, hide packs, and all manner of pouches filled with foodstuffs and other materials.

While the horses were being tested to the limits of their capacity and strength, they were very sturdy animals that did not easily wear down. Even so, Deganawida and the other sachems had insisted that caution be maintained with the animals. With so few horses available, the weary people could not succumb to the inviting temptation to overload the beleaguered creatures.

Even with the demand for conscious wariness, a few of the animals' burdens still threatened to become unwieldy. Clan matrons and others moved quickly to reprove some of the villagers, and implore them to either carry the excess materials, or to leave the packs and containers behind, if they could not capably bear them.

More troubling, a few of the horses had already been unburdened of their material loads, and the reason had nothing to do with any weaknesses of their own. They were diverted from their tasks to carry the frailest members of the tribes, who could not hope to keep up with the others.

Though there was no hesitation in helping the struggling, aged tribal members, a dangerous quandary faced the tribes, increasing with each horse that was shifted to help a human. The average villager did not have the endurance of a packhorse, nor did they have the strength. Precious supplies were slowly being left behind in the wake of the refugees, food and other items that could well prove vital to the survival of many in the days to come.

The realities facing the tribal people, as Deganawida proceeded along the side of the retreating throngs, were growing worse and worse. Even those that were young and hale were being pushed to the limits of exhaustion. Often, the healthy and hale sacrificed their own strength to help elders or small children unable to move forward on their own power. Their very kindness and sacrifice became the source of mounting threat to them. Such was the extreme ugliness of a time of war.

The uneven ground sometimes added further to the difficulties, becoming tortuous for the people when they moved up inclines. Conversely, downward slopes allowed for a little rejuvenation.

The only significant reprieve allowed to the tribal people was the fact that they were moving through a more ancient part of the forest. The older, long-established trees within that region had woven a dense canopy overhead, preventing sprawling undergrowth from creating even more obstacles to their passage. While the gloom around them did little to raise their downtrodden spirits, it was a small price to pay for not having to navigate through thick brush. The natural cover also enabled their movements to be better screened from the skies above, though few held any illusions that so many people on the march could mask their travel effectively.

All of the tribal people knew that the greatest threat was coming from behind them now. Deganawida had noticed the extreme edginess spread across the faces of those in the rear of the great retreat. Many of them cast regular, anxious glances over their shoulders, as if expecting the enemy to pour out of the trees behind at any given moment.

Seeing Deganawida, Ayenwatha, and the long column of robust Midragardan warriors heading in the other direction brought visible relief to many faces, especially those that appeared to be struggling the most. Deganawida noticed many eyes widen in curiosity and surprise at the sight of the well-armed Midragardans. Gunnar was the first of many hundreds of hardened, sturdy countenances that the tribal refugees set their eyes upon. Shields on their backs, spears and long-hafted axes clutched in strong hands, and strung bows over many a broad shoulder, the Midragardan warriors exuded strength and determination.

Deganawida was glad that the tribal people were being afforded the plenteous sight of Midragard's rugged warriors. It was one reason why he had them march along a path that took them right by the refugees, in addition to the fact that Gunnar's warriors would be placed in a good position for responding to any unexpected threat to the tribal people.

Whatever fears Deganawida, Ayenwatha, or any of the other tribal warriors with them harbored, they also kept up strong postures, displaying resolute outward appearances in front of the retreating exiles. Deganawida angled close enough to the tribal people to speak words of encouragement to many. He brought the Midragardan column to a halt towards the rear end of the exodus, to lend some assistance to the last section of refugees laboring to cross over a wide stream.

The fierce-looking Midragardan warriors showed themselves to be extremely gentle with a number of makeshift litters and cradle-boards. They kept the vulnerable, the old, the sick, and the newborn, out of the waist-high waters, as they enthusiastically contributed their strength to the endeavor.

The Onan sachem watched closely as two of the wolf-skins carried the ends of a litter above their heads. They brought an elderly Onan woman, who Deganawida recognized as being from his own village, over to her daughter on the other side.

Another wolf-skin waded through the modest currents as he bore a tightly-wrapped infant affixed to a cradle-board across to an overly relieved mother. Her diminutive stature would have made fording the river with the baby a most difficult task, with so few available to help in the rear of the exodus.

Deganawida did not know much about the wolf-skins, but he did know that they, along with the bear-shirts, were regarded as the fiercest of the Midragardans by far. It had not escaped his notice that the other Midragardan warriors regarded them with an almost mythical reverence. There was something very dangerous about the wolf-skins, though, the hint of a tremendous ferocity lurking just under their brooding visages.

Yet to see them so very gentle in their handlling of the weakest of the tribal people, a people who were not their own, revealed something else about the wolf-skins that contrasted sharply with the fearsome reputation that they carried.

The younger tribal people were awash with gratitude towards the unexpected assistance, being at the bitter end of their physical limits.

Deganawida could not stifle a smile as the young mother emotionally expressed her gratitude to the wolf-skin conveying her baby to her, tears of happiness running down her cheeks. Though the wolf-skin could not understand her words, he was enveloped in her meaning, and the harsh-looking warrior had an awkward, uncomfortable expression upon his face. While the wolf-skins could display a very benevolent aspect in their actions, Deganawida saw that they were not very adept at expressing it.

Deganawida still recognized that it was far from unhelpful that the wolf-skins, and the other Midragardans, exhibited such a toughened exterior. He knew that the sight of the confident demeanors of the Midragardans and tribal warriors would go forward with the refugees. The images of calm, strong faces on the men in the warriors' column would serve as a kind of reinforcement, and even rejuvenation, for what little strength and resolve that the hungry, sore, and exhausted refugees were drawing upon.

As the last of the refugees crossed the stream, Deganawida and the warrior column resumed their onward march. The forest swiftly grew silent around them. The tapestry of shadows echoed Deganawida's melancholy thoughts, as he returned to pondering their circumstances.

Day and night would no longer be merely divisions of time, to mark periods of labor and wakefulness, and periods of repose and rest. Instead, the dominions of sun and moons would melt into a desperate, increasingly burdensome continuum.

The previous night had been the first such instance of the tribal people's new, and daunting, reality, as the refugees had been cajoled onward despite a tremendous need for sleep and recovery. A couple of all-too-brief pauses had proved to be very difficult, as many had collapsed almost instantly into unconsciousness, wherever they had halted to take their short respite.

When the exodus had resumed, those that were asleep were unceremoniously roused from their slumber. If the refugees had any chance to gain some ground on the pursuing enemy, night remained their best advantage. The darkness of night strengthened the tribes' own attacks and efforts to frustrate the enemy's advances.

At the least, the skies above had largely been cleared of menace. The word that Midragardan sky warriors had driven off the Darroks and the Trogens had been an extremely welcome surprise to Deganawida. If the Darroks had been allowed to fly over the forested lands with impunity, the threats to the fleeing masses of tribal peoples would have been exceedingly dire, and the results absolutely devastating.

Unlike small bands of warriors who could easily seek cover in woodlands, a few thousand people could not blend into shadows and foliage. Using their new, dreadful method of warfare, the deadly rain from the Darroks would have inflicted staggering casualties upon the defenseless refugees.

Deganawida cast a furtive glance towards Gunnar, and felt a wave of immense gratitude towards the gritty, pale-skinned people from the far south. It was true that his people and the Midragardans had once shed each other's blood in abundance, but those days were buried in ages long past. The tribal people and the Midragardans now enjoyed friendship and trade, and had come to deeply respect each other. Their relations had reached the point where the masters of the sea had come very swiftly, and entirely willingly, in the Five Realms' hour of greatest need.

The Midragardans were such a mysterious people, but in many ways they were very similar to Deganawida's own. Like the people of the Five Realms, they harbored a staunch, abiding loyalty to their own ways and traditions. Their warriors were undeniably courageous, and from what the stories told, they came from a land of harsh winters that had done much to forge a toughened, robust people.

Deganawida hoped that he might find a way someday to demonstrate his great respect for them. He wanted to do no less for a people that risked their own blood to allow the Five Realms to preserve their lands, lives, and ways.

Eventually, the long column encountered a tribal war band of modest size, heading in the same direction as the refugees. Deganawida recognized the warriors as being a kind of rear guard for the refugees, a first line of defense and warning.

At the sight of them, Ayenwatha moved away from the column and spoke with a few of their number. Deganawida kept moving onward at the forefront of the combined Midragardan and tribal column.

Ayenwatha soon caught back up with Deganawida, bringing word that there was a fair distance yet to go before they came within range of the lines of battle. Deganawida was gladdened by the tidings, as it meant that the refugees were not under any imminent threats.

The column stopped for a few brief hiatuses, near creeks or streams. Deganawida watched as the Midragardans partook of the fresh waters of his lands, and ate a little of the salted fish that so many of them carried.

Deganawida allowed himself a small portion of the roast cornmeal that he kept in a hide pouch at his waist, consuming what was a staple of a tribal warrior on the path of war. Sweetened with the nectar of the maple tree, it tasted altogether wonderful in the face of the hunger that dwelled within him, even if he continued to ignore it.

Even with the short respites, the grueling gait of the march accumulated fatigue as the day's light began to fade. The gloom of the forest grew ever darker, and at last even the most optimistic among the warriors did not think that they could long sustain the pace that they had been enduring. Only the strange wolf-skins and the lone bear-shirt seemed to be physically unfazed, looking fresh, as if they had only just begun the march.

Gunnar and Ayenwatha finally called out for an extended rest, and the column drew to a halt, fanning out under the trees. Inwardly, Deganawida was immensely relieved, as his old muscles and joints had given all that they had to give for the day. He did not want to entertain any thought as to whether they would recover in time for the next march. It made him feel only marginally better as he saw Gunnar take in and release a long, slow breath, which gave outward evidence to the Midragardan's own fatigue.

Deganawida and Gunnar plodded over together towards the wide trunk of a tree, where Gunnar sat down heavily, leaning his back up against the bark surface. He set his shield down at his side, within easy grasp.

Deganawida slowly sat down cross-legged at Gunnar's side, his face tensing a little as he keenly felt the soreness in his back and knees. The wince ebbed from his face, as he gradually began to settle in.

At first, the two leaders were very quiet, content to let their minds and bodies ease further. Ayenwatha came over to join them after seeing to the organization of a few sentinels.

Gunnar looked over towards Deganawida, as Ayenwatha took a place on the elder sachem's other side. "We are not far now from the fighting. It is time to think of what must be done. We must find a way to locate the strong points of the enemy … the places where their forces have concentrated their greatest strength. Have your scouts located where such places may be?"

"The enemy has attacked us along many points," Ayenwatha replied grimly. "Their numbers are great, and they have been able to cross into our lands in strength at many places. Each loss we suffer is a heavy one, while the enemy can replace those who fall."

"We will soon see to that problem," Gunnar stated determinedly, with a look in his eye that closely resembled burning embers. "As soon as we can set Midragard's axes to the trunks of the Gallean trees, we will see if they can grow them faster than we can cut them down."

Deganawida did not doubt that there was no exaggeration to the sturdy Midragardan's claim.

A rueful smile surfaced on Ayenwatha's face. "May it be so, Gunnar, but even with your men, we cannot challenge them at every point."

"Then we decisively meet them at fewer points," Gunnar replied without hesitation.

Ayenwatha nodded.

"The Ulfhednar, the ones you call wolf-skins, and the Berzerk, will pursue the battle in their own way," Gunnar stated, "but the enemies that encounter them will wish that they had run headlong into five hundred of my other warriors."

"The matter of these wolf-skins and the bear-shirt ... a conversation that I wish to have with you when we have some time," Deganawida commented. "But my curiosities must wait. Now, we must each do what we can to keep the enemy away from the people of our tribes."

"Agreed," Gunnar replied, as his face took on a look of concern. "Many of your people are not holding up well. I looked upon many as we walked by, who do not look as if they can last much longer. Can they keep moving at the pace that you ask of them?"

Deganawida and Ayenwatha grew silent, as their countenances shadowed over.

"They must," Deganawida finally said, in a low voice. "Anything less is certain death."

Gunnar gave a low chuckle. "Is not death certain for all, anyway?"

Ayenwatha grinned. "What is certain depends on whether you believe death is a veil to cross, or an endless sleep."

"I sure hope that it is a veil to cross, or there is no hope of justice, for those who live with honor, or for those who do not," Gunnar answered a little more somberly. "I know little of this Palladium I hear so many speak of, but maybe it has a great warrior's hall too. I have known several with great honor that I could not bear to think met only nothingness ... and some other vile ones, that I would hate to think escaped their actions into nothingness.

"I do not think that the good of this world meet the same fate as the most vile," Deganawida said.

"It would be a very ugly world indeed, if that were true," Gunnar remarked. He then shrugged, and gave a slight sigh. "I can only choose my own path, whether it is an ugly world or not. And I choose to wield my sword for the good among your tribes, and the good among my own people. Yet I cannot deny that what has happened to your people shakes my hope in the All-Father."

"As great tragedy does to many of a good heart," Deganawida replied. "It is hard to believe that a Creator would tolerate such great evil, an evil that continues in generation after generation ... and many would say has grown worse."

"And not all of it of a man's doing," Gunnar said. "Failed crops ...disease...many things that do great evil are beyond the means of a man."

Deganawida nodded. "It makes this path in life difficult. Seems that there are only choices, where there are no answers."

Gunnar looked upward, and let out a long breath thick with frustration. "And the evils that plague the mind. I do not know whether this storm from the west will come to strike my own wife, my children, my brothers, father, sisters ...."

"Maybe somehow we can put a halt to it, in these lands," Ayenwatha offered in a low voice.

Gunnar glanced back down at the two tribal leaders, and Deganawida noticed that the stalwart Midragardan had a pained look glazing his eyes.

Gunnar spoke slowly, voicing a heavy inner burden, "It may yet be true that I have set my eyes upon my children and good wife for the final time. It is a very strange thing to think about, and one that I do not dwell upon, but it is always there, nonetheless."

Gunnar's expression shadowed further.

"And if it is the final time? Then it may be that if this storm does indeed come to the shore where my wife and children now live, I will not be standing there before them, to wield Golden Fury against those who would seek to harm them. Yet at the same time, I could not stay on that shore to wait and see if the storm would come, while it falls heavily upon your lands."

Gunnar clasped his hands between his knees, clenching them tightly, bowing his head towards the ground as he became silent. Deganawida could feel the anxiety tormenting the Midgragardan warrior. The man was not afraid of battle, or of risking death. His fears were concentrated in the thoughts of his family.

Deganawida did not want to think of how many tribal warriors had realized the fullness of such a fear, blood ebbing out into the soil of the woodlands, as their fading consciousness clung to final thoughts of wives and children. It was a horrific image to bring to mind, but it was something that no sachem of good conscience could shy away from.

Only a better world beyond that could reunite such warriors with those that they loved would bring any sense of goodness and beauty to the struggle of life, and the hardships of the world. Anything less would mean that life itself was ultimately senseless, and immersed in tragic, hopeless folly.

Faint and ephemeral, a part of Deganawida beckoned to him, as if to remind him of something long forgotten. He had experienced the odd feeling before, whenever doubts struck him particularly sharply.

It was an all too brief ray of light, one that inflamed burdened hopes, the radiance cloaked in an ambiguity that was tantalizingly close to the grasp of understanding. Yet just as he caught a wisp of the feeling, and reached out towards it with his focused attention, it always eluded his clutches like a dissipating smoke. Frustration, doubt, and sorrow, though, had no qualms about maintaining a clear presence within his besieged mind.

"This is truly a march filled with many pains, for all of us," Deganawida added softly, as his expression saddened under the weight of his own feelings.

As the air grew quiet around the three leaders, they each turned to their own thoughts.

Deganawida's contemplation centered once again upon the exiles. They were now laboring to move forward, somewhere off to the east, as his vivid remembrances of their strained, weary faces rose again in his mind.

In a way, all of the tribal exiles were warriors, and each and every one of them was fighting a battle. It did not matter whether they were a respected war sachem like Ayenwatha, one of the great clan matrons, or simply a young mother from a village, like the one that the wolf-skin had aided at the stream. All were engaged in a terrible struggle, from the strongest to the weakest, from the newborn to the eldest.

Yet it was the clan matrons that tended to occupy Deganawida's thoughts most often as of late. They were at the center of the five tribes' entire world, and the tremendous burdens that had been unceremoniously thrust upon them gave Deganawida many fears.

His concern for the revered clan matrons grew with every passing day, as many were of an advanced age. Stoically, and seemingly indefatigable, the clan matrons were striving to lift the spirits of everyone in the march, as Deganawida had observed time and time again. The clan matrons reflected every bit as much inner strength as that being showed by the warriors engaging the enemy in combat.

The deep, troubling worries were not unfounded, considering the place that the clan matrons had within the tribes. Their authority was not limited to enveloping their immediate family lines that they each headed within their own villages. In many ways the matrons were at the apex of both their own villages, and their greater tribe. Collectively, they were at the summit of the entire Five Realms.

The matrons held the exalted power to remove or place the deer antler headdresses upon the heads of sachems for the Grand Council. Selecting the fifty sachems of the Grand Council, and removing them whenever the matrons determined that Great Sachems were failing in their tasks, placed a tremendous responsibility into the hands of the eminent women.

The responsibility for designating, and ultimately continuing to evaluate, the members of the Grand Council flowed out of a very central core of authority that had been accorded to the great matrons within the tribal culture. Its nature spread far beyond the boundaries of a matron's own village.

The great matrons headed the revered clan societies that all of the tribal people belonged to. The various clan societies, in turn, were not confined to just one particular village or tribe.

Deganawida himself belonged to the Bear Clan. Though his memory of his younger years had regrettably misted over, he knew that he had gained his clan affiliation at birth, as was the way for all new children in the five tribes. The Bear clan existed among the Kanienke, Onondowa, Onyota, and Gayogohon, as much as it did the Onan.

Others of the animal-affiliated clans existed only among a few of the tribes, but all of the clans represented a type of bond that transcended village and tribe on several levels. The way of the sacred clans was ingrained into the very heart of the tribal people's identity and entire culture. It was through the clans that each village was organized. It was through the specific clans, the ones present within an individual village, that the matrons were identified.

This was the way of things that had led to the very day when the deer antler headdress was first placed upon Deganawida's own head. That sacred day had anointed him as a very special sachem from the Bear Clan in his village. He had been carefully selected, to be sent forth to serve in one of the fourteen permanent positions reserved for the Onan sachems on the Grand Council. That reserved place had bestowed him with a storied name, one that he had kept ever since.

In truth, his was the most preeminent position on the Grand Council. It hearkened back to the very founder of the Council itself, the legendary figure for whom Deganawida was named. His selection to the prestigious seat on the Grand Council was just one of the ways in which Deganawida's own life had been greatly touched, affected, and guided by the clan matrons.

There could be little doubt that the great clan matrons truly represented, and were imbued with, the spirit that bound the Five Realms together. There was also little denying that as the great clan matrons went, so did the morale of the tribes.

Above and beyond everything, the clan matrons would have to be protected and sustained, if the very foundations of the tribes were to survive. It was not a small burden, with the tribes moving into such a foreboding period of darkness. With the physical frailty of several of the matrons, the task would increasingly take on the appearance of hopelessness.

Gunnar reached out a hand, placing it firmly upon Deganawida's shoulder, breaking him out of his deep, morose thoughts with a slight start.

"We will be there in time, Deganawida," the Midragardan said firmly. The exasperation and sorrow that had clung to Gunnar's face before had since been replaced by a stony look of resolve. The Midragardan had obviously called upon the depths of his fortitude after giving voice to his innermost torments. "Deganawida, do not forget that the sky warriors will continue to give the enemy much to think about. We will soon be able to watch their movements, as they have watched yours."

"I had almost forgotten," Deganawida remarked, with a brief smile at the buoyant reminder from Gunnar. "I have so firmly come to believe that the skies would never be an ally that we could count on during this time."

"They will be," Gunnar reassured Deganawida with a fierce pride echoing within his voice. "The accursed Darroks have been driven off, and you have seen that the Harraks are now absent from the skies. Over three hundred Midragardan warriors upon Fenraren have survived the fighting. The steeds will be resting tonight, and they will be at your people's side tomorrow, ready to take part in the continued struggle."

"I wish that we could be at their side in the skies," Ayenwatha commented ruefully.

"How many of your valiant Brega steeds still survive, Ayenwatha?" Gunnar inquired. "They are indeed such magnificent steeds, who belong in the sky with as much honor as the Fenraren of our own lands."

It was no vain compliment, as Midragardans did not idly equate anything with themselves. Gaining the esteem of the hardy people of the south was no easy thing.

Ayenwatha shook his head, his face a look of resigned frustration. "So many died in fighting off the first assault from the Darroks. As with our people, the number of Brega in our lands has never been great, and the number trained for bearing riders even less. They were once a gift of the Onondowa to the Grand Council, another great light joined within our Sacred Fire. It was the Onondowa that first tamed them, but we have never been able to breed great numbers of the winged ones.

"Among all the tribes, we may have a hundred trained sky warriors remaining, but less than fifty steeds that are healthy, and can be ridden. As all of the tribes have provided sky warriors, many of these trained steeds were kept in our villages, and are being brought along in the march. But there are far too few of them left to risk any more losses … unless circumstances grow most desperate.

"There are a few more adults and young steeds in the breeding herd, but those are not trained for riding, or fighting."

"And what of this breeding herd now?" Gunnar asked Ayenwatha, bringing his gaze up to the war sachem's eyes.

"The breeding herd was kept within the territory of the Onondowa, where the Brega first came from. But I do not yet know what has become of the herd," Ayenwatha confessed.

"That is very ill-news, when we do not know what fate befalls a shining jewel among the Skiantha," Gunnar responded, in a despondent tone.

Gunnar tilted his head downward as he again clasped his hands together, looking highly distressed by Ayenwatha's uncertain tidings. Deganawida shared the Midragardian's great dismay, fearing any harm that might have come to the precious breeding herd.

The bear-like Brega were a creature unique to the lands of the Five Realms, exceedingly rare animals in the eyes of the broader world. They were renowned for their steadfast nature, and their courageous loyalty to their riders.

The idea that their full population might be threatened to extinction was debilitating enough to a Midragardan that sincerely respected such steeds. To men such as Deganawida or Ayenwatha, who had lived alongside Bregas all of their lives, and understood their revered place among the tribal people, it was a most horrifying prospect.

"I must then ask you about the breeding herd," Gunnar finally stated, his head still down, and his voice low and tense. "Can we find out what has become of them? Now that the skies have been regained, perhaps we can use our Fenraren to search them out … and if they find the herd, maybe something can be done. Our riders just need to know where the Onondowa sachems might be."

"To the best of our ability, Gunnar, sachems are sending word out that all who are not engaged in combat are to be moved to the south and eastern region of our lands," Deganawida replied.

The southern edges of the Five Realms, bordered by the tumultuous seas that separated them from Saxany's coastlines, were not under any imminent threat. They held the greatest potential in the Five Realms as a place of refuge. Aided by long strings of cliffs and tempestuous waters, a large part of the southern coastline had its own natural lines of defense. There were very few good places to land galleys, or lay anchor for sailing vessels.

Below the Shimmering River to the east, down south to where the coastline rounded and turned west to run along the narrow, turbulent straits, were a few remaining places where the Five Realms people could cling to desperate hope.

"If that word has been received by all of the Onondowa, and those who tend the breeding herd, I do not yet know," Deganawida continued. "Since our last Grand Council, we have not yet been able to take account of all the sachems who sit upon it. Our people have been cast out of their villages, and are scattered within our forests."

"Is there a place where all of your tribes know to gather? A common place that they will be moving towards? What if the Onondowa lands are being invaded as your western lands are? Could the breeding herd be cut off from you?" asked Gunnar, a little anxiously. "I have only traded along the Shimmering River, and am not familiar with your northernmost lands."

"We march to the east and south, and are trying to gather into one body, but there is not full consensus on a final gathering place," Deganawida replied. "But do not trouble yourself greatly, Gunnar. The lands of the Onondowa are not so easy for the invaders to travel through. It is why the invaders came through the lower hills to the west of here.

"The Giant's Furrow, and the swamplands to the north of it, make the Onondowa lands very difficult terrain for an army. If the breeding herd has not been brought to the south, or even if it is somehow blocked from reaching the south, it is not likely that it is under grave threat."

The Giant's Furrow, a deep, rocky gorge through which the strong Thunder River flowed, was a formidable boundary that had long been a blessing to the Onondowa. It alone was more than enough to deter the invaders from concentrating upon Onondowa lands.

The Swamps of Shadow to the north of it were impassable to those that did not know the pathways through them. If the Onondowa with the breeding herd were somehow cut off from the rest, they could sequester themselves deep within the swamplands.

"That brings a little more peace to the growing burdens of my heart. Long have I admired the nobility of your steeds," Gunnar commented. "Though I still wish to send Fenraren to search them out, as the loss of your breeding herd is terrible to even contemplate. And maybe a few of your sky warriors can help our riders look for likely places."

"I will see that your riders are accompanied by a couple of ours," Ayenwatha replied, with a nod of agreement.

"We will find the breeding herd, and make certain that it is reunited with your people," Gunnar declared in response, looking to both of the tribal sachems.

Ayenwatha then begged leave of them, to go look after the sentries, so that the ones who had been immediately assigned to the watch upon the column's halt could gain a little rest.

Deganawida stared off into the night for a few moments in silence, before he turned towards Gunnar. The Midragardan's bright eyes gleamed in the moonlight, as he took notice of Deganawida's gaze.

A foreboding feeling was interminably nagging at Deganawida's mind. He felt a compulsion to confide the speculations to Gunnar, curious to see whether the Midragardan perceived any sense of greater dangers himself. If Gunnar did, Deganawida wanted to know the man's thoughts on the matter.

"Gunnar, long have you and I shared in friendship. Long have our people held bonds of goodwill and trade. Please listen to my words with an open mind," Deganawida stated slowly. "I desire to know your counsel, if you would offer it."

Gunnar's expression grew somber, as he responded with a tone of piqued curiosity. "Of course I shall listen to you, Deganawida. You are both a true friend, and a true ally. Withhold nothing from me. What troubles you?"

Deganawida took a deep breath, and spoke in a low voice that was meant for Gunnar's ears only. "I see only a vast darkness ahead of us … something greater, far beyond this invasion. A matter of spirit, and not flesh."

"A matter of spirit?" inquired Gunnar.

"I see a malevolent power driving the forces that are attacking us," Deganawida replied. "It is like the blackest and most violent of storms is looming behind the hordes that beset us. It is something much more than this plague on our lands … and far older than even the Five Realms."

"You are speaking of … " Gunnar started to say, before hesitating, as if he did not want to give open voice to the thing that came to his mind. He finally added, at almost a whisper, "The Adversary, as my people would see it."

Deganawida nodded silently, in confirmation.

"And the One Spirit of your people? Sounds much like our All-Father? Do you think for a moment that we will be forgotten if this is a matter that goes beyond the ken of mortal men?" Gunnar responded. A trace of firmness emerged within the worrisome look that had crept onto his face. "Emmanu, and The All-Father, like your One Spirit, will not leave us undefended."

Deganawida looked upon Gunnar with a little amazement. Where Gunnar had earlier spoken of harboring doubts regarding the All-Father, the man had now given voice to a more simple level of faith, of a kind that so many Midragardans tended to carry.

For many of Gunnar's people, the faith of the Western Church was simply something expected of them by their jarls and kings. Embracing that faith had been the proclaimed order of the legendary King Olaf the White, many years in the past, which had broken age-old bonds that the Midragardans held with their elder gods.

A great number had been forced to outwardly accept the new faith. Many had done so grudgingly, while some accepted it as a matter of course. A considerable number had been dragged into it under threat of life and limb, but some held fast to their old ways, meeting violent, barbarous ends for their steadfast refusal.

Despite the purging, a few Midragardans had secretly clung to revering the old gods, establishing a legacy that spanned to the present day. Deganawida had long wondered whether Gunnar was one of those who quietly revered the old ways, but his simple, direct statement indicated that he was a man who had taken the new faith to heart, even if he still wrestled with doubts.

"No, I do not believe so," Deganawida responded. "But I wonder if we may be in the darkest days, spoken of in your prophecies. I know that it is said that the just and the honorable will be hunted down without mercy in those times … and that it will be a time like no other before. I cannot help but think of such a time, in the light of what my people are now going through."

Gunnar looked into Deganawida's eyes. Despite the relative absence of light, Deganawida could see the grave concern reflected within the depths of his gaze.

"There have been many such claims. There has always been war, and tidings of war, and there have always been storms and famine," Gunnar said. "Only the All-Father is said to know of the time spoken of in those prophecies."

"That is true, but the truth also remains that if the prophecies are not false, then the dark days will come," Deganawida countered. "I have long meditated on this feeling that has grown within me, and my heart tells me that the Unifier is no mere man … not even one of the great Wizards. No, I suspect that He is something much more … something more dangerous than you or I can even fathom."

"There have been other rulers whose hearts were governed by malice, Deganawida," Gunnar reminded him. "Though it gives me no pride to say so, Midragard has been a home to such rulers before."

"As has the Five Realms," Deganawida said. "As has every land upon the face of Ave. Wherever there are people, there have been those that have chosen the darker path."

"Then what gives this Unifier such greater importance?" Gunnar asked.

"What single ruler has ever been able cast a shadow across the world, like this Unifier has," Deganawida replied. "He has lived far beyond the years of mortal men, and shows no signs of age. It is known that he is not a Wizard, though it is said that He works great signs, and possesses incredible powers. Yet it is not this that speaks in the silence of my heart.

"No, it is the willingness of other rulers to cast aside their own ambitions of power to align with the Unifier. The pursuers of power do not easily put aside their own interests.

"It is also the reality that kings and rulers of many lands see the Unifier as the bringer of a shining new world. It is the willingness of so many lands to acclaim the Unifier as the one to put all of their hopes in to bring about peace, even though they all know He sends great wars upon others."

"Willingness? I would say that many have been forced," Gunnar said, with a hint of a growl. "That is why we are fighting now. We will not be forced to bend our knee to this usurper."

"And more have been forced, as time has passed, and His influence has grown … but in the beginning, this was not so," Deganawida said. "No, power swirled around the Unifier because of desire … and then, once that power was established, it began to be wielded, as it is being used now."

Deganawida recalled his reflections upon the Unfier. The fact that the Unifier had once called down a column of fire from the sky, in front of a great multitude, was not what had resonated most powerfully in earlier times. As fantastical as that singular event had been, engulfing a popularly despised troublemaker within a spectacular inferno, it was a much more subtle quality regarding the Unifier that lingered and endured in the minds of men and women.

Galleans living in the eastern regions of their kingdom, while trading with the tribal peoples, had oft spoken of their experiences with the Unifier. They had remarked about His striking, comely appearance, as well as the flooding of warmth and confidence that they had all felt while in His presence. Even if the observer was just one amid a numerous throng, it was a very common impression that the Unifier could somehow focus on each and every individual comprising a larger group; all at the same time.

Some attributed the peculiar sensation to some mystical art, but most held that The Unifier simply held the special favor of the All-Father. Galleans, by and large, deemed the Unifier to be blessed in abundance from the vaults of Palladium, as He had quickly empowered prosperity and stability in their own lands.

He had succeeded where even the Peace of the All-Father movement of the Western Church had not, empowering a rising peace that had soon spread across the western lands. The Peace of the All-Father movement had merely slowed some of the excesses of the nobles, and harsher levels of suffering incurred by the peasants during the incessant warring among Gallean lords. By contrast, the Unifier had brought many long, bitter feuds to a complete halt, washing away fiery acrimony that had burned for generations in many instances.

Many in the western lands would have been taken sorely aback at Deganawida's speculations, if offense was not taken outright. He was well aware that the populations of the lands under the shadow of the Unifier found it incomprehensible that the Five Realms and Midragard, as well as Saxany, had refused to acquiesce to the Unifier's bold vision for all of Ave.

Yet as a tree could be identified by the kind of leaf or fruit that grew from its branches, so could the Unifier's true nature be perceived in the actions that were being done on His behalf. The stones plummeting from the sky, and crashing down into tribal longhouses, indiscriminately shattering the bodies of man, woman, and child alike, were not the fruit of any being whose heart was aligned with the One Spirit.

The remembrances of the devastation inflicted upon his people inflamed tensions inside of Deganawida, as his mouth tightened. His dark eyes took on a sharper edge as he glanced towards Gunnar.

"No, this battle we now fight is just a small part of a much greater war, and we must not falter," Deganawida said. "We may be overcome by numbers, but we must stand as long as we possibly can. I will hold them back with my last breath, if that is what is asked of me."

"We shall hold them back, and we shall hold them back together," Gunnar swiftly returned, a fierce temperament surging to the fore. "And you must not lose heart. Never forget that even if these are the last days, even if they are the darkest that have ever graced this world, it shall not change the side that I stand with, and proudly wield Golden Fury for."

A slight smile pierced the stony countenance on Deganawida's face. "I know that you are true, my friend. Please understand that my heart grows heavier by the day. My tribal brothers and sisters are being slain, and driven farther from their homelands with each day. We are being forced from the lands that we have known our entire lives. I fear that there will be no end to this, as long as we still live."

"I fear that as well, my friend," Gunnar said, calming down a little. "And this shadow will not spare the homelands of my people. But we must not lose heart. The worse that it may all seem, the more we must believe in what we fight for."

The look of deep concern etched on Gunnar's face at the beginning of their conversation had transformed into a visage of grim determination, and now it changed again. A stoic, largely unreadable expression manifested, as the Midragardan grew quiet. After a little time had passed, without another word being said, Gunnar turned his head away from Deganawida, and stared out into the night.

Deganawida settled himself down onto the hard earth, and soon drifted off into the depths of a dreamless sleep. It seemed as if he had just blinked, before everyone was being roused to continue the march.

Judging by the position of the moons, Deganawida deemed it to be just past the middle of the night. It was still a long way until the mists of the pre-dawn wafted through the trees, but there was a decidedly crisper chill to the air.

Deganawida's sore muscles and stiffened joints complained loudly as he labored to limber up his old, aching body. The journey was resuming all too soon, at least for his own body's needs, but the column of warriors had to take full advantage of the shroud of night.

Ayenwatha came by and spoke for a few moments with Deganawida, and the old sachem could read the sympathy in the war sachem's eyes. The younger warrior was fully aware of the much greater burden being embraced by Deganawida, who did not enjoy the swiftness of recovery that those with fewer years did.

There were only a few Midragardans and tribal warriors that approached Deganawida's age, but even they were better prepared, as their bodies had been honed and conditioned on a more regular basis than the elder sachem. Yet none of them would have noticed any difficulties in Deganawida, as he gave off an untroubled outward appearance, despite bearing a plague of throbs and spasms within.

Deganawida availed himself of a few mouthfuls of water, and a little more of the maple-sweetened cornmeal, before the column started forward again. The ensuing, final segment of the march proceeded far better than Deganawida expected, as they found themselves journeying into a younger part of the forest.

While it was accompanied by a steep increase in the prevalence of brush, the thinner canopy overhead allowed for more light to break through from above. The faint light cast by the stars filling the night sky, and the sharp luminance of the pair of moons, was enough to reveal virtually all obstacles in their path.

The warriors of the Five Realms serving as scouts and pathfinders knew every contour and change in the terrain. It was an advantage gained from switching scouting duties over to whomever was from the villages within a given area. Years of hunting and tracking had given the men invaluable knowledge and experience that now greatly benefited the night march.

While regrettably too brief, the extended rest had still served to bolster Deganawida's spirit and energy. His mind, though vexed at the danger to his people, was not being weighed down further. There was nothing new to consider, or contemplate, at least until more information could be gained regarding the enemy's movements and attacks. When the sky began to lighten, and a dampness permeated the forest, Deganawida knew that it would not be much longer before they engaged the enemy in battle.

Realizing that, the steady, crunching trod of Midragardan footsteps upon the forest floor was welcome music to Deganawida's ears. At the very least, the people of the Five Realms would not be standing alone when the new day dawned.

LEE

Ryan planted a heavy, sideways kick into one of the soft mushroom stalks, breaking the monotony of his back and forth pacing within the underground forest. His foot plunged deep into the stalk, smashing through the softer outer surface, and causing the entire length to wobble and tilt.

Another well-placed kick sent the large stalk crashing down in the vicinity of three gallidils who were resting languidly along the bank of the underground river. The startled creatures hissed and snapped in alarm and irritation, whipping around in reflex. Scurrying on their short, stubby legs, they hastened toward the comfort of the river's dark waters. Within seconds, all but their eyes were submerged within the flowing liquid haven.

"Done acting like a child?" Lee asked Ryan, with palpable

indignation. "If I were you, I would want those things to be friends. We are in their territory."

He gestured off towards the gallidils, a couple of which were staring back at them from the water, drifting a little closer back toward the shore. Lee mused that the unwavering gazes of the creatures might well be conveying extreme annoyance, at the prospect of nearly having a fungal stalk dropped unceremoniously onto their long, massive heads.

"We don't know anything! We're stuck in this so-called kingdom. If that's what you want to call that pile of rocks. Who knows what's going on up there anymore?" Ryan exclaimed angrily, pointing upwards.

He started to angle towards the nearest stalk offering a promising target for his foot.

Lee threw his hands up in disgust, irritated with the youth's vandalism and tantrum. "Look, show some respect to their forest. We are here, whether we like it or not. We've got to deal with reality ... as we still haven't woken up from any dream, and we sure as hell haven't figured out how to get back home."

Lynn nodded in agreement, from where she stood to Lee's right. "I can't argue with that. We are the strangers here. We're not in much of a bargaining position, Ryan, and we should just be glad the Unguhur took us in. Things could be a lot worse."

Ryan whirled to face her, an irate expression across his face. He snapped, "And what have we heard? Nothing. We all know what is happening up above isn't nothing. Nothing wouldn't have made us come down here. Nothing wouldn't cause bunches of their warriors to head towards the surface in such a hurry. You've seen that with your own eyes. And that ... nothing ... may very well trap us in this hole. I would like to have at least a running chance if things are going really badly. A fighting chance, with our backs to rivers infested with those creatures, doesn't sound very good to me."

"Ryan's right about that," Erin added, looking over towards Lee, a sullen, petulant mien on her own face. "A lot of tensions flying around here, but he's got a point. Gunther went in to question that enemy prisoner. And you saw that Gunther found whatever that prisoner said important enough to leave right away ... imporant enough to take all of the adult Jaghuns with him, without even saying a word to us about any of it. Don't you think that might be because of something that could possibly trap us down here ... just like Ryan says?"

DREAM OF LEGENDS

The prisoner's capture had been quite a surprise. The man had suddenly been dragged in by a band of Unguhur warriors, who had just returned from surprising a party of Avanoran squires out foraging. The presence of the squires in the vicinity, though still a fair distance away from Gunther's homestead, was a troubling development.

The captured man had looked to be a rather ordinary Avanoran, but Gunther had reacted quickly when he had set his eyes upon him. Lee remembered looking back again at the man after observing Gunther's stark reaction. He recalled feeling that the man was not particularly exceptional in appearance, and was certainly not adorned richly. He had been clad in a simple woolen tunic and trousers, along with a pair of rather plain, leather shoes. A conical helm, beaten out of one piece of iron, rested upon his head.

Lee had found the man's hairstyle to be unusual, if not somewhat eccentric. It was a fashion whereby the man's head was shaved high up on the backside, such that his short-cropped, dark hair only graced the front half of his head.

Thinking back on it, Lee realized that it had indeed been the removal of the man's iron helm that had appeared to spark Gunther's interest. The only explanation was that the strange, distinctive hairstyle was representative of something highly troubling to the woodsman.

Gunther had made a remark about the man being from Avalos itself, and had immediately asked the Unguhur permission to question the man directly, in private. There had been no opposition to the request, and a couple of Unguhur had helped to drag the man away, with Gunther following close behind. They had disappeared into the interior of a ground level chamber. It had not been long after when Gunther had departed with his fully-matured Jaghuns to the upper surface.

Lee placed his hands on his hips, as he turned to face in the direction of the river, watching the current crawling along. He remained silent for many moments, before slowly shaking his head.

He replied in a much calmer voice, devoid of the harsh edge that it had carried a moment earlier. "We are at the edge of coming apart. I can see that now. I don't blame the way you feel. We all feel helpless, like we're moving around blind. This isn't our world, and this isn't a place we know anything about. With a war going on right around us, we're going to be at the mercy of others. We don't have a choice in that. So far, Gunther and these beings … these Unguhur … have not exactly tried to kill us. We are going to have to risk a little trust somewhere."

Ryan briskly walked over to face Lee, standing right in front of him, and looking him directly in the eye. Ryan's face, exhibiting more than a hint of anger, curled into a darkened scowl. The look was not that different from the one that Ryan had given the fungal stalk that he had kicked so violently.

"And what the hell are you going to do when those Avanorans from the Unifier are pouring through here? Are you going to fight them all off? No? I didn't think so. Then where ya gonna run to, Lee?" Ryan countered, in a mocking tone. "I, for one, do not want to be cornered in this murky cesspool, with a bunch of weird, primitive cave-dwellers, and those alligator-like things in the water."

Lee's disgust with Ryan's impertinence spiraled quickly. They were all wearing their blue stone pendants, and Ryan's insults towards their hosts could easily be understood, by any Unguhur overhearing the exchange.

"And what makes you think that there's going to be anything coming down here?" Lee asked him, straining to keep his composure under control. "It's not like there are big gaping passages down here. Doesn't take a big number to defend a passage like the one we came down. Whatever you might think of these Unguhur, they are not anything I would ever want to fight."

"You can feel it," Ryan retorted hotly, as if he could not believe that Lee still could not see his position clearly. "It is in the air. It is in the mood of the Unguhur. It is everywhere. And an Avanoran foraging party in the area? Yeah, I listened when Gunther figured out who was in that foraging party. Those were squires. I bet where there are squires, there are knights. I'm no military genius, but wouldn't that mean an army is near?"

"So what is your solution, Ryan?" Lynn interjected, apparently no longer content to remain on the sidelines of the exchange between the two males.

Ryan's head jerked in her direction, and a surge of hostility was reflected in the fiery look within his eyes. "What is my solution? Well, I'll tell you, since you can't figure it out for yourself. We've got to get out of here, and make our way far beyond this place. It's going to be conquered, I am telling you. Everyone living here has their heads in the sand. They aren't gonna stand a chance here. There's no real escape out of here, if the enemy seals off just a few key places. I've kept my eyes open."

"And where will we be going?" Lee queried, in a low, tense voice, raising the most obvious question. He did not think that Ryan had given that aspect much thought.

Cursing angrily, Ryan turned away, stomping off among the growths of the mushroom forest. He vigorously planted his fist deep into another stalk, sending chunks of the mushroom shaft flying, as the stalk snapped and toppled over.

"Maybe we'll have at least a running chance up there. There are at least a few more directions to go in. He's right about that," Erin stated. "We need to see what's happening."

She glared at Lee and Lynn, cursed under her breath, and broke into a jog after Ryan.

Lynn caught Lee's arm, just as he was about to go after Erin. She had spoken little during the entire argument, and her face was drawn in a taut expression, but he knew that she did not share the opinion of the other two. Lynn did not say a word until Erin disappeared among the high stalks.

"Come on, let's take a walk, and cool ourselves down," Lynn suggested tersely, as soon as they were alone.

Lee held her eyes for a moment, then nodded. The two started off across the spongy ground underlying the stalks. The towering mushrooms, a few of which came close to scratching the jagged cavern ceiling, loomed over them. A modest, bioluminescent glow emanated from the special fungi grown in patches all along the cavern walls, casting a soft, bluish light all around the large interior space.

Were it not for the circumstances, and nagging worries, Lee would have found the surroundings to be magical. The due diligence with which the Unguhur had molded and shaped their underground world, using natural means, was simply incredible.

The forest around them was not a naturally occurring phenomenon, any more than were the Unguhur's rock-carved terraces. The Unguhur, over many long years, had brought down tremendous quantities of organic material, and had carefully cultivated growths of specific fungi that could flourish within the sunless environment.

They had harnessed the use of the bioluminescent fungi, growing it in great enough quantity so that they did not have to use fires in a world where timber was undoubtedly in scarce supply.

An entire realm had been shaped and tended by the stout race of creatures. Lee was not about to underestimate the powerful, intelligent creatures when it came to defending that subterranean kingdom.

"I wish that things in this world weren't like they are … with the war, the constant threats, and our having to be in it," Lynn remarked wistfully, eyeing Lee. "I would love to just enjoy this place, and explore the things that are here, as long as we are stuck here. Does that make sense?"

"It is an amazing place. I never thought such a place could possibly exist," Lee replied, shaking his head. "And I agree with you. I would love to just enjoy this place while we're here. But we've got a mutiny in the works that we will have to deal with. And I'm not ready to give up on those two yet."

Lynn smiled. "Yes we do have an insurrection, and if you knew Erin like I do, you'd know how stubborn she can be. I bet you'd say the same about Ryan. It's probably why those two have gravitated together. But I don't think that going up there, to the surface, is going to bring us any more advantages than we have down here. At least we've got a few allies down here, who know a whole lot more about this world than we do. Up there, we might be on our own, and we don't know the lay of the land at all."

"That may be true, Lynn, but I also have to admit that Ryan could be right about some other things. The enemy might pour through here, and conquer the Unguhur. He's right, there aren't a lot of channels out of this underground city, especially if we get caught on the far shore of the lake in Oranim," Lee stated, looking up towards the rock ceiling with resignation.

As audacious as Ryan was, the young man had made some points that could not be argued against. Lee now knew what it meant when a person was described as being caught between a rock and a hard place.

"But then, what are the four of us going to do, if we get caught outside by the enemy's forces with nobody at our side? You are right, Lynn. At least here we have warriors who will help defend us," Lee continued.

He looked over towards Lynn, searching her face for any sign of her leanings on the matter.

Lynn halted in her tracks, and held Lee's gaze. It was as if a feeling she had been holding back for some time had finally broken free of its confinement. Her demeanor crumbled into sadness.

She almost sounded like she was begging him for answers when she replied. "Why are we here? What the hell brought us to this place? You know? At the least, back home in our world we didn't have to worry so much about whether we were going to be alive the next day or not. Did all of this just happen? No purpose at all? Can anyone tell us what is going on?"

"Lynn, I understand … I really do," Lee replied softly, sliding his right arm around her shoulders in a consoling fashion. He often found himself fighting internally to keep such disconsolate feelings at bay. "But we are here. We didn't choose to come here, and we can't change it. We just have to deal with things as they are. It's like a lot of things in life. You've got to think of it that way, whether we like it or not, or we're all going to lose our minds."

A frown welled up on Lynn's face, as lines of worry spanned her brow. "How are we ever going to get back? Are we going to get back at all? Are we stuck in this place forever?"

Reddening, her eyes filled up with moisture, and a few tears began making a slow trek down her cheeks. She looked to be an embodiment of hopelessness, and her hollow, empty stare was bereft of any speck of motivation.

"What is the point of even trying to fight," she muttered, weakly. "Let's just go to the Avanorans, and get things over with, Lee. Why not sooner than later? It's pretty much inevitable, isn't it?"

Erin had always shown much more emotion since Lee had met the two young women. It was the first time that he had seen Lynn in such a rattled, unguarded state, and the sight struck him very forcefully. Her breakdown left him dumbstruck, and for a brief moment, he felt entirely alone.

Her fears and sorrows were not unfounded. Nor were they things that he could not understand, in regards to his own condition of mind. He wished with all of his might that the biggest concern facing him right then was whether he had enough time to finish preparations before customers began trickling through the door of his restaurant. He longed for the times when his most common worries regarded whether the supplies for his restaurant would be accurate, and delivered on time. In the midst of such an unbelievably fantastical world, the things that were the most mundane suddenly held great appeal.

Uncertainty was perhaps the most threatening menace to the four of them. The pressures of uncertainty were like a volcano, gaining strength with every passing minute. It was a pressurized fiend that eventually had to break loose, one way or another. The foundations in Ryan and Erin were beginning to crack, and Lee now feared that Lynn was close to plunging beyond that point. While he had not yet become overwhelmed by the omnipresent uncertainties, he was not altogether convinced that he could endure the seemingly infinite marathon that they had all been thrust into.

As Lynn quietly sobbed, Lee wrapped his other arm around her, and hugged her close to him. It felt almost like a fatherly thing to do, even though his own father had rarely ever shown any outward affection to him. No words were needed from him, as Lynn knew very well that he shared the pain of their ordeal.

His own tribulation was going to be even more difficult. He realized that the moment he embraced Lynn. All of the others had been cut off from their families and friends, and Lee was not so blind that he could not see the gaping voids present in their younger lives. Even if they had estranged relations with their parents, or other figures of authority, the influence and presence of those figures was still in place.

Ryan might have often rebelled against the aunt in whose house he often stayed. Yet Lee knew that in the back of the young man's mind, Ryan drew some comfort from the fact that his aunt was always there for him. Here, in a daunting, strange world, Ryan had no such promise of comfort. The young man was perceptibly being loosened from his mental moorings.

In his heart, Lee reaffirmed his decision to accept a harder path, one of being the sort of person that the others could lean upon, and look to for some guidance. As a single man, he had not started a family of his own, but he could at least continue to try to bring a sense of family to the other three. He could never replace their families, but he might yet bring a little order into the chaos.

Lee knew that unity was perhaps the most important element to maintain if they were all going to have even the slightest chance of surviving. He was not naive enough to think that the worst was over. Far from such a perspective, he was pretty sure that much stormier seas lay ahead.

Holding Lynn snugly to himself, Lee began to wonder how he would be able to bridge the gap between himself and the other two. He also began to think of what they could seek to do, if Ryan and Erin turned out to be right about everything.

There were just so many things to consider, and unavoidable, onerous choices to make. Lee knew that the key to their very survival lay in keeping everything in its proper perspective, and, most of all, keeping a level head.

THE UNIFIER

The icy night winds whipped through the air, high up on the solitary, black mountain overlooking the vast city of Avalos. On a broad balcony, supported by thick, stone corbels, jutting out from the body of the great palace structure upon the citadel's seventh level, the Unifier stood silently, with His eyes raised intently skyward.

There were no guards, or other attendants about. Any uninvited eyes that might have strayed upon the open surface had long ago been cleared away.

A distant flock of serpentine flying creatures, wings outstretched, with thin tails trailing behind, glided along the powerful currents of the night winds. Their forms were sharply outlined by the light of the smaller moon. They were predators in their own right, but presented absolutely no threat to the figure on the balcony.

It was the Unifier's time of isolation, meditation, and supplication. Normally, He isolated himself within the special chapel that had been constructed deep inside the mountain, but this night He had opted to pray under the expansive, ebon skies.

"My Father, what should I do?" the Unifier called out, His words ascending into the black night. The stars flickered coldly, as an empty silence met His words.

He fell down upon His knees in humility, a look of measureless worry written upon His face. It was an expression that no human had ever beheld, but there was no use hiding His concerns before the immeasurably dark Power that He was so intimately united with.

As the words of the Unifier drifted off, the winds about the balcony slowly started to swirl, and were soon picking up in force. Though no clouds moved about in the starlit sky above, a massive, cloaking Shadow crossed over the balcony. It thickened, engulfing the forms of the Unifier and the balcony. The Shadow was a form in and of itself, and had not been caused by any physical element merely blocking light.

He knew immediately that it was not His Father that had manifested to His call, but rather one of the greater powers of the dark abyss, one that served dutifully at His Father's side.

The Sentience that had taken the form of the living Shadow was not the only essence that emerged. Flowing through and about the Unifier was a deep, freezing Presence, one that also encompassed the black Sentience in the air above.

"Seven Lands and Ten Great Rulers serve your bidding truly. You speak with His authority. The world sees that none can wage war against You," came a cold, deadly voice, filling the night air around the Unifier.

The Unifier immediately lowered His head in obeisance to the malevolent Sentience, and the Presence that transcended it, even as He felt the Presence's icy caress, and thorough permeation of His own being.

"Your power grows, as You do the work of the Master, Your Father, Our Lord," the voice continued in strong resonance. "Why do you cry out so?"

"Our enemies are proving more difficult to overcome than I believed they would be," the Unifier uttered in a deferential tone, knowing that nothing could be hidden from the Sentience, and certainly not from the Presence that had coalesced around them, and flowed within them.

"You will overcome them, those who serve our Enemy, for Your power is far too great for any power of this world," the Sentience stated firmly. "The Master will grant more of His power to Your Sorcerers, to aid you. Do not doubt that those who oppose You will find themselves consumed. More of the Master's servants have been released to come into this world, though it comes at a great price. Blood flows abundantly upon the Altar of Sacrifice, and it creates vulnerability in a place where we risked none before. These servants will be placed under Your command, from this moment forth, to comfort You, and to serve You, in the greater service of the Master."

The Unifier kept His eyes fixed downward. His words coursed with reverence and obedience, a tone that no mortal had ever heard from His lips. "I am grateful to the Master, my Father, to Whom I submit all that I am."

"Raise your eyes," the Sentience commanded Him.

Slowly, the Unifier brought His head and eyes upwards. A number of the stars in the sky, around a third of those in his field of vision, were now blocked out by the dark, billowing shape above Him.

"Behold, Your servants are here," the Sentience then stated.

Just to the right of the shapeless form, a strange, sinuous effect materialized in the air. It was similar to the look of ripples moving across a pool of water. Then, as if the sky was fashioned out of some tender fabric, the air itself split apart, revealing a widening hole teeming with fire and smoke.

A blistering heat blasted across the Unifier's face. Ghastly, bizarre sounds, of kinds never heard anywhere within Ave, mingled with hopeless, human-like cries, the latter imbued with tremendous pain and sorrow. The hellish chorus wafted out of the flaming hole, filling the Unifier's ears.

The rising cacophony and spectacle would draw no attention from others in Ave, as only the Unifier's senses had been enabled by the Presence to perceive the ethereal rift. Without warning, the hole was occupied with the massive head of a hideous, fearsome-looking creature.

Its broad, horned head contained white-hot eyes, and its mouth displayed rows of long, serrated teeth. The beastly figure's wide, bulging shoulders were adorned with the presence of dark, leathery wings, the tops of which rose high up from its back. In its left, clawed hand, it clutched a fiery, jagged sword.

With a lithe grace that belied its considerable bulk, the creature flapped its wings, and flew out of the gaping inferno. It drifted in a glide down to the surface of the platform with the Unifier.

Standing over three feet taller than the Unifier, the creature was a living quintessence of deadly intentions. Three other such creatures emerged in succession from the hole, all of them continuing over to stand alongside the first.

"As is above, so is below … The Accursed One sent His Archons to minister to His son, and so shall the Master send His own servants to minister to His only, begotten Son," the Sentience announced.

The Unifier's eyes remained transfixed, gazing in wonder upon the four monstrosities on the platform with Him. An eerie, shrieking cry cut through the night, prompting the Unifier to look back over towards

the tear in the sky. The high-pitched shrieks rose swiftly into a piercing crescendo.

The snout of a giant, serpentine creature emerged through the blazing hole. Its elongated neck was connected to a broad, scaly body, supported by an extensive wingspan. A horrible stench accompanied it, and its spiky teeth, each one as long as a dagger, glistened in the moonlight.

Riding on the back of the diabolical creature was a hooded figure, bearing a great black sword aloft in its right hand. Two small flames peered out from deep within the hood, a surreal gaze that seemed to penetrate through anything in its path.

The hooded cloak itself, the Unifier knew at once, was crafted out of skin, toughened and worked by abyssal arts to withstand the weapons of humankind better than any armor. It was a very intimate fabric, as at least some of the skin used to fashion the cloak had come from the one that now wore it.

With a simple crack of the black reins, the shrouded figure guided its infernal steed forward and upward, taking a slow, circular route in the air above the balcony. Three other similar flying creatures, each with cloaked riders mounting them, came forth, proceeding upwards to join the first one. When the last of the four was through, the rift in the sky suddenly collapsed, vanishing from sight, and leaving the sky undisturbed and silent once more.

The four great, winged creatures then descended, alighting upon an open expanse of ground spreading far outward, down before the balcony. The tall, horned creatures that had been earlier brought forth from the cleaved sky moved forward, spacing themselves apart along the balcony, while turning to face inward towards the Unifier. Riders, steeds, and horned figures alike waited in silence.

"Bow before the Son of your god!" the voice of the Sentience boomed.

The four riders upon the flying creatures dismounted, the last three drawing lengthy black swords from the scabbards at their sides before they all lay themselves prostrate before the Unifier. Faces pressed against the ground, they held their arms forth, with their black swords spanning their upturned palms, in a gesture rife with submission.

Three of the towering winged entities on the balcony immediately did likewise, their flaming swords not so much as singeing even one of the coarse hairs scattered across their rough, knotted skin. The fourth of the tall entities remained upright, its eyes appearing to burn more intensely than the others.

"You deny my order?" the Sentience inquired coldly of the fourth, as a coiling sensation stirred within the air.

The creature bellowed forth an ear-splitting roar, shaking its fiery blade upward, at the Sentience. The creature's mindset was naked and exposed to the Unifier, who was empowered to read deeply into the thoughts of anything subordinate to Him.

Its ample musculature bulged with the force of the anger and incredulity racing inside of it, enraged at being commanded to bow before a mere human entity. It had expected the Son of Jebaalos to have a different form, certainly something other than the pitiful body of a human.

Countless humans were held in bondage within the immense, nightmarish realms of Jebaalos. They were mere fodder for the amusement of a powerful creature of the lower realms, such as the demonic figure on the balcony was. It could not believe, or accept, that the human before it was actually the exalted Son of the Lord of Fire.

It quickly learned that it had made a terrible mistake in its prideful defiance. Flames accumulated in the air, converging into a mass that formed within the emptiness in front of the dense, shapeless manifestation of the Sentience. With blurring speed, the flames lashed out, proceeding to envelop the rebellious creature.

The searing flames instantly tore away at the thick flesh of the stricken, fourth creature, eliciting deafening cries of extreme pain. As the beast flailed helplessly and desperately, it cast its burning sword aside, throwing it out over the edge of the platform. The flames of the sword ebbed, as the sword itself dissipated like wisps of mist spread by robust winds.

The relentless fires whittled the mighty creature down to a small pile of ashes in just moments. A few light breezes scattered, and carried away, what little was left of the fearsome beast of the abyssal realms.

"And such is the fate of any that deny the will of the Master," the Sentience declared, as if to make a bold lesson of the gruesome display for the others still prostrated on the platform and farther below, on the ground.

The smoldering, dark circle that remained in the stony surface, where the powerful, demonic entity had stood only scant moments before, effectively served to accent the Sentience's foreboding words. There were no other challenges forthcoming from amongst the seven who were left, even if any had harbored similar, resistive feelings deep within.

The Unifier knew that they did not possess any such sentiments. They were all wise to His true nature, and had fully accepted Him as their Lord, and through Him they knew that they were continuing fervent obedience to Jebaalos.

"The four Arcamons before you, upon their steeds, have been given to You, as they are spirits most knowledgeable in the arts of war," the Sentience's voice proclaimed. "Their understanding is culled from the most brilliant war minds in all of Ave's history, most of whose souls are now claimed by the Master, and are now dwelling in His Kingdom. Use them to your advantage in gaining final victory over the Five Realms, over Saxany, and anywhere resistance to our Master yet exists.

"They are all former worshippers of the Master, granted their new forms over long ages, after their sentencing by the Accursed to our Master's Kingdom. They are warriors for whom there are few equals across the surface of this world. They have been granted to you as a reward for the devotion and service that You have given to the Master. Great power and sacrifice were used to pierce the Veil, and bring them through. As You know, the Sundering has not yet happened."

"I am duly honored," the Unifier replied with great reverence, knowing the rivers of blood that had flowed through the Altar of Sacrifice to empower such a breach of the Veil.

The expenditure of so much power was no small matter, as any direct action by Jebaalos within Ave required a high level of spiritual exertion. To bring through seven creatures of the abyssal regions into Ave, each in an incarnate form, required an unprecedented outpouring of power.

"The three remaining Archons are from the exalted legions placed under the command of Molech. They are warriors of the new armies that are forming even now, in deep realms of blood and fire, awaiting the Sundering. Know that there are many who are much greater than these, and innumerable ranks of their own kind, that are all now marshaling for the assault upon Palladium."

The Unifier looked upon the three warriors of Molech with a sense of wonder, imagining the kind of strength that was gathering within the Realms of Fire for the Final Battle. Like the Arcamons, they represented just a fraction of the vast powers that had been carefully gathered, and assiduously built up, since the Celestial War of the Schism.

The Unifier had no doubts that an army of the monstrous creatures could unleash a ferocious assault upon the legions of the Accursed. Their intimidating, fell appearance echoed the complex nature of the Great Archon in whose legions they served; the majestic titan of the nether realms, Molech.

The Unifier had no doubts that the Legionnaires of Molech were more than a match for any mortal warrior. The infernal creatures were overwhelming in terms of sheer strength, even compared to the most massive of Gigans.

"I must return to the Court of the Master, but You have been bestowed with an answer. Continue Your path, and the enslavement of this world shall be in Your hands," the Sentience avowed. "The Master will then join with You, and You shall rule at His side. Know that You shall rise with Him when He ascends to conquer the last horizon, when all Pallidium shall be laid low!"

The last words of the Sentience thundered, with an underlying abyss of defiance and rage. Slowly, the stars obstructed by the Sentience's manifestation began to reveal themselves again, as the dark, living Shadow faded out of the night skies. With its departure, the Presence that had saturated the area also ebbed.

As the Shadow and Presence vacated the area, the seven entities lying prostrate before the Unifier slowly began to rise. They continued to keep their eyes lowered in reverence, careful not to meet the gaze of their Master.

"Go into the world, Arcamons, and take account of the war as it is now," the Unifier ordered. "Seek to break the power of all who resist, that their lands may be conquered with swiftness. I desire to possess the Five Realms, Saxany, and Midragard, so that I can bring my Father's unity closer to embracing all the lands of Ave."

"As you wish," responded the deep, chorus-like voice from one of the four.

Without another word, the Arcamons sheathed their blades of obsidian-black, remounted their steeds, and took to the air. Rising on a sharp incline, they set forward swiftly. It was not long before their forms diminished, and blended into the distant, star-dotted horizons of the sky.

DREAM OF LEGENDS

The other three winged creatures remained dutifully in place. Their white eyes were anything but dull and lifeless. The Unifier could feel the scorching hatred churning deep within their molten gazes. The Legionnaires of Molech despised being in Ave, before the time of the Sundering that they bore a cavernous hunger for. They wanted nothing more than to assail the Archons of the All-Father directly, and gain vengeance for their brethren's ancient loss, and humiliation.

Feeding on ceaseless streams of antipathy, they had grown mightier, and even more terrible in fury, than many of those that had fought during that tragic age. They were more than ready to beset their greatest enemies, chafing to hurl their wrath towards the Archons from Palladium.

Yet they were firmly bound by the Unifier's command, which carried the authority of the One Who had sent Him, whether they wanted to be in Ave or not. Before The Unifier gave them any assignments, however, He wanted to amuse Himself a little, by witnessing the formidability of the great creatures.

"Guard!" the Unifier shouted into the night, even as He made a special summons from the depths of His mind.

He called to a being that had remained out of sight all throughout the night's events, at His strict order. It was several more moments before anything broke the thick stillness, but at last signs of movement transpired down on the ground, before the palace balcony.

A hulking shadow emerged, spreading across the area that the cloaked Arcamons and steeds had so recently stood upon. The mammoth form of a Gigan came into full view just a few moments later, trudging in the wake of the broad shadow. It was an exceptional brute among its rugged, hulking kind, bearing a wickedly-sharp axe of immense size.

In height and mass, the Gigan was easily the visual equal of the three demonic entities before the Unifier. The Gigan was advanced in its martial skill, as well as being further enchanted with Sorcerer's arts, such that the Unifier doubted that any warrior within Avalos would have stood much of a chance against the powerful beast. The Gigan had long been a personal guardian to the Unifier, quartered on the seventh level of the mountain citadel.

"Warrior of the Legions, come forth," the Unifier commanded, beckoning to the demonic entity farthest to His left, as His eyes fixed the creature rigidly.

The creature indicated strode forth obediently, its white-hot eyes locked on the Unifier, as it awaited His next command.

"If you are to be My personal warriors within this world, then you must defeat one of the greatest of warriors that already serves Me," the Unifier addressed the demonic being. "To the ground!"

Without hesitation, the Archon lifted up from the balcony, propelled by its powerfully flapping wings. It swooped down to alight on the ground, landing several paces away from the Gigan. The Gigan showed no fear, an expression like a leer coming to its protruded face, as it gripped its war axe more tightly.

"Kill it!" the Unifier then commanded the Gigan, as a bloodthirsty energy rushed through Him.

The specter of violence was always stimulating, and invigorating in the extreme, and the Unifier gazed in contentment and anticipation upon the unfolding scene of battle. With a loud, bellowing cry, the massive Gigan barreled straight ahead at the Legionnaire of Molech. Dexterously, it raised its massive war axe upward, readying to engage the sword-wielding Archon.

In a flash of movement barely perceptible to even the keen eyes of the Unifier, the demonic entity brought its flaming sword slicing through the air. The Gigan was able to bring the head of the huge war axe up, to partially block the slash, but the fire-sword cut straight through the exquisitely forged metal of the Gigan's axe blade.

The flaming sword raced without hindrance to separate the Gigan's head from its body. The large head tumbled to the ground, and rolled several paces away. The Gigan's jaws were still open, in the midst of its war cry, fully exhibiting its prominent, upward-jutting tusks from the end of the lower half of its gaping maw. The body of the Gigan wavered for an extended moment, before toppling heavily to the ground.

"I have seen your skill with my own eyes," the Unifier said approvingly, not regretting for an instant the death of the Gigan that had served so faithfully at His side for over five years. The creature had served its purpose, from its arrival to the last, violent moment. In its own failure, the Gigan had proven the much greater skill of the demonic entities. It was all that mattered to the Unifier. He was well-pleased with the gifts from his Father, as his eyes roved amongst the impressive trio. "Await me, warriors of Molech, for now."

Turning around, the Unifier strode back into the palace building, leaving the three horned Archons behind. In addition to the three Archons, vivid testaments to the Unifier's growing reign of mercilessness were left in His wake; a headless Gigan's body, sprawled out on the palace grounds, and a broad, amorphous, charred blemish in the stone surface of the balcony.

The Unifier found that His mood had improved considerably from the beginning of the night. He now felt fully rejuvenated, and was looking forward to the rest of the evening. While most in Avalos slept, there were nascent, intriguing plans for Him to dwell upon.

He had been given tremendous gifts from his infernal Father. He had not expected to have the service of such extraordinary creatures, immortals of exceptional powers, who would not be vulnerable to age or disease. The Unifier knew that He had been shown great favor by Jebaalos, in receiving such a boon of incredible proportions.

The Arcamons were a force unto themselves, as were the Legionnaires of Molech. The Unifier all but salivated at the possibilities beginning to unveil themselves within His mind.

GUNTHER

The light of day found Gunther and his pack of Jaghuns ardently searching amidst a sprawling congregation of death. All around them, multitudes of lifeless bodies lay strewn across the terrain. Gunther had seen such landscapes of death before, and was not deterred by the dour visions, as he looked diligently for even the slightest signs of life from the precious few who might still be saved.

The Jaghuns barked excitedly whenever they came across a Saxan that was still alive, whether languishing in pain, or unconscious, as the creatures roamed the blood-drenched ground surrounding the ridgeline and running down its long, western slope.

There were a few surviving Avanorans interspersed with the Saxans. Though Gunther bore great resentment, and not a small degree of hostility, towards the enemy, the solitary woodsman somehow managed to put his sense of honor ahead of his raw emotions, and aided them as well.

More than a few of the Avanorans displayed wide, frightened eyes at the sight of the large, thick-jawed Jaghuns. Their eyes enlarged even farther at the sight of the few Unguhur still lingering on the battleground.

"Hold yourself still, friend," Gunther urged in a low voice, tilting a half-emptied waterskin over, as he sprinkled a little wine into an open wound on the leg of a Saxan warrior. As the liquid touched the torn flesh, the man winced in pain, though he clenched his teeth and did not cry out.

Gunther had forced many things regarding his past out from his mind, hoping to someday forget his memories of things that once seemed utterly inseparable from who he was. Other things had been well worth retaining, the most valuable of them seeming to have been quite minor elements when Gunther had first come into knowledge of them.

Much of both kinds of elements had occurred during his time in Theonia, a land of regal splendor, complex intrigues, and magnificent opulence. Yet for all of its grandeur, Theonia also represented terrible betrayal, and sundering heartache, to Gunther. Even so, he had gleaned more than one thing during his tenure that had come to good use in the years since he had left the Empire far behind.

During those times, he had come across a physician from Gunther's own homeland who had spoken of wine as an effective treatment for open wounds. He was a well-traveled man, and very erudite. From the bonds of their shared homeland, Gunther had been able to open up a rich dialogue that had profited his learning greatly.

The physician had been a very firm believer in the teachings of a certain friar in Lombar, a man who had certainly gained unique experience as the son of a physician who had participated in one of the major Holy Wars in the Sunlands. In the few times since that Gunther had adhered to the physician's advice, he had found the things that he had learned to be infinitely more efficacious than the old salves and concoctions still passed down in western lands. The latter's origins derived from little more than folktale, and to Gunther's eyes had always been ineffectual.

Knowing that the enemy invading the Saxan lands was Avanoran had raised Gunther's hopes that a little wine could be located, when he had taken on the burden of searching the battleground. A few Unguhur had been dispatched to bring back any liquids that they could find still stored within the remains of the enemy's destroyed encampment.

As he had expected, a cask of strong wine was uncovered, presumably intended for the higher-ranking Avanorans amongst the enemy force. He had never been more grateful for the Gallean affinity for wine, or for the fact that Avanoran nobles were not opposed to indulging themselves, even while on a campaign.

The Saxan warrior continued to bite down on the leather strip that Gunther had provided for him, as more wine poured into the wound. The man was nearly overcome by the searing pain caused by the wine's increasing contact with the exposed, bleeding laceration.

"That should help you, so that you do not get a sickness later," Gunther assured the man, in a calm, confident tone. He then turned his attention towards a few Unguhur who were shadowing him, to assist where needed. "I am done with this man. Get this warrior back to a safer haven."

To Gunther's frustration, the hulking, gray-hided creatures were showing greater degrees of discomfort the longer that they remained in the direct light of day. Despite being underneath the leaves of the trees, they squinted incessantly, showing a real difficulty with adjusting to the wealth of light at mid-day on the surface of Ave.

The Unguhur warrior retrieved a litter fashioned out of a length of hide, looped and secured around two elongated wooden poles, a simple type of construct that Gunther had shown to them. Carefully, they moved the Saxan onto the litter, before two of the Unghuhur hunched over, and gripped the ends of the poles in their huge hands. Standing up, and lifting the man off the ground with extreme ease, they carried him away, to where he could rest down in the relative safety of the Unguhur Realm.

Gunther stood up himself, grimacing as he stretched his sore, stiffened back. His tightened back cracked and popped several times before he was through. Taking a couple of deep breaths, he wiped the thick sweat off of his brow, looking out across the debilitating vision of death surrounding him. His face was stony, and his eyes iron-hard, but deep within he was not unmoved by the sorrowful aftermath of the battle.

A couple of his Jaghuns were eagerly yapping and barking, indicating that yet another living being had been found in the carnage. Each and every such moment represented a small victory, of a kind that Gunther savored with gladness and gratitude.

A couple of the others from Gunther's four-legged entourage were diligently sniffing and pawing about in their continuing search for others. There was not much more left of the battlefield that they had not sifted through, a reality that dampened Gunther's spirits, as much as the discovery of survivors bolstered them.

Commanding his tired legs to move, Gunther plodded across the battlefield, to where the two Jaghuns were making their commotion. They had found another Saxan with breath yet in him, clad in a blood-stained mail shirt. The man had a significant wound near his midsection, where he had been pierced by a sword or lance that had since been removed.

The presence of a stout, well-crafted coat of mail, as well as the tri-lobed, silver-gilt pommel on the sword lying on the ground at his side, said more than enough about the warrior. The items indicated right away that the man was no common Saxan farmer or artisan, called forth by the mass levy of the General Fyrd.

Carefully, Gunther removed the Saxan's half-helm, a segmented construct of four iron plates set within an iron frame. Sounds of labored, erratic breathing emitted from the deeply unconscious man.

His thick beard and long locks were matted with sweat, blood and grime. The rounded face and broad, flat nose lent the man a rather kindly natural mien. Despite the circumstances, Gunther could imagine such a face regularly exhibiting expressions of jest and mirth before the battle.

He had encountered the burly, jovial type many times before in his life, drinking copious amounts of ale and booming with laughter. Gunther suspected strongly that this was a similar kind of man, as the etched lines in the Saxan's face were indeed conducive to laughter and smiles.

Yet the man also exhibited physical characteristics indicating the presence of a capable warrior. The broad shoulders of the man accented a powerful, bullish neck, all of which gave open testament to a great physical strength present within the unconscious warrior. Thick, powerful arms ended in massive, rough hands, of the kind that Gunther suspected could wield the most robust of weapons skillfully enough, though all now lay idly upon the ground.

In a tedious, careful fashion, Gunther began the onerous task of removing the battered, penetrated mail shirt. Underneath it was a woolen tunic that had been thoroughly soiled with the filth of battle. When he got down to the man's midsection, and peeled away the tunic, he got a much better look at the wound that had eliminated the warrior from the battle.

From the looks of the glistening, oozing wound, a spear had managed to penetrate through the mail, driving deep into the man's side. Gunther breathed a sigh of relief, as it looked as if the wound was not a mortal blow. The man had been incredibly fortunate, for if the blow had been just a few inches to the left he would have long since left the world behind.

"Water," Gunther called out to a lone Unguhur that hunkered in the shade of a tree nearby.

The Unguhur walked over to Gunther's side, and extended a waterskin towards him that had been filled up from a creek in the vicinity. Gently, Gunther cleaned off the wound, before rinsing it with some of the wine left within the other waterskin. When the wine touched the wound, the unconscious warrior was awakened with a start.

"Wha ... what?" the man stammered, his eyes widening with an element of fear, as well as pain from the sharp stinging that was undoubtedly radiating from the wine-cleaned wound.

Gunther put his hand out, shifting his speech back to Saxan, "Sssshhh! You are safe ... be still. It is lucky that we found you. I believe that you are going to survive. The wound that you received was not a killing blow, and it has been treated before it could fester ... I am Gunther, here with the Unguhur, who have come to your aid."

"The ... Unguhur?" the man iterated, with a look of momentary confusion. It was then that his eyes wandered past Gunther towards the tall Unguhur standing idly a few feet behind. A look of surprise and awe sprang upon his face. "What has happened? ... The battle? ... The Avanorans.... What has happened?"

"The Unguhur have helped the Saxans, the Avanorans have not won. We will speak of more later, but you are in the hands of friends, be assured of that," Gunther replied firmly. "First, you must rest."

The man's eyes reflected desperation, and an underlying stubbornness. His mind was clearly gaining in focus, and something was troubling him greatly. "No! I must know now ... please ... what has happened?"

Gunther replied, "In time, my Saxan friend."

"No!" the man shouted with desperation, his body trembling in pain at the sudden jostling. "I must know now! What has happened?"

Reluctantly, Gunther acquiesced to the man's wishes. "The battle is over ... we have only found a few who are wounded, and yet live, along this ridge. We do not know how many Saxans retreated or survived before we arrived. The Avanorans have been driven back, and their camp overrun. I am not sure that any force from the surface world won on this day."

To Gunther's surprise, the warrior's eyes suddenly reddened and a few tears leaked out, as the man exhibited a countenance rife with frustration and forlorn sorrow. Gunther was transfixed by the man's emotive expression, the mask of a dying hope.

"Aethelstan..." the man's lips barely mumbled, just above a whisper. "Aethelstan ... is he alive?"

Gunther was frozen by the name that came out from the mouth of the wounded warrior. Aethelstan, who had tolerated Gunther's eccentric presence in the outer forests of Saxany for so many years, had evidently been involved in the terrible battle.

Gunther's eyes immediately shifted over the long array of bodies that he had inspected. A horrible chill welled up in him at the mere thought that one of the helmeted, dead bodies could be that of a rarity in Ave; a man that Gunther could sincerely call a friend. A new fear raced through his veins, though he made an effort to keep his face steady for the benefit of the other man.

"There is no sign of Aethelstan, dead or alive," Gunther said quickly, straining not to choke on the emotion that threatened to grip him tightly.

The other man winced, whether from pain, recoil at the uncertain news, or from a combination of both.

"I must ... look ... for him," the other man said. His eyes closed, and he mercifully passed out again, leaving Gunther alone with the unsettling news.

Gunther finished binding the man's wounds, though he felt a great tension and anxiety as he did so.

"Get him to a place of rest," Gunther ordered the Unguhur when he was finished, standing up straight and staring down at the man beneath him, watching the Saxan's chest lift and fall with each breath.

Curtly, Gunther turned and called to his Jaghuns, consumed with the desire to know for certain what had become of Aethelstan. Of the small pack, he sent out four to search for any living beings just beyond the outermost boundaries of the fighting area. The others he kept with him, as he resumed attending to any living souls that could be found amid the bloodshed.

It took tremendous discipline to set his eyes upon any figure that wore mail or helm. Fear rose in intensity, with each and every dead face that he looked upon, garbed in anything that might possibly be worn by a Saxan thane.

As Gunther went across the battleground, his heart shook with the notion that at any moment one of the bodies found could be that of Aethelstan. His eyes wavered constantly, and were determinedly, and grudgingly, brought to bear on each area of fallen warriors. He was tormented by the dread of seeing Aethelstan lying still, devoid of breath, a truly noble man who Gunther had always seen as flowing with light and life.

A part of him turned in silent supplication to the All-Father. He prayed that the Jaghuns would either discover a surviving group of Saxans, or find a passage of retreat that would eventually lead Gunther to the still-living Aethelstan. A storm of tremendous regret and frustration engulfed him as he realized what was ultimately happening to him.

Though he had so fervently resisted, for many long years, he could not deny that he was being drawn back into the affairs of kings and emperors. He had sworn never to do so again, but now he had no choice.

Yet he could not betray the man that he was at heart, and then expect to live with himself, not for even one day.

EDMUND

Edmund, and the other two hale Saxan warriors, assisted by the heightened senses of their Himmeros steeds, kept a tight watch out of the cave opening. The atmosphere all around them was quiet and ponderous, each uncertain moment weighing upon their nerves.

The three of them had already shared their amazement that not one Avanoran warrior had yet crossed into the area in front of the cave. The end of the battle had been inevitable when they had fled with the unconscious Aethelstan. There was not a speck of doubt in any of them that the Avanorans had gained free reign throughout the forest by then.

As time crept on, hunger and thirst began to draw upon their reserves of willpower. After conferring, the three had decided that they could not risk a foray for sustenance, as long as they felt very strongly that they were in immediate danger.

A little hard bread, which was in one of the leather saddle-pouches carried by one of the Himmerosen, and some equally stout, rather dry cheese was divided up amongst them. They were able to wash it down with a little water from a skin. The meager fare was far from satisfying, and did very little to blunt the edges of their gaping appetites.

In short shifts, the Saxans afforded each other precious moments of rest. Aethelstan remained unconscious, drained and wounded from the arduous battle.

Edmund looked over towards one of the other Saxans, a man named Webba, who was now standing with him by the opening of the cave. Both men had taken their bows and quivers off of their sky steeds. Quivers hanging at their waists, and bows in hand, they would at least have some means of deterring an intruding, enemy presence from a distance.

"We cannot take to the skies, Webba," Edmund mused, in a low voice, looking out into the hushed woods. "There is little doubt that we would soon be overwhelmed. We cannot go along the ground recklessly, for we would be destroyed if a full force of the enemy swarms over us. We both know the outcome of the battle. Even so, I would risk something, were it not for Aethelstan … but I fear that we are now trapped."

Webba nodded grimly. A very pious man, and father of three well-mannered sons, he often served in Aethelstan's garrison in Bergton. Unsurprising to Edmund, his advice was religious in nature. "Pray, Edmund. That is something that you may do."

"You speak truly, and maybe the All-Father will deliver us yet," Edmund replied softly, smiling gently, and taking a deep breath to offset the pressures that he felt rising from their deteriorating prospects. With so much tugging at his mind, it took several moments to relax the tensions riddling his body.

Webba suddenly held up one hand, an abrupt gesture that at once quieted Edmund. With a finger, Webba pointed firmly just off to the right. Through the trees, a horrific sight brought a sudden, freezing chill to Edmund's heart.

Edmund felt a tingle of adrenaline race through him as he

witnessed multiple large forms moving among the trees, heading right in the direction of their hideout. Turning, he took a silent step back into the shadows of the cave, and carefully roused the last sky rider from his nap.

Edmund signaled to the man to stay silent, and to arm himself, before he rejoined Webba by the cave's opening. Slowly, Edmund drew an arrow and notched it. He raised the bow up, drawing the string back until it held a modest tension. To his right, Webba elevated his own bow and selected a target.

The two arrows were honed upon the point where the first massive form finally broke through the underbrush. The feline-like creature that broke through the trees, and gazed directly towards the cave, was paralyzing to behold. Edmund knew that it could be nothing other than a Licanther.

Three others emerged just behind the first. Their huge heads held an arsenal of formidable teeth within powerful jaws, including the two curving, sword-length monstrosities that protruded down from their upper lips. The immense, stabbing pair of teeth had given the creatures a legendary reputation that had worked its way into many fireside tales.

The creatures seemed to move almost effortlessly, their rippling musculature flowing in undulating precision, as they crossed the floor of the forest on their broad paws.

There was no sign of any Atagar with the robust cats, as Edmund would have expected, from what he had learned of the Avanoran forces arrayed against Saxany. This was clearly a pack that had somehow been set loose, whether for some unknown purpose, or due to the death of their rat-like masters.

The first Licanther kept a steely, cautious stare trained in their direction, as a couple of the others sniffed at the air and ground with obvious excitement.

Edmund recognized the particular path that they were following. It was the very approach to the cave that they had taken in escaping with Aethelstan.

There was no sense of outright recognition in the creatures at the moment. Nonetheless, they were heading in a direct approach towards the cave. Discovery would only be a matter of time. Recognized yet or not, the conflict between the two groups was imminent, and inevitable.

Edmund looked all around the incoming creatures, but there

appeared to be only four of the Licanthers. Even so, their numbers were considerable enough, as combined with their speed and power the creatures posed a monstrous threat to the three Saxans sequestered within the cave.

Even if their first arrows found their mark, Edmund knew that he and the other men would be vulnerable to the storm that would follow. Licanthers were reputed to be one of the most aggressive of the creatures that the enemy used for warfare. They were trained and used by the Atagar because of their fearlessness, and ferocity, facts that the well-read Aethelstan had briefed Edmund about.

Edmund and the two warriors with him leveled their aims, using eye contact with each other, and gestures of their heads, to make sure that they did not all target the same creature. They knew that they would have to take out at least three Licanthers with the first round of arrows, to have any chance to survive. The arrows would have to fly extraordinarily true for that scenario to happen, and Edmund did not want to consider how slim that chance was. He narrowed his own sights upon the huge Licanther in the lead of the oncoming quartet.

At any moment, he expected to hear sounds of agitation coming from the sky steeds behind him, as they caught the scents of the huge, predatory cats. The Himmerosen would fight back fiercely, and maybe, between the Saxans and their steeds, the Licanthers could be stopped from reaching the prone Aethelstan. Edmund was resolved to die if it prevented the sabre-toothed beasts from setting their claws and fangs on his friend.

A deafening, howling chorus abruptly rang out in the forest. The outburst of noise shattered the taut stillness, and caused the Licanthers to whirl about haphazardly, in confusion. Edmund and the others held their arrows, as the edges of the forest came alive with an eruption of motion.

Swift and raging, a number of sleek, massive forms poured from the depths of the forest. Edmund could not believe what his eyes were vividly revealing.

The creatures exploding out from the undergrowth were Jaghuns. Without a doubt, they were the very creatures raised by the woodland recluse that Aethelstan had long ago befriended, and often spoken of to Edmund.

There was a quality about them that was very reminiscent of

canine forms, but they were far larger, and undoubtedly stronger, than any dog that ever lived in Saxany. The Jaghuns were bearing down upon the surprised Licanthers, carrying the fight right to the feline creatures.

The Licanthers, stubborn and fearless themselves, were not ones for retreat. Their supple forms whipped about, and lunged forward to engage their rushing attackers.

Flurries of claws, and snapping jaws filled with sharp teeth, abounded, as the Jaghuns and Licanthers clashed. It was an even match, in terms of sheer numbers, as four Jaghuns had emerged from the forest to counter the Licanthers.

Eerie outcries from the animals, some sharp, and echoing great pain, filled the forest air. To Edmund's ears, it was a blood-curdling dissonance of primal rage and death.

The strengths of the Jaghuns, with their larger bodies and more powerful jaws, were set against those of the quicker Licanthers. The latter possessed an edge in the skilled use of their sharp claws, and in their slashing sabre-teeth.

One Licanther had been taken down quickly in the fighting, its throat seized and torn out by the crushing jaws of the largest Jaghun. As such, the Jaghuns immediately gained an advantage in numbers, which swiftly proved to be a critical factor in the short, furious struggle.

When the blistering melee came to an end, the foliage all around the scene of combat was sprayed with blood, as the last of the Licanthers twitched reflexively where it lay. A moment later, its body shuddered, as it fell into a breathless stillness.

All of the Licanthers had been slain, along with one of the Jaghuns. One of the other Jaghuns had suffered serious injuries, having been raked deeply along its left flank by a swiping claw. When the surviving Jaghuns lifted their heads up, they all displayed blood-stained muzzles, giving the already intimidating creatures an even more rabid appearance.

The remaining three Jaghuns, sniffing at the air, rapidly honed in upon the cave opening. After becoming very still, their eyes seemingly piercing the darkness of the cave mouth, the two that had been largely unscathed in the fighting turned about, and trotted back into the brush. The injured one of their number followed behind a moment later, exhibiting a noticeable limp as it favored its injured side. Loud barks could be heard shortly thereafter, followed by another series of howls.

"They know we are here," Webba stated, his eyes wide with fear.

"But they do not attack."

"Let us hope that the Woodsman is near," Edmund replied, in a low voice.

Edmund knew what it felt like to be utterly helpless. He did not know what to make of the strange behavior of the Jaghuns. They had been the Saxan warriors' saviors, but he had seen no sign of the reclusive Woodsman that he was sure the beasts belonged to. He also did not know whether the creatures regarded the Saxans differently than they had regarded the Licanthers.

With the Licanthers having been overcome so rapidly, he did not like the Saxans' chances at all, if they happened to be suddenly beset by the remaining Jaghuns.

"Should we go out of the cave, into the open?" Edmund posed to the others. "If the Woodsman is near, he will know that we are not of the Unifier's forces. I would not want a needless mistake made, because we gave no alert to the Woodsman."

"With not knowing how many of those creatures might be out there? And not knowing for certain if they can tell friend from foe? What if the Woodsman is not around?" Webba ventured, looking at Edmund as if the sky steed leader was losing his sanity. "If we are in the open, we are even more defenseless than in here."

"And what if they attack here, without really knowing who we are? Even one of them could overtake us, and kill us all. We need to find a way to give the Woodsman a chance to know who we are ... or whose side we are on," Edmund retorted. "It is not just our lives in the balance, but Aethelstan's as well."

Standing up, he threw his bow and arrow down, and proceeded directly out of the cave's mouth. Holding his hands up, palms out, he left the protective shelter of the shallow grotto. His heart raced with terror, but he knew that there was only one way to give advance evidence of his identity to the master of the Jaghun pack, if he was somewhere in the vicinity.

He trusted to the words that Aethelstan had told him about the Woodsman. Aethelstan had remarked how the creatures were exceedingly well-trained, and uncanny in their cleverness.

Over the many years that Edmund had served in the Select Fyrd of the Saxans, the creatures had never assaulted anyone from the realm. Edmund held tightly onto that singular notion, hoping that the Jaghuns had somehow been taught to differentiate friend from foe.

The howling continued to resonate through the trees as he exited the cave, but it gradually died down, as one moment passed anxiously into the next. Silently, and without warning, one of the Jaghuns came back out from the shadows of the forest growths, and approached Edmund cautiously. A second, the injured one, lumbered out a moment later.

Though Edmund's eyes darted about, there appeared to be no sign of the third.

While they moved carefully, the creatures showed no signs of aggression towards Edmund. One moved to his left, and one to his right, padding forward slowly. Unarmed, Edmund was rendered helpless if the beasts decided upon a concerted attack.

There was nowhere for him to run to, and he knew that he could not defend himself barehanded against two of the sizeable beasts.

The first of the creatures, the largest, drew up to Edmund, its great head even with the middle of Edmund's chest. In rapid inhalations, it sniffed Edmund, the distended nostrils conveying an array of scents back along the passages atop its broad, short muzzle. It moved its head around Edmund's arms, legs, and then back up again to his chest.

The feral eyes of the Jaghun were calm at the moment, the fires subsided from the furious battle with the Licanthers, one of whose mauled body lay less than ten strides away. Edmund's breath caught in his chest, as he awaited the Jaghun's verdict.

The tail of the Jaghun slowly began to wag, and the creature abruptly licked Edmund's exposed hand. Despite the friendly gesture, Edmund's heart leaped. He was still highly unsettled at the prospects of the Jaghun's long, sharp teeth being so close to his unprotected skin. His blood raced with the fear gripping him, as sweat beaded upon his brow.

The other Jaghun then limped up to Edmund, a little laboriously, just as the third of their number came out from the forest to join them. The one in front of Edmund seemed to sense his rising discomfort, and nudged his hand with its snout. Edmund, having owned dogs, recognized the canid gesture as being one of offered friendship.

He slowly reached out, and stroked the top of the head and neck of the formidable creature. He hoped the similarity to dogs continued to hold, as he scratched the creature lightly behind its ears. To his immense relief, the Jaghun's tail continued to wag.

"I think that it is okay!" Edmund pronounced in an even,

subdued voice, as he nervously smiled at the trio of Jaghuns.

Slowly, and with no small degree of trepidation, the other two Saxans emerged from the cave. They were quickly sniffed, inspected, and then greeted by the Jaghuns. After the other Saxans had evidently been accepted, the largest Jaghun started to race about, and bark incessantly.

"I think that they will lead us back to the woodland dweller," Edmund said, referring to Aethelstan's hermit friend. He finally began to relax his nerve-rattled edge, though his eyes did not stray from the Jaghuns.

"Then let us get our Himmerosen, and Aethelstan," Webba stated, starting back for the cave entrance with the other Saxan sky rider close behind.

After several moments passed, they returned with the steeds and Aethelstan. The great thane was being carried on the back of one of the Himmerosen.

The Jaghuns clustered about the Himmerosen, whose fidgety movements, and reflexive snorts and growls, indicated their extremely uncomfortable states. Their postures were defensive, and they were tensed to lash out at the first sign of a threat to them. It was only the firm commands and closer proximity of the two Saxan sky riders that kept the agitated steeds even mildly cooperative.

The Jaghuns, through their movements, effectively channeled Edmund and the others along, as they made their way from the cave and headed back towards the direction of the battlegrounds. Edmund, having remounted his own steed, rode quietly in the saddle of his Himmeros. He looked about in amazement at the formation of the Jaghuns now navigating the forest and guiding them, one set to each flank, and one positioned ahead.

The entire group maintained a steady pace, and only a short time passed before they reentered the outer boundaries of the battlefield. The sights greeting the Saxans were impossible to stomach, with the hundreds upon hundreds of dead bodies lying all about them. Carrion birds were already circling and landing for the onset of a gruesome feast.

Edmund thought that it was a very merciful stroke of fate that Aethelstan was unconscious. His own heart could not have been more downtrodden at the appalling scene of destruction. Each moment brought a sharp pang to his spirit, as he recognized many faces among the lifeless bodies spread across the ground.

DREAM OF LEGENDS

The three men could not help but marvel at the numerous giant beings now occupying the area. Due to Aethelstan's stories, Edmund guessed their nature at once. They were certainly the race of beings that the Saxan kings had long ago discovered, dwelling within and under their lands. The huge, humanoid beings, each holding a great spear in a massive fist, eyed the Saxans with suspicion, as they were ushered onto the battleground by the Jaghun escort. Without the Jaghuns accompanying the Saxans, Edmund knew that they would have received a less than pleasant greeting.

The two healthy Jaghuns bounded off, curling out of sight around a rise in the ground ahead. A series of excited barks soon came from the direction that they had gone. A few moments later, they reappeared. A broad-shouldered man, with a thick, dark beard, fatigue etched vividly across his face, strode along with them.

Edmund recognized him without any need of introduction. It was unmistakably the eccentric forest dweller. As if sight of the man triggered a memory, Edmund finally remembered that Aethelstan had said that the Woodsman's name was Gunther.

The man's eyes darted past the three warriors, and came to rest upon the fourth, unconscious figure that they bore along with them. His eyes stilled, and his face hardened, as he focused upon Aethelstan.

The great thane's chest rose and fell with breath. Almost instantly, a smile of radiant joy cracked the man's stony expression. A burst of energy coursed through his movements and features, as he ran swiftly up to the Himmeros bearing Aethelstan.

"He lives!" Gunther exclaimed buoyantly. "Praise the All-Father, he lives!"

"Yes," Edmund replied, as Gunther gently placed his hands upon Aethelstan, eyeing him closely, beginning to examine his wounds and bruises. "We got him out of the battle just before he would have been killed. He received some wounds during the fighting, and has not since regained consciousness."

"I thank you with all of my heart, for risking yourselves to get him free," Gunther responded, shooting a brief glance back at Edmund. "The world needs a mind such as his, and a man such as him, especially in these dark times."

Gunther looked away, towards a few of the tall creatures nearby, and then hesitated. He returned his attention to Edmund.

"I will speak more of them to you later. There is no time now. But these are the Unguhur, friends to the Saxans, who have stood by the Saxan people in this war. They share common cause with Saxany, and they are here to help us with those that have survived. Give them your trust, as they lend aid to us."

Edmund nodded, now understanding why the forest had not been flooded with Avanorans in the aftermath of the battle. It was not the Saxans that had stopped the invaders, as the shield wall had been collapsing when Edmund moved to rescue Aethelstan.

"We shall," Edmund replied. "Aethelstan has spoken of them to me before, and they are the reason why Avanoran warriors did not discover us in the cave that we took him to."

Gunther then gestured towards the Unguhur, one of whom was tending a stretcher made of hide and wooden poles. Several of the creatures came forward, and gently assisted Gunther, as he maneuvered Aethelstan from the Himmeros to the stretcher.

For creatures that looked so rough, bulky, and clumsy, they handled Aethelstan with diligent care. They placed the Saxan thane comfortably upon the stretcher.

"Aethelstan will need to rest in safety," Gunther said. "We do not know how many of the Avanoran force are left in the area. Where is this cave where my Jaghuns found you?"

"It is not far from here," Edmund said. He then added, "They overcame an unaccompanied group of Licanthers, who were approaching the cave entrance. If there were Licanthers out in the forest, then there must be some enemy forces still about."

"And still up there," Gunther stated, pointing up towards the sky with a grim expression.

It was then that the Woodsman focused upon the thick bloodstains covering the muzzles of the three Jaghuns. His eyes then moved to their bleeding wounds, especially the streaks of torn flesh plaguing the limping Jaghun.

An instant sadness came over his face, as he carefully looked over the group. Edmund realized that Gunther was just now becoming aware that one of his Jaghuns was not among the number gathered before him.

"How many?" came the whisper from the Woodsman. The question was filled with emotion.

Edmund knew what he was asking. "One."

Edmund had to turn his eyes away from the face of the Woodsman, as Gunther's loss fully dawned on him. The expression that came to the hermit's face was gut-wrenching to witness.

Edmund shifted his gaze up to the sky, but the sight that met him was anything but consoling. Far above, like distant specks, was the clear presence of a couple of Trogens slowly circling. At the very least, the Unifier's forces were keeping a close eye upon the area, and likely keeping appraised of the Unguhur interlopers that had so thoroughly interferred with their plans.

Edmund continued to watch the Trogens, prepared to be patient and give Gunther as long as he needed to recover from the shock of his loss.

"Must not be a large force on the ground, or they would have regrouped by now," Edmund suggested in a low voice to Webba, his eyes tracking the flying shapes high in the air.

"Be assured that they will be back, and no army will be here to stop them," Gunther said through clenched teeth, obviously fighting to keep his composure. His eyes had reddened, giving a sorrowful hue to the hollow look contained within them. Edmund could only imagine the emotions swirling beneath the surface. "You should go to the Unguhur Realm, where you will have refuge and allies. We must finish searching through the battleground, to find any survivors that may yet be lying among the dead ... and there have already been more than a few."

Edmund and the other two listened to Gunther's words quietly. As overwhelmed and exhausted as they all were, Edmund also knew that they had been among the lucky few to survive the terrible battle.

"It is good that we have a place of refuge to go to," Edmund said, knowing well that their best chance for survival lay firmly with Gunther and his underground friends.

"You have already suffered enough in this battle. You are not healers, and staying here will do you no good. The surviving men need you. Go with the Unguhur now, and I shall return later, when we have covered the entirety of this battlefield," Gunther said, instructing the Saxans with a steely voice, the tone as commanding as anything that they had ever heard spoken from Aethelstan's lips.

Despite the fact that the three warriors were able-bodied, Edmund knew what Gunther was truly thinking. Having to comb through the hideous field of war, sifting among their slain comrades and kin, would do nothing more than light the fires of a forge that would create an abundance of razor-sharp nightmares.

Edmund could see the weakened, wavering spirits in the men with him, who looked as if they were now just drifting within their minds. Edmund was already resigned to the reality that the terrible things that he had already seen would be cropping up to mar his dream world, haunting it with morbid visions.

Edmund also knew that the Woodsman had not even begun his mourning for the killed Jaghun, likely akin to the loss of a child for the solitary hermit. Gunther needed some time to himself as well.

A couple of Unguhur moved in to assist the three warriors along their new way, gesturing for the Saxans to follow the ones who were carrying Aethelstan's litter forward. Gunther remained behind, already returning his attention to the sorrowful tasks at hand. Edmund watched the Woodsman for a few moments longer, over his shoulder, as they moved away.

Gunther was resolutely committed to finding any warriors that yet held breath, saving whatever lives he could. Perhaps a few more bodies were still alive out on that battleground, with each passing moment a threat to the faint flicker of life remaining within them.

Edmund could only thank the All-Father for the heroic efforts of the Woodsman; a recluse who had only wanted to be left alone, and spared from the travails of humankind.

DRAGOL

Dragol awoke following an uneventful, yet still restless, sleep underneath the camouflage of a swathe of heavy brush. Strong beams of vibrant sunlight cascaded down to warm him, pouring through an opening in the forest's ceiling of branches and leaves.

Dragol had long ago conditioned himself to be a light sleeper. It was the only way for a warrior to survive within strange, threatening lands. He had roused himself to full consciousness several times during the night, most often due to the passage of various animals through the woodlands.

The movements of fauna were not necessarily a cause for comfort, even if it meant that the source of the shuffles, footfalls, and scrapings was not the tread of an enemy war party. Dragol was far from being familiar with the various types of animals inhabiting the region that he now traversed, and he was not about to underestimate any possible encounters. He had learned enough lessons during the many years spent in the harsh wilderness of his own lands to respect the elements of nature in lands that he had not been in for long.

It did not matter whether the beasts moving through the forest proved to be harmless or not, as any misguided assumption could have lethal consequences. Having come from a homeland containing a variety of very dangerous predators, Dragol knew that threats could come in all manner of sizes and forms.

The threats might not be limited to outright predators either. Many a Trogen had suffered agonizing deaths under the viciously-wielded tusks of a ferocious Blood Boar, after having unintentionally interrupted the robust, bristly creature's foraging.

Upon awakening, Dragol found that his body was wracked with soreness, and his muscles were stiffened from lying for hours upon the hard, uneven ground. Dirt, leaves, and other debris on the ground had pressed into his side and face, much of it sticking to him as he sat up. He took a moment to brush himself off.

He carefully stretched his limbs for a few minutes. The movements were accompanied by the audible pops of settled joints. He felt the deep extension of his muscles as he limbered up, a highly necessary activity before he could hope to search for some sustenance in a state of preparedness.

The new morning soon brought with it a little good fortune, revealed invitingly in its warming light. It was not long into his morning hike before he made a most welcome discovery, a stroke of sheer luck, something that Dragol had not recently been enjoying in abundance.

He had been moving into an area filled with younger, hardwood trees. The maturing trees had afforded extensive undergrowth to thrive, as the less-dense upper foliage allowed considerable amounts of sunlight through to the forest floor.

Dragol's path intersected with a narrow stream, which served beneficently in attracting a group of heavy-set birds, with fan-shaped tails. Dragol heard the birds well before he saw them, bringing him to a stop. Putting his shield down on the ground, Dragol quietly approached, taking cover where he could gain a more advantageous view of the creatures.

The birds' attentions were concentrated upon a few shrubs growing a short distance away from the near bank of the stream. The shrubs were loaded with an abundance of dark berries. Both birds and berries were inviting to Dragol's stomach, with the birds holding the greater attraction.

Dragol eyed one of the tantalizingly plump birds, a large one that had a distinctive black ruff on each side of the neck. Alone among the others, it had more than one white spot on each of its tail feathers, as opposed to the single spot on the feathers of the others. From his experience with other kinds of birds, Dragol judged the distinguishing characteristics to mark the creature as a male of its kind.

After a painstakingly stealthy, careful approach, Dragol was able to draw very close to the oblivious birds. A brief flash suddenly cut through the air, as sunlight glinted off of a speeding length of metal.

The black-ruffed bird was taken fully unawares, swiftly dispatched by a well-thrown, straight dagger. The force of the throw slammed its body against the ground, before the surrounding birds were even aware of their imminent danger.

The rest of the birds scattered in a flurry of panic, making quite a commotion as they flapped their wings and took off into the woods. The laws of nature would offer them no respite as they fled recklessly, as the forest was filled with a range of predators.

Dragol strode out from his hiding place, and walked over to the felled bird. He pulled his dagger free, congratulating himself on an exceptional throw, as his mouth began to water.

Deciding to risk a small fire, he put his trust into the fact that in a time of war, one singular, thin line of smoke was not likely to attract much attention. Even if it was sighted, it was just as likely to be spotted by Trogen sky riders as it was by any enemy sky riders. Furthermore, neither friend nor foe in the skies would have an easy landing site.

A fire was soon stoked, and a makeshift spit served to help Dragol prepare a most succulent, roasted fowl. As hungry as he felt, it took a lot of discipline to let the fresh, juicy meat cook thoroughly.

The well-cooked meat of the bird, coupled with the crisp, cool water of the flowing brook nearby, filled and renewed Dragol immeasurably. He also treated himself to several handfuls of the berries that had attracted the birds, feeling the almost-ripe fruit burst between his large teeth. While a little sour, the berries were a welcome find.

Once he had finished, his continuation of the journey was delayed a little, so that he could fill a small leather pouch, tied to the belt around his waist, as full as he could with the edible berries. It was not a frivolous task, providing reserves of sustenance just in case his luck in foraging or hunting was not so fortuitous later.

Late in the morning, he left the site of the hunt behind with a wellspring of energy. The simple meal had done much to replenish him, and to lift his spirits, as he searched out routes through the thicker brush.

After walking for about half a league, he came across an open space created by a small pond. He looked up into the sky, but saw nothing of interest. After taking a few moments to study the position of the sun, and estimate his bearings, he continued once again towards the south.

He moved slowly, sometimes laboriously, while he was traversing the congested brush. Years of experience derived from living in the midst of the forested mountains of his homeland manifested in Dragol's soft step, and guarded movements, as he navigated through some challenging swathes of growth. His progress was often slowed considerably, as he diligently pulled foliage back, and guided it back into place, to pass through it without spurring undue commotion.

He ignored the mounting scratches that he received from small thorns, as well as the little briars that occasionally clung to the surface of his clothing. He knew that it would have been much worse had he just blundered his way through. His caution spared him much of the stabbing and prickling of the brush. Yet limiting noise was far more important than any concerns for personal comfort.

Rested with a full stomach, Dragol's attentiveness was sharper, and it did not wane as he pressed forward. His acute sense of hearing and vision kept vigil for any sign of new dangers, a heightened sense that would not relax until he got himself safely back among his kind. He consistently reminded himself that any lapses, even for a few moments, could spell a violent, instantaneous death.

As had happened before, he began to get the distinct impression that something was watching his movements. He came to a halt, and his eyes darted about, as he thought of the carnivorous Pahyna and the old man, both of whom he had encountered the last times that he had experienced the uneasy feeling.

Irritation rose within him, as he could not believe his ill fortune. This time, if something like the four Pahyna appeared, he would not have a Harrak at his side to divide the attackers.

He kept silent, and admonished himself to keep a still mind. He was not yet certain of the nature of the threat, or even if there was really one to begin with. The ambiguity could create its own menace within the extreme wariness of his mind.

Even so, he was not about to start mistrusting his instincts. He slowly brought his shield from where it had been hanging on his back via the guige strap. He closed his grip firmly on the hilt of his longblade, and quietly drew it.

The sensation of being watched surged and ebbed over the next couple of hours. Sometimes, the feeling seemed to vanish entirely. At other times his hackles rose, to the point where he expected something to come into sight.

All around him, the contour of the terrain began to grow steeper, as the rolling hills turned into sharper inclines, on larger rises that more closely resembled small mountains. The younger hardwood trees gave way to a higher concentration of fir trees, even as the quantity of lower brush declined. He wound his way around the bottom of the taller inclines, noticing that his forward path was slowly rising.

After another couple of hours, Dragol came across a small waterfall, tumbling down from a rocky height off to his right. The water appeared to emerge from within the steep hillside, about a third of a way up the slope, though the source was hidden beyond his sight.

The water flowed downward in a few sparkling, intertwining rivulets that converged together, coursing over the lip of a rock outcropping. Once over the edge, the water broke into a glittering free-fall down into a small pool, collecting within a shallow basin of gray rock.

Skirting the outside of the lower basin, Dragol made his way to the opening of a small cave behind the waterfall. He felt the cool air and light mist touching his skin as he neared the falling water. Having worked up an ample sweat during his extended hike, the feeling was instantly pleasant, and soothing.

The broad part of the cave did not go very deep, narrowing quickly just a few paces inside. The outer part was just big enough for his large form to walk in, without having to lean over to any significant degree.

As he was inspecting the small cave, the impression of being under surveillance from the surrounding woods rose up again. It rapidly reached the point where his senses screamed that some kind of presence was imminent.

Resolutely, he gripped his longblade and shield. He turned, and walked back around the edge of the waterfall to stand on the left side of the basin.

"Who is there?" Dragol called out, with a growling edge to his voice, certain of his gut feelings. "Have you courage enough to stand forth? Come beasts, if you wish to try my blade once again. If not a beast, then announce yourself. You may try my blade as well."

His eyes became stony, as he waited for the flickers of movement indicating more woodland predators. With the shallow cave and waterfall behind him, and the water basin itself to work with, he was in a better defensive position than he had found himself in before. If there were multiple hunters, they could not attack him from all sides at once.

"It is only I, returning again, though I have no desire to try your blade," came a familiar voice, speaking in the Trogen language. It belonged to the last individual that Dragol had spoken with. "And I do have the courage to stand forth, make no mistake, though I would hope that you offer friendship instead."

The tension went out of Dragol's body, as he lowered his shield and blade. Walking from behind one of the trees beyond the basin was the older, white-bearded man, in the flowing, blue garments and wide-brimmed hat. Dragol watched him stride forward in silence, again struck by the strange, timeless look that seemed to be etched into the man's features and expression.

Beyond the shadows of the cave, the sunlight bathed the old man's face underneath the broad brim of his round-topped hat. The light made his long beard and snowy locks of hair shine brightly, as well as making his lone, blue eye sparkle radiantly.

Calm, confident, and relaxed, the old man walked around the rim of the basin towards where Dragol stood. As before, the man moved nimbly, displaying a level of dexterity that belied his seemingly advanced age. He looked up into Dragol's face as he drew close, his lone blue eye glittering with apparent amusement.

"Is it you that I have felt watching me?" Dragol inquired, a little indignant, and discomfited, at the second unannounced appearance of the strange traveler. "Have you been following me?"

"Like you, I am traveling through these woods. Both of us have our purposes, and neither of us has yet succeeded in our hopes. But no, I have not been following you," the elderly man replied, with a sincere expression on his face. He smiled amicably. "There are many dangers in these forests, from the war, and from the very fabric of life itself. You have probably felt many different eyes upon you, as you have moved through the trees of these lands, and they belong to living creatures that are in no way tamed. It is good that you are so alert."

Dragol was utterly perplexed, and was quickly growing weary of the man's cryptic ways. Trogens were not ones to tarry with riddles for long, becoming swiftly impatient with anything that was less than direct.

With some exasperation, Dragol queried, "Who are you, old man? I want to know! Why is it that you are in these woods?"

He shunned the idea of challenging the old man with violent intentions, as many humans in his position might have done to gain answers. That course of action was far from the Trogen way. Openly striking an unarmed, elderly man would do him great dishonor as a Trogen warrior. The strong sought out the strong, and only the truly weak bolstered themselves by preying upon the weak. It was one significant reason why he, and his fellow Trogens, so loathed the use of Darroks in the war.

His great instincts for threats and dangers from individual beings had never failed him before. He sensed that there was no threat whatsoever forthcoming from this old man. Yet all the same, the Trogen chieftain still wanted some answers.

The man smiled again, with a slight air of joviality. "I am not in these woods because of you, and the tasks that I am on take me away from you … but you have quickly become of great interest to me."

Dragol frowned, as his eyes narrowed, and he was confounded as to how he was going to get any answers out of the lone, highly confusing man. There simply had to be much more to the man than what he saw before him.

An old man with one eye, seemingly unarmed, would not fare very well in such dangerous forests. Dragol's own survival was not guaranteed, no matter how strong he was, and despite the fact that he was armed with a great shield and well-crafted Trogen longblade.

He asked the old man slowly, "What … are your tasks then?"

"I am a seeker now. I have been seeking for some that I know, and others that have come from a faraway place. I have found the ones from afar, and done what I could for them … but I cannot find the ones that I have known for many ages," the old man answered.

This time, the pleasant expression on the old man's face faded, replaced by a mien that was decidedly melancholy in nature.

"The ones that I know should have been aiding the fight against the invasion that brought you along with it," the old man continued.

Dragol did not miss that the man had not hesitated to imply that the forces that the Trogen had arrived with were in the wrong. Dragol could not help but respect the steadfast, direct manner of the old man in that regard.

After another moment, the old man's face darkened further, and a simmering anger pulsed just under the surface of his pale skin. For some unknown reason, Dragol felt the slightest tinge of fear. Quickly, be batted the feeling down, and inwardly admonished himself for feeling any intimidation from a very aged human.

"As we all have enemies, so I believe one of mine has something to do with the absence of the ones I seek," the old man finished, in a lower, tense voice.

"And why would I be of interest to you at all?" Dragol asked, after a few moments of uneasy silence had passed. He had no idea what the old man was talking about.

The old man's features then relaxed, and like the sun breaking free of storm clouds, a white smile came to his face. "If I gave you a direct answer, it would be too easy for you, Spirit of the Dragon."

The old man chuckled, as Dragol nearly growled in frustration. At the same time, the Trogen was caught completely by surprise, as the old man had known the literal meaning of the Trogen warrior's given name.

Dragol.

Spirit of the Dragon.

Few of those that learned the Trogen tongue ever learned all the meanings of names. It deepened the mystery surrounding the old man even further.

"As for myself, maybe it is time to reveal a little more to you," the old man stated.

The man slowly raised his arms out to either side, as a tremendous brightness surged, overcoming the cloaked form of his body. At its apex, the blinding light appeared to shatter into thousands of tiny shards of white light.

The intensity was such that Dragol had to quickly raise up his shielded arm, to simply protect his eyes from the overwhelming brightness. He blinked and squinted, trying to look around the shield and behold the magnificent vision before him. The tiny light shards fragmented further, before seeming to dissipate in all directions.

When they were gone from sight, the forest was empty once again. The elderly man was nowhere to be seen.

Dragol clenched his teeth in frustration, foiled again in the attempt to identify the strange traveler. The mystery was greater, not lesser as he had hoped, due to the event that had just happened.

Letting out a muffled grunt of anger, Dragol looked around the trees with a snarl on his face. He took a couple of deep breaths, as he struggled to reestablish his sanity, or at least a semblance of it. He could barely trust his senses anymore, or at least so it seemed. He waited a little while longer, but the old man did not reemerge, and the sensation of being watched was entirely absent.

With little else to do, Dragol finally decided to take a brief respite, and enjoy the cool, soothing air given off around the small waterfall. That was something he could understand fully, requiring no solving of riddles. He walked slowly back around the rim of the pool, and sat down on the smooth, damp rock of the cave opening.

He began to collect his thoughts, though he did not take his attention away from the forest around him. Setting the shield and longblade down, both easily within arm's reach, he untied the leather cords securing the small pouch at his waist.

Reaching in, he pulled out a few of the stored berries and put them into his mouth. The sweet, juicy bursts, tinged with a hint of sourness, filled his mouth with a pleasant flavor. He followed up the berries by cupping his hands, and drinking from the clear water near the edge of the pool.

The tensions gradually left his body and mind, as his senses appeared to align with the steady patter of the water, which fell down from above and came to rest in the pool. He felt the vapors from the cascading water blow across his face with each breeze, and very gradually he reached a feeling of serenity.

As much as Trogens were creatures of storm and fury, so were they also creatures of sunlight and tranquility. A cognizance of the order of things was just as importance as the most demanding physical challenges or tests.

The renewed sense of peace brought his thoughts back to the old man. He reflected upon what he knew of the man with a calmer, more revealing perspective.

His reflections were drawn towards the earlier exchange that he had with the old man, regarding the process of revelation. The old man had given him a simple example, likening it to the processes Dragol had undergone in learning the arts of the Trogen longblade.

The talk of unveiling realizations existing inside his heart was something that struck a familiar tone deep within Dragol. Trogens often spoke of how there were many things written into the very essence of their spirit, characteristics and inspirations that were a part of their innermost nature. They were the most basic of elements given to them by the Creator Spirit.

Every adolescent Trogen learned that there were many things that would be unlocked with the passage of time, as they passed from youth into full adulthood, and beyond. Life was a continuous process of awakenings, to the very end.

It was not that these revelations were in their fullest form from the moment that a Trogen was born, but were rather quietly growing, like crops in a field. The things that a Trogen did in life, and learned, were like the sun and rain that governed the growth in a cultivated field.

A proper focus and effort in life would tend such a crop bountifully, as it changed from a seed into a mature plant, ready for harvest. If a Trogen was wayward, or turned from a right path, the effect would be like an unrelenting drought, or flooding of a field of plants.

The difficult truth about life was that destructive processes could also be much quicker in their nature and effect. Such realities strongly echoed the truth that it was always swifter to tear something down than it was to build something up.

The process of crops had always served as a good analogy, in such a light. The hated Elven raiders had often ruined fields of rich abundance, right on the brink of harvest. In a similar way, a Trogen could rapidly become self-destructive, and destroy in moments what had taken years to cultivate. It was a daunting truth, one that always gave Dragol an impetus for self-restraint, as well as compelling periods of sober reflections, like the one that he was embracing now.

It was the process of coming to know oneself and one's purpose in life, and of harvesting one's inner growths. Dragol had always striven to give his own life adequate sunlight and water, even if he did not yet recognize the final form of the plant that would be his own, personal harvest. It was exactly what the old man appeared to be honing in upon. He was encouraging Dragol to know the yield of his own fields of life.

The old man was truly a mystery, to a maddening degree, but his enigmatic presence was not an entirely unwelcome development. To Dragol's understanding, the old man must have been intimately familiar with the rites and tenets of the Trogen race, in order to have such a close understanding of the more deep-rooted, subtler aspects of their kind. The keen understanding was very strange coming from a human, as most humans took the Trogens to be little more than barbarous beast-men.

Why the old man was returning to find him, or even had an interest in him to begin with, Dragol could not tell. Yet there was a firm reason for the encounters, as clearly they were not random in nature. Nor did Dragol believe that the old man's reasons for approaching him were insignificant, or even just something born from idle curiosity. The old man was revealing himself to Dragol slowly, for a definitive purpose.

Dragol suddenly fathomed that he was likely a mystery to the old man as well; even if Dragol believed that the old man had many more insights about him, than he did concerning the blue-robed man.

The old man had had an undeniable, calming presence about him that greatly intrigued Dragol. There had never been a feeling of a threat to his personal being, during any moment that he had spent in the old man's company. There was only the brief flash of fear, when the old man's emotions had surged with a temporal anger, though Dragol knew well that the flare of anger was not directed at himself.

The truth of the matter was that the more that Dragol pondered it, the effect had been quite the reverse. His sense of security had actually grown with each passing minute in the presence of the old man.

He could not really say why he felt an affinity for the old man, but it was there nonetheless. Perchance it was the quiet strength and confidence that emanated from the old man, radiance not unlike that from a trained, veteran Trogen warrior.

Possibly it was something else entirely. Perhaps there was even something very supernatural about the old man. At the least, the man obviously held magical abilities.

Whatever the reason was, Dragol could not be certain. Even the stranger aspects of the old man were not absolutes. Tricks of light were not conclusive, as human sorcerers, and even illusionists, could attain such knowledge and abilities. That the man moved with a fluidity and grace that did not reflect the years that his face seemed to show was also not necessarily decisive either.

Dragol had heard tales of such men before, such as those of holy men secluded in the deserts of the Sunlands. Others involved rumors of individuals from far distant, eastern lands, brought back on the lips of caravan traders returning westwards with new stores of spices and silks. Though very uncommon, the tales spoke of men of very advanced years, who had somehow held the erosion of time at bay in the workings of their bodies.

Whether the blue-robed man was a supernatural manifestation, a Wizard, or simply a human who had gained mastery of sorcerous arts, Dragol's instincts still told him that the old man held great power, and had to be respected.

"Who are you?" Dragol muttered, as he glanced skyward, as if that was the direction in which the old man could be found.

He silently beheld the leaves blowing about softly, on the swaying tree limbs far above him, letting the words of the question drift off into the air. A part of him almost expected that there would be some sort of audible answer. The only sounds to be heard were the gentle rustling caused by the wind, intermingled with the continuing splashes of water from the hillside waterfall. The forest seemed to be in as much of a state of repose as Dragol now found himself in.

Exposing his long, sharp teeth, Dragol rumbled with laughter that had a slightly manic edge to it. He began to wonder whether he was finally becoming crazed with the trials he was enduring, of living in a solitary state within enemy lands. He felt somewhat foolish, at seeing how consumed he was becoming with such a seemingly insignificant encounter. He could only hope that it was not an irrelveant one, as his mind drifted back along the echoes of time.

Dragol remembered one particular period in his upbringing as a Trogen of the Thunder Wolf clan. He had wished to prove himself worthy of being a full Trogen warrior, and had asked his clan's Chieftain, an old Trogen named Curaga, to provide a challenge by which Dragol could prove himself worthy.

Most Trogens making such a request would be sent forward with forces seeking to prepare ambushes and traps for the incessant Elven incursions. Others would serve as escorts with the hunting parties making forays into the highly valuable, and oft Elven-raided, territories of the Trogens' northwestern lands.

There were a few times when flare-ups with the Kiruvans to the south, or the Gigan clans to the east, provided other opportunities, but most of the time the young warriors risked, and proved, themselves against the deadly Elven blades.

Dragol had grown up with a constant, burning desire, to hurl the Elves out of the Trogen lands. With a state of peace holding between Trogens, Gigans, and the Kiruvan Prince of Chergrad, the Elves themselves had loomed as the primary chance that he longed for to prove himself within his clan.

Caruga had listened to the young Dragol's request impassively, and had then proceeded to send him forth on a challenge that had been completely unexpected.

Dragol had been sent alone for the span of two weeks into the harsh wilderness near to his home village, with little more than a dagger and a hide pouch containing a little smoked meat. The ensuing two weeks had been a most arduous experience, but a lasting lesson had begun to reveal itself to Dragol during the trial. The challenges in that wilderness were as much of a mental nature as they were physical.

Caruga had sent Dragol to a place close to his home village for a reason. As the strains of survival mounted, the temptation to return home, so tantalizingly close, often called out to him. The long hours without companionship or dedicated tasks caused time itself to grind on slowly.

Fashioning shelter, protecting himself, engaging in hunting, and doing a little foraging presented some difficulties, but when he looked back on the experience, it had been the mental tests that were the most daunting. Caruga was testing the willpower and fortitude within Dragol's mind, rather than measuring him against a physical danger.

Caruga had spoken with Dragol in private upon his return. The old Trogen chieftain had been very pleased that Dragol had both lasted for the full two weeks, and had also identified the true nature of the test.

The crusty, stoic demeanor of the old Trogen chieftain softened to Dragol's great surprise, as Caruga exuded a warm, and emotional, ebullience towards Dragol's achievement. The special test had spurred Dragol onto a path of rapid ascendancy within the Thunder Wolf Clan.

His mind had continued to be steadily conditioned over the following years. He had gradually inured himself to the powerful emotions that raced through all Trogens' blood, able to maintain a disciplined grasp on the realities around him.

He had consistently excelled in those areas, as well as in combat. With Caruga's blessing, he had risen quickly in stature within the Thunder Wolf clan, to become one of their highest-ranking warriors.

As much as he feared getting maimed or injured, and losing the ability to wield a longblade, he now held an equal fear of incurring any kind of damage to his mental resolve. He could see now that his adamant refusal to give in to the powerful impulses to chase after Gavnar and the others was another test that he had passed successfully. His discretion in not blindly following into Tirok's folly was bothering him far less. He was increasingly reconciled to the realization that he had indeed made the right choice.

Yet while one matter of concern eased in his mind, Dragol's encounters with the old man were still unresolved. The old man's presence seemed illogical, not entirely friend or foe, and with no discernible purpose. It was not impossible that everything was taking place in Dragol's mind.

The whole experience seemed ever more like the descriptions of the solitary Healers that lived among the Trogen clans. The Healers were said to have regular hallucinations of astounding natures, during their long sojourns into the lonely wildernesses.

Such tales were not relegated only to Trogens. They were also contained within the same stories that celebrated the vitality of the old hermits in the Sunlands, where the isolated men had also encountered strange, fantastical visions during their self-imposed exiles.

If the interactions with the peculiar woodland traveler were born out of sheer illusion, then there was something for Dragol to worry about.

The other prospect was that if the encounters were grounded in iron-solid reality, then Dragol had possibly come upon a crossroads of momentous revelation.

Until he knew which of the two possibilities that it was, he knew he had to respond as best he could, to every moment as he perceived it, come whatever may.

Dragol closed his eyes slowly, taking a deep breath, and exhaling. He envisioned the old man in the long blue robes, seeing the elderly human's gleaming blue eye as vividly as if the stranger was standing right in front of him.

'Often, we have already learned the answers to what we seek, only we have not realized how to ask ourselves the right questions to discover them within us.'

The words of the old man echoed in Dragol's mind over and over again. The soft strength in the voice continued to enamor Dragol. It held the gentle authority of a longtime mentor, neither domineering, nor wavering in purpose. The lesson was there for him to learn, just as it had been when he had left his home village, to accept the requested task from Caruga.

He grew very quiet, feeling the serenity reigning around him. Letting his eyes slowly open again, he took in the sight of the waterfall and trees beyond it.

The more that he listened to his heart, in the way that the Trogens tended to do, the more reassurance he found towards the strange traveler. A part of him harbored no doubts that he would be seeing the old man once again, perhaps very soon.

"I want to find the right question," Dragol murmured out loud, as casually if he was replying to the immediate presence of the old man. "If you can help me … then help me. Just tell me who you are, and what you are about. Why do you think I am anything more than what I am?"

The light, drifting breezes carried off Dragol's softly spoken words. Dragol could almost imagine the smooth, peaceful currents of air ushering the supplication carefully to the ears of the old traveler.

As easily and promptly as the old man seemed to be able to depart and appear, Dragol would not have been surprised if the old man was standing just twenty feet away. There was a palpable tinge of disappointment when several moments passed and no answer was forthcoming.

It was an unusual sort of feeling to have, but he believed the old man would not have remained hidden if he were there to hear Dragol's query. Furthermore, there was still no sensation of the kind that he had felt prior to the traveler's other appearances. Even so, Dragol had earnestly believed that the old man could somehow hear the spoken words.

Allowing himself an ephemeral, bemused smile, an expression not all that common amongst Trogen-kind, he raised his eyes upward again. He gazed through the deep green saturating the intertwining tree branches above and around him, taking in the smooth, silken expanse of the teal-colored sky farther above. Streaked with elongated swathes of white clouds, the sight held an aesthetic, enthralling attraction for him.

It seemed much more vivid and magical than he had ever noticed before, as if he had cleared away a veil, and recaptured some of the wonder of his early youth. In a sense, it was almost like looking up at the trees, clouds, and sky for the first time. In truth, though, he was looking up at a unique instance of the sky.

Sitting up straighter, Dragol chuckled to himself. There might well be a meaning to having an entirely new manner of perception. Then again, he had to concede that maybe his mind truly was losing the scope of reality that he had known.

Still, he had not bothered yet to wonder about whether new perceptions might bring with them an altogether new awareness. A new awareness might very well clear the mists away, removing that which clouded the nature of the particular questions that he needed to ask himself.

The answers that Dragol was seeking might not be all that far away, after all.

AYENWATHA

The presence of the Midragardans within the Five Realms was soon felt intimately by the invaders, as the allies of the five tribes reached the front lines of the fighting. The course of the battle was quickly turned to the defender's advantage, with the unexpected influx of seasoned warriors from the south.

Skillful Midragardan archers complimented the keen eyes of the Five Realms' own bowmen. The Atagar, utilizing the trees, were increasingly brought down with arrows, wherever they could be found.

The locating of enemy forces, positions, and their maneuverings was augmented tremendously by the availability of almost three hundred Midragardans mounted upon Fenraren. The airborne warriors owned the skies over the tribal lands, as they fanned out far over the woodlands. The sky warriors were boisterous and renewed, after having cleared the skies of Trogens and the massive Darroks only a day before.

A few loosed sporadic arrows from the great heights. While not overly accurate, and presenting no real practical threat, the arrows descending out of the upper skies did not go unnoticed by the enemy. The enemy was reminded starkly of their sudden vulnerabilities, and the arrows did much to slow the invaders down further.

Aided by a flow of new tidings from the sky warriors, Gunnar and Ayenwatha led a numerous contingent of Midragardans and tribal warriors in a powerful counter-attack. Their thrust was aimed right at a particularly large mass of enemy fighters streaming through the woods, near the central area of the invader's broad push. Midragardan sky warriors had identified the exact location of the concentrated enemy force, efficiently directing Ayenwatha, Gunnar, and the others to intercept it. Ayenwatha knew exactly where he was being guided by the scouts above, and hastily organized a plan with Gunnar to make use of the two allies' strengths.

They caught the enemy approaching on a stretch of ground that funneled down into a narrow passage running between a couple of low hills. A number of tribal warriors raced up the slopes of the flanking hills, continuing along them to gain ground just above the dense masses of Galleans now marching down below them.

The vanguard of the Gallean force had just passed through the confined stretch between the hills, and was spreading out on the other side, to proceed on their forward sweep through the woodlands. They moved with an easy, confident gait, having advanced without opposition since they had started out from their encampment that morning.

For the invaders, the woods had erupted, coming alive with a swelling roar and brandishing of steel. Almost immediately, seeing iron helms, round shields, and coats of mail, the invaders knew that they were being confronted by warriors who were not of the five tribes.

Before the enemy had time to draw up in battle order, the Midragardans charged them. Shocked by the presence of hundreds of Midragardan warriors screaming out in battle fury, and falling upon their forefront, the spreading line of enemy fighters beyond the hills was brought to a halt.

Galleans from urban militias, infantry, and even a few knights and sergeants tried to retreat. Some militia fighters fearfully abandoned their weapons, and fled at a full run.

A number of Galleans were engulfed as the initial wave of the attack crashed upon them. The knights within the encompassed pockets fought with desperate fury, though they were soon cut down by the vigorous attackers. Other knights screamed out harsh orders, to stiffen the wavering Gallean line a little further back, as the tight mass coming up behind them stalled in between the hills.

The sudden appearance of a numerous, strong, and well-equipped Midragardan force was much more than the enemy had ever anticipated. It was not much longer before panicked horn blasts could be heard, as the enemy signaled urgently for a full withdrawal.

"Drive them back!" Gunnar shouted, slaying a knight with an arcing, downward slash of his heavy sword.

He pulled the sword free, and thrust it out at an urban militia fighter wearing a padded gambeson. A look of terror was frozen on the Gallean's face, as Golden Fury drove into his exposed throat. The militia fighter dropped his polearm, and fell dead to the ground.

"For the One Spirit!" Ayenwatha cried out, eliciting an uproar from all the tribal warriors that had flowed in on the flanks of the Midragardans.

Brandishing their war clubs, spears, and hand axes, they hurtled into the panicking enemy ranks. The two leaders fought close together, with Ayenwatha on the inner edge of the tribal warriors on the Midragardan right flank, and Gunnar towards the outer edge of his warriors on that same flank.

Ayenwatha bludgeoned a Gallean spearman, hitting him flush on the side of his half-helm with a heavy, curved war club. The crashing sound of the impact covered most of the sickening snap that accompanied it, as the man's skull and neck gave way before the war club's potent force.

Exhilaration ran through Ayenwatha, as the defenders were finally taking the fight right to their enemies. Deganawida was somewhere behind them, with a small reserve of tribal warriors and Midragardans. The revered sachem was now a worry to Ayenwatha, because of his close proximity, but the older man had insisted on being present near to the fighting.

The old sachem had assured Ayenwatha that he would remain behind, and would not take unnecessary risks. In the fast changing fortunes of battle, Deganawida's promises were of little comfort, as a threat could emerge to the venerable sachem's life at any given moment.

Gunnar raised his sword high, waving it above his head, and called out to a group of Midragardans to form up with him. "Boar's head! Boar's head!"

The Midragardans in the center arranged into a formation that resembled the point of an arrow or spearhead, protruding out from their longer line. Gunnar, wielding Golden Fury, maneuvered to the apex of that point.

"Clamp the jaws upon them, Ayenwatha!" he called out over his shoulder. Once at the point of the boar's head formation, he led the group of warriors forward, tramping towards the thinning line at the center of the enemy resisting them. "We will pierce their line with the boar's head!"

Ayenwatha watched as the Midragardans tromped forward, in a tight, orderly unit, puncturing the enemy ranks, and instantly sending panic and chaos spiraling throughout the Gallean ranks.

Ayenwatha called for signals to be relayed swiftly to the warriors up on the hills, a little farther ahead. Once the signals had been conveyed, the warriors descended the slopes with whooping cries, coming down both sides, to strike at the bewildered Galleans coagulated within the narrow stretch of ground between the hills.

Attacked from both sides, divided and pressed from their front, the Galleans did everything that they could to hasten their retreat. Cleaving through the enemy, Gunnar's men were soon meeting up with Ayenwatha's warriors, eyes blazing as they closed off the main route of retreat for many enemy warriors now trapped behind them. In quickly passing moments, the tribal warriors from the slopes, and the fighters with Gunnar, began to strike at the rear of the trapped Galleans.

The Midragardans and tribal warriors arrayed at the forefront of the encircled enemy ranks redoubled their attacks at Ayenwatha's urging. The enemy force caught in front of the hills, and the one caught in the stretch of land between them, was soon whittled down.

The attackers had been turned into defenders with one bold, sweeping stroke. Morale dissipated rapidly amongst the Galleans, escalating the progress of the counter-attackers further.

As the last of the Galleans trapped before the hills were mopped up, Gunnar turned towards the narrow stretch of ground where he could see the back of the Gallean masses running away. They were falling into the woods on the other side of the hills, heading back in the direction from which they had marched.

"Onward!" shouted Gunnar, "Drive them out of the forest!"

Broad axes were raised high, and spears were leveled, as a jubilant roar filled the air. The Midragardans trotted forward, as incautious in their pursuit as the enemy had been in their forward push.

A sense of dread then clutched Ayenwatha's gut, as he saw so many warriors racing forward. The sight spurred his own feeling of panic, after Midragardan sky riders gliding overhead began to blast out urgent signals upon their horns.

Ayenwatha cried out to stop as many warriors as he could from going forward, tribal and Midragardan alike, knowing the sky riders had espied the cause for his uneasy feeling. Beyond the hills on the other side, the disciplined Avanoran knights had demonstrated their acute sense for the ebbs and flows of a battle. With the penetration, cut-off and encirclement of the forefront of the force, and the chaotic retreat by those immediately behind, they had rallied a number of crossbowmen and archers to prepare themselves for the inevitable pursuit.

A fair number of Midragardans were so caught up in the heat of combat, and first tastes of victory, that they strayed far into the grounds beyond the other side of the hills before they even began to sense that something terrible was amiss.

The air was filled a moment latter with a sibilant hissing.

The Midragardan warriors were riddled by a streaking host of bolts that punched through shirts of chain mail, as well as a flurry of arrows fitted with mail-piercing heads. Many Midragardans were knocked and spun off of their feet by the powerful bolts. Their anguished cries rang out to the skies, as they clutched at the shafts buried deep within the flesh of their bodies. A few more were killed trying to help wounded comrades, as all that could struggled desperately to retreat back down the channel between the hills.

Ayenwatha quickly sent tribal archers back up the slopes of the two hills, and soon some arrows of their own were beginning to fall among the reassembled enemy ranks. Fortunately, the enemy's overall stomach for fighting was gone, at least for the time being. They had been sorely bloodied by the unanticipated attack from the combined tribal and Midragardan forces.

When the Midragardans pulled back, and ceased their pursuit, the Galleans began an orderly retreat, abandoning the vicinity of the two low hills. Ayenwatha resisted any temptations at further pursuit. Overall, the defenders had attained a victory, though the Midragardans had been bloodied themselves at the end.

Ayenwatha was greatly relieved when he saw that Gunnar had survived the blunder at the end of the fighting. The big Midragardan had been amply anointed in the waters of battle, with blood and sweat covering his face. As he saw Ayenwatha striding up, he cast him a rueful grin.

"It is good to see you," Ayenwatha exclaimed.

"We were too reckless, a terrible lesson, and one to be remembered," Gunnar commented gruffly.

"Still a victory has been gained. The enemy was pushed back, and they lost many," Ayenwatha said, eyeing all of the bodies littering the ground nearby. He did not have to take any count to know that the bodies of invaders far outnumbered those of fallen defenders.

Gunnar nodded grimly. "Yes, a victory, but we had losses that did not need to be suffered."

Long, undulating wolf howls suddenly came upon the winds, bringing both men to an extended pause. An icy fear ran up Ayenwatha's spine, as a massive roar shook the forest just a moment later.

Ayenwatha looked off in the direction of the haunting sounds, as his brow furrowed. Most creatures of the forest should have long since fled the area, with so many humans moving about the vicinity.

Ayenwatha looked to his Midragardan friend with puzzlement etched on his face. There was something subtle and different about the tone of the howls from the calls of the wolves that lived in the tribal regions. The deep roar that had followed was undoubtedly bear-like, but yet different in tone from the vocalizations of the natural inhabitants.

"Seems that not everyone's day is done," Gunnar remarked, with a knowing grin. He nodded towards the area strewn with Gallean bodies. "I can only say that these invaders were probably the luckier, in regard to the opponents that they were made to face this day."

Ayenwatha looked towards Gunnar with a sense of amazement, as another huge roar, and more deep howls, resounded within the woodlands.

DEGANAWIDA

Both Bregas and Fenraren were used to ferry the exalted Great Sachems in, from points everywhere around the tribal regions. Some of them had been difficult to locate with the ongoing evacuation of the villages near the western border regions of the Five Realms. Many of the Great Sachems had never before flown upon sky steeds, but all understood the great urgency of the situation, and endured the unfamilar travel method as best they could.

The makeshift Grand Council was being held under the open sky, in a small clearing illuminated by the bright ambience of the afternoon sun. It was as ideal of a setting as could be had, given the less than ideal circumstances.

A Council Fire had been lit, the wood crackling to life from the flames of the Sacred Fire. The sachems from the Onan, Kanienke, and Onondowa sat to one side, while those from the Gayogohon and the Onyota were arrayed on the other. The Older Brothers and the Younger Brothers were together again, uniting the tribal family. An empty pole had been erected near to the fire, and, as nobody had yet spoken, no wampum belt had yet been hung upon it.

All fifty sachems of the Grand Council were in attendance, to Deganawida's great happiness and sheer amazement, as he had been watching them arrive with overriding anxiety, until the last was present. With their deer antler headdresses gracing their heads, their voices rose in unison, in a traditional expression of thanksgiving to the One Spirit.

Deganawida clutched the wampum belt that displayed the image of a man with an inner flame in his right hand. In the other, he gripped the bundle of five arrows signifying his honored status.

He drew strength from the familiar feel of the wampum, the sight of the sachems, and the sounds of chanting prayers and songs that filled the early portion of the Grand Council. It did much to soothe his troubled spirits, and evoked a state of mind that was better readied for the deliberation at hand.

Once the more ritualistic segment of the Council had been concluded, Deganawida slowly stepped forward into the midst of the fifty sachems.

"My Brothers, fortune has indeed been with us this past day," Deganawida began, as he walked closer to the blazing fire. His eyes methodically scanned the circumference of the gathering, taking in each and every sachem gathered. "The invaders have been slowed and stopped in many areas. They have been greatly wounded, but they will regroup and their attacks will resume soon. This Council has been called mainly for one purpose, in order to seek consensus on one matter.

"Gunnar, acknowledged war leader of our Midragardan brothers, desires to speak to the sachems of our Council about this matter. These are not ordinary times. Much is happening that is not in our traditional way. Please understand this, as he speaks to the Grand Council … and please listen to him. I ask Gunnar, friend to the Five Realms, now to come forth, to speak freely, and to tell us what he will."

Sitting just beyond the edge of the ring of sachems, Gunnar bowed his head somberly at Deganawida's acknowledgement. He slowly pushed himself up to his feet and walked forward, moving carefully through the sachems to where Deganawida was standing.

Deganawida laid a hand upon Gunnar's shoulder for a moment and nodded, before quietly moving back among the sachems and sitting down. Gunnar looked around at the Grand Council, as he readied himself to address the assembled Great Sachems.

Deganawida noticed that Gunnar had adhered to the fastidious attention to appearance that all the Midragardans tended to embrace. His hair was no longer matted and disheveled. The long locks were neatly combed out, as was his beard. His face held none of the caked blood and grime that had looked almost like tribal war paint at the end of the previous day's fighting.

He had even managed to get a change of tunic since the battle, perhaps borrowing the cleanest one that he could find among his warriors.

There was no question that the Midragardan chieftain had fought valiantly the previous day. The enemy advance had been halted for the first time since they had entered the woods. From all accounts, all of the Midragardans had fought with the skill and fury that had long ago fashioned their reputation for martial prowess.

Gunnar's hands descended as he produced a wampum medallion from a metal-framed leather pouch at his belt. It was a purple medallion, with a white image of the sun displayed upon it. Deganawida remembered when it had first been given to Gunnar, so very long ago, when the Midragardian chieftain had begun his long and amiable trading relationship with the Five Realms.

DREAM OF LEGENDS

The medallion symbolized good and truthful relations, and the particular wampum medallion that Gunnar now held was imbued with years of faithful and honest interactions with the tribes. His mere presence at the Council testified powerfully enough to the kind of relation that he had attained with the five tribes.

Gunnar held the medallion high. "I know some things of your ways, Great Sachems of the Grand Council. I know that it is a custom of a speaker to hang his wampum belt from the pole when addressing the Council, and then to take it from the pole when finished. As I wish to honor your ways, with what I can, and however I can, I bring this, my only wampum, which I have received myself from the Five Realms. I will use this as my belt, as what I come to say to you now is spoken with truth in my heart. If I err in your customs, please regard only my intent, and not my practice."

The gesture caught Deganawida a little by surprise, but he was very impressed with the Midgardan's keen insight. While wholly unexpected, the meaning of Gunnar's gesture would be understood, and it would be respected, and received well, by the Great Sachems.

It showed that Gunnar had not come to the Council with casual regard for the tribes, but was trying as much as possible to speak to them in a way that let them know that he truly cared for their plight.

His manner of speech itself would also reinforce his words, as many of the sachems were likely very surprised at hearing Gunnar's fluid mastery of the Quoian language.

Deganawida could remember the stumbling, crude period when Gunnar was first learning the tribal language. He often had to stifle a laugh, whenever Gunnar inadvertently had made a ludicrous statement, as he tried to gain a command of the Quoian tongue.

Other tribal members showed less discipline, falling into hilarity at some of the Midragardan's awkward, mistake-riddled comments. Thankfully Gunnar was always good humored, and laughed heartily with them when it was pointed out what he had actually said.

Yet Deganawida had always kept his own expressions of humor to a minimum, as he had a profound respect for the fact that Gunnar was working so hard to speak to the tribal people using their words. It had always showed that the Midragardan sincerely respected the people of the Five Realms.

Gunnar's diligence in learning had certainly produced a

prodigious harvest, as he rarely made a mistake anymore when speaking the tribal tongue. His hard-earned fluency now bolstered the integrity of the message he was delivering before the Grand Council.

Gunnar waited a few moments more after showing the wampum medallion, and moved to place it upon the empty pole before resuming his address. Once it was displayed upon the pole, his voice then carried the grave sincerity that loomed behind his portentous words.

"Brothers in the One that created all of us, the Unifier will surely come back, as Deganawida has said. They will be better prepared the next time, and will come back much stronger than before.

"They will seek to turn your own lands into a place to trap you, and destroy you to the last. They seek to drive you into the seas. I can offer help out of this, but it is a very difficult thing that I ask of you. If I thought that there was any another way, I would say so. But it is my advice that your people leave these lands for a time, and come with us upon our ships. We can reach the islands where my people have homesteads. They can be a haven for your people, for now.

"In time, we can plan a way to return, and look to take back these lands. I promise you that I will seek to gather more strength to help you. But with the men that I have brought, and the warriors available to you here, we cannot overcome the force that has come against us. Our sky riders have learned much more about what is arrayed against you. The enemy is far too strong, and grows stronger each day, while we will grow weaker."

Deganawida looked around at the sachems, quietly reading their faces. Gunnar had just asked them to do the seemingly unthinkable. Withdrawing from their villages and moving deeper into the woods was one matter. Fully abandoning the lands that they and their ancestors had occupied for thousands of years was quite another.

"We can be like a shield for your people, and fight as we move them towards the Shimmering River, where the longships are beached," Gunnar continued. "We can use the ocean as our ally. They will then have to come over the seas to get at us, whether we stay upon islands, or go onward to Midragard itself.

"Your tribes are bordered on land by kingdoms that look to your destruction. There is nothing to stop the invaders from coming into your lands, or having more supplies and warriors brought to them. We can defend much better in forcing them to have to cross water and land on another shore. Perhaps we can even deliver a crippling blow to any vessels they may try to send after us.

"As a chieftain among my people, this is my counsel to all of you. Please let me know what you decide. I desire to help you and your people in this time of terrible danger."

Gunnar then gave a low bow to the sachems of the Older Brothers on one side of the Sacred Fire, and then turned and bowed to the sachems of the Younger Brothers on the other. He quietly walked over, and took up his small wampum medallion from the pole, and continued back to where he had been sitting before Deganawida had summoned him. Without another word, he took a seat upon the ground and looked on with a solemn expression upon his face.

In the immediate aftermath of Gunnar's speech, Deganawida could see the logic of the Midragardan's words slowly seeping into the minds of the sachems. Gunnar had made a strong argument, and had taken care to present it in a way that showed his genuine respect for the tribes. It was the best advocacy that Deganawida could have hoped for, as he already agreed strongly with Gunnar's position.

Even so, it was not up to Deganawida to decide. He merely presided over the Council. He did not command it.

Deganawida got back up to his feet, and walked forward.

"Gunnar has spoken. Now, we must hear from each and every sachem that wishes to speak," Deganawida stated.

He took his place again at the edge of the circle among the other Onan sachems.

Wearing a buckskin cape, a Kanienke sachem named Sharenhowaneh, who was of the Wolf Clan, rose to be the first speaker upon Deganawida's invitation. He placed his wampum belt on the pole where Gunnar's medallion had been hung, retrieving it when he had finished speaking strongly in support of Gunnar's advice, and offer of help.

Many more wampum belts were added to the pole before the deliberations were finished. The sachems tended to be thorough and verbose, as the issue being discussed was unprecedented. As such, the Grand Council extended long into the day, and gradually approached the edge of evening.

Deganawida had begun to get worried, knowing that the Council would traditionally cease before evening took hold. The night was the dominion of the Dark Brother. The powerful evil Wizard, in league with witches and warlocks, was believed to wield his greatest powers during the dark, and could easily affect something like a Grand Council. Therefore, as a precaution, Grand Councils that went late were suspended until daylight returned again.

Fortunately, as the shadows lengthened, it finally reached a point where no other sachems rose up to speak. Deganawida quietly breathed a sigh of relief, as he rose to his feet once again.

"All who have spoken have had their say. Now, we must see what each sachem says in regards to this matter. Where do each of you stand, regarding moving the tribal people to the longships of our Midragardan allies, so that we can seek safer haven for a time?" Deganawida asked them.

A little anxiousness flitted within Deganawida. There could not be one objection if the tribes were to accept Gunnar's argument, and act upon it as one body. All fifty would have to give their assent.

One by one, the Grand Council sachems began to give their audible testaments regarding their inclinations. Deganawida's hopes rose by the time that half of the sachems had spoken their inclinations, seeing that the arguments from Gunnar were well on the way to being overwhelmingly supported.

Nevertheless, the procession of voiced agreements was not given with any semblance of enthusiasm. For many, there were a number of reservations and misgivings. Had a few of them not seen the first several sachems speak out in support, Deganawida had no doubt that they would have voiced opposition instead.

By the end, while admittedly on fragile ground, there was nonetheless a complete consensus. All fifty sachems of the Grand Council had committed to pursuing Gunnar's stated aims.

They were willing to depart their ancestral tribal lands in order to salvage the people from almost certain destruction. In his heart, Deganawida knew that they really had no other choice.

"None have voiced objection. The Five Tribes are in full agreement on this matter. We must all begin preparations to take our people to the Shimmering River," Deganawida stated after the last Grand Council sachem had spoken out.

While he was relieved that they had taken the wisest course of action in his view, it still gave him a heavy heart to actually speak the words aloud.

"But before we dismiss the members of the Grand Council, until night falls, let us use what time remains to discuss these preparations further," Deganawida added.

There were no objections, and the Council met until the last rays of the setting sun had emptied out across Ave. Only when night was about to claim full dominion did they finally cease.

During the rest of the extended Grand Council, a great heaviness lingered in the air, casting a somber pall over all the proceedings. Several of the sachems discussed in turn the necessary preparations to enact, so that the retreat could be maneuvered effectively towards the Shimmering River.

Deganawida did not have to read their thoughts to know that there was not one among them who was not hoping that they would soon wake up from it all, and find everything to be just a very bad dream.

A tremendous exodus lay ahead, something that no other generation among the Five Tribes had ever experienced before. It was wholly unprecedented, and there was nothing to draw from, or relate to, in all of the tribes' history.

A great and terrible burden lay upon all the sachems, as they would be leading their people into a future that was thickly laden with an impenetrable mist. The first step had been taken into that gray and shrouding uncertainty, and Deganawida knew that there would be many more to come.

section vi

WULFSTAN

Wulfstan gripped the leather hilt of his sword tightly, fingering the solid iron ring attached to the lobed pommel. He slowly traced the outline of the ring with his last finger, over and over again. The repetitive gesture reflected the nervous tension coursing throughout him, as he hungered for any shred of reassurance that things would somehow take a turn for the better.

Right next to Wulfstan, Cenwald stood with a taut grip of his own, applied midway along the shaft of his spear. His flesh seemed to bind with the scuffed, nicked wood. Cenwald's eyes were closed, as his mouth uttered silent prayers of supplication, beads of anxiety-ridden perspiration standing out upon the weathered skin of his broad forehead.

Wulfstan had been so relieved to see Cenwald after the swiftly alternating bouts of near victory and near destruction, finally culminating favorably when the formidable Andamooran flank had been decisively driven back. Cenwald was covered with scratches, bruises, and a modest gash, but nothing that left him with permanent injury, or likely threatened to fester with disease.

The battered Andamooran ranks had pulled back almost fully in the aftermath of the fierce fighting. A contingent of horse archers, and a few substantial formations of other cavalry, roamed the areas out in front of the Saxan right flank, if only to retain some residual honor while keeping an honest presence arrayed before their Saxan enemy.

The grassland before Wulfstan was now filled with the bodies of men and horses. A good number of them, man and beast alike, twisted and rolled in the agony of grievous injuries and open wounds. Far too many lay rigidly still. The ground beneath continued to slake its impassive, prodigious thirst on the innumerable small wellsprings of blood.

The mood of nearly all of the men gathered around Wulfstan was somber and drained. Far removed from the quiet fields and abundant forests of Sussachia, now perched on the western edge of their kingdom, an inevitable darkness was looming before them all.

As Wulfstan saw it, tasting the realization as a nauseous bile, the great armies of the Unifier were now settling into a war of attrition, one that they would eventually win. Until that happened, though, Wulfstan wanted only to be standing on his two feet, back at the very front edge of the fighting. At the very least, even his lone sword could help to slow that attrition and delay the inevitable; if only for a single moment longer.

Until further commands arrived, his desires would be restrained, as he was now forced into a bitter and chafing idleness.

A good number of men had been assembled and regrouped into a sizeable force behind the main shield wall. Many, like him, were from the heart of Sussachia, where Ealdorman Byrtnoth served as King Alcuin's highest authority. Others were from Ealdorman Oslac's lands in the Mittevald.

Ealdorman Aelfric was mustering all of them for some unspoken purpose, which Wulfstan believed would have to be revealed very soon, as the day was steadily growing older. It would not be much longer before night fell across the battlefield, and the fighting would most likely cease completely until the next dawn; unless a sudden breakthrough occurred.

Though it was a calm in the storm, the idleness was in itself a torment to Wulfstan's mind and constitution. He tried to occupy himself by looking over to where a force of light cavalry from Annenheim was in the process of mustering. The horse riders were gathering just a short distance beyond Wulfstan's contingent of northern Saxans under Ealdorman Aelfric's authority. Wulfstan wondered as to what the lightly armored, lance and shield bearing horse riders' purpose would be, in such late stages of the day's fighting.

An uproar of excited voices erupted suddenly around him, forcibly gripping his attention. Most of the men immediately around Wulfstan were looking and gesturing skyward, with eyes and expressions widened with a combination of sheer amazement and gaping fear. Following their riveted gazes, he watched the ominous approach of two enormous creatures, incredibly long of body, each supported by a pair of unbelievably vast wings.

"Darroks! Darroks!" a thane exclaimed loudly, as the two flying monstrosities drifted closer to the Saxan lines.

"May the All-Father be with us," Cenwald mumbled aloud at Wulfstan's side, his face a caricature of alarm and fear.

The two flying juggernauts cast massive shadows, which flowed smoothly across the ground under the creatures as they passed over the assemblage around Wulfstan. As he was engulfed in the darkness of their immense shadow, he looked up and marveled at the beasts passing right above him. It was hard to even imagine that something so huge could fly through the air.

His brow then furrowed as he watched them closely. He could tell that the creatures were lowering in altitude, noticeably heading from the upper sky towards the ground. They were soon well beyond the reserve muster of northern Saxans and light cavalry. A few moments later, Wulfstan judged that the Darroks had passed over the main Saxan encampment, and were now far behind the Saxan lines.

The giant flying beasts disappeared from his line of sight, and he could only wonder as to where they had made their final descent. Wulfstan knew that it could not have been very far beyond the encampment, and also recognized that the two creatures were now far removed from the Unifier's forces.

Yet they had not landed under duress, either. Their descent was done with pure intent. Whatever their purpose was, he knew that it did not bode well for the Saxans.

"I do not like this," Cenwald remarked after a long passage of uneasy silence, echoing the thoughts bandying about in Wulfstan's own mind.

"Nor I," Wulfstan replied in a low tone, his jaw clenching in the tension enveloping him.

He could hear the rising murmurs among the northern Saxans, as the others wrestled with the strange, unexpected sight. It was not much longer before the first signs of an answer to the strange mystery became manifest.

Several men came running into sight, streaking towards Wulfstan's throng from the direction of the main encampment. A few of them tripped over their own legs in their frantic haste, scrambling desperately back to their feet, and continuing forward with pressing urgency.

"The enemy comes! The enemy comes!" they yelled at the top of their lungs, eyes wide with panic.

Wulfstan's heart leapt up into his throat. He realized in that moment just what the huge flying creatures had been used for.

He knew that the encampment behind them held wounded warriors that had been dragged out of the battle. It also held a great number of non-combatants, gathered to aid the stricken fighters, and to attend to the needs of horses and warriors. The encampment contained the primary stores of foodstuffs, barrels of ale and water, additional weaponry, draft animals, and other elements so vital to a large force.

There was little doubt that Saxan scouts were all over the area behind the main battle lines, watching for any approaches by the enemy on horse or on foot. In both instances, whether a threat of enemy cavalry manifested, or a hard-pressed march of enemy foot soldiers, there would have been plenty of advance warning to muster a defense.

As it was, the enemy had landed a force by air, in an unprecedented manner, well within the far-flung ring of scouts. The enemy was positioned where there was little to nothing set between the landing monstrosities and the Saxan encampment. Well-guarded against ground based threats, the encampment was highly vulnerable to the daring maneuver.

"To the encampment! All Saxans, to the encampment, now! With all speed!" cried out a well-armed, mounted rider, waving his sword high in the air, as he urgently rallied the men around him.

Wulfstan recognized the stocky, bearded man as Ealdorman Oslac, having seen him several times moving among the Saxan men during the days leading up to the battle. Ealdorman Oslac had a reputation as a just, strong-hearted man among the people of the Mittevald, and that reputation spurred a vigorous response.

Wulfstan could tell which men hailed from the Mittevald in the surging response to his cries. Those from the Ealdorman's lands took up their arms with a zeal that testified to the motivation that Oslac's presence inspired within them.

Gripping their weapons, and faces determined, the mass of warriors around Wulfstan bounded forth, running in a loose, disorderly throng towards the encampment. Adrenaline sped through Wulfstan's veins, as they quickly crossed the last expanse of ground leading up to the outer ditch ringing the camp's perimeter.

Those in the lead of the body of warriors sprinted through the open gate set within the western section of the outer palisade. Wulfstan was among their number, having always been exceedingly swift of foot. Shield clenched securely on his left, and sword on his right, he pumped his arms vigorously, charging forward with urgency-fueled abandon.

A hissing sound cut the air, and a curt cry of pain emitted from one of the warriors running near to Wulfstan, as an arrow shaft embedded deep into his chest. The man pitched over to the ground, hitting it hard, and skidding a few feet to a halt where he lay still. Other sounds of agony burst out from others around Wulfstan, as deadly arrows fell in a tempestuous hail all about them.

"Shield yourselves!" Wulfstan cried out furiously, to any man that would listen. As he looked around, he saw that Cenwald was coming up just behind him.

He hurriedly shifted his sword into his shield hand, struggling with a makeshift grip as he slowed down a few steps, and allowed his comrade to catch up to him. He reached out and grabbed Cenwald by the upper arm, just as his friend drew up next to him. Wulfstan pulled Cenwald forward with him, nearly lifting the other man off of his feet.

Wulfstan's eyes could not lie as he took in the sight of the predicament facing the incoming Saxans; the situation they faced was daunting.

When the arrows had started to strike, the Saxans with Ealdorman Oslac had not yet proceeded far into the camp. There were only a few rows of tents left between the attacking enemy warriors and the greatest numbers of the wounded, most of whom were entirely helpless in their dire conditions. The rest, including the unarmed men and women serving as camp attendants, had little better prospects in the face of the determined enemy attack about to swallow them up.

Wulfstan moved quickly with Cenwald to take cover behind a large, four-wheeled wagon. He slammed forcefully against its stout wooden side, dragging Cenwald behind him. Cautiously, he peered out around the edge of the wagon, even as he winced in pain from the force of the impact against the rough, unforgiving wood. His shoulder throbbed as he reached over and took the hilt of his sword back into the familiar clutch of his right hand.

The shadowy forms of numerous enemy interlopers had drawn much closer, following the deadly barrage of missiles loosed by their brethren. A few of them broke into sight at last, brandishing broad, wicked-looking blades, and great wooden shields. The sight of the attackers came close to stilling Wulfstan's rapidly beating heart.

He saw at once that they were not human.

They were all much taller, and broader of build, than an average man. They were powerful, brutish creatures, with fierce countenances, as if feral dogs of war had been endowed with the bodies of very muscular men of considerable height.

There was only one creature, in all the lore and tales of the world that Wulfstan had ever heard, that held such a description. He was certain that they were the legendary Trogens, from their own faraway

570

homelands across an ocean to the east.

A feverish clash of steel erupted, and soared in ferocity as the Trogens poured through the tents and fell with fury upon the arriving defenders. One Trogen warrior suddenly moved past the corner where Wulfstan was crouched. The Trogen paused for a moment, momentarily unaware of Wulfstan and Cenwald's position by the large wheel of the wagon.

Without a moment's pause, Wulfstan stepped out behind the unsuspecting Trogen. He brought his sword up into an arc that crashed down into the exposed neck of the huge Trogen warrior. Wulfstan had to wrench the blade free with a hard yank, where it had embedded itself deep in the Trogen's flesh, as the body of the enemy warrior pitched over heavily to the ground.

An enraged roar from behind gave Wulfstan just enough warning to spin around and deflect a descending Trogen blade. The force of the fearsome blow was jarring, causing his knees to buckle. The creature rapidly leveled another heavy blow, which Wulfstan caught on his raised round shield. Wooden chunks and shards flew outward where the heavy blade cleaved into it.

The shield suddenly felt very heavy, as the blade had caught on the edge, if only for an instant. Yet it was enough time to give Wulfstan the opening that he badly needed.

He kicked up into the area of the creature's groin, connecting solidly. In the ensuing moment, when a flash of blinding pain gripped the Trogen, and held it within an instant of inaction, Wulfstan whipped his sword about and slashed at the side of the creature's head. His accuracy was deadly, connecting just beneath the iron half-helm that the beast-man wore.

Quickly, Wulfstan reached up to the edge of the empty wagon. He cast his sword and shield into the bed of the wagon, and jumped, hastily pulling himself up and over the edge.

"Cenwald, up here!" Wulfstan cried out, turning back towards his friend.

Thrusting his arm out, he grabbed Cenwald's forearm, and put all his effort into hoisting his comrade up. Cenwald needed little additional encouragement, frantically scrambling and gaining a foothold on the protruding end of the wheel's axle. He pushed upward, and flopped awkwardly over the top, tumbling down into the open bedding of the wagon.

Remaining low, Wulfstan achieved a better view of the chaotic battle swirling all around him. More and more of the towering Trogens were streaming into the area. Wulfstan cursed the ease with which such a strong force had gotten behind their lines, carried directly over the main Saxan force and dropped right behind the largely defenseless encampment.

Resistance was mounting quickly, though. Warriors from Sussachia and the Mittevald mixed in with light cavalrymen from Annenheim, as the Saxans started to form a stout line of defense, facing the Trogen onslaught.

The worsening problem for Wulfstan was that the Trogens had largely overrun the area that he and Cenwald now found themselves in. The main defensive line was forming well behind the wagon that the two Saxans were huddled in.

He looked about, as another of the long, wide blades of a Trogen shattered the wood of the wagon, unbearably close to where his head had been. A spear instantly shot over the top of his shoulder from behind, catching the Trogen squarely in the face.

"That, I owe you for," he called back to Cenwald, who was holding the other end of the spear's ash haft. Though there was fear splayed on his comrade's face, there was also a determined strength.

Wulfstan looked around again, seeing that there were a substantial number of wagons and carts arrayed around them. They were pulled close enough together that an idea sprouted in his mind.

"Let us try it! We are dead if we stay here!" Wulfstan yelled urgently. "Follow me! Let's use the wagons to work away from here!"

Taking a couple of steps, he built up some momentum and leapt upward, his foot catching and propelling himself forward from the edge of the raised wagon side. The inertia carried him towards a wagon immediately behind them, clearing the top of its side. He came down with heavy thuds as his feet struck the timber of the bed, but managed to keep his footing underneath him.

He turned and waited for Cenwald to follow, helping him up when he fell to his knees following his own jump. The two men then cleared another wagon in a like manner, and then jumped down to the hard ground.

Wulfstan and Cenwald found themselves on the edge of the area where the wounded from the battle were being quartered. He looked into a sea of terrified, helpless faces, but there was also the presence of courage.

Many of the monks, Sisters, and others that had been dressing the warrior's wounds had chosen not to try and flee, and many of the wounded had propped themselves up. Grabbing whatever was available, from a few formal weapons, to smaller knives, and even simple tools, they were readying to meet whatever end fighting.

"Behind you!" cried out one of the Sisters to Wulfstan, her face a mask of sudden panic.

The huge shadow of a Trogen loomed over him, a scarred brute that had followed them across the wagons, and was still standing in the bed of the last one in the line. It was armed with a long lance, which it now thrust rapidly towards Wulfstan. The Saxan ceorl spun around as the lance point darted past, feeling the shaft of the weapon brush against the links of his mail shirt.

He hacked down with all of his might on the extended arm of the Trogen. The beast-man howled in agony, stumbling over the edge of the wagon to crash onto the ground.

An injured warrior, who still retained full command of both of his legs, and Cenwald fell in swiftly together upon the fallen Trogen. Their weapons rose and fell several times, taking no chances as they finished the grisly task.

Wulfstan saw that the situation facing the quarters of the wounded was tenuous at best. The hastily formed line of Saxans close by was all that kept a considerable number of Trogens from implementing untold disaster upon hundreds of injured warriors and camp attendants. Yet as Wulfstan had done, the Trogens could still cross over the massed wagons, and Wulfstan had to get word of the danger to the Saxan fighters.

"Cenwald, stay here, with all who can bear arms, and watch for others!" he cried out to his comrade. He loped forward, keeping his eyes alert for any signs of disturbance.

A shadow then darted over the ground just ahead of him, bringing him to a brief halt, as he looked up to see what the source of it was. Wulfstan immediately rushed forward, bringing his sword into a downward slash, and slaying another Trogen warrior as it leapt to the ground from another wagon. He was grateful that the burly creature was unaware of him, affording him the advantage of complete surprise.

Some Saxans whirled towards him as he neared the main line

of defenders. Seeing that he was human, they quickly lowered their weapons.

"Some are coming over the wagons, and a few warriors need to go to ward the wounded in this camp," he cried out to them.

A grizzled thane, clad in half-helm and blood-streaked mail, nodded with a grim expression, evidently needing to ask no questions. The thane looked around, and called out forcefully to several men near him.

Wulfstan did not wait for further response, his message effectively delivered. He looked behind him, towards the quarters of the wounded. He saw with horror that Cenwald and the few capable, wounded Saxans were already overwhelmed.

A few Trogens had broken through their thin defense, making it past the heavily-engaged Saxans. The merciless creatures brought heavy maces, lances, great blades, and peculiar, long-hafted weapons, used like two-handed axes, down upon several semi-conscious, Saxan fighters situated upon makeshift ground coverings, including blankets, cloaks, and straw-filled pallets. A few of the Saxan warriors weakly tried to defend themselves, but their efforts were in vain, as they were easily overpowered by the immense strength of the Trogens.

The carnage would mount rapidly, if it were not stopped immediately. Seeing nothing but rage through his burning sight, Wulfstan desperately rushed forward, without another thought, embracing full combat with the Trogens. As he neared one of the marauders, he instinctively felt something lunge towards him, just before he heard the guttural war cry of his assailant.

Wulfstan leaned forward, and pushed off his right foot, seeing a blurring shape descending upon him out of the periphery of his left eye. He knew that a strike was already in motion, speeding at him from behind. There was not even a moment to spare, as a weapon closed the remaining gap, wielded in a swift, deadly arc.

Wulfstan then felt a crushing blow to his upper back, hurtling him onto the ground. The impact had not caught him squarely, having missed Wulfstan's head. It had also lost much of its power, extended well beyond its apex of strength when Wulfstan had leaned and burst forward at the last instant.

Nonetheless, even overextended and awry, it was still a heavy blow, wielded with brute force by a Trogen warrior. The only good fortune was that it was not an edged weapon, like their lengthy blades and the strange, long-hafted weapons, which may well have cleaved his mail shirt.

Rolling over, he used his sword to block the second blow from the huge mace, as it whipped back around to claim his life. He caught the stroke in time, the thunderous force reverberating throughout his body.

The pain in Wulfstan's back was intense, and there were flashes before his eyes as his very consciousness flickered in and out. The mace was pressed down hard upon his sword, as the jubilant Trogen reached back with a free hand and began to withdraw a long, single-edged dagger from a leather scabbard at its waist.

Wulfstan cried out as the Trogen growled menacingly, feeling the enemy warrior's hot, fetid breath upon his face. The sharp canines of the Trogen were bared at him, within a ferocious, snarling visage, as Wulfstan struggled with everything that he had left to resist the much stronger opponent. A part of him expected at any moment for the broad jaws of the creature to snap at him.

The arm wielding the mace had him pinned in place. It would only be a moment more before the Trogen had the dagger in hand, and Wulfstan knew that he could do little to stop what was about to come.

With a hissing sound filling the air for an instant, just above Wulfstan's head, the Trogen appeared to instantly freeze in place. Its expression did not even change, as it crumpled toward the ground, an arrow protruding from the top of its left shoulder. It had died immediately, as the arrow had pierced its heart in a penetrating, downward thrust.

Wincing from the thudding pain coursing through him, Wulfstan nearly doubled over. He raised his head, and turned to see a man holding an empty bow out in front of his chest, the weapon clenched in his left hand.

Out of the corner of his eye, he also espied the form of another Trogen striding around the end of a nearby tent, raising its blood-covered blade as it stormed forward with lethal intent. The enemy warrior was almost within range of the injured bowman that had just clearly saved Wulfstan's life.

With nothing more than sheer adrenaline, a lifting force that ignored the ferocious throbbing in his back, he rose briskly to his feet. Wulfstan lunged forward in a desperate, reckless attempt to reach the

Trogen, without having any conscious regard for himself.

Fortunately, the Trogen's attention was fully intent upon the bowman on the ground. The enemy warrior did not see the onrushing Wulfstan until he was already upon the creature. The two adversaries engaged in a short, furious sword fight. Their exchanges lasted through several thunderous clashes of forged iron, until the slightly better skill of Wulfstan finally gained the upper edge over the sheer strength of the Trogen.

Even so, the fight did not end before another significant blow was suffered by Wulfstan. A slashing stroke by the Trogen warrior grazed him, opening a bleeding gash in his upper left arm. Several links of his mail shirt were burst apart by the enemy's enraged blow, which preceded the sword stroke from Wulfstan that ended the exchange. Wulfstan choked the fiery pain down, and turned back towards the injured warrior that he had just defended.

Wulfstan's chest heaved with heavy breath, and his arms seemed to contain the weight of boulders. His left upper arm continued to suffer the scorching touch of the open wound, while the Saxan warrior's back pulsed with a terrible ache.

He looked around for any new dangers. The thane that had responded to his warnings had arrived with several hale Saxan warriors, and the few Trogens that had made it among the wounded had been driven out. To his great relief, he saw Cenwald with a couple of the new arrivals, as the area before the edge of the wagons was secured. The sight was a tremendous relief, as he knew that he would not have survived another combat.

He turned back to face the bowman again.

"If we get past this battle, my debt to you is more than I can ever give in a lifetime," Wulfstan said, gradually regaining his breath.

"Be glad I would not let go of my bow," the other man replied with a slight grin.

The bow-carrying warrior slumped down fully upon the earthen-hued cloak he had been lying on, wincing painfully. His thick, red hair was matted, and his large eyes could not mask the sharp ache that was continuously being generated from his body, caused by the large wound underneath the ragged strips of blood-stained, wool-cloth bandages wrapped snugly around his side.

One of his leathery hands still grasped his bow tightly, the bulging forearm muscles pulsing with the throbs of pain wracking him. His other hand was reaching down towards a quiver of arrows, in a labored effort to draw one of the feather-fletched shafts out.

"Your name?" the man asked, pulling an arrow free of the quiver.

"Wulfstan, son of Ealdred, from Sussachia," Wulfstan replied, as he kept his eyes searching for any remaining Trogens that might have escaped their notice.

"Then we are not far apart, Wulfstan," the man said slowly, in a purposeful manner, forcing a smile through the clouding pain of his wounds. He spoke with no small amount of effort, pausing to take several deep breaths. "I am Sebright. Just a simple woodworker … from the village of Raven's Nest. No, not from Sussachia as you … but we are on the very borders of your lands. Might be that just a few trees are between my village and the lands under Ealdorman Byrtnoth. You make me glad now that I have spent many years hunting with a bow."

"It is the greatest misfortune that it takes wars to bring new friends together," Wulfstan observed.

"But there is cause to celebrate," Sebright said, with another grimace interrupting the smile on his face.

Wulfstan thought for a moment that the man was also delirious, in the light of the irrefutable circumstances surrounding them. He responded with a tone of incredulity, "Celebrate?"

"Right here … is your reason, something to always keep in mind, in times such as this," Sebright uttered confidently. With his right hand he reached up and gestured to a small, silver pendant hanging about his neck. It was the spear-shaped symbol of Emmanu. "Look to the skies if it seems darkest. He will return. Believe it, Wulfstan. That hour is drawing near, as the world is shackled in madness."

Wulfstan smiled gently, not wanting to offend the man. Times had always been dark in the history of the world. The course of Saxan history alone had been filled with challenges, as tyrants and kingdoms alike had risen and fallen. He had listened to many such stories over the years, from gleeman and family alike.

He just felt lucky that Saxany had been strong for hundreds of years, enough to withstand the inevitable onslaughts against it. Though he was not so certain about the current times, Wulfstan now believed that Sebright was probably another one of the doomsayers who were said to crop up at the end of centuries, millennia, and during great wars.

The wound that he had suffered had probably added a small dose of madness as well to the man's sense of reason, taking him to its embrace.

Wulfstan had undergone the Three Immersions, and had attended the village church regularly, but that did not mean Sebright was prophetic. Emmanu was always said to be on the verge of return, even though each century continued to pass into yet another century, without even a hint of the possibility.

"He will come again," Wulfstan echoed, a statement that he struggled greatly to believe could even possibly be imminent.

He hoped that he had at least humored the man that had saved his life, not entirely finding the moment appropriate to engage in a discussion of this sort.

"He will," Sebright responded, matter-of-factly. The archer's eyes darted about. "The threat here is now gone. You should go see to your other comrades."

Wulfstan shook his head. "I am staying here, among you and those here. There's nobody to stand among all of you if any of those creatures break through again."

In all truth, Wulfstan was the only able-bodied warrior currently standing in the midst of well over a hundred badly wounded Saxans. The recently arrived thane and other Saxans had clearly bolstered what little defense could be placed near to the line of wagons, but it would not take many Trogens to break through to the wounded again. Wulfstan had no way of knowing just how large the force of Trogens was. He would almost have to be a second line of defense by himself.

Farther away, the Saxan line seemed to be thickening, bolstered by more incoming warriors. Some Saxan archers were now levying their arrows towards the Trogens, whose advance was stalled by the increasing weight of the defender's numbers.

Wulfstan watched the monks, priests, Sisters, and others resuming their work on the wounded, seeing a determination and courage that was equal to that of any warrior.

A middle-aged Sister held the hand of a man, and looked into his eyes without wavering, as he shuddered and succumbed to a terrible stomach wound, laying her hand upon his sweat and blood matted forehead with a mother's gentleness. She looked right into his eyes as he expired, showing no trace of discomfort, holding on to him till several moments after his spirit had fled his body.

Her lips moved as she whispered some private, silent prayer, getting up and moving in her grimy, blood-stained tunic to attend to yet another grievously wounded man, who also looked to be entering his final moments. Wulfstan inwardly knew that she would continue as long as there was a warrior in danger of dying alone, making certain that they did not.

A great yell arose from the Saxan line behind him, mixing with several deep, short horn blasts from the rear of the camp, where the Trogens had entered. The horn blasts had a deeper, different tone than the Saxan ones, and Wulfstan had no doubts as to what they meant. The Trogens were falling back. Wulfstan turned his head in time to see the Saxan line pressing forward, driving hard against the retreating Trogens.

Wulfstan took a deep breath. Another grave threat had been beaten back, the second such in just one day, but Wulfstan had no illusions that it would be the last in this terrible battle.

Several armed Saxans were being dispatched to search among the wagons, to look for any Trogens that might still be hiding. Wulfstan opted to stay among the wounded as long as he could, as he was now injured himself.

Some time later, a kindly-faced monk brought Wulfstan an ash-wood cup. It was filled with a rather poor quality ale, but Wulfstan received it with great enthusiasm nonetheless. He warmly thanked the monk, who nodded back, with a brief smile of acknowledgement, and moved away to other tasks. To Wulfstan, at that moment, it was as if the drinking vessel was a glass cup from Ehrengard, filled with the finest ale, set at the table of a wealthy Saxan thane.

With daylight ebbing towards darkness, Wulfstan doubted that anything more would be asked of the Saxans that had responded to the emergency defense of the encampment. Sebright, exhausted, and fully free of the threats, fell quickly into a deep sleep as Wulfstan watched over him.

The skies were soon cast with a decidedly reddish hue, and Wulfstan recalled the old saying of the Venerable Ethelwulf of the Jarrede Monastery. The legendary churchman and chronicler had once said that a reddish sky at the onset of night heralded the promise of a clear day on the morrow.

Wulfstan hoped that the All-Father would forgive him for outright disagreement with one of his highest, and most renowned,

Saxan servants. With all those who had fallen on that day, Wulfstan did not see how the coming day could ever be seen as clear, no matter what the weather might be.

Rather, he believed, the battle was simply so terrible that even the ground could not hold the blood that had been spilled. The sky itself looked to have had been stained with the baleful dye of war.

He also mused over the common notion among his people that the blood of the Saxans had been much stronger in days of old. After what he had witnessed that day, he disputed that saying as well. It was hard to conceive of stronger blood than that which ran in the veins of the Saxan warriors standing courageously on the battlefield that day, and those other Saxans whose unyielding will served the dying and wounded within the encampment.

Many horns were sounded in the distance, where the main battlefront was. The sonorous blasts were Saxan in tone, and were clearly signaling the end of the day's hostilities, as the first signs of the cessation of battle started to appear.

Wulfstan slowly strode among the tents of the encampment, working his way gradually back to where the contingents from Sussachia were situated. He endured the pain from his injuries, simply glad that they did not hinder him from moving.

Guards and lookouts were being posted at the rear of the camp, as streams of exhausted soldiers began to enter the boundaries of the encampment. Notched axes, torn mail, gouged and shattered shields, and other various mementos of the ferocious combat were commonly seen among the battered, blood-smeared men returning to the confines of the war camp.

Wulfstan finally reached his tent, and sat down outside the opening. Now that the fighting was done, a part of him was given over to the needs of hunger. He scraped up some pieces of hard bread, using the remaining ale in his cup to soften it to a level that he could chew.

Gradually, more of the warriors that had been in the assemblage prior to the Trogen attack filed back around Wulfstan. Several gave him nods or smiles that held sparks of gladness that he was healthy and alive, even as he returned the expressions in a like manner. The sparks could not take to flame, though, dampened as all of them were by the reality that many others would not be returning to their tents that evening.

Cenwald slumped down heavily next to Wulfstan, his face filled with weariness, and his spear holding several new nicks and scrapes. Overall, he was none the worse for wear, having made it through the end of the day without incurring serious injury. Wulfstan gave him a light pat on the back, as his friend sat down next to him.

They were allowed to light fires, and eat a meager fare of hard bread, which they dipped into a grain-and-vegetable pottage to soften. The provisions were accompanied with a modest serving of salted fish, and some more poor quality ale. It was a much lesser repast than that which they had enjoyed on previous nights in the camp, but after the long, tiring day, it tasted as if it were a sumptuous feast.

There was little to no conversation among the men, as each nursed his hunger, thirst, and various physical or mental troubles in private. Wulfstan found his mind returning to wondering over the purpose of the assemblage that had been taking place prior to the arrival of the Darroks.

The mystery did not linger for long. The purpose was soon explained to them by Aelfric himself, who presently came into the camp, and dispersed several of his thanes among the weary men. They summoned all those who had previously been mustering towards the end of the day together once again, except for those greatly wounded in the defense of the encampment.

Aelfric waited for them to gather within an open space, standing near to a large campfire. His face, reddish in the firelight, was grim of countenance as he spoke to them in the last vestiges of twilight.

Aelfric spoke of a free-holding lord named Godric, who held a sizeable fortress and attendant lands on the outer borders of Saxany. The use of Godric's fortress, situated as it was near to the south and west of the battlefield itself, had to be denied to the enemy ranks. Diligent scouts had ascertained that there were still routes available to reach the fortress, despite the presence of the invasion forces.

A force was now to be sent, under the cover of night, to reach Godric's lands. Their task was to entreat with Godric directly, to gain his cooperation to allow his fortress to be garrisoned.

Among those being gathered, a larger faction, including riders, would be involved with scouting and protection on the perimeters. Some of these would act within the areas that were now being heavily patrolled by the enemy, creating diversions if the need arose. A smaller group would be sent on foot to navigate the route through the dense woodlands to the actual fortress itself. It was a task fraught with danger, but one that the Saxan leader saw as entirely necessary.

After Aelfric concluded his address, everyone was mercifully allowed a short nap. Wulfstan and the others within the assemblage walked back to their tents and campfires in relative silence, most lost in the depths of a murk born of their dark thoughts and great fatigue.

When he reached his tent again, Wulfstan removed his mail shirt. He gave a low groan as he slid the protective iron links up and over his head, aggravating the tender area of his upper back and his slashed arm in the process. He then took off his half-helm, and set it down beside him, before pulling off his tunic.

He savored the relief of the cooling night air as it settled all over his body. With no threat of rain, he eschewed the small interior of the ridge tent. He sprawled out before the tent opening on the ground, under the night sky, feeling the soft grasses underneath his head. He wasted little time before falling into unconsciousness.

Once again, he found himself in the midst of a mysterious dream, featuring an old man dressed in the garb of a priest of Emmanu. The old priest carried within his hands an ornately bound codex, dressed richly with gold and gems. The priest had kindly, blue eyes, and though advanced in age his hair was a luxuriant black. His voice was gentle, but imbued with a great strength.

"To the skies, Wulfstan. Go farther, and seek the one that can help your people."

Wulfstan awoke with an abrupt start, peering upward at a worried, familiar face. Cenwald was leaning over him, having reached down to lightly nudge him.

"Are you okay?" Cenwald asked. "It looked as if sleep was troubling you. The night force has begun to assemble. We will gather beyond the western camp gate. All would be awakened soon enough."

"I do not fault you, Cenwald. Even so, this sleep is far too short," he lamented, for the short draught of sleep had brought an enormous thirst to the fore.

"Will your injuries allow you to travel?" Cenwald asked him.

"I will bear the pain, it does not prevent me from movement," Wulfstan replied somberly.

Stretching his tightened muscles, he sat up, carefully pulling his tunic back on. He winced with the pulsating pain coursing through his upper back, knowing that he would be nursing a very sore area there for quite some time from the Trogen mace blow. He slowly replaced his old half-helm on his head, tying the leather straps underneath his chin, to secure it firmly.

"Time to do what we must," he said resolutely, forcing a smile of encouragement through the icy feeling gripping him, born of fatigue and the countless losses and sufferings that he had witnessed on the previous day.

Those gleemen who would someday be singing great songs of that day, and the rest of the battle to come, might well render heroic tributes to the Saxan warriors. Wulfstan would expect nothing less, for they deserved to be remembered in glory, but the costs that purchased that glory were a horrific burden that Wulfstan was only beginning to understand.

After adjusting the fit of his sword and scabbard, and pulling his shield up, he walked with Cenwald through the chilly night. His rigid muscles gradually became more supple as he moved. Wulfstan paused a couple of times to twist his torso and limber up his back, which ached even more from the short respite on the hard ground, and the accumulation of the previous day's exertion.

They continued through the teeming campfires, which silhouetted the forms of a great many slumbering men. They finally exited the western gate of the camp, and followed some others that he recognized from the Sussachia contingent. They headed to where the small force that he was to join was now mustering.

On his way outside the camp's entrance, he noticed a large number of warriors from Bretica heading out silently towards the battlefield itself. They were carrying an array of digging implements, from iron-edged wooden spades to sharp iron picks, affixed to long wooden hafts. A few of them led draft animals, the horses and oxen pulling carts and wagons in their wake.

He regarded them curiously for a few moments, wondering what their purpose was, before continuing on his way towards the growing assemblage.

More than one initiative was evidently being undertaken by the Saxans during that restless night.

AELFRIC

Aelfric partook of a light meal and some thin ale, as his stomach would not take much more after the harrowing day of battle. The dark tent, whose gloom was only partially offset with the glow from a couple of braziers, was filled with silent, reflective men. A number of them were simply grateful that they still drew breath.

"Too many … far too many," Aelfric stated leadenly, with a heavy heart.

"Aelfric, the Andamoorans are not likely to strike hard if they array for battle tomorrow," suggested a tall man with sharply chiseled features, and dark, wavy locks of coarse hair.

"And were it not for you, Einhard, our right flank would not even be available to array tomorrow," Aelfric responded somberly, taking a deep breath.

Many Saxans, such as Ealdorman Byrtnoth's levies, had been caught out in the open when the Avanorans had made their deft adjustment. Even Count Gerard's formidable Bretican cavalry had been in grave danger of being cut off, as they had pressed to the far recesses of the Andamooran ranks.

Quite possibly, the battle itself had come dangerously close to being decided in those precarious moments. Such were the incredible shifts within a battle.

"And of tomorrow? My men are preparing a surprise for the Avanorans, one used by our people before, in the center," Count Gerard then announced. "Their Andamooran left flank has been mauled, but their right and center are still very strong, and there are many that they have yet to bring into this fight."

"And many that we have not," Aelfric added, glancing at the stoic, powerfully-built figure standing just a few paces away. "Aldric? Would you care to say how tomorrow will begin?"

"We will be striking the Avanoran reserve, where many of their great barons are, at first light," Aldric stated confidently, as if it was an event that had already occurred.

Aelfric had no doubts that within Aldric's mind, it truly had happened. Such was the supreme conviction dwelling within the determined Saxan.

A murmuring broke out in the tightly crowded tent at Aldric's words, as all of them knew that it indicated that a full strike by their stalwart, sky steed commander was going to be undertaken.

"And what if the flying monstrosities return?" another thane asked. "We were not prepared for the attack today on the camp."

"I do not think they will repeat themselves. Many of their men and other creatures have expended themselves heavily today, and I look for them to try new ways tomorrow," Aelfric answered.

He had little doubt that the enemy would expect them to be wary for another similar strike, and in truth they would be, with some additional men held back to guard the wounded. There would be enough to hold off any attack at the palisade's edges until reinforcements arrived. The enemy would not be able to pour uncontested through the camp's eastern gateway, as they had done in the brazen attack that day.

"Then what are our goals?" Count Leidrad inquired, his face awash with deep concern. "The Halmlander must be broken."

Aelfric had spent a good amount of time on the Saxan left flanks, and shared Count Leidrad's anxieties. The first day had largely been a parry by the enemy, but the second day would likely be a thrust, or crushing slash.

The Ehrengardians on the enemy's right had been content to harry them with arrows and bolts, and unleash a few mounted skirmishes from behind their living fortification of Halmlander mercenaries. All of the Saxans who had been on the left flank felt strongly that the second day would see a much heavier blow delivered by the warriors of Ehrengard and their loathsome mercenaries.

It was likely that the day's debacle among the Andamoorans had caused a ripple all the way down the enemy lines, thereby preventing a stronger attack by Ehrengard on the first day. The Avanorans had probably been forced to break off their original contrivances. With the left and center distracted, the risks of committing the right flank had likely been too high for the tenuous state of agreement governing the command of the Ehrengardians, held delicately amongst their often-fractious princes and bishops.

Aelfric was much relieved that the woods to the left and right of the plains were highly difficult to pass through, even in peaceful times. They were now even harder to navigate, with the presence of ubiquitous barricades erected along any path that might even be slightly conducive to horses. It was a younger woodland terrain, filled with brush and undergrowth alongside the trees, making even progress on foot quite ponderous.

The thought of the forest, especially to the south and west of their position, brought his mind back around to the small band of skilled woodsmen who had been dispatched to look in upon Godric.

He had no great hopes for Godric's loyalty, but the truth needed to be known. Only then could the Saxans know to the fullest extent what position the enemy was in. Many among them hoped that Godric would make a bold stand, at least in closing the gates of his large fortress.

He would not have to withstand a long siege. The enormous invading army could not remain stagnant for long, and certainly could not endure long delays. It was an army that had been built to break through in a rapid, decisive blow.

If it could not break through, then it would be too unwieldy to sustain itself. A starving army would swiftly become its own greatest enemy.

In a sense, all the Saxan hopes relied on the voracious needs of such a juggernaut of men, horses, oxen, and other creatures.

ALDRIC THE STORMBLADE

Aldric's warriors took a wide, circuitous route under the concealing cloak of darkness, most accompanying him to the north, while a smaller force of sky riders headed directly towards the south.

It was almost fitting that Aldric's own force was able to reach one of the small tidal islands, of the kind that dotted the northwest waters off the shoreline and continued along the northern coasts of Saxany. They were places where legendary monks had lived contemplatively, some in their small, seaside monasteries and others in hermitages situated upon the tiny islands. It was also where some of the worst Midragardan raids in coastal waters had occurred, before the ocean in that region had become too restless for ship travel.

The flowing and ebbing tides either made them into fully surrounded islands when in, or exposed land bridges when out. Aldric had heard some talk that the Avanorans had a huge, fortified monastery in such a place, which had been dedicated to the warrior Archon Mikhael.

The knowledge had struck him as odd, as he doubted that such blood-lusting warriors of Avanor could ever honor the quiet spirit required of such a sanctified location.

The Saxan sky steed commander was badly in need of some of the stabilizing tranquility that the monks cultivated in such environments. Aldric's mind and heart were like two slow-burning embers, waiting to touch some kind of kindling, to burst forth into a full inferno. He had initially disagreed with Aelfric, but the Saxan thane had turned out to be correct.

The enemy sky steeds had conducted their movements with great caution, largely keeping out of the battle, and hovering in the skies over their side of the battlefield. The absence of the Saxan sky steeds, and their unknown whereabouts, had neutralized what would have quickly become an enemy advantage born of sheer numbers.

Toward the end of the first day, the incident with the landing of Trogen warriors, using the behemoths called Darroks, had been most unexpected, and was perhaps the hardest aspect of the first day for Aldric to live with. A part of him wondered whether the strike had been done with the purposeful intent to draw the Saxan sky riders forth. It was all that he could do to exercise restraint.

He was now relieved that Aelfric had seen fit to listen to his bold suggestion. They now knew where the enemy reserve was lining up, held in the back and center of the vast, frontal formations. That reserve undoubtedly held the most important Avanorans, who would be the most important individuals amongst the entirety of the enemy force.

With the Andamooran's mauled, another heavy blow, one suffered by the elite of the Avanorans, might well tilt the favor of battle towards the Saxan cause.

The timing would have to be about perfect, as the sun made its presence known in the east. It would be a maneuver in the form of a great hook. The Saxan sky riders under Aldric would come in from the north, in between the reserve and the frontal deployments of the enemy.

They would then make a sharp turn back to the west, to strike at the reserve formations with the sun at their own backs, and in their enemy's eyes. With the attack coming right out of the skies, the enemy could not help but look directly up into a large, blinding, and unforgiving sun.

If timing was exceptional, that maneuver was to be preceded by a smaller diversionary force coming out of the woods on the far right flank of the enemy. Aldric had urged the others to be sure to be within striking range the minute that the horizon was lined with the first rays of the rising sun.

His own final approach would be occurring just after that point, and if all went as he had planned, they would be among the Avanoran reserves well before the enemy sky steeds could respond in force.

He could not dwell on what might come thereafter, as he knew that desperate and unconventional methods had to be done if there was to be any possibility of stemming the martial titan now facing them on the Plains of Athelney.

There was only one vision to cling to, as his Himmeros steadily pumped its great wings, carrying him ever closer to the intended strike; getting into the midst of the Avanoran reserve, and delivering an enormous, shattering blow.

GUNTHER

Gunther, broken emotionally, and exhausted physically, from working his way through hundreds upon hundreds of bodies on the battlefield, stumbled into the cool darkness of the passageway leading down into the relative sanctuary of the Unguhur's subterranean lands. His hair matted with sweat, and his face and hands smudged with dirt and blood, Gunther bore on his body the signs of the burdensome, grievous tasks that he had undertaken that day.

His Jaghuns padded along with him, their tails down, and one of them walking with a discordant gait, as it struggled with the wounds suffered in the fight with the Licanthers. They were reflections of their despondent master, and their movements were entirely devoid of the confidence and energy that they normally displayed. They had been able to muster excited barks when coming upon survivors, but now only sorrowful whines passed from their muzzles. They did not stray far from the woodsman, keeping close company with the man that had raised all of them from the moment of their first breath.

Gunther was barely able to make it through the main cavern, pausing every so often to lean against one of the tall stalks of the underground forest. His spirits were debilitated, lending him no motivation to spur his leaden legs forward. A few of the Unguhur workers nearby offered to assist him, but he wordlessly waved them off, as finally he trudged slowly down to the waterline of the wide, underground stream. The Jaghuns halted each time that he did, and they did not move again until he had taken a step, as they accompanied Gunther down to the waterway.

It seemed as if he were moving through a dark dream. Everything seemed so surreal, and his spirits were almost entirely emptied of the spark of life. The gruesome, painful sights that he had pushed to the far recesses of his mind had stormed back ten-fold.

He was caught in a mountain avalanche, not knowing whether he was tumbling down towards a cliff's edge or not. No matter how much he resented it, and had fought it, the world had pulled him right back into the midst of its madness. Even more maniacal, the world had bluntly thrust him into the most ugly and degrading failures of mankind, in the form of the bloody war now underway.

He had seen the loathsome face of war before, but had never drawn himself so closely to the numerous, individual faces of it as he had that day.

His legs somehow carried him forward, as his stained leather shoes sank into the soft footing beneath. A lone Unguhur raft pilot, who was down by the moored objects, spared him the need to navigate his own raft. Gunther did not know whether he even spoke a word to the raft pilot, but the Unguhur must have sensed his great need. He accompanied Gunther and his Jaghuns onward, taking them through the water-carved tunnel that led on to the vast underground lake and Oranim.

The woodsman rode in dejected, exhausted silence as the Unguhur's stone city loomed on the far shore of the lake. He almost fell into slumber on the raft's surface, lulled by the smooth passage across the waters. When they had reached the shoreline before the city, the Unguhur raft pilot nudged him as gently as he could with his massive, stone-grey hands.

"Thank you, " Gunther muttered in the language of the Unguhur, rousing himself slowly to full wakefulness, shaking his head to bring about some sense of clarity.

His Jaghuns disembarked from the raft, one less in number than had started out on the grim sojourn. Most of them leapt to the solid ground, but the injured one whined and yipped as it gingerly stepped from the raft. The sight stabbed into Gunther, as he sorrowed over the agony of the creature, as well as the death of its comrade, both the result of his choosing to become involved in the world of humankind again.

Gunther stared after the limping Jaghun as he set his feet upon the ground, and set off along the shoreline, listening to the echoes of distant voices and splashes, as large bodies broke the surface of the lake. Sound moved so very differently in the depths of the caverns than it did on the surface, but his ears had already begun to meticulously separate individual noises within the subterranean world.

Skirting a few Unguhur youth who were running along the edge of the lake, he continued up to the wide, rock-carved steps leading towards the lower level of the mass of terraced, stacked dwellings. The way had already become familiar to him, and he made no mistakes in finding the chambers that had been given over to the use of the refugees.

He left the Jaghuns with their other brethren in a lower chamber. His return had ignited a rush of enthusiasm, as the younger ones eagerly yapped at his heels, wagging their tails excitedly in their outright oblivion to his exhausted condition. He could not find it in him to begrudge their affectionate kindness, as he leaned over, rubbing and scratching their little heads for a few moments.

His face still remained expressionless, no matter how hard he wished to force a smile. The young Jaghuns were fortunate creatures in a way, as they had not registered the loss of one of their number, and would not bear the same pain that Gunther carried in his heart.

Moving carefully, as the youthful Jaghuns continued tussling about his legs, he moved over to the center of the chamber and ascended the ladder up to the next level. He shuffled forward across the roof and continued into the opening of the chamber in front of him. Once inside the entryway, he leaned his longbow against the wall to the right, setting his quiver down on the stone floor next to it.

Dire fatigue was swiftly enveloping him, as every muscle in his body seemed to constrict. He paused for a moment, his normally powerful body now swayed with a severe paucity of energy. He slowly removed his baldric, and let it clatter to the floor, with his sword still sheathed in the attached scabbard.

He slumped down upon the mats spread across the stony

floor. He did not even bother to pull the hide coverings over him, as he collapsed in a tired heap. In just moments, he was mercifully sent adrift into the numbing ocean of a dreamless sleep.

It was a tiny respite granted by his drained physical and mental condition. A thousand new personal demons had been created that day, adding their numbers to the legions that had existed before. A host of sleepless nights and nightmares pounded at the gates of his mind, but the abyss of unconsciousness had him confined for a few, short, precious hours.

The time passed altogether too quickly. As if echoes from another world, faint voices reached out to him through the murky depths of black sleep. The voices reminded him of the world that he had left behind, calling him back to cognizance.

When he became aware of them, his first impulse was to ignore them, and give himself over to the darkened embrace of forgetfulness. His world had been turned upside down, and his soul was spinning out of control in the midst of the horrors that he had done everything to avoid. The gray mists of nothingness beckoned invitingly, and there was even a part of him that did not really care if he ever woke up into the terrible world he had left behind.

Yet like a last ember stoked by a breeze, the part of him that was resolute and persevering heard the distant, clarion calls. Though only having a shred of willpower to grasp onto, that latter part of him clenched onto it with an iron grip. He willfully made the gradual ascent back into full consciousness, emerging the victor over the swirling, debilitating impulses that fought for control within him.

What had sounded like crisp voices belonged to one source, which rose steadily in clarity and volume, as he left the haven of oblivion. At the end, as he was on the cusp of waking, the sound filled his head like a booming din, conjuring a biting ache inside his head.

"What!" he barked out irately, mustering a burst of aggravated energy.

He heard the sound of shuffling feet, as someone moved backwards across the stone floor.

"Gunther?" inquired a startled, soft voice from the dim shadows beside him. It took Gunther a moment to register that the voice belonged to the outlander named Lynn. "Gunther, I really need to speak with you. I'm so sorry for waking you … but it is important. I promise I would not have done it otherwise."

A part of him wanted to lash out, and command her to leave him alone. Fatigue had eroded his already thin patience for the travails of others, especially those that he had already paid a great price for.

He could not deny that there was an edge to her voice, which told him right away that something was indeed very wrong. He had awoken to find himself cast right into another dilemma. The world was relentless in its merciless cruelty.

Almost hating himself for it, he knew that he was the one choosing to embroil himself continually in the things that he had expressly sought to avoid. Gunther had arrived in the woodlands of western Saxany with a precise, dedicated purpose, when he had used axe and adze to cut the first timbers of his remote, woodland dwelling.

The gruff woodsman took a deep breath to temper the scathing fires of agitation that had arisen in him. Of the four outlanders, Lynn was definitely not the one that would be prone to needlessly rousing him. The young, headstrong male, and the moody female, Ryan and Erin, were much more likely to do something like that. The realization of that contrast was just enough to help him regain a vague semblance of rational control over his embattled emotions.

"What is it, Lynn? What is so important" he muttered thickly, through dry lips.

Slowly, he opened his eyes, the lids feeling as if they were made of stone. He gave a silent prayer of thanks to the All-Father, that the bright rays of daylight were not able to penetrate through the caverns to his sleeping quarters.

He could see the wide-eyed expression on Lynn's face, and her hands were clenched together in front of her, faintly shaking.

"I think that Ryan and Erin left the caverns," Lynn told him, following a nervous pause, before she drifted off again into silence.

The words struck Gunther fully awake, as if a whip had been lashed against his bare skin. He sat up with an abrupt start, causing Lynn to flinch.

"Gone? What happened? How do you know for sure?" he asked quickly, almost blending the questions together in his haste for immediate answers.

The sudden urgency produced a throbbing ache and dizziness within his drained head.

"They both have left this city," Lynn replied. A look of worry and sorrow was prevalent upon her face, as he stared at her. "They wanted to go to the surface, to see the day again. Maybe it's our fault, as Lee and I talked about how nice it was to breath the open air again, when you took us above earlier.

She looked down at the ground forlornly.

"What else? Do you know anything at all about where they went?" Gunther prodded her.

Slowly, Lynn brought her eyes back up, though she had not ceased her trembling.

"They told us that there was probably nothing to worry about ... the battle above was over, and that there were other places in the forest that wouldn't have enemy forces. They really believed there wouldn't be any real danger above right now.

"Then they left, and were gone for a long time. Lee and I tried looking for them. We couldn't find them, and then we got the help of the Unguhur. They put a search out, and found one who had guided Ryan and Erin on the underground streams, to a place where there is a passage that took them out to another part of the forest."

Gunther shook his head, as he bitterly cursed his ill fortunes, his mounting irritation spreading abundantly across the features of his face. His countenance darkened, as he thought of the foolishness that so many people always seemed so eager to embrace.

Ignorance combined with stubbornness had brought a great number of people to their doom over the course of humankind's history. Gunther had long ago stopped trying to fathom the rationale by which fools set about their ill-advised tasks, especially within the confines of his own land and time. Gunther was not about to start trying to understand foolishness brought over from a strange, unknown world, one that he had not even heard of until his encounter with the four now in his care.

Though he knew that neither Ryan nor Erin were anything like himself, he could not help but imagine what his own decisions would have been like, if he had been one of them. Had he been taken to another world against his will, and found himself blessed with a guide and protector, one that knew both the nature and land of that strange new world, he would have likely remained on his knees in extended thanksgiving to the All-Father. He would never have questioned anyone who kept him safe in the midst of an unfamiliar world, especially one caught up within widespread wars and turmoil.

Muttering further curses under his breath, he forced himself to stop worrying about what he would have done. The decision made by the two outlanders had never been his. No amount of agonizing over what would have been his own choice would change the circumstances.

"Then I suppose we must find them," Gunther responded matter-of-factly, for there was nothing else sufficient to say, and he was not going to take out his ire on the messenger.

"What can we do?" Lynn asked him.

"Not much, but their idiocy will be putting others in trouble … myself, perhaps the Unguhur, and perhaps yourself and Lee," Gunther said with grim certitude. His tone then sharpened. "Do not forget that, if you ever ponder such foolhardy notions."

Lynn shook her head emphatically. "No, Gunther. I'm sorry. Please don't think that we don't appreciate you. Erin and Ryan are being very rash, and what they've done is their choice alone. One is still young, and the other I can't understand sometimes. But it's certain that both of them are being very, very stupid."

"Rash and stupid … either reason can get you killed in these woodlands, even if there were no invading army," Gunther remarked darkly, though not intending to mock her assertions.

Slowly, he drew himself up into a sitting position, and cringed with the motion. He would have thought such stiffness of body and muscle to be for someone twice his age. He moaned softly, as all extremities of his joints, and all the length of his muscles, seemed to cry out at once. It had been a long, long time since he had taxed his body to such an extreme.

The causes for his body's weakened state flashed through his head. The war had not been of his own making. It was not of the Saxans' making either, but he had foresworn taking part in the conflicts of kings and empires.

He had paid dearly for the several hours spent over the course of a couple hellish days, sifting through the numerous bodies. On countless occasions, he had lifted dead corpses, some still in their mail armor, to uncover others beneath, as he made certain that any who still had even a frail breath of life in them were not abandoned.

In some way that he could not yet fully fathom, the urgency of that horrible task was somehow expected of him, if he considered himself a true follower of the All-Father. Now, faced with responding to yet more ill-advised follies, something similar was being asked of him. As tired as he was, there was nothing to do but respond.

Gunther winced again as he stood up on his sore feet, still in the leather shoes whose soles were now nearly worn to their end. He leaned back, and twisted side to side, trying to ease the cracks and pops out of his weary body. There was little else to do but to put on his baldric, which was the only thing he had taken off when he had returned to Oranim. Even his belt, with his seax and affixed pouches, still remained wound around his dirty tunic, just above his breeches.

When he was finished stretching, he looked over at Lynn, who was standing patiently. At the very least, he could console himself that she had not been acting foolishly, and that she shared his ire towards the others.

"Let us go find those two fools," he said, striding past her and out through the chamber's entry way. "But do not expect me to give them a warm welcome when we find them."

"I don't plan to give them a warm one either," Lynn replied.

When they exited the chamber, he saw Lee standing at the far edge of the rooftop, looking out over the underground city. Lee turned towards them as he heard them emerge, a drawn, tired look on his face.

"I didn't know that they would be dumb enough to leave on their own," Lee said, with an undercurrent of apology.

"People make their own choices," Gunther retorted, pausing a second before adding, "and they are responsible for those choices. So if they come to an ill end before we reach them, then they are the only ones to blame."

Neither Lee nor Lynn contradicted him, both continuing to look very downcast.

"We will not delay further. Take me to the fellow who guided them to the passageway," Gunther said, walking over to the opening in the roof where the ladder descended down to the next chamber. His Jaghuns, having heard his approach, were already stirring, and milling around the base of the ladder.

Gunther fingered the hilt of the sword at his side, perhaps for emphasis, as he paused at the top of the ladder. "Out in these forests, there are many creatures that can endanger your life. If you go, we stay close together. Is that clear?"

One glance told him that he had their full cooperation.

With the remaining mature, healthy Jaghuns in his wake, Gunther strode down towards the shoreline. Regaining his stride, Gunther outdistanced the other two easily, prompting them to break into a mild jog just to catch up with him.

They did not have far to go, as Lee and Lynn pointed out the particular Unguhur that had conveyed Erin and Ryan to the passageway leading to the world above. It took a couple of moments to board all of them, Jaghun and human, and they set off across the lake. They worked their way to an area of the cavern located far to the right of the tunnel leading back to the underground forest beneath Gunther's abode.

The Jaghuns appeared eager for the adventure, as they paced the drifting rafts. At a few points, they cast fidgety looks towards a pair of immense gallidils, cruising slowly along the surface in the vicinity. One was a behemoth of its kind, so large that it drew wary glances from their Unguhur guides. The huge creature possessed a back as wide as the raft, and a length that was many times longer than the watercraft.

The scaly giant paid them little heed, intent on gliding to other parts of the underground lake, and the streams and rivers beyond, where bountiful fish and other creatures supplied the needs of its considerable appetite.

They finally entered the stream exiting the right side of the cavern. The ceiling of the passageway was much lower than the one leading to the underground forest was, such that the tall Unguhur had to crouch as they worked their way down the smaller channel.

It was clearly a passage that was well-traversed by the Unguhur. There were many areas in the clefts, folds, and niches of the rock where the familiar bluish-light emitted from luminescent fungus patches cultivated to provide ambience. In the tighter confines of the tunnel, the light cast a strange pall over the water, raft, and travelers, as they continued on past several other offshoots and confluences over the course of a couple of leagues.

The Unguhur pilot presently slowed, and deftly navigated them off to the left as the passage widened on that side. He brought the raft to rest against a rough, thin shelf of rock at the stream's edge. A thick, pungent scent reached Gunther's nostrils, as they heard flitting sounds within the depths of the shadows above them.

Scattered about the upper ceiling of the adjacent small cavern were a fair number of bats. Gunther gestured to the others to keep their silence, not wanting to suddenly arouse the horde of tiny creatures nesting in the high reaches of the rocky ceiling.

The Unguhur gestured at an opening off to the left, accessible by the rock shelf. The opening was marked with more of the luminescent fungi. Gunther nodded in response, and signaled for Lynn and Lee to follow him. The Jaghuns were unloaded a moment later. The beasts stared upward towards the bats, though Gunther hushed them before they made any loud noises.

As they entered the passage to the surface, Gunther found that it was just big enough for a single Unguhur to move through. From the look of the two sides of the passage, it was also clear that some stone had been cut away, to further widen it.

After working their way through the damp passageway, ascending upwards on a pronounced incline, they found themselves in a small cave entrance that exited out of a hillside, just beneath a wide rock overhang.

The light of day again cascaded down through the leaves of the trees, the overhead sun having reached its zenith, at the summit of midday. Lynn, Lee, and even Gunther had to pause for a few moments, to take in several deep breaths of the fresh, clean air when they emerged from the cave's mouth. Gunther blinked and squinted as his eyes readjusted to the daylight.

The Jaghuns took to the natural settings with open enthusiasm. They were not creatures that could ever be entirely happy down in the dank, moist, shadowy underground world that the Unguhur had fashioned. They looked elated to be surrounded by forest and sky once again. They bounded sprightly down from the cave mouth, sniffing the air, trotting around the trees, and circling back to where Gunther and the others stood.

"I wish that I could let them run free for awhile," Gunther commented, watching the creatures with a little regret. "Perhaps we will find your companions soon, and this will all be nothing more than a nice respite for my Jaghuns."

His face did not crack a smile, as he looked around him. He took out some hemp-line, and set about restringing his longbow. As welcome as he found them, the woods were nonetheless a very unpredictable place, and precautions always had to be taken. It was not called a wilderness region without reason.

"I would think they would not go too far away," he continued. He finished stringing the bow, and called out some signals to the Jaghuns, making a deliberate, sweeping hand gesture towards the trees before them.

The Jaghuns fanned out wide in the area before the cave, lowering their muzzles and sniffing the ground diligently. Examining the bow, and tugging on its line, Gunther started down from the mouth of the cave towards them. The creatures then appeared to hone in upon one track in particular, and padded away towards the trees.

"Come, we have fools to find," he said to Lynn and Lee, before trotting off into the forest after the Jaghuns.

The Jaghuns' forms disappeared amidst the trees ahead, pulled forward by their broad snouts, rooting assiduously along the ground's surface to follow the distinctive scents that they had picked up.

FRAMORG

Framorg rarely slept soundly, but the night following the first day of battle had been entirely devoid of rest. There had been a meeting of the various commanders that had lasted well into the night.

His own initiative had been well recognized, as the Trogens had achieved at least a moral victory on the heels of the near disaster that had been incurred on the Andamooran left flank. Framorg did not doubt that his daring maneuver had injected a great wariness into the planning of the Saxans.

The collapse of the Andamoorans had caused a great shift in overall plans, as the Avanoran heavy cavalry had been suddenly diverted to stem the advance of the Saxans against the left flank of the allied forces. From what Framorg could assess, the failure of the Andamoorans was more of a result of robust, spirited Saxan fighting, than it was due to any shortcoming on the part of the northwesterners.

The Andamooran Emir's pride had still been stung greatly. At the evening's meeting, Abu Yaqub Battuta had listened quietly to the deliberations with a terse, angered expression upon his face, of kind that could only have been carved by great tensions inside of him. Framorg could understand the eminent man's look far better than any spoken words could have attested to.

With little purpose in vainly trying to pursue more rest, Framorg decided to take his warriors up into the sky a little earlier than the previous day. He harbored a little reticence, though, as they would be slightly exposed in the moments of time when they would be facing directly into the rising sun's first rays.

In the cool mists at the edge of morning, Framorg visited for a few private moments with his great Mountain Bear. Barondas was a living embodiment of Framorg's clan symbol, and the sight of the creature always gave him renewed inspiration. He gazed fondly upon the enormous form of the noble creature, which held a mind-boggling level of strength within its great bulk.

Framorg reflected that he would have to be like a Mountain Bear, if the second day was to be any different from the first. Strong, bold, and fearless, he would have to rise up, and confront all enemies, no matter their number.

He spoke a few words to the massive beast, stroking Barondas's fur affectionately, and giving it a few hunks of fresh meat that he received from a Trogen warrior who had procured it earlier, upon his order. Giving the creature a final pat on its flank, as the great bear finished off one of the ample pieces of meat, Framorg straightened up, and looked into the sky.

The day's light had just begun to form a crease on the edge of the eastern horizon, where the dark's barricades were about to be steadily pushed back by the ascent of the rising sun. The air was peaceful, as Framorg gathered and assembled his main force of Harrak-mounted Trogens.

The large force of Harraks flew out in orderly fashion with Framorg in the lead, as they streaked towards the frontal regions of the battlefield, passing over the assembling, awakening camp.

The main formations on the ground were already arraying for battle, settling into the three distinctive contingents, with the central Avanoran reserve set a modest distance behind the lines at the center. From the sky, Framorg could observe the deploying ranks easily enough, from flank to flank.

Nervous, frantic horn blasts suddenly resounded from the far right of the Trogen formation. Framorg bellowed out a sharp command that brought all of the Trogens to slow their steeds, into a disciplined hover. Framorg spurred Argazen around and darted off down the line of Harraks.

"The enemy sky steeds! They come!" a Trogen called out to him, pointing emphatically.

To Framorg's great amazement, the Trogen was pointing behind them, to the immediate south, off the right side of their airborne flank. True to the sky warrior's word, there was a throng of incoming enemy warriors visible in the distance, flying low, and rapidly approaching the outer edges of Ehrengard's encampment. It was a sizeable war band, but nothing remotely threatening to the masses of Ehrengardian fighters comprising the overall right flank of the allies.

The large force of Trogens in the sky with Framorg reacted quickly. They had just begun to start off to intercept the attack, when something tugged strongly at Framorg's mind. He snapped his head around, to gaze back down their lines to the direct north.

Instinct governed his action, as much as intuition informed it. In the dimness of the onset of dawn, what he was looking for was hard to see, but the enemy was doing exactly what he might have done, if he were in the same position as them.

Waves of enemy riders saddled upon Himmerosen were skimming just above the tree-line, far behind the Trogens' position to the left, coming in from the north. It was a much larger force than the one that had begun to divert the Trogen force to the south. The second, more numerous force would soon arrive over the open ground among the three main bodies of warriors, Andamooran, Avanoran, and Ehrengardian, and the powerful, concentrated Avanoran reserve positioned at the middle of the three formations.

"Downward! Do not stop!" Framorg called out with urgency, having full conviction in his rapid judgement.

He reached across and drew out his longblade as he guided his Harrak into an immediate, diagonal descent, building up a blurring speed that caused Framorg to tuck the longblade close into his body for the time being. He could will his steed to go no faster, and watched helplessly as the enemy sky riders swiftly closed the gap with their intended target.

Now behind the three frontal formations, the enemy riders banked sharply towards the west, as if they were one body. They hurtled down in the face of the central Avanoran reserve, clearly the planned destination for the large force, and also the reason for the smaller diversionary group.

Even worse, the sun's first rays were breaking directly in the faces of the allies. Framorg knew that it was no coincidence. Whoever commanded the enemy forces had timed the attack perfectly, and he could not help but admire the deftness of the strategy, and the precision of the execution.

The enemy sky riders fell upon the reserve ranks of the Avanorans with a vengeance. The claws and bites of their fierce, well-trained Himmeros steeds added to the mayhem, as the first Saxan fighters to make contact thrust their spears down vigorously into the stunned, blinded Avanorans.

Framorg found as he continued to descend that he could not begrudge his admiration for whoever had conceived the enemy's strike. It was truly a brilliant maneuver, heralding the presence of a very worthy adversary.

The light of the new day was now mercifully at Framorg's back, but he could see that the Avanoran reserve was in a terrible situation, as they stared directly into the sun. Blinded and thrown into chaos, the Avanorans scrambled erratically to respond to the deadly Saxan storm emerging right out of the sun's rays.

Framorg clenched his teeth, gripped the hilt of his longblade tightly, and suffered the seemingly endless moments that it was taking to reach the fray. There was little else that he could do. The Saxans had undertaken a daring ruse, and had caught even the Trogens by complete surprise.

WULFSTAN

Wulfstan and the other warriors edged forward cautiously on their bellies, to the crest of a small hill. When they had reached the top, Wulfstan and a couple of the others crept carefully forward the last few feet, and peered over.

His heart was beating a little closer to normal. The harrowing, winding journey to the hills outside the fortress in view before them had been accomplished successfully, even if done under the clouds of constant threat.

The small band of warriors that had traversed the forest was

STEPHEN ZIMMER

entirely made up of skilled woodsmen, all of whom knew how to survive, and move elusively, within a woodland environment. Some were men who were important enough to send in such a delegation, but none were of such importance that their failure would greatly hurt the Saxan defense out on the Plains of Athelney.

All were from the Select Fyrd, ceorls of different means who were known for their skills in tracking, hunting, archery, and other areas that could prove useful to the covert, risk-laden delegation. The largely beardless faces amongst the small war band indicated their younger nature, as the sojourn was fraught with a high level of stressful, tiring physical exertion, and had to be pressed forward with the greatest of haste.

Movement and concealment were of the highest priority, an increasing difficulty under skies regularly patrolled by the enemy's Trogen sky riders. The war band traveled very lightly, wearing no helm or mail shirt, either of which could glint inopportunely in the reflecting light of moon or sun. A few of the northerners wore ridged, forward pointing caps, but most let their hair flow freely.

Their woolen clothes were all of earthen, dull colors, off-whites and browns, the garments blending well with the shadows and trees of the woodlands that they traveled through. They carried only leather pouches at their waists, a single-edged seax, and their principle weapons, opting to leave their large round shields behind with their mail and helms, the shields a liability with their cumbersome size, and reflective iron bosses.

The night sky, with modest cloud cover, had capably shrouded their clandestine movements as they skirted around the territory being patrolled by the forces from Ehrengard. A couple of men who lived in the immediate region helped lead the group along the shadowy trails through the brush and trees of the thicker forest region located to the south and west of the battlefield.

There were no herepaths in the younger woodlands, by which an army could march through, and the forest itself presented an obstacle to a large force. It had been left that way long ago, so that any armies threatening the Saxan lands would be forced into the Plains of Athelney, or be made to face a highly vulnerable, plodding passage through the dense forest growths.

While the invaders had sent raiding and foraging parties into the area, the Saxans' intimate knowledge of the forest lent a great advantage to the small war band. Those that were native to the land knew the natural pathways that enemies would have had to scout out endlessly, so as not to be stuck within an obstructive labyrinth of thorns and brush. With a surety of direction, the Saxan war band was able to maintain a brisk pace, covering well more than four leagues through the thick forest-growth.

The stout fortress belonging to the alloidal lord Godric now stood before their eyes, at journey's end. The fortress's high, palisaded walls crowned a tall earthen rampart that sloped sharply downward, completely ringing the circular perimeter. It was a fort designed in the old way, reflecting methods of the former Southern Kingdom. Four gates set at equal distances from each other pierced the fortress, effectively dividing the interior into wedge-shaped quarters.

Within the main walls of the fortress, they could identify a more streamlined enclosure, filled with a variety of timber buildings with sharply-sloped roofs. A large hall with gable ends stood out prominently amongst all of the sundry buildings, a structure that Wulfstan surmised was the main hall of Godric himself. A number of guards bearing spears, and a few with curving longbows that were strung and at the ready, could be seen walking slowly along the inner perimeter of the palisade-crowned rampart.

The final instructions given to the Saxan warriors involved the existence of a specific underground tunnel, one that all of their hopes rested on. The information also imparted some of the history and lore of the fortress to Wulfstan, and those others of the group who were not from the immediate area.

The fortress might have been bequeathed as a freehold in past times, but one small aspect of its construction had been acutely remembered, and passed down quietly, within a few certain families in the Saxan Kingdom. That carefully transferred heritage of knowledge was about to demonstrate its value.

Wulfstan had to concede that the storied southern king Clovis II had possessed excellent foresight in the moment that he had initially bestowed the fortress and lands upon Conrad the Ironheart. In the instance that a day of treachery or grave threats beckoned towards the larger kingdom, if the freehold was ever held by someone as suspect in their integrity as Godric, Clovis II had taken a precaution. He had seen to it that the future generations would have a valuable piece of knowledge at their behest, to utilize during a dark hour such as the present time.

If the tunnel was still fully in place, and had not ever been discovered and blocked by its occupiers, the continued diligence of a small group of related nobles down the long ages would have made possible a gift of hope to the present Saxans. It was now undeniably the darkest hour that the Saxans had ever faced, and each possible advantage at hand was worth more than many towering piles of silver.

"The question is simply where the tunnel entrance is, exactly," Wulfstan said in a low voice to the men close at his side.

"Should we spread out now?" a warrior on his left side asked. "We know the general area."

"Not yet," Wulfstan said, shooting a serious glance at the warrior. "We need to watch this place, closely, for as long as we can spare. From what we have come to know of this Godric, there are no certainties regarding his loyalties. They may have already been given to our enemies, and we need to see if we can tell."

The other warrior nodded to him in apparent agreement, and went back to a mode of silent observation. Over the course of the next hour, as the morning sun crawled ever higher into the sky, the small group of Saxans remained almost motionless, in their places on the hill's summit.

Wulfstan's eyes scanned the wide, open ground surrounding the base of the fortress, studying the land and its features carefully. To the immediate west of the fortress, there were cleared fields that likely belonged to the nearest village. There was no sign of any activity within the fields, which did not surprise Wulfstan entirely. The villagers were likely to have gone into hiding at the presence of such vast armies as those now invading Saxany.

The villagers were wise to choose seclusion in any instance. Whether an army in the vicinity was friend or foe, there were always individuals within any force who were both capable and willing to commit atrocities, such as spilling blood over a little bread, a haunch of meat, or a cask of ale. That did not even begin to take account of the pervasive lusts of humankind that erupted viciously within the chaos of a war.

Men with shadowy hearts tended to swiftly avail themselves of the breakdown of order, escaping from their own hatred of life by visiting great evils upon others. The harsh reality was that the value of life always tumbled precipitously during a time of war, and Wulfstan could not begin to find fault in those who still valued it enough to flee.

As for himself, he valued life as much as they did, but knew that he was both readily able and highly motivated to strike back against those who did not. Not everyone in possession of good intentions could be said to be in such a position, mostly due to a lack of necessary skills.

It was a regrettable truth borne out over long ages of warfare. Many a peasant villager had the inspiration to oppose barbarity, but few had the capability. Such a reality had resulted in a sad litany of tragedy, filled with flames, gorged lusts, and blood.

Off in the distance to the east of the fortress there was a large contingent of mounted warriors coming within sight, with pennons flying from the ends of several of their lances. The mass of riders were still at a far enough range that Wulfstan could not make out the specific designs on the pennons, but he was all but certain as to whom the riders belonged to.

Another hour passed by, with no significant activity perceptible around the fortress. Godric's men kept pacing along the wall-walks, and several individuals could be seen moving among the buildings within the enclosure, but there was nothing to indicate the presence of anything unusual.

A few of the men in the band of Saxans began to get edgy as time passed, looking up regularly towards the cloud-streaked skies for signs of enemy sky riders. Wulfstan then heard the light shuffling of cloth against the dew-dampened grass, just as he felt a body pull up right beside him.

"What do you wait for?" Cenwald whispered to Wulfstan. "The longer we stay, the greater the chance we may be discovered."

"I am waiting for certainty. It would appear that few trust this Godric," Wulfstan replied evenly, glancing over to Cenwald. He then added, "And we should not become lax in this. We may be free now, but we are far from our encampment and army, and the moment that we go into that fortress we will place ourselves in Godric's power. Let us first see in whose influence that power lies."

Whether Cenwald's growing impatience invoked something or not, the sight of a broad shadow crossing the expanse of ground before the hill subsequently grabbed their attention. The dark patch glided along the ground's surface, moving speedily towards the fortress.

Looking upward, Wulfstan espied the distinctive form of an

armed Trogen mounted upon a Harrak. The sky rider was coming in at a very low altitude from the east, where the armies of the Unifier were fiercely engaged with the massed Saxan forces.

The position of the Saxan observers on the hilltop was a fortuitous one, as they were located almost directly to the south of the fortress. With the upper contour of the hill that they were prostrate behind, they were afforded a good measure of concealment, and were well-hidden to the eyes of the low-flying rider.

The sky rider would have only caught sign of them if he had been carefully scanning the hilltop, but the summit was clearly of little concern to the Trogen. The sky rider's eyes were fixed ahead on the fortress, as the Harrak swooped in on a fairly level plane.

The Harrak then angled even lower, as the rider guided the creature down sharply. The sky steed came within bow-shot of the high ramparts at last, without its rider showing any kind of care, or even signal of some kind. Significantly, no alarm was forthcoming from within the fortress either, nor were any arrows loosed in defense of it.

The guards on the walls paused in their walking for a moment, idly watching the Harrak's passage just over their heads into the midst of the fortress. Rider and steed disappeared from Wulfstan's sight as they landed upon the ground within the inner fortress, close to one of the four gates.

"There, some other riders," Cenwald then whispered, a little excitedly, drawing Wulfstan's attention towards about a half-dozen figures mounted on horseback that were sauntering up the winding path leading to the eastern gate.

One of the men was flying a pennon near the blade end of a long spear. The pennon was largely rectangular in shape, with the longest edge vertical. From the side opposite the spear shaft, there were three, elongated, triangular tendrils that streamed out to their endpoints. Most of the pennon was yellow in color, save for a vertical blue strip that formed the right edge of the rectangular portion. The middle of the triangular extensions was also that same blue color, the other two being yellow.

"Avanoran," Wulfstan murmured to Cenwald tensely, taking note of the pennon whose appearance and coloration he had so recently learned about, under very life-threatening circumstances.

He watched as the gate swung open to allow the riders unimpeded access to the interior of the fortress. The calm, unopposed entrance of the sky rider and the mounted warriors into the fortress made a clear, unobstructed statement concerning the situation at hand. It told Wulfstan everything that he needed to know, confirming the worst of his fears.

"That explains everything, and answers the certainty that I sought," Wulfstan said in a low, edgy voice, the lines on his neck popping above the skin's surface, as he clenched his jaw in hot irritation. All of the fears and rumors that he had ever heard about Godric had manifested before his eyes. "You see, caution is sometimes very advised. Now we know that a traitor is surely at hand."

Wulfstan fell into a stony silence, passing on the word for all of the others to wait just a little longer. There would be no need to send any sort of delegation to the perfidious lord, but there was always need for information on an enemy.

All of the years that Saxany had allowed Godric, and those who preceded him, running all the way back to Conrad the Ironheart, to flourish, had counted for absolutely nothing in the darkest of hours. When the entire Saxan realm was under grave threat, and needed the loyalty of the allodial freehold the most, Godric had discarded the years of support, friendship, and trade, on a calculated gamble.

The realization was maddening, and a burning desire for retribution coalesced inside Wulfstan. He began to foment a rough idea involving the tunnel, one that just might deliver Godric the reward that he so richly deserved for his duplicity. Wulfstan was not a commander in the group, such that he could order any attack, but he could put forth a suggestion for the others to consider. Having a good idea of the mettle of the men who he had traversed the forest with, he felt that there was a good chance that any workable idea to strike a blow at Godric would be well-received.

Wulfstan had to think quickly, but he did so clearly, and without any inner conflict, as there was no doubt as to what side Godric had cast his lot with. The tunnel had to be found very soon, and fires would have to be started swiftly from within.

Food supplies would be the most valuable target, as Godric had likely hoarded a substantial supply from the nearby villages under his dominion. Wulfstan knew that it would not go to the people on Godric's land, but would feed the hunger of the invaders. The timber buildings that served as stores for such foodstuffs and supplies would have to be identified before the Saxans moved into the fortress.

Keeping to his belly, Wulfstan began to back down the hill, in order to summon the war band together. There remained a matter of consensus, before any final evaluation of the fortress's buildings and layout could take place for a possible raid. Agreement to a strike on the fortress would also decide the necessity of searching out the tunnel entrance.

He had gotten no more than a couple body lengths down the slope when Cenwald's agitated voice called out to him from above.

"Wulfstan, more come, quickly, get up here!" Cenwald whispered hurriedly, looking fleetingly back to him, and gesturing sharply for him to come back up with impetus.

Wulfstan got to his hands and knees, and scurried up the short length, forsaking meticulous caution and falling flat on the ground next to Cenwald. He peered back in the direction of the fortress.

"Up, there, to the right," Cenwald directed him, pointing. "Look at that!"

Like a cloud breaking up into several tendrils, a massed contingent of Trogen sky riders were rapidly descending from the upper skies. They were approaching along a similar route to that of the lone rider that had arrived just moments before.

"The new day is bringing many surprises," Wulfstan muttered darkly, keeping his eyes fixed on the scene unfolding before him.

As if instinctively, Wulfstan's eyes shot back over towards the place where the small group of horsemen had been sighted. His eyes alighted upon another, much larger force of mounted riders, just a second before Cenwald urged him to look upon the newly-arriving, swiftly moving contingent.

A realization dawned on him, even as Cenwald called his attention to the fact that the horse riders were cantering as a full body directly towards the eastern gate of the fortress. The rumbling of the steeds' hooves pounding across the ground flowed like a muffled thunder.

A large number of the incoming Trogens swarmed around the same gate that the horse-mounted force was heading towards, and faint cries of alarm erupted suddenly from the wall-walks. There was no time to gather any significant defense, as Godric's men had plainly been caught unawares. A raid was taking place, though not one that Godric or his men had apparently expected.

Harraks dipped and swooped around the wall-walks, while others dropped down behind the wall. A few others broke away to beset other areas of the wall-walk, darting and flying about the high ramparts.

The tall wooden gates then slowly swung open from the inside, as the horse riders continued their approach along the ground. Drawing closer to the fortress, the riders shifted from a canter to a full gallop as they streaked towards the opening. They were now close enough for Wulfstan to see that the pennons flying in the riders' midst were identical to the ones carried by the small group that had freely entered just moments prior.

The light of day gleamed off helms, mail, and weapons, the sparkling, deadly stream coursing uninhibited towards the gaping entrance. The mass of riders covered the last expanse of ground swiftly, and with lances lowering the lead elements issued through the open gate, virtually unopposed.

The clash of arms and shouts of fighting had broken out from within, but it would be no contest. Wulfstan knew that Godric's men were doomed. In a lightning strike, the Trogens and horse-mounted warriors were seizing the fortress, and everything within it. There would be no bartering, as Godric probably had hoped. The fortress was a possible liability that the enemy was not going to tolerate, not to mention the inviting prospects of acquiring sizeable stores of foodstuffs and other supplies. Godric had been deceived, even as he had deceived the Saxans.

The need to search for the entrance to the old tunnel was rendered unnecessary, almost at the same moment that the tunnel's continued functionality was revealed. Three figures appeared to hastily emerge from the very earth, as an opening suddenly manifested well beyond the fortress's high ramparts to the south, right before the eyes of the Saxan observers.

Breaking into a run, as if pursued by a pack of wolves, the three figures raced across the open ground just to the west of Wulfstan's position. They carried swords and shields with them, and he had a deep-seeded suspicion as to who would be among the first to flee the attack.

Reflexively, and spurred by his great ire, Wulfstan stood and bounded off to the west, racing along the top of the ridgeline. He put himself on a direct line to intercept the three warriors, whom he guessed were heading for the refuge of the wild forestlands spread just in back of the Saxan position. Wulfstan altered his course slightly, to descend behind the crest of the ridge, so that the oncoming trio would not be able to see him.

The three men aided his cause, as they called out to each other several times in panicked exhortation on the other side of the hill. Honing in upon their voices, Wulfstan adjusted his approach until he was certain that he was in their path. He lowered himself into a crouch, waiting and listening carefully to the gasps, grunts, and heaving breathing of the three men scrambling to climb up the slope on the other side.

The three men nearly tumbled over the top of the ridgeline in their manic haste. They were feverish in demeanor, choked with fear, and gasping for air, such that they were a little off balance as their forms were outlined starkly against the morning sky.

Wulfstan moved quickly, thrusting his leg out at the nearest man, who tripped over his shin and crashed into the ground. The sudden impact provoked an audible gasp, as the air was knocked out the surprised warrior. The man's hands opened up, and his sword and shield went flying out from his grip.

The other two men had run right by Wulfstan's position, staggering and striding down the hill as they picked up speed and struggled frenetically to keep their balance.

Wulfstan scurried forward and pressed his right knee down heavily into the middle of the fallen warrior's back. He used his left knee to pin the man's left arm down, while using his right arm to immobilize the man's right. His free left arm clutched his seax tightly, the point placed at the base of the fallen man's neck.

"Hold! Hold!" the man cried out desperately, as the point of Wulfstan's seax elicited a small drip of blood from where the sharpened tip pressed down into his skin. The man then stammered, "I am Godric, of nobility, I can pay you."

Wulfstan could not suppress an ironic smile. "You do not look so noble to these eyes, though I believe you will pay dearly."

Speaking one of the five main dialects used in the northern areas of Saxany, Wulfstan drew a quick response from Godric.

"You are a north Saxan? Get me back to the lines, quickly. We have been overcome, invaded," Godric sputtered out.

"You are coming with us, as you are going to answer for your treason against us," Wulfstan said, letting his weight press heavier on his knees. Godric groaned in pain underneath him.

Wulfstan's single-minded focus on Godric might have exposed him to danger, as he had completely forgotten about the other two warriors that had raced by him. Fortunately, both would be of little consequence, as they had been surrounded and confronted by several of Wulfstan's fellow warriors, who had followed in his wake after he had raced down the ridgeline.

Cenwald had a big smile on his face, as he held a spear point towards one of Godric's companions. "What do you think we should do with them?"

"I was not expecting to take prisoners, but we are not going to let these three walk away. Killing this one would be too much of a mercy. Get this dung pile bound and gagged, right away, as well as those two, with whatever we can find to bind them well," Wulfstan spat out with disgust, voicing an order that the others were all too happy to oblige with.

As their belts were being used for pouches, seax sheaths, and the like, the Saxans had to get a little creative. Cenwald grinned, as he slipped his seax out from his sheath, and set about unwinding the fabric strips that were bound tightly around the lower length of his trousers. "I've got my wininga, Wulfstan. I think that I can live with some loose folds about my legs for the march back."

Using the seax, he cut the long strips where needed, and soon had fashioned both bindings and a gag for Wulfstan's principle prisoner. Some more material came from a couple of the other warriors, and the three prisoners were soon well-secured, with only their legs freed up for the return journey.

"There is nothing more we can do here, let's get moving and press hard for our lines," Wulfstan urged, as soon as they were done with the prisoners.

The band of Saxans headed back for the woods, moving to the south, away from the ridge. Though tired, they had gotten a little respite while waiting on top of the ridgeline. The couple of men who knew the forest well moved to the forefront to serve as guides.

The march back was conducted a little quicker, as visibility was far better than at night. The men with the prisoners had no problem prodding them forward, and the group made steady progress on the circuitous route back towards the waiting sanctuary of the Saxan lines.

Though the journey back was undertaken at a brisk gait,

Wulfstan's mind drifted towards thoughts of the ongoing battle, and the strange dreams that he had been having. His eyes looked up to the sky, wherever it showed through the wider breaks in the tree branches.

He went through scenario after scenario in his head, hoping that he could think of some way to envision the turning of the tide of battle. There just had to be some shred of hope to cling to, a ray of light to offset the darkness of the withering attrition that Wulfstan feared the Saxan forces were encompassed by.

Yet try as he might, his heart grew heavier after the morning's events. The Saxan prospects had just gotten worse.

Godric's fortress was now firmly in enemy hands, bringing a prodigious quantity of stored food, the fruits of the combined labor of many surrounding fields and villages, into the hands of the invaders. The fortress would also serve as a solid base, as it was far larger than many of the outposts dotting the western marches of Saxany, and was situated so ideally in relation to the Plains of Athelney.

As he was mired in his melancholy thoughts, the Saxans then skirted a large clearing, one where Wulfstan gained a clear, unobstructed look up into the sky.

A steady procession of clouds was lazily drifting by overhead. The clouds came in a variety of masses and lengths, broken by patches of silken, open sky, but it was a more distant, distinctive sight that suddenly drew his gaze. His eyes focused right in upon it, even as a light-headed feeling passed over him.

To most, even among those with farseeing eyes, it would have looked like just another layer of clouds. In comparison to the mass of the lower layers, it was much farther up, and beyond any reasonable level that any veteran sky warrior would have even dared to fly.

Wulfstan drew to a rigid halt for a few moments, peering fixedly upwards, as a tingling sensation passed throughout his body. The Saxans around him continued onward, although a few stared at him quizzically as they passed by.

Hunting had long ago taught him the value of keeping a steady, observant gaze, of the nature that would reveal even the slightest of movements against an immobile background. The skies were far from being like a deer moving against a still background, consisting of forest undergrowth and trees. It was a very different kind of vision spread above him. Yet the solid, unbroken, aqua sky enabled Wulfstan to ably contrast the lower cloud levels with the higher plane; the one that contained the conspicuous element that had so suddenly grasped his attention, and sent his head to the verge of spinning.

The lower clouds continued along on their gentle passage, as did a second formation of clouds that could be distinguished just a little higher up than the first. They were passing towards the east, buoyed forward by the air currents coming up from the southwest.

Wulfstan kept his eyes affixed studiously to the sight, focusing on the visible movements of those cloud layers, as the full force of undeniable cognizance struck him profoundly.

Well beyond the second formation of clouds was a white patch that was perceptibly moving in an altogether different direction than the cloud layers below it. It was also moving at a much slower rate, almost as if the amorphous white mass was not in motion at all, but Wulfstan's trained eye could detect a very slight drift towards the north. The movement contrasted visibly with the motions of the cloud layers far beneath it. He had seen that distant white mass before; for many years, in fact.

"Wulfstan, let us get back," Cenwald interjected, having returned from the front of their group, to come stand at his side.

Wulfstan broke his gaze away momentarily and looked over, seeing that the others had all moved past him. He understood that Cenwald likely reflected the opinions of many in the small band. He did not doubt that they were all very impatient to return to the Saxan lines at the Plains of Athelney.

All of them, Wulfstan included, desired the comparative safety of the massed Saxan armies, as opposed to marching through woodlands that were most likely being infiltrated and scouted by enemy war bands, of much greater size than their own.

Wulfstan glanced past Cenwald's shoulder, to where a few of the other Saxans bringing up the rear of their short column had come to a stop. Several strides beyond Cenwald stood a lean, limber warrior named Eadric, who hailed from the westernmost edges of Sussachia. At Eadric's side was a stocky southern warrior who served in the western marches, a round-faced man named Eudes. Eadric's angular face was stoic in its appearance, but great anxiety was written openly across Eudes's wide face.

Eudes shared one of the more onerous tasks in the war band, that of guiding the Saxans to Godric's fortress and back. At the present time, Eudes's mission was relatively close to being immaculately fulfilled, without having lost so much as one man out of the entire group.

The achievement of such a successful conclusion to the sojourn was a real, imminent possibility, now easily within sight. That such an end was at hand would make any strains harbored by Eudes all the worse.

Everything was now viewed in light of the glaring reality that a large enemy force could have come upon the Saxan force at any point during the sojourn, and might yet at any given moment. The Saxan guide was definitely not eager to endure any delays, especially so tantalizingly close to the bloodless completion of their journey.

It was a sentiment that Wulfstan could readily appreciate, even if he had not closed his eyes to the harder, more discomfiting truths surrounding their delegated task. He had no illusions regarding how he and his companions were seen and valued, or what was expected of them, even if the ones that sent them did not openly admit, or recognize, the truth of it themselves.

The contingent of Saxans had been sent to learn whatever they could of the fortress and Godric's standing, risking little else but several ceorls, and a few capable peasants, in the eyes of those that commanded them. The mission was seen as a chance to uncover an opportunity to turn to the Saxan's advantage, without being in danger of incurring any significant losses. It was much more of an exploration, rather than a succinct expectation, which said much about the status of those who had been sent to pursue the endeavor.

Wulfstan viewed the whole ordeal much differently. In his own eyes, none of the individual warriors in the war band were in any way expendable. They were as valuable to him as the greatest count, ealdorman, thane, or even king, as he saw things.

None of those with him, though, no matter how much he valued their lives, would understand his sudden, compelling skyward distraction, empowered by years of vivid, recurring dream images. Neither would they be in much of a mood to make an effort.

He nodded slowly towards Eadric, Eudes, and Cenwald, as he did his best to come out of his seeming trance. "My apologies. Something drew my attention … but it is nothing."

Eadric nodded, with a slight smile breaking through his impassive mien. His voice was buoyant, filled to the brim with a youthful confidence. "No worries. I've been watching for sky raiders all through this march. I've seen nothing. With the battle on the plains, and the fortress taken, few will be looking for the likes of us … and it is not far till we are back."

"And we should get back as soon as we can," Wulfstan replied firmly, returning the smile in a friendly manner, while he started forward towards them. He could see the great relief on Eudes face, as they all turned to resume the march.

The group proceeded to pick up its pace, pushing and cajoling the three prisoners along with them. Wulfstan chanced a few more furtive glances up at the sky, whenever there was a break in the foliage above.

The brief glimpses he got of the sky were frustrating, as he could not get his mind off of the unusual, yet intimately familiar, white patch. A long, slow-moving embankment of clouds had momentarily obscured the peculiar mass, which seemed to be perched on the highest edge of the firmament.

He did not doubt himself for a moment, nor did he accept that the spectacle was any mere trick of the eye. The strange white patch was decidedly different from anything above in the skies. The faraway sight was something other than the regular clouds that he had observed countless times before; it was moving on its own force, in another direction.

The dreams and the stories that Wulfstan had known for so many years had now been conjoined with something visible and real. A rush of excitement rippled throughout his body, even as he wrestled with the absurdity he felt at taking the dreams and stories so seriously.

That white patch, ostensibly beyond reach in the sky, was the very image he had seen many times before in the embrace of deep slumbers. He had never been one to lie to himself, and he was not about to start now. The white patch represented something much more than any clouds, or other heavenly body. It beckoned to him as the place where great creatures of legend could be encountered, if such heights could ever be attained.

Through the years, he had always wondered if the repeating vision in his nights had been something triggered by the stories of the great, legendary entities whose symbol was still carried by the Saxan royalty. Whether folktales from a gleeman, or accounts written upon an old parchment affectionately saved in a monastery, the tales all agreed that the winged giants were still reputed to exist in dazzling abodes drifting far above the surface of the world.

Since their inception, the reputed abodes had never been intended to be reached by humans, or any living beings who inhabited the surface of Ave so far below. They were said to exist far beyond the highest clouds that the various Skiantha steeds, like the Himmerosen and Harraks, could reach.

The dwellings were said to be like distant islands in the sky, providing a haven for the undying beasts of ancient lore. Wulfstan knew that if the incredible beasts did truly exist, then they represented a great hope.

Most of their mythical kind were held to be benevolent. The stories spoke of how they were serving a self-imposed exile, which had been bound with the combined power of the great Wizards, in the early ages of the world.

It was said that the ones in the high havens were loyal to the Almighty, choosing to endure exile rather than to risk their standing before the Creator, following an ancient age of great upheaval and terrible wars. Wulfstan gleaned that the beasts feared becoming pawns of dark purposes, unknowingly being manipulated to serve the purposes of Jebaalos, rather than the Creator to whose allegiance they were pledged.

Such beings, as far as Wulfstan could see, had to have a keen sense of justice. There was no way that they would easily allow or tolerate innocent lands to fall completely under a malignant shadow, especially when they had banished themselves to avoid even the risk of such an occurrence.

He thought back upon the many dreams he had experienced over the long years. In his mind's eye, in the depths of many nights while his body was still, he had often soared from the surface of the world towards the same, beckoning white mass that his conscious eyes had now perceived. He always remembered a feeling of being driven by the gentle voice that permeated his mind, the one that he heard inside his entire being each and every time that he experienced the recurring dream.

'Bring them into the world.'

In many of the dreams, he had glanced downward, towards the ground, from his high vantage. The world underneath him was always revealed to be a maelstrom of smoke and fire, creeping menacingly, and unrelentingly, towards his homelands.

The white mass had always become blinding in its brightness, as he ascended at a rapid, increasing speed. The sensation of great warmth and peace had flooded through him, as if to reassure him that the ascent was something that he had to do.

What looked to be a white cloud mass from the ground never turned out to be clouds at all, but was instead a floating landscape of hills and undulating plains, of the purest white that he had ever laid his eyes upon. Everything there seemed to consist of a light, soft substance, which sank in a few inches with each step he took.

The dream always ended with an immense shadow looming over him, as he slowly turned around to look up towards a shiny, silvery creature of enormous proportions. What the creature was, he could not say, as he was always stymied in remembering the detail of that part of the dream.

In the dreams, the voice always faintly repeated the phrase once last time, 'Bring them into the world', before Wulfstan was returned back to waking consciousness.

He had spoken of the repeating dreams to Father Dunstan several times before. To his surprise, Father Dunstan had never laughed or scoffed at the unusual night visions, but had merely cautioned him to keep his wits, and sense of discernment.

According to Father Dunstan, there was nothing to say that the Almighty would not use dreams to communicate with a person, and, in fact, the older Sacred Writings carried many stories of such dreams. Yet there was nothing to confirm that it was a sacred message, and, as such, Father Dunstan wanted Wulfstan to be very careful. According to the priest, Jebaalos was also capable of working dark influences through dreams.

On one occasion, the priest did make a passing reference to a legend that the Elder were said to reside in a place fashioned out of some ethereal substance. Such an environment was interpreted to reflect the purity of the stringent covenant that the great beasts were said to have engaged in, so many years ago.

The echoes of that particular memory reverberated in Wulfstan's mind, as he agonized impatiently for the sprawling cloud mass overhead to pass by and reveal the white patch once again. A part of him felt that if he stopped looking for it, the patch might vanish.

"Is everything okay?" Cenwald inquired, with a very concerned expression on his face.

"Just deep in thoughts, nothing more," Wulfstan replied, forcing an amiable grin to his face as they continued onwards.

DRAGOL

Dragol stepped forward with cautious stealth, his eyes fixed upon the large animal lapping water at the natural basin just ahead of him. The long, white fangs of the creature flashed as its tongue dipped and flicked at the clear waters, where they pooled at the end of the waterfall. The waterfall itself obscured Dragol's current position, but he was very careful not to shuffle or scrape his leather shoes against the rock footing underneath him.

Massive of head and stout of shoulder, it was a beast that was constructed with incredible bodily power. Its sinewy, muscular legs hinted at a capability for explosive speed, as the talons at their end announced a capacity to inflict mortal wounds with one strike.

It was the second sizeable animal that Dragol had come upon in the woodlands, adding to his encounter with the small pack of Pahyna. There was only the singular beast this time, as opposed to the four Pahyna that had stalked him before, but there would be no easing of his vigilance.

Hunting a hunter was nothing new to Dragol, but it did lend much more caution to his approach. At the moment, he had the advantage of surprise, and he needed to retain it. Against a creature such as this, it gave him his best chance by far.

His position within the shallow cave was precarious. If he chose to remain silent, and try to avoid the creature, he was aware that there was always the possibility that it would still pick up his scent and come after him. If he did attack, he also understood that he had to bring it down immediately, or face a terrific struggle, whose final outcome was definitely not for certain. In the truest sense of the words, it was a simple matter of killing or being killed.

He had chosen his weapon, as the hilt of his longblade rested in the scabbard at his side. Slowly, he lifted his dagger up in his right hand. His target was much larger than the plump bird that he had slain earlier, which demanded an even more precise throw. He steeled his nerves. If he missed, or just wounded the predator, he would have to draw his longblade out with the quickest of haste.

Without a sound, he hurled the dagger at the creature's extended head. His aim was true, as the dagger thudded on impact, embedding itself deeply into the side of the beast's skull. The killing throw occurred so quickly that not the slightest sound came from the beast, except for the thump of its heavy body, as it collapsed on the spot where it had been standing.

Dragol drew his great longblade, trotted forward, and severed the head from the body as an extra precaution. He was not about to gamble with a creature as formidable as the one before him, and take the success of his strike for granted.

With swift efficiency, Dragol carved himself out some portions of meat from the carcass. He took time to fix a small fire, and prepare a few chunks of meat on a spit, keeping his eye on the surrounding woods just in case there might be more unwanted visitors. While the juices of the meat hissed and popped on the crude spit that he fashioned, he took up his position behind the waterfall again.

He breathed a sigh of relief. He should have kept in mind that a good watering site, such as the one he was resting in, would be an inviting location for predators. It was simply fortunate that he kept alert enough to have heard the creature padding out of the brush, before it began to drink from the pool.

Yet there was a favorable aspect to the encounter. At the very least, he would not have to go hunting or foraging in the immediate future.

A voice broke the silence, almost as soon as Dragol had settled into a comfortable position to survey the surrounding area.

"A good hunt!" called the exuberant voice of the old, white-bearded stranger. "The bounty of this land will provide food for your body. The bounty of other things will provide food for your spirit."

Dragol looked around quickly, raising his blade in defensive reflex. His eyes came to rest on the elderly traveler, right as the man moved out from the trees to his left. The man walked with a brisk, youthful gait towards the pool of water, his deep blue robes swishing the tops of the grass with each step. It was clear that he did not really need the gnarled, twisting walking staff that he carried with him.

"No danger ... no trouble, my friend," the man said calmly, before grinning, "Or have you forgotten about me so quickly?"

With a little embarrassment, the Trogen warrior realized that he was still holding his longblade up in a combat stance. Dragol also noticed that the old man had not so much as flinched when he brought the blade up. He lowered the blade, turning it and sliding the weapon back into its leather-covered sheath.

"I remember," Dragol replied, "And I had little choice with a creature like this. It was good fortune that I heard it coming, long before it reached the water."

"It was good that you did," the old man commented more seriously, looking to the remaining carcass. "Hyaeds are among the fiercest predators that these woods have to offer. It is good that you came across a lone one as well. While uncommon, they are known to hunt in packs."

Dragol inwardly shuddered at the thought of taking on a pack of such creatures alone.

"Perhaps you should get moving. It will not be long before scavengers want at this meat," the old traveler advised him.

"I was just about to eat a little of this meat, and go," Dragol stated, eyeing the tall, elderly man. "But it seems you have come back here. Can you tell me who you are yet?"

"Just an old fellow, traveling through these parts, on some business I have in these lands. And still no favorable outcome yet. Or perhaps my hopes should be in you. It would seem we still walk upon a similar path," the old man replied, with an amused grin.

"You pick a dangerous time to be doing anything. War is all about this place," Dragol remarked, as he walked back over to the roasting meat on the spit.

He took it off the fire, pulling out his dagger, as he turned back to face the old man. "I have plenty here. Surely you get hungry sometimes."

"You would suppose that I do, but I never seem to work up much of an appetite," the old man replied, as Dragol proceeded to cut off some smaller chunks of the meat. "But if you have a little wine, I would gladly accept that."

Dragol rumbled with laughter at the old man's remark about wine. He hardly bothered to chew the meat, as he put the first piece into his mouth, and followed it immediately with another chunk. He savored the flavor of each bite, instantly amenable to the taste.

"Good meat?" the old man queried. "I know a couple of gray

furred rogues that would gladly indulge in the rest of that carcass over there."

Dragol glanced curiously at the old man, who was now sitting cross-legged on the ground. "So wars do not concern you at all?"

"Wars are for the young. Surely an old man, with no weapons, and no chest of gold, or pouch filled with silver coins, is of little concern," the old man replied. "I just have this old walking staff. Should not be much of a threat to hordes of warriors with axes and swords."

"Then you know little of your fellow humans, once the bloodlust is upon them," Dragol commented darkly.

He did not bother to point out the fact that the old man was wearing a shining, golden ring that held a magnificent, luxuriant blue stone in it. The ring alone would evoke a response from marauding warriors bent on plunder and loot.

A somber expression then spread across the old man's face. "Perhaps I do, but I have means of dealing with such things ... or at least of avoiding such problems."

"Ever more questions," remarked Dragol irritably, cutting off another strip of meat for himself.

He thought back to the man's demonstrative vanishing amid a thousand shards of light. The old man was doubtlessly speaking the truth, but Dragol had a feeling that there was a lot more to the old man than just his disappearance amid a burst of light.

"Have you found more questions?" the old man responded inquisitively, a searching look in his single eye.

"Just a short while ago, I was asking the wind to take my plea for help to you," Dragol replied, wiping grease off his lower jaw with the back of his hand.

"And I may have even heard you," the old man replied, with a sparkle dancing in his eye.

"Then I will ask you one of the questions again now ... because if you did hear, I still have no answer. Why do you think I am anything more than what I am?" Dragol inquired, in a low, somber tone.

The old man smiled, as if inwardly amused with some thought that was percolating within him. "You are what you are, in truth. It is more of a matter of what you will reach out to do."

His gaze lowered to Dragol's chest. "That is a Thunder Wolf tooth, yes?"

Dragol nodded, and replied with a hint of melancholy. "We have relics of them, even if their howls can no longer stir our spirits in the night."

"Incredible creatures," the old man remarked.

"Do you know much of wolves?" Dragol asked him.

A bemused smile drifted across the old man's face. "Yes, wolves have been a very close part of my life. Both friend and foe."

"I have heard stories of the Midragardans … the ones that came up the rivers and settled among the people to the south of our lands, long ago," Dragol said. He noticed that the old traveler's eyebrow raised at the mention of Midragard. For the moment, he decided to keep the observation to himself. "I heard a story once about a great wolf, who wished to be a friend, but was betrayed and bound for all time."

"Yes, that is a tale well-known in Midragard," the old man stated, and there was a palpable tinge of sadness at the edges of his voice.

"We have a similar tale, of the first Thunder Wolf who befriended the Trogens. Only the ending is different, as we embraced the Thunder Wolves from the first day. They came down from the storm-shrouded mountains … and they lived among us, as we did among them," Dragol said, staring off into the woods, as the gentle forest breezes caressed his face. His heart always felt a little heavier when he spoke of the revered creatures who gave identity to his clan. "All of our own stories tell of incredible loyalty. They were our friends, they were steeds, guardians, and so much more."

He paused for a moment, and picked up the moon-shaped pendant in his hand, staring down at the wolf image and the sharp tooth situated within it.

"And this is what is left, after what the Elves have done to us. This is what drives us into this war," Dragol said, his voice taking on a harsher edge, with the saddened anger creeping towards the boundaries of his own psyche.

"So you fight in a war that is not of your liking?" the old man asked. "You fight against those who are not your enemies? I thought this was not the Trogen way."

Dragol's face darkened, in an abrupt flare of heated anger, which subsided a moment later as he thought further about the question. He responded as his ire simmered down. "When the first Trogens came into the world, the Elven kind already had built up their own lands, and sailed upon the seas. Before the first Harrak was tamed, the Elves had long been sky riders. I will match my courage and blade against any of them, but we have always been under a great burden.

"Build a ship? Thirty Elven warships would be there the moment it was put into the waters of the sea. Take twenty sky steeds, upon new riders, beyond our mountains? A hundred Elven warriors on sky steeds, with hundreds of years of training on them, would be upon us.

"Our kind had just begun to settle in our lands, when they came with warships, sky steeds, sorcerers, armor, and blades. We fight them hard now, within our lands, but until we can cross those seas in force, they will continue to hold many of us in bondage, laboring in their mines. They will continue to occupy lands that they took from us ... and they will continue to raid us, to keep us weakened, and diminished."

The old man seemed to become lost deep in thought as Dragol finished his answer. His gaze was still set towards the ground when he replied, almost under his breath. "Fair of countenance, and deadly of intent. Among the First Born of Ave, they feel they are greater in the Creator's eyes than the other high races of creatures. Such arrogance and power combined is indeed a dangerous thing. Dragol, I am very sorry for what your kind has gone through."

"Then you know why I fight this war," Dragol concluded starkly. "Even if it takes us on paths away from the Trogen way of things."

"And yet what have the tribal peoples of the Five Realms, or the Midragardans, ever done to the Trogen kind?" the old man riposted sharply, his gaze rising to grip Dragol within its strong embrace. "Is this war so unlike what the Elven kind have done to your race?"

Dragol felt a hot flush run through him again, though he kept his emotions under control. "It is not easy for me, but after many, many centuries of what we have been through, we have seized upon the one chance to cross those seas, to set our brothers and sisters free, and to end the torment on our lands. I do not deny you that it is an evil path we walk now. It has the most bitter taste for us, but if we do not do this, we let a far greater evil continue to prevail."

The old man made no reply, and seemed content to let Dragol brood on the words that both of them had spoken. It was as if he was letting Dragol turn the words of their conversation over in his thoughts, and Dragol did not doubt that the old man had a certain conclusion in mind.

Dragol was determined that the old man could wait as long as he wanted, as there was nothing to really conclude. The war against the Five Realms was very distasteful, and Dragol could admit to that, but the necessity involving his own kind was paramount, to gain aid in their long struggle against the Elves. He simply could not see any other way for the Trogens.

Despite the sensitive questions, Dragol found that he was feeling a growing affinity for the human stranger. The old man was one of the few humans to engage him in the manner that they engaged one another. Most others that he had been among regarded the Trogens as barbaric brutes, little more than walking beasts. At the very least, Dragol was grateful that the old man had shown him enough respect to desire the thoughts in his mind.

Dragol held up a chunk of meat, and extended it towards the old man, wanting to further diffuse the insecurity that the old man's words had conjured up in him. "I may not give the answers that you wish, but you may share in my food, old one."

"I am still quite fine, and I will be sure to tell you when I am not," the old man replied politely, with a smile. "I do thank you for your kindness. You will likely need the food much more than I."

"I see no pack, and you show no weapons. Do you ever eat? Or are you like those holy men who go for long with little or no food, to show their faith?" Dragol asked, as he bit into the tough meat, tearing off another sizeable chunk.

"You could say that … in a way," the old man replied. "It is not often that I just get to sit and enjoy good conversation. If I could just stay and converse with you for a time, it would be food enough for my needs."

Then he added, with a chuckle and a light grin, "Unless, of course, you perchance have some wine on you. I am quite fond of that wonderful liquid."

"It is good talking with you, as well," Dragol admitted with a slight shrug, exasperated at the man's apparent lack of normal human needs. "Most human kind do not bother doing so with Trogens, and do not master our tongue as you have. But I do not have any … wine … I have never tasted it, but have heard it is well liked among the Avanorans."

The old man laughed. "It flows like a river with them. I will have to get you to try it someday."

Dragol made no reply, focusing instead on the cooked meat remaining in his hands. He was feeling particularly ravenous after his sleep in the woods, and the exertions of the previous days. It did not take very much longer for him to finish the meat that was in his hands, and the remaining portion that had been cooking over the fire.

The old man did not disturb him while he ate. Instead, he grew silent, and shut his eyes, sitting quietly as if in deep meditation. When Dragol had finally consumed the last morsel of meat, the old man's eye calmly opened, as if the final swallow was some kind of cue.

"So, where are you going from here?" the old man asked Dragol, his timbre casual.

Dragol looked up for a second, catching the penetrating gaze of the old man's deep blue eye. He was not entirely convinced that the old man's question pertained to simply his physical plans in the forest.

"I do not know," Dragol answered. "I just have to find my way back."

"Mind if I travel with you for awhile?" the old man asked calmly.

Dragol thought about the request for a moment, before slowly nodding. The man had given him no reason to worry about traveling with him, but all the same, Dragol knew that the old man was not a friend to the forces invading the lands of the Five Realms. "You can travel with me if you wish, but know that I am trying to make it back to my own kind."

The old man smiled. "There are many paths back to one's own kind. You are not limited to just one road."

"Your ways are maddening, old man," Dragol grumbled, nonplussed.

"All things in time," the blue-cloaked traveler remarked brightly.

"And you are not worried about traveling with one of the enemy?" Dragol asked him.

"Are you my enemy?" the elderly man asked him pointedly.

"Only if you choose to make me so," Dragol responded evenly.

"Then no," he replied. "So I am not worried in the least."

"Then it is best that we set off while there is still good daylight remaining," Dragol responded, adding a glance upwards, towards the sun, for emphasis.

He got to his feet, cutting a little more meat off of the Hyaed carcass to take along with him, placing the pieces into one of the large leather bags he carried. When finished, he cleaned off his dagger, and placed it back into the sheath hung horizontally on the right side of his waist.

He retrieved his shield from where he had left it near the cave opening, cursing himself again for allowing it to get out of arm's reach. He had not been able to avail himself of it when the Hyaed had emerged from the forest to drink at the pool. Even so, he felt a distinct sense of optimism. The old man's relaxing presence was truly affecting the hulking Trogen.

Dragol then walked slowly over to the old man, who had just gotten to his feet.

"Do you know your way through these woods?" Dragol asked him.

"I have traveled here before," the old man answered, a reply that neither confirmed nor denied his level of familiarity with the particular woods around them.

Dragol looked off through the trees, and up at the sky peeking through the branches overhead. "I want to head towards the south, and try to see what I can from the hilltops. Maybe I can find some sign of other Trogens. As long as we can get out of these woods without being killed."

"Then let us head towards the south," the old man concurred amiably, giving no response to the second part of Dragol's statement.

Dragol started off slowly, so that the old man could keep up with him. He then started to increase his gait, making sure that the old man could still match his stride. Before long, he was walking at a forced march speed, as the old man effortlessly strode alongside him.

"You keep your body in good condition. You seem to have better physical ability than humans half your age," Dragol commented, marveling at the old man's exceptional heartiness.

The old man smiled, and laughed merrily. "And probably some younger than that. Few humans realize that there are things in this world that go far beyond age, and the merely physical aspects of life."

Again, Dragol had the distinct sense that the old man's comments were not strictly confined to the issue that Dragol had brought to light.

"You are not just talking about the physical, and you are not just physical, are you?" Dragol challenged his new traveling companion, deciding to put himself out on a limb.

The old man's wry smile was an answer in itself. "You are

perceptive, Dragol. In time you will know more, but you are right in both of your queries."

Dragol regarded the old man for a moment, allowing himself to look deeper into the old man's eye. He had looked into the eyes of thousands of warriors, and he knew very well how to read the look in an eye. Time after time, he had ferreted out hostilities, rebellious flares, and deception, all because he had bothered to study the nuances within a gaze.

The look in the old man's eye, as he let himself reach into its depths, took him off guard. There was absolutely no hint of a threat there, or any hidden natures. Even so, there was a quiet strength that pulsed just beneath the surface. It was the type of strength that Dragol could respect, for it centered upon fortitude, and unwavering commitment. He also felt that the old man's eye contained a look that he had only seen in two individuals in his entire life; his mother and his father.

He also felt unusually secure in the old man's presence, an uncanny sense that was almost as if there would be no attacks or threats that could harm him, as long as the old man was with him. The perceptions were utterly strange, but Dragol was not about to quibble, stranded as he was within a land whose inhabitants would give him a less than enthusiastic greeting.

Dragol shook his head, and his lips pulled back in the Trogen version of a smile. It was all mystifying, but, then again, nothing in life had ever made much sense to the stalwart Trogen.

section vii

AELFRIC

The second day advanced without respite out on the Plains of Athelney, as a maelstrom spread wide under the cool, clear skies hovering above the battlefield. The Saxan reserve force gathered around the great dragon standard of King Alcuin remained firmly in place, under the leadership of Prince Aidan, allowing Aelfric to rove freely behind the long lines of the steel-bristling shield wall. He had just finished inspecting the Saxan right flank, giving great scrutiny to the condition of the enemy opposite it.

The Andamoorans had arrayed a solid line of rectangular, hide shields, seeming content to present a forest of spears, gripped by the veiled men who kneeled down just behind the shields. A few passes of horse archers at the edge of their arrows' range was about the only gesture of offense from the badly mauled Andamooran ranks.

Aelfric had little doubt that the enemy's left flank would be licking its wounds after suffering tremendous casualties during the previous day's fighting. They were not likely to take any unnecessary chances, whittled down as they were. The stalemate was beneficial to Aelfric, giving him one less thing to worry about, so that he could turn his focus more squarely towards the other areas of the battle.

Guiding Midnight, he trotted back towards the center of the Saxan line, nodding in acknowledgement of the many men hailing him as he passed by. Only a handful of his household retinue rode along with Aelfric, as most were positioned at the heart of the shield wall.

The Avanorans had been forced to divert their efforts on the previous day, but no such repeat would be likely on the new one. With the invader's weakened left flank, Aelfric expected a powerful thrust to come from the enemy center.

A group of heavy cavalry, mounted upon horses wearing bards of scale armor, were clustered together a short distance ahead of him, with one of their number set a few paces forward from the rest. Aelfric drew up the reins as he approached them, eliciting a curt snort from Midnight.

Count Gerard II stared out silently over the battlefield, gazing off in the direction of the massed Avanoran ranks, just opposite his force. His face was impassive, but the look in his eye was forged of iron.

"They are going to move upon us soon," Count Gerard commented, as Aelfric neared him, keeping his face fixed forward. "I think you will enjoy this, if they choose to try the methods that won them the kingdom of Norengal."

"Those monstrous beasts they ride, if you can call them horses, can surely shove our men back, if that's what you mean," Aelfric said, reflecting on what he knew of the Avanoran methods of war.

The Avanorans' heavy horse would not charge into a solid spear wall. No horse, even the most frothing, cantankerous war stallion, could be coaxed into anything so blatantly suicidal. That only left a few options if the Avanorans hoped to employ their formidable knights on horseback.

One option was to punch holes in the shield wall using men on foot. Once breaches were made, mounted cavalry could then exploit them, a tried and true method that was certainly within their capabilities.

There was another tactic, and it was the one that Count Gerard was apparently expecting; a disciplined formation, slow, deliberate, and cohesive. One where the ends of their extended lances would be pushed against the Saxan shields, with the force generated by the brawny war stallions that they rode.

Breaches would be created with the exceptional physical power of the war destriers, jostling and shoving the men in the shield wall back and aside. The horses could be cajoled into cooperating with such a tactic, and their strength would be too much for any normal man to long withstand.

Aelfric was still more than a little perplexed at Count Gerard's manner earlier that morning, especially the Count's unyielding insistence that he bring the bulk of his cavalry to assemble at the Saxan center. He had gotten Aelfric to promise not to send the Saxan forces forward in the center, under any circumstances, at least beyond where some conspicuous white stones had been placed on the ground far in front of the shield wall. Aelfric knew that Count Gerard was anticipating the enemy to attack the center with near certitude, and he also understood that there was a tactical countermeasure in place.

The blaring of multitudes of war horns called Aelfric's attentions back to the battlefield. A forest of knightly pennons and baronial gonfalons were surging towards the Saxan center. At the moment, there was a screening line of heavy infantry, archers, and crossbowmen, but they were not a cause for concern. The real nexus of the force was contained in the sleek, muscular forms of the warhorses, and the glinting armor of their knightly riders.

Aelfric found that he was getting more acclimated to the shaking of the ground, though he could see the jarring effect that it had on the morale of the peasant levies arrayed behind the shield wall. The sight of their extreme agitation gave him some cause for concern. There had been many replacements put into the shield wall for the second day of fighting, with so many thanes and household guards falling on the first. Most replacements on the face of the shield wall were still well-equipped thanes and ceorls, but it would not be much longer before simple peasants would be asked to hold shields, to ensure a continuous, unbroken line.

Aelfric banished the fears rising up within him, as that moment was not yet upon the Saxan defenders. Turning his head, he looked off towards the left, to see whether he could gain some hint as to what was transpiring on the left Saxan flank.

The forces of Ehrengard were again deployed in a conservative posture. On the Ehrengardianardan far right was the enormous, shielding hedge of Halmlander pikemen, like the bristling back of some giant porcupine, curled to protect an assemblage of knights sheltered within the underbelly of its center.

Masses of infantry, like an adjacent shield wall, provided a further line of protection all the way down to the center where the Avanorans were positioned. As before, large pockets of the kettle-helmed archers and crossbowmen emerged to the fore of the line, to loose sporadic volleys of arrows and bolts at the Saxans opposite them. Ranks of heavy cavalry behind both infantry and missile troops appeared content to remain in place under their fluttering banners.

For the time being, the Ehrengardians would not likely be a major concern, though the dense, spiky formation on their far right continued to worry Aelfric greatly. He reverted his attention back to the center. Peering ahead at the oncoming lines of Avanorans, he quietly took several steady, slow breaths. He could see a large number of Saxan archers gathered behind the shield wall, and knew that the enemy forces would be well-greeted when they reached the barrier of overlapping, wooden shields.

Arrows had been dutifully collected wherever they had remained intact, after descending in the enemy rain on the first day of fighting. Weaponry, shields, and armor had been stripped from fallen enemies, as non-combatants labored to pull as many of the Saxan dead from the battlefield as they could. Often, they came within just paces of their counterparts from the enemy encampments, though the tense truce that allowed for dealing with the wounded and slain held in place.

Aelfric was grateful for the diligence taken in adhering to his wishes for that first night. The Saxan archers would have a prodigious quantity of arrows to use in the second day's fighting, both from their own stores, as well as those collected from the enemy. It was one small reward gleaned from enduring the seemingly endless volleys of the previous day. Many of Saxans had already notched their first arrows of the day on their bows, anxiously awaiting the commands to set them free.

The Avanorans proceeded at a tight canter, controlled and relatively slow, as they drew closer to the Saxan lines. At a unified horn blast, as if in one motion, their great lances were lowered from their upright positions. The lances were secured in the couched technique that was such a distinguishing characteristic of the Avanoran knights.

To Aelfric's eyes, it looked like a solid wall of steel approaching upon a foundation of muscle, as horse and rider readied themselves to connect with the shields of the Saxan lines. They were just about within reach of the Saxan arrows, and Aelfric expected to hear their own horn signals and shouts resounding soon enough.

Aelfric glanced over at the Bretican noble at his side. A smile was spreading across Count Gerard's face, breaking into a chuckle as the plainly amused Count of Bretica looked upon the furrowed brows of worry surmounting Aelfric's rigid, tensed expression.

Looking at Aelfric the whole time, Count Gerard spoke loudly, to one of the horsemen in attendance upon him. "Ready the signals."

"Now I think that I just might have an idea as to what your men were heading out to do last night," Aelfric said, as his brows gradually relaxed.

He looked back out to the battlefield, his sight focusing in upon the white stones placed along a roughly even line. The stones were within the range of the Saxan bows, and though that might have factored into their placement, Aelfric knew that they signified something much more ominous for the enemy ranks.

He looked back to Count Gerard, as the corners of his own mouth turned up in a subtle smile. The Count now had one of the most wry grins that he had ever seen, winking to Aelfric, before turning his head back towards the battlefield

"Just an extra precaution for your center. My men took care of it last night, as you noticed. I hope you do not mind my initiative in this matter," Count Gerard stated, as he settled himself in his saddle. He hefted up his circular shield, where it had been hanging from a guige strap on his left side. Reaching across his body, he drew his sword out, and held it high. "I will see you in a little while. It is time to greet these Avanorans properly."

It was about that moment that Count Gerard's plan manifested. Aelfric's spirit leaped, as he saw a considerable number of horses and riders in the forefront of the Avanoran ranks suddenly go tumbling down, falling out of his sight. He recognized that they had fallen into pits, which had been dug under Bretican supervision, carefully covered by turf, and marked by the small white stones.

The Avanorans had encountered no pits the previous day, and were pressing a direct attack from the onset on the second. The pits were a brilliant move on the part of Count Gerard, and Aelfric wished that he could take a moment to congratulate the man's genius.

The Count had already moved onward, and horns were sounding among his own horsemen, as those manning a few areas of the Saxan shield wall parted aside to allow the riders through. Aelfric's gratitude would have to wait for later, as there was an Avanoran harvest to reap.

Confusion was rampant up and down the Avanoran lines. The back ranks, and those few knights in the front that had not fallen into one of the pits riddling the ground, jerked in panic on their reins, pulling their steeds to an abrupt halt.

Many of those who had fallen into the pits were badly injured in the avalanche of horses and men. Cries of man and beast emitted from the hollows, some pitiful, and others full of rage. A few knights who had freed themselves from their mounts were trying to scramble out of the pits, just as the Bretican cavalry emerged from the Saxan lines and counter-attacked the Avanorans with brazen ferocity.

The clash of steel erupted, swelling into its own chorus as a host of swords danced. Avanoran knights swiveled their mounts about to meet the unexpected onslaught, and to acquit themselves honorably. Sergeants and squires pressed forward wherever they could to aid the knights that they so dutifully accompanied and served.

The Avanorans were not the only ones to press forward, as many thanes recognized the stagnation and severe disruption in the Avanoran advance. The advantage that the Avanorans held moving in tight, coordinated units had been cast into disarray. With masses of horses and men jammed together and constricted, without coordination, an irresistible opportunity arose.

Aelfric dismounted quickly, as he watched the development unfolding, hurrying towards the shield wall the second that his shoes touched the ground. He called out to a number of his household guards and thanes, joining with a large throng hastening forward to the Saxan shield wall.

A cluster of his elite household warriors surrounded him, as he moved with alacrity out onto the battlefield. They bore their long-hafted axes eagerly, intent on inflicting great damage to the Avanoran invaders. Raising his own sword high, Aelfric passionately exhorted them, as he felt the upsurge in adrenaline, conveying a tempest of fury throughout his body.

The knights in the pits were at a terrible disadvantage as the Saxans on foot reached the edges of the earthen cavities. Swinging long axes, or thrusting and slashing broad-bladed spears downward, the Saxan defenders slew many of the hapless knights, delivering torrents of blows.

"The mounts! Go for the mounts!" a thane close to Aelfric cried out to some of the axe-bearing men, who obliged the order with great rapidity.

The great war axes, wielded by the powerful household guards, could behead a horse, and several fearsome blows did just that. Many knights cried out in a terrible rage as their mounts were cut out from under them. Many steeds pawed, reared, and kicked out with tremendous force behind their sharp hooves, claiming more than a few of their Saxan attackers, as the battling soared towards a feverish crescendo.

A few particularly unfortunate knights were pinned securely under the bulk of fallen horses, but others moved with a strength purchased by desperation, and pulled themselves free. In the swirling battle, with the ranks so tightly contracted together, and so many bodies creating obstacles on the ground, the Avanoran squires could not bring forward replacement mounts.

One knight cut and thrust at Aelfric, as he thundered into the eye of the storm alongside his men. He had fully expected the style of attack, as the Avanoran knights, with their tapering sword blades, were every bit as likely to thrust as they were to slash. Aelfric caught the first strike with his blade, and the latter with his shield. He fired back a heavy sword blow that crashed into the knight's shield, a flat-topped design, rounded of corner and curved in at the sides, that was red with several black lines crisscrossing its surface. The knight was garbed in a close-fitting, black, sleeveless surcoat over his chain mail armor, and Aelfric could feel the cold, deadly stare coming from behind the rigid face visor.

Back on the offensive, the knight pressed forward with three more rapid strikes. The last was a blurring-fast thrust that scraped along the edges of Aelfric's mail shirt, on his right side, grazing the iron links just under his arm pit. The strike had gotten past Aelfric's sword and shield, but a slight twist of his body had both saved him, and given him an opening to capitalize on.

Aelfric immediately moved his body forward, and a little to the left, bringing his raised iron shield boss into the fight as an offensive weapon. He drove it up vigorously, shoving the iron piece towards the knight's head, putting his full weight behind it. The stout shield boss smashed into the right side of the knight's face, just behind his visor, crashing into chain mail links and staggering him.

Aelfric whipped his sword down low, bringing the heavier, wider blade underneath the knight's shield, and into his mail-shrouded leg. As the heavy Saxan blades were adapted more for impact than for slicing, the robust blow delivered a serious injury, causing the knight to drop instantly to the ground with a loud outcry.

It took only a couple of moments longer to finish the grisly task, though Aelfric had to bring his defenses up fast, as an enraged squire, hate boiling on his face, struck down at him from his mount. The long, thin spear tip, prime for piercing chain mail armor, narrowly missed Aelfric's body.

War was war, and without a good position to cut at the squire, Aelfric brought an arcing blow up from below, into the neck of the squire's steed. Aelfric jumped backwards as the steed toppled to the ground with a mortal wound, trapping the squire's leg underneath, as the man's face turned swiftly from hate to unbridled terror. Aelfric did not let the man suffer much longer in such a state, bringing an end to the squire's life with one more deadly blow.

By the time that the call came to return to their own lines, Aelfric's shield was jagged at several places along its outer rim, his sword was generously nicked and bloodstained, and a part of his mail shirt had suffered many broken links. He trudged back wearily, with the consoling knowledge that the damage done to his equipment had been far less than what he had inflicted upon the enemy.

At least two men that he was sure were knights had fallen under his blade, in addition to four lesser fighters who were likely a mix of squires and sergeants. Several others had been either wounded, or had been caught up in the surges of the fighting and taken away from the reach of his blade.

Those of his household guard around him had hewn a plentiful harvest while amongst the forest of Avanorans. Their axes were blood-soaked, and only a few of them had been killed, or taken injury in return. Most had remained close to Aelfric throughout the fighting, circling around him tightly as the calls rang out to pull back to the shield wall.

The Avanorans were now retreating themselves, in an orderly, controlled fashion that demonstrated their great discipline. Well-coordinated units were fighting together in rear-guard type actions, while the ranks behind them hurried to retreat.

Aelfric plodded on leaden legs across the last stretch of ground to the shield wall. He was out of breath, shoulders and arms aching from all the exertion, and the impacts of absorbed blows, but his mood was very much uplifted.

He stopped for a moment, to aid a wounded household guard struggling along to his right side. Aelfric allowed the man to put his left arm around the ealdorman's shoulder, hastening to slide his own sword back into his scabbard, so that he could concentrate on supporting the injured warrior. The man had taken a gash to his thigh, and was weakening fast, but had not suffered a mortal wound. The household guard would likely be fine with some further rest and attention.

Aelfric would still say a few prayers for the Saxan warrior. Any kind of wound suffered in battle was still a threat to survival, with the festering, corrupting possibilities that time often brought to an injured warrior in a battle's wake.

Entering through the parted shields, he called out loudly for some of the men in the deeper ranks to assist the wounded household guard back to the main camp. There, at the least, monks, nuns, and priests more skilled in the treatment of wounds could help the man. He imparted a few words of encouragement to the veteran warrior, as two wide-eyed levy men bore up the injured man's weight on either side, carefully starting back towards the encampment.

DREAM OF LEGENDS

Turning around, Aelfric looked off across the wide battlefield, gazing over the fully reconstituted Saxan shield wall. The Avanorans were continuing their fallback, and their cavalry were now shielded behind a solid wall of infantry, archers, and crossbowmen. Aelfric could not help but give another nod of respect to their coordinated retreat, positioning themselves in such a cohesive order, after suffering a fair number of losses.

Nothing of further concern had occurred on either the left or right flanks. The Andamoorans had remained in place. The Ehrengardians had not remained entirely inert, but had made no significant moves.

As he looked on, he witnessed a small cluster of mounted knights returning from an unsuccessful sortie against the Saxans. The knights of Ehrengard were now moving toward the far right end of the Ehrengardian flank, hurrying to gain the protection of the Halmlander pikemen.

There was no question that the action in the center was by far the most important on the battlefield. Perhaps the strongest element of the invader's army had been engaged and repelled. In many ways it was a tremendous achievement, testifying to both Saxan wits and temerity.

Aelfric took several deep breaths, as sweat streamed down his face, hunching over in his fatigue and letting his shield rest on the ground. His chest heaved as he labored to get air into his lungs.

"Did you approve of my surprise?" inquired an exuberant voice.

Though he remained stooped over, Aelfric brought his eyes up to see Count Gerard, mounted on horseback before him. The burly, bearded man's face, with his prominent, aquiline nose, echoed the visage of his war steed, an ironic sight that almost caused Aelfric to laugh. As things stood, he was highly elated over Count Gerard's initiative, and battened down his momentary amusement.

He knew that the Avanorans would have been able to jostle holes in the shield wall had those brawny destriers been able to put their full force behind the knights' extended lances, and push forward. Having been so close to the Avanoran stallions, Gerard's own impressive steed clearly appeared lesser by comparison.

The destriers carried a foreboding appearance with their ferocious demeanor, and sharp, wickedly powerful hooves. With noticeably long manes, substantially heavy fore and hindquarters, and an ample span of strong, muscled back stretched between their saddle's pommels and cantles, the heavy war horses of the Avanorans were like big barbarians amongst the race of equines. They were exceptional steeds, bred for the art of war, well-suited to the stout flow of martial blood running steadily through the veins of their Avanoran masters.

Having those brutes resisted by men holding shields was not something that Aelfric had ever wanted to test. It was an even more dour thought to imagine those stallions thundering down upon mere peasant levies, behind breaches in the shield wall.

"Approve?" Aelfric finally replied, with a grin. "Thrilled, and greatly relieved, I would say, Gerard."

Count Gerard smiled. "That should take a little fight out of them for the day, but they will not fall for that twice."

"No they won't," Aelfric agreed, slowly straightening up, as his breath returned to him. "But they should be stymied for a short while. Go and get your men and mounts some rest, and a little to eat and drink, while you can."

The enemy tide had ebbed into the oceanic mass of invaders, but it would soon return. In what form, Aelfric had no way of knowing, but the fact that they had withstood a major attack by the Avanorans boded well for their chances of surviving one more day.

AYENWATHA

Sweat, blood, and desperation poured from the allied ranks of defenders. They had persisted in weathering the relentless onslaught hurled at them by the renewed Gallean forces, but it was becoming more unbearable with every passing moment.

Wherever they could deploy in any numbers, the Gallean ranks trudged stalwartly forward. Under the resolute leadership of their knights, they were lethally methodical. Gallean crossbowmen and archers loosed deadly barrages of arrows and bolts, while disciplined ranks of Gallean warriors pushed forward in tight lines of shields and lances. Wherever there was significant resistance, the invaders were augmented by the fast-moving Atagar in the boughs of the trees, and the huge, lumbering Gigans upon the ground.

"Keep faith!" Ayenwatha shouted out to his fellow warriors, as he landed a crushing blow on a Gallean with the balled wooden head of his war club.

He had no time to spare, as he ducked under the vicious sword slash of an oncoming Gallean knight. With a vigorous swing of the small axe in his left hand, he sent the attacker into the embrace of the afterlife.

Straightening up, and looking swiftly for the next closest threat, he yelled out, "Hold strong, my brothers!"

A little farther down the line, Gunnar fought with great fury, providing a fountain of inspiration to the sorely beset ranks of defenders around him. His men yelled defiantly, adding to the higher-pitched, vibrant war cries coming from the tribal warriors. Between Ayenwatha's and Gunnar's resolve, the wavering spirit of the defenders was kept from breaking.

The terrain was such that the battle around the two leaders was conducted on uneven, and often hazardous, footing. Trees, fallen trees, brush, the contours along the bases of hills, and other natural features of the forested hills afforded an array of obstacles, helping to lend further chaos to the swirling fighting.

In some areas, the natural features were to the defender's advantage. The forested slope of a nearby hill afforded a small batch of tribal bowmen adequate cover, as well as a good vantage from where they could pick out their targets from a great number of options.

"We cannot hold this ground forever!" Ayenwatha shouted, as he worked to approach Gunnar.

He narrowly avoided a lance thrust from a Gallean fighter. A short, dart-like arrow whizzed by his head an instant later. Glancing up, he saw the Atagar that had loosed it, perched in a tree a short distance away, just behind the enemy line of battle.

He gestured towards the partially hidden creature with his war club, hoping someone would see it, yelling out, "There! Up the tree! The rat-man! In the tree!"

With a dexterous maneuver, he then felled the human spear bearer with blows from both axe and club. To his immense relief, a tribal archer heeded his warning, felling the Atagar with just one arrow.

Ayenwatha saw the rat-like being crumple, and fall lifelessly to the ground below. His heart skipped a beat as he saw that the arrow had been loosed just in time, as the Atagar had just trained another of its own missiles upon Ayenwatha. Its small bow, and the notched arrow, descended harmlessly to the forest floor alongside their felled bearer.

"No, we cannot hold for long," Gunnar responded tersely,

wetting his blade with the blood of another Gallean.

The careless Gallean had occupied himself too much with another Midragardan and left himself sorely exposed, a common mistake in a whirling melee. The hard-pressed Midragardan warrior that Gunnar freed up nodded in acknowledgement of the assistance, and briefly raised his beard-bladed long axe, in a gesture of salute and gratitude towards Gunnar.

With a powerful overhand swing, the fighter then brought the axe plummeting down over the shield of another Gallean warrior. The Midragardan caught the top of the shield with the lower extension of the axe. The shield was lodged firmly between the axe haft and the unusual-looking portion of the blade, where the bottom point had been sheared off to form a flat edge, giving it the bearded profile by which its type was known.

With a double-handed yank on the haft of his axe, the Midragardan ripped the shield back, leaving the Gallean highly vulnerable. A tribal warrior next to the axeman saw the opening and wasted no time. Loosing a shrill war cry, the warrior's arm arced through the air as he smashed the end of his war club into the helmed side of the Gallean's head, downing the man instantly.

As Gunnar had freed up the Midragardan warrior, so had the Midragardan freed the tribal warrior, who was being beset by the shield-bearing Gallean. Such was the synergy in the tumult of a battle, a stark reality played out in scant moments before Ayenwatha's eyes. It was a sobering sequence to witness, as it underscored the truth that dangers in such a boiling atmosphere were always multiplied.

"Gunnar, we must fall back!" Ayenwatha declared hurriedly.

His heart raced as his eyes scanned the fighting before him. He cried out and gestured with desperation to a couple of archers, to bring their aim around to focus on a huge Gigan that was now tromping into view through the trees.

The Gigan was only about a hundred paces away. The ponderous juggernaut had just bludgeoned a Five Realms warrior with one deadly swipe of its great mace. Ayenwatha could not conceive of the force in the tremendous blow, lifting the hapless warrior off his feet, and effectively shattering his body, such that he landed upon the ground in a gruesomely distorted manner.

The powerful creature bellowed out a bone-rattling war cry,

kicking the broken body aside, as it trudged forward to engage the defenders a short distance from where Ayenwatha stood. The archers needed little encouragement, quickly letting their shafts fly at the creature, and eliciting wrathful shrieks, as a couple of iron tips found a home within its toughened flesh.

In frustration, the creature turned the round shield of a Midragardan warrior into a mass of timber shards with another thundering blow. The creature roared as it stomped its broad foot down on the head of the man, who had collapsed to the ground under the incomprehensible force of the blow. Having seen all manner of wounds incurred in battle, Ayenwatha was nevertheless sickened by the sound of the crushing stomp, and the ghastly sight that followed in its wake.

Another Midragardan with a long-hafted broad axe opened up a modest gash on the creature's thigh. A tribal warrior barreled forward, lodging his spear into the side of the Gigan, with all the force that the man could muster.

The Gigan roared in rage, snapping off the haft of the spear, and swiping its mace towards the axeman. The Midragardan fell back just a scant moment before the massive iron head swooshed through the place where he had just been standing. The Gigan backed up a stride, as another tribal archer's missile burrowed into its left shoulder.

The axemen had a stunned look upon his face. Ayenwatha had no doubts that the Midragardan, feeling the potent rush of air from the passage of the huge mace, just mere inches from his face, was utterly relieved to see the Gigan retreat.

The creature staggered farther back, even as a couple more arrows landed in its body. Ayenwatha knew that it would take even more arrows to bring it down, though a small victory had been achieved, as the huge beast withdrew from the fighting, heading deeper into the forest to nurse its wounds.

"We must fall back!" Ayenwatha reiterated to Gunnar.

"I do not know if we can," Gunnar finally replied. "We are very hard pressed."

The words were more than prophetic in Gunnar's own case, as the Midragardan rounded about in haste. The ensuing events happened in a blur of speed, though to Ayenwatha's experienced eyes everything stood out clearly.

Two Galleans breaking away from a cluster of combatants surged forward, one bearing a spear, the other a sword, and both carrying long, triangular shields. With his own round shield, Gunnar blocked a sword strike, while he cleaved through the haft of the other attacker's spear with his sword.

Turning in the same motion, he struck the swordsman down with an upward, diagonal slash. Gunner then threw a hard kick back into the bearer of the broken spear. The forceful blow caught the man squarely in the side of his knee, and collapsed him to the ground, where another Midragardan wielding a long spear skewered the fallen Gallean.

As was the precarious nature of battle, Ayenwatha had not been given any time to get himself into position to help his Midragardan friend.

"They come from behind! They come from behind!" erupted a frantic call.

Out of the corner of his eyes, Ayenwatha saw a wide-eyed Five Realms scout, out of breath, running in great haste towards their position. He exuded panic and anxiety, covered in sweat from his feverish pace.

"Tell us now! What has happened?" Ayenwatha shouted quickly to the scout, as he drew up to them.

He did not look directly at the scout, keeping his own wits and eyes alert for other attackers. Turning abruptly to the side, he hurled his short-hafted axe at a Gallean. The man had just disarmed a Five Realms warrior, and was about to land a killing thrust with his spear. The well-thrown axe deprived the enemy warrior of his victory, in an instant swing of fortune that turned the Gallean's impending triumph into a lethal defeat.

The sorely winded scout, now having come to a full stop, gulped in breaths of air. Sweat streamed down his flushed skin, and Ayenwatha could see that the man had undergone a tremendous amount of exertion to reach him. Yet there was no time to allow the scout to recuperate.

"Hurry now!" Ayenwatha exhorted the warrior sharply. "Out with it!"

"A fleet of boats came up the river … enemies … so many! They overwhelmed and destroyed Midragard's ships…" the scout announced, before pausing to regain his wind.

"The fleet?" Ayenwatha prodded him in disbelief, as the scout prepared to speak again.

"The longships are lost … none could escape … except by land.

Great numbers of enemy warriors have landed … many places. And farther down the river … they swarmed over the ships … and are now coming inward!" the warrior hurriedly stated, inhaling a long breath as he finished. "I…"

The warrior gasped in abrupt shock, cut off by an arrow streaking in from the enemy ranks. He wavered for a moment with eyes wide, and then fell forward, first to his knees, and then toppling face first into the ground. The shaft of the arrow, buried in his chest, snapped as he fell.

Gunnar had his shield raised towards the enemy, maneuvering over to stand between Ayenwatha and the approximate position of the archer. Ayenwatha moved in closer behind Gunnar in the wake of the arrow, his eyes darting amid the chaos to espy the one that had felled the scout.

Gunnar's movements were strong, and without hesitation, but he had heard the scout's news clearly enough. He looked sickened by it, but gritted his teeth, and remained steadfast in the fight.

The fragments of ill news brought Ayenwatha's own thoughts to an instant halt. He knew very well which river the scout was referring to. There was only one that mattered in the area where the battle was taking place; the Shimmering River, where Gunnar's fleet had come up from the sea, and where all of the tribal people were now heading. It was the very place where all of their slim hopes had resided.

The enemy had deftly maneuvered behind the defenders. The invaders were closing in, to clamp their jaws down upon the tribal people, a powerful, gaping maw that was filled with teeming ranks of iron-forged, razor sharp teeth.

Ayenwatha took a deep breath, deliberately claiming a shred of composure amid the tumult and fading hopes. He could not give in to despair, even if it now permeated his being. There was one need that was imminent in light of the dire tidings. One particular man needed to know of the dilemma right away.

"I must tell Deganawida of this ill-fortune, now!" Ayenwatha called to Gunnar.

"Go, Ayenwatha! We'll hold! None of these devils are moving past here now!" growled Gunnar. Ayenwatha could see immense anger boiling up within the Midragardan, a potency reflected in his fiery gaze.

Ayenwatha knew that the venerable sachem was somewhere just down the line of battle from where they were standing. The stubborn sachem still refused to be too far removed from the tribal warriors. Deganawida's adamant insistence to stay near the warriors was a blessing and a curse, with many sound reasons in support of both perspectives.

Looking around, Ayenwatha saw a discarded spear, lying on the ground a few paces to his right. Fortunately, it was a tribal warrior's spear, the balance and feel of which Ayenwatha was well familiar with. As with most things in the Five Realms involving iron, the blade end was of Midragardan make, while the crafting of the spear shaft, and the manner of fitting the blade to the shaft at the end, was tribal.

Grabbing up the spear, to replace the axe that he had thrown, Ayenwatha left the protection of Gunnar's shield, racing swiftly down the general area of the fighting.

The cries and shouts of men, and the snarls and bellows of combatants not human, swirled all around him, as he nimbly skirted around the trees. He eyed a small hill off to the right, set back from the hostilities. He picked up his speed, pumping his arms as he streaked towards the lower part of the slope.

Deganawida was standing just in back of a group of archers, who were screened by a larger throng of tribal warriors, whose fierce countenances were covered in black and red war paint. Several of the latter warriors had donned the rather unique wooden armor known among the tribes, a long, mantle-like arrangement of wooden rods tied tightly together. Placed over a warrior's head, one long section of rods descended in front, and another in back, of the wearer, hanging down to below the knees. The ones with the wooden armor also bore shields of a similar make, rectangular constructs of several timber rods lashed together.

Ayenwatha was very glad to see them all unscathed, without any wounded amongst them. He had personally gathered the protective group together, arranging them in a manner that mimicked the Midragardan methods of war, with shield-bearers in front, and archers behind. He had insisted that a stout defense be placed around the revered, Grand Council sachem, as he could not dislodge the stubborn sachem from the battle site himself.

The bared chest and arm muscles of the tribal archers bulged, growing taut with the strings of their pulled bows, poised at the very edge before the shafts were set free onto deadly flight paths. The instant that they recognized Ayenwatha, their muscles relaxed, as the tension on the bows was eased.

Deganawida stared quietly at Ayenwatha with a grim mien, as he trotted up to the band of warriors. Ayenwatha knew that the sachem was well aware that his personal presence during the thick of the fighting was an ill omen in itself.

Ayenwatha wasted no time as he halted in front of Deganawida. He proceeded without delay to the matter at hand, relating the dreadful news brought to him by the scout.

Deganawida, whose composure was legendary, did not so much as flinch at the highly-troubling report. His steely, dark eyes shielded the feelings and thoughts that Ayenwatha knew were storming all throughout the sachem's heart and mind.

Having slowed down after hustling to reach Deganawida, Ayenwatha's own thoughts were increasingly oppressed. The five tribe's appalling predicament drove him deeper into despair, as he grasped about for any possible options.

"We must hold this line, for a time," Deganawida stated, in his smooth, resonant voice, only a few moments after Ayenwatha had finished delivering the ill-news. "If they are coming from behind, then the lands towards the eastern cliffs, and just to the south, are the only answer for us. If we tried to go to the north, we will be driven straight into the lands of hostile tribes.

"We must get this message to our people immediately. Tell the sachems and matrons among the refugees that there is no other way. We must move south with haste. May the One Spirit shine light upon our innocent ones, and give strength to those that defend them."

A pained look then spread within the eyes of Deganawida as he spoke the last words. His lower tone of voice reflected his abiding concern over the non-combatants of the tribes, something that Ayenwatha knew resonated throughout every fiber of the sachem's being.

Ayenwatha believed he could even feel the mystical sachem's wrenching apprehension over the fate of their people. It was like a surging emanation from his mentor's body, wave upon wave increasing with intensity as the moments passed. Ayenwatha knew that there was no member of any of the tribes that held the same ardor for the land and people that Deganawida did.

In some ways, Ayenwatha wondered if Deganawida had somehow inherited the deep passion along with his name, when he had received the latter when being placed on the Grand Council. Deriving as it did from the ancient, legendary Wizard that had taught the Great Law, and formed the First Grand Council, perhaps a special connection was transferred to those who had succeeded to the particular council position bearing the Wizard's name.

The apprehensive feeling engulfed Ayenwatha fully, as if his spirit was keenly attuned to that of the old sachem. His heart also burned intensely for the land and people, needing little to stoke its flames.

"We will get the tribes moving … with no delay," Ayenwatha promised, with renewed determination, and a sense of pressing urgency. He looked straight, and unblinking, into Deganawida's eyes. "I will go now, by myself, to see that this is done."

"Take a Brega, to save you time. I know that some are being held close by, to the rear of this place, and down in between some hills. I do not know if they come from among the Onan," Deganawida replied. He turned, and pointed off through the trees, down to where some higher rises in the land could be seen through breaks in the foliage. "Around the second of those hills."

Ayenwatha nodded, turned, and broke into another run that took him down behind the battle lines.

A small shield wall of Midragardans protected the narrow pass between the two steep hills looming just in back of them. The Midragardans were hunched behind their overlapping shields, and several fervently called out warnings to Ayenwatha, the instant that he emerged into the open ground behind them.

Ayenwatha heard the whistling air, and unnerving swishes, as arrows and bolts raced past him. The sounds were intermingled with several thwacks, thuds, and other sounds of driving impacts, as iron embedded itself into the wood of shields and trees.

Ayenwatha darted to the side, and turned his body sideways behind the trunk of an aged maple tree, gaining shelter for the moment. There was no realistic way of averting the deadly hail, as there was no time to spare, to take a more circuitous route to reach the Brega. The battle's momentum could change in an instant, and the message that he had from Deganawida was absolutely vital. The situation facing the masses of tribal refugees was precarious at best.

Closing his eyes for a brief moment, Ayenwatha offered up a silent petition to the One Spirit. Inhaling a deep breath, as his heart pounded, he bounded forth, holding onto his wits, even as a rush of fear flowed over him.

Another swishing sound cutting through the air, and the subsequent thud immediately ahead of him, caused Ayenwatha to snap to a sudden halt. His heart nearly stopped, for only a scant stride in front of him, set evenly in line with his head, was the newly-buried shaft of an arrow.

The fickle line between life and death had come dangerously close to being crossed for Ayenwatha. He shook himself out of his fleeting shock, reaching deep into his reserves of willpower to move forward again.

Adroitly, he ran through the rest of the perilous zone with a zealous impetus to pass through it unscathed. Fortune smiled on Ayenwatha, as he reached a more undisturbed tract of forest, where the ground sloped upward.

His eyes swiftly identified a few tribal archers, and other warriors who had taken refuge higher on the steeper slope. All were looking at him as he kept his stride and raced towards them.

"Brega! Brega!" he cried out, his legs straining as he pressed up the slope. "I need to find them, now!"

"Here!" came an answering shout, from a tall, lean warrior. "Follow me!"

The warrior led him on a course that wrapped around the side of the slope. It was moderately difficult to keep his footing, as fast as he was running, but they hurriedly covered the remaining ground, reaching the opposite side of the hill without incident.

A few warriors with bows and arrows already notched emerged from the foliage, as if they had formed out of the very trees and brush. The red and black painted faces fixated sternly upon Ayenwatha, and he knew that every arrow was trained on his body.

Ayenwatha would have almost felt pity for an enemy stumbling into such a reception. As with the group around Deganawida, the bows were lowered as the warriors recognized one of their tribal brethren.

"Ayenwatha!" one of the warriors called out quickly, recognizing him.

"Brega! I need a steed! I must take word from Deganawida onward! It cannot wait even a moment!" Ayenwatha declared loudly, looking towards the man that had spoken.

"Come with me," the warrior answered.

The Onan warrior led Ayenwatha past the newly-emerged throng of warriors, and they angled downward, heading into a modest gully. Another small group of armed, vigilant warriors was gathered there. Just behind them was a loose assemblage of Brega, about twenty in number. He saw at once that the creatures were already saddled, which was a great relief.

"Which steed is the best on land? Who knows these steeds?" Ayenwatha called out, as they descended towards the Brega. He hoped that at least one of the warriors was more than a ward, and was a rider.

A little anxiety struck him, as he did not readily recognize any of the warriors within sight. Most were from different tribes, and any Onan gathered there were from villages farther removed from his own. The widespread chaos of the war was intermingling the tribes, though ironically the close cooperation among the members of different tribes reflected the ancient Wizard's foundational idea that the Five Tribes were of one family.

After a moment, a warrior from just out of the edge of Ayenwatha's sight strode into view, emerging from the shadows of a great oak tree. His eyes momentarily scanned the collection of Brega. Walking forward, he laid his hands on the reins of one of the creatures, and looked towards Ayenwatha.

The Brega was not the largest of the group, but well proportioned. The creature's fur had a lustrous sheen, and there was an alert look in its eyes.

"Of these, Horizon is the best on land," the warrior said to Ayenwatha, extending the reins. "I have been among these steeds, and know them well."

"What is your name? That I might remember it," Ayenwatha asked, as he reached to accept the proffered reins.

"Red Skies, of the Gayogohon, of the Beaver clan," the warrior answered. He patted the neck of the Brega with obvious affection, a tell-tale detail that Ayenwatha's eyes did not miss.

"This is the steed that you ride yourself," Ayenwatha stated, as he realized the truth.

The warrior nodded somberly. "And the one that I know will bear you well."

"The Young Brothers have brought me good fortune this day,

Red Skies of the Beaver Clan," Ayenwatha remarked, placing his hand on the warrior's shoulder, as he moved to mount the creature.

Ayenwatha knew very well how a rider felt about a favorite steed, and the kind of trusting bond that grew between man and Brega in an uncertain environment such as the upper skies. A rider had no wings and was extremely vulnerable, fully dependent on the steed in the lofty, often turbulent heights of the air. The kind of relationship that was subsequently formed could never be taken lightly. Red Skies had shown Ayenwatha the sincerest form of trust.

Settling into place, Ayenwatha said in a low, grateful tone, "Know that what I do is of the greatest urgency. I take word from Deganawida, first Onan Sachem of the Grand Council. I thank you, Red Skies, and shall not forget this gift of trust! May we see each other soon, on a better day!"

Without further delay, he urged the creature forward. Ayenwatha guided the Brega away from the warriors and the others of its winged kind, heading eastward into the forest, and away from the battle.

The Brega stepped with excellent balance, and was clearly well-rested, judging from the explosive acceleration that occurred as Ayenwatha prompted the creature to go faster and faster. Ayenwatha inwardly commended Red Skies' selection, comprehending immediately that the winged-beast moved as well, or better, than any land-based steed or forest creature could have.

The creature bounded through the forest with the confident command of body and dexterous agility of a deer. The trait was not commonly found among the Brega, as many ran in a very ungainly manner when pressed to sustain themselves at speed along the ground. It could only be imagined how graceful Horizon was when aloft, soaring in the air over the Five Realms, where the Brega were at their finest.

The forest rushed past Ayenwatha. He had to keep his wits focused to guide the Brega, though it was becoming readily apparent that the creature was harmonized with the signals given to it through the legs and reins of its rider.

The Brega navigated smoothly through the trees, crossing the uneven terrain at an exceptional speed. The sure-footed pace of the Brega allayed much of the trepidation that Ayenwatha would normally have had, at chancing the unpredictable hazards of forest ground. Even so, Ayenwatha could barely endure each moment that passed, wishing that he were already dispersing the warning and exhortation from Deganawida to the mass of tribal refugees.

A new, horrid notion began to tug at the back of his mind, adding to the weighty concerns plaguing him. The strange, foreign humans, Janus, Erika, Antonio, Kent, Mershad, Derek, and Logan, were quartered at Eirik's homestead, which was not far from where the Shimmering River met the sea. If a mass of enemy ships had come up the Shimmering River, then they could easily have reached the small island. He could only hope that the longships had already come and taken them on to Midragard.

He wished that he knew their whereabouts or fate, but he also knew that he could not spare the time to find out. Ayenwatha could only worry about what had become of them. Yet neither could he lie to himself. Because the enemy had come up the river, if the foreigners had not yet departed for Midragard, then they were undoubtedly exposed to great danger.

Mercifully, the time passed quickly, as the Brega covered the last remaining distance to the main body of refugees. A number of alert warriors, watching over the perimeter of the rear areas, appeared at his approach.

Seeing the Onan war sachem upon a Brega, and recognizing his urgency, perplexed and anxious expressions emerged on several of their faces. Ayenwatha did not pause to satisfy their curiosity, heading onward without breaking his mount's stride.

Fortunately, the masses of refugees had been brought to a halt for a sorely needed respite. Ayenwatha slowed the Brega to a trot as he made for the center of the sprawling, temporary encampment, which covered a broad expanse of hilly ground. Countless makeshift shelters were in evidence, thrown up hastily for cover by the tribal people.

The attentions of old men and women, children, several younger adults, and even a loose throng of barking dogs were drawn towards the incoming warrior astride the Brega. It was all a blur to Ayenwatha, as he arrived in the middle of the camp, a cleared out space where a few of the Grand Council sachems were sitting together.

All four of the older men gathered there stood up at his approach. Ayenwatha pulled the Brega to a halt, a few feet away from the elder Council members. Ayenwatha nodded towards them, in a gesture of respect.

"Ayenwatha, war sachem of the Onan, what matter brings you to us, in the midst of this terrible assault?" one of the men asked, another Onan Grand Council sachem named Skanawaadi, who was of the Turtle Clan. It was plain that there was no time for any formalities.

"A large enemy force has landed by river. They have taken the fleet of the Midragardans up the Shimmering River. These forces are coming from behind us, while the larger force presses their attack against our front," Ayenwatha announced to the sachems.

Dismay clouded their faces further, with each troubling word from his lips.

"I have come by request of Deganawida. The people of our tribes are advised to head swiftly to the lands near the eastern cliffs. It is the only place that may yet be free from the enemy trap. We cannot go north, as we would be pushed into enemy lands. It is best to waste no time with this, for there is very little time for the warriors holding the invaders back. Our fighters, and those that help us, are heavily beset, even as I speak to you now."

The four somber faces around him did not change in expression, and the men said nothing for several ponderous moments. Each moment seemed like a year, as Ayenwatha awaited their response.

"Then we must get the people moving … it is wise to do so immediately," one of the four stated to Ayenwatha resolutely, a sharp-nosed sachem with leathery skin. Ayenwatha recognized him as Kanokareh, one of the Onondowa Grand Council sachems, a man that was well-respected amongst all the tribes.

Kanokareh looked to the other three sachems, who each nodded assent in turn, reaching a unified consensus without deliberation. Turning, Kanokareh gestured towards three warriors that were standing idly towards the edge of the cleared area. The warriors ran swiftly to him, and listened intently as he instructed them. Kanokareh dispatched the warriors to begin the process of spreading the word around the camp that preparations had to be made to leave immediately.

Unease was evident upon the warriors' faces as they hurriedly moved off, to attend to their given task.

"How long do we have? Do you have any estimations?" questioned another of the four older sachems, one whom Ayenwatha did not recognize.

Ayenwatha shook his head. "No, I do not. Our war bands at the front lines of the fighting should be able to delay those who invaded from the west, but there is nothing to deter the forces that are coming up from behind. There are no warriors to spare. I would advise that everyone who can handle a weapon, or even hold one, be armed, for they may all need to use them."

The admission came heavily to Ayenwatha's heart, but he could not avoid the difficult truth. The forces available to him were stretched as thin as they could possibly be to oppose the main invasion force.

He had spoken truly to the sachem. Nobody could be spared, even if Ayenwatha understood that arming the refugees would ultimately prove futile, if even a modest force of trained enemy warriors descended upon them. It would be like Firakens among deer, and the result would inevitably be a tremendous slaughter.

The older man nodded with a grim expression, and Ayenwatha did not doubt that he understood the implications as well. Ayenwatha glanced around, and noticed that a pulsating energy was already rippling through the camp as the word carried by the warriors was disseminated rapidly. Agitated voices could be heard everywhere, some calling out with great urgency. People were working to collapse the makeshift tents and shelters, gathering together whatever belongings they could carry.

"I must return to my brothers at the front lines of the fighting. We will bleed for every moment that can be gained to give you. I hope to see all of you at the cliffs," Ayenwatha stated, lowering his eyes and head towards the four sachems.

"May the One Spirit protect you," Kanokareh replied in a low voice.

Tightening the reins, and tensing his thighs, he turned the Brega, and guided it away from the four sachems as he made his way back through the camp. He did not allow Horizon to accelerate beyond a trot, as the creature had been given such a short respite following the frenzied dash from the front lines. Ayenwatha desired to spare the noble creature a little exertion, by pursuing a more contained pace along the return path.

Yet once they had cleared the boundaries of the camp, the creature sprang forward lithely, as if it had not exerted itself at all that day. The return trip seemed to be much quicker than the initial journey, though Ayenwatha knew that they could not possibly have traveled faster.

The only plausible explanation was that he was now unburdened of his charges from Deganawida. He was relieved by the fact that he had accomplished the task of warning the masses of refugees, and had gained their acquiescence to Deganawida's counsel. Each passing moment no longer felt like an eternity, even if his heart was still heavy.

The band of tribal warriors guarding the small group of Brega appeared visibly relieved at his swift reappearance, perhaps knowing the connotation. Dismounting, he patted Horizon on the neck, taking a moment to savor the exquisite steed, before turning to look for Red Skies.

He did not have far to look. Red Skies's stoic face had taken on a little anxiety since Ayenwatha had departed. The relief in the man at the sight of his returned steed was obvious, another testament to the deep bond between rider and steed.

Red Skies approached Ayenwatha, and the war sachem handed the reins over to the tall warrior.

"Red Skies, I can find no words to say how special this Brega is," Ayenwatha said approvingly.

The corners of the warrior's lips turned up into a slight grin. "I thought that you would be satisfied with Horizon."

Ayenwatha smiled, and patted Horizon on the back.

"May we fly together soon, during a day of peace," Ayenwatha said to Red Skies, before giving Horizon a couple of last strokes on its neck, and turning away.

The warriors parted, as Ayenwatha moved through them.

"Be on alert! All of you! The fighting is not far from here!" Ayenwatha urged all within hearing, calling out over his shoulder, as he strode up the slope of the hill.

He continued around the hillside, carefully working his way back towards the area that had suffered the hail of arrows and bolts. The line of Midragardans was still in place, spanning the two rises. The ground before them was littered with bodies, both of enemies and allies. The air was eerily still, save for the faint sounds of battle drifting along the air currents from afar.

Ayenwatha paused for a moment, looking past the Midragardans, but could see nothing among the trees before them. The enemy had withdrawn, and he hoped that it proved that their supply of arrows and bolts was not inexhaustible. Again, he closed his eyes and offered up another silent prayer, one that contained thanksgiving and a plea for favor.

Though expecting a less-threatening return passage, he nonetheless girded his courage and ran forward, zigzagging amongst the trees as an added precaution. He crossed through the area without incident, as not even one enemy missile disturbed the stillness surrounding him. Were it not for the ubiquitous bolts and arrows sticking out of the ground and trees, one would have been hard-pressed to believe that the area had recently been part of the feverish woodland struggle.

The sounds of combat ahead grew as he continued at a loping jog, past the second rise. Farther beyond were flurries of movement, as the ebb and flow of invaders and defenders alike came into view, filling up his vision.

Raising his war club in one hand, and spear in the other, Ayenwatha charged forth, running towards the deadly chaos. The proud Five Realms warrior hastened to the fight, and the cause of his people.

A fire blazed within him as he eyed the enemy. Like Gunnar, his despair transformed into a tempestuous battle rage, as he determined not to let a single enemy warrior get by them that day. Every moment possible had to be purchased for the refugees, and like any other tribal warrior, Ayenwatha was more than willing to pay for it with his own blood.

GUNTHER

The search dragged onward, several hours passing without avail. The trails picked up at the entrance to the cave had been lost in the bed of a stream, dashing Gunther's hopes for an immediate discovery of the two wayward outlanders. It was still daylight, and, judging by the sun's position, a reasonable portion of the day yet remained, a boon for which Gunther was highly grateful.

The two outlanders were not skilled in wilderness craft. Even if they shared Gunther's skills, the region of the forest that they had ventured into carried a variety of potent dangers. As it was, at best, they were bumbling about in wild, perilous territory, with a number of denizens that represented lethal threats.

Just as his rising frustrations began to sink their tendrils even deeper into his psyche, one of the male Jaghuns started to bark excitedly.

It was circling a small patch of ground, within the midst of a grassy clearing.

Gunther jogged over to where the Jaghun was trotting with its nose at ground level. "What is it, Fang?"

Lowering himself down to one knee, he leaned over, and examined the ground carefully. The Jaghun pressed its nose into the earth, sniffing and whining. Where the nose touched, Gunther beheld the faint outline of a footprint. Looking closely, he discovered a companion to it, and then a second set. They were human tracks, of the size that would most likely belong to the young male.

Whistling, Gunther summoned the rest of the Jaghuns to him, as well as Lee and Lynn. Fang and the other Jaghuns moved a little further off from the spot, pacing in a direct line leading to the edge of the clearing. Fang's companions also began to bark energetically.

They had found a trail again.

"Find them," Gunther urged the formidable trackers, with a sweeping gesture that they had come to know long ago.

The gathering of Jaghuns wasted no time, loping along the pathway that Fang had uncovered, as they set off into the trees to find the two errant humans.

"I just hope that those two fools are still safe," Gunther muttered acidly, as Lynn and Lee caught up with him.

Lee rolled his eyes, as he nodded back to Gunther, a look of exasperation on his face. Lynn's own expression was not far removed from Lee's.

Lee, Lynn, Gunther, and all of the Jaghuns had been put at terrible risk, and not just from the unforeseen dangers of forested wildlands. The further they moved away from the underground city of the Unguhur, the more vulnerable they became if an enemy force should come across them.

Gunther had a chance to fight off any beast of the forest, but he could not drive off an entire host of warriors. He only hoped that he could maintain his composure, once they found Ryan and Erin, as his blood boiled with the realization of how reckless the two foreigners were.

"Thinking about wringing their necks?" Lynn asked Gunther, to which he nodded his head sharply in the affirmative. She then added curtly, "Same here."

"Add me to your number," Lee offered.

The three continued on in a hardened silence, keeping their attention focused upon the progress of the Jaghuns moving just ahead from them. Another hour passed in that manner, as they crossed a vast expanse of ground.

The scenery changed little. Similar types of trees and foliage populated the area around them, and the land maintained its low-rolling contours. A few creeks, one of which was broad enough to make crossing it a slight challenge, cut through the forest floor, and intersected the trail.

None of the waterways impeded their headway, or obstructed the tracking. Once they had crossed the larger stream, the Jaghuns were quickly able to pick up the trail on the opposite bank, and resume the pursuit.

Gunther remained close to Lee and Lynn, who were dropping behind gradually as fatigue began to slow their stride, until the Jaghuns were finally out of sight in front of them. He had wanted to remain within visual range of the Jaghuns, but was loathe to leave the sides of the two remaining otherworlders.

Having two of the foreigners missing was bad enough; to have all four of them out of his sphere of supervision would be intolerable. Both to their credit, and Gunther's relief, the two with him endured, and did not complain in the least, moving forward with a stoic determination.

Periodically, Gunther uttered sharp calls, which were answered by the unseen Jaghuns ahead in curt barks. The few exchanges helped Gunther to maintain his orientation, whenever he was in the slightest doubt of their direction. As the light of day started to shift, beginning its gradual descent towards the depths of night, a sudden commotion arose among the Jaghuns.

Gunther knew his Jaghuns exceedingly well, and he quickly recognized that the tones of their frantic barks were laced with a hint of fear. In one motion, he lunged forward, setting off at a full run, drawing his sword out of its scabbard as he raced onward. Lynn and Lee broke into a run after him, though he rapidly increased the distance with his long, loping gait.

As Gunther approached the area where the Jaghuns were located, he heard a frenzied yapping and barking, sometimes breaking into something akin to a crazed human's laughter. The surreal sound nearly paralyzed him in his tracks, for he knew very well what sort of creature made such distinctive, blood-curdling noises.

It was perhaps one of the worst of possibilities that could be faced in the Saxan woodlands, an encounter with predators not altogether common. He whirled about to face Lynn and Lee, urgently raising his left hand to get them to stop.

"Stay back ... it is Hyaeds! If you wish to live, you will stay here!" Gunther shouted harshly at them, his own eyes unable to hide the fear that gripped him with the recognition.

Gunther turned, and reevaluated his approach, sliding his sword back into the scabbard and taking his strung bow from his shoulder. He drew an arrow out from his quiver and jogged forward, just as the pained outcry of a Jaghun reached his ears. The agonized cry spurred him forward, to the point of recklessness, as the singular thought of coming to the aid of his beloved creatures consumed him. He had suffered too much loss already, and his emotional wounds were raw and bleeding.

A terrible sight met his eyes, as he burst into view of his Jaghuns. The image that greeted him would remain forever emblazoned in his mind's eye. There was scant time to think; only the need to react.

Altogether, there were four Hyaeds. Often a solitary hunter, the presence of so many together presented an even worse dilemma to Gunther. He had encountered one of their fearsome kind nearly two years before, barely surviving the incident. He had fervently hoped never to cross the path of even one of the beasts again, much less the four that he was now compelled to confront.

The Hyaeds had extensive, powerful bodies, the largest being just over ten feet in length. Their bodies were carried upon lengthy, muscular legs, each ending in broad paws, the latter enhanced by a set of deadly claws. Each one of the creatures rose easily to more than four feet at the shoulder, the greatest of them being closer to five feet.

Gunther knew that he could not hope to run away, even if he had wanted to leave the two foolish otherworlders, and abandon them to the hands of fate and the All-Father. These were creatures capable of tremendous bursts of speed, running swiftly on their toes. He had long since passed beyond the range in which he could have sought to evade the beasts. He had no choice left but to fight, if he wanted even the slimmest chance to survive.

He eyed the monstrous predators with a cool, iron gaze, one that was a necessity in order to keep his composure and wits about him. His steady arms and hands raised the bow up, and drew the arrow smoothly back, ready to loose it in an instant.

Thick, powerful necks flowed from the Hyaeds' chiseled shoulders directly into an extended muzzle. Their jaws were arrayed with an arsenal of glistening teeth, displayed vividly within their snarling visages.

Gunther knew that those jaws clamped down with awesome force, capable of crushing bone with ease. Their jaws were made even deadlier by the fact that they possessed more than one pair of sheering teeth, located a little farther back of their prominent canines. These additional sheering teeth were a unique marvel that Gunther had never seen on any other type of creature in his extensive travels. He knew very well what the sheering teeth were used for, and what they were capable of, in a creature with the power of a Hyaed.

The eyes of the Hyaeds were set a little forward on their elongated skulls, with large, spade-shaped ears set farther back, on either side of their heads.

They were not hyenas, nor wolves, nor lions, but to Gunther's eyes had something reminiscent of each of those formidable carnivores. They were fearsome adversaries, against which even the strongest of his Jaghuns were no match in a direct conflict.

The circumstances of the overall situation began to become clearer, as Gunther assessed the quartet of Hyaeds more carefully. One large, older male and two younger male Hyaeds had been brought together by the fourth Hyaed; a female in the full bloom of the mating season of their kind.

Where a ferocious combat might otherwise have occurred between the males over her attentions, differences had been put aside at the inviting prospect of easy prey that had wandered so fortuitously into their territory.

The predators were clustered at the base of an oak tree. A quick glance upward betrayed the presence of two very terrified humans, a young man and woman huddled amid the highest branches that would support their weight.

Yet the attention of the Hyaeds was no longer focused on the trapped prey. A fight was already underway, creating the worst sight of the scene before him, as Gunther's Jaghuns had already moved in to intervene.

Two of the Hyaeds, the two young adult males, had driven one of his Jaghuns to the ground. Working as a tandem, they snapped their powerful jaws down upon the hapless Jaghun, using their powerful bulk to pin their quarry down. The Jaghun cried out in terrible pain, struggling furiously against the overwhelming assault. One of the Hyaeds locked its jaws down upon the Jaghun's neck, and a sickening, crunching sound could be heard, as the Jaghun's struggles ceased, along with its life.

The sight enraged Gunther, pushing him to madness, as all sensibilities darted away from him in less than an instant. Bellowing out a thundering cry, he loosed his arrow at the one whose bite had snapped the Jaghun's neck. Gunther then threw down his bow, drew his sword, and rushed furiously at the slayers of his Jaghun.

Both Hyaeds whirled away from the slain Jaghun to face the human interloper that so brazenly dared to attack them. The menacing creatures moved with a great swiftness, despite their considerable mass. They bared their teeth at Gunther, and their blazing eyes bored into him.

The burning pain from Gunther's arrow, lodged deeply in its left shoulder, infuriated one of the Hyaeds. It caused the creature to turn its head to snap at the offending arrow, in the wake of the penetrating impact. The sliver of delay allowed Gunther the barest of opportunities, in which to strike at the other Hyaed, before being forced to engage both of them.

Gunther seized that opening without delay, slashing down desperately at the muscled hide covering the nearest creature's right shoulder. The sharp sword sprayed open a long gash, out of which streamed a dark flow of blood. The creature howled in pain and madness, shifting back on its haunches, and swiping its great right paw at him.

Gunther jumped backwards, as the tips of the beast's talons came within just inches of slashing him across the chest. Bringing his sword back around, he brought it crashing down on the creature's thick neck. The blow was well-delivered, embedding deep into the creature's flesh, and going almost half-way towards beheading it. The Hyaed abruptly toppled to the ground, as its spinal column was severed by a cold steel edge.

Gunther's remaining Jaghuns, while he was delivering the killing blows to the one younger male, had moved in to snap at, and maneuver around, the other two Hyaeds.

The older male and the female stalked the Jaghuns in their own turn, feinting lunges from time to time, and continuing their chorus of unsettling, high-pitched cries. The Hyaeds were trying to position

themselves for a prime moment, in which the chance presented itself to fall upon the harassing Jaghuns, whose exceptional quickness was all that kept them from being torn apart. The surreal cries were now intermingled with a horrific, highly unsettling sound, generated by the grinding of their teeth as they sought to intimidate Gunther's Jaghuns.

The Hyaed with the arrow lodged in its shoulder recovered its control, bounding over the dead Jaghun, and past the fallen Hyaed. Gunther had to twist immediately on reflex, falling heavily to the ground as the beast sprang forward, flinging its bulk towards him.

Gunther fell flat against the earth, feeling a brush of air across his face, and hearing the incensed cry of the creature as it missed its prey. The Hyaed landed beyond him on its paws, and whirled about, baring its gleaming sharp teeth. Its snout wrinkled into a menacing snarl, as its eyes seared into Gunther with a storming rage.

Gunther rolled over and scrambled to his feet, spurred by the surety that he was much slower than the beast attacking him. With all of his might, he raised his sword up and brought it rushing down without delay, knowing that the creature was unbearably close.

The ensuing blow was more than he ever could have hoped for. It landed squarely on the head of the Hyaed, whose jaws were already stretched wide in anticipation of a crushing, killing bite.

The steel edge cleaved through the bone of the beast's skull, burying itself into its brain and slaying the Hyaed instantly. The creature's tongue lolled out over its still-glistening muster of blade-like teeth, as it collapsed heavily onto the ground. With a strong heave, Gunther pulled his sword free.

It had all happened within a whisk of time, yet the blood-chilling sense of danger had seemed to last forever. Regaining more of his wits in the midst of his battle rage, Gunther bounded over to retrieve his bow from where he had thrown it down. He still had a few arrows remaining in his quiver, and he risked a couple of moments to notch one.

Pulling back the arrow, he trained his sights on the last two Hyaeds, who were still being held at bay by the relentless harassment of his Jaghuns. The stalemate provided him with his choice of targets, and he hoped that the huge creatures continued to hesitate, and did not move to engage his remaining Jaghuns. Of the two Hyaeds, Gunther preferred to keep his concentration focused on the massive, older male, instead of the female.

Keeping his hand steady, it was as if he assimilated his entire being into an unbroken continuum with the bow, arrow shaft, iron tip, and intended target. Everything was an extension of himself, even the air between him and the Hyaed. As he had done a hundred upon a hundred times before, he loosed the arrow, with the kind of exceptional, sharply honed skill that made it appear as if he delivered the arrow's point by hand to his desired target.

The shaft flashed across the clearing, and burrowed deep into the chest cavity of the large male. With its teeth still grinding, the beast slumped ponderously to the ground, as the fires were extinguished within its eyes.

Gunther dexterously switched back to his sword again, knowing that he was within just a couple strides' reach of the last remaining Hyaed. There would be no chance to notch another arrow.

Instinct for preservation prevailed in the female. The creature was now faced with being outnumbered, having already witnessed the three formidable males silenced permanently, and severed from any possibility of courting her as a mate.

Backing up slowly, the female spun, and vaulted in the other direction. Her legs churned rapidly as she propelled herself into the depths of the forest. The Jaghuns darted forward in her wake, snapping the empty air where she had just been. They halted just beyond the base of the tree, canny enough not to give chase recklessly.

The area was now cast with an eerie silence, made even more disquieting by its suddenness. Gunther took a deep breath, and looked back towards the broken body of the fallen Jaghun.

The creature was a male named Arrow, who had always raced through the woodlands with the grace and directness of the object for which the creature had been named. Images of Arrow, vibrant, alive, and bounding through the foliage, as if nothing in all the world could hinder the creature, flooded Gunther's shaken, grieving mind. The living kaleidoscope of memories contrasted starkly with the still, lifeless, and broken form sprawled on the ground before him.

Thoughts and emotions racing, as the weight of yet another terrible loss was heaped upon him, he gazed hotly up into the tree, to where Ryan and Erin were still crouched. His fiery look threatened to spark a conflagration in the wood of the tree.

He gripped the hilt of his sword tightly, and all of his muscles tensed, as he visibly shook with the tremors generating from within. It appeared that he was readying to try and cleave through the trunk of the tree, in one blow. A fearsome madness danced in his eyes, as his psyche strained to corral the delirious impulses brought forth by extreme sorrow and fury.

"Get down ... now!" Gunther thundered at them, his voice shaking with his surging anger. He left no room for any questions or debate, glaring at the tree-bound pair with a look that was dangerously close to murderous in its ferocity.

Meekly, and clearly frightened as they beheld his countenance, Ryan and Erin started climbing slowly down the branches. Gunther ripped his attention away from them, knowing that he was on the very brink of snapping, and trotted back over to the fallen Jaghun. Kneeling down, he hugged the body of the slain beast, a practice that was becoming all too common.

Unseen by the other humans, a couple of tears welled up and broke free. They crawled down his sweaty, blood-stained face, wetting the musky, blood-matted fur of Arrow's body where the drops touched.

He offered up a fervent prayer to the All-Father for the soul of his Jaghun, defying some of the priests that he had heard, who claimed that only humans possessed souls. To Gunther, it was unfathomable how such loving, loyal creatures as his Jaghuns could have anything less than a soul. When his supplication was finished, Gunther quietly set about making a makeshift funeral pyre.

Gathering wood and stone, he had to pause for a moment, wiping his eyes as they leaked from the overflow of heart-rending emotions within him. His brooding, mournful silence pervaded the air with a great heaviness, one that was not disturbed by any that witnessed him, whether human or beast.

He gently laid the body of Arrow down upon the wood, and then brought flames to life within it. The flames spread steadily, and the body of the Jaghun was quickly consumed, the smoke rising above the trees and climbing towards the heavens.

In his own mind, Gunther imagined Arrow bounding once again, in a land where no harm would ever come to the creature. With a little effort, he could envision a forest where the very leaves glistened with the light of undying life, blinking back more tears as he was left behind in such a miserable world of decay and sadness.

At the very least, Arrow's body would not be left to rot and decay, no matter what the Western Church felt about the old world's funeral practices. Gunther's body might one day lay in the ground, according to the Church's teaching, but those of his Jaghuns would not.

In a way, he thought of the burning pyre as conveying Arrow's body over into the next world, where it would exist forever, incorruptible. The light shining from that thought provided a singular, precious drop of comfort within the sprawling fires of his bereavement.

"Won't that attract something?" Ryan tentatively asked, from where he stood a few feet away. The youth eyed the smoky tendrils swirling up into the sky.

Gunther slowly turned his head towards Ryan. The sight of the youth rekindled his ire, which swelled quickly. The woodsman's body trembled, until his pent-up anger could be held back no longer.

Stomping over to Ryan, his right arm shot forward, and he threw the young man to the ground in an outburst of violent force. Ryan skidded, and his startled, fearful outcry could not finish passing his lips before his throat was seized in Gunther's left hand.

"Do I care?" Gunther hissed at the young man, applying more force to his grip. Ryan squirmed and gagged, but was helpless against the overpowering force applied by the woodsman. "Would this have happened … if it was not for you, and that other dimwit?"

Gunther spat the words out, each one feeling like hot bile in his mouth. There had been no good reason for his Jaghun to die. Arrow was filled with vitality, coming into the bloom of his prime. Gunther had raised the Jaghun since the day of his birth in the woodlands. Like the others, the creature had a unique, special personality that Gunther had come to know well.

The death was needless, inarguably avoidable, and had the two otherworlders had even the slightest bit of sense Arrow would still be alive down in the Unguhur Realm. Gunther had given of himself for the Saxans, and for the otherworlders, and he now found himself continuing to pay a price that was far too high for his liking.

Pulling his knife out in a blur of movement, he pressed the tip of it against Ryan's exposed neck, just above the point where he was choking him. Ryan was wide-eyed, desperate and panicked, and his face was wracked with sheer terror. His staggered breaths were curt, as he peered back into the visage of a grief-crazed, enraged man. The youth blanched as he took in the look growing within the depths of Gunther's eyes, trembling fearfully and whimpering. There was no doubt that the youth knew that his life was teetering in the balance.

"Please, Gunther … Ryan is foolish, and he is young … he did not intend any of this … please forgive him," Lee interjected, pleading in a low voice, moving to within a couple of feet of Gunther's right side.

Gunther did not so much as twitch, keeping his focus bearing down hotly on the foolish lad pinned on the ground before him. He pressed his knife in a little harder, pricking the youth's skin, and holding it there for a long moment. A thin trickle of blood worked its way from the knife's bite, meandering in rivulets down the left side of Ryan's neck.

"A life for a life, yes?" Gunther growled dangerously. "Is that not what the old writings say?"

"Please Gunther … don't do this!" Lynn begged Gunther, from his other side, raw passion saturating her words. "They are stupid, not evil. Please don't kill him, I beg you."

Erin made no move to draw any closer to Gunther, or to attract his attention. She watched his fearsome reaction to Ryan from a distance, with pure, wide-eyed horror splayed across her face.

After pressing the metal point to the very edge of penetrating deeper into the flesh of Ryan's neck, Gunther swiftly withdrew the blade, and replaced it in the sheath at his side. Without another word, he released Ryan, stood up, and whistled to his Jaghuns. He did not spare a single glance or word to the four otherworlders.

The Jaghuns regrouped around their caretaker, emitting whining sounds that carried a distinctive, forlorn quality. The saddened master and beasts strode off in the direction from which they had come, heading back towards the cave entrance leading to the Unguhur Realm.

Gunther did not pause to see whether the four otherworlders followed him, and at the moment he hardly cared. Grief had overwhelmed him, almost to the point of changing him irrevocably. That shook him more than anything else, as he began to realize what he had nearly done.

He knew that a momentous, inner struggle loomed, one that would determine whether or not he could keep the foundations of his spirit from crumbling.

WULFSTAN

Returning on a long, looping route through the dense woods, the band of Saxan warriors finally emerged a short distance behind the front lines of the titanic battle. They had encountered a few Saxan scouts and patrols as they drew closer, but fortunately had evaded those of the enemy in the contested region.

Wulfstan had found the Saxans warding the forest to be both anxious about the ongoing battle, and elated to see the return of the small party. It was obvious from their reactions that they had not expected to see Wulfstan and his companions again.

In the light of day, Wulfstan could appreciate the Saxan efforts that had been undertaken within the forest. Any stretch that would have been passable by larger groups or mounted warriors had been heavily barricaded, utilizing masses of felled trees and branches.

Time and time again, Wulfstan's group had passed by the obstacles, and he could understand why the enemy had attempted so little through the woods. It would have been an outright killing zone, and no amount of numerical superiority would have given much of an advantage in such treacherous environs. Cavalry would easily have become bogged down, and subsequently cut to pieces, in such an environment.

The trees also negated any advantages that the enemy may otherwise have enjoyed from the air. There were few areas to land steeds, and the thick foliage of the upper branches prevented effective surveillance.

Truly, with such a large army in the field, the enemy's only viable option was to come right at the Saxans through the Plains of Athelney. That the enemy had to take a direct approach was of little consolation, though, as the enemy had an ocean of force to hurl at Saxany's shores.

As they walked out of the woods, and back into the full embrace of the sun, Wulfstan was filled with mixed emotions. It had been a successful journey, but the battle itself was far from over. Even more troubling was the undeniable reality of the strange sight that he had witnessed in the sky, a vision directly related to the recurring dreams that he had been having in ever greater intensity.

The Saxan band worked their way to a rendezvous point, where their helms, mail, and other potential encumbrances on the woodland mission had been discarded until their return. Several of the light horsemen from Annenheim that had been used to scout for, and guard, Wulfstan's group on their outward foray were now warding the pile of items. With broad smiles and vigorous shouts, they hailed his band. It took only a few moments more for their eyes to fall on the conspicuous prisoners being conveyed along in the group's midst.

Wulfstan felt a sense of relief, as he put his mail shirt on, and placed his half-helm back on his head. As close as he was to the ongoing battle, he felt much more secure with the mail and helm returned to his possession, almost as if he had been sent naked on the woodland sojourn.

Once they had retrieved their items, the small party took a long walk as they were escorted well behind the Saxan lines, and guided towards the main encampment. Wulfstan's heart ached as he saw badly wounded men stumbling back of their own accord, or being aided by what few individuals could be spared to attend to the stream of stricken men limping and trudging in from the fighting to the west.

Far to his left, the horizon was inundated with a dark mass of warriors, banners, and flags, reaching as far as his eyes could see. The battle itself was raging furiously. The air was filled with a terrible din, a cacophony that swelled and ebbed, as choruses of horns called out new commands to various contingents on both sides.

The booming war drums far down the lines, where the Andamoorans were located, brought a chill to Wulfstan's spine. A flood of vivid, gut-wrenching recollections from just a day prior blazed through his mind. He closed his eyes, and took a deep breath to settle his rattled nerves.

From what he could tell, the general lines of the Saxans still seemed to be holding, and the great dragon standard of the King still soared proudly in the winds from its high shaft. That the standard was still in the center, and behind the lines, was a very reassuring sight. Prince Aidan had not yet engaged the reserves, which could only suggest that the day had not yet gone badly.

At last, Wulfstan, Cenwald, and the others walked through the entrance to the encampment. They quickly sought out a couple of Aelfric's men who had been assigned to wait for them, should they return. Like the Saxan men that they had encountered in the forest, the two men were overjoyed at their return. Their spirits were made even more boisterous by the quarry that the small band had brought back with them.

Wulfstan had to calm one of the men down, when the identity of Godric was revealed, in the first moments after a portion of the tale of what had transpired was told. Aelfric's warrior walked up and spit right into Godric's face, and would have struck him a heavy blow, but Wulfstan caught the man's arm in time, and forcibly held him back before his balled fist could connect with Godric's jaw.

"None of us disagree with your urges, but stay your hand. I am sure Aelfric will see to his justice, let us not bloody our hands with such a poisonous wretch," Wulfstan said firmly, keeping an iron grip on the man's forearm.

The Saxan glowered at Wulfstan for an instant, but finally simmered down, though he was far from being in a tranquil mood as the three prisoners were led away. Wulfstan was exceedingly glad to rid his hands of the prisoners, as Godric's mere presence raised his own ire, and sorely tested his reserves of discipline and patience.

Nothing within him could reconcile how a man could become such a traitor to the land that had made his own good fortune possible. Wulfstan was glad that treachery had been Godric's reward, even if the act had given a sizeable fortress, a quantity of foodstuffs, and some villages over to the enemy, to be used as a base or foothold in Saxan lands.

Wulfstan looked around the camp, endeavoring to turn his thoughts to other matters. All around him were an overwhelmed mass of priests, monks, Sisters, camp attendants, and a fair number of peasants, most of whom were from the villages in the immediate region. All were heavily engaged in their grisly, dour labors, doing everything in their power and ability to tend to the seemingly unending stream of wounded being brought in from the battlefield.

Almost to a man or woman, their faces were weighed down with fatigue. He recognized some of the faces from the previous day, and had little doubt that they had exerted themselves all through the night to aid as many as they could. Most had clearly done so without regard for themselves, as one glance at a number of them revealed several who were not far from outright collapse.

The Sister that he had witnessed comforting the dying continued in her grim task, with the same sense of gentleness that he had observed before. He did not even want to consider how weary she must have been in her spirit, much less contemplate her physical debilitation.

Though the sight saddened him, there was a certain inspiration that he gleaned from watching her display of quiet determination. She refused to give in to her growing burdens, bringing light through her kind smiles and words as she labored to soothe the terrified, pain-wracked men she attended. Wulfstan was grateful for the spark of inspiration, as he needed as much of it as he could get, given the morose surroundings.

A number of the bodies lying on the ground no longer held any life within them, mixed among those who still struggled to hold breath in their lungs. There was blood everywhere, and the air was filled with a noxious stench. Moans, cries, and occasional screams of horrible pain formed an unholy chorus that flooded the air.

Wulfstan's own assignment had been filled with dangers, and had required tremendous endurance, but he knew that the non-combatants attending the wounded, whether religious or not, had been given perhaps the hardest of all tasks. He was aware that a great majority of them readily embraced it, even if the sights that they were seeing, and the screams that they were hearing, would scar them at the core of their spirits.

He felt his eyes moisten as he looked upon the wounded Saxan men, and regarded the resolute faces of the overwhelmed attendants straining to help them. He did not turn his eyes away, wanting to remember the images if ever his own resolve should waver.

He silently watched as an old, gray-haired priest slowly traced out the sign of the Sacred Spear and passed his hands over the eyes of a man who finally succumbed to his battle wounds. Not far from the old priest, Wulfstan observed another of the Sisters holding another dying man's hand, as she looked into his eyes without blinking. The man's body shook violently, and then he went still, his grip relaxing as his spirit fled his body.

Very likely a father and husband, Wulfstan could tell by the man's plainer clothing that he was probably a villager who had come with the General Fyrd. The man would never see his home village or his family again.

The compassionate Sister had not flinched as she gave him a connection and comfort in those final moments. Like with the other Sister, Wulfstan could not imagine the strength of character that it took to endure such tragic, sorrowful moments, selflessly giving comfort to the suffering, dying men. To Wulfstan, the strength in the Sister was amazing to behold.

Close to her, a young man, who could not have been over sixteen or seventeen, cried out in anguish as a monk worked to bandage a horrific gash in the young man's side. Even if the bleeding could somehow be stopped, Wulfstan knew that the young man was probably beginning a terrible descent into slow torment, as sickness and disease took root at the site of the injury. Even the smallest of battle-wounds could prove fatal, and the young man exhibited a wound that was anything but minor.

A dark, malevolent mood seemed to permeate and condense in the air around Wulfstan. The battle had not yet been lost, but an unimaginably terrible cost was being exacted from the Saxans. A weakness came to Wulfstan's knees, as he continued to watch the flow of men being carried, dragged, or propped up on another's shoulder, as they were added to the miserable, suffering assemblage within the camp.

Burning, salty tears came to his eyes, as he thought of what he had seen on the battlefield, and what he was looking at around him. The mental scars being formed were ones that he was sure would never fully heal.

Even more disheartening, those being brought back to the camp were perhaps the luckiest ones among the condemned. Wulfstan knew that there were many that even now lay alone, where they had fallen out on the field of battle. Where the fiercest fighting was raging, all too many were stranded out in the open, as others were prevented from reaching them.

He had set his eyes in quick glimpses on such men as he had fought his way back to the Saxan lines the previous day, after the Avanoran cavalry had fallen upon them. Cut off, and impossible to reach, many had found no succor during their last, gasping moments. They merely lay helpless where they had been struck down, with their life force slowly ebbing out through wounds inflicted by arrow, crossbow bolt, axe, sword, or lance.

A few were pulled out when night fell, during the time when a shaky understanding held concerning the removal of the dead and wounded from the battlefield. Yet most died where they had lain, having remained far too long on the field unattended, passing well beyond any slim hope of recovery.

Wulfstan was not ashamed of the deep emotions rippling throughout him, and could see that the men around him were stirred to the center of their souls by such devastating sights.

"Give me a moment," Wulfstan said to Cenwald, his voice hollow and weakened. He turned and walked into the midst of the wounded.

Cenwald, who was also choked with emotion, merely gave a slow nod in reply. In the midst of everything, out of thousands of combatants around him, Wulfstan's worries were focused on one, singular warrior who had been among the mass of wounded.

Sebright was still where Wulfstan had last seen him. To Wulfstan's elation, Sebright was both alive and alert. The wounded man's immediate burdens had been made a little easier. He could see that the dead bodies around Sebright had, for the most part, been removed. That was a relief, as Wulfstan could only imagine how distressing it must have been to be lying side by side with lifeless bodies, as those near the front of the camp were now doing.

To his further relief, he also noticed that there were a number of armed peasants, and even a few mailed warriors, likely culled from the rear reserves, who were now watching over the wounded. After the harrowing incidents of the previous day, the Saxans were clearly taking no chances.

A couple of Himmerosen could also be seen flying at a low altitude, off in the skies beyond the rear of the camp. Their presence reassured Wulfstan even further.

"You are back ... and in one piece, I might say," Sebright called out upon seeing Wulfstan, waving to him with a grin.

Sebright sat up, propped himself against the wheel of a cart, and glanced over to where a monk nearby was fixing some cloth bandages to the arm of a young man.

Wulfstan walked up to him, his smile cracking his now tear-stained, wearisome face. "Yes, back, and still in one piece, thanks to the Almighty ... and I can see that the All-Father has also smiled favorably upon you."

"I would rather be back in those lines, but I couldn't stand to fight," Sebright replied, with heavy regret in his voice. "How have you fared since we last enjoyed the enemy's visit to our camp?"

"I would say well, if you consider what we were asked to do," Wulfstan replied, still grinning at the welcome sight of his recently-forged friend. He knelt down, gently laying his hand on Sebright's left shoulder "I brought back a traitor, we did not lose any men, and you appear well. It has gone as well as I could have hoped. I probably should be getting back to the battle lines. If we can just somehow survive this awful war

... then you and I can sit down together, and speak of a number of things over some northern Saxan ale."

"Northern Ale ... would taste like the waters of life right now," Sebright remarked.

"Northern Ale, eh? Perhaps I should share with you some of our Southern vintages ... wine, of course ... though I must admit that I never have tasted that which pours from silver vessels at the tables of counts and dukes," interjected a man listening in to their conversation from the right. He spoke in a thick voice, having just emerged from sleep, and his heavy eyes showed that he was not far from returning to it. He grimaced as a stab of pain rippled from the considerable gash on his right leg, as he shifted his body weight. He gave a light chuckle a moment later, remarking wistfully, "What I would not give for just one cup of either your ale, or my wine."

"I think most everyone on this battlefield would be in agreement with you," Wulfstan replied, and then added with a smile, "Then we shall have to invite you as well, when this nightmare is all over."

"That ... I would like," the man said, and his eyes fluttered as he drifted back towards a merciful sleep.

Wulfstan looked again to Sebright.

"So how do we finish this war and find ourselves surviving it? That is the real question left to us now. How do you think we can?" Sebright queried, his expression tinted with a saddening sense of fatalism.

It was clear that Sebright's spirits had taken a downturn since Wulfstan had last seen the man. With what he had been constantly surrounded, Wulfstan could not blame him.

Regarding the question of survival, Sebright was most likely correct in wondering how a Saxan could hope to survive the war that was breaking out over their lands. In truth, it was the only question that most men could ask, when faced with such terrible circumstances.

Wulfstan could see that the wounded man did not expect a good end to the battle at hand. It pained him sorely to see Sebright's hopes dimmed so much since the fight with the Trogens in the encampment. Yet the wounded man had been made to endure another night, and much of a day, surrounded by increasing numbers of wounded and dying Saxans.

Wulfstan frowned, shaking his head slowly. He could not willingly lie to his new friend. "I do not know how. I fear that this field is not going to be held much longer. We have fought hard and well, but the enemy's numbers are far too great."

"I am no ealdorman, or southern count, but even I know we cannot hide behind the walls of towns, if we make it off of this field of battle alive. We will be isolated and strangled one by one, until all resistance to the Unifier is choked to death," Sebright remarked darkly. He stared upwards, and his chest heaved with a pronounced breath. "Alas, what wicked times have fallen upon us."

As if confirming Sebright's laments, a roaring outcry suddenly ripped back towards them from the far horizon, tearing through the air with great force. It was accompanied by a discernible rise in horns blasting out waves of unified signals. The sounds were breaking out from somewhere near the central area of the shield wall, according to Wulfstan's estimation.

The surge carried strongly over the steady, hellish chorus of drums, horns, and other battle din that had formed into an incessant, droning background that Wulfstan had grown partially numbed to. The anomalous outburst of noise from the battlefield caused Wulfstan to shudder, as he knew very well how fragile the course of a battle could be. He had been caught up in the shifting currents himself, and the sounds pouring into his ears might well be heralding the onset of a great doom upon the Saxans.

"Ours or theirs? And what does it mean? I wish I knew," Wulfstan remarked dourly, struggling to keep the worst of his worries at bay.

Conscious efforts were largely useless, as his subconscious was a maelstrom born from the essence of obsession. A sharp pang of anxiety lanced through him as he worked in vain to stifle the ongoing fears, of the kind that he and so many other Saxans carried with them during the extended battle.

Any number of things could be occurring, as shifts of fortune and newly engaged tactics governed the ebbs and flows of the fighting. Wulfstan's greatest worry narrowed down on one particular situation, a crisis which would spell defeat for the Saxans; the full breaching, or breaking, of the shield wall.

Wulfstan knew that the Avanorans were deployed in the center of the battlefield, and also that they carried the greatest war reputation onto the Plains of Athelney, amongst all the combatants involved. He looked off in the distance nervously, wondering if their heavily armored knights had finally broken through the Saxan resistance. He tensed, as he listened for the thunder of hooves that would accompany such a disaster.

"This is no good," Sebright commented, outwardly dismayed at the new waves of sounds. "If this army is destroyed here, then our whole realm is as good as conquered."

"You speak truly, but what other choice is there for us?" Wulfstan asked Sebright. "This is where the battle must be fought. There is nothing more to call up in our lands, levy or otherwise. I did not even think there could be this many people in the entire world, when our contingents arrived in this very camp. The enemy must be fought here, before they could reach any of our provinces and villages."

"No more levies here? Then maybe elsewhere … we should send a summons to the Midragardans, you or I. We should tell them that they would be ill-advised to tarry, as this threat is a threat to them as well," Sebright responded, in a tone of voice that, strangely enough, was not entirely in jest.

He chuckled bitterly after he had said the words. A grim expression gripped his countenance, as he looked into Wulfstan's haggard face.

"Truly, if there was some way to get out a cry for help, to send a message … then that is where I would go. The tales say that the warriors of Midragard are masters of the oceans, and it is said that they have no love for the Unifier either. But there is no way to reach out to Midragard, or to anyone that would help us," Sebright muttered in a low voice.

"And what of our ealdormen and counts, even if there was such a way? I am sure they would take no time to counsel with a mere ceorl, especially with all of the things on their minds right now," Wulfstan stated, with the fullness of sincerity girding his voice.

Sebright looked at him with an odd expression, as if trying to fathom what was behind the sudden change of tone within Wulfstan's voice.

"If there was such a way, to cry out for help, it should be taken with, or without, counsel. There is no more time for talking. The hour is desperate. It is a time for action by any that could possibly change these events," Sebright replied, in a slow, deliberate tone. His eyes then looked off, with a faraway gaze. "Yet I fear there is no ceorl that knows of anything that the ealdormen and counts have not thought or spoken of … but if there was one…"

Sebright drew into an extended silence, letting the thought trail off without a firm conclusion.

An idea had been building rapidly in Wulfstan's mind. It was a notion strengthened by his strange dreams, by the tales that he had heard throughout his whole life, and most of all by the physical, undeniably real sight that he had beheld, on the return from Godric's fortress, in the skies above Saxany.

He looked skyward again, his gaze drifting across the heavens. A tension formed in his gut, as expectation wrestled with skepticism. After a few moments, the former prevailed in the contest.

His eyes rested once again upon what looked to be a pure white patch, far above the first layers of clouds. He knew without reservation that it was the very same patch that he had seen during the recent journey back. There was no mistaking the vision that matched that of his dreams with perfection.

"Do you see that?" Wulfstan asked Sebright slowly, pointing upwards. "There, above the main clouds."

Sebright looked up, squinting a little, as he stared. He was quiet in his intensity, as he scrutinized the sky. At last, he spoke, "You mean that big, whitened cloud? The one that looks to be way above the others?"

Wulfstan smiled as resolution filled him, from the innermost core of his being to the outer hairs on his skin. In that singular moment, the idea that had tugged at the edges of his mind crested into an impetus to act.

It was a most dangerous thought, a seemingly whimsical notion that might very well result in his personal death. Furthermore, he could not deny that his conception was perhaps something that was rooted in insanity. It was an amalgamation of hope, recklessness, courage, inspiration, and many other elements that were hard to grasp with absolute surety.

Yet if the bizarre idea succeeded, a new chance could be given life. A fresh hope, to bring outside help to the beleaguered Saxans, would be born.

Most importantly, if it did fail, it would only cost the Saxan cause the life of one lone ceorl. A single ceorl could not change the battle as it now stood, as Wulfstan had come to understand. That was one lesson of his inclusion in the party sent to scout Godric's fortress, as each of those who had been sent out had been men who could be risked on such an uncertain venture. Yet if the slim chance that Wulfstan saw before him led to something more, then one ceorl could possibly change the parameters of the battle, and perhaps affect the very balance itself.

Wulfstan knew that nobody would take his initiative seriously, not even Sebright. But he was ready to move forward, and set his feet down upon a new, dangerous, and strangely inviting path. His heart felt harmonious with the impulse.

"I need to gain the use of one of the Himmerosen," Wulfstan stated, matter-of-factly.

"What are you thinking?" Sebright replied, with an incredulous mien.

"If I told you, or anyone, all would surely think that I have been struck with madness. It may not be my status to make such a choice, but I have made it anyway," Wulfstan answered resolutely.

"Is there a ceorl that knows of something that the ealdormen and counts have not tried?" Sebright then asked, in a very deliberate voice, looking hard into Wulfstan's eyes.

"There may be, though I cannot prove it," Wulfstan replied, as a slight grin bloomed on his lips. "So, do you have any thoughts on Himmerosen?"

Sebright looked off to the right. "There was some big attack by our forces early this morning. I do not know what happened, but I have noticed some steeds straggling in throughout the passing of the day."

He gestured in the direction that he was staring. "They were taken off, somewhere that way. From what rumors I heard, the attack set off a big fear among the enemy, but it also caused a lot of damage to our sky riders."

"They say they are like horses, in some ways," Wulfstan replied, voicing the words similar to a question.

"That is what they say, but I would not know myself. I have little experience with horses, and none with the sky steeds," Sebright replied. He then shrugged. "What villager gets to ride horses often, much less the noble sky steeds?"

Wulfstan grinned at Sebright again, feeling a firm sense of purpose, as he patted his new friend gently on the shoulder. He rose to his feet, and looked off in the direction where Sebright had indicated that the Himmerosen were being quartered.

He turned his head, and looked back down to Sebright. "Stay

strong, and get yourself through all of these storms, Sebright. May we share some Northern Ale together, and maybe some of the southern wine from our resting friend's lands, in a time of peace."

"Good luck, Wulfstan. May the All-Father watch over you, and keep you in His care," Sebright replied, as Wulfstan turned to walk away. He then added, from behind Wulfstan, in a low voice that the Saxan warrior could not hear, "You are a ceorl with as much nobility in you as any count or ealdorman of Saxany … that ever was, is, or will be, my friend."

Wulfstan started off at a brisk stride, working his way through the masses of tents, carts, stores of materials, and other camp elements. He passed through a quarter where a small number of carpenters, leather workers, blacksmiths, and other artisans kept up a diligent labor in repairing weapons, horse harness, and other ongoing needs of the army. In the tense atmosphere, attending to their tasks during the ongoing battle, nobody paid Wulfstan much attention as he trekked by their temporary workshops.

Sebright proved to have been observant, as Wulfstan soon came upon the sight of a number of the winged beasts that he was searching out. All of them were tethered. A few were eating food, others were drinking water out of buckets, and still others were lying in repose on the ground.

Wulfstan had never approached a number of Himmerosen so closely before. He was struck by how much they resembled a pack of huge war dogs, in many ways. The contours of their bodies were more elongated than blocky, but the creatures still had a rugged appearance that began with their large heads, and broad, powerful jaws. A few of the creatures eyed him warily as he approached the cleared space that they were being kept in, and he could sense the innate intelligence within their alert gazes.

A small number of Saxan guards were watching over the Himmerosen, from the edges of the space. A few other men were amongst the creatures, seeing to the various needs of the beasts, whether brushing their coats, ferrying more water or food in, or resetting saddles and harnesses. Though the steeds were resting, it was clear that they were being kept in a state of readiness.

A diminutive man was coming up right behind Wulfstan, as he idly watched the scene before him, drawing his attention as he heard the man's footsteps shuffling along the grass. The man bore a saddle along with him, and had the impassive look of a worker conducting routine chores.

"Can I ask you a question?" Wulfstan asked, as the man neared.

The man blinked at the unexpected interruption, and eyed him for a second, slowing down and drawing to a stop. "I suppose so … but be quick, as I have much to do here."

Fidgety, and brimming with impatience, the man looked expectantly at Wulfstan through his small, deep-set eyes.

"Are there any really strong, rested steeds here?" Wulfstan finally asked, glancing towards the Himmerosen.

"A few reserve mounts. But most of the others have little energy, after the fighting this morning," the man replied tersely. He then started to turn to go.

"Wait, just one thing more," Wulfstan urged.

"Yes?" the man replied acerbically. "Be quick about it."

"Do they really ride like horses?" Wulfstan asked. "I have always wanted to know that."

"A strange time to be curious. As to your question, I just tend to them, I don't ride them. Might ask that fellow there, he is about to go on patrol soon, " the man said, indicating a lean man, of medium height, who was talking to a couple of the spear-bearing sentries nearby. The attendant then added, with an air of great impatience. "Now, if you will excuse me."

Without another word, or waiting for Wulfstan's reply, he scurried off, lugging his saddle along with him towards the gathering of Himmerosen.

Wulfstan's attention was already focused on the other man, talking with the sentries. He eyed the sky rider for a few moments. The man was probably a little older than he was, perhaps by around five years. He was dressed in a dark tunic and light brown trousers, his legs wrapped snugly in bandelettes.

A segmented iron helm rested upon his head. The iron frame band crossing over the top of the helm featured a raised iron decoration, fashioned into the figure of a boar with bright tusks of copper.

The adornment had a thick line of true boar's bristle mounted down the length of its back, accentuating its prominence atop the helm. The nasal guard in the front was inlaid with a Sacred Spear of pure silver, the point of it oriented upwards.

The crest ornament alone identified the man as a northerner like Wulfstan. The boar was one of the symbols long cherished by the old kingdom of the north, and even hailed from the times before the western faith had taken its first steps into their land.

The sky rider had a relaxed posture, with a narrow face, a small mouth bordered with full lips, and a short, rounded nose. He had a light brown moustache, and was otherwise devoid of facial hair, except for a stubble of growth that created a faded shadow across the surface of his face. His brown eyes were calmly oriented upon Wulfstan, as he approached him.

"Are you getting ready to go on patrol?" Wulfstan queried.

"Yes," the sky rider replied. "Within this very hour. Is there something you need?"

Wulfstan nodded. "Yes, something very important. Can I speak with you for a moment."

The two guards, both probably ceorls themselves, as they were clad in mail, helm, and had quality shields and weaponry, glanced between Wulfstan and the sky rider.

"I'll be back in a moment, and I'll finish my tale," the sky rider remarked to them. They nodded back, as he walked a few paces away with Wulfstan, where they could speak with more privacy. Looking to Wulfstan, he asked, "And I must ask you first, by what name are you called?"

"I am Wulfstan, of Sussachia, a ceorl of the lands of Ealdorman Byrtnoth," Wulfstan said, introducing himself.

"And I am Ulfcytel, from Wessachia, a thane of Ealdorman Morcar's lands, not far at all from yours," he replied in an amicable manner. Wulfstan found himself taking an instant liking to Ulfcytel.

"Wessachia is a long march from my home area," Wulfstan remarked. "I have yet to visit your province."

Ulfcytel grinned lightly. "It may be that distances seem shorter to a sky rider … you will have to forgive me for the manner in which I estimate such things."

"I imagine so," Wulfstan commented. He took a deep breath, and fixed the sky rider with a solemn look. "I know that you have little time. I also have little time, and an urgent task lies ahead of me. I am no sky rider, but time demands that I need a steed."

The other man's eyes widened considerably at the entreaty. It was clearly not the kind of request that he had been expecting. "You mean to ride a sky steed? And I sense that you have never ridden before?"

"Is it true that it is not unlike riding upon a horse, in some ways?" Wulfstan queried. His tone strongly conveyed that this was no jest, of any sort.

"In some ways, yes, but in others it is entirely different," Ulfcytel said, regarding Wulfstan with an expression that displayed both caution and curiosity. "And no person can say how a man reacts when going up into the skies. I have seen many good warriors that wished to be sky riders, who were unable to master their fears when taken away from solid footing."

"Then it is my risk to take," Wulfstan replied, holding Ulfcytel's gaze. "Can you tell me something of the use of the reins? In guiding the sky steeds?"

Ulfcytel shook his head. "Even if I did, you could not take one of the steeds out of here. I do not have such authority."

Wulfstan could only speak the truth in response.

"This is a desperate time, Ulfcytel of Wessachia. You do not need me to tell you that … your own eyes tell you that truth. I was sent forth by Ealdorman Aelfric on a long journey last night, into land held by the enemy, and I have returned. I now have a task even more important, one that may bring hope to all of us. There is no time to seek out the greater thanes such as Aelfric, and I can only do this if I have a sky steed to ride. Know that this task will not take me into enemy lands, and I will return from it as well."

"You cannot just take a sky steed, Wulfstan," Ulfcytyel responded, in the kind of manner that displayed the sky rider's disbelief that he even had to say the words aloud to Wulfstan.

"Do you not keep spare mounts?" Wulfstan pressed.

Ulfcytel grew silent for a moment. When he finally spoke again, his voice was laden with sorrow. "Great tragedy has befallen us this morning, and there are several more steeds than trained riders in this camp now."

"I heard something of the fighting, after I had returned," Wulfstan replied in a sympathetic voice. "Though I know little of what happened, I am very sorry to hear of any losses, as I have come to know loss well in the past couple of days."

Ulfcytel gaze bored into Wulfstan, and his voice was suddenly tense. "And what is this matter that cannot wait?"

Wulfstan refused to give a falsehood to Ulfcytel, but he also did not choose to offer overly much in the way of explanation. He hoped that a vague answer would suffice, as full details would have the other thinking him to be lost in the grip of madness.

"I am going to try and summon some more help, from a source that none of our leaders has yet considered. I do not have time to try and convince them, nor would they give me the time, as they are now in the thick of the battle. That is why every moment counts, and why I am at your mercy, Ulfcytel," Wulfstan said.

"Are you certain that the leaders of this army have not considered whatever it is that you wish to do?" Ulfcytel asked.

"Thanes ... counts ... ealdorman ... none of them would try what I am to try, nor would they even think of what I wish to do. I have my reasons for keeping my own confidence on this. I am just one man, and would be asking you for just one steed, in order to gain a chance to bring great help to the Saxan defense," Wulfstan said, his voice taking on a pleading tone.

"You appear convinced of this path that you wish to take, and I do not doubt your sincerity," Ulfcytel stated, staring at Wulfstan intently, with a tense expression.

"It is a chance, nothing less, and nothing more. But it will not take a steed away from a rider, and will only risk the life of one man ... a man who is willing to risk it. And you and I both know that many more men fall with each minute that passes," Wulfstan continued.

The answer must have seemed reasonable enough to Ulfcytel, or at least it had connected to something personal, deep within him. The sky rider did not refuse Wulfstan outright, as he seemed to become lost for a moment in his private thoughts.

There was probably not one Saxan anywhere on the Plains of Athelney that day who would not welcome a new influx of support, during such a desperate time. Ulfcytel was no exception.

"Wulfstan of Sussachia, do you speak the truth in this? Do you really seek a new source of help? One that will matter?" Ulfcytel questioned him, his rigid gaze locked onto Wulfstan's eyes.

Wulfstan did not so much as blink.

"Help that would not come from any other place, currently in the minds of those in authority over us," Wulfstan answered firmly. "And yes, one that would matter greatly, if this help can indeed be gained."

"Have you ridden horses before?" Ulfcytyl asked.

Wulfstan inclined his head. "I have."

Slowly, Ulfcytel's head tilted up and down in a slow nod, as he emerged from the depths of his rumination. It was clear that strong misgivings still tugged at the mind of the Saxan sky rider.

"I will take you with me, when I go up for my patrol of the rear areas. Know that this choice of yours is likely folly, but I will not stand in the way, if you truly think that you can find us some significant help. We have lost enough already," Ulfcytel said, the look in his eyes becoming momentarily downcast.

"I cannot say whether my task will come to any good, but it will do no harm, and will not burden our army any worse … thank you, Ulfcytel," Wulfstan responded, feeling relieved.

"I will not be able to make you a skilled rider. I only can give you what you need to survive a flight. You will follow my instructions very carefully, every word," Ulfcytel said, in a sharper tone.

Wulfstan nodded resolutely. "I will."

"Then wait here, and I will call you when I am ready," Ulfcytel said. He shook his head again, as if he could not believe what he had just acquiesced to. "You are fortunate that I am going alone on patrol, for even if one other was with me, I do not doubt that you would be denied … perhaps we should set to flight now, before good sense comes over me."

Walking away, Ulfcytel went back over to the two sentries, where he talked with them for a short while longer. He then walked into the midst of the Himmerosen, striding towards one steed in particular. He rubbed the side of its neck, and looked the winged creature over, as if evaluating its condition.

Ulfcytel straightened up, glanced over towards Wulfstan, and summoned him over. He then called out for some of the camp attendants. When they had come over to him, he instructed them to saddle and prepare the harness on the mount that he had been inspecting, one whose name was Spirit Wing. He exhorted them to make haste, and the camp attendants nodded dutifully, hurrying off.

While he and Wulfstan were waiting, he talked with Wulfstan about the Himmerosen, their nature, and the means of riding upon one in the sky. Ulfcytel proceeded very carefully over the basic methods of getting the Himmerosen to rise, to drop, to speed up, to slow down, or to turn to the left and right.

With the exception of rising and lowering in elevation, the general techniques were not all that different from those used with horses. Those similar techniques would guide the steed when it walked upon land as well. The close relation of most of the techniques to riding a horse came as a very welcome relief to Wulfstan, and he realized that it was probably one of the major elements in Ulfcytel's decision.

As Wulfstan harbored a little experience with riding horses, he was not worried about retaining a majority of the instructions. Only the unfamiliar, primary elements involved in guiding the steed higher or lower once airborne, and the impending sensation of flight, would be of any significant challenge.

Wulfstan then strolled along with Ulfcytel as the sky rider proceeded over to another Himmerosen, which enthusiastically greeted the sky rider with anxious whines and several licks upon his face. Ulfcytel pressed his head to the forehead of the steed, while rubbing both sides of its broad head with his hands, demonstrating genuine affection for creature. He then took up the steed's reins and held them loosely, as it was already saddled and harnessed.

"This is my steed, Cloud Runner," Ulfcytel said. "He and I have soared across Saxan skies far too many times to count, and he has always brought me back to Saxan ground safely."

Wulfstan could hear the strong resonance of the rider's great esteem for his steed through the words. It was plainly evident that a powerful bond existed between the two of them.

It was not much longer before the two camp attendants approached them, leading a fully harnessed, saddled Spirit Wing forward on tethers. They brought the Himmerosen up alongside Cloud Runner.

The two creatures looked rested and healthy enough, with a luxuriant sheen to their black and brown coats. A spry look was reflected in their eyes, and their postures were firm and proud. Wulfstan's steed was just a little shorter, and slightly narrower of back, than Ulfcytyl's, minor differences that could only be noted when the two creatures were standing side by side.

"I took the liberty of choosing for you a steed that has good speed, and most excellent endurance," Ulfcytel commented. "The fastest of our steeds must remain with the trained warriors, but this one will allow you to travel as far as any of their kind could. As you heard, his name is Spirit Wing ... not too different of a name from Prince Aidan's own horse ... but it is a proper name, as I believe this one could reach Palladium itself if it tried."

Wulfstan worked to take the comments in stride, though the Saxan sky rider had unintentionally struck very close to the essence of his upcoming mission. Endurance was exactly what Wulfstan needed in a sky steed, and he could not help but think that the All-Father had just given him a bountiful grace with the particular steed that Ulfcytel had selected.

"I want you to know that I am not seeking to go quite that far. I do intend to stay in the world," Wulfstan replied, in jest, with a light-hearted smile.

"I hope you do as well," Ulfcytel responded, with an easygoing laugh.

At Ulfctyel's encouragement, Wulfstan placed his left foot in the stirrup and hoisted himself up into the saddle. It was a movement that was more awkward than mounting a horse, as the saddle itself sat a little forward of the creature's great set of wings.

In a practical sense, it was like he was seated on a six-limbed creature, positioned where the saddle was arranged close to the front limbs, at the base of the Himmeros's burly neck. The location of the saddle, and some marked differences in the design of the saddle as compared to those used on horses, required a little adjustment on Wulfstan's part. Otherwise, the feeling of sitting upon the creature was relatively familiar, not all that far removed from the sensation of being astride a horse.

Turning his head, he looked down the length of the creature's body, studying the broad wings that were now partially outstretched. He marveled at the sculpted, pronounced musculature attached to those wings.

The awareness of what he was about to attempt was beginning to fully dawn on him, accelerating rapidly as he looked at the wings. Wulfstan began to feel his heart rate rise, the beats quickening as a feeling of lightheadedness came over him.

In only a few moments he was going to be experiencing flight, for the first time in his life. Even more daunting, everything he sought to do depended upon his acclimating immediately to the act of flying.

He had no way of knowing how he would react, once in the sky. As Ulfcytel had said, some who were excellent, brave warriors while on the ground could not adjust to the vastly different environment of flight.

Wulfstan would not know the answers for himself until he was already in the air. He wrenched his thoughts away from the troubling uncertainty, knowing that worrying about it could profit him nothing.

Ulfcytel had mounted by then, and brought his steed around to face Wulfstan's. Ulfcytl guided Wulfstan through the securing of the additional leather straps that would hold him in the saddle, in the instance that the steed had to make any sudden movements, or go upside down.

Wulfstan tightened the straps and buckled their ends, gaining a little more confidence from the feeling of being anchored into the saddle. Ulfcytel then questioned Wulfstan briefly on the various methods for guiding the steeds in the air. Wulfstan answered the veteran sky rider to the other's satisfaction.

"Are you ready?" Ulfcytel asked him, at the end of the questioning.

Wulfstan nodded, taking a deep breath. It was much more a matter of necessity rather than readiness, but what had to be done, had to be done. "As ready as I am ever going to be, with the time we have available to us."

"Then let us take to the skies," Ulfcytel said, with a hint of exuberance.

Turning his steed, Ulfcytel guided it forward. Wulfstan followed, as they worked their way over to a long stretch of open ground. Following Ulfcytel's instigation, Cloud Runner sprang forward, and then leaped up, towards the sky, pumping its wings furiously. The creature began to ascend slowly, with each flex of its wings.

Wulfstan took another deep breath, and uttered a silent prayer to the Almighty. Gripping the reins, he let out a long, extended breath. Then, he executed the motions to command the steed to take flight, as he had been instructed, and followed in the wake of the sky rider.

Wulfstan's sky steed bounded forward and then leaped. A rush of adrenaline manifested with the explosion of movement, and escalated within Wulfstan, as the Himmeros' wings clung to the air and lifted them off of the ground. His stomach felt queasy, and he had to close his eyes for a moment to avoid becoming too disoriented. He felt a strong, constant pull at his back, causing him to brace his feet in the stirrups and hold onto the reins firmly. The air beat incessantly against his face while the steed's wings pumped vigorously, and he felt immensely glad for the securing straps as the Himmeros went into a steep incline.

Opening his eyes, he was relieved that all he could see ahead of him was Ulfcytel, and the cloud-draped skies above. He craned his neck back, and kept his eyes fixed forward. He knew the ground was falling away behind him, and he did everything that he could to resist the temptation to turn his head and look.

The steed climbed higher and higher. Wulfstan was not worried about determining where they were, as he placed his full trust in Ulfcytel. He tried to concentrate on the rhythmic, powerful beats of the Himmeros' wings, feeling the exceptional power of the steed just underneath him.

Even though he had been airborne for only a handful of moments, he completely understood why the sky riders had always been said to be insatiably loyal, and virtually inseparable, from their steeds. Wulfstan's life was now in a very fragile state, completely held in the dominion of his steed. If anything amiss happened to the steed, he would be rendered entirely helpless. He had never experienced such an extreme dependency before, save for his infancy in the hands of his parents.

Quickly, he repressed the daunting thoughts, and grasped anxiously at lighter things to occupy his mind. The effort was largely futile, as his rattled nerves forced any comforting notions to vanish. Though the final verdict was not yet determined on his own accord, he knew that he could never cast aspersions on anyone that found flight to be something to avoid.

The climbing sensation seemed to go on forever. The unsettled feeling in his stomach persisted, and a faint dizziness continued to shroud him.

Wulfstan had begun to wonder if it would ever end, when he finally noticed Ulfcytel's steed level out, and break out of its sharp climb. Wulfstan clenched the reins and pressed his heels against the sides of his steed, as he closed in on the altitude that Ulfcytel was maintaining.

Using the instructions that Ulfcytel had given him, he successfully guided Spirit Wing into evening out its course of flight. The steed glided forward, drifting gracefully on the air currents, and the taut pressure eased from Wulfstan's back as he was brought into a vertical, sitting position. Wary to keep his eyes away from the ground so far below, he riveted his gaze onto the back of Ulfcytel's dark tunic.

After a moment, he closed his eyes, feeling the crisp winds flowing across his face. Eventually, he knew that he would have to face the stark realities of flight, as Ulfcytel would not be with him for his mission, or his eventual return. It was also ludicrous to think that he could find his way back to the Saxan encampment without looking out over the ground.

Slowly, calling upon his willpower, he forced his eyes to open, lowering his gaze slightly from Ulfcytel's back. He turned his head so that the sky rider was no longer in his field of vision. The light of day flooded into his eyes, bringing along with it a host of new, amazing sights. It was a perspective like none other that he had ever experienced before.

It was like the entire world had opened up around him. He had never thought such a wondrous sight could be experienced, as he looked out over endless leagues of hills, forests, streams, and plains, spreading in all directions.

The view far transcended everything that he had ever seen before, even from the summit of the highest hill or mountain that he had climbed in the past. Almost forgetting to breathe, he chanced a glance directly downward.

His breath caught in his lungs. Everything below him was displayed in extreme miniature, even the large, forested hills that took so long to skirt when traveling on the ground. It was a stunning, wholly unprecedented way of looking upon the world, and Wulfstan felt a little envy underneath his fears. The sky riders were certainly afforded a tremendously astounding experience, each and every time that they took their steeds into the skies.

"To the right," Ulfcytel shouted from up ahead of him, bringing Wulfstan's attention back into focus.

Wulfstan guided Spirit Wing in a curving turn to the right, straightening out again just behind Ulfcytel. The sky rider gestured for Wulfstan to come up to him, and slowed his steed down long enough to let Wulfstan's pull up alongside.

"Different from what you have been used to, is it not?" Ulfcytel inquired, in a raised voice that cut through the air blowing over his body.

"Incredible," Wulfstan replied, his eyes wide with the thrill of it.

"Look down, to the right," Ulfcytel suggested.

Wulfstan turned his head and looked. The battle was sprawled out across the land, in the distance. The two armies appeared like two

vast shadows on the undulating plain.

"It looks like we have held!" exclaimed Ulfcytel, his words echoing with spirited fervor at the pronouncement.

Peering more attentively, Wulfstan could ascertain that the farther, and much larger, of the great shadows, which he knew at once was the invading army, was slowly crawling back, away from the other shadow. There was only one conclusion to draw from the sight.

The enemy was retreating from the battlefield, en masse. It meant that the day's fighting was likely over, and it was apparent that the Saxan lines still held on the battlefield.

From the great heights he could see the locations of the enemy encampments off in the distance, a monstrosity of tents that was significantly larger than the square-shaped encampment on their own side.

"Whatever task you are on, do not stray too close to the enemy," Ulfcytel admonished Wulfstan sternly "You would be no match for a Trogen warrior upon a Harrak, and there are a great number of both that way."

"I will not be going that way, not at all," Wulfstan replied.

A kind smile came to Ulfcytel's face. "May your flight be true, Wulfstan, and may you find the help that you are looking for. We will have to part ways now, as I must keep some eyes on those dark storm clouds far below."

Ulfcytel cast a glance downward, in the direction of the shadowy masses marking the position of the enemy invaders.

"Ulfcytel, thank you for trusting in me, a man that you have not known before," Wulfstan said, in all sincerity and gratitude.

"I have been a good judge of men throughout my life, and I see no reason why my senses should begin failing me now," Ulfcytel replied. His gaze then became a little narrower, as his voice evened out. "Do not disappoint me in this."

"If this task comes to success, then know that you have been a great part of it," Wulfstan stated. "Without you, I could not take this path."

"It is simply good to see such courage in one man," Ulfcytel said. "That I will not impede. Fly to success in your quest!"

Raising his right hand to bid him well, Ulfcytel guided his steed sharply off to the left, leaving Wulfstan by himself. After just a few moments, Wulfstan felt isolated. There was little else but the sounds of the steed's flapping wings, and the winds whipping brusquely about his ears.

Banking his own steed off to the left, Wulfstan was careful to put some more distance between himself and the battlefield. His mission was reckless enough, and he did not need to endanger it further by being needlessly careless.

He took Ulfcytel's words to heart regarding the dangers of encountering enemy sky riders. If he was caught out in the open sky by trained, veteran sky warriors, especially by the powerful brutes whose kind had nearly killed him in the attack on the Saxan encampment, then he was as good as dead.

Wulfstan craned his neck all around, scanning the upper skies for the unique, white patch he had sighted from the ground. He espied it rather quickly, set against the blue sky with nothing to obstruct his view of it. Fortuitously, he saw that it was located up and even farther to the left of him, situated well away from the battle lines. Seeing it from the higher altitude, the patch looked much larger in size.

Even so, he could tell that it was still a very long distance away. Steadying his nerves, and letting out another extended, relaxing exhalation, Wulfstan said one more silent prayer to the Almighty. He then guided Spirit Wing to the left, angling up into another steep incline. The heavy, pulling sensation returned to his back, and again he braced his feet more forcefully in the stirrups.

He kept his eyes fixed on the white patch as he soared into the upper skies on the back of the winged steed, wrestling with the numerous feelings sweeping through him. The enemy was now of little concern. Wulfstan's assessment of the skies, and his own proximity to the battle lines prior to the ascension, had shown that the enemy forces were far away. Furthermore, they had probably suffered a high enough cost in the day's fighting, such that they would not be inclined to follow a lone rider well behind the Saxan lines; and certainly not one who was recklessly striving for the uppermost heights.

The dizzying flight continued to pull him farther and farther away from the battlefield and encampments. His head was rigidly set forward, steadfastly refusing to look below, as he set all of his thoughts upon his intended destination. He was not about to turn back, and there was little sense in courting more fears that would only serve to distract or disrupt.

Wulfstan clenched the reins even tighter, as he decided to lean forward and tuck his head in closer to the neck of the beast. It was as if he subconsciously wanted to fuse himself into the creature, and acquire the inner security that would come with being a living part of a beast with wings. He was painfully conscious of the reality that his own natural form did not possess the necessary tools for flight.

A layer of clouds was drifting into sight, directly ahead of him, now crossing his path. From below, it looked to have a rather flat-bottomed underside, like a great, stretched cloak, bearing along with it some accumulations of a kind of puffy, light-gray effluvium. In some ways, it resembled the thick fogs that cloaked the hills and valleys of his homeland in the ambience of a cool, misty morning.

Wulfstan kept himself steeled, as the Himmeros continued to rapidly ascend, gaining increasing height until the misty wisps of the first cloud layer caressed and wrapped around both man and Himmeros alike. Wulfstan and Spirit Wing then plunged into the heart of the cool vapors. His world became an impenetrable mass of light gray, until he abruptly burst forth into the embrace of sunlight once again.

While looking very flat on the bottom, the cloud mass held a spectrum of varying contours on the other side. In many places, the formations stretched upward, towering above him like great hills, while other areas of the cloud mass were comprised of lower, undulating textures, such as the particular location where he had passed through the vaporous substance.

It was an amazing vista to behold, and his eyes were mesmerized for several moments as he looked out over the rolling, cloud-landscape. Obstructing his view of the land far below, the sight also brought a bit of comfort to his raw, rattled nerves.

Inspired by his passage above the first cloud layer, Wulfstan focused his resolve to an even greater degree, as he looked up towards the white patch beckoning to him from farther above. Eager to traverse the remaining distance to it, he spurred the Himmeros onward.

"Spirit Wing, reach that pure white cloud, the one you see far ahead," Wulfstan urged the steed in a loud voice.

He knew that while the beast might not understand his words, it might sense his intentions in some subtle way, and perhaps derive some impetus from them. Animals often appeared to possess a sixth sense, and

Wulfstan was not about to underestimate the perceptiveness of such an incredible creature as Spirit Wing.

It took a short while for them to reach the next level of clouds, and Wulfstan nearly avoided having to pass through them. They were prominent, puffy masses, scattered all about the high altitude, as if amorphous blotches of white had been woven randomly into an aqua tapestry. The bodies of the towering, vaporous formations were much more vertical than horizontal, and were separated by wide swathes of unsullied, blue-green sky.

Wulfstan saw the unique white patch marking his destination looming ever larger ahead of him, but his angle of approach ended up taking him through one of the dispersed, bulging masses of vapor. The passage through the towering expanse took a little longer than going through the lower mass had. Wulfstan and his steed broke out into the open again, just short of the uppermost reaches of the soaring cloud mass.

As they continued to climb upward, he began to notice some disturbing changes occurring within his immediate environment. The cooling of the air about him had not been bothersome before, but an icy, discomfiting chill had begun to take root.

They were approaching a broad, third layer of clouds. The layer ahead was already in a position to intersect with their path, as its vanguard blotted out Wulfstan's view of his snow-white objective. During the same period, his breathing began to become much more labored, and his heart rate sharply increased.

Unease drifted to the forefront of his mind, and he refocused the force of his thoughts towards the oncoming layer of clouds. The third layer looked to be more of a long, linear array of billowing white clouds. As the clouds themselves were an incredible phenomenon to experience, and he needed something to concentrate on, Wulfstan determined to observe them a little closer, as he passed through their midst.

At the very least, the clouds could offer him some distractions from the mounting anxieties plaguing him from within. His diagonal ascent took him straight into the body of the clouds, and he felt the cool dampness engulf him.

When he had entered the third mass of clouds, the world again became an enveloping, unblemished sheet of gray, for several moments. In some ways, it was like existing within a realm of absolute, formless nothingness until he was freed back into the sunlight.

Looking down on the layer, it appeared to his eyes to be solid and dense, to the degree that it almost seemed strange that he had been able to pass through its midst at all. As before, he found that he was grateful for that density, as it completely blocked out the sight of the land far, far below.

Beyond the third cloud layer, there was nothing left before him but the growing, snow-white patch, and the blue-green, silken firmament beyond it. The biting cold continued to increase in its intensity, almost at the same rate as the air thinned. An urgency developed in Wulfstan, as he started to feel the efforts of the Himmeros underneath him noticeably become more strained.

Even more alarming, Wulfstan's own vision was starting to distort, and a pervasive feeling of disorientation was spreading over his body. It was a very alarming development, adding briskly to his fears, as his steed struggled to continue onward. He wondered if he had been a total fool in trusting to his instincts, but he was not about to concede.

"Keep strong, keep strong!" he exhorted the increasingly beleaguered creature, injecting confidence into his tone, even though he was not at all certain about their fate.

He prayed silently to the All-Father, with great urgency in his heart, that both he and the steed could keep enough breath in their lungs to reach the gleaming white patch.

Ignoring his racing heartbeat, as his lungs strove futilely to draw adequate breath in the sparseness of the air, Wulfstan continued imploring the steed to keep pressing upward. For him, the white patch was now his entire universe, more valuable than the world below him, and even more important than his concern for his own well-being. Getting to that white mass was his consuming, irrevocable goal, for it was only through the attainment of that altitude that even the possibility of his hopes could begin to be realized. It was the only place where he could find out whether or not his instincts and dreams held any truth to them.

Higher and higher, Spirit Wing climbed bravely onward. Wulfstan had unwittingly passed through altitudes that no other Saxan had dared to travel. The dizzy sensations continued to rise inside of him, as the breathable air became ever more scarce. At times, it seemed like the white mass above him was dancing atop a blue-green surface. His mind vacillated between cognizance of what he was doing, and an empty blankness that seemed oddly inviting.

He shook his head vigorously, and fought with all the force of his will not to give into that nihilistic seduction. He clung onto consciousness with every bit of strength that he had left inside of him, knowing that it was the slim thread holding him to life.

With little warning, random patches of darkness started to pulse before his eyes, as a particularly light-headed feeling showered over him. His Himmeros began to snort and whine in the thin air, as its own breathing became laborious in its intensifying exertion.

The whiteness was closer than before, but still seemed to be at a dauntingly far distance. Wulfstan could only hope that his steed somehow understood the desperate nature of their ascent, and the tremendous need to reach that whiteness. In a fully lucid moment, Wulfstan greatly feared that the creature's sense of self-preservation would probably cause it to turn away from their course.

Digging his heels in, and renewing his tight grip on the reins, Wulfstan did everything that he could to convey to the steed his feverish desire to reach that swathe of whiteness.

"Get there ... Spirit Wing ... reach for that place ahead with everything you have. You must reach ... that ... place ... " Wulfstan said, his voice starting to slur and trail off.

Wulfstan then felt himself spiraling into the abyssal depths of unconsciousness. He fought valiantly against the inner descent, resisting to the utmost limit of his remarkable willpower, before finally being forced to succumb to the overwhelming, unforgiving powers of nature.

He drifted faster, before plummeting helplessly into the blackness, oblivious to whether his steed was still striving forward, or had joined him in the dark embrace. His last thought was that he hoped that the Almighty would forgive his recklessness, and see that he had only been trying to find a way to help the people of his land.

DEGANAWIDA

Deganawida walked alone, proceeding quietly towards the end of the last contingent of refugees. Farther behind him were the warriors protecting the rear of the great exodus. It was one of the few moments in the day that Deganawida had been able to gain a degree of solitude, though every perspective that he took revealed nothing but a gaping, beckoning darkness.

Deganawida was lost deep within his thoughts, and utterly weary of spirit, body, and mind. Despite the urgency of the situation, and the constant threat from the pursuing invaders, the stalwart clan matrons, supported by the sachems and headmen of the villages, and the Great Sachems of the Grand Council, had done the impossible. They had managed to keep an orderly calm instilled in the mass migration, as it moved ever farther into the southeastern forests of the tribal lands.

Word had long since spread that the Midragardan ships had been overtaken in the Shimmering River. It was common knowledge that the enemy held the river, and was steadily pressing along two fronts. The newly-arrived forces were marching upon the refugees from the north, while the main invasion force continued up behind them from the west. There were no illusions about the situation; the multitudes of survivors were being herded towards a finite boundary.

Scouts were ranging far and wide through the woodlands. They took great risks to keep a broad perimeter warded around the huge body of exiles, so that any hostile menace would at least be detected early enough that advance warnings could be delivered to the refugees.

Whatever weapons could be gathered had been passed out among all that could hold them, including even the older children. Deganawida knew that the weapons would avail the refugees little to nothing, if the iron-sheathed enemy knights were to fall amongst them. Even so, he also knew that the feel of a weapon in one's hand brought some intrinsic reassurances with it, and bolstered teetering courage. In those areas alone, there was great value to the decision to distribute the weapons among the throngs of refugees.

The only consolation in taking to the lands south of the Shimmering River was that the tribal people did not risk being pushed into the territory of hostile tribes. Yet the immediate future was now limned clearly enough, as the edge where land and the ocean met marked a place of destiny.

With a deepening frown, Deganawida shook his head, as one method of hunting deer was evoked in his mind. Setting up temporary camps, tribesmen erected triangular wooden enclosures close by, which were then concealed with branches and other brush. Working in small groups, the hunters would then make their way a good distance from the front of the enclosures, and begin flushing any deer in the area out, driving the deer ahead of them. The creatures were finally herded into the masked enclosures, where the animals were trapped. It was a very effective method of hunting, often resulting in the harvest of a hundred or more deer over the course of a single hunt.

In a dark way of looking at it, the tribes were now facing a plight similar to that of the deer, with the enemy forces being the hunters. In this instance, the triangular enclosure was the land itself, with the boundaries defined by the open sea. The five tribes were being herded into a most deadly trap, facing no better fate than that of the hapless deer caught within the wooden enclosures.

Deganawida could only wonder where the Wizards who held affinity for the tribal lands had gone. It seemed as if the only will that prevailed among Wizards associated with the tribal lands was that of the reviled Dark Brother. The hour had long ago grown desperate, and yet there was no sign of the benevolent Light Brother, who had so often manifested to help the tribal peoples in much less trying times.

Even worse, the Wizard that Deganawida's own name was derived from had not yet appeared, despite a promise made so many ages ago. After setting up the first Grand Council, and teaching the Great Law, the Wizard named Deganawida had departed from the view of the tribal peoples. He had not left before giving a promise to the Five Tribes; that he would return if the peace should ever fail. All that the tribes had to do was call out his name in the midst of a gathering storm.

"Deganawida, from whom I received my own name, I call out to you, as the Five Realms, and the Great Law, may soon fall into darkest night," Deganawida suddenly said aloud. "The peace has never been more threatened. We cannot survive what is coming. We need you to return to us in this terrible hour."

Debris crunched and snapped under the multitude of steps from the tribal people proceeding forward just ahead of him. His ears sifted out the low sounds of conversation, carried on the breezes that swayed the branches of the surrounding trees.

If he had expected something profound to happen at that moment, as he was the very one that had inherited the traditional place honoring the Wizard Deganawida on the Grand Council, he was to be sorely disappointed. As he continued forward, drawing closer to the refugees, everything stayed as it was, with no sounds or sights of anything unusual.

A spark of anger lit his spirit aflame.

"Deganawida! The peace is failing, and you promised to return to us in our desperate hour! Can you not hear us?" Deganawida said, a little louder, his voice taking on a hint of accusation.

Deganawida wished bitterly that he were a Wizard, one of the legendary immortals who could do something extraordinary in the momentous hour. Yet he was just a man, even if he had acquired a few exceptional talents and skills over the course of his long life.

But even as a man, he wished that he could gain some sign from the One Spirit. Whether a great vision, or a small symbol, he just wished that he could see even the slightest glimmer of light within all the suffocating darkness shrouding his people and lands.

Though he had seen nothing in the way of signs, he did not lash out at the One Spirit in anger, as some tended to do under trying circumstances. He knew that in the mortal world, for reasons that he could not fathom, tragedy and fortune fell like rain upon all humankind; the wicked and the innocent alike.

It was one aspect of life that he had chosen to simply accept, lest he kindle resentments at the terrible plight of humans. The matter of the current threat, enveloping each and every surviving tribal member, nonetheless battered Deganawida's conscience relentlessly.

The tormenting thoughts were abated for a moment, as Deganawida was distracted from his reflections. A warrior came trotting into sight, from the trees ahead. Deganawida welcomed the diversion, as it kept him from dwelling upon the abyss that they were all being shoved towards.

The warrior was a young Onan, from a village on the northernmost edges of the tribe's territory. His eyes did not hide the anxiety present within him, though his face mustered a smile, as he lowered his eyes in respect to Deganawida.

"Deganawida, I have been sent to ask you to come, and eat. A bear has been brought down, a bear of great size and strength, larger than any that the ones that hunted it have ever seen," the warrior informed him, with an undercurrent of enthusiasm. "Scouts came across the tracks of this bear as they found better paths to the south. They were fresh tracks, and it did not take long for the hunting party to find the creature.

None were hurt when they took the great beast. No greater quarry could have been discovered. All see this as a great blessing, and all ask that you come and eat of this great bounty."

Deganawida smiled at the young warrior. In the face of all their ongoing trials and hardships, the suffering exiles wanted him to indulge in a meal, of a kind cherished in their culture. In better times, the meat of a bear held great significance within the tribes, often used in sacred ceremonies.

Bear meat was a cause of celebration, which was a feeling that seemed so very far removed from Deganawida's heart at the moment. Yet he could not deny the fact that his stomach felt otherwise regarding the prospect of consuming bear meat. He had partaken of quite enough corn meal, even sweetened as it was with the syrup made from the boiled sap of the maple tree.

Only that afternoon, as he had opened up a bark container to withdraw a small portion of dried fish, he had inwardly lamented that the tribes could not soothe their hardships with the gifts of their own lands. They were being forcibly prevented from harvesting the abundant eel and salmon that made their visits to the rivers of the tribal lands every spring.

The tribes had been reduced to scraping up whatever they could find along the sorrowful trail. It just so happened that they had discovered a bear on that pathway.

"All know that you would not wish to partake of a meal such as this, at a time like this. Yet all insist that you accept this gift. You need your strength too, Deganawida," the warrior said in a gentle tone, when the sachem did not respond immediately.

"I do not wish to take this meat. Distribute it to the others, who need its sustenance more than I do," Deganawida said evenly.

"They knew that you would ask this, and have said that none will eat, if you do not. They will leave this meat behind, untouched, if none of it passes the lips of Deganawida," the warrior responded, a little more firmly.

"That would be a very foolish thing to do," Deganawida said. "You have acquired meat that can feed many, and bring strength to a multitude of weary limbs and hearts."

"Then all will make a fool's choice," the warrior replied somberly.

Deganawida placed a hand on the upper left arm of the warrior, and looked the young man in the eyes. He knew that even if his people were under the worst of famines, they were stubborn enough of will to walk away, and leave the meat of ten bears to waste, if they were determined on a certain course.

"I will accept. But only if this meal is shared with the oldest, and those that are struggling the most. They must share in this meal, if I am to take part in it. That which is not eaten, distribute among as many as you can, for whatever uses can be made of what remains," Deganawida replied. "This is what I ask, in return for accepting this gift."

Deganawida knew that many would benefit beyond the food itself. As the tribal practice was with all types of prey, whether deer, beavers, bear, or anything else, uses were found for all manner of bodily elements.

Coating the skin with bear grease helped to keep bothersome insects away in warmer weather. The skins of bears made for wondrous fur blankets. Little to nothing of the kill would be wasted, and Deganawida wanted to make certain that all gifts from the animal were put to use, for those that needed them the most during such a time of great necessity.

The warrior nodded, his dark eyes holding Deganawida's gaze without blinking. "Yes, Deganawida. It shall be as you ask."

"Then I will forgo cornmeal and dried fish this night, and accept this generous gift from my Onan brothers and sisters," Deganawida answered, nodding to the warrior.

As he walked with the warrior towards the promised meal, he realized that for a few precious moments, his growing feeling of despondency had been lifted. The unexpected development of the bear meat, and the offering of it to him by his fellow Onan, was, he abruptly recognized, a sign. It was something for him to hold onto during his tremendous ordeal, a glimmering beacon of the purest light; an enduring radiance that was not consumed by the ravenous darkness surrounding it.

AETHELSTAN

Aethelstan lowered himself into a sitting position, easing close to the edge of the elevated tier of stone. He looked out over the drop to the sloping ground far below, leading to the shoreline of the cavern-lake. His eyes traveled out across the waters, which were tinted with the pale blue of the glowing patches of light that were so abundant in the Unguhur Realm.

A few rafts could be seen out on the lake surface. The Unguhur on them worked patiently, with long spearing implements in hand, to draw food from the murky depths.

Here and there, drifting along the surface, Aethelstan could see the forms of the huge, reptilian creatures that shared the Unguhur's world. None of his men ventured close to the water because of the creatures, and all had expressed gladness that the habitat of the waterborne beasts did not extend to Saxan rivers. He could not disagree, as even with the far distance he felt a tingling of his nerves at the sight of the massive predators. Yet the Unguhur seemed to be entirely unconcerned with the creatures, living side by side with them.

He stared off towards the mouth of an underground waterway, where it left the enormous cavern by means of a wide, high tunnel. It was the largest offshoot from the underground lake that he could see. He watched as one of the Unguhur rafts disappeared into its midst, wondering about the task occupying the creature piloting it.

There was so much for him to learn regarding his generous, and very strange, hosts. He had only the scraps and shards of stories, legends, and a few accounts to work with when he was brought down into their subterranean world. He was absorbing as much as he could about their ways, but the realm of creatures who did not see the sun during the day, or gaze towards the moon at night, was very different in essence from the things of his own life experience.

A number of thoughts were spinning throughout his troubled mind, as he gazed out across the dark waters, pondering the Saxans' current predicament. Of those who had taken refuge among the Unguhur, there were just over two hundred Saxan survivors who were entirely self-sufficient in their health. Nearly seventy or so others were like Aethelstan, in need of some minor assistance, not yet free from the dangers of battle wounds, but healing rather well. There were about twenty-five that would need significant aid for some time to come.

Many of the latter group were not likely to survive the coming days, as a few of them were already in the clutches of feverish torments, with their wounds putrefying and spreading their malignancy rapidly.

The overall realization of the Saxan contingent's condition was like a cold sword cleaving deep into his soul. Less than three hundred men remained out of an initial force of a few thousand.

As the force had been assembled from the immediate region, including much of Wassachia and the Wesvald, it was certain that every survivor with Aethelstan had suffered a great personal loss in the battle; whether a friend, a brother, a father, or some other manner of kin. There would not be one soul in the midst of the terrible ordeal that did not mourn the loss of someone close to heart. In such a cold, harsh light, Aethelstan knew that every single man in the underground haven was deeply wounded, whether in spirit, physically, or both.

Even worse, with the urgency of the situation, there had been no time for burials. Every Saxan was well-aware that their comrades had been left to decay, and the bellies of scavengers out on the surface. It was one matter that Aethelstan wished he could broach with the Unguhur, but he did not yet know what their own practices were, involving their dead.

He had seen nothing in the way of tombs during his short tenure in Oranim, or any sign that the Unguhur committed the bodies of the dead to fire. He had not been able to query the Woodsman regarding the Unguhur's ways, as he was the only human that might know the answer. Compounding the issue was the fact that Aethelstan was not yet comfortable interacting directly with the Unguhur, and did not want to inadvertently cause offense to his hosts, so soon after arriving in their realm.

Abandoning the bodies of the brave Saxans wrenched Aethelstan's gut, at a very intimate level. He did not want to open the gates to his own personal losses. So many that he considered trusted friends and comrades had fallen, and many of the slain were related to him in blood. He had to stifle the flood of emotions that threatened to break out inside him. A time for mourning and remembrance would come later. He had to keep his composure and focus for the sake of the men that yet survived.

One thought superseded all others. He had to get as many of the remaining Saxans as possible back to the embraces of their loved ones.

It was the same goal that he held from the first moments that the horns had called out the signal to begin the long march out from the gates of Bergton, the last morning that he had set his eyes upon his own wife and children.

The way would be far from easy, even if the Unguhur had destroyed the enemy encampment, and broken the force that had been sent against the shield wall. The thrust of the enemy had been blunted for the time being, but there was little denying that the enemy's living spearhead would soon be re-forged. The Saxans that were left in the region, led by Aethelstan, could not hope to stop another large enemy force.

The Unguhur were admittedly very formidable beings, and had managed to turn the tide of a disastrous fate, but the Avanorans would adjust to their presence in due time. Aethelstan did not want to be around when the enemy enacted a solution to the problem of dislodging the Unguhur. He and the remaining Saxans would be like dry grass before a brush fire when the enemy's designs were unfurled.

His raw instincts told him that the Avanoran solution would be simultaneously brutal, overwhelming, and immensely effective. Such was the well-attested nature of Avanor and the Unifier, when it came to the ways of war.

"Aethelstan?" queried a familiar voice, from a few paces behind him.

"Yes, Edmund?" Aethelstan responded, without turning his head. He heard the scuffling of Edmund's shoes against the stone as his friend walked up to his side.

"I came to see if everything is well with you," Edmund replied. The sky warrior had steadfastly been at Aethelstan's beck and call, ever since the great thane had been rescued from the battle.

"Physically yes … mentally, and spiritually, no," Aethelstan responded heavily.

"What have you decided to do?" Edmund asked. "I know that you do not want to tarry here overlong."

"I do not know yet," Aethelstan confessed. "There are many who cannot yet leave this place, due to their wounds. We cannot leave them behind with the Unguhur, because this is going to be a dangerous place to be, very soon. You know that, and I know that. That was decided when the Unguhur Realm intervened in the Unifier's affairs."

"Yes, I do know that, and I think most of the men do as well," Edmund replied evenly.

"What do you think?" Aethelstan said, turning his head to eye Edmund. His friend had a pensive look on his face. "What course of action should we be considering?"

"I have no easy answers," Edmund said. "It is a dark day for everyone, everywhere, I am afraid. Down here in the lower world, under the skies in Saxany, or wherever someone in Ave is trying to be free."

"I fear you are right," Aethelstan said, shaking his head regretfully. "We can only seek to make the best decision that is available to us, Edmund."

"And there are precious few choices left to us now," Edmund responded.

Aethelstan dropped his gaze, and clasped his hands firmly together. Though he was looking in the direction of the glimmering lake surface, he focused his gaze on nothing, as his mind was enveloped with concerns. He wondered whether the main force of the Unifier was still being held at bay, back out on the Plains of Athelney, or whether they had broken through to begin an orgy of destruction throughout the Saxan lands.

Frustration welled up swiftly, as there was no way of discerning which one of the developments presided at the moment. He only knew that he could do little if the enemy had broken through the great shield wall. Three hundred drained, battered warriors could not make a difference against thousands upon thousands of enemy troops, who enjoyed a constant stream of supply and reinforcement.

Even if the shield wall still held, little comfort could be gained. There was always the possibility of another large force being sent to maneuver through the forests to the northeast of the Plains of Athelney, to outflank the main Saxan army. There would be no stout Saxan shield wall to try to stop such a force in the future. The only one that could have been arrayed was now irrevocably broken, the remnants of which had been salvaged by the Unguhur and a lone, reclusive woodsman.

"What do you know of the Unguhur's willingness to cooperate? They have the strength to hold the channel leading up from that strange forest of theirs, if a mind like yours is lent to them for the sake of strategy," Edmund suggested. "It is my observation that their khan and khanum, Treas and Vuriant, are receptive to us, and they are certainly hostile towards the Unifier. Perhaps we can make an arrangement with them, to make use of your knowledge of Avanor's methods. They might even be persuaded to come to the aid of the main army."

Aethelstan did not feel entirely hopeful about the prospects of being placed in tacit command of another kingdom's warriors, especially ones that were not human to begin with. Even further, he held little enthusiasm towards the idea, as his heart was burdened enough by the costs of leading his own kind.

As reluctant as he had been to approach the Unguhur about their beliefs and burial practices, there was also the worry that the Unguhur would find the proposition arrogant and presumptuous, if not entirely ridiculous. From their perspective, the Saxans had just been crushed in battle with the Avanorans, and it had been the Unguhur who had emerged victorious in combat with the invaders. They would probably feel that it was the Saxans who needed the Unguhur to guide them.

"Perhaps, Edmund, but it is a far thing to grasp for. We may very well transgress the goodwill of our hosts, even if unintentionally. But what else is left to us?"

"We have to leave here, and I think it would be best to retreat to a higher terrain, perhaps the lands to the north and east," Edmund said.

The sky warrior's reply struck a note of harmony inside Aethelstan, as the suggestion was the option that he had been considering the most. The area that Edmund spoke of ran along the northeastern borderlands of Saxany for a considerable distance. It consisted primarily of a broad mountain range, populated with rises that ranged from modest to immense in size.

The mountains were covered with stout trees, thick shrubbery, and dense brush, the latter two elements being significant impediments to the passage of large numbers on foot. Within the high ground, using the sporadic, narrow mountain passes that funneled any marching force into choke points, the Saxans under Aethelstan could easily maintain a defense against an enemy horde many times larger.

"If the enemy is not already trying to navigate that route," Aethelstan said, after an extended pause.

"No, it is not practical to conduct an invasion there, and our scouts are constantly watching over that region for any sign of a threat. If an enemy force tried to move through there, they would likely be cut to pieces, even by a hastily gathered defense," Edmund returned. "At the very least, any force moving towards there would have been detected early, and word of their movements would have reached us here quite a while ago."

"And what of the Unguhur?" Aethelstan queried. "What is your counsel regarding them?"

"We can tell them where we are going, and why we have no other choice. It is their own choice as to whether they would accompany us or not," Edmund said. "You can do no more than share what you know."

"I will think on this matter for a time," Aethelstan said. "I do not wish to bring our new allies an ill-fate."

"An ill-fate would have befallen them later, if they had not chosen to come to our aid," Edmund said. "The Unifier does not long suffer those who do not bend their knee to Him, in one form or another."

Aethelstan quietly listened to Edmund's wisdom. The sky warrior was correct in his assessment, but it did not negate the fact that the Unguhur had accelerated the Unifier's direct attention by helping the Saxans. The Unguhur had to be warned about the imminence of the peril that was likely coalescing right at that moment to strike at them.

Already, he had begun to think of the issues that would be raised among the Unguhur. Their kingdom and its subterranean environs served as the only places that they had known for untold generations. The surface world was something very foreign to the underground-dwelling race, in the same way that their world was alien to the Saxans. Additionally, all of their kingdom's natural advantages and routes were well-known to the Unguhur, and unfamiliar to any surface enemy, giving them a considerable advantage within any pending combat that took place in their demesne.

But they were not familiar with the ways of the Unifier. If anything, they were probably naïve about the Unifier, and had no appreciation for the immense power wielded out of Avanor. Aethelstan was not sure that they would blindly trust him, when he informed them of the Unfier's renowned ability to adapt to any presented obstacle; and come forth with an overwhelming solution. It was that widespread reputation that had made the Saxan decision to stand and fight so bold in the eyes of a few, and so foolish in the eyes of a great many.

The Avanorans were lords of war. In that sense, the Unifier was effectively a god of war, holding the martial reins of the Avanorans, and now many others, in His hands.

When pondering the notion of a journey by the Unguhur to the northeastern mountains, there were also logistics to consider. Access to the ocean waters, and the streams located within the hills, coupled with the small game inhabiting the area, would produce enough food to sustain a larger group of humans.

The enormous Unguhur, with their stature and numbers, were another matter entirely. The vast mushroom forests and underground streams, teeming with fish and other quarry, were certainly adequate for their needs. The Unguhur would find the higher lands to be otherwise. Sparse and challenging in the longer term, the mountainous territory would be unable to sustain any significant numbers of the large creatures.

Aethelstan did not see much hope when it came to pleading with the Unguhur, to get them to avoid the doom that would inevitably fall upon their realm, but he knew that he would have to try. Despite the improbability of convincing them of the mounting danger, and the strong possibility of angering them unwittingly, he resolved himself to make an effort. He had to give the brave souls that had saved him and his men the best explanation of the situation that he could, and pray fervently that they would listen to his words, give them credence, and then heed them.

"Go to their khan and khanum, and petition them for an audience, as soon as possible," Aethelstan stated. "I must endeavor to open their eyes. I can do no less than that for those who have helped us so unconditionally."

Edmund nodded. "At once, Aethelstan."

Turning, his friend headed off with brisk strides towards the heart of the great Unguhur city of Oranim. Athelstan quietly watched his friend depart. Even though a decision had been rendered, regarding a course of action for the Saxan survivors, his hopes were lifted no higher.

The things weighing heavily on his heart were waiting patiently, and mercilessly, to beset him upon his return to solitude. It was as if a deep shadow fell across him, as he turned his eyes back towards the view of the expansive lake, as the vanguard of his mounting sorrows and fears reached their claws out towards him.

WULFSTAN

Wulfstan's eyelids fluttered, and he awoke slowly to the feeling of soft, silken breezes caressing his face. His eyes were filled with the purest white that he had ever seen.

A mystical ambiance surrounded him. He wondered whether he had expired in his mortality, and had entered into the heavenly realms of the All-Father. The atmosphere evoked all of the types of legendary images concerning the celestial realms of Palladium, including the accounts described by everyone from the simplest of village priests to the most erudite of monks, the latter of the kind that Wulfstan's uncle had oft interacted and traded with.

The thought of being alive in the bosom of the afterworld was instantly sobering. It brought Wulfstan to a state of full alertness, as he lifted his back off the ground, and subsequently pulled his knees up so that he was in a more comfortable sitting position.

At that moment, he heard the quork of a startled raven, turning just in time to witness its black form flying off with haste. He stared after the raven, as the dark bird sped low across a scene that was as fascinating as it seemed to transcend reality.

Delicate vapors wafted over a broad terrain composed of the cushioning, white substance that he was currently sitting upon. Hills and valleys of the white material could be seen stretching to the horizon, as well as a randomly strewn variety of other strange shapes and formations.

To Wulfstan's eyes, the sight resembled the winter wonderlands that he had known several times in his own life, when the skies draped the hills and fields of Wessachia in thick blankets of snow. Yet the impossibility of that notion, and a dawning realization, threatened to make his mind spin.

Wulfstan had a little idea as to what the environment around him was not; and he had more than an inkling as to what it was.

He knew that he could not be on a simple cloud, of the types that he had traversed on the back of the winged steed. He remembered quite well how he and the Himmeros had flown through them without incident during his desperate ascent.

No matter what its appearance looked like when gazing down from above, no cloud could support the weight of a man or beast. The clouds felt like the mists and fogs that shrouded the woods on the ground, and posed no obstructions whatsoever to his passage in flight. Wulfstan knew with certainty that he could not sit on one.

As he scanned the area, looking to the left and right, his gaze fell upon the form of his Himmeros, lying nearby. Spirit Wing's body was heaving, smoothly and steadily, with each relaxed breath. The creature was curled up, fast asleep, with its wings tucked snugly into its sides.

The sight bestowed a feeling of relief over the smattering of guilt that lay deeper within Wulfstan. He knew that he had pressed the poor animal harshly, beyond all its known limits of endurance. While the larger part of him did not regret the action, as it was undertaken to help Saxany avert a terrible doom, he was nonetheless gladdened by the knowledge that the Himmeros was unharmed.

It was then that he emerged fully from the initial shock of his strange surroundings. He brought more focus upon the reason that he had set off on the risky, and likely foolhardy, flight in the first place.

The footing underneath the leather soles of his shoes was extremely unusual, like nothing that he had ever felt before. It had a little give and bounce, as he lifted his knees slightly and set his feet back down, feeling the odd sensations derived from pressing against the unfamiliar surface.

Carefully, he got to his feet. He turned around in place, to take a look behind him. The white terrain in that direction held no rises, and it did not spread to the horizon. Rather abruptly, the low span of white came to an end about fifty paces from where he now stood.

Slowly, Wulfstan walked over towards the edge. When reaching it, as if on the brink of a cliff's boundary, he got down to his belly, crawling the last few paces so that he could peer over the edge without feeling wholly insecure. Despite the reassurance from having his body supported, his stomach churned as he gazed downward.

There were stratified layers of clouds scudding by far below, designating a mind-boggling distance that culminated in solid ground. Nothing about the land was distinct from the lofty heights, and Wulfstan wasted no time trying to identify any specific places. It was like looking down upon a vast cloak fashioned with greenish hues. The movements of the clouds, themselves imbued with misty, shifting qualities, gave evidence that they were what they appeared to be, entirely unlike the surreal substance that Wulfstan now rested his weight upon.

As he looked down at one group of randomly sprinkled clusters, he realized that he was gazing upon the second level of clouds that he had passed through during his long climb upward. It was then that he wondered whether his whimsical, desperate idea, born of dreams, and adhered to with a fanatical effort, had somehow come true.

At that moment, he heard a low rumble.

The snow-like ground, if the unfamiliar substance could be termed in such a way, shook underneath Wulfstan, in a slow, rhythmic fashion. Edging back a few paces from the lip of the enormous drop, he got back to his feet, feeling the powerful vibrations through his shoes. Carefully, with more than a little trepidation clenching his gut, he rotated his body and head around, facing towards the source of the low-pitched resonance. Off in the distance, striding out from behind one of the ubiquitous, hill-like formations, was a living spectacle that froze Wulfstan in place.

By then, the rumblings had roused the Himmeros from its deep, restful sleep. With a nervous grunt, Spirit Wing swiveled its head towards the swelling noise. Seeing what Wulfstan was witnessing, the Himmeros' head snapped back immediately, its gaze orienting upon the place where the Saxan was standing. Shifting about, and getting its paw-like feet braced underneath it, Spirit Wing lurched up agilely, and hastily loped back to where Wulfstan gazed in awestruck wonderment.

As if instinctively, Wulfstan's hand shot out, grabbing Spirit Wing's tether forcibly before the creature could entertain any notions of escaping off the edge of the terrain behind them. The Himmeros' eyes were brimming with fear, and the agitated creature shifted about, tugging at the leather cording, as Wulfstan desperately tried to calm the terrified beast. It whined and whimpered, as Wulfstan had to anchor his legs to resist the creature's pull.

"Spirit Wing! Hold here with me, it's alright … it's going to be alright," he said to the Himmeros, somehow keeping his voice from shaking.

There was nobody to soothe Wulfstan, though, and his eyes could not mask the fright spiraling within him as he glanced back towards the colossal vision approaching them. His mouth twitched in his extreme anxiety, while his very breath was trapped in his chest. A cold, clammy feeling spread through him, and his chest constricted further, as he resisted the initial, compelling impulse to simply mount the Himmeros and fly far, far away.

Another force inside him resisted the urges. He had come for a stated purpose, believing that he had reason to trust his instincts, dreams, and the recognition of the anomalous white patch in the upper reaches of the sky. That intended ambition revolved around an uncertain hope; that an ancient race of creatures, immortalized through song and tale, did truly exist in a heavenly exile.

Though of ancient origin, the songs and tales he had heard indeed resonated with truth, as the evidence before Wulfstan's eyes could not be denied. Breathtaking and terrifying at once, the monstrosity approaching him caused his mind to grapple to comprehend what his eyes continued to reveal to him.

Bright, silvery wings, vast in size, and shining resplendently in the light cascading down without hindrance from above, were carried outstretched, lending the regal bearer of them an exalted appearance. An elongated, supple body, whose scales shone with a silvery hue, was conveyed forward upon robust, well-developed legs. Pronounced lines of muscles, each contour appearing to be skillfully etched and sculpted into the creature's flesh, wound their way down the length of the appendages to end in sets of extensive claws. The talons themselves looked wickedly sharp, like giant, curving sabers fastened into its broad feet.

Despite its incredible size, the creature proceeded forth with a grace of motion that was extraordinary to behold. The protracted, capacious head of the beast emerged smoothly from its thickset neck, the latter continuing in similar fashion from its base into the main portion of its body. The harmonizing line of its neck and head were carried on an even level with the upper spinal ridge running along the length of its back, giving the titanic creature a rather flattened profile. The magnificent beast had a prominent tail, one that comprised a significant portion of its overall length.

Enveloped in a swirling, pulsing amalgam of paralyzing fear, astonished incredulity, and sheer wonder, Wulfstan could do no more than watch as the beast strode resolutely towards him. Each step of the creature shook the ground underneath, building in force as it drew steadily closer. The winged colossus loomed ever larger, each stride continuing to fill up the field of Wulfstan's vision. It was of a scale that Wulfstan would have previously thought to be unfathomable. At last, it seemed as if there was nothing else in the world, save for the silvery titan rising up before the awed Saxan.

Wulfstan had never imagined anything dwelling in the world of Ave that could be so incredible. Even after having witnessed the immense

Darroks, he could not have envisioned something so gigantic and elegant as the living legend before him.

The creature appeared far larger than the fabled stories described. It was a stunning, overwhelming revelation, as Wulfstan knew full well that tales commonly tended to exaggerate in their claims.

The height alone of the gargantuan creature was staggering to behold, even in comparison to the Darroks. Like the Darroks, its wings were enormous in proportion to its body. Even with the great scale of the wings, the structure of the creature's body exuded an inherent level of physical strength that truly was inconceivable to Wulfstan.

He had always accepted the fascinating tales about the ancient creatures as reflecting some distant truth, in that the mythical beasts had gone into exile under the perception that they were too powerful to continue residing in the world of humankind. Now that he was witnessing the unobstructed reality with his own eyes, he understood such reasoning more clearly than ever before. There was nothing in the world that could be much of a threat to such a formidable beast, save for great sorcery, or perhaps an incredible weapon, of siege engine size.

Tilting its huge head downward, the monstrous being fixed Wulfstan with an encompassing, mesmerizing gaze, which seemed to swallow up his comparatively diminutive form within its depths. The dark round pupils of its eyes were like portals to a shrouded abyss, beckoning to realms as vast and mysterious as they were dangerous and foreboding. Most notably, there was an ancient, surreal aura around the creature, one that went far beyond its impressive physical presence.

The great jaws of the creature, wide enough that several humans could easily stand within them, spread apart, as it opened its mouth. An abundant forest of serrated, backward curving teeth was unveiled, each and every glistening tooth a deadly weapon by itself.

"Young human of the lands below," the majestic creature stated.

It spoke evenly in the common tongue of the Saxans, startling Wulfstan even further. The words were carried within a deafening voice, one that was as deep and regal in tone as it was capable of resounding all throughout the wide expanse around them. Wulfstan listened enraptured, and with great trepidation, as the creature continued its address to him, using his own language.

"What brings you to try to reach the Forbidden Dominions? No man can come here of his own volition," the creature thundered. "Even the Wizards are banned from these realms, as we banned ourselves from yours and theirs. I trust that you were not trying to destroy yourself, for such is foolishness.

"I could only believe that you were seeking us. Were it not so, you and your loyal steed would have died after a terrible descent. Know that your steed reached only a little farther than you, before it could go onward no longer. Others of my kind may have allowed you to fall, for the divide between our kinds has long been set. I chose not to let you die, as I wanted to hear the reason for your foolishness for myself. Be grateful that I am considered to be of good humor among my kind."

Wulfstan nodded nervously, knowing very well what the legendary creature was that now towered over him, a fact confirmed even more by what it had said. Faced with the undeniable reality of its existence, his heart and courage wavered. He struggled within a wave of confusion and fear, and it seemed as if his wits had entirely abandoned him. The creature silently regarded him with its absorbing eyes, patiently waiting for the human to respond.

"The Elder, yes … I was … it is desperate in Saxany below. And I knew that I must … try to find your kind," he stumbled, trying in vain to sound confident, and to raise his voice, as the sound of it was so tiny and minute in comparison to that of the Elder Dragon.

"Collect your wits about you," the venerable dragon replied, with an unmistakable hint of amusement at his discombobulated state. "Yes, I am of the Elder. You have heard of our kind. Or you would not know that name, or have come to this place. Then you should also know well that our kind is no longer involved in the world of mankind, until the End of Days comes. We are bound by the Oath, made during the waning days of the First Age of this world.

"Now tell me again, and delay no further, why did you undertake such a reckless effort to reach my sanctuary?"

Wulfstan could feel the scrutiny coming from the creature like an increasing pressure, as he scrambled for the best way to answer the awe-inspiring beast.

"We need your help," Wulfstan blurted out quickly, shouting up at the Elder.

The words were simple but direct. They were also bluntly honest. He paused for a moment, taking a few deep breaths as he tried to gain some small measure of confidence.

DREAM OF LEGENDS

Despite the massive, fearsome features of the Elder Dragon, Wulfstan realized that the creature's voice, demeanor, and aura, while grand in scope, were not meant to intimidate him. It was hard not be frightened in its awesome presence, but he could see that the creature was trying to take a soothing posture with him, as best as such a majestic creature could do.

It was no simple-minded beast, governed solely by hunger, fatigue, and primal urges for mating, but rather an ancient intelligence, with a perspective and lifespan that was extraordinary just to comprehend. Such a creature was now personally regarding Wulfstan, with more than a passing interest. As before, it waited patiently for him to collect himself, and his thoughts.

"I fear the End of Days are upon us … at least in some ways. I know no Wizards … and I am no great man among the Saxan people below. I am just a ceorl, driven by desperation, who came here only on faith in old tales, a glimpse of this place from below, and recurring dreams I have had for a long, long time. I also came because of what the tales say, about what the Elder once stood for," Wulfstan responded, finding a better grasp of his thoughts and composure.

Catching his breath for a couple of moments, as he was straining his lungs to give volume to his words, he continued, "Even if not the End of Days, it is the end of the world that I know, and that a great many know. An evil power has risen in the world below, wielded by a Man said to be of fair appearance and gifted with wisdom. That power is not of the All-Father, as it casts a dark and bloody shadow wherever its touch falls. This one Man is taking all power to Himself, and now moves to control all lands and kingdoms."

The Elder listened to him attentively, and paused for a moment before responding to Wulfstan's statements.

"Many who have heralded the End of Days are now spirits separated from the dust that once cloaked them. None can say when the End of Days is to occur, but the One that brought days into being," the dragon replied somberly. "Did you ever wonder if I know of this Man you speak of, or what your war is about?"

If the dragon were not so fearsome, and Wulfstan not so fearful, he would probably have been able to detect the tinges of amusement present in the latter part of the question. Instead of sensing the dragon's subtle humor, the Saxan ceorl had a sickening feeling come over him,

thinking only that the dragon might not have bothered to take account of the affairs of mortals over the ages. The dragon perhaps did not even care who was considered good or evil in the wars of humankind that took place on Ave's surface, at least until the End of Days.

"You ascended here on a hurried judgement," the Elder Dragon stated firmly, before Wulstan could begin to muster a reply. The beast lowered its great head a little closer to Wulfstan, as it continued speaking in a slower, more purposeful tone. It was as if the creature wanted to emphasize each and every word to Wulfstan. "Be assured … our kind do watch over the passing of the world, and I do know what besets your world because of this … Man … as you understand Him to be. I speak of the One that you know as the Unifier, which is the name that humans in all realms call Him. I also believe that you did not come to me for just wisdom or knowledge. You have come to seek the help of the Elder in your affairs … have you not?"

Wulfstan nodded slowly in the affirmative, wholly relieved that the Elder had openly voiced the singular, most important question he had carried inside of him to the upper skies. There was no room to be anything less than direct with the Elder, now that the momentous subject had been broached.

Straightening up, and craning his neck, he looked directly into the eyes of the Elder. He tried to convey his deep sincerity as he answered, "Yes. All of the legends of your kind that I have ever heard speak of your faithful allegiance to the All-Father. I do not come to ask you to fight our war. It is just that we have no time left to us … the darkest hour our land has ever faced has come, and we must find help if we can, and warn others in this world, such as those from Midragard. I know of no other who can help us do this, as we have little time. It was a choice of trying to find you, or to do nothing, and watch Saxany and all those I love be destroyed. I could not choose to do nothing."

The Elder Dragon hesitated for a few seconds. For a brief moment, the creature's gaze shifted, looking past him as if taking a glance into the depths of time itself. Wulfstan sensed something in the Elder's detached look, and believed that he detected the presence of some kind of inner pain on the part of the dragon.

"Only part of what you have heard about us remains true. Once, the things that you heard were all true, and the things of that age formed the knowledge recorded in the tales that were passed down. Most of our kind are still in allegiance to the All-Father, and continue to accept the Ban willingly," the Elder Dragon stated, with the faraway look yet lingering within its great eyes.

The creature then appeared to become lost in inner reflections for another moment or two, before bringing its eyes back down to look upon the small human before it.

"Since the ancient times, a few of our kind have turned their hearts to the Lord of the Deep Darkness, Jebaalos. They resent the Ban, and seek for a way to break the Oath. Their hearts darken, and their rage grows with each day that passes in this world. There are some among our kind that fear that these others are readying themselves in a hidden manner, to fight for the Unifier … though I do not know how they will withstand the binding formed by the Oath. Strange and wicked times are upon us, both your kind, and ours. As to your desire … yes, I will assist you in any way that I can, though know that I am still bound by the Oath, which is no small thing."

The great Dragon's voice then softened a little, as it finished, "There is a rare valor dwelling in you, human … even if it is a reckless one. You harbor a courage that is not common in this troubled age."

Wulfstan was struck to the point of being dumbfounded by the creature's extensive response. Not only had his gut instincts regarding the existence of the Elder turned out to be accurate, but the dragon had swiftly, and openly, agreed to assist him.

He had achieved everything that he had sought on a fragile hope and whim, having left the surface of the world that he knew far behind, with only the faintest ghost of a chance to inspire him onward. Wulfstan was utterly stunned at the quick acquiescence of the legendary creature to his petition.

"Time is no friend to you now, as you have said. And I know myself well enough after many millenia, to know that I am not hasty in the directions I choose," the great dragon then continued, as if perceiving Wulfstan's amazement at its cooperation. "You show wisdom in speaking of Midragard. Only the lands of Midragard can be of any help to you now, and they must also be warned. They bend no knee to the Unifier, and are a strong and proud people. They saved many of my kind's smaller brothers and sisters, the ones that yet live in the lower world. For this reason alone, the people of Midragard are owed a debt."

"Smaller brothers and sisters?" Wulfstan asked, curiosity spurring him to inquire.

"The dragons of your world, who live there even now," the Elder replied. "There is no time to speak further on this, as I must take you to Midragard with no delay."

"To Midragard? Now?" Wulfstan responded, bewildered by the declaration.

"It is the only land that may be able to bring aid to your people, and that is why you sought my help ... so what benefit is it to you to wait any longer?"

"There is none," Wulfstan admitted, shouting the answer back up to the dragon.

"Another thing ... I can hear you well enough, if you speak in a normal manner, as you would among other humans. Our senses are exceptional," the creature then informed him, with no trace of haughtiness in its booming voice.

"I will," Wulfstan yelled up in response, before catching himself. He then resumed a vocal level that would be considered conversational around a cook fire back in the Saxan encampment. "I mean, I will."

"That should spare your lungs and voice a little," the dragon replied, with another flare of subtle mirth. "So do you wish to tarry further?"

Wulfstan shook his head, and then replied. "No, I am ready to go with you."

"We are about to go forth, and I still do not know your name, human," the dragon replied, with obvious amusement. "What is the name by which you are called?"

"Wulfstan," he returned. "Son of Ealdred. From Sussachia, a province of Saxany."

"I am known as Bevriedak, of the Elder, though I am afraid that I do not hail from any place, unless you deem this part of the Forbidden Dominions to be so," the huge dragon replied. "Well met, Wulfstan. Now let us waste no more time. I will have to take you and your steed within my claws, as you could not breathe the air beyond this haven. It would be death for you beyond the edge of this place, where the ground gives way to the open sky."

The dragon lifted up its front right claw, and slowly extended it forward. As it set its clawed foot downward, the dragon rotated it so that the underside of the foot faced upward, to enable Wulfstan and his steed to climb up to its surface.

Wulfstan turned towards the Himmeros, which had remained at his side throughout the verbal exchange. He had not thought of the steed during the conversation, though his clenched hand was still taut upon its tether.

In some ways, he was very surprised that the brawny steed had not tried to bolt away. Perhaps Spirit Wing had sensed the dragon's non-threatening intentions from the beginning, on a level that Wulfstan had not initially perceived. It was the only reason that he could think of why Spirit Wing had not made for the edge, and dragged him along in its wake.

Whether or not the Himmeros had been reassured, at least enough not to try and run away, Spirit Wing still exhibited great trepidation regarding the notion of approaching the dragon. Defiantly, it dug its paws firmly into the white, spongy surfacing, locking its legs as Wulfstan tried to coax the nervous creature towards the opened, offered underside of the dragon's claws. He could not entirely blame the Himmeros for its reluctance, as the Elder's sharp talons looked far more deadly than any sword or axe ever forged upon a skilled blacksmith's anvil.

Wulfstan then turned his head back up and around, as he heard the sonorous voice of the dragon calling out again. This time, the sounds coming from the dragon's mouth were unintelligible, though from their timbre and pattern Wulfstan guessed them to be some manner of words. He knew at once that the words were not intended for him, in any way. His eyes narrowed, and his brows furrowed in confusion, as the dragon continued to speak in the strange, unknown tongue. The language was harmonious and flowing in its cadence, and it made the dragon's voice lighten even further from the deep, imposing tone that it had used to address Wulfstan.

The Saxan's attention was diverted once more, as the rigid tether holding the Himmeros close to him suddenly slackened. Inexplicably, Spirit Wing brushed right by him towards the open, extended claws, showing not one sign of its former apprehension.

In a few moments, the Himmeros was tugging Wulfstan forcibly towards the claw. With a stronger yank, Spirit Wind lifted him off of his feet, and pulled him a couple of steps forward, bringing him out of his momentary stupor.

"The language of the First Age, spoken by the servants of the

All-Father," the Elder dragon explained to Wulfstan, resuming the Saxan speech once again. "I will speak to you later of it as well. But know that it is a tongue good for speaking to all manner of creatures brought into this world by the All-Father."

With some effort, Wulfstan was able to find footholds and handholds in the leathery roughness of the dragon's skin. The grips that he was afforded enabled him to clamber up onto the surface of the upturned claw. He strode to the middle of the great claw, where the Himmeros now stood in a relaxed manner. He flinched slightly, as the giant talons of the dragon closed in slowly, to fully encase their bodies.

The dragon brought its claws together delicately, until Wulfstan and the Himmeros were held relatively snugly near the center. Wulfstan then shifted and rotated, as he felt the dragon carefully turning its clenched talons over, while keeping its right foreleg lifted up off the ground.

A moment later, he was jostled abruptly, as the great bulk of the creature lurched forward. The dragon stepped forward somewhat awkwardly on its three unencumbered feet. After a few more paces, Wulfstan felt the dragon come to a halt. He knew that they were on the outermost edge of the floating snow-land, at the very cusp of the dizzying, plunging fall to the distant ground.

His heart started racing, as he felt the tension rippling through the dragon's body. He had a good idea of what was about to happen, and did not want to think about it at all.

The Elder's body rocked backward, just before its rear legs propelled its massive bulk forward in a strong leap, springing the great dragon far from the edge that Wulfstan had so carefully, and timidly, looked over just a short while before. There was a gliding sensation for a couple of moments, before a brief, sharp dip, as the creature's vast wings stretched out and seized on the air. The sound of the dragon's wings beating through the air, stirring up a tempest in their own right, filled Wulfstan's ears. He felt his stomach grow queasy with the unpleasant sensations coming over him, and felt that it would not be much longer before he began to retch.

As if in reflex, he clutched tightly onto the neck of the Himmeros, which was now lying by his side. As Wulfstan's hands grabbed fistfuls of its fur, Spirit Wing whined and fidgeted in the darkness of the dragon's hold. Wulfstan trembled in fear as the dragon's body alternately rose and fell, doing his best to endure as the creature worked to attain a level of equilibrium in its flight.

Gradually, the sharp fluctuations of motion steadied significantly, as the dragon settled down into a rhythmic trajectory. Wulfstan was grateful for both the darkness of the talon-enclosure, and for the imminent presence of the sky steed. He could take some succor from Spirit Wing's company, while not being faced outright with the altitude that they were being carried at.

He rested his head against the Himmeros, making himself as comfortable as he possibly could, given the circumstances. The sky steed's coarse fur lay against his right cheek, and the musky scent of it filled his nostrils.

Wulfstan's stomach continued churning a little, although the nausea did not advance into an overwhelming degree of sickness. He felt his heart leap, to varying degrees, as the dragon continued bobbing in its flight. Sometimes he felt a sudden, sharp drop, and at other times he felt the dragon abruptly rising up, or sliding quickly to one side or the other, buoyed by the shifting, sudden winds, powerful enough to affect a body as immense as the Elder's. A cold sweat eventually broke out on Wulfstan's forehead, and a clammy feeling encompassed him, as he struggled to steel his nerves to the unpredictable lurches.

After what seemed like an eternity of being buffeted about, there was an extended period where Wulfstan felt the dragon's wings pumping more furiously. With what little experience he had gained in flying, he recognized the sensation as coming from a steady climb in height. When the dragon leveled out its flight once again, their progress went much smoother than before. As squeamish as Wulfstan was feeling, it was a very welcome development.

As high as they had been on the floating white mass, where Bevriadak dwelled, Wulfstan could not believe that they had not yet run into the upper firmament; the lofty place where the stars were said to be positioned in the night. The explanation was probably just a simple matter, in that his judgement of spatial distance was rendered ineffective by the unblemished smoothness of the upper firmament. Perhaps there was a much greater distance to it than he had initially fathomed.

Even so, he knew that they were flying at an altitude that was far, far beyond anything that could be reached by a living creature of the world below. The comprehension of that sobering notion evoked his gratitude once more, over the fact that he and the Himmeros were being conveyed in a state of complete darkness. He was certain that his nerves and mind would not be able to handle the view currently spread out beneath the dragon's claws.

It took him well over an hour to wrestle his anxieties down to a point where he stopped worrying about every slight shift in turbulence. The makeshift carriage created by Bevriedak's closed claw was rough to endure for an extended journey, but Wulfstan was not about to complain.

After a short while, he noted the dragon climbing up a little higher. He then closed his eyes, resting his weight fully against the Himmeros' body. The sky steed was now breathing easily, evidently having come to acceptable terms with the manner of their travel. Wulfstan was not nearly as relaxed as the steed, as he still felt tightness in his gut, and a skip in his heartbeat with pronounced movements of the dragon, but he found himself slowly acclimating.

Though Wulfstan had little way of knowing what time it was outside, or even how much distance they had covered, he knew that he had no major concerns to contend with. For all intents and purposes, it was a miracle that he had even reached Bevriedak. Lightning had struck twice in the same place, as Wulfstan had been successful in securing the dragon's cooperation.

It still seemed unbelievable that he was going to Midragard in the willing company of an Elder, a living legend out of story and song. But this was not another instance of his recurring dreams.

A dream of legends had guided him to a tremendous reality, breathing and living, soaring through the uppermost skies of Ave.

Wulfstan would soon be able to reach out for help, to come to the aid of his beleaguered homeland, just as his wildest hopes had aspired to do. Against all probability, a chance still existed. It had grown much stronger since the moment that Wulfstan had decided to risk everything, and take to the skies on the back of a Himmeros, holding fast to a dream and trusting his instincts. Already he had achieved a tremendous success, as the great wings of an Elder had lifted him above the impossible, and were carrying him ever closer to the possible.

ABOUT THE AUTHOR

Author and Filmmaker Stephen Zimmer was born in Denver, Colorado, and currently resides in Lexington, Kentucky.

His literary works include two epic-scale series, The Rising Dawn Saga, and the Fires in Eden Series. His short fiction includes "In the Mountain Skies", a steampunk story included in the *Dreams of Steam* anthology from Kerlak Publishing (edited by Kimberly Richardson).

In the world of movies, his work as a director and screenwriter includes the supernatural thriller *Shadows Light* and the horror short film *The Sirens*. He also directed the forthcoming fantasy short film *Swordbearer*, which is based upon the H. David Blalock novel *Ascendant* (Sam's Dot Publishing).

Stephen's online home is at
www.stephenzimmer.com
and his blog, Fantastical Musings, is located at
stephenzimmer.blogspot.com.
Those with FaceBook are invited to friend him at
www.facebook.com/sgzimmer

Check out the following pages to see more from

All Seventh Star Press titles available in print and an array of
specially priced eBook formats.

Visit www.seventhstarpress.com for further information.

Connect with Seventh Star Press at:
www.seventhstarpress.com
seventhstarpress.blogspot.com
www.facebook.com/seventhstarpress

Coming Soon

**brings you an amazing YA fantasy series
from award-winning author Jackie Gamber.**

**The Leland Dragon Series arrives in 2011,
with Book One, <u>REDHEART</u>, in early 2011,
and Book Two, <u>SELA</u>, in the summer of 2011.**

If you enjoyed the Fires in Eden series, be sure to check out Stephen Zimmer's epic urban fantasy series, The Rising Dawn Saga....

Epic Urban Fantasy-The Rising Dawn Saga

A shadow falls across the world, and realms beyond, as a war that has raged since the dawn of time itself draws closer to a decisive clash. As groups aligned with a movement called The Convergence speed up their efforts to bring about a global economic and legal order, resistance mounts after the host of a syndicated radio show, Benedict Darwin, discovers the true nature of a virtual reality device that has come into his possession. The Rising Dawn Saga will take you into mythical, supernatural realms as it unfolds, as the most unlikely of individuals rise to confront powers that have existed since before the world began.

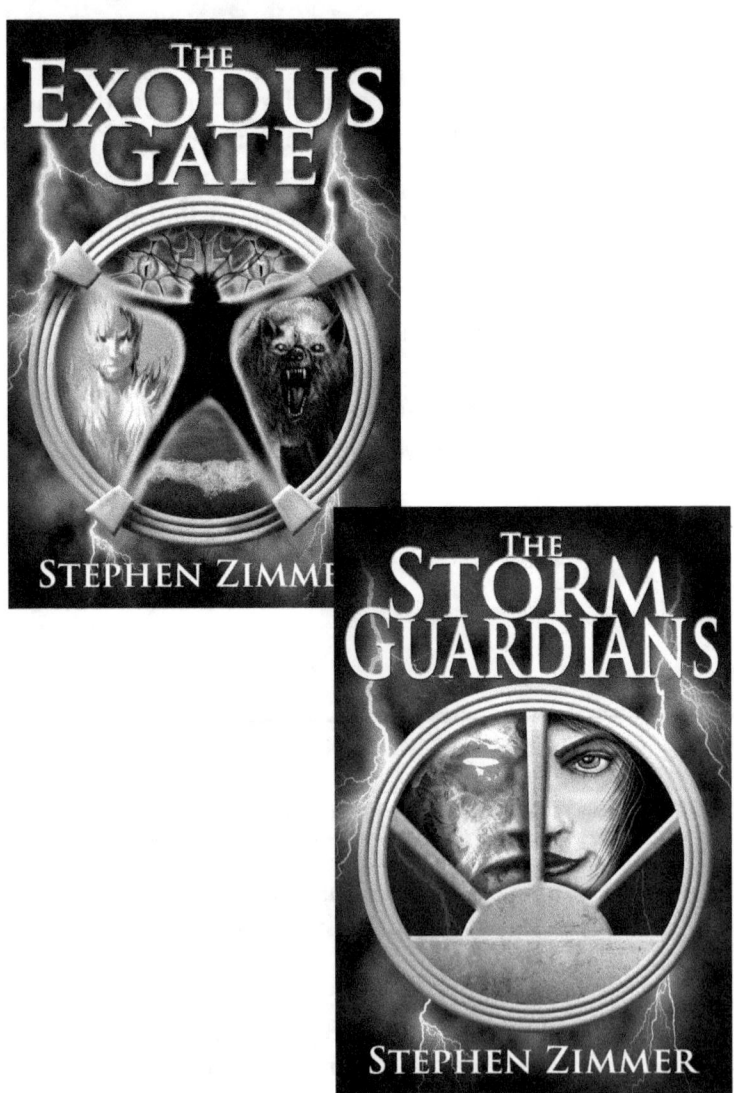

Book One: The Exodus Gate
ISBN: 978-0615267470

"With *The Exodus Gate* author Stephen Zimmer sets the stage for an adventurous new science fiction fantasy series that is sure to entertain the reader from beginning to end. Zimmer has weaved a tale of fantastic realms populated with exotic creatures. Keep a sharp eye out for this new series."
-Mark Randell, Yellow30 Sci-Fi

"…a book that Fantasy Book Review recommends for lovers of thoughtful-fantasy. It is also a book with an ending that is near-prophetic, written as it was before the world's economic meltdown."
-Fantasy Book Review

Book Two: The Storm Guardians
ISBN: 978-0982565636

"This novel transports me from my bedroom to the edge of an upcoming storm — a battle to be fought by incredible villains and noble heroes of all forms. I love Zimmer's imagination, as each of his creatures play a pivotal role in the bigger picture. Unfortunately, for every auspicious being there is an ominous beast lurking in the shadows. Zimmer's weave of fantasy and religious fables leaves the reader sated"
-Bitten By Books

"The scope of *The Storm Guardians* is massive, opening up and expanding on the conflict only hinted at in *The Exodus Gate*. The intrigue and action promised in the first book is fully developed and mercilessly exhibited. T*he Storm Guardians* is a non-stop thriller that lives up to the promise of *The Exodus Gate* and points at an even more amazing denouement in the final book of the series. Once again, Zimmer has used his command of cinematic imagery to give us a spectacular vision of war both heavenly and hellish. Two thumbs up on this one."
-Pure Reason Book Review

Now Available from Seventh Star Press, Steven Shrewsbury's hard-hitting, heroic fantasy novel THRALL, featuring illustrations and cover art by fantasy artist Matthew Perry!

Trade Paperback ISBN: 9780983108634
Hardcover ISBN: 9780982565650
eBook ISBN: 9780983108641

FOR GORIAS LA GAUL...
DELIVERANCE WILL COME

Set in the mists of ancient times, *Thrall* tells the story of Gorias La Gaul, an aging warrior who has lived for centuries battling the monstrosities of legend and lore. It is an age when the Nephilum walk the earth, demonic forces hunger to be unleashed, and dragons still soar through the skies ... living and undead. On a journey to find one of his own blood, a young man who is caught in the shadow of necromancy, Gorias' path crosses with familiar enemies, some of whom not even death can hold bound.

Thrall is gritty, dark-edged heroic fantasy in the vein of Robert E. Howard and David Gemmell. It is a maelstrom of hard-hitting action and unpredictable imagery, taking place within an incredible antediluvian world. In Gorias La Gaul, *Thrall* introduces an iconic new character to the realms of fantasy literature. Thrall invites the reader to go on a perilous journey where it is not a matter of whether one has the courage to die, but whether one has the courage to live.

All Seventh Star Press titles available in print and an array of specially priced eBook formats. Visit www.seventhstarpress.com for further information.

www.ingramcontent.com/pod-product-compliance
Lightning Source LLC
Chambersburg PA
CBHW070533030726
47505CB00001B/28